Praise for Kristin Hannah

"Marvelous . . . a touching love story . . . You know a book is a winner when you devour it in one evening and hope there's a sequel. . . .This page-turner has enough twists and turns to keep the reader up until the wee hours of the morning."
            —*USA Today* on *On Mystic Lake*

"Excellent . . . an emotional experience you won't soon forget."
            —*Rocky Mountain News* on *On Mystic Lake*

"A shining triumph that is not to be missed . . . hauntingly beautiful and richly emotional."
            —*Romantic Times* on *On Mystic Lake*

"The Phrase 'page-turner' is redefined. . . . A clean, deep thrust into the reader's heart . . . unfolds tenderly and with suspense . . . In Hannah's world, nothing can be taken for granted and triumph must be earned, with hard work, truthful reckoning, and tears."
            —*Publishers Weekly* (starred review) on *On Mystic Lake*

"Hannah is superb at delving into the characters' psyches and delineating nuances of feeling."
            —*Washington Post Book World* on *Summer Island*

"An all-night reading affair . . . You won't be able to put it down. . . . [*Angel Falls* will] make you laugh and cry."
            —*The New York Post* on *Angel Falls*

"A tearjerker . . . about the triumph of family . . . perfect reading for hopeless romantics."
            —*Detroit Free Press* on *Angel Falls*

By Kristin Hannah
(published by Ballantine Books)

A HANDFUL OF HEAVEN
THE ENCHANTMENT
ONCE IN EVERY LIFETIME
IF YOU BELIEVE
WHEN LIGHTNING STRIKES
WAITING FOR THE MOON
HOME AGAIN
ON MYSTIC LAKE
ANGEL FALLS
SUMMER ISLAND
DISTANT SHORES
BETWEEN SISTERS
THE THINGS WE DO FOR LOVE
COMFORT AND JOY

On Mystic Lake
&
Summer Island

On Mystic Lake

&

Summer Island

TWO NOVELS

Kristin Hannah

BALLANTINE BOOKS · NEW YORK

2005 Ballantine Books Trade Paperback Edition

On Mystic Lake copyright © 1999 by Kristin Hannah
Summer Island copyright © 2001 by Kristin Hannah

Published in the United States by Ballantine Books,
an imprint of The Random House Publishing Group,
a division of Random House, Inc., New York.
Originally published as two separate works by Crown
Publishers, a division of Random House, Inc.

BALLANTINE and colophon are registered trademarks
of Random House, Inc.

Published by arrangement with Crown Publishers, a division
of Random House, Inc.

ISBN 0-345-48684-6

Printed in the United States of America

www.ballantinebooks.com

OPM 9 8 7 6 5 4 3 2 1

On Mystic Lake

To Barbara Kurek.
My mother couldn't have chosen a better
godmother for me . . .

To the men in my life, Benjamin and Tucker . . .

And in memory of my mother, Sharon Goodno John.
I hope they have bookstores in Heaven, Mom.

Acknowledgments

Some books are battles. Others are wars. To my generals—Ann Patty, Jane Berkey, and Linda Grey—thanks for always demanding my very best; to Stephanie Tade, thanks for believing in this book from the very beginning; to Elisa Wares and the wonderful team at Ballantine Books, thanks for your continued support and encouragement along the way; to my comrades—Megan Chance, Jill Marie Landis, Jill Barnett, Penelope Williamson, and Susan Wiggs—thanks for always being there, for listening and laughing and everything in between; and to my guardian angel, my *über*-agent, mentor, and friend, Andrea Cirillo, thanks for everything.

Part One

The true voyage of self-discovery lies not in seeking new
landscapes but in having new eyes.
—MARCEL PROUST

Chapter 1

Rain fell like tiny silver teardrops from the tired sky. Somewhere behind a bank of clouds lay the sun, too weak to cast a shadow on the ground below.

It was March, the doldrums of the year, still and quiet and gray, but the wind had already begun to warm, bringing with it the promise of spring. Trees that only last week had been naked and brittle seemed to have grown six inches over the span of a single, moonless night, and sometimes, if the sunlight hit a limb just so, you could see the red bud of new life stirring at the tips of the crackly brown bark. Any day, the hills behind Malibu would blossom, and for a few short weeks this would be the prettiest place on Earth.

Like the plants and animals, the children of Southern California sensed the coming of the sun. They had begun to dream of ice cream and Popsicles and last year's cutoffs. Even determined city dwellers, who lived in glass and concrete high-rises in places with pretentious names like Century City, found themselves veering into the nursery aisles of their local supermarkets. Small, potted geraniums began appearing in the metal shopping carts, alongside the sun-dried tomatoes and the bottles of Evian water.

For nineteen years, Annie Colwater had awaited spring with the breathless anticipation of a young girl at her first dance. She ordered bulbs from distant lands and shopped for hand-painted ceramic pots to hold her favorite annuals.

But now, all she felt was dread, and a vague, formless panic. After today, nothing in her well-ordered life would remain the same, and she was not a woman who liked the sharp, jagged edges of change. She preferred things to run smoothly, down the middle of the road. That was where she felt safest—in the center of the ordinary, with her family gathered close around her.

Wife.

Mother.

These were the roles that defined her, that gave her life meaning. It was what she'd always been, and now, as she warily approached her fortieth birthday, it was all she could remember ever wanting to be. She had gotten married right after college and been pregnant within that same year. Her husband and daughter were her anchors; without Blake and Natalie, she had often thought that she might float out to sea, a ship without captain or destination.

But what did a mother do when her only child left home?

She shifted uneasily in the front seat of the Cadillac. The clothes she'd chosen with such care this morning, navy wool pants and a pale rose silk blouse, felt wrong. Usually she could take refuge in fashionable camouflage, by pretending to be a woman she wasn't. Designer clothes and carefully applied makeup could make her *look* like the high-powered corporate wife she was supposed to be. But not today. Today, the waist-length brown hair she'd drawn back from her face in a chignon—the way her husband liked it, the way she always wore it—was giving her a headache.

She drummed her manicured fingernails on the armrest and glanced at Blake, who was settled comfortably in the driver's seat. He looked completely relaxed, as if this were a normal afternoon instead of the day their seventeen-year-old daughter was leaving for London.

It was childish to be so scared, she knew that, but knowing didn't ease the pain. When Natalie had first told them that she wanted to graduate early and spend her last quarter in London, Annie had been proud of her daughter's independence. It was the sort of thing that seniors at the expensive prep school often did, and precisely the sophisticated sort of adventure Annie had wanted for her daughter.

Annie herself would never have had the courage for so bold a move—not at seventeen, not even now at thirty-nine. Travel had always intimidated her. Although she loved seeing new places and meeting new people, she always felt an underlying discomfort when she left home.

She knew this weakness was a remnant of her youth, a normal by-product of the tragedy that had tainted her childhood, but understanding her fear didn't alleviate it. On every family vacation, Annie had suffered from nightmares—dark, twisted visions in which she was alone in a foreign land without money or direction. Lost, she wandered through unfamiliar streets, searching for the family that was her safety net, until, finally, sobbing in her sleep, she awoke. Then, she would curl into her husband's sleeping body and, at last, relax.

She had been proud of her daughter's independence and courage in choosing to go all the way to England by herself, but she hadn't realized how hard it would be to watch Natalie leave. They'd been like best friends, she and her daughter, ever since Natalie had emerged from the angry, sullen rubble of the early teen years. They'd had hard times, sure, and fights and hurt feelings, and they'd each said things that shouldn't have been said, but all that had only made their bond stronger. They were a unit, the "girls" in a household where the only man worked eighty hours a week and sometimes went whole days without remembering to smile.

She stared out the car window. The concrete-encrusted canyons of downtown Los Angeles were a blur of high-rise buildings, graffiti, and neon lights that left streaking reflections in the misty rain. They were getting closer and closer to the airport.

She reached for her husband, touched the pale blue cashmere of his sleeve. "Let's fly to London with Nana and get her settled with her host family. I know—"

"Mom," Natalie said sharply from the backseat. "Get real. It would be, like, *so* humiliating for you to show up."

Annie drew her hand back and plucked a tiny lint ball from her expensive wool pants. "It was just an idea," she said softly. "Your dad has been trying to get me to England for ages. I thought . . . maybe we could go now."

Blake gave her a quick look, one she couldn't quite read. "I haven't mentioned England in years." Then he muttered something about the traffic and slammed his hand on the horn.

"I guess you won't miss the California traffic," Annie said into the awkward silence that followed.

In the backseat, Natalie laughed. "No way. Sally Pritchart—you remember her, Mom, she went to London last year—anyway, Sally said it was way cool. Not like California, where you need a car to go anywhere. In London, all you do is get on the Underground." She poked her blond head into the opening between the two front seats. "Did you take the Underground when you were in London last year, Dad?"

Blake slammed on the horn again. With an irritated sigh, he flicked on his turn signal and jerked the car into the fast lane. "Huh? What was that?"

Natalie sighed. "Nothing."

Annie squeezed Blake's shoulder in a gentle reminder. These were precious moments—the last they'd see their daughter for months—and, as usual, he was missing them. She started to say something to fill the silence, something to keep from thinking about the loneliness of a house without Natalie, but then she saw the sign, LAX, and she couldn't say anything at all.

Blake pulled onto the exit ramp and drove into the dark silence of the underground parking lot, killing the engine. For a long moment, they all sat there. Annie waited for him to say something fatherly and important, something to mark the occasion. He was so good with words, but he merely opened his door.

As always, Annie followed his lead. She got out of the car and stood beside her door, twirling her sunglasses in her cold, cold fingers. She looked down at Natalie's luggage— a single gray duffle bag and a green canvas Eddie Bauer backpack.

She worried that it wasn't enough, that it was too un-wieldy . . . she worried about everything. Her daughter looked so young suddenly, her tall, thin body swamped by a baggy denim dress that stopped an inch above her scuffed black combat boots. Two metal clips held her long, silver-blond hair away from her pale face. Three silver earrings formed a curved ladder up her left ear.

Annie wanted to manufacture a conversation—toss out bits of advice about money and passports and the importance of always being in a group of kids—but she couldn't do it.

Blake walked on ahead, carrying the two lonely pieces of luggage, as Natalie and Annie followed silently in his wake. She wished he'd slow down and walk with them, but she didn't say anything—just in case Natalie hadn't noticed that her dad seemed to be in a rush. At the ticket counter, he handled everything, and then the three of them headed for the international terminal.

At the gate, Annie clung to her navy handbag as if it were a shield. Alone, she walked to the huge, dirty window. For a split second, she saw herself reflected in the glass, a thin, flawlessly dressed housewife standing by herself.

"Don't be so quiet, Mom. I can't take it." The words contained a tiny wobble of anxiety that only a mother would hear.

Annie forced a laugh. "Usually you guys are begging me to keep quiet. And it's not like I can't think of a million things to say right now. Why, just yesterday I was looking at your baby picture, and I thought—"

"I love you, too, Mom," Natalie whispered.

Annie grabbed her daughter's hand and held on. She didn't dare turn toward Natalie, afraid that her heartache would show. It was definitely not the image she wanted her child to carry like a bit of too-heavy baggage onto the plane.

Blake came up beside them. "I wish you had let us get you first-class tickets. It's such a long flight, and the food in coach is horrible. Christ, you'll probably have to assemble your own beef pot pie."

Natalie laughed. "Like you would know about the food in coach, Dad."

Blake grinned. "Well, it's certainly more comfortable."

"This isn't about comfort," Natalie answered. "It's about *adventure*."

"Ah, adventure," Annie said, finding her voice at last. She wondered how it felt to have such big dreams, and once again she was envious of her daughter's independence. Natalie was always so sure of who she was and what she wanted.

A voice boomed over the loudspeaker. "We will now begin boarding flight three-five-seven, with service to London."

"I'm going to miss you guys," Natalie said softly. She glanced at the plane, chewing nervously on her thumbnail.

Annie placed a hand on Natalie's soft cheek, trying to memorize everything about this moment, the tiny mole beside her daughter's left earlobe, the exact hue of her straight blond hair and blue eyes, the cinnamon sprinkling of freckles across her nose.

Annie wanted to implant it all into her memory so she could pull it out like a treasured photograph over the next three months. "Remember, we'll call every Monday— seven o'clock your time. You're going to have a great time, Nana."

Blake opened his arms. "Give your old dad a hug."

Natalie hurled herself into her father's arms.

Too soon, the voice came over the loudspeaker, announcing the boarding of Natalie's row.

Annie gave Natalie one last long, desperate hug—not nearly long enough—then, slowly, she drew back. Blinking away tears, she watched Natalie give her ticket to the woman at the doorway, and then, with a last, hurried wave, her daughter disappeared into the jetway.

"She'll be fine, Annie."

She stared at the empty doorway. "I know."

One tear, that's how long it took. One tear, sliding down Annie's face, and her daughter was gone.

Annie stood there long after the plane had left, long after the white trail of exhaust had melted into the somber sky. She could feel Blake beside her. She wished he'd take her hand or squeeze her shoulder or pull her into his arms— any of the things he would have done five years ago.

She turned. In his eyes, she saw her own reflection, and the misty mirror of their life together. She'd first kissed him when she was eighteen years old—almost Natalie's age—and there'd never been another man for her in all the years since.

His handsome face was as serious as she'd ever seen it. "Ah, Annie . . ." His voice was a cracked whisper of breath. "What will you do now?"

She was in danger of crumbling, right here in this sterile, crowded airport. "Take me home, Blake," she whispered unevenly. She wanted her things around her now, all the reminders of who she was.

"Of course." He grabbed her hand and led her through the terminal and into the garage. Wordlessly, they got into the Cadillac and slammed the doors shut. The air-conditioning came on instantly.

As the car hurtled down one freeway after another, Annie felt exhausted. She leaned back heavily in her seat and stared out the window at this city that had never become her city, although she and Blake had moved here right after college. It was a sprawling labyrinth of a town, where gorgeous, elaborately appointed dowager buildings were demolished daily by a few well-placed charges, where men and women with no appreciation for art or beauty or constancy set fire to fuses that blasted tons of sculptured marble and glass into piles of smoking, belching rubble. In this city of angels, too few noticed the loss of one more landmark. Before the collapsed building had even cooled, developers swarmed City Hall, climbing over one another like black ants for permits and easements. Within months, a sleek, glass-faced child of a building would rise higher and higher into the smoggy brown sky, so high that Annie often wondered if these builders thought they could access heaven with their leveraged millions.

She was seized by a fierce, unexpected longing to return home. Not to the crowded, affluent beauty of Malibu, but to the moist green landscape of her youth, that wild part of western Washington State where mushrooms grew to the size of dinner plates and water rushed in silver threads along every roadside, where fat, glossy raccoons came out in the light of a full moon and drank from mud puddles in the middle of the road. To Mystic—where the only sky-scrapers were Douglas firs that had been growing since the American Revolution. It had been almost ten years since she'd been back. Perhaps she could finally talk Blake into a trip now that they were no longer tethered to Southern California by Natalie's school schedule.

"What do you think about planning a trip to Mystic?" she asked her husband.

He didn't look at her, didn't respond to her question, and it made her feel stupid and small. She pulled at the large diamond stud in her ear and stared outside. "I was thinking about joining the Club. God knows I'll have more time on my hands now. You're always saying I don't get out of the house enough. Aerobics would be fun, don't you think?"

"I haven't said that in years."

"Oh. Well . . . there's always tennis. I used to love tennis. Remember when we used to play doubles?"

He turned off the freeway and eased onto the twisting, traffic-clogged Pacific Coast Highway. At the gated entrance to their road, he waved to the guard and passed into the Colony, the beachfront jewel of Malibu. Rain beaded the windshield and blurred the world for a split second, before the wipers swept the water away.

At their house, he slowed, inching down the brick-paved driveway. He stopped in front of the garage.

Annie glanced at him. It was odd that he hadn't pulled into the garage. Odd that he hadn't even hit the door's remote control. Odder still that he'd left the car running. He hated to leave the Cadillac out in the rain. . . .

He's not himself.

The realization sanded the hard edges from her anxiety, reminded her that she wasn't as alone as she felt. Her high-powered, ultra-competent husband was as fragile as she was right now.

They would do it together, she and Blake. They would

get each other through this day, and all the empty-nest days and nights to come. They had been a family before Natalie, and they would be one again, just the two of them. It might even be fun, like the old days when they had been best friends and partners and lovers . . . the days when they went out dancing and didn't come home until the sun was peeking up from the horizon.

She twisted around to face him, and brushed a lock of hair from his eyes. "I love you. We'll get each other through this."

He didn't answer.

She hadn't really expected him to, but still the awkward silence stung. She tucked the disappointment away and opened the car door. Tiny shards of rain slipped through the opening, mottling her sleeve. "It's going to be a lonely spring. Maybe we should talk to Lupita about planning a barbecue. We haven't had an old-fashioned beach party in years. It'd be good for us. God knows it's going to be weird walking around the house without—"

"Annie." He said her name so sharply that she bit her tongue in the middle of her sentence.

He turned to her, and she saw that there were tears in his eyes.

She leaned over and touched his cheek in a fleeting, tender caress. "I'm going to miss her, too."

He looked away and sighed heavily. "You don't under-stand. I want a divorce."

Chapter 2

"I meant to wait to tell you . . . at least until next week. But the thought of coming home tonight . . ." Blake shook his head and let the sentence trail off.

Very slowly, Annie closed the car door. Rain hit the windshield and ran in streaks down the windows, obscuring the world outside the car.

She couldn't have heard right. Frowning, she reached for him. "What are you talking about . . ."

He lurched against the window, as if her touch—the touch he'd known for so long—were now repugnant.

It all became real suddenly, with that gesture he wouldn't allow. Her husband was asking for a divorce. She drew back her hand and found that it was trembling.

"I should have done this a long time ago, Annie. I'm not happy. I haven't been happy with you in years."

The shock of it was unlike anything she'd ever experienced. It was everywhere, spreading through her in wave after numbing wave. Her voice was tangled deep, deep inside of her, and she couldn't find the frayed start of it.

"I can't believe I'm saying this," he said softly, and she

heard the choked-up thickness of his breathing. "I'm seeing someone else . . . another woman."

She stared at him, her mouth hanging open. He was having an *affair*. The word sank through her, hurting all the way to the bone. A thousand tiny details slipped into place: dinners he'd missed, trips he'd taken to exotic locations, the new silk boxer shorts he'd started wearing, the switch in colognes from Polo to Calvin Klein after all these years, the love they made so rarely . . .

How had she been so blind? She *must* have known. Deep inside, in some primitive feminine core, she must have known what was happening and chosen to ignore it.

She turned to him, wanting to touch him so badly it was a physical ache. For half her life, she'd touched him whenever she wanted, and now he had taken that right away. "We can get over an affair. . . ." Her voice was feeble, not her voice at all. "Couples do it all the time. I mean . . . it'll take me some time to forgive you, time to learn to trust, but—"

"I don't want your forgiveness."

This couldn't be happening. Not to her. Not to *them*. She heard the words and felt the pain, but it all had a dizzying sense of unreality about it. "But we have so much. We have *history*. We have Natalie. We can work this out, maybe try counseling. I know we've had problems, but we can get through it."

"I don't want to try, Annie. I want out."

"But *I* don't." Her voice spiked into a high, plaintive whine. "We're a *family*. You can't throw twenty years away. . . ." She couldn't find the words she needed. It terrified her, the sudden silence she found in her own soul; she was afraid there were words that could save her, save them, and she couldn't find them. "Please, *please* don't do this. . . ."

He didn't say anything for a long time—long enough for her to find a strand of hope and weave it into solid fabric. *He'll change his mind. He'll realize we're a family and say it was just a midlife crisis. He'll—*

"I'm in love with her."

Annie's stomach started a slow, agonized crumbling.

Love? How could he be in love with someone else? Love took time and effort. It was a million tiny moments stacked one atop another to make something tangible. That declaration—love—and everything it meant diminished her. She felt as if she were a tiny, disappearing person, a million miles away from the man she'd always loved. "How long?"

"Almost a year."

She felt the first hot sting of tears. A year in which everything between them had been a lie. Everything. "Who is she?"

"Suzannah James. The firm's new junior partner."

Suzannah James—one of the two dozen guests at Blake's birthday party last weekend. The thin young woman in the turquoise dress who'd hung on Blake's every word. The one he'd danced with to "A Kiss to Build a Dream On."

Tears stung Annie's eyes, turned everything into a blur. "But after the party, we made love. . . ."

Had he been imagining Suzannah's face in the darkness? Was that why he'd clicked off the bedroom lights before he touched her? A tiny, whimpering moan escaped her. She couldn't hold it all inside. "Blake, please . . ."

He looked helpless, a little lost himself, and in the moment of vulnerability, he was Blake again, her husband. Not this ice-cold man who wouldn't meet her gaze. "I love her, Annie. Please don't make me say it again."

The sour remains of his confession tainted the air, left her with nothing to breathe. *I love her, Annie.*

She wrenched the car door open and stumbled blindly down the brick walkway to her house. Rain hit her face and mingled with her tears. At the door, she pulled the keys from her handbag, but her hand was shaking so badly she couldn't find the lock on the first try. Then the key slipped into the slot and clicked hard.

She lurched inside and slammed the door shut behind her.

Annie finished her second glass of wine and poured a third. Usually two glasses of chardonnay left her giddy and reeling and trying to remember song lyrics from her youth, but tonight it wasn't helping.

She walked dully through her house, trying to figure out what she'd done that was so wrong, how she'd failed.

If only she knew that, maybe then she could make it all right again. She'd spent the past twenty years putting her family's needs first, and yet somehow she had failed, and her failure had left her alone, wandering around this too-big house, missing a daughter who was gone and a husband who was in love with someone else.

Somewhere along the way, she'd forgotten what she should have remembered. It was a lesson she'd learned early in life—one she'd thought she knew well. People left, and if you loved too deeply, too fiercely, their swift and sudden absence could chill you to the soul.

She climbed into her bed and burrowed under the covers, but when she realized that she was on "her" side of the bed, she felt as if she'd been slapped. The wine backed up into her throat, tasting sour enough that she thought she would vomit. She stared up at the ceiling, blinking back tears. With each ragged breath, she felt herself getting smaller and smaller.

What was she supposed to do now? It had been so long since she'd been anything but *we*. She didn't even know if there was an *I* inside of her anymore. Beside her, the bedside clock ticked and ticked . . . and she wept.

The phone rang.

Annie woke on the first ring, her heart pounding. It was him, calling to say it was all a mistake, that he was sorry, that he'd always loved her. But when she picked up the phone, it was Natalie, laughing. "Hey, Mom, I made it."

Her daughter's voice brought the heartache rushing back.

Annie sat up in bed, running a weak hand through her tangled hair. "Hi, honey. I can't believe you're there already." Her voice was thin and unsteady. She took a deep breath, trying to collect herself. "So, how was your flight?"

Natalie launched into a monologue that lasted for a steady fifteen minutes. Annie heard about the plane trip, the airport, about the strangeness of the London Underground, and the way the houses were all connected together—like, San Francisco, you know, Mom—

". . . Mom?"

Annie realized with a start that she'd lapsed into silence. She'd been listening to Natalie—she truly had—but some silly, pointless turn in the conversation had made her think of Blake, of the car that wasn't in the garage and the body that wasn't beside her in bed.

God, is that how it's going to be from now on?

"Mom?"

Annie squeezed her eyes shut, a feeble attempt to escape. There was a white, static roar of sound in her head. "I . . . I'm right here, Natalie. I'm sorry. You were telling me about your host family."

"Are you all right, Mom?"

Tears leaked down Annie's cheeks. She didn't bother to wipe them away. "I'm fine. How about you?"

A pause crackled through the lines. "I miss you guys."

Annie heard loneliness in her daughter's voice and it took all of her self-control not to whisper into the phone, *Come home, Nana. We'll be lonely together.*

"Trust me, Nana, you'll make friends. In no time at all, you'll be having so much fun that you won't be sitting by the phone waiting for your old mom to call. June fifteenth will come much too quickly."

"Hey, Mom, you sound kinda shaky. Are you going to be okay while I'm gone?"

Annie laughed; it was a nervous, fluttery sound. "Of course I will. Don't you dare worry about me."

"Okay." The word was spoken so softly Annie had to strain to hear it. "Before I start crying, I better talk to Daddy."

Annie flinched. "Dad's not here right now."

"Oh."

"He loves you, though. He told me to tell you that."

"Yeah, of course he does. So, you'll call Monday?"

"Like clockwork."

"I love you, Mom."

Annie felt tears flood her throat again, squeezing until she could hardly talk. She suppressed a fierce urge to warn

Natalie about the world, to tell her to watch out for lives that fall apart on a rainy spring day without warning. "Be careful, Natalie. Love you."

"Love you."

And the phone went dead.

Annie placed the handset back on the base and crawled out of bed, stumbling blindly into her bathroom. The lights came on like something out of an Oliver Stone movie. She stared in horror at her reflection. She was still wearing her clothes from the airport, and they were wrinkled into something she didn't recognize. Her hair was stuck so tightly to her head it looked as if she'd used Elmer's glue as conditioner.

She slammed her fist onto the light switch. In the blessed darkness, she stripped down to her bra and panties and left the wrinkled clothes in a heap on the tile floor. Feeling tired and old and swollen, she walked out of the bathroom and crawled back into bed.

She could smell him in the fabric of the sheets. Only it wasn't him. Blake—her Blake—had always worn Polo. She'd given him the cologne for Christmas every year; it came already wrapped for the holiday in a green gift box at Nordstrom. She'd given it to him every year and he'd worn it every day . . . until Calvin Klein and Suzannah changed everything.

Annie's best friend showed up bright and early the next morning, pounding on the front door, yelling, "Open up in there, goddamn it, or I'll call the fire department."

Annie slipped into Blake's black silk bathrobe and stumbled tiredly toward the front door. She felt like hell from the wine she'd drunk last night, and it took considerable effort simply to open the door. The expensive stone tiles felt icy cold beneath her bare feet.

Terri Spencer stood in the doorway, wearing a baggy pair of faded denim overalls. Her thick, curly nimbus of black hair was hidden by a wild scarlet scarf. Bold gold hoops hung from her ears. She looked exactly like the gypsy she played on a daytime soap. Terri crossed her arms, cocked one ample hip, and eyed Annie. "You look like shit."

Annie sighed. Of course Terri had heard. No matter how much of a free spirit her friend claimed to be, her current husband was a dyed-in-the-wool lawyer. And lawyers gossiped. "You've heard."

"I had to hear it from Frank. You could have called me yourself."

Annie ran a trembling hand through her tangled hair. They had been friends forever, she and Terri. Practically sisters. But even with all they'd been through together, all the ups and downs they'd weathered, Annie didn't know how to begin. She was used to taking care of Terri, with her wild, over-the-top actress lifestyle and her steady stream of divorces and marriages. Annie was used to taking care of everyone. Except Annie. "I meant to call, but it's been . . . difficult."

Terri curled a plump arm around Annie's shoulder and propelled her to the overstuffed sofa in the living room. Then she went from window to window, whipping open the white silk curtains. The twenty-foot-tall, wall-to-wall windows framed a sea and sky so blue it stung the eyes, and left Annie with nowhere to hide.

When Terri was through, she sat down beside Annie

on the sofa. "Now," she said softly. "What the fuck happened?"

Annie wished she could smile—it was what Terri wanted, why she'd used the vulgarity—but Annie couldn't respond. Saying it out loud would make it too real. She sagged forward, burying her puffy face in her hands. "Oh, God . . ."

Terri took Annie in her arms and held her tightly, rocking back and forth, smoothing the dirty hair from her sticky cheeks. It felt good to be held and comforted, to know that she wasn't as alone as she felt.

"You'll get through it," Terri said at last. "Right now, you think you won't, but you will. I promise. Blake's an asshole, anyway. You'll be better off without him."

Annie drew back and looked at her friend through a blur of stinging tears. "I don't . . . want to be without him."

"Of course you don't. I only meant . . ."

"I know what you meant. You meant that it will get easier. Like I'd trust your opinion on this. You change husbands more often than I change underwear."

Terri's thick black eyebrows winged upward. "Score one for the housewife. Look, Annie, I know I'm harsh and pessimistic, and that's why my marriages fail, but remember what I used to be like? Remember in college?"

Annie remembered, even though she wished she didn't. Terri used to be a sweet little Pollyanna; that's why they'd become best friends. Terri had stayed innocent until the day her first husband, Rom, had come home and told her he was having an affair with their accountant's daughter. Terri had had twenty-four hours' notice, and then *wham!* the checking account was gone, the savings had been mysteriously "spent," and the medical practice they'd built together had been sold to a buddy for one dollar.

Annie had been with Terri constantly back then, drinking wine in the middle of the day, even smoking pot on a few occasions. It had made Blake insane. *What are you doing still hanging around that cheap wanna-be, anyway?* he used to say. *You have dozens of more acceptable friends.* It had been one of the few times Annie had stood up to Blake.

"You stayed with me every day," Terri said softly, slipping her hand into Annie's and squeezing gently. "You got me through it, and I'm going to be here for you. Whenever you need me. Twenty-four hours a day."

"I didn't know how much it hurt. . . . It feels like . . ." The humiliating tears burned again. She wished she could stop them, but it was impossible.

"Like your insides are bleeding away . . . like nothing will ever make you happy again? I know."

Annie closed her eyes. Terri's understanding was almost more than she could bear. She didn't want her friend to know so much; not *Terri,* who'd never held a marriage together for more than a few years and couldn't even commit to owning a pet. It was terrifying to think that this was . . . ordinary. As if the loss of twenty years was nothing at all, just another divorce in a country that saw a million breakups a year.

"Look, kiddo, I hate to bring this up, but I have to. Blake's a hotshot attorney. You need to protect yourself."

It was bruising advice, the kind that made a woman want to curl up into a tiny, broken ball. Annie tried to smile. "Blake's not like that."

"Oh, really. You need to ask yourself how well you know him."

Annie couldn't deal with this now. It was enough to realize that the past year had been a lie; she couldn't fathom the possibility that Blake had become a complete stranger. She stared at Terri, hoping her friend could understand. "You're asking me to be someone I'm not, Terri. I mean, to walk into a bank and clean out the money, *our* money. It's so . . . final. And it makes this about things . . . just things. I can't do it to Blake. I can't do it to *me*. I know it's naive—stupid, even—to trust him, but he's been my best friend for more than half my life."

"Some friend."

Annie touched her friend's plump hand. "I love you for worrying about me, Terri. Really, I do, but I'm not ready for this advice. I hope . . ." Her voice fell to a whisper. She felt hopelessly naive when she looked into Terri's sad, knowing eyes. "I still hope I don't need it, I guess."

Terri forced a bright smile. "Maybe you're right. Maybe it's just a midlife crisis and he'll get over it."

They spent the next few hours talking. Time and again, Annie pulled a memory or an anecdote out of the black hat of her marriage and tossed it out, as if *talking* about her life, remembering it, would bring him home.

Terri listened and smiled and held her, but she didn't offer any more real-world advice—and Annie was thankful. Sometime around noon they ordered a large lamb sausage pizza from Granita's, and they sat on the deck and ate the whole thing. As the sun finally set across the blue Pacific, Annie knew that Terri would have to go soon.

Annie turned to her best friend. Finally, she asked the question that had been hovering for the better part of the afternoon. "What if he doesn't come back, Terri?" She said it so quietly that, for a moment, she thought the words were buried in the distant sound of the surf.

"What if he doesn't?"

Annie looked away. "I can't imagine my life without him. What will I do? Where will I go?"

"You'll go home," Terri said. "If I'd had a dad as cool as Hank, I would have gone home in an instant."

Home. It struck her for the first time that the word was as fragile as bone china. "Home is with Blake."

"Ah, Annie." Terri sighed, squeezing her hand. "Not anymore."

Two days later, he called.

His voice was the sweetest sound she'd ever heard. "Blake . . ."

"I need to see you."

She swallowed hard, felt the sudden sting of tears. *Thank you, God. I knew he'd come back.* "Now?"

"No. My schedule's kind of tight this morning. As soon as I can break free."

For the first time in days, Annie could breathe.

When Blake stared at the soaring white angles of the house, he felt an unexpected pang of loss. It was so beautiful, this home of theirs, so stunningly contemporary. A real showpiece on a street where teardowns routinely cost five million dollars and nothing was too expensive.

Annie had conceived, created, and designed this place. She'd taken the view—sea and sand and sky—and translated it into a home that seemed to have grown out of the hillside. She'd chosen every tile, every fixture; all through the house were incongruous little items of whimsy—an angel here, a gargoyle there, a ratty old macrame plant hanger in the corner of a room with thousand-dollar-a-square-foot wooden paneling, a family photo in a home-made shell frame. There was no place inside that didn't reflect her bubbling, slightly off-center personality.

He tried to remember what it had felt like to love her, but he couldn't anymore.

He'd been sleeping with other women for ten years, seducing them and bedding them and forgetting them. He'd traveled with them, spent the night with them, and through it all, Annie had been at home, baking recipes from *Gourmet* magazine and picking out paint chips and tile samples and driving Natalie to and from school. He'd thought sooner or later she'd notice that he'd fallen out of love with her, but she was so damn trusting. She always believed the best of everyone, and when she loved, it was body and soul, forever.

He sighed, suddenly feeling tired. It was turning forty that had changed his outlook, made him realize that he didn't want to be locked in a loveless marriage anymore.

Before the gray had moved its ugly fingers into his hair and lines had settled beneath his blue eyes, he thought he had it all—a glamorous career, a beautiful wife, a loving daughter, and all the freedom he needed.

He traveled with his college buddies twice a year, went on fishing trips to remote islands with pretty beaches and prettier women; he played basketball two nights a week and closed the local bar down on Friday nights. Unlike most of his friends, he'd always had a wife who under-stood, who stayed at home. The perfect wife and mother—everything that he thought he wanted.

Then he met Suzannah. What had begun as just another

sexual conquest rolled into the most unexpected thing of all: love.

For the first time in years, he felt young and alive. They made love everywhere, all times of the day and night. Suzannah never cared what the neighbors thought or worried about a sleeping child in the next room. She was wild and unpredictable, and she was smart—unlike Annie, who thought the PTA was as vital to world order as the EEC.

He walked slowly down to the front door. Before he could even reach for the bell, the hand-carved rosewood door opened.

She stood in the doorway, her hands clasped nervously at her waist. A creamy silk dress clung to her body, and he couldn't help noticing that she'd lost weight in the past few days—and God knew she couldn't afford it.

Her small, heart-shaped face was pale, alarmingly so, and her eyes, usually as bright and green as shamrocks, were dull and bloodshot. She'd pulled her long hair into a tight ponytail that accentuated the sharp lines of her cheekbones and made her lips look swollen. Her earrings didn't match; she was wearing one diamond and one pearl, and somehow that little incongruity brought home the stinging pain of his betrayal.

"Blake . . ." He heard the thin lilt of hope in her voice, and realized suddenly what she must have thought when he called this morning.

Shit. How could he have been so stupid?

She backed away from the door, smoothing a nonexistent wrinkle from her dress. "Come in, come in. You . . ." She looked away quickly, but not before he saw her bite down on her lower lip—the nervous habit she'd had since she was young. He thought she was going to say something, but at the last minute she turned and led the way down the hallway and out onto the huge, multitiered deck that over-looked the Colony's quiet patch of Malibu beach.

Christ, he wished he hadn't come. He didn't need to see her pain in sharp relief, in the way she kept smoothing her dress and jabbing at her hair.

She crossed to the table, where a pitcher of lemonade—his favorite—and two crystal glasses sat on an elegant silver tray. "Natalie's settling in well. I've only talked to her once—and I was going to call again, but . . . well . . . it's been hard. I thought she might hear something in my voice. And, of course, she'll ask for you. Maybe later . . . while you're here . . . we could call again."

"I shouldn't have come." He said it more sharply than he intended, but he couldn't stand to hear the tremor in her voice anymore.

Her hand jerked. Lemonade splashed over the rim of the glass and puddled on the gray stone table. She didn't turn to him, and he was glad. He didn't want to see her face.

"Why did you?"

Something in her voice—resignation, maybe, or pain—caught him off guard. Tears burned behind his eyes; he couldn't believe this was *hurting*. He reached into his pocket and pulled out the interim settlement papers he'd drafted. Wordlessly, he leaned over her shoulder and dropped them on the table. An edge of the envelope landed in the spilled lemonade. A dark, bubbling splotch began to form.

He couldn't seem to draw his eyes from the stain. "Those are the papers, Annie. . . ."

She didn't move, didn't answer, just stood there with her back to him.

She looked pathetic, with her shoulders hunched and her fingers curled around the table's edge. He didn't need to see her face to know what she was feeling. He could see the tears falling, one after another, splashing on the stone like tiny drops of rain.

Chapter 3

"I can't believe you're doing this." Annie hadn't meant to say anything, but the words formed themselves. When he didn't answer, she turned toward him. Sadly, after almost twenty years of marriage, she couldn't bear to meet his eyes. "Why?"

That's what she really wanted to understand. She'd always put her family's needs above her own, always done everything she could to make her loved ones feel safe and happy. It had started long before she met Blake, in her childhood. Her mother had died when Annie was very young, and she'd learned how to seal her own grief in airtight compartments stored far from her heart. Unable to comprehend her loss, she'd focused on her grieving father. It had become, over the years, her defining characteristic. Annie the caretaker, the giver of love. But now her husband didn't want her love anymore, didn't want to be a part of the family she'd created and cared for.

"Let's not rehash it again," he said with a heavy sigh.

The words were like a slap. She snapped her head up and looked at him. "Rehash it? Are you *joking*?"

He looked sad and tired. "When did you ever know me to joke?" He shoved a hand through his perfectly cut hair. "I didn't think about what you'd . . . infer from my phone call this morning. I'm sorry."

Infer. A cold, legal word that seemed to separate them even more.

He moved toward her, but was careful not to get too close. "I'll take care of you. That's what I came to say. You don't have to worry about money or anything else. I'll take good care of you and Natalie. I promise."

She stared at him in disbelief. "February nineteenth. You remember that date, Blake?"

His million-dollar tan faded to a waxen gray. "Now, Annalise—"

"Don't you 'now, Annalise' me. February nineteenth. Our wedding day. You remember that day, Blake? You said—you *vowed*—to love me till death parted us. You promised to take care of me on that day, too."

"That was a long time ago."

"You think a promise like that has an expiration date, like a carton of milk? God . . ."

"I've changed, Annie. Hell, we've been together more than twenty years; we've both changed. I think you'll be happier without me. I really do. You can focus on all those hobbies you never had time for. You know . . ." He looked acutely out of his depth. "Like that calligraphy stuff. And writing those little stories. And painting."

She wanted to tell him to get the hell out, but the words tangled with memories in her head, and it all hurt so badly.

He came up beside her, his footsteps clipped and harsh on the stone flooring. "I've drafted a tentative settlement. It's more than generous."

"I won't make it that easy for you."

"What?"

She could tell by his voice that she'd surprised him, and it was no wonder. Their years together had taught him to expect no protest from Annie about anything. She looked up at him. "I said, I won't make it easy for you, Blake. Not this time."

"You can't stop a divorce in California." He said it softly, in his lawyer's voice.

"I know the law, Blake. Did you forget that I worked beside you for years, building the law firm with you? Or do you only remember the hours *you* put in at the office?" She moved toward him, careful not to touch him. "If you were a client, what advice would you give?"

He tugged at his starched collar. "This isn't relevant."

"You'd tell yourself to wait, spend some 'cooling off' time. You'd recommend a trial separation. I've *heard* you say it." The words tripped her up in sadness. "Jesus, Blake, won't you even give us that chance?"

"Annalise—"

She kept tears at bay one trembling breath at a time. Everything hung on the thread of this moment. "Promise me we'll wait until June—when Natalie gets home. We'll talk again . . . see where we are after a few months apart. I gave you twenty years, Blake. You can give me three months."

She felt the seconds tick by, slicing tiny nicks across her soul. She could hear the even, measured cant of his breathing, the lullaby that had eased her into sleep for more than half her life.

"All right."

The relief was overwhelming. "What are we going to tell Natalie?"

"Christ, Annie, it's not like she's going to have a heart attack. Most of her friends' parents are divorced. That's half of our goddamn problem, all you ever think about is Natalie. Tell her the truth."

Annie felt her first spark of true anger. "Don't you dare make this about motherhood, Blake. You're leaving me because you're a selfish prick."

"A selfish prick who's in love with someone else."

The words cut as deeply as he intended them to. Tears burned behind her eyes, blurred her vision, but she'd be damned if she'd let them fall. She should have known better than to fight with him—she had no practice, and hurtful words were his profession. "So you say."

"Fine," he said in a clipped, even voice, and she knew by the tone of it that this conversation was over. "What do you want to tell Natalie and when?"

This was the one answer she had. She might be a complete failure as a wife and lover, but she knew how to take care of her daughter. "Nothing for now. I don't want to ruin this trip for her. We'll tell her . . . whatever we need to . . . when she gets home."

"Fine."

"Fine."

"I'll send someone over tomorrow to pick up a few of my things. I'll have the Cadillac returned on Monday."

Things. That's what it came down to after all these years. The bits and pieces that were their life—his toothbrush, her hot rollers, his album collection, her jewelry—became just things to be divided up and packed in separate suitcases.

He picked up the envelope from the table and held it out to her. "Open it."

"Why? So I can see how generous you've been with *our* money?"

"Annie—"

She waved a hand. "I don't care who owns what."

He frowned. "Be sensible, Annie."

She looked at him sharply. "That's what my dad said to me when I told him I wanted to marry a skinny, dirt-poor, twenty-year-old kid. *Be sensible, Annie. There's no rush. You're young.* But I'm not young anymore, am I, Blake?"

"Annie, please . . ."

"Please what—please don't make this hard on you?"

"Look at the papers, Annie."

She moved closer, stared up at him through her tears. "There's only one asset I want, Blake." Her throat closed up and it became hard to speak. "My heart. I want it back in one piece. Have you given me that in your precious papers?"

He rolled his eyes. "I should have expected this from you. Fine. I'll be living at Suzannah's house if there's an emergency." He pulled out a pen and wrote on a scrap of paper from his wallet. "Here's the number."

She wouldn't take the piece of paper from him. He let go and it fluttered to the floor.

Annie lay perfectly still in her king-size bed, listening to the familiar sound of her own breathing, the steady rhythm of her own heart. She wanted to pick up the phone and call Terri, but she'd already leaned on her best friend too much. They'd talked daily, for hours and hours, as if talking could ease Annie's heartache, and when their conversations ended, Annie felt more alone than ever.

The last week had passed in a blur, seven endless days since her husband had told her he was in love with someone else. Each lonely night and empty day seemed to hack another bit of her away. Soon, she'd be too small for anyone to notice at all.

Sometimes, when she awoke, she was screaming, and the nightmare was always the same. She was in a dark room, staring into a gilt-edged mirror—only there was no reflection in the glass.

Throwing back the covers, she climbed out of bed and went to her walk-in closet. She yanked open her lingerie drawer and pulled out a big gray box. Clasping the box to her chest, she moved woodenly back to the bed. A lifetime's collection of photographs and mementos lay at her fingertips, all the favorite pictures she'd snapped and saved over the years. She went through them slowly, savoring each one. At the bottom of the box, she found a small bronze compass, a long-ago gift from her father. There was no inscription on it, but she still remembered the day he'd given it to her, and the words he'd said: *I know you feel lost now, but it won't last forever, and this will make sure that you can always find your way home again . . . where I'll always be waiting.*

She clutched the bit of metal in one hand, wondering when and why she'd ever taken it off. Very slowly, she slipped it around her neck again, then she turned to the photographs, beginning with the black-and-white ones, the Kodak trail of her own childhood. Small, dog-eared photos with the date stamped in black across the top. There were dozens of her alone, a few of her with her daddy. And one of her with her mother.

One.

She could remember the day it was taken; she and her mom had been making Christmas cookies. There was flour everywhere, on the counter, on Annie's face, on the floor. Her dad had come in from work and laughed at them. *Good God, Sarah, you're making enough for an army. There's just the three of us. . . .*

Only a few months later, there were only two of them. A quiet, grieving man and his even quieter little girl.

Annie traced the smooth surface of the print with her fingertip. She'd missed her mother so often over the years—at high school graduation, on her wedding day, on the day Natalie was born—but never as much as she missed her now. *I need you, Mom,* she thought for the millionth time. *I need you to tell me that everything will be all right. . . .*

She replaced the treasured photograph in the box and picked up a colored one that showed Annie holding a tiny, blotchy-faced newborn wrapped in a pink blanket. And there was Blake, looking young and handsome and proud, his big hand curled protectively around his baby girl. She went through dozens more pictures, following Natalie's life from infant to high school senior, from graham crackers to mascara.

Natalie's whole life lay in this box. There were countless pictures of a smiling, blue-eyed blond girl, standing alongside a succession of stuffed animals and bicycles and family pets. Somewhere along the way, Blake had stopped appearing in the family photos. How was it that Annie had never noticed that before?

But Blake wasn't who she was really looking for.

She was looking for Annie. The truth sank through her, twisting and hurting, but she couldn't give up. Somewhere in this box that held the tangible memories of her life, she had to find herself. She went through print after print, tossing aside one after another.

There were almost no pictures of her. Like most mothers, she was always behind the camera, and when she thought she looked tired, or fat, or thin, or ugly . . . she ripped the photo in half and ditched it.

Now, it was as if she'd never been there at all. As if she'd never really existed.

The thought scared her so badly, she lurched out of bed, shoving the photographs aside with a sweep of her hand. As she passed the French doors, she caught sight of a disheveled, desperate-looking middle-aged woman in her husband's bathrobe. It was pathetic what she was becoming. Even more pathetic than what she'd been before.

How dare he do this to her? Take twenty years of her life and then discard her like a sweater that no longer fit.

She strode to the closet, ripping his clothes from their expensive hangers and shoving them in the garbage. Then she went to his study, his precious study. Wrenching the desk drawer open, she yanked everything out.

In the back of one drawer, she found dozens of recent charge slips for flowers and hotel rooms and lingerie.

Her anger turned into an honest-to-God fury. She threw it all—charge slips, bills, appointment reminders, the checkbook register—in a huge cardboard box. On it, in big bold letters, she wrote his name and office address. In smaller letters, she wrote: *I did this for twenty years. Now it's your turn.*

Breathing hard, feeling better than she had in days, she looked around at her perfect, empty house.

What would she do now? Where would she go? She touched the compass at her throat and she knew.

Perhaps she'd known all along.

She'd go back to the girl she'd seen in those rare black-and-white photos . . . back to where she was someone besides Blake's wife and Natalie's mother.

Part Two

In the midst of winter, I finally learned that there was in me
an invincible summer.
—ALBERT CAMUS

Chapter 4

After hours of flying and driving, Annie was finally steering her rental car across the long floating bridge that connected the Olympic Peninsula to the rest of Washington State. On one side of the bridge, the waves were in a white-tipped frenzy; on the other side, the water was as calm and silvery as a newly minted coin. She rolled down the window and flicked off the air conditioner. Sweet, misty air swept into the car, swirling tiny tendrils of hair across her face.

Mile by mile, the landscape rolled into the vivid greens and blues of her childhood world. She turned off the modern freeway and onto the two-lane road that led away from the shore. Under a purplish layer of fog, the peninsula lay hidden, a pork chop of land ringed by towering, snow-capped mountains on one side and wild, windswept beaches on the other. It was a primitive place, untouched by the hustle and bustle of modern life. Old-growth forests were draped in skeins of silvery moss, and craggy coastlines were sheltered from the raging surf by a towering curtain of rock. At the heart of the peninsula was the

Olympic National Park, almost a million acres of no-man's-land, ruled by Mother Nature and the myths of the Native Americans who had lived here long before the white pioneers.

As she neared her hometown, the forests became dense and dark, covered still in the early spring by a shimmering, opalescent mist that concealed the serrated tips of the trees. It was the time of year when the forests were still hibernating, and night fell before the last school bell had rung. No sane person ventured off the main road until early summer; legends were told and retold of children who did and were never seen again, of Sasquatches who roamed the thickets of this wood at night, snatching up unsuspecting tourists. For here, in the deepest reaches of the rain forest, the weather could change faster than a teenage girl's mind; it could turn from sunshine to snow in a heartbeat, leaving nothing but a blood red rainbow that wept into ebony at the edges.

It was an ancient land, a place where giant red cedar trees grew three hundred feet into the sky and fell into utter silence, to die and reseed among their own, where time was marked by tides and tree rings and salmon runs.

When Annie finally reached the town of Mystic, she slowed her speed, soaking in the familiar sights. It was a small logging community, carved by early, idealistic pioneers from the great Quinault rain forest. Main Street ran for only six blocks. She didn't have to reach its end to know that at Elm Street the rutted asphalt gave way to a puddled, pockmarked gravel road.

Downtown wore the shabby, forgotten look of a white-haired old man left out in the rain. A single, tired stoplight guided nonexistent traffic past the huddled group of brick-

and wood-fronted stores. Fifteen years ago, Mystic had been a booming town supported by fishing and logging, but the intervening years had obviously been hard ones that had driven merchants to more lucrative communities and left in their wake several vacant storefronts.

Rusted pickup trucks were parked at an angle behind thirty-year-old meters; only a few people in faded overalls and heavy winter overcoats could be seen on the sidewalks.

The stores that were left had down-home names: The I of the Needle fabric shop, the Holey Moses Doughnut counter, the Kiddie Corner consignment clothing store, Dwayne's Lanes bowling alley, Eve's Leaves Dress Emporium, Vittorio's Italian Ristorante. Each window displayed a placard that read THIS ESTABLISHMENT SUPPORTED BY LOGGING—a resentful reminder to distant politicians, living in pillared homes in faraway cities, that logging was the lifeblood of this region.

It was an exhausted little logging town, but to Annie, whose eyes had grown accustomed to steel and concrete and glass, it was gorgeous. The sky now was gray, but she could remember how it looked without the cover of clouds. Here, in Mystic, the sky started deep in the palm of God's hand and unfurled as far as the eye could see. It was a grand land of sublime landscapes, with air that smelled of pine needles and mist and rain.

So unlike Southern California.

The thought came unwanted, a stinging little reminder that she was a thirty-nine-year-old woman, perched on the edge of an unwanted divorce. That she was coming home because she had nowhere else to go.

She tried not to think about Blake or Natalie or that big, empty house perched precariously above the beach. Instead, she remembered the things she didn't mind leaving behind—the heat that always gave her a headache, the cancer she could feel lurking in the invisible rays of the sun, the smog that stung her eyes and burned her throat. The "bad air" days when you were advised to stay indoors, the mud slides and fires that took out whole neighborhoods in a single afternoon.

Annie had roots in this county that went deep and spread far. Her grandfather had come here almost seventy years ago, a block-jawed German with an appetite for freedom and a willingness to use a saw. He had carved a good living from the land and raised his only son, Hank, to do the same. Annie was the first Bourne in two generations to leave this soil, and the first to get a college education.

She followed Elm Street out of town. On both sides of the road, the land had been cut into bite-size pieces. Modular homes huddled on squares of grass, behind yards cluttered with broken-down cars and washing machines that had seen better days. Everywhere she looked, Annie saw the evidence of logging: trucks, chainsaws, and signs about the spotted owl.

The road began its slow, winding crawl up the hillside, thrusting deeper and deeper into the forests. One by one, the houses receded, giving way to trees. Miles and miles of scrawny, new-growth trees huddled behind signs that read: CLEARCUT 1992. REPLANTED 1993. There was a new sign every quarter mile or so; only the dates were different.

Finally, she reached the turnoff to the gravel road that meandered through fifteen acres of old-growth timber.

As a child, this woodland had been her playground. She had spent countless hours climbing through the dewy salal bushes and over crumbling nurse logs, in search of treasures: a white mushroom that grew only by the light of a red moon, a newborn fawn awaiting its mother's return, a gelatinous cache of frog's eggs hidden in the bogs.

At last, she came to the two-story clapboard farmhouse in which she'd grown up. It looked exactly as she remembered: a gabled, fifty-year-old structure painted a pale pearl gray with white trim. A whitewashed porch ringed the whole house, and baskets of winter-spindly geraniums hung from every post. Smoke spiraled up from the brick chimney and merged into the low-slung layer of gray fog overhead.

Behind it, a battalion of ancient trees protected a secret, fern-lined pond. Moss furred the tree trunks and hung in lacy shawls from one branch to another. The lawn melted down toward the silvery ribbon of a salmon stream. She knew that if she walked across the grass, it would squish between her toes, and this time of year, the stream would sound like an old man snoring in his sleep.

She maneuvered the rented Mustang to the parking area behind the woodshed and shut off the engine. Grabbing her purse, she walked up to the front door.

Only a moment after she rang the bell, her father opened the door.

The great Hank Bourne—all six feet three inches and 220 pounds of him—stood there for a second, staring at his daughter with disbelieving eyes. Then a smile started, buried deep in his silvery-white mustache and beard.

"Annie," he whispered in that scratchy, barrel-chested voice of his.

His arms opened for a hug, and she launched herself forward, burying her face in the velvety folds of his neck. He smelled of woodsmoke and Irish Spring soap and of the butterscotch hard candies he always kept in the breast pocket of his work shirt. Of her childhood.

Annie let herself be carried away by the comfort of her father's embrace. At last, she drew back, unable to look at him, knowing he'd see the tears in her eyes. "Hi, Dad."

"Annie," he said again, only this time she heard the question he didn't ask.

She forced herself to meet his probing gaze. He looked good for his sixty-seven years. His eyes were still as bright and curious as a young man's, even tucked as they were in folds of ruddy pink skin. The tragedies he'd endured appeared only occasionally and quickly retreated—a shadow that crossed his wrinkled face when a stoplight turned red on a rainy day, or when the heartless sound of an ambulance's siren cut through the fog.

He tucked a scarred hand—cut long ago by the unforgiving blades at the lumber mill—into the bib of his faded denim overalls. "You alone, Annie?"

She flinched. The question contained layers and layers. There were so many ways to answer.

He looked at her so intensely she felt uncomfortable, as if he were seeing into her soul, into that big house on the Pacific Ocean where her husband had said, *I don't love you, Annie.*

"Natalie left for London," she said weakly.

"I know. I've been waiting for you to call with the address. I thought I'd send her something."

"She's staying with a family called Roberson. It's raining every day, cats and dogs from what I und—"

"What's going on, Annie Virginia?"

She swallowed the rest of her sentence on a gulp of

breath. There was nowhere now to go except forward. "He . . . he left me, Dad."

He looked hopelessly confused. "What?"

She wanted to laugh and pretend it was nothing, that she was plenty strong enough to deal with this, but she felt like a kid again, tongue-tied and lost.

"What happened?" he asked softly.

She shrugged. "It's an old story. He's forty . . . and she's twenty-eight."

Hank's lean, wrinkled face fell. "Oh, honey . . ." She saw him search for words, and saw the sadness fill his eyes when he came up empty. He moved toward her, pressed a dry-skinned palm against her face. For a heartbeat, the past came forward, slid into the present; she knew they were both remembering another day, long ago, when Hank had told his seven-year-old daughter that there'd been an accident . . . that Mommy had gone to heaven. . . .

She's gone, honey. She won't be coming back.

In the silence that followed, Hank hugged his daughter. She laid her cheek against the comforting flannel of his plaid work shirt. She wanted to ask him for some words of advice, some comforting thought to take to her lonely bed-room and curl up into, but they'd never had that kind of rela-tionship. Hank had never been comfortable handing out fatherly wisdom. "He'll be back," he said quietly. "Men can be pretty damn stupid. But Blake will realize what he's done, and he'll be back, begging for a second chance."

"I want to believe that, Dad."

Hank smiled, apparently bolstered by the effect of his words. "Trust me, Annie. That man loves you. I knew it the first time I saw him. You were too young to get married, I knew, but you were a sensible girl, and I said to myself, now *there's* a boy who's going to take care of my daughter. He'll be back. Now, how about if we settle you into your old bedroom and then bring out the old chessboard?"

"That'd be perfect."

Hank reached out and grabbed her hand. Together they walked through the sparsely decorated living room and up the rickety stairs that led to the second floor.

At Annie's old bedroom, Hank turned the knob and pushed the door open. The room was a wash of yellow-gold wallpaper lit by the last lavender rays of the fading sun; it was a young girl's floral print, chosen by a loving mother a lifetime ago, and never changed. Neither Annie nor Hank had ever considered peeling the paper off, not even when Annie had outgrown it. A spindly white iron double bed dominated the room, its surface piled high with yellow and white quilts. Beside a narrow double-hung window sat a twig rocker, the one her father had made for her on her thirteenth birthday. *You're a woman now,* he'd said, *you'll be wanting a woman's chair.*

She had spent much of her youth in that chair, gazing out at the endless night, clipping photographs of celebrities from a *Teen Beat* magazine, writing gushy fan letters to Bobby Sherman and David Cassidy, dreaming of the man she would someday wed.

He'll be back. She wrapped Hank's words around her, letting them become a shield against the other, darker thoughts. She wanted desperately to believe her dad was right.

Because if he was wrong, if Blake didn't come back, Annie had no idea who she was or where she belonged.

Chapter 5

The night had passed in fitful waves. On several occasions, Annie woke with a start, the remnant of a sob floating in the darkness around her, the sheets coiled about her legs, damp and sour smelling. She'd spent the past four days wandering around this old farmhouse like a lost spirit, feeling restless and bruised. She rarely ventured far from the phone.

I made a mistake, Annie. I'm sorry; I love you. If you come home to me I'll never see Suzannah again. She waited for the call all day, and then, at night, she collapsed into a troubled sleep and dreamed about it again.

She knew she should do something, but she had no idea what. All her life she'd taken care of people, she'd used her life to create a perfect setting for Blake's and Natalie's lives, and now, alone, she was lost.

Go back to sleep. That was it. She'd burrow under the down comforter again and sleep. . . .

There was a knock at her door. "I'll be out in a while," she mumbled, reaching for her pillow.

The door swung open. Hank stood in the opening. He

was wearing a red and blue plaid flannel shirt and a pair of bleached, stained denim overalls—the makeshift uniform he'd worn to the lumber mill for almost forty years. He was holding a tray full of food. Disapproval etched his face, narrowed his eyes. He carefully set down the tray and crossed the room. "You look like hell."

Stupidly, she burst into tears. She knew it was true. She was thin and ugly and dirty—and no one, including Blake, would ever want her again. The thought made her sick to her stomach. She clamped a hand over her mouth and raced to the bathroom. It was humiliating to know that her father could hear her retching, but she couldn't help it. Afterward, she brushed her teeth and moved shakily back into her room.

The worry in Hank's eyes cut like a knife.

"That's it," he said, clapping his hands together. "You're going in to see the doctor. Get your clothes."

The thought of going out, of *leaving*, filled her with horror. "I can't. People will . . ." She didn't even know what she was afraid of. She only knew that in this room, here in her little girl's bed, she felt safe.

"I can still throw you over my shoulder, kiddo. Either get dressed or go into town in those pajamas. It's up to you. But you're going to town."

She wanted to argue, but she knew her father was right, and frankly, it felt good to be taken care of. "Okay, okay." She made her way slowly into the bathroom and re-dressed in the same rumpled clothes she'd worn on her trip up here. Putting her hair up was way too much for her; instead, she finger-combed it and covered her bloodshot, baggy eyes with sunglasses. "Let's go."

* * *

Annie stared out the half-open window of her dad's Ford pickup. Behind her head, the empty gun rack clattered against the glass.

He maneuvered the vehicle expertly between the potholes in the road and pulled up in front of a squat, brick building. A handpainted sign read MYSTIC MEDICAL CLINIC. DR. GERALD BURTON, FAMILY PRACTITIONER.

Annie smiled. She hadn't thought about old Doc Burton in years. He had delivered Annie into the world and seen her through almost two decades of colds and ear infections and childhood accidents. He was as much a part of her youth as braces, proms, and skinny-dips in Lake Crescent.

Hank clicked off the engine. The old Ford sputtered, coughed, and fell silent. "It seems odd to be bringing you back here. I'm suddenly afraid I missed a booster shot and they won't let you start school."

Annie smiled. "Maybe Doc Burton will give me a grape sucker if I'm good."

Hank turned to her. "You were always good, Annalise. Don't you forget it."

His words brought it swelling back inside her, sent her falling back into that big house by the sea where her husband had told her he loved another woman. Before the sadness could get a good hold, she squared her shoulders and opened her door. "I'll meet you at . . ." She glanced around, wondering what was still around.

"The riverpark. You used to love it down there."

"The riverpark," she said, recalling all the evenings she had spent down at the bank, crawling through the mud, looking for fish eggs and dragonflies. With a nod, she climbed down out of the truck, hitched her bag over her shoulder, and strode up the concrete steps to the clinic's front door.

Inside, a blue-haired old lady looked up at her. Her name tag read, HI! I'M MADGE. "Hello. May I help you?"

Annie suddenly felt conspicuous in her rumpled clothes, with her hair hanging limp and lifeless around her face. Thank God the sunglasses hid her eyes. "I'm Annie Colwater. I'd like to see Doctor Burton. I think my father made an appointment."

"He sure did, darlin'. Have a seat. Doc'll see you in a jiff."

After she filled out the insurance forms, Annie took a seat in the waiting room, flipping idly through the newest issue of *People* magazine. She hadn't waited more than fifteen minutes when Dr. Burton rounded the corner and strolled into the waiting room. The ten years she'd been gone showed in the folds of red skin along his neck and in the amount of hair he'd lost, but he was still old Doc Burton, the only man in all of Mystic who religiously wore a tie to work.

"Well, Annie Bourne, as I live and breathe."

She grinned up at the old man. "It's been a long time."

"So it has. Come, come." He slipped an arm around her shoulder and led her into the nearest examining room. She hopped up onto the paper-covered table and crossed her feet at the ankles.

He sat in a flecked, yellow plastic chair opposite her, eyeing her. Coke-bottle-thick glasses magnified his eyes to the size of dinner plates. She wondered how many years ago he'd started to lose his vision. "You don't look so hot."

She managed a smile. Apparently his vision wasn't all

that lost. "That's why I'm here. Hank said I look like hell—he figured it must be a disease."

He let out a horsey laugh and opened a manila folder, poising a pen on the blank page. "Sounds like Hank. Last time I saw him he had a migraine—and he was sure it was a brain tumor. So, what's going on with you?"

She found it hard to begin. "I haven't been sleeping well . . . headaches . . . sick to my stomach . . . that sort of thing."

"Any chance you could be pregnant?"

She should have been prepared for the question. If she'd been ready, it wouldn't have hurt so much. But it had been years since any doctor had asked the sensitive question. Her own doctors knew the answer too well. "No chance."

"Any hot flashes, irregular periods?"

She shrugged. "My periods have always been irregular. In the last year, I've skipped a couple of months completely. Frankly, it's not something I worry about—missing a period. And yes, my own gynecologist has warned me that menopause could be just around the corner."

"I don't know . . . you're a little young for that. . . ."

She smiled. "Bless you."

He closed the chart, laid it gently across his lap, then looked up at her again. "Is there something going on in your life that would lead to depression?"

Depression.

One word to describe a mountain of pain. One word to steal the sunlight from a person's soul and leave them stranded in a cold, gray landscape, alone and searching for something they couldn't even name.

"Maybe."

"Would you like to talk about it?"

She looked at the old man. The gentle understanding in his rheumy eyes took her down a long and winding road, and at the end of it, she was twelve years old again, the first girl in her class to menstruate. Hank hadn't known what to say, so he'd bundled her up, taken her to Doc Burton, and let the doctor handle her fear.

Tears stung her eyes and slipped unchecked down her cheeks. "My husband and I recently separated. I haven't been . . . handling it very well."

Slowly, he pulled his glasses off, laid them on top of his papers, and tiredly rubbed the bridge of his beaked nose. "I'm sorry, Annie. I see too much of this, I'm afraid. It happens in little ole Mystic as often as it does in the big city. Of course you're blue—and depression could certainly explain sleeplessness, lack of appetite, nausea. Any number of symptoms. I could prescribe some Valium, maybe start you on Prozac. Something to take the edge off until you come out on the other side."

She wanted to ask him if he'd known a woman who came out on the other side . . . or one whose husband had changed his mind . . . but they were such intimate and revealing questions, so she remained silent.

He slipped the glasses back onto his nose and peered at her. "This is a time when you want to take dang good care of yourself, Annie. Depression isn't a thing to trifle with. And if it all gives you too many sleepless nights, you come on back around. I'll give you a prescription."

"Pills to take the place of a lover?" She forced a grim smile. "Those must be some drugs. Maybe I'll just take a handful now."

He didn't smile. "Handful isn't a word I like to hear, and

sarcasm doesn't sit pretty on a lady's tongue, missy. Now, how long are you sticking around?"

She felt a wash of shame, as if she were ten years old again. "Sorry. I have to go . . . home in mid-June." *Unless Blake calls.* She shivered inwardly at the thought. "I guess I'll be here until then."

"Mid-June, huh? Okay, I want to see you on June first. No matter what. I'll set you up with an appointment, okay?"

It felt good to have someone care about her progress. "Okay. I'm sure I'll be better by then."

He walked Annie out of the clinic. Patting her shoulder, he reminded her again to take care of herself, then he turned and disappeared back down the hallway.

Annie felt better as she left the clinic and headed across town to the park. The crisp spring air rejuvenated her, and the sky was so blue and bright she had to put her sunglasses back on. It was one of those rare early spring days that held all the promise of summer. She passed a huge chainsaw-cut statue of a Roosevelt elk and wound through the park, kicking through the last black winter leaves that clung to the dewy grass.

She found Hank sitting on the same wooden bench that had always been alongside the river. She sat down beside him.

He handed her a Styrofoam cup of steaming hot coffee. "Bet you haven't had a decent cup of coffee since high school."

She curled her fingers around the warm cup. "I *do* have a latte machine, Dad."

They sipped their coffees in silence. Annie listened to the comforting, familiar sound of the rushing water.

He pulled a croissant out of a paper sack and handed it

to her. Her stomach rebelled at the thought of eating, and she waved it away.

"What did the doc say?" Hank asked.

"Big surprise . . . I'm depressed."

"Are you pissed off yet?"

"Last night I pictured Blake being eaten by piranhas—that seems angry, don't you think?" He didn't answer, just stared at her until, more softly, she said, "I was for a while, but now, I'm too . . . empty to be angry." She felt tears rise and she couldn't stop them. Humiliated, she looked away. "He thinks I'm nothing, Dad. He expects me to live off alimony and be . . . nothing."

"What do you think?"

"I think he's right." She squeezed her eyes shut. "Give me some advice, Dad. Some words of wisdom."

"Life sucks."

She laughed in spite of herself. It was exactly what she would have expected him to say, and even though it didn't help, the familiarity of it was comforting. "Thanks a lot, Dad. I ask for wisdom and you give me bumper stickers."

"How do you think people come up with bumper stickers?" He patted her hand. "Everything is going to work out, Annie. Blake loves you; he'll come around. But you can't keep spending all your time in that bed. You need to get out. Do something. Find something to keep you busy until Blake gets his head out of his ass."

"Or hers."

"Nice comment from my little girl. Here's one for you," he said with a smile. "When life gives you lemons, make lemonade."

She pictured the pitcher of lemonade she'd made for

Blake, and then the big splotch of it that had bled across the settlement papers. "I don't like lemonade."

His look turned serious. "Annie Virginia, I think you don't know what you like, and it's about time you found out."

She knew he was right. She couldn't go on the way she had been, waiting for a phone call that wasn't going to come, crying constantly.

"You've got to take some risks, honey."

"I take risks. I don't floss every day, and sometimes I mix florals and plaids. Once I wore white shoes *after* Labor Day."

"I mean—"

Annie laughed—the first real, honest-to-God laugh since the shit hit the fan. "Haircut."

"What?"

"Blake always liked my hair long."

Hank grinned. "Well, well. I guess you're a little angry after all. That's a good sign."

Lurlene's Fluff-n-Stuff was not the kind of salon Annie usually patronized. It was an old-fashioned, small-town beauty parlor housed in a Pepto Bismol–pink Victorian with glossy white gingerbread trim. A porch wrapped around the front of the house, offering shade to three pink wicker rocking chairs.

Annie parked beneath a hot pink sign that read: PARKING RESERVED FOR LURLENE'S CUSTOMERS ONLY. VIO-LATORS WILL BE SUBJECT TO A CUT AND PERM. As she followed a walkway of heart-shaped cement stones up to the front porch, a tinny rendition of "It's a Small World" seeped from a single black speaker by the door.

She stopped, suddenly afraid. She'd had long hair forever. What was she thinking—that a pair of scissors could recapture her youth? *Calm down, Annie.* She took a deep breath, draining away everything except what she needed to take a single step forward, to walk up those steps and get a haircut.

She had almost reached the top step when the front door whooshed open and a woman appeared. She had to be at least six feet tall, with a pile of Lucille Ball red hair that pooched up to the doorway. Someone had poured her statuesque body into a pair of sparkly red spandex pants (either that, or it was a coat of glitter paint). A tight-fitting angora sweater in a black-and-white zebra print strained across breasts the size of the Alps. A huge zebra earring dangled from each ear.

The woman moved—an excited little shiver rippled along her whole body, right down to the gold Barbie-doll mules that encased her canoe-size feet. "You must be Annie Colwater. . . ." She pronounced it *Colwatah* in a Southern drawl as thick and sweet as corn syrup. "Why, darlin', I been waitin' on you! Your daddy said you wanted a makeover—why, I couldn't believe my ears. A makeover in *Mystic*!" She bounded down the creaking steps like a Rose Bowl float. "I'm Lurlene, sweetie. Big as a moose, you're thinkin', but with twice the fashion sense. Now, sugah, you come on in. You've come to the right place. I'll treat you like a queen." She patted Annie and took hold of her arm, leading her up the steps and into a bright, white and pink room with a few wicker-framed mirrors. Pink gingham curtains shielded the view and a pink hook rug covered the hardwood floor.

"Pink is my color," Lurlene said proudly, her drawl

spinning the sentence into *pink is mah colah.* "The twin shades of cotton candy and summer glow are designed to make you feel special and safe. I read that in a magazine, and ain't it just the God's truth?" She led Annie past two other customers, both older women with their gray hair twined on tiny multicolored rods.

Lurlene kept up a steady chatter as she washed Annie's hair. *Oh, Lordie, I ain't seen this much hair since my Disco Barbie doll.* After she'd clamped a fuchsia plastic cape around Annie's shoulders and settled her into a comfortable chair in front of the mirror, Lurlene peered over Annie's shoulder. "You sure you want this cut? Most women'd give their husband's left nut for hair like this."

Annie refused to give in to the flutter of nerves that had settled somewhere in the region of her stomach. No more halfways. Not anymore. "Cut it off," she said evenly.

"Of *course* you're sure," Lurlene said with a toothy grin. "Somethin' shoulder length, maybe—"

"All of it."

Lurlene's painted mouth dropped open. "Off? As in . . . *off*?"

Annie nodded.

Lurlene recovered quickly. "Why, darlin', you're gonna be my crownin' achievement."

Annie tried not to think about what she'd done. One look at her own chalky, drawn face in the mirror, with her hair slicked back from her thin face, was enough to make her slam her eyes shut . . . and keep them shut.

She felt a tug on her hair, then a snip of steel blades, and a whoosh of hair fell to the floor.

Snip, whoosh, snip, whoosh.

"I shore was surprised when your daddy called. I've

heard stories about you for years. Kathy Johnson—you recall her? Well, Kath and I went to beauty school together. 'Course Kath never actually finished—something about the scissors bothered her—but we got to be best friends. She told me tons o' stories about when y'all were kids. I reckon you'n Kathy were wild and crazy."

Kathy Johnson.

It was a name Annie hadn't heard in years. *Kathy and Annie, friends 4-ever. 2 good 2 be true.* That's what they'd written in each other's yearbook, what they'd promised as the end of high school neared.

Annie had always meant to keep the friendship up, to stay in touch, but somehow she never had. Like so many childhood friendships, it had dwindled to nothing. Christmas cards for a few years, and then even that had stopped. Annie hadn't heard from Kathy in years. The separation had started before high school was over, when Nick proposed to Kathy.

Nick.

Annie could still remember the day she'd first seen him. Junior English. He'd walked in arrogantly, his blue eyes challenging everyone in the room. He was wearing ragged Levi's and an overwashed white T-shirt, with a pack of cigarettes rolled up in his sleeve. He wasn't like anyone she'd ever seen before, with his wild, too-long black hair and don't-mess-with-me attitude. Annie had fallen in love on the spot; so had every other girl in the room, including her best friend, Kathy.

But it was Kathy he had chosen, and with that choice, Annie had tasted the first salty wounds of a broken heart.

She smiled at the memory, faded and distant as it was. Maybe she'd go see them, try to kick-start the old camaraderie—God knew it would be nice to have a friend right about now. If nothing else, they could laugh about the old days. "How are Nick and Kathy?"

The scissors abruptly stopped clipping. "You ain't heard?"

"About what?"

Lurlene leaned down in a cloud of rose-scented perfume. "Kathy died about eight months ago."

Annie opened her eyes. A pale, chalky woman with hacked-off hair stared back at her from the oval mirror. She slammed her eyes shut again. When she found her voice, it was thin and soft. "What—"

"I been helpin' out as much as I can—baby-sittin' an' such, but that child of his, Isabella, well . . . she just ain't right in the head anymore. Got herself kicked out of school yesterday. Can you imagine that? A six-year-old gettin' kicked outta school? Just what're they thinkin', I ask you? They all know about her mama. You'd think a little pity'd be in order. Nick's been lookin' for a nanny, but he finds fault with everyone I send him."

"How did it happen?" Annie's voice was a whisper.

"Just called her into the principal's office and said, kiddo you're outta school." Lurlene made a tsking sound. "That child don't need to get rejected again. What she *needs* is a daddy. 'Course a rabbit's a better parent than he is right now—and they eat their young. I wish I could do more for 'em, but Buddy—that's my husband—he says he raised his kids, all five of 'em, with his ex-wife, Eartha—you know her? She lives down around Forks. Anyway, Buddy don't want to go through *that* again, not marryin' Eartha, I mean, but raisin' kids. And I've never had kids, what do I know about it? I mean, I can give her a durn fine cut and perm, and even paint her little nails, but I don't know about much else. I don't mind watchin' her after school—she's actually quite a help around the place—but she scares me, if the truth be told, what with her problems and all."

It was all coming at Annie so fast. She couldn't make herself really comprehend it. *Kathy.*

How could Kathy be dead? Only yesterday they'd been best friends, playing together in the schoolyard at recess in elementary school, giggling about boys in junior high, and double dating in high school. They had been friends in the way that only girls can be—they wore each other's clothes and slept at each other's houses and told each other every little secret. They promised to always stay friends.

But they hadn't taken the time and energy to stay in touch when their lives went down separate roads . . . and now Kathy was gone. Annie hadn't *meant* to forget Kathy. But she had, and that's what mattered now. She had gone to Stanford, met Blake, and exchanged the past for a future.

"Nicky's fallin' apart, pure and simple," Lurlene said, snapping a big bubble of gum. "Him and Kathy bought the old Beauregard house on Mystic Lake—"

The Beauregard house. An image of it came to Annie, wrapped up in the tissue-thin paper of bittersweet memories. "I know it. But you still haven't told me how Kath—"

The hair dryer blasted to life, drowning out Annie's question. She thought she heard Lurlene still talking, but she couldn't make out the words. Then, after a few minutes, the dryer clicked off. Lurlene set the scissors down with a hard click on the white porcelain tile counter.

"Lordie, you do look fine," Lurlene squeezed her on the

shoulder. "Open your eyes, honey, and take yourself a peek."

Annie opened her eyes and saw a stranger in the mirror. Her brown hair was so short there was no curl left. The pixie cut emphasized her drawn, pale skin, and made her green eyes look haunted and too large for the fine-boned features of her face. Without lipstick, her unsmiling mouth was a colorless white line. She looked like Kate Moss at fifty—after a lawn-mower attack. "Oh, my God . . ."

Lurlene nodded at her in the mirror, grinning like one of those dogs that sit in the back windows of cars. "You look just like that young gal that nabbed Warren Beatty. You know who I mean—the one from *The American President.*"

"Annette Bening," said one of the ladies across the room.

Lurlene reached for her camera, a disposable. "I gotta get me a picture of this. I'll send it in to *Modern Do* magazine. I'll win that trip to Reno for sure." She hunkered down in front of Annie. "Smile."

Before Annie could think, Lurlene popped the photo and straightened, chewing on the scarlet tip of her acrylic nail. "I'll bet there ain't a hundred women in the world who can do justice to that haircut, honey, but you're one of them."

All Annie wanted was to get out of this room without crying. *It'll be all right. It'll grow back,* she told herself, but all she could think about was Blake, and what he would say about what she'd done when—*if*—he came back to her. Shakily, she reached for her handbag. "How much do I owe you?"

"Nothin', honey. We've all had bad weeks."

Annie turned to Lurlene. In the woman's heavily mascaraed eyes, there was real, honest-to-God understanding.

If she hadn't felt so sick, Annie might have managed a smile. "Thanks, Lurlene. Maybe I can return the favor sometime."

Lurlene's painted face cracked into a toothy grin. "Why, honey, this here's Mystic. You hang around long enough and a favor's gonna come beggin'." She bent down and grabbed a big green fishing tackle box from the corner. It hit the tile counter with a clatter and the lid snapped open. Inside was enough makeup to turn Robin Williams into Courtney Love. Lurlene grinned. "Now, are you ready for your makeover?"

Annie gasped. She could picture it—her face with more color than a Benjamin Moore paint wheel. "N-No thanks, I'm in a rush." She popped to her feet and backed away from the chair.

"But, but—I was gonna make you look like—"

Annie mumbled a hurried thank you and ran for the door. She escaped into her rented Mustang and cranked up the engine, barreling out of the driveway in a spray of gravel and a cloud of smoke. She made it almost a mile before she felt the sting of tears.

It wasn't until almost fifteen minutes later, as she drove past the corner of the World-of-Wonders putt-putt golf course, with her hands white-knuckled around the steering wheel and tears leaking down her cheeks, that she remembered the question that had been left unanswered.

What had happened to Kathy?

Annie drove around Mystic, down the rain-rutted back roads, up the bare, harvested hills, until the tears on her cheeks had dried to thin silver streaks. She knew she had to put on a happy face when she saw her dad. Finally, when she'd regained some measure of self-control, she went home.

Hank was seated in one of the old butter-yellow chairs beside the fireplace. A book of crossword puzzles lay open on his lap. At her entrance he looked up. The smile on his face fell faster than a cake when the oven door was slammed. "Holy hamhock," he said slowly.

Annie couldn't help laughing. "I've been cast in *G.I. Jane*, the sequel."

Hank's laugh started slowly, gathering strength. "It looks . . . good, honey."

"Good? I wanted to look younger, but I didn't want to look like an *infant*."

Hank got to his feet and opened his arms. The magazine fell to the floor in a flutter of paper. "Come here, honey."

Annie walked into his embrace and let him hug her. When he drew back, he reached into his breast pocket and pulled out a small, wrapped piece of candy. Butterscotch. He'd always thought those candies would help Annie through the dark times. He'd given her one when her mom died. *Here, honey, have a piece of candy.* For years afterward, whenever she smelled butterscotch, she looked around, expecting to see Hank.

Smiling, she took the candy and unwrapped it, popping it in her mouth. It rolled around on her tongue, tasting of sweetness and memories.

He touched her cheek. "Real beauty is on the inside."

"That's something women say to each other, Dad. Trust me, men don't believe it."

Hank gave her a crooked grin. "I believe it, and last time I looked, I'm a man. And I think your haircut is stunning. It'll just take a little getting used to."

"Well, I *feel* like a new woman, and that's what I wanted."

"Of course it is." He patted her shoulder. "Now, how about a rousing game of Scrabble?"

Annie nodded and let him lead the way. He pulled the Scrabble box out from the armoire in the corner of the living room, where it had probably been sitting since the last time they'd played—twenty years ago. He dusted off the box and set out the board on the coffee table.

Annie stared at her seven smooth wooden squares, trying to come up with a word to start the game. "So, Dad, you didn't tell me about Kathy Johnson."

He didn't look up. "Didn't I? I thought I wrote you about it. Or maybe I told you when I was down for Christmas?"

"No."

He shrugged, and she could tell that he wasn't going to look up. "Oh, well. I guess you know now. That Lurlene's the mouth that roared in Mystic. Sorry you had to find out about it that way."

Annie could tell that Hank was uncomfortable. He kept pulling at his collar, though it wasn't even buttoned to his neck, and he was staring at his letters as if they were the original ten commandments. He was not the kind of man who liked to discuss death. Anyone's. But certainly not the untimely death of a woman he'd watched grow up.

Annie let the subject rest. Forcing a thin smile, she plucked up four letters and started the game. Anything she wanted to know about Kathy's death, or her life, would have to come from somewhere else.

Chapter 6

Nick Delacroix stood in his front yard in the pouring rain, staring down at the limp, sagging, half-dead cherry tree he'd planted last year. Slowly, he fell to his knees in the muddy grass and bowed his head.

He hadn't cried at his wife's funeral, or yesterday when his daughter had been kicked out of school, but he had the strangest goddamn urge to cry now—and over this stupid little tree that wouldn't grow. He pushed to his feet and then turned away from the tree, walking tiredly back up to the house.

But when he was safely inside, with the door slammed shut behind him, he couldn't forget about that damned tree.

It was all because of yesterday; it had been a bad day— and in the past eight months he'd had enough of them to know.

His Izzy had been kicked out of school.

At the thought, the anger came crawling through him again. When the anger faded, all he had left was shame.

Yesterday, his Izzy had stood in the principal's office, her brown eyes flooded with tears, her full, little girl's lips quivering. Her pink dress was stained and torn, and he'd known with a sinking feeling that it had been like that when she'd put it on. Her long black hair—once her pride and joy—was a tangled bird's nest because no mother's hand had combed through it.

He'd wondered fleetingly, absurdly, what had happened to all those pretty ribbons she'd once had.

We can't have her in school anymore, Mr. Delacroix. Surely you see that?

Izzy had stood there, motionless. She hadn't spoken—but then, she hadn't spoken in months. That was one of the reasons they'd expelled her . . . that and the disappearing. A few months ago, she'd started to believe she was disappearing, one tiny finger at a time. Now she wore a small black glove on her left hand—the hand she could no longer see or use. Recently she'd begun to use her right hand awkwardly, as if she believed some of those fingers were "gone" now, too.

She hadn't looked up, hadn't met Nick's eyes, but a single tear had streaked down her cheek. He'd watched the tear fall, hit her dress, and disappear in a tiny gray blotch.

He'd wanted to say something, but he had no idea how to comfort a child who'd lost her mother. Then, like always, his inability to help his daughter had made him angry. It had started him thinking that he needed a drink—just one to calm his nerves. And all the while, she had stood there, too quiet and still for a six-year-old, staring at him with a sad, grown-up disappointment.

He picked his way through the living room, stepping over containers from last night's takeout. A lonely housefly buzzed lazily above the scraps. It sounded like the roar of a lawn mower.

He glanced down at his watch, blinking until his vision cleared. Eight-thirty.

Shit. He was late to pick up Izzy. Again.

The thought of facing her, letting her down again, seeing that tiny black glove . . .

Maybe if he had a little drink. Just a short one—

The phone rang. He knew even before he answered that it was Lurlene, wondering where he was. "Heya, Lurl," he drawled, leaning tiredly against the wall. "I know, I know, I'm late. I was just leaving."

"No hurry, Nicky. Buddy's out with the boys tonight— and before you jump down my throat, Izzy's fine."

He released a sigh, unaware until this moment that he'd tensed up. "You don't care that I'm late, and Izzy is fine. So, what's up?"

Her voice fell to a stage whisper. "Actually, I was callin' with an interestin' bit o' gossip."

"Good God, Lurl. I don't give a shit—"

"I met an old friend of yours today—you care about *that* don'tcha? And I have to say, she ain't nuthin' like I expected her to be. Why, to hear you and Kath—oops! I didn't mean to mention her, sorry—anyway, she was just as sweet as cream butter. I wouldn't even have known she was rich. She was that everyday. Like Miss Sissy Spacek. I saw her on *Oprah* the other day and you woulda thought that lady was no differ'nt'n you or me."

Nick tried to keep up with the conversation, but it was spiraling beyond his control. "Sissy Spacek was in your salon today? Is that the point?"

Lurlene's musical laugh skipped up and down the scales. "You silly, of *course* not. This is Mystic, not Aspen.

I'm talkin' about Annie Bourne. She's back in town, visitin' her daddy."

Nick couldn't have heard right. "Annie Bourne is back
in town?"

Lurlene babbled on about haircuts and cashmere sweaters
and diamonds the size of grapes. Nick couldn't keep his
focus. *Annie Bourne.*

He mumbled something—he had no idea what—and
hung up.

Jesus, Annie Bourne. She hadn't been home in years; he
knew that because Kathy had waited futilely for phone
calls from her old best friend.

Picking his way through the debris in his living room,
he went to the fireplace and grabbed a picture off of the
mantel. It was one he'd seen daily but hadn't really looked
at in years. A bit faded, the colors sucked away by time and
sunlight, it was of the three of them, taken in the last rosy
days of the summer before their senior year. Annie and
Kathy and Nick. The gruesome threesome.

He was in the middle, with an arm around each girl. He
looked young and carefree and happy—a different boy
from the one who'd lived in a cramped, dirty car only a few
months before. In that perfect summer, when he'd first
tasted the rain-sweet elixir called normal life, he'd finally
understood what it meant to have friends, to *be* a friend.

And he had fallen in love.

The photograph had been taken in the late afternoon,
when the sky was a deep and unbroken blue. They'd spent
the day at the lake, shrieking and laughing as they dove off
the cliffs into the water. It was the day he'd first understood
it would have to come to an end, the day he realized that

sooner or later, he'd have to choose between the two girls he loved.

There had never been any doubt about whom he would choose. Annie had already applied to Stanford, and with her grades and test scores, everyone knew she'd be accepted. She was on her way in the world. Not Kathy. Kathy was a quiet, small-town girl given to blue moods . . . a girl who needed desperately to be loved and cared for.

He still remembered what he'd told Annie that day. After the life he'd lived with his mother, he knew what he wanted: respect and stability. He wanted to make a difference in people's lives, to be part of a legal system that cared about the death of a lonely young woman who lived in her car.

He'd told Annie that he dreamed of becoming a policeman in Mystic.

Oh, no, Nicky, she had whispered, rolling over on the blanket to stare into his face. *You can do better than that. If you like the law, think big . . . big . . . you could be a supreme court justice, maybe a senator.*

It had hurt him, those words, the quiet, unintentional indictment of his dreams. *I don't want to be a supreme court justice.*

She'd laughed, that soft, trilling laugh that always made his heart ache with longing. *You've got to think bigger, Nicky-boy. You don't know what you want yet. Once you start college—*

No college for me, smart girl. I won't be getting a scholarship like you.

He'd seen it dawn in her eyes, slowly, the realization that he didn't want what she wanted, and that he wouldn't reach that far. He didn't have the courage to dream big dreams.

All he wanted was to help people and to be needed. It was all he'd ever known, all he was good at.

But Annie hadn't understood. How could she? She didn't know the gutters he'd crawled through in his life.

Oh, was all she'd said, but there'd been a wealth of new-found awareness in the word, a tiny unsteadiness in her voice that he'd never heard before. After that, they had lain side by side on the scratchy green blanket, staring up at the clouds, their bodies an infinitesimal distance apart.

It was so simple to him back then. He loved Annie . . . but Kathy needed him, and her need was a powerful draw.

He'd asked Kathy to marry him just a few months before graduation, but it didn't matter by then, because Annie had known he would. They tried, after the engagement, to keep their friendship together, but inevitably they'd begun to drift apart. It had become Nick-and-Kathy, with Annie a bystander. By the time Annie left for college, amid a shower of promises to keep in touch, Nick had known there would be no lifelong friendship, no gruesome three-some anymore.

By the time he got back from Lurlene's, it was almost nine-thirty. Well past a six-year-old's bedtime, but Nick didn't have the heart to put her right to bed.

Izzy sat cross-legged on the floor in front of the cold, black fireplace. It had always been her favorite spot in this house; at least, it had been in the old days when there was always a fire crackling behind her, always a wave of gentle heat caressing her back. She was holding her rag doll, Miss Jemmie, in one arm—the best she could do since she'd begun "disappearing." The silence in the room was overwhelming, as pervasive as the dust that clung to the furniture.

It shredded Nick into helpless pieces. He kept trying to start a conversation with his daughter, but all his efforts fell into the black well of Izzy's silent world.

"I'm sorry about what happened at school, Izzy-bear," he said awkwardly.

She looked up, her brown eyes painfully dry and too big for the milky pallor of her tiny face.

The words were wrong; he knew that instantly. He wasn't just sorry about what had happened at school. He was sorry about all of it. The death, the life, and all the years of distance and disappointment that had led them to this pitiful place in their lives. Mostly, he was sorry that he was such a failure, that he had no idea where to go from here.

He got up slowly and went to the window. A glimmer of moonlight skated across the black surface of Mystic Lake, and a dim bulb on the porch cast a yellow net across the twin rocking chairs that hadn't been used in months. Rain fell in silver streaks from the roofline, clattering on the wooden steps.

He knew that Izzy was watching him warily, waiting and worrying about what he would do next. Sadly, he knew how that felt, to wait with bated breath to see what a parent would do next. He knew how it twisted your insides into a knot and left you with barely enough oxygen to draw a decent breath.

He closed his eyes. The memory came to him softly, unintentionally, encoded in the percussive symphony of the rain, the plunking sound of water hitting wood. It reminded

him of a day long ago, when a similar rain had hammered
the rusty hood of his mother's old Impala . . .

He was fifteen years old, a tall, quiet boy with too many
secrets, standing on the street corner, waiting for his
mother to pick him up from school. The kids moved past
him in a laughing, talking centipede of blue jeans and
backpacks and psychedelic T-shirts. He watched envi-
ously as they boarded the yellow buses that waited along
the curb.

At last, the buses drove away, chugging smoke, changing
gears, heading for neighborhoods Nick had never seen, and
the school yard fell silent. The gray sky wept. Cars rushed
down the street in a screeching, rain-smeared blur. None of
the drivers noticed a thin, black-haired boy in ragged, holey
jeans and a white T-shirt.

He had been so damned cold; he remembered that most
of all. There was no money for a winter coat, and so his
flesh was puckered and his hands were shaking.

Come on, Mom. That was the prayer he'd offered again
and again, but without any real hope.

He hated to wait for his mother. As he stood there,
alone, his chin tucked into his chest for warmth, he was
consumed by doubt. How drunk would she be? Would it be
a kind, gentle day when she remembered that she loved
him? Or a dark, nasty day when the booze turned her into a
shrieking, stumbling madwoman who hated her only child
with a vengeance? Dark days were the norm now; all his
mother could think about was how much she'd lost. She
wailed that welfare checks didn't cover gin and bemoaned
the fact that they'd been reduced to living in their car—a
swallow away from homelessness.

He could always read her mood immediately. A pale,

dirty face that never smiled and watery, unfocused eyes meant that she'd found her way to a full bottle. Even though he went through the car every day, searching for booze like other kids searched for Easter eggs, he knew he couldn't stop her from drinking.

He rocked from foot to foot, trying to manufacture some body heat, but the rain hammered him, slid in icy, squiggly streaks down his back. *Come on, Mom.*

She never came that day. Or the next. He'd wandered around the dark, dangerous parts of Seattle all night, and finally, he'd fallen asleep in the garbage-strewn doorway of a tumbledown Chinese restaurant. In the morning, he'd rinsed out his mouth and grabbed a discarded bag of fortune cookies from a Dumpster, then made his way to school.

The police had come for him at noon, two unsmiling men in blue uniforms who told him that his mother had been stabbed. They didn't say what she'd been doing at the time of the crime, but Nick knew. She'd been trying to sell her thin, unwashed body for the price of a fifth of gin. The policemen told Nick that there were no suspects, and he hadn't been surprised. No one except Nick had cared about her when she was alive; no one was going to care that another scrawny, homeless drunk, turned old before her time by booze and betrayal, had been murdered.

Nick buried the memory in the black, soggy ground of his disappointments. He wished he could forget it, but of course, the past was close now. It had been breathing down his neck ever since Kathy's death.

With a tired sigh, he turned and faced his utterly silent child. "Time for bed," he said softly, trying to forget, too, that in the old days—not so long ago—she would have mounted a formal protest at the thought of going to bed without any "family time."

But now, she got to her feet, held her doll in the two "visible" fingers on her right hand, and walked away from him. Without a single backward glance, she began the long, slow climb to the second floor. Several of the steps creaked beneath her feather weight, and every sound hit Nick like a blow. What in the hell was he going to do now that Izzy was out of school? She had nowhere to go and no one to take care of her. He couldn't stay home from work with her, and Lurlene had her own life.

What in the hell was he going to do?

Twice during the night, Annie awoke from her solitary bed and paced the room. Kathy's death had reminded her how precious time was, how fleeting. How sometimes life snipped the edges off your good intentions and left you with no second chance to say what really mattered.

She didn't want to think about her husband—*I love her, Annie*—but the thoughts were always there, gathered in the air around her, crackling like heat lightning in the darkness of her room. She stared at her face in the mirror, studying the haircut, trying to figure out who she was and where she belonged. She stared at herself so long, the image changed and twisted and turned gray, and she was lost in the blurry reflection of a woman she'd never known.

Without Blake, she had no one who'd witnessed the past twenty years of her life. No one but Hank who could remember what she'd been like at twenty-five or thirty, no one with whom to share her lost dreams.

Stop it.

She glanced at the clock beside the bed. It was six

o'clock in the morning. She sat down on the edge of the bed, grabbed the phone, and dialed Natalie's number, but her daughter was already gone for the day. Then she took a chance on Terri.

Terri answered on the fifth ring. "This better be important," she growled.

Annie laughed. "Sorry, it's just me. Is it too early?"

"No, no. I love getting up before God. Is everything okay?"

Annie didn't know if things would ever be okay again, but that answer was getting stale. "I'm getting by."

"Judging by the hour, I'd say you weren't sleeping well."

"Not much."

"Yeah, I pretty much paced and cried for the first three months after Rom-the-shit-heel left me. You need to find something to do."

"I'm in Mystic; the choices are a bit limited. I suppose I could try my hand at beer-can art. That's a big seller up here. Or maybe I can learn to hunt with a bow and arrow and then stuff my own kills."

"It's good to hear you laugh."

"It beats crying."

"Seriously, Annie. You need to find something to do. Something that gets you out of your bed—or into someone else's. Try shopping. Go buy some new clothes. Something that changes your look."

Annie rubbed her shorn hair. "Oh, I've changed my looks all right. I look like Rush Limbaugh on Phen-fen."

They talked for another half hour, and when she hung up, Annie felt, if not stronger, then at least better. She roused herself from her bed and took a long, hot shower.

Dressing in a white cashmere boat-necked sweater and

winter-white wool slacks, she went downstairs and cooked Hank a big breakfast of scrambled eggs, orange juice, pancakes, and turkey bacon. It wasn't long before the aroma drew her dad downstairs.

He walked into the kitchen, tightening the gray cotton belt around his ankle-length robe. He scratched his scruffy white beard and stared at her. "You're up. Are you out of bed for long, or just roving until the headache starts again?"

The perceptiveness of the question reminded Annie that her father had known tragedy and had more than a waltzing acquaintance with depression himself. She pulled some china plates from the old oak breakfront in the corner and quickly set two places at the breakfast table. "I'm moving on with my life, Dad. Starting now. Starting here. Sit down."

He pulled out a chair. It made a grating sound on the worn yellow linoleum. "I'm not sure feeding a man is a big leap forward."

She gave him a crooked grin and took a seat across from him. "Actually, I thought I'd go shopping."

He plucked up a mouthful of egg in his blunt-edged fingers. "In Mystic? Unless you're looking for the ideal steelhead lure, I don't know how much luck you'll have."

Annie stared down at her eggs. She wanted to eat—she really did—but the sight of the food made her faintly nauseous. She hoped her dad didn't notice. "I thought I'd start by getting a few books. This seems like a good time to catch up on my reading. Hell, I could get through *Moby-Dick* in my spare time. And the clothes I brought won't work up here."

"Yeah, white's not a very practical color up here in mud-land." He poured a blot of ketchup alongside his eggs and peppered everything. Reaching for his fork, he glanced across the table at Annie. She could tell that he was doing his best not to grin. "Good for you, Annie Virginia." Then, softer, "Good for you."

Mystic dozed beneath a bright spring sun. The town was full of activity today, with farmers and housewives and fishermen scurrying up and down the concrete sidewalks, in a hurry to get their errands done while the clouds were slim and spread out beneath a pale blue sky. Everyone knew that those same clouds could suddenly bunch together like school-yard bullies, releasing a torrent of rain so vicious that even a full-grown eagle couldn't take flight.

Annie strolled down Main Street, peeking into the various stores, a couple of times pushing through a half-open door. Invariably a bell tinkled overhead and a voice called out, *Hiya, miss. Fine day, isn't it?* At the Bagels and Beans coffee shop, she ordered a double tall mocha latte, and she sipped it as she moved down the street.

She passed stores that sold trinkets for tourists, hardware, fabric, and fishing tackle. But there wasn't a single bookstore. At the H & P Drugstore, she picked up the latest Pat Conroy bestseller but couldn't find anything else that interested her. There wasn't much of a selection. It was too bad, because she needed a manual for the rest of her life.

At last, she found herself standing in front of Eve's Leaves Dress Emporium. A mannequin smiled down at her from the display window, wearing a bright yellow rain slicker and matching hat. Her awkwardly bent elbow held a sign that read: *Spring is in the air.* Multicolored silk flowers sprouted from watering cans at her booted feet, and a rake was slanted against one wall.

Annie pushed through the glass door. A tiny bell tinkled at her entrance.

Somewhere, a woman squealed. "It *can't* be!"

Annie looked around for the owner of the voice. Molly Block, her old high school English teacher, came barreling through the maze of rounders, her fleshy arms waving.

"Annie?" she said, grinning. "Annie Bourne, is that you?"

"It's me, Mrs. Block. How are you?"

Molly planted her hands on her wide hips. "Mrs. Block. Don't make me feel so old, Annie. Why, I was practically a *child* when I taught your class." She grinned again, and shoved the wire-rimmed glasses higher on her nose. "It's grand to see you again. Why, it's been years."

"It's good to see you, too, Molly."

"Whatever brings you up to our neck of the woods? I thought you married a hotshot lawyer and were living the good life in smoggy California."

Annie sighed. "Things change, I guess."

Molly cocked her head to the left and eyed Annie. "You look good; I'd kill to be able to wear that haircut, but I'd look like a helium balloon. That white cashmere won't last long in this country, though. One good rainstorm and you'll think you left the house wearin' a dead rabbit."

Annie laughed. "That's the truth."

Molly patted her shoulder. "Follow me."

An hour later, Annie stood in front of a full-length mirror. She was wearing a nineteen-dollar pair of jeans (who knew they still made jeans at that price?), cotton socks and tennis shoes, and a baggy UW sweatshirt in a utilitarian shade of gray.

The clothes made her feel like a new woman. She didn't look like the thirty-nine-year-old soon-to-be-ex-wife of a hotshot California lawyer; she looked like an ordinary small-town woman, maybe someone who had horses to feed and porches to paint. A woman with a life. For the first time, she almost liked the haircut.

"They suit you," Molly said, crossing her beefy arms and nodding. "You look like a teenager."

"In that case, I'll take everything."

While Molly was ringing up the purchases, she rambled on and on about life in Mystic, who was sleeping with whom, who'd gone bankrupt over the spotted owl fiasco, who was running for city council.

Annie glanced out the window. She listened vaguely to the small-town gossip, but she couldn't really concentrate. Lurlene's words kept coming back to her, circling, circling. *Kathy died eight months ago.* She turned back to Molly. "I heard . . . about Kathy Johnson . . . Delacroix."

Molly paused, her pudgy fingers plucking at a price tag. "It was a true shame, that. You all used to be awfully close in high school." She smiled sadly. "I remember the time you and Nick and Kathy put on that skit for the talent show—you all sang some silly song from *South Pacific.* Nicky wore that outrageous coconut bra, and halfway through the song you all were laughing so hard you couldn't finish."

"I remember," she said softly, wondering how it was she'd forgotten it until this very second. "How's Nick doing since . . . you know?" She couldn't bring herself to actually say the words.

Molly made a tsking sound and snipped the price tag from the jeans with a pair of scissors. "I don't know. He makes his rounds and does his job, I guess—you know he's a cop, right? Don't see him smile much anymore, and his daughter is in pretty bad shape, from what I hear. They could use a visit from an old friend, I'll bet."

After Annie paid for her new clothes, she thanked Molly for the help and carried her purchases out to the car. Then she sat in the driver's seat for a while, thinking, remembering.

She shouldn't go to him, not now, not spur-of-the-moment, she knew that. A thing like this needed to be thought out. You didn't just go barging into a strange man's life, and that's what he was: a stranger. She hadn't seen Nick in years.

Besides, she was broken and battered herself. What good could she be to a man who'd lost his wife?

But she was going to go to him. She had probably known from the second Lurlene mentioned his name that it was inevitable. It didn't matter that it didn't make sense; it didn't matter that he probably wouldn't remember her. What mattered was that he'd once been her best friend, and that his wife had once been her best friend. And that she had nowhere else to go.

It was approaching nightfall by the time Annie gathered the nerve to go see Nick. A winding brown ribbon of road led to the Beauregard house. Towering old-growth trees bracketed the road, their trunks obscured by runaway salal bushes. Every now and then, through the black fringe of forest, she could see a glittering silver reflection of the lake. The last few rays of gray sunlight fell like mist through the heavy, moss-draped branches.

It wasn't raining, but tiny droplets of dew began to form on the windshield. In this, the land of ten thousand waterfalls, the air was always heavy with moisture, and the lakes were the aquamarine hue of glacial ice. Some, like Mystic Lake, were so deep that in places the bottom had never been found, and so remote that sometimes, if you were lucky, you could find a pair of trumpeter swans stopping by on their migratory patterns. Here, tucked into the wild, soggy corner of this secret land, they knew they would be safe.

The road twisted and turned and finally ended in a big circular dirt driveway. Annie parked next to a police squad car, turned off the engine, and stared at the beautiful old house, built back at the turn of century, when woods were solid and details were hand-carved by master craftsmen who took pride in their work. In the distance, she could hear the roar of the mighty Quinault River, and she knew that this time of year it would be straining and gnawing at its bank, rushing swollen and headlong toward the faraway shores of the Pacific Ocean.

A pale yellow fog obscured half of the house, drifting on invisible currents of air from the lake. It crept eerily up the whitewashed porch steps and wound around the carved posts.

Annie remembered a night when this house had been spangled in starlight. It had been abandoned then; every broken window had held jagged bits of shadow and moonlight. She and Nick had ridden their bikes here, ditched them alongside the lake, and stared up at the big, broken house.

I'm gonna own this house someday, Nick had said, his hands shoved deeply in his pockets.

He'd turned to her, his handsome face cut into sharp angles by the glittering moonlight. She hadn't even seen the kiss coming, hadn't prepared for it, but when his lips had touched hers, as soft and tentative as the brush of a butterfly's wing, she'd started to cry.

He had drawn back, frowning. *Annie?*

She didn't know what was wrong, why she was crying. She'd felt foolish and desperately naive. It was her first kiss—and she'd ruined it.

After that, he'd turned away from her. For a long time, he'd stared at the lake, his arms crossed, his face unreadable. She'd gone up to him, but he'd pulled away, mumbled something about needing to get home. It was the first and last time he'd ever kissed her.

She brushed the memory aside and fixed her thoughts on the here and now.

Nick and Kathy had fixed up the old house—the windows were all in place, and sunshine-yellow paint coated everything. Hunter-green shutters bracketed each window, but still the whole place looked . . . untended.

Last year's geraniums and lobelia were still in the flower boxes, now a dead, crackly bunch of brown stalks. The grass was much too long and moss had begun to fur the brick walkway. A dirty cement birdbath lay on its side amid gargantuan rhododendrons.

And still it was one of the most beautiful places she'd ever seen. The new spring grass was as green as emeralds and as thick as chinchilla fur; it swept away from the building and rolled gently to the blue edge of the lake. Behind the house, swollen clouds hung suspended in a sky hammered to the color of polished steel.

Annie tucked her purse under her arm and slowly crossed the squishy wet lawn, climbing the white porch steps. At the oak door, she paused, then took a deep breath and knocked.

No answer.

She was just about to turn away when she heard the slow shuffling of feet. Suddenly the door swung open, and Nick was standing in front of her.

She would have recognized him anywhere. He was still tall, over six feet, but time had whittled the football star's muscles to a whipcord leanness. He wasn't wearing a shirt, and the dark, corrugated muscles of his stomach tapered down into a pair of bleached Levi's that were at least two sizes too big. He looked as tough and sinewy as old leather, with pale, lined skin stretched across hollowed-out cheeks. His hair was ragged and unkempt, and something—either time or grief—had sucked its color away, left it the silvery hue of a nickel when struck by the sun.

But it was his eyes—an eerie, swimming-pool blue— that caught and held her attention. His gaze flicked over her, a cop's look that missed no detail, not the brand-new tomboy haircut or the newly purchased small-town clothes. Certainly not the Buick-size diamond on her left hand. "Annie Bourne," he said softly, unsmiling. "Lurlene told me you were back in town."

An uncomfortable silence fell as she tried to figure out what to say. She shifted nervously from side to side. "I'm . . . sorry about Kathy."

He seemed to fade a little beneath the words. "Yeah," he answered. "So am I."

"I know how much you loved her."

He looked as if he were going to say something, and she waited, poised forward, but in the end he said nothing, just cocked his head and swung the door open wider.

She followed him into the house. It was dark—there were no lights on, no fire in the fireplace—and there was a faint musty smell in the air.

Something clicked. Brilliant white light erupted from a shadeless lamp; it was so bright that for a moment she couldn't see anything at all. Then her eyes adjusted.

The living room looked like someone had dropped a bomb on it. There was a scotch or whiskey bottle lying beside the sofa, a drop of booze puddled at its mouth; open pizza boxes littered the floor; clothes lay in heaps and on chairbacks. A crumpled blue policeman's shirt hung across the television screen.

"I don't seem to spend much time at home anymore," he said into the awkward silence. Reaching down, he grabbed a faded flannel shirt from the floor and put it on.

She waited for him to say something else, and when he didn't, she glanced around. The sprawling living room was floored in beautiful oak planks and dominated by a large brick fireplace, blackened by age and smoke. It looked as if there hadn't been a fire in the hearth in a long, long time. The few bits and pieces of furniture—a faded brown leather sofa, a tree-trunk end table, a morris chair—were scattered haphazardly around the room, all wearing tissue-thin coats of dust. A stone archway led into a formal dining room, where Annie could see an oval maple table and four scattered chairs, their seats cushioned by red and white gingham pads. She supposed that the closed green door led to the kitchen. To the left, an oak staircase hugged the brightly wallpapered wall and led to a darkened second floor.

Annie felt Nick's gaze on her. Nervously, she picked an invisible lint ball from her sleeve and searched for something to say. "I hear you have a daughter."

Slowly, he nodded. "Izzy. Isabella. She's six."

Annie clasped her hands together to keep from fidgeting. Her gaze landed on a photograph on the mantel. She picked her way through the rubble on the floor and touched the photo. "The gruesome threesome," she said, smiling. "I can't remember this one. . . ."

Lost in her own memories, Annie vaguely heard him pad out of the room. A moment later, he was back.

He came up behind her, so close she could feel the warmth of his breath on the back of her neck. "Would you like a drink?"

She turned away from the fireplace and found him directly behind her, holding a bottle of wine and two glasses. For a second, it startled her, then she remembered that they were grown-ups now, and offering a glass of wine was the polite way to entertain a guest. "A drink would be great. Where's your daughter? Can I meet her?"

An unreadable look passed through his eyes. "She's staying with Lurlene tonight. They're going to see some cartoon at the Rose theater with Buddy's granddaughters. Let's go sit by the lake." He grabbed a blanket from the sofa and led her out of the house. Together, not too close, they sat down on the blanket.

Annie sipped at the glass of wine Nick had poured for her. Twilight slipped quietly through the trees in blood-red streaks. A pale half moon rose slowly upward, spreading a blue-white veil across the navy-blue surface of the lake. Tiny, silvery peaks rippled against the shore, lapped against the pebbly ground. Memories sifted through the air, falling like rain to the ground around them. She remembered how easy it had once been with them, as they sat together at sporting events, watching Kathy cheerlead at the sidelines; how they'd all squeezed together in vinyl booths to eat greasy hamburgers and fries after the games. They'd known how to talk to each other then—about what, she couldn't recall—but once she'd believed she could tell him anything.

And now, all these years later, with the bumpy road of their separate lives between them, she couldn't think of how to weave a fabric of conversation from a single thread.

She sighed, sipping her wine. She was drinking more than she should, and faster, but it eased her awkwardness. A few stars came out, pinpricks of light peeking through the purple and red twilight sky.

She couldn't stand the silence anymore. "It's beautiful—"

"Nice stars—" They both spoke at the same time.

Annie laughed. "When in doubt, mention the weather or the view."

"We can do better than that," he said quietly. "Life's too damned short to spend it making small talk."

He turned to her, and she saw the network of lines that tugged at his blue eyes. He looked sad and tired and infinitely lonely. It was that, the loneliness, that made her feel like they were partners somehow, victims of a similar war. So, she put the small talk aside, forgot about plundering the shared mine of their teenage years, and plunged into intimacy. "How did Kathy die?"

He sucked down his glass of wine and poured another one. The glittering gold liquid crested at the rim of the glass and spilled over, splashing on his pant leg. "She killed herself."

Chapter 7

Annie stared at Nick, too stunned to respond. "I . . ." She couldn't say the pat *I'm sorry*. The words were too hollow, almost obscenely expected. She gulped a huge swallow of wine.

Nick didn't seem to notice that she hadn't spoken—or maybe he was grateful for it. He stared out at the lake, sighing heavily. "Remember how moody she used to be? She was teetering on the edge of despair even then—her whole life—and none of us knew it. At least, *I* didn't know it . . . until it started to get bad. The older she got, the worse it became. Manic-depressive. That's the technical term. She started having episodes right after her twentieth birthday, just six months after her folks were killed in a car accident. Some days she was sweet as pie, then something would happen . . . she'd cry and lock herself in a closet. She wouldn't take her medication most of the time, said it made her feel like she was breathing through Jell-O." His voice cracked, and he took a huge, gulping swallow of wine. "One day, when I came home from work early, I found her standing in the bathroom, crying, knocking her head against the wall. She just turned to me, her face all smeared with tears and blood, and said, 'Hi, honey. You want me to make you lunch?'

"I bought this place to make her happy, hoping maybe it would help her remember what life used to be like. I thought . . . if I could just give her a home, a safe place where we could raise our kids, everything would be okay. Christ, I just wanted to help her . . ."

His voice cracked again, and he took another drink of wine. "For a while, it worked. We poured our hearts and souls and savings into this old mausoleum. Then Kathy got pregnant. For a while after Izzy was born, things were good. Kathy took her medication and tried . . . she tried so hard, but she couldn't handle a baby. She started to hate this place—the heating that barely worked, the plumbing that pinged. About a year ago, she gave up the medications again . . . and then everything went to hell."

He finished his second glass of wine and poured another. Shaking his head, he said softly, "And still, I didn't see it coming."

She didn't want to hear any more. "Nick, you don't—"

"One night I came home from work with a quart of butter brickle ice cream and a rented video and found her. She'd shot herself in the head . . . with my gun."

Annie's fingers spasmed around the stem of her glass. "You don't have to talk about her."

"I *want* to. No one else has asked." He closed his eyes, leaning back on his elbows. "Kathy was like the fairy tale—when she was good, she was very, very good, and when she was bad, you wanted to be in Nebraska."

Annie leaned back beside him, gazing up at the stars.

The wine was making her dizzy, but she was glad; it blurred the hard edges of his words.

He gave her a tired smile. "One day she loved me with all her heart and soul, and the next day, she wouldn't even speak to me. It was worst at night; sometimes she'd kiss me, and other times she'd roll toward the wall. If I even touched her on those nights, she'd scream for me to get away. She started telling wild stories—that I beat her, that Izzy wasn't really her child, that I was an imposter who'd murdered her real husband in cold blood. It made *me* . . . crazy. The more she pulled away, the more I reached out. I knew I wasn't helping, but I couldn't seem to stop myself. I kept thinking that if I loved her enough, she'd be okay. Now that she's gone, all I can think about is how selfish I was, how stupid and naive. I should have listened to that doctor and hospitalized her. At least she'd be alive. . . ."

Without thinking, Annie reached for him, touched his face gently. "It's not your fault."

He gave her a bleak look. "When your wife blows her brains out in your bed, with your baby daughter just down the hall, believe me, *she* thinks it's your fault." He made a soft, muffled sound, like the whimpering of a beaten pup. "God, she must have hated me. . . ."

"You don't really believe that."

"No. Yes. Sometimes." His mouth trembled as he spoke. "And the worst part is—sometimes I hated her, too. I hated what she was doing to me and Izzy. She started to be more and more like my mother . . . and I knew, somewhere down inside, I knew I wasn't going to be able to save her. Maybe I stopped trying . . . I don't know."

His pain called out to her, and she couldn't turn away.

She took him in her arms, stroking him as she would have soothed a child. "It's okay, Nick. . . ."

When he finally drew back and looked at her, his eyes were flooded with tears. "And there's Izzy. My . . . baby girl. She hasn't said a word in months . . . and now she thinks she's disappearing. At first it was just a finger on her left hand, then her thumb. When the hand went, she started wearing a black glove and stopped talking. I've noticed lately that she only uses two fingers on her right hand—so I guess she thinks that hand is disappearing, too. God knows what she'll do if . . ." He tried to smile. She could see the superhuman effort he was making simply to speak, but then he failed. She could see when the control slipped away from him, tearing away like a bit of damp tissue. "What can I do? My six-year-old daughter hid under her bed one night because she heard a noise. She wanted to go to her mommy and get a hug, but thank God, she didn't. Because her mommy had put a gun to her head and blown her brains out. If Izzy had walked down the hall that night, she would have seen bits and pieces of her mommy on the mirror, on the headboard, on the pillow. . . ." Tears streaked down his unshaven cheeks.

His grief sucked her under, mingled somewhere in the darkness with her own pain. She wanted to tell him that it would all be okay, that he would survive, but the words wouldn't come.

Nick gazed at her, and she knew he was seeing her through the blur of his tears. He touched her cheek, his hand slid down to coil around her neck and pulled her closer.

She knew that this moment would stay with her forever, long after she wanted to forget it. She would perhaps wonder later what had moved her so—was it the shimmering of the stars on the lake, or the way the mixture of moonlight and tears made his eyes look like pools of molten silver? Or the loneliness that lay deep, deep inside her, like a hard square of ice pressed to her broken heart.

She whispered his name softly; in the darkness it sounded like a plea, or a prayer.

The kiss she pressed to his lips was meant to comfort; of that she was sure, a gentle commiseration of understood heartache. But when their lips touched, soft and pliant and salty with teardrops, everything changed. The kiss turned hot and hungry and desperate. She was thinking of Blake, and she knew he was thinking of Kathy, but it didn't matter. What mattered was the heat of togetherness.

She fumbled with the buttons on his shirt and pressed her hands beneath the worn flannel as quickly as she could, sliding her open palms against the coarse wiry hairs on his chest. Her hands moved tentatively across his shoulder, down his naked back. Touching him felt secret and forbidden, dangerous, and it made her *want* . . .

With a groan, he wrenched his shirt off and tossed it aside. Annie's clothes came next. Her gray sweatshirt and bra sailed across the wet grass like flags of surrender.

Cool night air breezed across her bare skin. She closed her eyes, embarrassed by the intensity of her desire. His hands were everywhere, touching her, rubbing, stroking, squeezing, sliding down the curve of her back. In some distant part of her mind, she knew that she was getting carried away, that this was a bad idea, but it felt so good. No one had wanted her this badly for a long, long time. Maybe forever . . .

They became a wild, passionate tangle of naked limbs and searching mouths. Annie gave in to the aching pleasure of it all—the hard, calloused feel of his fingers on her face, her breasts, between her legs. He touched her in places and ways she'd never imagined, brought her body to a throbbing edge between pleasure and pain. Her breathing shattered into choppy, ragged waves, until she was gasping for air and aching for release. "Please, Nick . . ." she pleaded.

She clung to him, feeling the damp moisture of tears on her cheeks, and she didn't know if they were his or hers or a mingling of the two, and when he entered her, she had a dizzying, desperate moment when she thought she would scream. . . .

Her release was shattering. He clung to her, moaned, and when she felt his orgasm, she came again, sobbing his name, collapsing on his damp, hairy chest. He gathered her into his arms, stroking her hair, murmuring soft, soothing words against her ear. But her heart was pounding so hard and her pulse was roaring so loudly in her ears she had no idea what he said.

When Annie fell back to earth, amid a shower of stars, she landed with a thud. She lay naked beside Nick, her breathing ragged. Overhead, the sky was jet-black and sprinkled with starlight, and the night smelled of spilled wine and spent passion.

Very slowly, Nick pulled his hand away from hers. Without the warmth of his touch, her skin felt clammy and cold.

She grabbed one end of the blanket and pulled it across

her naked breasts, sidling away from him. "Oh, my God," she whispered. "What have we done?"

He curled forward, burying his face in his hands.

She scouted through the wet grass and grabbed her shirt, pulling it toward her. She had to get out of here, now, before she fell apart. "This didn't happen," she said in a whispery, uncertain voice. "This did *not* happen."

He didn't look at her as he scooped up his clothes and hurriedly dressed. When he was armored again, he stood up and turned his back on her.

She was shaking and doing her best not to cry as she dressed. He was probably comparing her to Kathy, remembering how beautiful his wife had been, and wondering what the hell he'd done—having sex with a too-thin, too-old, too-short-haired woman who had let herself become such a nothing. . . .

Finally, she stood. She stared down at her own feet, wishing the ground would open up and swallow her. "I better get—" She'd been about to say *home*, but she didn't have a home any more than she had a husband there waiting for her. She swallowed thickly and changed her words. "Back to my dad's house. He'll be worried—"

At last, Nick turned to her. His face was lined and drawn, and the regret in his eyes hit her like a slap. God, she wanted to disappear. . . .

"I've never slept with anyone but Kathy," he said softly, not quite meeting her eyes.

"Oh" was all she could think of to say, but his quiet admission made her feel a little better. "This is a first for me, too."

"I guess the sexual revolution pretty much passed us by."

Another time it might have been funny. She nodded toward her car. "I guess I should get going."

Wordlessly, they headed back to the car. She was careful not to touch him, but all the way there, she kept thinking about his hands on her body, the fire he'd started deep inside her, in that place that had been cold and dead for so long. . . .

"So," he said into the awkward silence, "I guess Bobby Johnson was lying when he said he nailed you after the Sequim game?"

She stopped dead and turned to him, fighting the completely unexpected urge to laugh. "*Nailed* me?"

He shrugged, grinning. "He said it, not me."

"*Nailed* me?" She shook her head. "Bobby Johnson said that?"

"Don't worry—he said you were good. And he didn't even *imply* a blow job."

This time she did laugh, and some of her tension eased. They started walking again, across the wet grass, to her car. He opened the door for her, and it surprised her, that unexpected gesture of chivalry. No one had opened a car door for her in years.

"Annie?" He said her name softly.

She glanced up at him. "Yes?"

"Don't be sorry. Please."

She swallowed hard. For a few moments, Nick had made her feel beautiful and desirable. How could she feel sorry about that? She wanted to reach out for him again, anything to stave off the cold loneliness that would engulf her again the moment she climbed into her rented car and closed the door. "Lurlene told me you were looking for a nanny . . . for Isabella. I could watch her . . . during the day . . . if that would help you out. . . ."

He frowned. "Why would you do that for me?"

The question saddened her; it was full of mistrust and steeped in a lifetime's disappointments. "It would help *me* out, Nick. Really. Let me help you."

He stared at her a long time, that wary cop's look again. Then slowly, pointedly, he took hold of her hand and lifted it. In the pale moonlight, the three-carat diamond glittered with cold fire. "Don't you belong somewhere else?"

Now he would know what a failure she was, why she'd come running back to Mystic after all these years. "My husband and I have recently separated. . . ." She wanted to say more, tack a lighthearted excuse on the end of the glaring, ugly statement, but her throat closed up and tears stung her eyes.

He dropped her hand as if it had burned him. "Jesus, Annie. You shouldn't have let me act like such a whiny ass-hole, as if no one else in the world had a problem. You should have—"

"I *really* do not want to talk about it." She saw him flinch, and was immediately sorry for her tone of voice. "Sorry. But I think we've had enough shoulder-crying for one night."

He nodded, looking away for a minute. He stared at his house. "Izzy could use a friend right now. I'm sure as hell not doing her any good."

"It would help me out, too. I'm a little . . . lost right now. It would be nice to be needed."

"Okay," he said at last. "Lurlene could use a break from baby-sitting. She and Buddy wanted to go to Branson, and since Izzy's out of school . . ." He sighed. "I have to pick Izzy up from Lurlene's tomorrow. I could meet you at her house—she lives down in Raintree Estates—you remember where that is? Pink house with gnomes in the front yard. It's hard to miss."

"Sure. What time?"

"Say one o'clock? I can meet you there on my lunch break."

"Perfect." She stared up at him for another long minute, then turned and opened her car door. She climbed in, started the engine, and slowly pulled away. The last thing she saw, out of her rearview mirror as she drove away, was Nick looking after her.

Long after she'd driven away, Nick remained on the edge of the lawn, staring down the darkened road. Slowly, he walked back into the house, letting the screen door bang shut behind him. He went to the fireplace and picked up the photograph of the three of them again. He looked at it for a long, long time, and then, tiredly, he climbed the long, creaking staircase up to his old bedroom. Steeling himself, he opened the door. He moved cautiously inside, his eyes adjusting quickly to the gloom. He could make out the big, unmade bed, the clothes heaped everywhere. He could see the lamp that Kathy had ordered from Spiegel and the rocking chair he'd made when Izzy was born.

He grabbed a T-shirt from the floor, slammed the door behind him, and went down to his lonely couch, where he poured himself a stiff drink. He knew it was dangerous to use alcohol to ease his pain, and in the past months, he'd been reaching for that false comfort more and more.

Leaning back, he took a long, soothing drink. He finished that drink and poured another.

What he and Annie had done tonight didn't change a thing. He had to remember that. The life she'd stirred in him was ephemeral and fleeting. Soon, she'd be gone, and he'd be left alone again, a widower with a damaged child who had to find a way to get through the rest of his life.

There was a light on in the living room when Annie pulled up to her dad's house. She winced at the thought of confronting him now, at two o'clock in the morning, with her clothes all wrinkled and damp. God, she probably smelled like sex.

She climbed out of the car and headed into the house. As she'd expected, she found Hank in the living room, waiting up for her. A fire crackled cheerily in the fireplace, sending a velvet-yellow glow into the darkened room.

She closed the door quietly behind her.

Hank looked up from the book he was reading. "Well, well," he said, easing the bifocals from his eyes.

Annie self-consciously smoothed her wrinkled clothes and ran a hand through her too-short hair, hoping there was no grass stuck to her head. "You didn't need to wait up for me."

"Really?" He closed the book.

"There's no need to worry. I'm a hell of a long way from sixteen."

"Oh, I wasn't worried. Not after I called the police and the hospital."

Annie sat down on the leather chair beside the fireplace. "I'm sorry, Dad. I guess I'm not used to checking in.

Blake never cared . . ." She bit back the sour confession and forced a thin smile. "I visited an old friend. I should have called."

"Yes, you should have. Who did you go see?"

"Nick Delacroix. You remember him?"

Hank's blunt fingers tapped a rhythm on the cover of the book, his eyes fixed on her face. "I should have expected you'd end up there. You three were as tight as shoelaces in high school. He's not doing so good, from what I hear."

Annie imagined that Nick was a delectable morsel for the town's gossips. "I'm going to help him out a little. Take care of his daughter while he's at work, that sort of thing. I think he needs a breather."

"Didn't you two have sort of a 'thing' in high school?" His gaze turned assessing. "Or are you planning to get back at Blake?"

"Of course not," she answered too quickly. "You told me I needed a project. Something to do until Blake wakes up."

"That man's trouble, Annie Virginia. He's drowning, and he could take you down with him."

Annie smiled gently. "Thanks for worrying about me, Dad. I love you for it. But I'm just going to baby-sit for him. That's all."

"That's all?" It wasn't a question.

"You told me I needed to find a project. What am I supposed to do—cure cancer? I'm a wife and mother. It's all I know. All I am." She leaned forward, ashamed that she couldn't tell him the whole truth—that she didn't know how to be this alone. So, she told him the next best thing. "I'm too old to lie to myself, Dad, and I'm too old to change, and if I don't do *something* I'm going to explode.

This seems as good as anything. Nick and Izzy need my help."

"The person you need to help right now is you."

Her answering laugh was a weak, resigned little sound. "I've never been much good at that, now have I?"

Chapter 8

Annie threw back the covers and stumbled out of bed, the gauzy filaments of a nightmare wrapped around her. It was the same dream she used to have years ago, and she'd begun lately to have it again. She was trapped in a huge mansion, with hundreds of empty rooms everywhere, and she was searching desperately for a way out.

Her first thought when she woke was always *Blake?* But, of course, he wasn't beside her in bed. It was one of the many aspects of her new life to which she would have to become accustomed. There was no one to hold her after a nightmare.

It was getting harder and harder for her to believe that Blake would ever come back to her, and the loss of that transient hope made her feel as hollow as a reed sucked dry by the summer heat.

Tears stung her eyes. Last night she had broken her marriage vows for the first time in her life; she had shattered the faith she'd made with the only man she'd ever loved. And the hell of it was, he wouldn't care.

* * *

Nick was just getting ready to sign off for his lunch break when the call came in, a domestic disturbance on Old Mill Road.

The Weaver place.

With a sigh, Nick radioed the dispatcher and asked her to put a call in to Lurlene. He wouldn't make his meeting with Annie and Izzy.

Flicking on his siren and lights, he raced down the rutted strip of asphalt that led out of town. He followed Old Mill Road along the winding curves that sidled along the Simpson tree forest, over the concrete bridge above the choppy silver rapids of the Hoh River, and came at last to the driveway. A lopsided, dented mailbox, rusted to the color of Georgia mud, hung precariously from an arched piece of weathered driftwood. He turned cautiously down the road, a narrow, twisting swatch cut by hand from the dense black forest around it. Here, deep in the rain forest, no sunlight penetrated the trees; the foliage had a dark, sinister cast even in the middle of the day. At the end of the mud lane, a half-acre clearing butted up against a hillside of dense evergreen trees. Tucked into the back corner of the clearing a rickety mobile home squatted in the mud. Dogs yelped and barked at his entrance.

Nick radioed the dispatcher again, confirming his arrival, and then he hurried from the squad car. With one hand resting on the butt of his gun, he splashed through the puddles that pocked the driveway and charged up the wooden crates that served as the front steps. He was about to knock when he heard a scream from inside the trailer.

"Police!" he yelled as he pushed through the door. It

swung inward and cracked on the wall. A shudder reverberated through the room. "Sally? Chuck?"

Outside, the dogs went wild. He could imagine them straining on their chains, snapping at one another in their desperation to attack the trespasser.

He peered through the gloomy interior. Avocado-colored shag carpeting, littered with beer cans and ashtrays, muffled the heavy sound of his boots as he moved forward. "Sally?"

A shriek answered him.

Nick ran through the dirty kitchen and shoved through the closed bedroom door.

Chuck had his wife pinned to the fake wood paneling. She was screaming beneath him, trying to protect her face. Nick grabbed Chuck by the back of the neck and hurled him sideways. The drunken man made an *oofing* sound of surprise and stumbled sideways, cracking into the corner of the pressboard bureau. Nick spun and grabbed him again, cuffing him.

Chuck blinked up at him, obviously trying to focus. "Goddamn it, Nicky," he whined in a low, slurred voice. "What in the fuck are you doing here? We was just havin' a argument. . . ."

Nick holstered a fierce, sudden urge to smash his fist into Chuck's fleshy face. "Stay here, goddamn it," he said instead, shoving Chuck so hard he crashed to the floor, taking a cheap Kmart lamp with him. The lightbulb splintered and left the tiny room in shadows.

Nick rested his hand on his baton as he cautiously made his way to Sally. She was leaning against the wall now, her torn, stained dress splattered with blood. A jagged cut marred her lower lip, and already a purplish bruise was seeping across her jaw.

He couldn't readily recall how many times he'd been here, how many times he'd stopped Chuck from killing his wife. It was a bad situation, this marriage, and had been long before Chuck got laid off at the mill, but since then, it had become a nightmare. Chuck spent all day at Zoe's Tavern, sucking down beers he couldn't afford and getting mad. By the time he crawled off his bar stool and made his stumbling way home, he was as mean as a junkyard dog, and when he pulled his broken-down pickup into his driveway, he was ready to do some serious damage. The only one around was his wife.

Nick touched Sally's shoulder.

She made a gasping sound and cringed. "Don't—"

"Sally, it's me. Nick Delacroix."

She slowly opened her eyes, and when she did, he saw the bottomless well of her despair, and her shame. She brought a shaking, bruised hand to her face and tried to push the blood-matted hair from her face. Tears welled in her blackened eyes and streaked down her battered cheeks. "Oh, Nick . . . Did the Robertses call you guys again?" She edged away from him and straightened, trying to look normal and in control. "It's nothing, really. Chuckie just had a bad day, is all. The paper company isn't looking for any employees. . . ."

Nick sighed. "You can't keep doing this, Sally. One of these days he's going to kill you."

She tried to smile. It was a wobbly, unbalanced failure, and it tore at Nick's heart. As always, Sally made him think of his mother, and all the excuses she'd made for alcohol over the years. "Oh, no, not my Chuckie. He gets a little frustrated, is all."

"I'm going to take Chuck in this time, Sally. I want you to make a complaint."

Chuck lurched from his place at the corner, stumbling into the bed. "She won't do that to me, willya, honey? She knows I don't mean nothing by it. It's just that she makes me so damned mad sometimes. There wasn't nothin' in the whole house to eat when I got home. A man *needs* somethin' to eat, ain't that right, Nick?"

Sally glanced worriedly at her husband. "I'm sorry, Chuckie. I didn't expect you home s'early."

Defeat rounded Nick's shoulders and washed through him in a cold wave. "Let me help you, Sally," he said softly, leaning toward her.

She patted his forearm. "I don't need no help, Nick. But thanks for comin' by."

Nick stood there, staring down at her. She seemed to be shrinking before his eyes, losing weight. The ragged cut of her cotton dress was too big for her; it hung off her narrow shoulders and lay limply against her body. He knew as certainly as he knew his own name that one day he would answer one of these calls and Sally would be dead. "Sally—"

"Please, Nick," she said, her voice trembling, her eyes filling with tears. "Please, don't . . ."

Nick turned away from her. There was nothing he could do to help her. The realization caused an ache deep inside him, and left him wondering why in the hell he did this job. There was no success, or damned little of it. He couldn't do much of anything to Chuck unless Chuck killed his wife, and of course, then it would be too late.

He stepped over an upended laundry basket and took

hold of Chuck's collar. "Come on, Chuck. You can sleep it off downtown."

He ignored Chuck's whining and refused to look at Sally again. He didn't need to. Sally would be following along behind them, whispering words of apology to the husband who'd broken her bones, promising to be "better" when he came home, vowing to have dinner on the table on time.

It didn't sicken Nick, her behavior. Unfortunately, he understood Sally. He had been like her in his youth, had followed his mother around like a hungry dog, begging for scraps of affection, taking whatever affection she would occasionally fling his way.

Yes, he understood too well why Sally stayed with Chuck. And he knew, too, that it would end badly for both of them. But there was nothing he could do to help them. Not a goddamn thing except to throw Chuck in jail to sleep off his drunk, and wait for the next domestic disturbance call on Old Mill Road.

Izzy Delacroix lay curled in a tight little ball on Lurlene's guest bed. The pillow didn't smell right—not the right smell at all. That was one of the things that made Izzy cry almost every night. Since her mommy went to Heaven, nothing smelled right, not the sheets or the pillows or Izzy's clothes.

Even Miss Jemmie didn't smell like she was s'posed to.

Izzy clutched the doll to her chest, stroking her pretty yellow hair with the two fingers she had left on her right hand, her thumb and pointy finger.

At first it had sorta scared her, when she'd figured out that she was disappearing. She'd started to reach for a crayon, and halfway there, she'd noticed that her pinky finger was sort of blurry and gray. The next day it was invisible. She had told her daddy and Lurlene, and she could tell by the way they looked at her that it scared them, too. And that icky doctor—it had made him look at her like she was a bug.

She stared at the two fingers that remained on her right hand. *It's goin' away, Mommy.*

She waited for an answer, but none came. Lots of times, she imagined her mommy was right beside her, and she could talk to her just by thinking the words.

She wished she could make it happen right now, but it only seemed to happen at special times—at the purply time between day and night.

She needed to talk to her mommy about what had happened the other day. It had been so bad. One minute, she'd been looking at the pictures in her book, and the next thing she knew, there was a scream inside her. She knew it wasn't good to scream in school—the other kids already thought she was stupid—and she'd tried really, really hard to keep her mouth shut. She'd clenched her hands into tight balls and squeezed her eyes shut so hard she'd seen stars in the darkness.

She had felt so scared and so lonely she couldn't breathe right. The scream had started as a little yelp that slipped out. She had clamped a hand over her mouth but it hadn't helped.

All the kids had stared at her, pointing and laughing.

And the scream had come out. Loud, louder, loudest. She'd clamped her hands over her ears so she couldn't hear it. She'd known she was crying, but she hadn't been able to stop that, either.

The teacher had grabbed Izzy's gloved hand, squeezing

around all that nothingness. It had made Izzy scream harder that she couldn't feel anything.

"Oh, pumpkin, it's not invisible," Mrs. Brown had said softly; then she'd gently taken Izzy's other hand and led her down the hallway.

And the scream had gone on and on and on.

She had screamed all the way down the hall and into the principal's office. She had seen the way the grown-ups looked at her—like she was crazy—but she couldn't help herself. All she knew was that she was disappearing, one finger at a time, and no one seemed to care.

As quickly as the scream had come, it went away. It left her shaken and weird-feeling, standing in the middle of the principal's office, with everyone staring at her.

She had inched her way into the corner, wedged herself between a yucky green sofa and the window. The grown-ups' voices kept going, talking about her, whispering. . . .

Everyone cared about why she didn't talk anymore, that's all. That Dr. Schwaabe, all he cared about was why she didn't talk, and Izzy heard Lurlene and Buddy. They acted like she couldn't hear because she didn't talk. Lurlene called her "poor little thing" all the time—and every time she said it, Izzy remembered the bad thing, and she wished Lurlene would stop.

Then, like a knight out of one of Mommy's fairy tales, her daddy had walked into the principal's office. The grown-ups shut up instantly, moved aside.

He wouldn't have come to the school if she hadn't started screaming, and for a second, she was glad she'd screamed. Even if it made her a bad girl, she was glad to have her daddy here.

She wanted to throw herself in his arms, say, *Hi, Daddy,*

in that voice she used to have, but he looked so sad she couldn't move.

He was so handsome; even since his hair had changed color after the bad thing, he was still the most handsome man in the world. She remembered what his laugh used to sound like, how it used to make her giggle right along with him. . . .

But he wasn't really her daddy anymore. He never read her stories at night anymore, and he didn't throw her up in his arms until she laughed. And sometimes at night his breath smelled all mediciney and he walked like one of her wobbly toys.

"Izzy?" He said her name softly, moving toward her.

For one heart-stopping minute, she thought he was going to touch her. She wormed her way out from the corner and baby-stepped his way. She leaned toward him, just a little teeny bit, but enough so maybe he'd see how much she needed him.

He gave a sharp sigh and turned back to face the grown-ups. "What's going on here, Bob?"

Izzy almost wished for the scream to come back, but all she felt was that stinging quiet, and when she looked down, another finger was gone. All she could see on her right hand was her thumb and pointy finger.

The grown-ups talked a bunch more, saying things that she wasn't listening to. Then Daddy went away, and Izzy went home with Lurlene. Again.

"Izzy, sweetheart, are you in there?"

She heard Lurlene's voice, coming through the closed bedroom door. "Come on out, Izzy. There's someone I want you to meet."

Izzy wanted to pretend she hadn't heard, but she knew

there wasn't any point. She just hoped Lurlene wasn't going to give her another bath—she always used water that was way too cold and got soap in Izzy's eyes.

She sighed. *Miss Jemmie, we gotta go.*

She clutched the doll with her good arm and rolled out of bed. As she walked past the vanity, she caught a glimpse of herself in the mirror. A short, skinny girl with dirty black hair and one arm. Her eyes were still puffy from all that crying.

Mommy never let her look like this.

The bedroom door swung open. Lurlene stood in the opening, her big feet smacked together, her body bent at the waist. "Good morning, sweetheart." She reached out and tucked a tangled chunk of hair behind Izzy's ear.

Izzy stared up at her.

"Come on, pumpkin."

Wordlessly, Izzy followed her down the hallway.

Annie stood in the entryway of Lurlene and Buddy's triple-wide mobile home, on a patch of pink carpet.

Lurlene's husband, Buddy—*nice ta meetcha*—sat sprawled in a burgundy velour Barcalounger, with his feet elevated, a *Sports Illustrated* open on his chest, his right hand curled around a can of Miller. He was watching Annie carefully.

She shifted from foot to foot, trying not to think about the fact that she wasn't a psychiatrist, or that the child's trauma was a dark and bottomless well, or that Annie herself was lost.

She knew that love was important—maybe the *most* important thing—but she'd learned in the past weeks that it wasn't a magic elixir. Even Annie wasn't naive enough to believe that every problem could be solved by coating it in love. Some pain couldn't be assuaged, some traumas couldn't be overcome. She'd known that since the day her own mother had died.

"Nick ain't comin'. Did Lurlene tell you that?"

Annie frowned and glanced at Buddy. "Oh. No. I didn't know."

"He don't never show up when it matters." He took a long slug of beer, eyeing Annie above the can's dented rim. "You're taking on a hell of a job, you know. That Izzy's as unscrewed as a bum valve."

"Nick told me she hasn't spoken in a while, and about the . . . you know . . . disappearing fingers."

"That ain't the half of it. She's got the kind of pain that sucks innocent bystanders under and drowns 'em."

In other words: *you're out of your depth here, city girl.* Annie knew how she must appear to him, with her cheap jeans that still showed the manufacturer's creases and the tennis shoes that were as white as new-fallen snow. She went to tuck a lock of hair behind her ear, but there was no hair there. Embarrassed, she forced a smile. "That rain yesterday hurried spring right along. Why, at my dad's house, the daffodils are busting out all over. I thought maybe—"

"Annie?"

It was Lurlene's voice this time. Annie slowly turned.

Lurlene appeared at the end of the hallway, clad in a neon-green sweater and a pair of skintight purple faux snakeskin leggings. She clashed with everything in the house.

A child hung close to her side, a small girl with big brown eyes and hair the color of night. She was wearing a too-small pink dress that had seen better days. Her thin legs stuck out

from the hemline like twin beanpoles. Mismatched socks—
one pink, one yellow—hugged her ankles and disappeared
into a pair of dirty Beauty and the Beast tennis shoes.

A little girl. Not an assortment of psychological problems or a trauma victim or a disciplinary problem. Just a
plain, ordinary little girl who missed her mother.

Annie smiled. Maybe she didn't know about traumatic
muteness and how the doctors and books and specialists
thought it should be treated. But she knew about being
afraid, and she knew about mothers who disappeared one
day and never came back.

Slowly, with her hand out, she moved toward the girl.
"Hey, Izzy," she said softly.

Izzy didn't answer; Annie hadn't expected her to. She
figured Izzy would talk in her own sweet time. Until then,
Annie was just going to act as if everything were normal.
And maybe, after what Izzy had been through, silence was
the most normal thing in the world.

"I'm Annalise, but that's a mouthful, isn't it. You can
call me Annie." She kneeled down in front of the little girl,
staring into the biggest, saddest brown eyes she'd ever
seen. "I was a good friend of your mommy's."

A response flickered in Izzy's eyes.

Annie took it as encouragement. "I met your mom on
the first day of kindergarten." She smiled at Izzy, then
stood and turned to Lurlene. "Is she ready to go?"

Lurlene shrugged, then whispered, "Who knows? Poor
thing." She bent down. "You remember what we talked
about. Miss Annie's goin' to be takin' care of you for a
while, durin' your daddy's work hours. You be a good girl
for her, y'hear?"

"She most certainly does *not* have to be a good girl," Annie said, winking at Izzy. "She can be whatever she wants."

Izzy's eyes widened.

"Oh." Lurlene pushed to her feet and smiled at Annie. "God bless you for doing this."

"Believe me, Lurlene, this is as much for me as anyone. See you later."

Annie looked down at Izzy. "Well, Izzy. Let's hit the road. I'm positively dying to see your bedroom. I'll bet you have all kinds of great toys. I *love* playing Barbies." She led the way to the car, settled Izzy in the front seat, and clicked the seat belt in place.

Izzy sat in the passenger seat, strapped tightly in place, her head tilted to one side like a baby bird's, her gaze fixed on the window.

Annie started the car and backed out of the driveway, steering carefully past a crowd of ceramic gnomes. She kept talking as she drove, all the way past the Quinault Indian reservation, past the roadside stalls that sold smoked salmon and fresh crabs, past a dozen empty fireworks stands. She talked about anything and everything— the importance of old-growth trees, the viability of mime as an art form, the best colors, her favorite movies, the Girl Scout camp she and Kathy had gone to and the s'mores they'd made at the fire—and through it all, Izzy stared and stared.

As Annie followed the winding lake road through towering trees, she felt as if she were going back in time. This rutted, gravel road, spackled now with bits of shade, seemed a direct route to yesterday. When they reached the end of the road, Annie found herself unable to move. She

sat behind the wheel of the car and stared at the old Beauregard place. Nick's home, now.

I'm going to own this house someday.

It had sounded like a silly dream to Annie then, all those
years ago, a bit of glass spun in a young man's hand.
Something to say on a starlit night before he found the
courage to lean down and kiss the girl at his side.

Now, of course, she saw the magic in it, and it cut a tiny
wound in her heart. Had she even *had* a dream at that
tender age? If so, she couldn't remember it.

She pulled into the gravel driveway and parked next to
the woodpile. The house sat primly in the clearing before
her. Sunlight, as pale and watery as old chicken broth,
painted the tips of the lush green grass and illuminated
the daffodil-yellow paint on the clapboard siding. It still
looked forlorn and forgotten, this grande dame of a Victorian house. In places the paint was peeling. Some of the
shingles had fallen from the gabled roof, and the rhododendrons were crying out to be cut back.

"I'll bet that used to be a fort," Annie said, spying the
broken boards of a treehouse through the branches of a
dormant alder. "Your mom and I used to have a girls-only
for—"

Izzy's seat belt unhooked with a harsh click. The metal
fastener cracked against the glass. She opened the door
and ran toward the lake, skidding to a stop at a picket-
fenced area beneath a huge, moss-furred old maple tree.

Annie followed Izzy across the squishy lawn and stood
beside the child. Within the aged white fence lay a beautiful square of ground that wasn't nearly as wild and overgrown as everything else on the property. "This was your
mom's garden," she said softly.

Izzy remained motionless, her head down.

"Gardens are very special places, aren't they? They aren't like people . . . their roots grow strong and deep into the soil, and if you're patient and you care and you keep working, they come back."

Izzy turned slowly, tilted her head, and looked up at Annie.

"We can save this garden, Izzy. Would you like that?"

Very slowly, Izzy reached forward. Her thumb and fore-finger closed around the dead stem of a shasta daisy. She pulled so hard it came out by the roots.

Then she handed it to Annie.

That dried-up, hollowed-out old shoot with the squiggly, hairy root was the most beautiful thing Annie had ever seen.

Chapter 9

Izzy clutched Miss Jemmie under her arm; it was the best she could do without all her fingers. She lagged behind the pretty, short-haired lady.

She was glad to be home, but it wouldn't last long. The pretty lady would take one look at Daddy's mess in the house and that would be that. Grown-up girls didn't like dirty places.

"Come on, Izzy," the lady called out from the porch.

Izzy stared up at the front door. She wished her daddy would suddenly shove through that door and race down the creaky old porch steps like he used to, that he'd sweep Izzy into his big, strong arms and spin her around until she giggled, kissing that one tickly spot on her neck.

It wouldn't happen, though. Izzy knew that because she'd been having the same dream for months and months and it never came true.

She remembered the first time her daddy had brought them out here. That was when his hair was black as a crow's wing and he never came home smelling like the bad place.

That first time had been magic. He had smiled and laughed and held her in his arms. *Can't you just see it, Kath? We'll plant an orchard over there . . . and fill that porch with rocking chairs for summer nights . . . and we can have picnics on the grass. . . .* He'd kissed Izzy's cheek then. *Would you like that, Sunshine? A picnic with chicken and milkshakes and Jell-O salad?*

She'd said, *Oh, yes, Daddy,* but they'd never had a picnic, not on the lawn or anywhere else. . . .

The front door creaked open, and Izzy remembered that the lady was waiting for her. She trudged reluctantly up the porch steps. The lady—Annie; she had to remember that the lady's name was Annie—clicked on the lamp beside the sofa. Light landed in streaks on Daddy's mess. Bottles, pizza boxes, dirty clothes were lying everywhere.

"As Bette Davis would say, 'What a dump.' Your father certainly doesn't win the Felix Unger award."

Izzy winced. That was it. Back to Lurlene's for chipped beef on toast. . . .

But Annie didn't turn and walk away. Instead, she picked her way through the junk and flung open the curtains in a cloud of dust. Sunlight poured through the two big picture windows. "That's better," she said, glancing around. "I don't suppose you know where the brooms and dustpans are? A bulldozer? How about a blowtorch?"

Izzy's heart started beating rapidly, and something felt funny in her chest.

Annie winked at her. "I'll be right back." She hurried out of the living room and disappeared into the kitchen.

Izzy stood very still, barely breathing, listening to the rapid fluttering of her heart.

Annie came back into the living room carrying a black garbage bag, a broom, and a bucket of soapy water.

That strange feeling in Izzy's chest seemed to grow bigger and bigger, until she almost couldn't breathe. Slowly, she moved toward Annie, waiting for the lady to throw her hands up and say, *It's too goddamn much work, Nicky,* like her mommy used to.

But Annie didn't say that. Instead, she bent over and picked up the garbage, one piece at a time, shoving it into the black bag.

Cautiously, Izzy moved closer.

Annie didn't look at her. "It's just junk, Izzy. Nothing permanent. There's nothing done here that can't be undone. My daughter's room used to look like this all the time—and she was a perfectly lovely teenager." She kept talking, and with each unanswered sentence, Izzy felt herself relaxing. "Why, I remember this place when I was a little girl. Your mom and daddy and I used to peek in the windows at nighttime, and we'd make up stories about the people who used to live here. I always thought it was a beautiful, wealthy couple from back East, who walked around in tuxedos and evening gowns. Your dad, he thought it was once owned by gamblers who lost everything in a single hand of cards. And your mama—why, I can't recall what she used to think. Probably something romantic, though." She paused long enough to smile at Izzy. "Maybe when the weather warms up, we could have a picnic on the lawn. Would you like that?"

Izzy felt the weirdest urge to cry. She wanted to say, *We could have milkshakes and Jell-O salad,* but she didn't. She couldn't have, even if she'd really tried. Besides, it was just one of those things grown-ups promised even when they didn't mean it.

"In fact," Annie said, "we could have a mini-picnic today. When I get the living room cleaned up, we'll have cookies and juice outside—iced raisin cookies and Maui punch. That sounds good, don't you think? 'Yes, Annie, I think that would be terrrrrific.' That's my Tony the Tiger impression. Natalie—that's my daughter; she's almost a grown-up now—she used to love Frosted Flakes. I'll bet you do, too."

Izzy bit back an unexpected smile. She liked the way Annie didn't wait for her to answer. It made Izzy feel like she wasn't so different, like not talking was as okay as talking.

Tiny step by tiny step, she inched sideways. When she reached the sofa, she sat down, ignoring the dust that poofed up around her. Bit by bit, the garbage disappeared, and after a while, it began to look like home.

Annie tapped lightly on Izzy's bedroom door. There was no answer. Finally, she pushed open the door and went inside. The room was small and dark, tucked under an overhang in the roofline. A charming dormer reached outward, capturing the last pink light of day behind pale, worn lace curtains. The walls were done in a beautiful lavender-striped paper, and a matching floral print covered the bed. A Winnie-the-Pooh lamp sat on a white bedside table.

Nick and Kathy had probably planned this room and saved for it, wanting to create the perfect place for their child. Annie could remember the dreams that came with pregnancy, and the endless details of hope. Much of it started with the nursery.

Annie didn't know much about manic-depression, or how it had twisted and changed Kathy, but she knew that Kathy had loved her daughter. Every item in this room had been lovingly chosen, from the Little Mermaid nightlight to the Peter Rabbit bookends.

She crossed the clothes-strewn wooden floor to the bed. Izzy's dainty profile made a beautiful cameo against a faded yellow Big Bird pillowcase. A fuzzy purple blanket was drawn taut across her shoulders and tucked gently beneath her chin. The doll—Miss Jemmie, Lurlene had said—was sprawled on the floor, her black button eyes staring up at the ceiling. Izzy's tiny, black-gloved hand lay like a stain on the lavender lace bedspread.

Annie hated to wake the sleeping girl, but she was a big believer in routine. Children needed to know where the limits were and what rules governed. She'd put Izzy down for a nap at two-thirty—and was surprised when she actually fell asleep. Now, at four o'clock, it was time to wake up.

She bent down and jostled the little girl's shoulder. "Wake up, sleepyhead."

Izzy made a tiny, mewling sound and snuggled deeper under the covers.

"Oh, no, you don't. Come on, Izzy."

One brown eye popped open. Izzy used two fingers on her right hand to push the covers back. Blinking and yawning, she sat up.

"I thought you'd like to take a bath before your daddy gets home." Annie smiled and held up the bag of treats she'd brought with her. "I got you some new clothes and a few surprises—Lurlene told me what sizes to get. Come on." She helped Izzy out of bed and led her to the bathroom, where she quickly ran some water into the tub.

Then she knelt in front of the child.

Izzy eyed her warily.

Annie looked down at Izzy's gloved hand. "Don't you just hate it when parts of you start disappearing? Now, hands up."

Izzy dutifully raised her right arm. Her left arm hung limply at her side, the black-gloved fingers completely slack.

Annie sat back on her heels. "How, exactly, do we undress the invisible parts? I guess, if I just peel your jammies back . . ." Slowly, she pulled the sleeve along the "invisible" arm. Then she reached for the glove.

Izzy made a choking sound and wrenched away from her.

"Oh, sorry. The glove can't come off?"

Izzy stared intently at a spot somewhere behind Annie's left ear.

"I understand. There is no glove, is there, Izzy?"

Izzy bit down on her lower lip. She still didn't look at Annie.

Annie stood. Carefully taking Izzy by the shoulders, she steered the child toward the bathtub and helped her into the warm water. Izzy hugged the side of the tub, where her left arm hung limply over the edge.

"That's not too hot, is it?" Annie asked. "No, Annie, that's just right. Just exactly the temperature I like."

Izzy stared at her.

Annie grinned. "I can carry on a conversation all by myself. When I was a girl—I was an only child, too—I used to do it all the time."

Annie poured bubble bath into the falling water. Izzy watched, apparently awestruck, as airy white foam bubbled up around her.

Then Annie lighted a trio of votive candles she'd found in the kitchen. The sweet aroma of vanilla rose in the air. "Sometimes a girl needs a romantic bath—just for her. Okay." She reached into her brown bag. "Look at my goodies. I've got Johnson's baby shampoo, Pocahontas soap, a Hunchback of Notre Dame towel, and a Beauty and the Beast comb. And this *darling* play suit. It's lavender with little yellow flowers—just like your mom's garden will be—and a matching yellow hat."

She kept up a steady stream of dialogue, asking questions and answering them herself as she washed Izzy's long hair and lathered and rinsed her body, and finally helped her out of the tub. She wrapped the tiny girl in a huge towel and began combing her hair. "I remember when my daughter, Natalie, was your age. No bigger than a minute. It used to make my heart ache just to look at her." She wove Izzy's hair into a pair of perfect French braids and finished them off with two yellow satin bows.

"Turn around."

Dutifully, Izzy turned.

Annie dressed her in new white cotton underwear and helped her into the lavender blouse and overalls. When she was finished, she guided Izzy to the full-length mirror in the corner.

The little girl stared at herself for a long, long time. Then, very slowly, she lifted her right hand and touched the satin ribbons with her forefinger. Her rosebud mouth wobbled uncertainly. She bit down hard on her lower lip. A single tear trickled down Izzy's flushed pink cheek. Just one.

Annie understood. It was what she'd been hoping for, at

least in part. That Izzy would see herself as she used to be. "I bet you always used to look like this, didn't you, Izzy?"

She placed a tender kiss on Izzy's forehead. The child smelled of baby shampoo and new soap. Like little girls everywhere.

Then, Annie sat back on her heels and looked steadily in Izzy's eyes. "You know how you share your toys with a friend, and you have more fun than if you were playing all by yourself? Sometimes that's true of sadness, too. Sometimes if you share it, it goes away."

Izzy didn't respond.

Annie smiled. "Now, I could use some help in the kitchen. I've started dinner, but I can't find the dishes *anywhere*. Maybe you could help me?"

Izzy blinked.

Annie took that as a yes.

Together, they went down to the kitchen. Izzy walked dutifully toward the table and sat down. Her little feet dangled above the floor.

Annie talked the whole time she made dumplings, stirring batter and dropping it into the simmering chicken stew. "Do you know how to set the table?" she asked as she put the lid on the big metal pot.

Izzy didn't answer.

"This isn't going to work, you know, Miss Izzy." Annie picked up a spoon and handed it to the girl. "Here you go—this is for you."

Izzy used her thumb and forefinger to take hold of the spoon. She stared at it, then frowned up at Annie.

"One shake of the spoon is yes. Two shakes is no. That way we can talk . . . sort of in code, without ever having to say something out loud. Now, do you think you could show me where the plates are?"

Izzy stared unblinking at the spoon for a long, long time. Then, very slowly, she shook it once.

"Hey, Nicky, I hear Hank Bourne's daughter is back in town."

Nick glanced up from his drink. There was a headache pounding behind his eyes, and he couldn't quite focus. He'd had it all day, ever since the fiasco at the Weaver place. He'd booked Chuck and thrown him in a cell, but already Sally had been to the station to make sure that no charges were leveled at her husband. Already she'd told the desk sergeant that she'd fallen down the stairs.

Nick thought that if he stopped in at Zoe's for a quick drink—just one to steady his nerves—he'd be okay to face Annie and Izzy at home. But, like always, one drink led to another and another and another . . .

What he'd seen in Sally's eyes opened a wound in his soul, a dark, ugly place that was bubbling with painful memories.

He closed his fingers around the glass and took another long, soothing pull of the scotch. "Whatever you say, Zoe."

Joel Dermot scooted closer to him. "I remember Annie Bourne. Her and my daughter, Suki, used to be in Girl Scouts together."

Nick closed his eyes. He didn't want to think about those days, long ago, when the three of them had been best friends. When he thought of those days, he remembered how much he used to care about Annie, and then he wound up thinking about the previous night, when she'd been in his arms, naked and wild, fulfilling all the fantasies he'd ever had about her. The memory invariably pushed him down a long and treacherous road, a road that made him question all the choices he'd made along the way. How he'd chosen Kathy because she needed him . . . and how he'd let her down, and how loving her had ruined him. Then he'd find himself having dark, dangerous thoughts— like what would his life have been like if he'd chosen Annie, or what it *could* be like if she were the kind of woman who would stay in Mystic.

Another man's wife.

Nick shot unsteadily to his feet, in a hurry to outrun that thought. Tossing a twenty-dollar bill on the bar, he turned and hurried out of the smoky tavern. He jumped into his patrol car and headed for home. By the time he pulled into his driveway, he felt as if he'd driven a thousand miles over a corrugated road. His body ached, his head hurt, and he longed for one more drink to ease the way.

What in the hell would he say to Annie now, after what had happened between them?

Slowly, he got out of the car, walked across the gravel walkway and up the sagging porch steps, and went inside.

Annie was stretched out on the sofa. When the door clicked shut behind him, she sat up and gave him a bleary-eyed smile. "Oh," she said. "I guess I fell asleep."

Her beauty left him momentarily speechless. He backed up a step, keeping as much floor as possible between them. He glanced away. "Sorry I'm late. I . . . meant to show up at Lurlene's, but we had an emergency call, and, well . . ."

She threw the blanket back and got up. Her clothes were wrinkled, and there was a network of tiny pink lines across her right cheek. "It's no problem. Izzy and I had a good time today. I think we're going to get along great."

He wanted to say something that would ease his guilt and make her think well of him. He had a ridiculous urge to talk to her about what had happened today, to share with another human being that he was shaken, that something had spilled out of him today, and he didn't know how to retrieve it, or how to put it back where it belonged. But that kind of intimacy was so alien to him that he couldn't imagine how to begin.

She plucked her purse from the coffee table. She was careful not to look at him for too long. "If you want . . . I could make you and Izzy a nice dinner tomorrow night. I think she'd like that."

"That would be great. I'll be home at six o'clock."

She edged past him but stopped at the door, turning back. "From now on . . . if you're going to be late, I'd appreciate a phone call."

"Yeah. I'm sorry."

She gave him a last smile and left the house.

He stood at the window, watching her drive away. When the tiny red dots of her taillights disappeared around the bend in the road, he slowly climbed the stairs and went into the guest bedroom, the one he'd moved into eight months ago and still used when he didn't fall asleep on the couch. Stripping out of his blue uniform, he slipped into a pair of ragged old sweats and tiredly walked down the hallway. Outside Izzy's door, he paused for a moment, gathering his strength.

A tiny nightlight glowed from the wall next to her bed. It was Winnie-the-Pooh's face in vibrant yellow. He picked up her favorite book—*Where the Wild Things Are*—and lowered himself slowly to the edge of her bed. As the mattress sagged beneath his weight, he froze. Izzy wiggled in her sleep, but didn't waken.

He opened the book, staring down at the first page. In the old days, when he'd read to her every night before bed, she'd curled her little body so trustingly against his, and cocked her smiling face up. *Daddy, what're yah gonna read me tonight, Daddy?*

He squeezed his eyes shut. It had been a long time since he'd remembered her habit of saying *Daddy* at the beginning and end of every sentence. He leaned down slowly, slowly, and kissed the softness of her forehead. The little-girl scent enveloped him, made him remember giving her bubble baths. . . .

He let out a long, slow breath. Now, all he did was read to her when she was asleep, just a few pages from her favorite book. He hoped the words soaked through her sleeping mind. It was a tiny, stupid way of saying he loved her; he knew that. Still, it was all he seemed to have left.

He read the book in a soft, singsong voice, and then gently placed it back on the bedside table. "Goodnight, Izzy-bear," he whispered, placing a last kiss on her forehead.

Back downstairs, he went to the kitchen and poured himself a stiff drink. He kicked open the front door and slumped onto a chair on the porch.

It came to him then, as he'd known it would. He could recall suddenly how it had smelled at the Weaver house, of bacon and Lysol, and how a thin strip of linoleum had been peeling up from the edge of the kitchen floor. He remembered the bruise on Sally's cheek, how it had been spreading already, seeping like a spot of blood through a bit of tissue paper.

Once, long ago, he had believed he could rescue people like Sally. He'd thought that when he put on his uniform, he would be invincible. God, he'd been such an idiot, believing in the words that meant so little today: honor, respect, justice. He'd actually thought that he could save people who had no desire to be saved.

But life had taught him a lot. Between his job and Kathy, his idealism had been hacked away, bit by bit, until now there was nothing left but rusted scraps. Without it, he didn't know who he was.

He took a long drink and leaned back in the chair, looking up at the night sky. He was startled for a moment to realize that outside, everything was still as it should be. The lake still glittered in the moonlight. Night still fell softly across the mountaintops and through the forests. Soon, dawn would come, chasing darkness to distant corners of the globe.

Once, he'd watched such things with wonder. He'd thought in those days that his needs were simple and easily met. He'd wanted only his family, his job, his home. He'd imagined that he would grow old in this house, sitting in this chair on his porch, watching his children grow up and move on. He'd thought then that age would pull the black from his hair, and that it would take years. He hadn't known then that grief and guilt could age a man and turn his hair silver in the span of a single season.

He drank until his head began to spin, until his vision blurred. The empty bottle slipped through his numb fingers and rolled away, clattering down the steps one by one to land silently in the grass.

* * *

The next morning, Izzy woke to the sound of her mommy's voice. She kicked the covers away and sat up, blinking. *Mommy?*

At first, all she could hear was the rain. In the old days—before the bad thing—she'd loved that sound, the way it rattled on the roof. She looked out the window, disappointed to see nothing out there but pink and yellow sunlight. No rain.

Mommy?

There was no answer, just the creaking sound of the house. Izzy slipped on her favorite bunny slippers and crept out of her bedroom. She moved silently down the stairs, hoping not to wake her daddy. He was asleep on the couch, with one arm flung across the coffee table and his bare feet sticking out from the end of his blue blanket.

She tiptoed past him, her heart thudding in her chest as she eased the front door open and closed it silently behind her. She stood on the porch, looking out. A pink mist floated across the lake. *Mommy?*

She walked through the grass, to the edge of the lake. She squeezed her eyes shut and pictured her mommy. When she opened her eyes, her mommy was there, standing in the middle of the water, too far away for Izzy's hands to reach.

Mommy didn't seem to move, but all at once, she was beside Izzy, so close that Izzy could smell her perfume.

It's okay now, Izzy. Her mom's voice mingled with the breeze. Somewhere, a bird squawked and flew up from the brush, flapping its wings as it rose into the sky.

It started to rain for real, a slow pattering shower that kissed Izzy's hair and fell on her lips. She saw that the rain was tinted, a million rainbow-hued flecks landing on the surface of the lake. But on the other side of the water, it wasn't raining.

It's okay now, Mommy said again. *I have to go.*

Izzy panicked. It felt as if she were losing her mommy all over again. *Don't go, Mommy. I'm disappearin' as fast as I can.*

But her mommy was already gone. The multicolored rain stopped falling and the mist went away.

Izzy waited and waited, but nothing happened. Finally, she went back into the house. Crossing the living room, she wandered into the kitchen and started making herself breakfast. She got out the Frosted Flakes and the milk all by herself.

In the other room, she heard her daddy wake up. She'd seen it a bunch of times, and it was always worse when he fell asleep in the living room. First he'd sit up on the sofa, then he'd grab his head and make a little moaning sound. When he stood up, he always hit his shin on the coffee table and yelled a bad word. Today was no different.

"Shit!"

Izzy hurried to put the pink tablecloth on the table—the one her mommy always used for breakfast. She wanted her daddy to notice how smart she was, how grown up. Maybe then he'd finally look at her, touch her . . . maybe he'd even say, *Heya, Sunshine, how did you sleep?* That's what he used to say in the mornings, and if he talked to her, maybe she could find her own voice, answer, *I'm fine, Daddy-O,* and make him laugh again. She missed hearing him laugh.

That's all she really wanted. She had given up on lots of the other things that used to matter. She didn't care if he told her he loved her. She didn't care if he kissed her good night on the forehead, or took her on picnics, or twirled her around in his big, strong arms until she squealed. She just wanted him to look at her the way he used to, as if she were the most important person in the world.

Now, he hardly ever looked at her. Sometimes, he looked away so fast, she'd get scared and think she had finally disappeared. But it was never true; she was always there, most of her anyway, except her hand and a few fingers. He just didn't like to look at her anymore.

He stumbled into the kitchen and came to an unsteady stop. "Izzy. What are you doing up?"

She blinked at him in surprise. *You c'n do it,* she thought. *Just answer him. I'm makin' you breakfast, Daddy.* But the words tangled in her throat and disappeared.

"Frosted Flakes," he said with a thin smile. "Annie will love that." He went to the refrigerator and poured himself a glass of orange juice.

He headed toward her. For one heart-stopping moment, she thought he was going to pat her shoulder and tell her she'd set the table real pretty. Or that *she* looked pretty—just like she used to look, with her hair all braided. She even leaned slightly toward him.

But he moved on past, and she had to squeeze back tears.

He looked at the table again. Not at her. "I don't have time for breakfast, Izzy-bear." He touched his forehead and closed his eyes.

She knew he had a headache again—the same one he'd had ever since Mommy went to heaven. It scared her, thinking about that. It always scared her to see how sick her daddy looked in the mornings. She wanted to tell him that she would try harder to be a good girl, that she'd stop disappearing and start talking, and eat her vegetables and everything.

Her daddy smiled—only it wasn't his real smile. It was the tired, shaky smile that belonged to the silver-haired daddy—the one who never looked at her. "Did you have a good time with Annie yesterday?"

Izzy tried and tried but she couldn't answer. She saw how her daddy looked at her, like he was gonna cry, and it made her ashamed of herself.

Finally, he sighed. "I'm gonna go take a shower. Annie should be here any minute."

He waited a second—as if she were going to answer—but she didn't. She couldn't. Instead, she just stood there, holding two bowls, and watched him walk away.

Later, long after he'd left for work, Izzy sat down on the sofa, her knees pressed together and Miss Jemmie asleep in her lap. Annie came bright and early and started cleaning the house again. All the time Annie was working, she talked to Izzy. She talked so much that sometimes Izzy couldn't listen to it all.

Izzy liked the way her house looked now, after Annie had finished cleaning it up.

It made her feel safe.

She closed her eyes, listening to the soothing sound of the broom. It made her think of her mommy, and all the times she'd sat by herself, looking at a book while her mommy cleaned the house.

Before she knew it, a sound had slipped from her mouth. It was a faint *schk-schk* noise, the same sound that the broom was making on the floor.

Her eyes popped open. It shocked her to hear her own voice after all this time. Even if it wasn't words, it was *Izzy*.

She thought that part of her—the talking part—had dried up and disappeared, just like her hand and arm. She hadn't meant to stop talking, but one day after her doctor's appointment, she had opened her mouth to speak and nothing had come out. Nothing.

It had terrified her, especially when she realized that she couldn't change it. After that, everyone treated her like a baby and pretended she couldn't hear, either. It had made her cry, the way they all looked at her, but even her crying had been silent.

Annie was different. Annie didn't look at Izzy like she was a broken doll that belonged in the trash.

Annie looked at her the way her mommy and daddy used to.

Izzy smiled, and the sound kept coming, softly, barely louder than the sound of her own breathing. *Schk-schk-schk.*

Chapter 10

The county courthouse had been built a hundred years ago, when Mystic had been a booming log town, when the inlets were swollen with miles of trees waiting to be piled onto locomotives and employment was always high. It was an imposing building of hand-cut gray stone, fronted by dozens of double-hung windows and placed squarely in the middle of a flat green lawn. Precisely trimmed rhododendrons and azaleas outlined the brick walkways. A Washington state flag fluttered in the spring breeze.

Nick stood on the courthouse steps, leaning back against one of the stone pillars that flanked the huge oak doors. He flipped through a slim notebook, reminding himself of the facts of an arrest that had taken place more than a month ago. Testifying was part of his job, but it wasn't something he liked to do—especially not in family court, where everything usually came down to broken families and lost souls.

Today it was Gina Piccolo. He'd known Gina since she was a little girl. He remembered her only a few years back, when she'd had the lead in the junior high production of

Oklahoma! She was a bright, sunny girl with jet-black hair and shining eyes. But in the past year, she'd gone more than a little wild. At fourteen, she'd fallen in with the wrong crowd, and she wasn't a bright-eyed girl anymore. She was a sullen, nasty, baggy-clothed young woman with a logger's mouth and a penchant for trouble. Her parents were out of their minds with worry—and it didn't help that she'd recently started dating a seventeen-year-old boy. Nothing her parents said seemed to make a difference.

And so Nick was here, preparing to make a statement to the judge about Gina. He checked his watch. Court reconvened in ten minutes. He flipped through his notes again, but he found it difficult to concentrate.

It was a problem that had plagued him for the past four days—really ever since Annie Bourne had shown up in his life again.

Already Izzy was improving. She wasn't talking, of course, and she still believed she was disappearing, but Nick could see the changes. She was interacting, listening, smiling . . . and the reasons were obvious.

Annie was just so damned *easy* to be around. That was the problem—for Nick, anyway. Memories of their love-making were everywhere, and Annie fascinated him—the way she squinted when she smiled, the way she kept tucking nonexistent hair behind her ear, the way she shrugged helplessly when she screwed something up.

Most of the time, he couldn't look at her; he was afraid that the wanting would show in his eyes.

With a sigh, he flipped his notebook closed and headed inside the courthouse toward courtroom six.

Gina was waiting by the door, wearing baggy black jeans and an oversized black sweatshirt that hung almost to her knees. Her once-black hair was streaked with pink and purple highlights, and a silver ring pierced her nose.

She saw him, and her eyes narrowed. "Fuck you, Delacroix," she said. "You're here to tell them to put me away."

Where did they get all that anger? He sighed. "I'm here to tell Judge McKinley what happened on February twenty-sixth."

"Like you would know anything about that—or me. I was framed. That wasn't my coke."

"Someone put it in your pocket?"

"That's right."

"If that's the way you want to play it, Gina, fine. But honesty would be a smarter course."

She tapped her thigh nervously. "Yeah, like you would know about honesty. You cops make me sick."

"You're young, Gina—"

"Screw you."

"And like all young people, you think you're a pioneer, the first person ever to find the great undiscovered country. But I know you. I've been where you're going, and believe me, it isn't pretty."

"You don't know shit about the real world. You're a cop . . . in *Mystic*." She pulled out a cigarette and lit up. Her gaze cut to the no-smoking sign behind her and she grinned, daring Nick to do something.

He saw the challenge in her eyes as she exhaled a stream of smoke. He cocked his head toward the open doors. "Follow me."

Without looking back, he crossed the hall and went outside. He was mildly surprised to find that Gina had followed him. He sat down on the top step.

She sat cross-legged a few feet away. "Yeah? What?"

"When I was your age, I lived on the streets."

She snorted. "Uh-huh. And I'm one of the Spice Girls."

"My mom was an alcoholic who used to prostitute herself for booze. It was a lovely life . . . normal for an addict with no formal education and no particular job skills. She dropped out of school at sixteen when she got pregnant with me. My old man dumped her pretty fast—and she didn't have anywhere to go after that."

Gina went very still. The cigarette sagged in her black-painted lips. "No way," she said, but this time there wasn't much conviction in her voice.

"We couldn't afford to pay rent—that's another thing addiction does. It takes your money, fast, then your will and your pride. Pretty soon you don't care that you live in an old Chevy Impala and that your son has no winter coat. All you care about is getting high or drunk. You'll sleep under a sheet of newspaper on a park bench and not even know you're freezing or that some time in the middle of the night you threw up all over yourself."

"You're trying to scare me."

"You're damn right I am. The road you're on leads three places, Gina—to a park bench or a jail cell or a coffin. You think about it."

She slowly lifted her gaze to his. He could see that she was scared. For a split second, he thought she was going to reach out for help.

Come on, Gina, he thought. *You can do it.* He pulled a business card from his pocket and handed it to her. "Call me. Anytime."

"I—"

"Hey, Gino, what're you doin' talkin' to that jerk in blue?"

Gina drew back as if stung and lurched to her feet. The white business card fluttered to the gray stone steps at her feet. She turned and waved at the green-haired boy who was bounding up the courthouse steps. Chains jangled from his ears and pockets, and a thin silver hoop glittered in his eyebrow. He slipped an arm around Gina and pulled her close. Taking the cigarette from her mouth, he took a long drag and exhaled slowly. "You're here to send Gino to lockup, aren't you?"

Nick stared at the boy, Drew Doro. A bad seed who'd first come into contact with the law at age ten, when he'd burned down his family garage. Two years ago, his parents had quietly, and with broken hearts, given up on him. It was only a matter of time before this kid was doing time in Monroe. He was Gina's first boyfriend.

"I'm here to give the family court judge my opinion, Drew. That's all. It's not a trial." He glanced at Gina. "Not yet, anyway."

Gina took a step toward Nick. The uncertainty in her eyes reminded Nick that underneath all that black mascara and attitude, she was still just a kid, scared and trying to find her way in a confusing world. "What are you gonna tell the judge?"

He wished he could lie to her right now, tell her what she wanted to hear. "I'm going to tell her that you present a threat to yourself and others. You left me no choice."

The uncertainty was replaced by a flash of pure hatred. "Screw you, Delacroix. It wasn't my coke."

Slowly, Nick stood. "If you need help, Gina . . . you know where to find me."

"Why in the hell would she need *your* help?" Drew laughed. "She's got tons of friends who really care about her. You're just a low-rent cop in this backwater dump of a town. All you're good for is getting cats outta trees. Come on, Gina."

Nick watched them walk away. He hadn't expected Gina to listen to him. Hoped, perhaps—it was that uncontrollable surge of hope that had chewed viciously through his life. He couldn't seem to completely walk away from it.

He'd had the same talk with a dozen teens over the years and none of them ever listened. None of them ever changed. Most of them died young and violently and far away from the families who loved them.

Just once, he thought dully. It would be nice to actually protect and serve. Just once.

He saw Gina, loitering outside the front door, finishing her cigarette.

"You remember that park bench," he called out.

Gina's answer was an all-too-familiar hand gesture.

By the time Nick finally got home from work—late, as usual—Annie was exhausted. She drove home and stumbled into bed. Almost immediately, she fell into a deep sleep, but sometime in the middle of the night she awoke and reached out for Blake.

Once awake, she couldn't fall back asleep again. It was an unfortunate symptom of her depression that she was tired all the time, but she rarely slept well.

As usual, she spent the hours until dawn trying not to think about the big empty house on the Pacific, and the man who had been a part of her life for so long. The man who'd said, *I love her, Annie.*

She went into the kitchen and ate a bowl of cereal, then she picked up the phone and called Natalie—an unscheduled call. She listened to her daughter's stories about London for several minutes, and then quietly told her about the move to Mystic. *To see Hank and help out an old friend,* she'd said.

Natalie had asked only one question: "What does Daddy say?"

Annie had forced a fluttery laugh that sounded false to her own ears. "You know Dad, he just wants me to be happy."

"Really?"

It made Annie feel inestimably old, that single, simple question that seemed to know too much. After that, they'd talked for almost an hour, until Annie could feel bits and pieces of herself returning. It anchored her to talk to her daughter, reminded her that she hadn't failed at everything in her life.

At the end of the conversation, she made sure Natalie had Hank's phone number in case of an emergency, and then she hung up.

For the next hour, Annie lay in her lonely bed, staring out the window, watching the darkness until, at last, the sun came to brush away the bruising night.

It was thoughts of Izzy that gave Annie the strength to get up, get dressed, and eat something. The child had become her lifeline. Izzy touched something deep and elemental in Annie, and it didn't take a two-hundred-dollar-an-hour psychiatrist to understand why. When Annie looked down into Izzy's frightened brown eyes, she saw a reflection of herself.

She knew the hand Izzy had been dealt. There was

nothing harder than losing a mother, no matter what age you were, but to a child, a girl especially, it changed everything about your world. In the years since her mom's death, Annie had learned to talk about the loss almost conversationally, the way you would remark upon the weather. *My mother died when I was young . . . passed away . . . passed on . . . deceased . . . an accident . . . I really don't remember her. . . .* Sometimes, it didn't hurt to say those things—and sometimes the pain stunned her. Sometimes, she smelled a whiff of perfume, or the vanilla-rich scent of baking sugar cookies, or heard the tail end of a Beatles song on the radio, and she would stand in the middle of her living room, a woman full grown, and cry like a little girl.

No mother.

Two small words, and yet within them lay a bottomless well of pain and loss, a ceaseless mourning for touches that were never received and words of wisdom that were never spoken. No single word was big enough to adequately describe the loss of your mother. Not in Annie's vocabulary, and certainly not in Izzy's. No wonder the girl had chosen silence.

Annie wanted to say all of this to Nick, to make him understand all that Izzy must be feeling, but every time she started to speak, she had an overwhelming sense of her own presumptuousness. When she looked into Nick's pale blue eyes, or at his grief-whitened hair, she knew that he understood all too well.

They were still awkward around each other. Uncertain. For Annie, at least, the memory of their passion underscored every look, every movement, and if she spoke to him too intimately, she found that it was difficult to breathe evenly. He seemed equally unnerved around her;

and so they circled each other, outfitted more often than not with false smiles and pointless conversations.

But slowly, things had begun to improve. Yesterday, they had spent ten minutes together, standing at the kitchen counter, sipping coffee while Izzy ate breakfast. Their conversation crept along the perimeter of their old friendship, dipping now and then into the shared well of their memories. In the end, they had both smiled.

It had given Annie a new strength, that single moment of renewed friendship, and so, today, she pulled into the driveway a half hour early. Grabbing the bag of croissants she'd picked up from the bakery and the bag of surprises she'd bought for Izzy, she climbed out of her car and went to the front door, knocking loudly.

It took a long time, but finally Nick answered, wearing a pair of ragged gray sweatpants. Swaying slightly, he stared down at her through bloodshot eyes.

She held up the bag. "I thought you might like some breakfast."

He stepped back to let her in, and she noticed that he moved unsteadily. "I don't eat breakfast, but thanks."

She followed him into the house. He disappeared into the bathroom and came out a few minutes later, dressed in his policeman's uniform. He looked sick and shaky, with his silvery hair slicked back from his face. The lines under his eyes were deeply etched, as if they'd been painted on.

Without thinking, she reached for him, touched his forehead. "Maybe you should stay home . . ."

He froze, and she could see that he was startled by the intimacy of her touch. She yanked her hand back, feeling the heat of embarrassment on her cheeks. "I'm sorry. I shouldn't—"

"Don't," he said softly. "I have trouble sleeping, is all."

She almost went to him then, almost started a conversation that wasn't for her to begin. Instead, she changed the subject. That was always the safest thing—to keep it strictly about Izzy. "Will you be home for dinner?"

He turned away, and she knew he was thinking about the last two nights. He'd been too late for dinner both nights. "My schedule—"

"It would mean a lot to Izzy."

"You think I don't know that?" He turned to her, and in his eyes was a bleak desperation that wrapped around her heart. "I'm sorry—"

He shook his head, held a hand up, as if to ward her off. "I'll be home," he said, then he pushed past her and left the house.

Their days together followed a comfortable routine. Annie arrived early and spent the day with Izzy, playing, reading, walking around the forest. In the early evening, she made a hot dinner for the two of them, and afterward, they played board games or watched videos until bedtime.

Every night, Annie tucked Izzy into bed and kissed her good night.

Nick consistently missed dinner, forgot to call, and showed up around nine o'clock, smelling of smoke and booze. Even when he promised to be home, as he did almost every night, he didn't make it.

She was tired of making excuses for him. Once again, it was bedtime and this beautiful child was going to have to go to bed without a kiss from her father.

She glanced at Izzy, who stood now at the big picture window, staring out at the falling night. She'd been

stationed there for almost thirty minutes, no doubt listening for the quiet purr of her dad's patrol car.

She went to Izzy and knelt beside her on the hardwood
floor. She chose her words with care. "When I was a little
girl, my mom died. It made my daddy and me very quiet
for a long time. When my dad saw me, all he could think
about was my mama, and the hurt made him stop looking
at me."

Izzy's brown eyes filled with tears. Her lower lip trembled
and she bit down on it.

Annie reached up and caught a single tear on the tip of
her finger. "My daddy came back to me, though. It took a
while, but he came back because he loved me. Just like
your daddy loves you."

Annie waited for Izzy to respond—so long the waiting
became noticeable. Then she smiled and pushed to her
feet. Her knees popped and cracked at the suddenness of
her movement. "Come on, pumpkin. Let's get you to bed."
She started to walk toward the stairs.

Izzy fell into step beside her. Annie slowed her steps to
match the child's as they climbed the stairs. Halfway up,
Izzy inched closer and slid her hand into Annie's. It was
the first time Izzy had touched her.

Annie clung to the tiny fingers, squeezing gently. *That's
it, Izzy . . . keep reaching out. I won't let you fall.*

Upstairs, after Izzy brushed her teeth, they knelt beside
the bed together. Annie recited the "Now-I-lay-me" prayer
and then tucked Izzy into bed, kissing her forehead. After a
quiet moment, she went to the rocking chair by the
window and sat down.

The chair made a soft *ka-thump, ka-thump* on the
wooden floor. Her gaze moved from Izzy to the window.

She stared out at the glittering moonlit lake, listening to the slow evening-out of the girl's breathing.

As so often happened, the nightly ritual made Annie remember. When her own mother had died, she'd been much too young to handle her grief. All she knew was that one day her world was bright and shining and filled with love, and the next, everything fell into a gloomy, saddened, tear-stained landscape. She could still recall how much it had scared her to see her father cry.

That was when the blueprint of her life had been drawn. She'd become a good little girl who never cried, never complained, never asked uncomfortable questions.

It had taken her years to grieve. Her first year away from home had been incredibly lonely. Stanford was no place for a small-town millworker's daughter. It had shown her—for the first time—that she was poor and her family uneducated.

Her love for Hank was the only reason she stayed at that big, unwelcoming school. She knew how much it meant to him that she was the first Bourne to attend college. And so she kept her head down and her shoulders hunched and she did her best to fit in. But the loneliness was often overwhelming.

One day she started her car, and the sound of the engine triggered something. The memory was as unexpected as a snowstorm in July. All at once, she felt her mother beside her in the car, and Annie's Volkswagen "Bug" had become the old station wagon they'd once had, the one with the wood-grain strip along the side. She didn't know where they'd been going, she and her mom, or what they'd talked about, and she realized with a sharp, sudden pain that she couldn't recall the sound of her mother's voice. The more she tried to slip into the moment, to immerse herself in the memory, the more flat and one dimensional it had become.

Until that moment, she had actually—naively—thought she'd overcome the death of her mother, but on that day, more than ten years after they'd placed her mother's coffin in the cold, dark ground, Annie fell apart. She cried for all the missed moments—the nighttime kisses, the spontaneous hugs, the joy that would never be as complete again. She grieved most of all for the loss of her childhood innocence, which had been taken on a rainy day without warning, leaving behind an adult in a child's body, a girl who knew that life was unfair and love could break your heart, and mostly, that nothing was worse than being left behind by the one you loved.

It took her several days to master her grief, and even then control was tissue-thin, a layer of brittle ice on a cold, black body of water. It was not surprising that she fell in love almost immediately after that. She had been a walking wound of loneliness, and caretaking was the only way she knew to fill the void in her soul. When she met Blake, she showered him with all the pent-up longing and love that was inside her.

Annie slowly got out of the rocker and tiptoed to the bed. Izzy was sleeping peacefully. Annie wondered if the child was blessed with dreams in which Kathy appeared; Annie herself was rarely so lucky.

She was halfway down the stairs when the phone rang. She jumped down the last few risers and dove for the phone, answering it on the third ring. "Nick?"

There was a moment of silence, then a woman's voice said, *"Nick?"*

Annie winced. "Hi, Terri."

"Oh, no you don't, don't you dare act like this is a normal conversation. Who in the hell is Nick and where are you? I called Hank and he gave me this number."

Annie sank onto the sofa and tucked her knees up underneath her. "It's nothing, really. I'm baby-sitting for an old friend and he's late getting home."

"I had *hoped* you'd changed. A little bit, at least."

"What do you mean?"

"You just spent twenty years waiting for a man to come home—now you're waiting for another man? That's insane."

It *was* insane. Why hadn't Annie seen that on her own? It made her angry suddenly, both that she'd lost the ability to really get mad, and that she'd allowed herself to take from Nick what she'd spent a lifetime accepting from Blake. Excuses and lies. "Yeah," she muttered more to herself than to Terri. "I only have to take this kind of shit from men I'm in love with."

"Well, that answers my next question. But what—"

"I've got to run, Terri. I'll call you later." Annie could still hear Terri's voice as she hung up the phone. Then she punched in another number.

Lurlene answered on the second ring. "Hello?"

"Lurlene? It's Annie—"

"Is everything all right?"

"Fine, but Nick isn't home yet."

"He's probably down at Zoe's, havin' a drink—or ten."

Annie nodded. That's what she'd suspected as well. "Could you come watch Izzy for a little while? I want to go talk to him."

"He ain't gonna like that."

"Be that as it may, I'm going."

"Give me ten minutes."

After she hung up, Annie went upstairs and checked on Izzy again, then she hurried back downstairs and paced the living room. True to her word, Lurlene showed up in ten minutes, wearing a puffy pink chenille bathrobe and green plastic clogs.

"Heya, honey," she said quietly, stepping into the house.

"Thanks for coming," Annie said, grabbing her purse off the coffee table. "This won't take long."

Chapter 11

Annie stood on the sidewalk below a cockeyed pink neon sign that read: *Zoe's Hot Spot Tavern*. It sputtered and gave off a faint buzzing sound.

Clutching her handbag, she went inside. The tavern was bigger than she'd expected, a large rectangular room, with a wooden bar along the right wall. Pale blue light shone from tubes above a long mirror. Dozens of neon beer signs flickered in shades of blue and red and gold. Men and women sat slumped on bar stools, drinking and talking and smoking. Every now and then, she heard the thump of a glass hitting the bar.

Way in the back were two pool tables, resting beneath pyramids of fluorescent lighting, with people bent over them, and others standing alongside, watching. Someone broke up a rack of balls and the sound was a loud *crack* in the darkness.

Keeping her back to the side wall, she edged deeper into the place, until she saw Nick. He was at a table in the back corner. She pushed through the crowd.

"Nick?"

When he saw her, he lurched to his feet. "Is Izzy—"

"She's fine."

"Thank God."

He was unsteady on his feet as he backed away from her. He stumbled and plopped into his chair. Reaching out, he grabbed his drink and downed it in a single swallow. Then he said softly, "Go away, Annie. I don't . . ."

She squatted beside him. "You don't what?"

He spoke so quietly she had to strain to catch the words. "I don't want you to see me here . . . like this."

"Did you know that she listens for you every night, Nick? She sits beside the front door for as long as her little eyes can stay open, waiting to hear your footsteps on the porch."

"Don't do this to me . . ."

Her heart went out to him, but she didn't dare stop, not now when she'd finally found the courage to begin. "Go home to her, Nick. Take care of your little girl. This time you have with her . . . it goes away so quickly, don't you know that? Don't you know that in a heartbeat, you'll be packing her bags and watching her board a plane for somewhere far away from you?"

The look he gave her was sad and hopeless. "I can't take care of her, Annie. Haven't you figured that out? Christ, I can't take care of anyone." In an awkward, jerking motion, he pushed to his feet. "But I'll go home and pretend. It's what I've been doing for the past eight months." Without looking at her, he tossed a twenty-dollar bill on the table and walked out of the bar.

She rushed after him, trying all the way through the crowded bar to figure out what to say to him. At the curb outside, he finally stopped and looked at her. "Will you do me one more favor?"

"Anything."

A quick frown darted across his face, made Annie wonder why he'd expected to be let down. Why was it so hard for him to believe that she wanted to help him?

"Drive me home?"

She smiled. "Of course."

The next morning, Annie arrived at Nick's house an hour early. She slipped through the unlocked door and crept up the stairs. She checked on Izzy, found her sleeping peacefully, then went to Nick's bedroom. It was empty. She went down the hall to a guest room and pushed the door open.

The curtains were drawn, and no sunlight came through the heavy Navajo-print drapes. Against one wall was an old-fashioned four-poster bed. She could just make out Nick's form beneath a mound of red wool blankets.

She should have known that he didn't sleep in the master bedroom anymore.

Annie knew it was dangerous to enter his room, a place where she didn't belong, but she couldn't help herself. She went to his bed and stood beside him. In sleep, he looked young and innocent; more like the boy she'd known so long ago than the man she'd recently met.

It came to her softly, whispering on the even, quiet sound of his breathing, how much she had once loved him. . . .

Until the night she saw him kiss Kathy.

She needs me, Annie, don't you see that? he'd said afterward. *We fit.*

I can fit with you, Nicky, she'd pleaded softly.

No. He'd touched her cheek, and the gentleness of his touch had made her cry. *You don't need someone like me, Annie Bourne. You're off to Stanford in the fall. You're going to set the world on fire.*

"What are you doing here so early?"

With a start, Annie realized that he was awake, and that he was looking at her. "I . . . I thought you might need me."

Frowning, he sat up. The covers fell away from his body, revealing a chest that was covered with coarse black hair.

She waited for him to say something, but he just sat there, his eyes closed. His skin had a waxy, yellow cast, made even more noticeable by the tangle of silvery-white hair and the blackness of his eyelashes. A fine sheen of sweat had broken out on his forehead and upper lip.

She pulled up a chair and sat beside the bed. "Nick, we've got to talk."

"Not now."

"You've got to make a better effort with Izzy."

He looked at her finally. "I don't know how to help her, Annie. She scares me." The words were spoken softly, and they were steeped in pain. "I mean to have one drink with the boys after work, but then I start thinking about coming home . . . to my empty bedroom and my disappearing daughter, and one drink turns into two. . . ."

"You'd be fine if you'd stop drinking."

"No. I've always been shitty at taking care of the women I love. Ask Kathy about it."

Annie fought an unexpected urge to brush the hair away from his face—anything to let him know that he wasn't as alone as he felt. "You couldn't make her well, Nick."

He seemed to deflate. A low, tired sigh slipped from his lips. "I'd rather not talk about this now. I don't feel good. I need—"

"Izzy loves you, Nick. I understand your broken heart—at least to the extent anyone can understand such a thing—but nursing it is a luxury. You're her father. You simply don't have the right to fall apart. She needs you to be strong. But mostly, she needs you to be *here*."

"I know that," he said softly, and she could hear the heartache in his voice, the hushed admission of his own failure. "I'll be home for a family dinner on Friday night. It'll be a beginning. Okay? Is that what you want from me?"

Annie knew that it was another lie, a promise that would be broken. Nick had lost faith in himself, and without it, he was in a turbulent sea without any sense of direction, waiting to be sucked under the current once again.

"It isn't what I want from you that matters, Nick," she said softly, and in the deep sadness that seeped through his eyes, she knew that he understood.

If Izzy stood very, very still, she could feel her daddy in the house. There was the faintest smell of him, the smoky smell that always made Izzy want to cry.

She hugged Miss Jemmie to her chest and inched out of her bedroom. She heard voices coming from her daddy's new room, and for a split second, it sounded like it used to, before the bad thing.

But it wasn't Mommy who was talking to him.

Mommy was up with the angels, and down in the ground, and once you went to those two places, there was no coming back. Daddy had told her that.

She crept down the darkened hallway and went downstairs.

Everything looked so pretty; there were fresh flowers in a vase on the table, and the windows were open. Her mommy would have liked the way it looked now.

She opened the big wooden front door and went out onto the porch.

A pink sun was hanging just above the tops of the trees, and she knew it would soon rise into a blue sky. But it was still too early, and a layer of soft hazy fog clung to the sides of the lake and peeked out from the trees. Her heart started beating faster and she had trouble breathing.

She cast a quick glance back inside to make sure no one was watching, then slipped past the screen door. Birds chirped from the high branches of a big old tree as she made her way across the wet grass.

Ducking into her hiding place in the forest, she stared hard at the fog. *Mommy?*

She listened really, really close. After a few moments, she heard it, the whisper-soft answer of her mother's voice.

Hey, Izzy-bear, are yah busy?

Her eyes popped open. In the wavering gray fog, she saw a woman's outline, golden hair and all.

I'm disappearin', Mommy, just like you.

Her mommy's voice was a sigh that sounded like the breeze. She felt her touch, a gentle ruffling of her hair. *Oh, Izzy-bear . . .*

For the first time, her mommy sounded sad, not happy to see her at all. She peered into the mist, saw her mommy's blue, blue eyes through the gray. Red tears fell from her mommy's eyes, like tiny drops of blood. *It's getting harder for me, Izzy, coming to see you.*

Izzy felt a rush of panic. *But I'm comin' as fast as I can!*

She felt it again, the softness of her mother's hand in the

coolness of the breeze. *It won't work, Izzy-bear. You can't follow me.*

Tears stung Izzy's eyes, blurred everything until she couldn't see anything anymore. She blinked away the tears.

The fog was moving away from her.

She ran after it, following the pale cloud to the edge of the lake. *Mommy, don't go, Mommy. I'll be good this time . . . I promise I'll be good. I'll clean my room and brush my teeth and go to bed without a sound . . . Mommy, please . . .*

But sunlight hit the surface of the water and cut through the fog until there was nothing left of it.

She knelt down on the cold, gravelly bank and cried.

Nick limped out of his bedroom. It had taken him forever to dress in his uniform, and buttoning the collar was flat impossible. With one hand on the wooden wall for support, he made his way down the hallway. Clutching the slick wooden handrail, he went down the stairs, one painful step at a time.

His body felt as brittle as a winter leaf. Sweat crawled across his forehead and slid in cold, wet streaks down his back.

It was a miracle that he reached the bottom of the stairs without falling or puking. Still holding the banister in a death grip, he paused, sucking in air, trying to keep the bile from rising in his throat. Tears stung his eyes from the effort.

He blinked and forced the nausea away.

When he reopened his eyes, he noticed the changes Annie had made in his home. A fire leaped and danced in

the gray river-rock opening. The two leather chairs had been shined up and now sat opposite the sofa, and between them the rough-hewn wooden coffee table glowed a beautiful reddish brown. On the table was a polished silver water pitcher full of fern fronds and white blossoms.

He had often dreamed of a room just like this one, filled with the sounds of laughter . . . instead of the hushed silences and sudden outbursts that had been Kathy's way.

With a heavy sigh, he moved away from the stairway.

That's when he saw his Izzy. She was standing beside the big windows that overlooked the lake; golden sunlight created a halo around her face. Time drew in a sudden breath and fell away, leaving Izzy as she once was, a porcelain doll dressed in pretty clothes, with satin ribbons in her braided hair.

She looked at him from across the room, her eyes wide.

"Hey, Izzy," he said, trying to smile. "You look gorgeous."

She blinked and didn't move.

He wet his dry lips. A bead of sweat slid down his temple.

Just then, Annie came bustling out of the kitchen, carrying a steaming pot of coffee and a covered serving dish. At the sight of him, she stopped dead. "Nick! This is wonderful, you can join us for breakfast."

The thought of breakfast sent his sour stomach into revolt.

"Izzy, go help your daddy into the sunroom. I've got breakfast set up in there. I'd better add another place at the table."

She apparently had no idea he was about to throw up. She just kept on talking—about what, he had no idea—and fluttering between the kitchen and the sunroom. Her chatter buzzed like gnats around his head.

"Annie, I don't—"

"Izzy," she said again. "Go help your daddy. He doesn't feel well." And she was off again, scurrying toward the sunroom.

Izzy looked up at him when they were alone in the room. Her brown eyes were wide with uncertainty.

"I don't need help, Izzy," he said. "I'm just fine, really."

She looked at him a moment longer, then slowly she moved toward him. He thought she was going to walk past him, but at the last second, she stopped and looked up at him.

It killed him to see the fear in her eyes, and that damned black glove almost did him in. Annie was right. He *had* to be a better father. No more drinking to dull the memories and sugarcoat his failures. He had to take care of his baby. Feeling awkward and unsure, he smiled down at her. "Come on, Izzy-Bear. Let's go."

Slowly, he covered her one bare hand with his larger, calloused one. Together, they walked toward the sunroom. His steps matched hers perfectly. It was sadly silent between them, the daughter who no longer spoke and the father who had no idea what to say.

Annie was beaming when they walked in. The sunroom looked like a picture from one of those women's magazines. There was a bright blue tablecloth on the rickety plank table, with a centerpiece of huckleberry and dogwood in a crockery vase. Plates were heaped with scrambled eggs and pancakes. Beside the three empty plates were glasses of milk and orange juice.

"Sit down," she said to both of them. She helped Izzy into a seat and scooted her close to the table.

Nick slowly sat down, trying to ignore the drums beating inside his head.

"Just coffee for me," he croaked. "I feel like shi—" He glanced at Izzy. "I feel bad. A headache, is all."

Izzy's eyes told him that she knew all about Daddy's *headaches*. Guilt came at him hard, riding on the crest of shame.

He reached for the pitcher of orange juice, but his aim was off. He whacked the vase with his fist, sent it flying. Water sprayed everywhere, evergreen boughs flopped across the eggs, dripping. The vase hit the floor with a loud *craaack*.

Nick squeezed his eyes shut. "Shit," he moaned, cradling his throbbing head in his hands.

"Now, don't you worry a bit about that. Everyone has accidents—don't they, Izzy?" Annie stood up and dabbed at the puddles with her napkin.

He turned to Annie, ready to tell her that he had to get the hell out of here, but her smile stopped him. She looked so damned . . . hopeful. He couldn't bear to disappoint her. He swallowed the thick lump in his throat and wiped the sheen of sweat from his brow with a weak hand.

Annie gave him a broad smile and began dishing out food. She served herself a man-size portion of eggs and a stack of pancakes a logger couldn't finish.

He tried to concentrate on that, her food—anything besides his headache and the tremors that quaked through his limbs. "Are you going to eat all that?"

She laughed. "I'm from California. I haven't had an egg in fifteen years, and lately I've been eating like a pig. I'm hungry all the time." Still smiling, she poured syrup over the whole god-awful mess and began eating and talking, eating and talking.

Nick curled both shaking hands around a thick porcelain coffee cup. When he thought he was steady enough, he brought the cup to his lips and took a slow, thankful sip. The hot coffee soothed his jittery nerves and took the shine off his headache. Slowly, slowly, he leaned back in the chair and let himself be carried away by the comforting buzz of Annie's voice. After a while, he managed to eat a bit of breakfast. Through it all, Annie talked and laughed and carried on as if they were a family who ate breakfast together every morning, instead of a silent, disappearing child and her hungover father. She acted as if it were normal, what Nick and Izzy had become.

He couldn't take his eyes off Annie. Every time she laughed, the sound moved through Nick in a shiver of longing, until he began at last to wonder how long it had been since *he* had laughed, since his Izzy had laughed . . . how long since they'd had something to laugh about or a moment together in which to find joy. . . .

"I thought we'd go to the Feed Store today and buy some gardening supplies," Annie said brightly. "It's a good day to get that flower garden into shape. Why, if the three of us worked, it would take no time at all."

Gardening. Nick recalled how much he used to love working in the yard, planting bulbs, raking leaves, snipping dead roses from the thorny bushes. He'd loved the triumph of watching something he'd planted and watered and nurtured actually *grow.* He had always loved the first buds of spring, but this year they'd come without his even noticing. All he'd noticed was the spindly, bare cherry tree he'd planted after Kathy's funeral.

"What do you think, Izzy?" Annie said into the thick silence. "Should we let your dad help?"

Izzy picked up her spoon, holding it in two tiny

fingers—the only ones his baby thought she had left—and shook it so hard it cracked on the table.

Annie gazed at him across the flowers. "That means your daughter would love to garden with you, Nick Delacroix. Can she count on you?"

Nick wanted to pretend it was that easy, a few spoken words at a breakfast table and everything could be made right again. But it had been a long, long time since he'd been that naive. Even as he nodded, he knew that it could end up being a lie. Another promise made by a man who'd kept too few.

Chapter 12

Nick sat in his squad car on the edge of downtown Mystic. Beyond the six short blocks, Mount Olympus rose like something out of a fairy tale, its snow-capped peak brushed up against the swollen gray underbelly of the sky. Leaves scudded across the rough concrete sidewalk, pushed along by a chilly breeze. As always, the town looked beaten and forlorn, tired around the edges. A steady stream of gray white smoke issued from the mill's distant stack, leaving behind the acrid, pulpy scent of wood.

He used to love walking these streets. He'd known everything about the people he was sworn to protect: when their daughters were getting married and their sons were preparing for bar mitzvahs, when their grandparents were moved into nursing homes and when their kids started day care. He'd always taken pride in how well he did his job; he knew that by checking up on these people every day, he contributed to their sense of well-being.

He knew he'd been letting everything that mattered slip away from him, but he was terrified to start caring again. What if he failed Izzy once more? She needed so much from him, his brown-eyed little girl, and Nick had an ugly habit of failing those he loved. Even when he tried his best. It was *his* fault Izzy was disappearing, *his* fault she didn't feel safe or loved; he knew that. If he'd been a stronger man, a better man, he could have helped her through the grief, but he hadn't been able to do a damn thing. Hell, he couldn't even help himself, and he sure as hell hadn't helped Kathy.

It would be difficult, finding his way back, but Annie was right. It was time. For the first time in months, he felt a stirring of hope.

He eased out of the car and took a first cautious step into his old life. He merged quietly into the crowd of late-afternoon shoppers. All around him, people were moving, darting into stores, coming back out with paper bags and parcels. He noticed the sounds of everyday life. Car doors slamming, horns honking, quarters clicking into parking meters.

Every person he saw waved at him, said "Heya, Nick" as he passed, and with each greeting, he felt himself coming back to life. It was almost like the old days, before Kathy's death. Back when his uniform had always been clean and starched, and his hands had never trembled.

He walked past the stores, waving at shopkeepers. At the kids' clothing store, he saw a beautiful little pink dress in the window. It was exactly what Izzy needed. As he opened the door, a bell tinkled overhead.

Susan Frame squealed from her place at the cash register and came at Nick like a charging bull, her pudgy pink hands waving in the air. "Good Lord, I can't believe it's you."

He grinned. "Hi, Susan. Long time no see."

She swatted him on the shoulder and laughed, her triple chins jiggling. "You haven't been in here in ages."

"Yeah, well . . ."

"How are you doing?"

"Better. I saw that little girl's dress in the window—"

She clapped her pudgy hands together. "Ooh-ee, that's a beautiful thing. Perfect for Miss Isabella. How old is she now?"

"Six."

"Ooh, I'll bet she's growing like a weed. I haven't seen her since her mama—" She shut up abruptly and took him by the arm, propelling him through the store. He let himself be carried away by her steady, comforting stream of words. He wasn't listening to her; she knew it and didn't care. She seemed to sense that it was a major event for him to be here.

She plucked the dress off the hanger. It was a pink and white gingham with a white lace underskirt and a pale blue yoke embroidered with tiny pink and white flowers. It reminded him of Kathy's garden—

Come out here, Nicky—the tulips are coming up—

It hit him like a blow, the memory. He winced and squeezed his eyes shut. *Don't think about the flowers . . . don't think about her at all. . . .*

"Nick? Are you feeling well?"

A little unsteadily, he pulled a twenty-dollar bill from his pants pocket and tossed it on the counter. "The dress is perfect, Susan. Can you wrap it up?"

She answered, but he wasn't listening. All he could think about was Zoe's, and how a single drink—just one— would calm the shaking in his hands.

"Here you go, Nick."

It seemed only a second had passed before she was back beside him, waving a big lavender-wrapped package beneath his face. He wet his dry lips and tried to smile.

Susan touched his shoulder. "Nick, are you all right?"

He nodded, though even that simple action seemed to take too long. "I'm fine. Fine. Thanks." Gripping the package, he pushed through the glass door and went outside.

It had started to rain, big nickel-size drops that splashed his face. He glanced longingly toward Zoe's.

No. He wouldn't go that way. He'd finish out his rounds and head home. Izzy and Annie were waiting, and he didn't want to disappoint them. Taking a deep breath, he straightened his shoulders and kept moving down the street, his hand resting lightly on his baton. With each step, he felt better, stronger.

He returned to his patrol car and got inside, ducking out of the hammering rain. He reached for the radio, but before he could say anything, a call came out.

Domestic disturbance on Old Mill Road.

"Shit." He answered the call, flicked on his siren, and headed out of town.

When he reached the Weavers' driveway, he knew it was bad already. Through the falling rain and the curtain of trees, he could see the distant red and yellow blur of lights. He raced up the bumpy road, his heart beating so fast he couldn't draw an even breath.

The mobile home was surrounded by cars—two patrol cars and an ambulance.

Nick slammed the car in park and jumped out. The first person he saw was Captain Joe Nation, the man who had given Nick a place to live all those years ago.

Joe was walking out of the trailer, shaking his head. The

long black and gray braids he wore swayed gently at the
movement. Across the clearing, he caught sight of Nick,
and he stopped.

"Joe?" Nick said, out of breath already.

Joe laid a thick, veiny hand on Nick's forearm. "Don't
go in there, Nicholas."

"No . . ."

"There's nothing you can do now. Nothing anyone
can do."

Nick shoved past Joe and ran up the muddy driveway,
splashing through the puddles. The door fell away beneath
his shove and crashed against the wall.

Inside, several people were milling about, searching for
clues in the green shag carpeting. Nick pushed past them
and went into the bedroom, where Sally lay on the bed, her
thin floral dress shoved high on her rail-thin legs, her face
bloodied almost beyond recognition. A red-black blotch of
blood seeped across her chest and lay in an oozing puddle
across the wrinkled gray sheets.

Nick skidded to a stop. It felt as if pieces of him were
crumbling away. He knew he was swaying like an old
Doug fir in a heavy wind, but he couldn't stop. He was
thrown back suddenly to another time, another place,
when he had had to identify a similarly beaten body . . .

"Goddamn it, Sally," he whispered in a harsh, fractured
voice.

He went to her, knelt beside her bed, and brushed the
bloodied, matted hair away from her face. Her skin was
still warm to the touch, and he could almost believe that
she would wake up suddenly and smile and tell him that it
was nothing.

"Don't touch her, sir," said someone. "The evidence . . ."

Nick drew his shaking hand back and got awkwardly to his feet. He wanted to pull her dress down—give her that final dignity at least—but he couldn't. No one could do anything that mattered for Sally anymore. Now it was time for detectives and photographers and pathologists.

He turned blindly away from the bed and stumbled through the cluttered trailer, emerging into the rainy day; everything looked exactly as it had ten minutes ago, but nothing felt the same.

Joe came up to him, pulled him away from the trailer. It felt strangely as if it were years and years ago, back when Joe had met a skinny, freezing fifteen-year-old boy at the bus station in Port Angeles. "There was nothing you could do, Nicholas," he said. "She didn't want our help."

Nick felt the life slowly, inexorably draining out of him. Buried images of another night, not long ago, were oozing to the forefront of his mind, images that were also stained in blood and violence and tragedy. He'd spent eight months running from the images of that night, burying them deep in his subconscious, but now they were back, killing him. "It's too much," he said, shaking his head. "Too much."

Joe patted his back. "Go home, Nicholas. Go home to the little girl who loves you and your beautiful house on the lake and forget about this."

Unable to move, Nick stood there, gripping the butt of his gun, standing in the rain, knowing there was only one thing that could help him now.

Nick hadn't shown up for dinner again.

Annie had tried to pretend it meant nothing. She'd made a great show of cheeriness for Izzy, but she knew that the child wasn't fooled. No amount of cookie dough or knock-knock jokes could make Izzy stop looking outside. . . .

Annie held the girl in her lap, gently rocking back and forth in a rocking chair on the porch. She hummed a quiet song and stroked Izzy's silky hair.

She could feel a tiny tremble in the child's body, and if she listened very, very carefully, she could hear the unasked questions in Izzy's in-drawn breaths.

"Your daddy will be back soon, Izzy," she said softly, praying it was true. "He loves you very much."

Izzy didn't move, didn't respond.

"Sometimes grown-ups get confused . . . just like kids do. And your dad's confused right now. He doesn't feel like he belongs anywhere, but if we're patient, and we give him time, I think he'll figure it out. It's hard to be patient, though, isn't it? Especially when the waiting hurts."

Annie's voice faded. She closed her eyes and leaned back in the rocker, listening to the rhythmic scraping of wood on wood and the plunking echo of rain on the porch roof.

"He loves you, Izzy," she said at last, perhaps more to herself than to the silent child. "I *know* he loves you."

It took her a moment, but Annie realized there was a sound coming from the child, a tiny, reed-thin whisper that sounded like *png-png-png*.

She was mimicking the sound of the rain hitting the tin roof overhead.

Annie smiled.

Izzy was trying to find her way back.

Izzy felt the scream starting again. It was way down deep inside her, in that dark place where the night-mares lived. Every time she closed her eyes, she saw her mommy, and she remembered what she'd heard. *You can't follow me . . . can't follow me . . . can't follow me . . .*

What if that were true? What if she disappeared into the fog and still couldn't find her mommy? A tiny, whimpering cry escaped her lips.

She was scared. It was one of those nights when nothing good happened in her sleep and she woke up with tears on her cheeks. She kept dreaming about that doctor, the one with the pointy nose and the thick glasses who told her that she had to talk or else she wouldn't get over her mommy. It had scared her so much, those grown-up words that she hardly understood. The last thing she'd ever said was to him. *I don't want to get over my mommy. . . .*

Her whole body was shaking.

She didn't want to scream again.

She threw the covers back and slithered out of bed, walking barefooted to the closed door. There, she stopped. She stared down at her own hand, at all that nothingness around her thumb and forefinger. She wished suddenly that she wasn't disappearing, that she could just reach out and grab that old doorknob and twist it hard.

With a sigh, she used her two fingers to turn the knob. It took a while, but finally, she got the door open.

She poked her head out and saw the dark hallway.

Her daddy's room was to the left, just three doors down, but she knew he wouldn't be there. She'd heard Annie talking to Lurlene. They thought she was gone, but she wasn't. She'd been hiding in the corners, listening.

Her daddy was in the bad place, the place that made him smell like cigarettes even though he didn't smoke, the place that made him come home with that scary look in his eyes and slam his bedroom door shut. The place that made him walk funny.

She crept down the hallway and peeked over the railing, and saw Annie asleep on the sofa.

Annie, who held Izzy's hand and brushed her hair and acted like it didn't matter at all that she didn't talk. Annie, who was going to make her mommy's garden grow again.

Very slowly, she went down the stairs. The steps felt cold beneath her bare feet and made her shiver, but she didn't care. Once she started walking, she felt better. The scream slipped back into the dark place.

She almost wanted to say something, call out Annie's name, maybe, but it had been so long since she'd even wanted to talk, it felt weird. She couldn't even remember what her voice sounded like anymore.

She tiptoed to the sofa. Annie was asleep, with her mouth open. Her short hair was smashed to one side of her head and stuck straight up on the other.

Izzy wasn't sure what to do. When she was little, she used to climb into her mommy and daddy's bed whenever she was scared, and it felt so good, so warm. Mommy would curl Izzy up in her arms and tuck the blanket around them both, and Izzy would go to sleep.

Annie made a quiet snoring sound and stretched out, leaving a big empty space along the edge of the sofa. Just enough space for Izzy.

Izzy cautiously peeled back the scratchy blue blanket and gingerly crawled onto the couch.

She lay stiffly on her side, hardly breathing. She was afraid Annie would wake up and tell her to go back to her room. But she didn't want to be alone in her room. She was scared of the dark in there.

Annie made another quiet sound and rolled toward Izzy.

Izzy clamped down on her breath and went perfectly still.

Annie curled her arm protectively around Izzy's body and pulled her close.

Izzy felt as if she were melting. For the first time in months, she felt as if she could breathe right. She snuggled backward, poking her bottom into the vee of Annie's bent body, so they were like two spoons pressed together.

With a quiet, happy sigh, she closed her eyes.

In the early hours of the morning, Annie woke to the scent of baby shampoo and the feel of a small, warm body tucked against hers. It brought back a flood of memories— days long ago and a child that was now far away and hadn't been a baby in years. She gently stroked Izzy's sweaty hair and kissed her small, pink ear. "Sleep well, princess."

Izzy snuggled closer. A quiet sound answered Annie, so quiet she might have missed it if they'd been outside or if it had been raining or she had been talking.

In her sleep, Izzy laughed.

Annie glanced at the clock on the mantel. It was five-thirty in the morning. Very gently, she peeled back the blanket and climbed over Izzy. Hugging herself against the chill morning air, she walked over to the window and stared out at the lake. Dawn was a pink brush stroke across the serrated black treetops.

"Damn you," she whispered.

This time, Nick hadn't come home all night.

Chapter 13

The phone rang at five forty-five in the morning. Annie reached over Izzy and answered softly, "Hello?"

"Hello. Annie Bourne, please."

She frowned, trying to place the male voice. "This is she."

"This is Captain Joseph Nation, of the Mystic police force."

Annie's stomach clenched. She eased away from the sleeping child and sat down on the cold floor. "It's Nick . . ."

"He was in an accident last night."

"Oh, my God. Is he—"

"Fine. Apart from a few bruises and . . . a hell of a hangover, he's going to be fine. He's at Mystic Memorial."

"Was he driving?"

"No. He was smart enough to get a ride home with someone—but not smart enough to pick a sober driver."

"Was anyone else hurt?"

Captain Nation sighed. "No. They hit a tree out on Old Mill Road. The driver walked away without a scratch, and

Nick just bonked his head a good one. He has a slight concussion. He was lucky . . . this time. I'm calling because he's going to need a ride home from the hospital."

Annie glanced over at Izzy, sleeping so peacefully on the sofa. She couldn't help remembering the way Izzy had waited and waited for a daddy who didn't come home— because he was getting drunk again.

Enough was enough. Slowly, she answered, "Oh, I'll come get him all right."

Nick moaned and tried to roll over, but the covers were tangled around his legs so tightly he couldn't move. Slowly, so as not to punish his already throbbing head, he pushed to his elbows and looked around. Lights stabbed through his brain, and somewhere a radio was blaring.

He was lying in a narrow, metal-rimmed bed. Fluorescent tube worms crisscrossed the ceiling, sending blinding pyramids of light into the white-walled room. A bright yellow privacy curtain hung in folds from ceiling to floor.

He closed his eyes and thumped back onto the narrow bed, flinging an arm across his face. He felt like shit. His head hurt, his eyes ached, his mouth was dry, and his stomach felt as if it had been scraped clean by a rusty scalpel. His whole body was shaking and weak.

"So, Nicholas? You back among the living?"

All in all, it was not a good sign to wake up in a hospital bed with your boss standing beside you. Even worse when that boss was as close to a father as you'd ever known.

Joe had offered Nick the first real home of his life. Nick had been young and scared and ready to run; his mother had taught him early that policemen were the enemy. But he'd had nowhere else to go. His mother's death and Social Services had given him no options.

You must be Nicholas, Joe had said that day. *I've got a spare bedroom . . . maybe you wouldn't mind hanging out with me for a while. My daughters have all gotten married and Louise—my wife—and I are sorta lonely.* And with those few welcoming words, Joe had shown Nick the first frayed edges of a new life.

Nick pushed up to his elbows again. It hurt to move; hell, it hurt to breathe. "Hey, Joe."

Joe stood quietly beside the bed, staring at Nick through sad, disappointed eyes. Deep wrinkles lined his forehead and bisected his round, dark-skinned cheeks. Long, gray-black hair hung in two skinny braids that curled against the blue checked polyester of his shirt. "You were in a car accident last night. Do you remember it? Joel was driving."

Nick went cold. "Christ. Did we hurt anyone?"

"Only you . . . this time."

Nick sagged in relief. He rubbed a trembling hand over his face, wishing he could take a shower. He smelled like booze and smoke and vomit. The last thing he remembered was taking a drink at Zoe's—his fourth, maybe. He couldn't remember getting into Joel's car at all.

With a high-pitched scraping sound of metal on linoleum that almost deafened Nick, Joe pulled up a chair and sat down next to the bed. "You remember the day we met?"

"Come on, Joe. Not now—"

"*Now.* I offered you everything I had to give. My home, my family, my friendship—and this is what you give me in return? I'm supposed to watch you turn into a drunk? If

Louise—God rest her soul—were alive, this would kill her. You blacked out, you know."

Nick winced. That was bad. "Where?" It was a stupid question, but it seemed important.

"At Zoe's."

Nick sank back onto the bed. In public. He'd blacked out in public. "Jesus Christ," he moaned. He could have done it in front of Izzy.

He didn't want to think about that. He threw the covers back and sat up. At the movement, his stomach lurched and his head exploded. He cradled his head in his hands and leaned forward, staring at the floor through burning eyes until he could breathe again.

"Nicholas, are you all right?"

Slowly, he looked up. It came back to him in bits and pieces: Sally Weaver . . . all that blood . . . Chuck's wailing voice, *it's not my fault.* . . . "Remember when you talked me into going into the academy, Joe? You told me I could help people like my mother. . . ."

Joe sighed. "We can't save 'em all, Nicholas."

"I can't do it anymore, Joe. We don't help people. All we do is clean up bloodstains. I can't . . . not anymore. . . ."

"You're a damn fine cop, but you have to learn that you can't save everyone—"

"Are you forgetting what I came home to last year? Hell, Joe, I can't save anyone. And I'm sick to fucking death of trying." He climbed out of bed. He stood there like an idiot, swaying and lurching in a feeble effort to stand still. His stomach coiled in on itself, just waiting for an excuse to purge. He clutched the metal bed frame in boneless, sweaty fingers. "You'll be getting my resignation tomorrow."

Joe stood up. Gently, he placed a hand on Nick's shoulder. "I won't accept it."

"It's killing me, Joe," he said softly.

"I'll agree to a vacation—for as long as you need. I know what you're going through, and you don't have to do it alone. But you do have to stop drinking."

Nick sighed. Everyone said that. *I know what you're going through.* But they didn't know; how could they? None of them had come home to his blood-spattered bedroom. Even Joe, who had been a full-blown alcoholic before his eighteenth birthday, and who had grown up in the blackened, marshy shadow of a drunken father. Even Joe couldn't completely understand. "You're wrong, Joe. In the end, we're all alone."

"It's that kind of thinking that got you into this mess. Believe me, I know the alcoholic-kid's code: don't tell, don't trust. But you've got to trust *someone,* Nicholas. There's a whole town here that cares about you, and you have a little girl who thinks you hung the moon. Stop thinking about what you've lost, and think about what you have left. You want to end up like your mother, half starved on a park bench, waiting to be killed? Or maybe you want to be like me—a man with two beautiful daughters who moved to the East Coast to get away from their drunken father." He pulled a business card out of his pocket and handed it to Nick. "When you're ready to sober up, here's the number for you to call. I'll help you—all of us will—but you have to take the first step by yourself."

"You look like warmed-over shit soup."

Nick didn't even look at Annie. "Nice language. They teach you that at Stanford?"

"No, but they did teach me not to drink and drive."

He glanced around, ran a shaking hand through his dirty, tangled hair. "Where's Izzy?"

"Ah, so you do remember her."

"Goddamn it, Annie—"

"We—your *daughter* and I—were worried about you last night. But you don't care about that, do you?"

Suddenly he was tired, so tired he didn't think he could stand up much longer. He pushed past her and stumbled out of the building. Her Mustang was parked in the loading zone in front of the electronic glass doors. Half falling, he grabbed onto the cold metal door handle and stood there, his eyes closed, concentrating on each breath.

He heard her walk past him. Her tennis shoes made a soft scuffing sound on the cement. She wrenched her car door open, got inside, and slammed the door shut. He wondered dully if she had any idea how loud it sounded to a man whose head was ticking like a bomb ready to go off.

She honked the horn, and the sound sliced painfully through his eardrums. He opened the door and collapsed onto the red vinyl seat with a haggard sigh.

The car lurched onto the rutted road. She sped up at every bump and pothole in the road, Nick was sure of it. He clung to the door handle for dear life, his knuckles white and sweaty.

"I spoke with your police captain, Mr. Nation, while you were getting dressed. He told me you were taking some time off from the force. And he mentioned your blackout."

"Great."

She made a low, whistling sound. "And what's that on your shirt front? Vomit? Yes, yes, what a high time you must have had yourself. God knows, it's better than being at home with your daughter."

He winced and closed his eyes, feeling shame sink deep into his gut. Joe's words came back to him. *You want to end up like your mother? Or maybe you want to be like me?* He thought about Izzy, and how she would remember him, and where she would go when she had the chance . . . he thought about what it would be like if she left him.

He slanted a look at Annie. She was sitting perfectly erect, her hands precisely placed at the ten o'clock and two o'clock positions on the steering wheel, her gaze focused on the empty road in front of them. "Would you do me a favor, Annie?"

"Of course."

"Take me to the Hideaway Motel on Route Seven," he said quietly. "And watch Izzy for a few days."

She frowned. "The Hideaway? It's a dump, and why—"

He felt as if he were treading water in the deep end of a swimming pool full of dark, murky water. He couldn't handle an argument; not now. "Please don't argue with me. I need some . . . time."

She cast a quick, worried look at him, then turned back to the road. "But Izzy—"

"Please?" The word came out soft and swollen, unmanly, but he couldn't help it. "Could you please stay with her while I get my act together? I know it's a lot to ask . . ."

She didn't answer, and for once the silence was uncomfortable. After a mile she flicked on her signal and turned off the highway. Within minutes, she had pulled into the parking lot at the Hideaway Motel. A neon sign flickered in the window. It read: SORRY. VACANCY. That pretty much summed it up.

"Here we are, Nick. I don't know . . ."

"Home sweet home," he said, smiling weakly.

She turned to him then, and there was a softness in her expression that he hadn't expected. She leaned toward him, gently brushed the hair from his eyes. "I'll help you. But you'd better not screw up this time, Nicky. That beautiful child of yours doesn't need to lose her daddy, too."

"Christ, Annie," he whispered in agony.

"I know you love her, Nick." She leaned closer. "Just meet me halfway. Trust me. Or better yet, trust yourself."

Even as he told himself he'd fail again, he didn't care. He wanted the second chance she was offering. He was tired, so tired, of being lonely and afraid. The words *I want to try* weighed heavily on his tongue, but he hadn't the strength to give them a voice. He could remember too many other times he'd wanted a chance . . . and the times his mother had said, *Trust me, Nicky, I mean it this time*. He had long ago gotten out of the habit of trusting people.

He climbed out of the car and stood there, watching her drive away. When she was gone, he jammed his hands into his pockets and turned toward the motel. Fishing his credit card out of his front pocket, he signed the register and got himself a room for the night.

The room was small and dark and smelled of urine. Dirty brown walls ran in a perfect square around a sagging double bed. A gray woven bedspread covered a lumpy mattress. A curtainless window looked out onto the neighboring building's cement brick wall. Gold shag carpet, peeled away in places to reveal the bubbling blue foam pad, lay untacked atop a cement floor.

He could see the closet-size bathroom behind a wood-grain plastic door that hung awkwardly from broken hinges. He didn't have to go inside to know that there was a white plastic shower and beige toilet, and that rust ran in rings around the sink's metal drain.

He sat on the bed with a tired sigh. He had been living less than half a life for so long, and now even the half he'd clung to was slipping through his shaking, numb fingers like crumbled winter leaves. He knew that he'd been wrong to drink, that he'd gone down the wrong road when he first reached for a bottle. The booze was sucking him dry, and when it was finished with him there would be nothing left except a skinny, freezing old man on a park bench. . . .

On the far wall, a cockroach scurried up alongside the brown plastic molding and disappeared beneath a framed picture of Mount Olympus.

Finally, after eight months of drifting, he'd come to the end of the line. There was only one thing that might make a difference. He reached into his pocket and pulled out the card Joe had given him.

Annie kept Izzy busy all day, but as the night began to fall, she couldn't pretend anymore. She read Izzy a bedtime story after dinner, then pulled Izzy into her arms. "I need to tell you something, Izzy," she started softly, trying to find the right words. "Your daddy is going . . . to be away for a while. He's sick. But he'll be back. He loves you more than the world, and he'll be back."

Izzy didn't respond. Annie didn't know what to say, what words could soothe this situation. She held Izzy for a long, long time, humming tunes and stroking her hair, and then, finally, she sighed. "Well, it's bedtime." She pulled away from Izzy and got to her feet. She started to head for the stairs, but Izzy grabbed her hand.

Annie looked into the sad, frightened brown eyes, and it broke her heart all over again. "I'm not going anywhere, honey. I'm right here."

Izzy held on to her hand all the way up the stairs and down the hall, and into the bathroom. In the bedroom, she still wouldn't let go.

Annie looked down into the girl's huge brown eyes. "You want me to sleep with you?"

A quick smile darted across Izzy's face. She squeezed harder and nodded.

Annie climbed into Izzy's tiny twin bed, without bothering to brush her teeth or change her clothes. She left the Little Mermaid nightlight glowing next to the bed as Izzy snuggled close.

Annie stroked Izzy's soft cheek, remembering suddenly how much she'd missed talking about her mom when she was young. After the accident, no one ever mentioned her: it was as if she'd never existed in the first place. And so, Annie had begun, day by day, to forget. She wondered if poor, quiet Izzy was facing the same fears.

She pulled up a memory of Kathy, concentrating until she could *see* Kathy, sitting in that old rocking chair on her porch. "Your mom had the prettiest blond hair I ever saw; it was the color of a ripe ear of corn. And it was so soft. When we were little, we used to braid each other's hair for hours. Her eyes were almost black, the deep midnight color of a night sky, and when she smiled, they crinkled up in the corners like a cat's. You remember that?"

Annie smiled. It was funny the things she could recall all these years later. "Yellow was her favorite color. She wore it in every school picture for years. And to her first dance—that was in eighth grade—she wore a yellow cotton dress with a deep blue satin trim that she'd made herself. She was the prettiest girl in the school."

Izzy twisted around to see Annie. There were tears in her eyes, but she was smiling.

"You'll never forget her, Izzy. You remember her laugh? The way it used to spike up at the end, just before she started snorting? And the perfume she liked to wear? And the feel of her hand in yours? You remember how it used to feel to snuggle in her lap and hear her read you a bedtime story? All of that is your mom. My mom's been gone a long, long time, and I still think of her every time I smell vanilla. I still talk to her at night, and I believe she hears me." She brushed a lock of black hair from Izzy's earnest little face. "She hears you, honey. She just can't answer, is all. But that doesn't matter. You snuggle under your blankets with Miss Jemmie and close your eyes and remember one thing about your mom—just one—and the next thing you know, she'll be in bed beside you. You'll feel yourself getting warmer, or you'll see the moonlight get a little brighter, or the wind will moan a little louder, and you'll know. In her own way, she's answering you." Annie took Izzy's cheeks in her hands and smiled down at her. "She's always with you."

She held Izzy close and talked and talked and talked, laughing every now and then, and occasionally wiping a tear from her eye. She talked of girlhood pranks and loves lost and found, and wedding days; she talked of babies being born and growing up, and of Natalie. She talked about Nick, and how strong and handsome he had been and how much he loved Kathy, and how sometimes grief sent a person into a deep, cold darkness from which there seemed to be no escape.

She was still talking when night fell and plunged the room in darkness, when Izzy's breath took on the even wheezing of a deep and peaceful sleep.

Spring chased away the last vestiges of winter, threw its bright colors across the rain forest. Dainty crocuses, hyacinths, and daffodils bloomed in beds, along walkways, and in pockets of sunlight in the damp, needle-strewn forest floor. The birds returned, sat together on telephone wires, and dove for bits of string on the road. Jet-black crows hopped across the lawn, cawing loudly to one another, and used the driveway as a landing strip.

Against her father's pointed advice, Annie had packed a small suitcase and moved into Nick's house. It had proved to be a blessing, for although the nights were still long and lonely, she found that she now had someone to help her through it. She was no longer alone. When she woke in the middle of the night, her heart pounding from familiar nightmares, she climbed into bed with Izzy and held her tightly.

They spent all their time together, she and Izzy. They went to town, baked cookies, and made jewelry boxes from egg cartons. They concocted elaborate care packages for Natalie and mailed them every few days. They worked out of kindergarten and first-grade workbooks, to ensure that Izzy was still learning what she needed for school. And every evening, Nick called to say good night.

Today, Annie had special plans. It was time to revive Kathy's garden.

She stood at the wobbly white picket fence that framed

the garden, and Izzy was beside her. The earth was a rich brown, soggy to the touch from last night's heavy rain. Here and there, puddles winked with a strange, silvery light.

Annie set down her big cardboard box and began extracting her tools: spades, hand shovels, trowels, scissors. "I wish I'd paid more attention to the gardeners at home," she said, spying a big lump of brown twigs that looked promising. "That must be something good—or it's the biggest individual pile of weeds I've ever seen. And see how they're growing in clumps—that surely must be a good sign. I think cutting it back will help; at least that's what Hector at the Feed Store said. Come on, Izzy." She led her across the necklace of stepping stones that formed a meandering trail through the large garden. They stopped at the patch of dead stuff.

Annie knelt. She could feel the moisture seeping from the soil into her pants, squishing cold and clammy against her skin. Pulling on a pair of gloves, she attacked the dead plant and yanked a handful out by the roots. "Bulbs," she said with a triumphant smile. "I knew it."

She turned to Izzy, gave her a self-satisfied look. "I knew it was a flower all along. Never questioned it, no sirree."

She separated and replanted the bulbs, then attacked the dead stalks of perennials with her clippers, hacking everything down to ground level. "You know what I love about gardening? Paying someone to do it for me." She laughed at her own joke and kept working. She pulled up everything that looked like a weed and divided and replanted all the bulbs. At last, she turned to the roses, carefully pruning the thorny branches. As she worked, she hummed. She tried to think of a song that Izzy would know, but all she could come up with was the alphabet song, and so she sang it in her wobbly, off-key voice. "A-B-C-D-E-F-G . . . H-I-J-K . . . L-M-N-O-P."

She frowned suddenly and looked down at Izzy, keeping her gaze averted from the tiny black glove. "My goodness, I've forgotten the alphabet. Not that it matters, of course. It's just a song and I'm sure I'll remember it in no time. "L-M-N-O-P. Well, there I go again, getting stuck on P."

Izzy reached slowly for a trowel. It took her a while to pick it up with only two fingers, and after the first fumbling attempts, Annie couldn't watch.

She kept singing. "H-I-J-K . . . L-M-N-O-P . . . darn it. There's that block again. Oh, well. I think we're about done for a while. I'm starving. What do you say we—"

"Q."

The spade fell from Annie's hand and hit the ground with a thunk. She looked at Izzy, who was still kneeling in the dirt, awkwardly pulling up weeds with her two "visible" fingers as if nothing had happened. The moment bloomed, full of beauty and possibilities.

Izzy had spoken.

Annie released her breath in a slow sigh. *Stay calm, Annie.* She decided to act as if speaking were as normal as not speaking. "Why, I do believe you're right. L-M-N-O-P . . . *Q*-R-S . . ."

"T-U-V."

"W-X-Y . . . and Z." Annie felt as if she would burst with pride and love. She forced herself to keep digging weeds for a few more minutes. She wanted to shriek with happiness and pull Izzy into her arms, but she didn't dare. She didn't want to scare Izzy back into silence.

"There," she said at last. "That's enough for now. My arms feel like they're going to fall off. Jean-Claude—that was my personal trainer in California—he would be so proud of me right now. He always said I didn't sweat. I said if I wanted to sweat, I wouldn't wear color-coordinated clothes that cost a fortune." She wiped a dirty hand across her slick forehead. "I have lemonade in the fridge, and some leftover chicken from last night. What do you say we have a picnic dinner out here? I could make us milkshakes . . ."

When Izzy looked up at her, there were tears in her eyes.

At last, Annie pulled the little girl into her arms.

Chapter 14

Cigarette smoke swirled in a thick blue haze beneath a ceiling of stained acoustical tiles.

Nick stood in the open doorway of a long, narrow room in the windowless basement of the Lutheran church. Two wood-grain Formica tables hugged the back wall, their surfaces covered with coffeemakers and Styrofoam cups and boxes stacked with packaged sugar and instant creamer. There was a crowd of people at the Coke machine, and an even larger crowd at the coffeepot. The smell of burnt coffee mingled with the bitter stench of the cigarettes.

People sat in folding metal chairs, some comfortably stretched out, some perched nervously on the edge of their seats. Nearly all of them were smoking cigarettes.

He didn't know if he could go through with this, if he could stroll into this smoky room and throw his vulnerability on one of those cheap-ass tables and let strangers dissect it. . . .

"It's harder than hell the first time. All the tension of first sex, with none of the fun."

Nick turned and saw Joe standing behind him.

188

The older man's shoe-leather-brown face was creased into a relieved smile. "I hoped you'd show up. It was sort of a shock to my system after all those years of hoping you'd *never* show up."

"I'm sorry to disappoint you, Joe," Nick said.

Joe laid a hand on Nick's shoulder and squeezed gently. "I'm *proud* of you, Nicholas. Not disappointed. Life's thrown a lot of curves your way—enough to crush a weaker man. I couldn't be prouder of you if you were my own son. If Louise were here, she'd say, 'Give that boy a hug, Joseph,' and I think I will."

It was the first time Joe had ever hugged him, and Nick didn't quite know how to respond. For as long as he could remember, he'd thought there was something wrong with him, something essential missing at his core, and he'd spent a lifetime waiting to be unmasked. He'd shielded himself from the people he loved—Kathy, Izzy, Louise, and Joe—afraid that if they saw the real Nick, they'd turn away. But Joe had seen the truth, seen all of Nick's weaknesses and failures, and still he was here, claiming Nick as his son.

When Joe drew back, his black eyes were moist. "It's going to get tougher before it gets better. You've just jumped into the deep end, and you'll think you're drowning. But I'm here to keep your head above water."

"Thanks, Joe." He didn't say *for everything,* but he could see that Joe understood.

"Come on," Joe said. "Let's sit down."

They headed into the room. Over the next few minutes, more people wandered in, some talking among themselves, others noticeably silent.

Nick shifted in his seat. His feet tapped nervously on the floor. The repetitive sound only increased his anxiety.

"It's okay, Nick," Joe said quietly. "Why don't you get yourself some coffee."

"Right." He surged to his feet and cut across the room. Fishing a few quarters from his pocket, he got a Classic Coke and snapped the tab, drinking greedily.

Feeling a little better, he went back to his seat and the meeting got under way.

A man introduced himself: "Hi, I'm Jim. I'm an alcoholic." The crowd of people answered back like good Catholics on Sunday, "Hi, Jim."

Jim stood in the front of the room and started talking. First there was the "God grant me" prayer, then stuff about meetings and twelve steps and more on serenity.

A young woman stood up suddenly. She was tall and rail-thin, with bleached yellow-white hair and skin the color of candlewax. Obviously shaking, she stepped past the row of chairs and stood in front of everyone.

She looked as if she hadn't eaten in a year, and Nick had been a cop long enough to recognize the signs of long-term drug use. No doubt needle marks ran like train tracks up the insides of her pale arms. She took an endless drag off her cigarette and exhaled heavily. "I'm Rhonda," she said, nervously eyeing the crowd, "and I'm an alcoholic and an addict."

"Hi, Rhonda," said the crowd on cue.

She sucked in another lungful. "Today's my seventh sober day."

There was a round of applause; a bunch of people yelled "Way to go, Rhonda!"

Rhonda gave a wan smile and stubbed her cigarette out on the ashtray in front of her. "I've tried this before—lots of times. But this time'll be differ'nt. The judge said if I can stay clean for one year, I can see my son again." She paused and wiped her eyes, leaving a black tail of mascara down one white cheek. "I used to be a normal girl, going to junior college, working part-time as a waitress in a ritzy restaurant. Then I met this guy, Chet, and before I knew it, I was guzzling tequila and backing it with mountains of coke."

She sighed, stared dully at the open door. "I got pregnant, and kept drinking. My Sammy was born small and addicted, but he lived. I shoulda been there for him, but all I thought about was getting high and drunk. My son wasn't enough to make me quit drinking and snorting." Her lower lip started to shake, and she bit down on it. "Nooo, I had to drive drunk. I had to hurt someone." She sniffled hard and regained a measure of control. "So, here I am, and this time I mean it. I'm gonna do anything to see my son again. This time I'm gonna get clean and stay clean."

When Rhonda was finished, someone else started talking, then another and another. They all used different words, but the stories were the same, tales of loss and pain and anger. Hard-luck stories and bad-luck stories from people who'd been through hell on earth.

Nick was one of them, he knew it by the close of the meeting, and there was a strange comfort in admitting that, in knowing he wasn't the only one in the world trying to wrestle with a bottle of booze.

Izzy couldn't sleep. She went to her window and stared outside. Everything was dark and scary-looking. The only light was tiny white flecks on the black lake. Annie said those were stars fallen from the sky.

She turned away from the window. All week long, ever since Annie had told her that her daddy wasn't coming home, she'd been scared. Yesterday, she'd stood at the window for a long time, waiting. So long that Annie had come up to her.

I don't know when he'll be coming home, Izzy. That's what Annie had said to her. *You remember I told you that your daddy was sick? The doctors say he needs a little time—*

But Izzy knew the truth about doctors. Her mommy had seen lots and lots of them, and none of them ever made her mommy feel better.

They wouldn't help her daddy, either.

Izzy hadn't been able to stop crying. *I miss him* was all she said to Annie, but there was a lot more she didn't say. She didn't say that she'd been missing him for a long, long time, and she didn't say that the man with the silver hair wasn't really her daddy—because her daddy never got sick and he laughed all the time. She didn't say that she thought her real daddy had died when her mommy died, and that he wouldn't ever be coming back.

Izzy crept down the stairs and sneaked outside. It was raining gently, and a mist floated on the top of the grass, so thick that she couldn't see her feet.

"Mommy?" she whispered, hugging herself. She closed her eyes and concentrated really, really hard. When she opened her eyes, she saw her mommy, standing alongside the lake. The vision was shimmery and out of focus. Mommy stood with her shoulders rounded and her head cocked at an odd angle, as if she were listening for footsteps, or the sound of a bird's call in the middle of the night. The rain turned all sorts of colors, red and yellow and pink and blue.

You should be sleeping, little girl.

"Daddy's sick again."

Her mom made a quiet sound, or maybe it was a breeze, kicking up along the water. *He'll be okay. I promise.*

"I miss you, Mommy." Izzy reached for her. There was a whisper of something not quite solid against her fingertips, a brushing of heat. She closed her hand around . . . nothing.

The touching days are gone for me, pumpkin.

"Mommy, I love you, Mommy."

I'm sorry, Izzy-bear. God, I'm so sorry . . .

Izzy reached out, but it was too late. Her mom was gone.

An unusual wave of heat rolled across Jefferson County. Flowers unfurled and reached skyward for the precious sunlight. Baby birds squawked from nests in green-budded trees. It still rained each night, but by dawn, the world was a sparkling, gilded jewel.

Annie made sure that Izzy was busy all the time. They colored Easter eggs, baked cookies, and drew pictures for Nick—presents for the day he would return. They shopped on Main Street and bought Natalie hokey presents from the rain forest: pens with ferries in them, slug cookbooks, postcards of Lake Mystic. They doubled their reading efforts, until Annie was certain that Izzy was ready to go back to school. But when she mentioned this hope to Izzy, it scared her. *I don't wanna go back. They'll make fun of me.* Annie had let the issue rest there, knowing that it wasn't her decision anyway. She hoped that when Nick came home, they could convince Izzy to return to school.

But for now, their routines were comforting. Izzy was talking regularly; it no longer seemed hard for her to remember the words. They were gaining strength from each other.

Annie had finally learned to sleep alone. She knew it didn't sound like much, but to her, it was momentous. Sometimes, when she left Izzy and crawled into her empty bed, she didn't even think about the man who used to sleep with her; sometimes she went for whole days without thinking about him. Oh, the ache was still there, and the loneliness, but day by day, she was learning that she could survive without him. She still didn't want to, but she knew now that she could.

Every Monday, like clockwork, she called London and heard about Natalie's week. In her daughter's voice, she heard a burgeoning maturity that filled Annie with pride. Natalie wasn't a child anymore, and when she learned of the divorce, she would be able to handle it.

And Annie finally understood that she could handle it, too. Last night, when Terri had called (after ten minutes of grilling Annie about who this *Nick character* was and why Annie was staying at his house), she had finally settled down and listened to Annie, and when the conversation was over, Terri had said quietly, *Of course you can handle it, Annie. You're the only one who thought you couldn't.*

Easter Sunday arrived wrapped in clouds and drenched in rain, but Annie refused to let the uncooperative weather ruin her plans. She dressed Izzy warmly and drove her to Hank's, where the three of them had a huge brunch and a world-class egg hunt. Then they went to church services in town. Afterward, Annie and Izzy drove back to the house, and Annie gave her a small, wrapped gift. "Happy Easter, Izzy."

Izzy tried to open the package with her two good fingers, and the failing effort pinched at Annie's heart. "Here, I'll do it, sweetheart. It's hard when your fingers are gone."

Annie unwrapped the shiny paper, then placed the box on the coffee table.

Biting back a grin, Izzy flipped open the box top. Inside, on a bed of white tissue paper, was a bronze medallion the size of a quarter, resting on a coil of thin silver chain. At Izzy's frown, Annie took the compass from the box and placed it in Izzy's hand.

"When I was a girl, I thought I was lost all the time. Then my dad gave me this compass, and he told me that if I wore it, I'd always know where I belonged." Annie sighed softly. She hadn't kept wearing the compass. Instead, she'd gone all the way to California and lost her sense of direction again. If only there were some internal mechanism that pointed unerringly to the true north of our selves. It was so damned easy in life to get lost. "So," she said at last, "do you want to learn how it works?"

Izzy nodded.

"I knew you'd say that. Okay, grab your boots and rain gear, and I'll show you."

With a quick smile, Izzy ran to the coat closet and grabbed her still-wet coat and hat. Within moments, they were both dressed in rain gear, with rubber boots and big floppy hats. Annie quickly explained to Izzy how the compass worked, and when she was convinced that Izzy understood, she slipped the compass around the girl's neck. "Let's go exploring."

Outside, the weather was horrible. Stuttering gusts of

wind blew across the lake, sending silvery ripples onto the gravel shore. Diamond-drops quivered on the tips of the yellow daffodils and tulips that lined the walkway and grew in clumps in the window boxes.

They veered away from the lake, took their heading, and started down the wide, needle-carpeted trail that led into the rain forest. On either side, the immense wooded sentinels stood guard, catching most of the raindrops on their broad, leafy shoulders. A cool mist swirled along the forest floor, so thick in some places that Annie couldn't see her tennis shoes. At every bend in the trail, Izzy stopped and checked her compass.

By midafternoon, Izzy had a sense for true north, and the quiet confidence that came with knowledge.

They walked down one trail and then another and another. Suddenly, the trees opened up, and they found themselves in an overgrown clearing deep in the oldest part of the rain forest. Tucked in one corner was an old ranger station, obviously abandoned for years. Its shingled roof was furred with moss, and gray fungus peeked out from cracks in the log siding. Scratches from a black bear's claws marked the unhinged door.

Izzy blinked up at her. "Can we go in?"

Annie looked questioningly at the cabin. Unfortunately, there was a lot more mother in her soul than explorer. But when she saw the excitement in Izzy's eyes, she couldn't say no. "Okay, but go slow . . . and don't touch anything icky."

With a shriek, Izzy raced for the cabin. Annie hurried along behind her. Together, they eased through the broken door.

Inside, buried under a gauzy net of spiderwebs and dust,

were two twin beds, complete with musty blankets; a flimsy, handmade wooden table and two chairs; and a long-forgotten black iron woodstove.

Annie felt like Daniel Boone. She wandered to the old stove and picked up a dusty coffee can, turning it over.

Izzy let out a squeal and pulled something out from under the bed. "Look!" She thrust her hand at Annie.

It was a silver coin, dated 1899.

"Oh, my," Annie said, touching the metal. "That's a treasure indeed. You'd best put that in a safe place."

Izzy frowned, then very solemnly looked up at Annie. Wordlessly, she shoved the coin toward her.

"It's yours, Izzy. Don't give it to me."

"Annie? You'll always be here, won'tcha, Annie? That makes you a safe place."

Annie knew she should force the coin gently back into Izzy's small hand. She should give the child the gift of honesty. *I'm not safe, Izzy. Not really. This isn't my life at all. . . .*

But then she looked into Izzy's liquid brown eyes and she was lost. "Always is a lot longer than you'll need me, Izzy, but I'll keep the coin until you're ready to give it to your daddy, okay?"

" 'Kay. Don't lose it." Izzy grinned and nodded and started to run for the door. Halfway there, she skidded to a stop and turned around. She was staring at her right hand.

"Izzy, what is it?"

Slowly, Izzy turned. Frowning, she stuck her right hand up in the air. "I can see all my fingers on this hand again."

"Oh, Izzy . . ." Annie went to Izzy and knelt beside her, pulling the child into her arms. But Izzy was stiff and awkward, and she couldn't seem to take her eyes away from her hand.

Izzy started to cry. "She said I couldn't follow her."

Annie stroked the child's soft, soft cheek and smiled. "Who said that?"

"Mommy. I . . ." She bit her quavering lower lip and looked away.

"Tell me, Izzy," Annie said softly. "I can keep a secret."

"Promise?"

"Promise."

Izzy stared at Annie for a long, silent moment, then said quietly, "I . . . I see her sometimes . . . in the fog. I was disappearin' to be with her . . . but last time I saw her . . ." Huge tears welled in Izzy's eyes and spilled over, streaking down her pink cheeks. "Last time she said I couldn't follow her."

Annie's heart squeezed into a tight little fist. She took Izzy's hand and led her outdoors. Side by side they sat on the rickety, moss-haired porch of the cabin.

"You can't follow your mom, Izzy, and you know why?"

Izzy turned to her. "Why?"

"Because it would break your mommy's heart. She's up in heaven now, and she wants to watch you grow up. She wants you to have fun and make friends and go to school—to do all the things she did when she was a little girl. She wants to see you wear a pretty white dress on your wedding day and hold your own baby in your arms." Annie sighed. "She wants so much for you, Izzy."

"How do you know she's watchin' me?"

Annie smiled at her. "*You* know. In your heart. That's why you see her in the fog. You know she's watching over you, and when it rains . . . that's when she's missing you. The rain is her tears, and the sunshine is her smile."

Izzy stared out at the trees a long, long time. "I miss her, too."

Annie curled an arm around Izzy's narrow shoulders and drew her close. "I know, baby."

They sat that way for a long time. The rain softened the world into the muted blues and greens of a Monet painting. Then, finally, Annie smiled brightly and tapped on Izzy's right hand. "Why, I do believe you're right, Miss Izzy. I can see those fingers just as clear as a bell. I say we drink a toast."

"I like my toast with jam."

Annie laughed. "I don't have toast, but I have lemonade. And if we don't eat soon, I'm going to start chewing on your coin. I think it's time to head home."

Izzy laughed, and it was such a high, clear, heartbreakingly beautiful sound that Annie let herself forget the tiny strand of worry.

If nothing else, she'd given Izzy back her voice and her smile . . . and now one hand was visible again. Maybe tomorrow, that glove would come off the left.

For now, that was enough.

Chapter 15

It was raining on the day Nick came home.

He paid the cabdriver and got out of the car, watching the town's only taxi drive away.

He flipped up the collar of his Levi's jacket and hunched his shoulders against the driving rain. Tucked under one arm was the ragged, wrinkled bag of clothes and toiletries he'd purchased to get him through his time away from home. Rain thwopped the sack, but it couldn't be helped. Day had just rounded the bend into a lavender evening, and there was a slight chill in the air. The gravel road that led to the house went straight for about a quarter of a mile, then turned sharply around a triangular patch of Douglas fir trees. Beyond that, it disappeared into the misty mauve shadows along the lake.

He could have had the cab drive him to the front door, but he needed the time to approach slowly.

Blinking against the rain, he began the long walk home. To his left, the lake reflected the twilight sky. Glossy green leaves, rhododendron, azalea, trillium, and salal hemmed the road on either side, creating a shadowy tunnel that led him ever closer to the house.

At last, he turned the corner. Soft, golden light poured through the windows of his home. The chimney puffed smoke into the purple sky. It was how he'd always imagined it. . . .

This house had seized his imagination from the start. He could still recall the night Annie had brought him here. Kathy had the flu, so Nick and Annie had gone to the carnival alone, and afterward, she'd brought him here, to the "haunted" house by the lake.

He'd first seen this house through her dreamer's eyes. She'd lit a fire inside his soul that night, and this old house had become the physical embodiment of that dream. Perfect for a boy who'd lived in a car for two years and eaten breakfast from Dumpsters.

It had taken him years, but he'd finally saved enough money to buy the place. It had been summer then, August, when he'd signed the papers and written the downpayment check. Yet even on that hottest day of the year, this road had been cool and shaded, and a breeze had swept along the banks of the lake. He had gazed into the distance at Mount Olympus, which stood as an immense granite triangle thrust high, high into the robin's-egg-blue sky, with only the barest hint of snow left to dust its jagged crown.

The memory was as sharp as broken glass. He'd raced to bring Izzy and Kathy here, but it was night by then and shadows lay thick and dark along the porch rails.

He'd grabbed Kathy's hand and dragged her through the murky, musty interior.

Can't you just see it, Kath? This'll be the sunroom— where we'll have breakfast . . . and that's the kitchen, they don't make stoves like that anymore . . . and check out that fireplace—I bet it's one hundred years old. . . .

He smelled hope and home and possibilities.

She smelled must and dirt and work.

How had he failed to notice? And why hadn't he stopped talking long enough to ask her opinion? Why had he just thought, *she's having one of her bad days,* and let it go at that?

With a tired sigh, he straightened his shoulders, crossed the grass, climbed the porch steps, and knocked on the front door. The wet sack of his useless new belongings hit the floor beside his feet, forgotten.

There was a flurry of footsteps behind the door, and a muffled "just a minute," then the door opened and Annie stood before him.

The silence between them was deafening; every sound seemed amplified, the rhythmic thunking of the rain on oversized leaves, the quiet licking of waves on gravel.

He wished he could smile, but he was afraid. He looked away, before she could see the sudden longing in his eyes.

"Nick." It was just a whisper of sound; he imagined he could feel the moist heat of her breath on his neck. Slowly, slowly, he looked at her.

She was standing so close he could see the smattering of freckles that lay along her hairline, and a tiny white scar that bisected one eyebrow. "I've been going to AA twice a day," he said quickly, without even adding a mumbled hello. "I haven't had a drink since you dropped me off at the motel."

"Oh, Nick, that's wonderful. I—"

It was as if she suddenly realized how close they were

standing. In the pale glow of the porch light, he saw a sweet blush color her cheeks.

She broke eye contact and cleared her throat, moving back a respectable few feet. "Izzy is in the family room. We were painting. Come on in."

"Painting. Sounds fun. I wouldn't want to—"

"You can do this, Nick." She took hold of his hand—her grasp was solid and comforting—and pulled him into the house. The door banged shut behind him.

The house smelled clean, and somewhere a radio was playing, but he didn't have time to really notice the changes she had made. She was pulling him down the hallway.

Her "family room" was what Nick used to think of as the shit room. Years ago, probably in the fifties, somebody had tried to remodel this room on a skimpy budget. Pressboard wood paneling hid the log walls underneath, and mustard-colored carpet covered the hardwood floor. The only nice thing in the room was a big old brick fireplace, in which Annie had a fire going.

The French doors that led onto the back porch were open. A cool, early evening breeze ruffled their gauzy white curtains, and the rain was a silvery veil between the house and the falling night. Multicolored jars and paintbrushes cluttered a portable card table. Spilled paint lay in bright blemishes on the newspaper that protected the carpet.

Izzy stood with her back to them, one gloved hand hung limply at her left side. There was a huge easel in front of her, with a piece of white paper pinned in place. He could see splashes of color on the paper, but her body blocked the picture.

He realized suddenly that Annie was gone. His hand felt cold and empty. Turning slightly, he saw her in the hallway. She gave him a quick thumbs-up and disappeared.

He sighed. Turning back toward the room, he took a cautious step inside. He expected Izzy to spin around and stare at him, but the carpet muffled the sound of his steps, and she kept on painting.

"Izzy." He said her name softly, as if a quiet voice could somehow soften the surprise.

She dropped a baby-food jar full of blue paint. The colorful liquid splashed across the newspaper. Slowly, clutching her paintbrush, she turned around.

She looked like an angel. She was wearing a paint-stained pair of yellow overalls, but there were no streaks of color on her hair or face. Her jet-black hair lay in two evenly plaited braids, tied at the ends with bits of yellow ribbon.

She looked like she used to.

It was that thought, more than anything, that brought him fully into the room. His knees felt weak, and fear was a cold knot in his stomach, but he kept moving, going toward his little girl, who stood so silently beside the easel, her big brown eyes fixed on his.

Beside her, he knelt. His knees squished in the puddle of blue paint.

She looked down at him, her eyes unblinking, her pink lips drawn in a serious line.

Only a few years ago, she would have leapt into his arms and smothered him with kisses. Even when he'd had a hangover, or after a fight with Kathy, Izzy had always adored him. She'd never looked at him like she did right now—with the wary, worried expression of an animal that was ready to flee at the first hint of danger.

He realized with a sudden tightening in his chest how much he'd missed her kisses . . . the sweet smell of her hair . . . the gentle softness of her hand as she slipped it into his.

"Hey, Sunshine," he said, his eyes avoiding the tiny black glove that evidenced his failure and her heartbreak.

It was his pet name for her—given on the first day she'd smiled and he'd said it was like sunshine after a rain. He hadn't called her Sunshine in a long time. Since Kathy's death, and probably even before that.

She remembered. A little jumping smile tugged one side of her mouth.

There were so many things he could say to her right now, promises he could make, but in the end, he knew it would only be words. Promises made by a man who'd broken too many to be trusted.

One day at a time; that was one thing AA definitely had right.

That was how he'd lost his daughter—one moment at a time—and that was the only way to get her back. He couldn't ask for her trust; even though she'd probably give it to him freely, he had to *earn* it. One day at a time.

In the end, he made no promises. Instead, he said only, "What are you painting?"

She cocked her head toward the paper and stepped back. It was a colorful smearing of squiggly lines and globs of falling paint. Because he'd seen her artwork before, he could make out Izzy's self-portrait: she was the tiny, big-headed stick figure in the corner with the floor-length cascade of black hair. Someone—probably Annie, judging by the spiked brown hair—stood beside her, wearing a broad brush stroke of a smile. Above the two stick figures was a bright yellow sun bracketed by writhing red rays.

Nick grabbed a clean paintbrush from the card table and dipped it into a jar of brown paint. Trying not to spill—although he had no idea why he bothered—he carefully maneuvered the paintbrush to the paper. "Can I add something?"

She stared up at him. Then slowly she nodded.

He drew a quick, misshapen circle alongside Annie. Another four strokes and he had a body of sorts. "This is Daddy," he said, without looking at her. Then he added eyes, a nose, and a flat line of a mouth. "I don't need to paint the hair—it's almost the same color as the paper. We'll just imagine it." Lowering the brush, he looked at her.

Her gaze was level and steady. Two oversized front teeth—her only grown-up teeth—nipped nervously at her lower lip.

"Is it okay if I come home, Izzy?" He waited a lifetime for her answer, a nod, a blink, anything, but she just stood there, staring at him through those sad, grown-up eyes in her little-girl's face.

He touched her velvet-soft cheek. "I understand, Sunshine."

He started to get to his feet.

She grabbed his hand.

Slowly, he lowered himself back to his knees. He stared at her, losing himself in the chocolate-brown eyes that had once been his world. In that instant, he remembered it all—walking down the docks with her, looking at boats, dreaming about sailing around the world someday. . . . He remembered how it had felt to hold her hand and laugh with her and swing her in his arms on a beautiful, sunny spring day.

"I love you, Izzy," he said, remembering then how simple it used to be.

Nick stood on the porch, his legs braced apart, his arms crossed. He was hanging onto his world by a fraying thread. Dinner had been a tense affair, with Annie's cheerful chatter punctuated by awkward silences. He'd noticed that Izzy was using her right hand again—and not in that pathetic two-fingered way.

Every time he looked at his daughter, he felt a hot rush of shame, and it took all his self-control not to turn away. But he hadn't taken the coward's road tonight, and that was something of a triumph. He'd looked Izzy square in the eye, and if he flinched at the wariness in her gaze, he did it inwardly, so she couldn't see.

Behind him, the screen door screeched open and banged shut.

It took him a second to find the courage to turn around. When he did, Annie was standing there, alongside the old rocking chair that had been Nick's gift to Kathy when Izzy was born.

Annie's fingers trailed lightly across the top rail, and her wedding ring glittered in the orange glow of the outdoor bulb. The size of the diamond reminded Nick once again of how different her world was from his. As if he needed reminding.

She was holding a small designer suitcase.

"Izzy has brushed her teeth. She's waiting for you to

tuck her in." Her voice was as soft and cool as a spring rain, and it soothed the ragged edges of his anxiety.

She was standing close to him, her arms at her sides. Even with that Marine-issue haircut, she was beautiful. A tired gray UW sweatshirt bagged over a pair of oversized jeans, but it didn't camouflage her body. Suddenly he could remember her naked, recall vividly how she'd lifted her arms and pulled off her shirt . . . the moonlight kissing her breasts. . . .

"Nick?" She took a step toward him. "Are you all right?"

He forced a weak laugh. "As well as a drunk who has stopped drinking can be, I suppose."

"You're going to make it." She started to reach for him, and he leaned slightly toward her, needing that touch more than air, but at the last minute, she drew back. "It's not easy to start over. I know . . ."

He saw the haunted look in her eyes and wondered what he'd done to her, the man who'd put that egg-size diamond on her left hand. He wanted to ask, but it felt wrong, presumptuous, to probe her wounds. "You saved my life, Annie. I don't know how to thank you."

She smiled. "I always knew you'd be back for her, you know. It wasn't much of a risk. I could see how much you loved Izzy."

"Such optimism." He glanced out at the darkened lake. "I loved Kathy, too, and look what happened." He sighed and leaned back against the porch rail, staring out at the yard. "You know what haunts me? I never really understood my wife. The sad thing is—I do now. I know what hopelessness feels like; before, I thought I did, but I was skimming the surface. She used to tell me that she couldn't feel the sunlight anymore, not even when she was standing in it, not even when it was hot on her cheeks." It surprised Nick that he could talk about his wife so easily. For the first time, he remembered *her*, not the illness or the crumbling of their marriage over the last few years, but Kathy, his Kathy, the bright-eyed, big-hearted girl he'd fallen in love with. "She didn't want to live in the darkness anymore. . . ."

When he turned back to Annie, she was crying. He felt awkward and selfish in the wake of her grief. "I'm sorry . . . I didn't mean to upset you."

She gazed up at him. "You're so lucky."

"What?"

"It doesn't matter how you felt about Kathy by the end, or since the end. You obviously loved her. No matter what she did, or why she did it, she must have known." Her voice fell to a throaty whisper. "Most people are never loved like that in their whole lives."

He knew he was going to ask the question, though he shouldn't. He stepped toward her, a heartbeat closer than was safe. "How about you? Have you known that kind of love?"

She gave him a fleeting, sad little smile and looked away. "No. I have loved that way . . . but been loved . . . I don't think so."

"You deserve better than that."

She nodded and nonchalantly wiped her eyes. "Don't we all."

Silence fell between them, awkward and uncomfortable. "Annie—"

She stopped and turned to him. "Yes?"

"Maybe you'd like to come over tomorrow—spend the day with us."

"I'd like that," she answered quickly, then she looked away.

"Thank you." His voice was soft, and came as close to a kiss as he dared.

"You're welcome, Nicky." There was another moment of awkwardness as she stared up at him. "You should know that Izzy started talking while you were gone."

Nick frowned. "She didn't talk to me."

Annie touched his arm in a brief, fleeting caress. "She will. Give her time."

He couldn't meet Annie's gaze. Instead, he stared out at the lake.

She moved nervously from foot to foot, then said, "Well, I should be getting home. . . ."

"See you tomorrow."

She nodded and hurried past him. With a quick wave, she climbed into her Mustang and drove away.

Nick watched her taillights, two bright red dots in the darkness of the forest, until she turned the corner and was gone. Reluctantly, he went back into the house and climbed the stairs. Outside Izzy's room, he paused, then knocked.

Answer, baby . . . you can do it.

But there was no response. Slowly, he turned the knob and opened the door.

She was sitting up in bed, her right arm curled around Miss Jemmie. The black glove on her left hand was a tiny blotch against the white and lavender lace comforter.

He went to the bed and sat down beside her.

Silence spilled between them, and every heartbeat plucked at the fragile strands of Nick's self-confidence. "I thought I'd read you a story."

She let go of Miss Jemmie and pulled a book out from under the covers, handing it to him.

"Ah, *Where the Wild Things Are.* I wonder how Max has been doing lately. He probably turned into a warthog."

Izzy made a small, hiccuping sound, like a hacked-off laugh.

Curling an arm around her tiny shoulders, he drew her close. With the book open on his lap, he began to read. He used his best storyteller voice, the one Izzy had always loved.

And as he slipped into the familiar story, he felt for the first time as if he might have a chance.

But it was not so easy. For the first week, Nick was shaky and short-tempered and afraid that if he made one wrong move, he'd end up back on a bar stool at Zoe's. Every moment of every day was an agonizing test of his will.

He rose early, needing a drink, and went outside to chop wood, where, still needing a drink, he stood for hours, chopping, sweating, wondering if today was the day he'd fail.

Annie arrived every day with a smile on her face and an activity planned. By sheer force of will, she was turning the three of them into a patchwork family, and it was that connection that kept Nick going to his AA meetings every day. He'd be damned if he'd let Annie and Izzy down.

Now, he was driving to the four o'clock meeting. He slowed the car to a crawl at Main Street, his hands curled tightly around the steering wheel. It had started to rain about five minutes ago, and the suddenness of the storm had forced the pedestrians inside, left the town rainy-day quiet. Only a few scattered cars filled the row of empty stalls.

Except at Zoe's. In front of the tavern, there was a steady line of cars. He knew from experience that every bar stool would be occupied. He stared at the tavern's murky windows, hearing in his head the quiet clinking of the glasses and the sloshing of scotch over ice cubes.

He licked his dry lips and swallowed thickly, trying not to imagine how sweet a shot of scotch would taste right now. He still couldn't imagine the rest of his life without booze, but he could manage this one day.

He eased his foot down on the accelerator and sped up. He felt every inch of road as he drove past Zoe's, and by the time he reached the Lutheran church, the shaking had receded a bit and the sweat was a cold, drying trail on his skin.

He pulled into the paved lot behind the church and parked beneath a Rainier Beer billboard. Taking a second to collect himself, he pocketed his keys and went inside.

By now, the room was full of familiar faces, and it was oddly comforting to step through the open door.

Joe grinned at him, waved him over to a seat.

Nodding, Nick quickly got himself a can of Coke, then took the empty seat beside Joe.

"Nicholas, are you okay? You look pale."

"I don't know," he answered, thankful in a small way that AA had given him that—the ability for the first time in his life to be honest. This room, among these strangers-who-would-be-friends, was the one place where he could haul his vulnerability and his failings out of the pocket of his soul and throw them under the glaring light of scrutiny. There was some comfort in that, he knew now. Honesty helped. Admitting that the addiction was stronger than he was helped even more.

He was hanging on by a thread at home. Wherever he went, whatever he said, he felt Izzy's eyes on him. She was waiting for the inevitable screw-up.

She hadn't spoken a word to him yet, and this time, the silences were worse than before, because she was talking to Annie—though he'd never heard it. Not once had he heard the sweetness of his little girl's voice.

Mealtimes were bad, too. Sometimes, when he reached for the fork, his hand was shaking so badly that he had to plead a headache and run for the dark isolation of his bedroom.

He gave Joe a weak smile. "Trying is a hell of a lot harder than not trying, you know?"

"It always is, Nicholas. You know I'm here for you. We all are."

Nick took the statement at face value and was thankful for it. "I know."

The meeting got under way. One by one, the people around him spoke up—those who wanted to share their burden—revealing their anniversaries and their failures and their hopes and dreams. As always, they came around, finally, to Nick.

He thought about saying something. *Hi, I'm Nick. I'm an alcoholic. I haven't had a drink in twenty-three days.*

But, in the end, like all the other times, he couldn't quite manage it.

Chapter 16

Their days followed a familiar pattern. Monday through Friday, Annie showed up at Nick's house bright and early. He made pancakes and eggs for breakfast, and then the three of them spent the day together. Rain or shine, they were outside, fishing along the crumbling rock banks of the river, riding bikes on the trails around the lake, or window-shopping on Main Street. Today they had hiked deep into Enchanted Valley, and now, several hours and even more miles later, each of them was exhausted. Poor Izzy had fallen asleep almost before her head hit the pillow.

Annie leaned down and kissed Izzy's forehead, murmuring a quiet good night.

" 'Night, Annie," Izzy mumbled back, her eyes closed.

Annie drew back. This was the time of the week she hated most. Friday night. She wouldn't see Nick and Izzy again until Monday, and though she enjoyed the time she spent with Hank, she couldn't wait to get back here Monday morning. She didn't often let herself think about how much she liked Nick and Izzy, or how *right* it felt to be with them. Those thoughts led her down a dark and twisting road that frightened her, and so she pushed them away, buried them in the dark corner that had always housed her uncertainties. She had come to the sad realization that Blake wasn't going to change his mind, that she wasn't going to receive the apologetic phone call she'd fantasized about for weeks. Without even that slim fantasy to cling to, she was left feeling adrift. Sometimes, in the midst of a lovely spring day, she would stumble across her fear and the suddenness of it shocked and frightened her.

Those were the times when she turned to Hank—but his comforting words *he'll be back, honey, don't you worry, he'll be back* didn't soothe Annie anymore. She couldn't believe in them, and somehow the not believing hurt more than the believing ever had. Terri was the only one who understood, and a phone call to her best friend, often made late at night, was the only thing that helped.

She started to turn away, when she noticed something through the window, a movement. She pushed the patterned lace curtains aside.

Nick was standing down alongside the lake, his shadow a long streak across the rippling silver waves. As usual, he'd helped with the dinner dishes, read Izzy a story, and then bolted outside to stand alone.

He was as lonely as she was. She saw it in his eyes all the time, a sadness that clung even when he smiled.

He was trying so hard. Yesterday, he'd spent almost two hours playing Candy Land with Izzy, his long body crouched uncomfortably across the multicolored board. Every time Izzy smiled, Nick looked like he was going to cry.

Annie had never been as proud of anyone as she was of

him. He was trying to do everything right—no drinking, no swearing, no broken promises. Nothing but soft, sad smiles and time spent with the little girl who still studied him warily and didn't speak to him.

So often, during the day, she was reminded of Blake, and the kind of father he'd been. Never there, physically or emotionally, for his daughter, taking so much of his life for granted. It was partially Annie's fault; she saw that now. She'd been part of what their marriage had become. She had blindly done everything he'd asked of her. Everything. She'd given up so much—everything of herself and her dreams; she'd given it up without a whimper of protest . . . and all because she loved him so much.

Her life, her soul, had faded into his, one day, one decision at a time. Little things . . . nothing by themselves . . .

A haircut she didn't have because Blake liked her hair long, a dress she didn't buy because he thought red was a tramp's color.

She'd done what they "agreed" she should do. She'd stayed home and become the perfect suburban wife and mother, and in her quest for quiet perfection, she'd let Blake become a bad husband and bad father. And all the while, she'd thought she was the perfect wife. Only now she saw how wrong she'd been: she'd made all those sacrifices not out of strength and love, but out of weakness. Because it was safer and easier to follow. She had become what she'd set out to be, and now she was ashamed of her choices. But still she had no true understanding of where she would go from here.

Alone. That was all she knew. Wherever she went from here, it would be as a middle-aged woman alone.

She wished she had Nick's strength, his willingness to shove past his fear and *try*.

She touched the glass softly, feeling the cool smoothness beneath her fingertips. "You're going to make it, Nick."

And she believed it.

She closed the bedroom door behind her and went downstairs. Plucking her purse from the sofa, she headed for the door. Outside, the cool night air breezed across her cheeks.

She stared across the blackened lawn at Nick. It was at times like these, at the quiet end of the day, that memories of their lovemaking floated to the surface of her mind.

She closed her eyes for a moment and remembered the feel of his hands on her naked skin . . . the softness of his lips . . .

"Annie?"

Her eyes popped open. He was in front of her, and when she looked at him, she was certain that it was all in her eyes: the naked, desperate need for companionship and caring. She was afraid that if she spoke to him, if she said anything, and heard the soft tenor of his voice in response, she would be lost. She was vulnerable now, longing to be held and touched by a man . . . even if it was the wrong man . . . even if she wasn't truly the woman he wanted.

She forced a quick, nervous smile. "Hi, Nick . . . 'bye, Nick. I've got to run."

Before he could answer, she ran to her car.

But a mile later, all alone in her car, listening to Rod Stewart's scratchy-voiced song about his heart and soul, and an attraction that was purely physical, she was still remembering. . . .

*   *   *

Saturday morning, Izzy stood on the porch in her bright new overalls and rain boots, watching her daddy. He was kneeling in the yard, beside that tree they'd planted on the day of her mommy's funeral. The skinny cherry tree that wouldn't turn green, not even now when everything around it was blooming. It was dead, just like her mommy.

Her daddy was all hunched over, like a character from one of her books, wearing dirty gloves that made his hands look like bear claws. He was yanking up weeds from around the baby tree, and he was humming a song, one Izzy hadn't heard in a long time.

All of a sudden, her daddy looked up and saw her. He gave her a big smile and pushed the silvery hair away from his face. The glove left a big streak of brown mud across his forehead. "Heya, Izzy-bear," he said. "Wanna help me pull up weeds?"

Slowly, she moved toward him, past the row of primroses Annie had planted last week. He was still smiling when she came up beside him.

All she could think was that her daddy was back and she wanted a hug more than anything in the world, but she was afraid. What if he didn't stay again? She almost said something to him, she even opened her mouth and tried.

"What is it, Izzy?"

The words wouldn't fall out. They were jammed in her throat behind a big old lump. *Come on, Izzy,* she told herself, *just say, "Hi, Daddy, I missed you."*

But she couldn't. Instead, she reached out her hand and pointed to the trowel that lay on the ground. He bent down and picked up the big fork, handing it to her slowly. "It's okay, Sunshine," he said softly. "I understand."

I love you, Daddy. Tears stung her eyes; she was sad and embarrassed that she couldn't force herself to say the words. She squeezed her eyes shut before he could see the stupid, babyish tears. Then she took the trowel and moved in beside him.

He started talking, about the weather and flowers and the beautiful day. He talked so long she forgot she was embarrassed and sad and that she was a stupid little girl who couldn't talk to her daddy anymore.

Sunday was the kind of day that tricked people into moving into this damp, soggy corner of the world. The kind of day when hapless tourists who stumbled into the rain forest tended to draw in deep breaths of awe and then find themselves driving their rental cars slowly past real estate offices. Almost involuntarily, they reached for pamphlets about cabins for sale, and called their faraway families with stories of the most gorgeous land they'd ever seen.

When Nick flung back the living room curtains and looked outside, he was as awestruck as any foreigner. A bright yellow sun had just crested the trees; lemony streamers of light backlit the forest and gave it a translucent, otherworldly glow. Lake Mystic swallowed the surrounding images and held them against its blue mirrored surface. On the far bank, a single gray heron stood on one leg, proudly surveying his domain.

It was a perfect day for a father-daughter outing. He hurried up the stairs and woke his sleeping child. He helped her brush her teeth and get dressed in warm woolen clothes. While she was sleepily making her bed, he went downstairs and packed a picnic lunch—smoked salmon bought fresh from the Quinault tribe at the local roadside stand, cream cheese and crackers for him, and peanut butter and jelly sandwiches and string cheese for Izzy. Annie had left a quart of homemade lemonade, and he poured it into a thermos, then crammed everything into a picnic basket.

Within the hour, they were driving down the winding coastal road that seemed to bisect the world. On one side stood the darkest, densest of all American woodlands, and on the other, the crashing wildness of the Pacific Ocean. Along the coastal side, the evergreen trees had been sculpted by a hundred years of gale winds; their limbs bent backward in an unnatural arc.

Nick parked in one of the turnouts that were designed to showcase the view to tourists. Taking Izzy's hand, he led her down the trail toward the beach.

Below them, huge, white-tipped waves crashed against the rocks. When they finally dropped onto the hard-packed sand, Izzy grinned up at him.

The silver-blue ocean stretched out for a thousand miles away from the land. Sometimes, the wind along this stretch of the Pacific howled so hard no man could draw a breath, but today it was almost preternaturally quiet. The air was as crisp and delicious as a sun-ripened apple. Cormorants and kingfishers and seagulls cawed and wheeled overhead, landing every now and then on one of the wind-sculpted trees that grew atop house-size rocks in the surf.

Nick set the basket down on a gray boulder near the land's end. "Come on, Izzy."

They ran across the sand, laughing, creating the only footprints for miles, searching for hidden treasures: sand dollars, translucent quartz stones, and tiny black crabs. Around a bend in the coastline, they stumbled into a knee-deep mass of tiny blue jellyfish, blown ashore by the wind—a sure sign to old-timers that tuna would appear off the coast this summer.

When the sun reached its peak in the sky and sent its warmth through their layers of wool and Gortex, Nick led Izzy back to where they'd begun. He threw a huge red and white blanket over the hard sand and unpacked the basket. They sat cross-legged on the blanket and ate their lunch.

All the while, Nick told stories—about the Native Americans who had first combed this beach, hundreds of years before the first white settlers appeared; about the wild parties he had attended in high school on this very same stretch of sand; about the time he'd brought Kathy here when she was pregnant.

Once, he'd thought that Izzy was going to say something. She'd leaned forward, her brown eyes sparkling, her lips trembling.

He'd put down his glass of lemonade. *Come on, Izzy-bear.* But in the end, she'd held back. Whatever had made it to the tip of her tongue was lost.

That silence was worse than the others, somehow. It lodged in his heart like a steel splinter; he felt it with every in-drawn breath afterward. But he forced a smile and went on with another story, this time about a night long ago when he and Annie had climbed to the top of the town's water tower and painted GO PANTHERS on the metal sides.

At the end of their picnic, they loaded up the basket with their leftovers and made their slow, silent way back up to the car. They drove home in the last fading rays of the setting sun. Nick found it difficult to keep talking, to keep spilling his soul into the stony silence that surrounded them, but he forced himself to do it. When they passed

Zoe's, the need for a drink rose in him, relentless as the surf. He hit the gas harder and they sped beyond the tavern.

When they pulled into the driveway, day had given way to a pink and gold evening. He held Izzy's hand as they quietly made their way back into the house.

"What do you say we play a game?" he said, shutting the door behind him.

Izzy didn't answer, but scampered away. In a few moments, she appeared again, with the big, multicolored Candy Land box mashed to her tiny chest.

He groaned dramatically. "Not that—anything but that. How about Pick-up Sticks?"

A tiny smile tilted her mouth. She shook her head.

"You think I don't want to play that because I never win, but that's not true. It's because I fall into a coma. Come on—Pick-up Sticks. Please?"

She gave him a grin that bunched her cheeks. Her index finger thumped on the Candy Land box.

"Okay. One game of Candy Land, then Pick-up Sticks."

She released a giggle, and the simple sound of that soothed the ragged edges of his nerves. He quickly made a fire, then they set up the board in the middle of the living room floor.

One game turned into another and another. When Nick had finally lost his fine motor skills, he tossed the tiny blue and yellow board pieces into the oblong box. "I give up. You're the queen of Candy Land. No one can beat you. Come on, Izzy-bear, it's dinnertime. Even *cooking* is better than this game." He got slowly to his feet—he'd lost half the bloodflow into his legs—and staggered to a stand.

She lurched up and grabbed his hand. Worry furrowed her brow.

He smiled down at her. "It's okay, honey. I'm just old, and old people wobble a bit. Remember Grandma Myrtle? She used to totter around like a broken toy."

Izzy giggled.

In the kitchen, they sat at the big plank table and ate store-bought macaroni and cheese until their skin took on the orange glow of whatever passed for cheese in that little white packet. Izzy helped Nick wash and dry the dishes and put them away, and then they went upstairs. He helped her into her nightgown, brushed those incredibly tiny white teeth of hers, and together they climbed into her narrow twin bed.

He pulled the tattered copy of *Alice in Wonderland* off the bedside table. Curling an arm around Izzy's tiny shoulders, he drew his daughter close and began to read.

When he closed the book, her eyes were heavy and she was more than half asleep. "Good night, Sunshine," he said softly, kissing her forehead. Slowly, he drew back and stood up.

She reached out suddenly and grabbed his hand. He turned back, stared down at her. "Izzy?"

"Daddy?"

For a second, he couldn't breathe. It was the first time he'd heard her sweet child's voice in almost a year. Slowly, slowly, he sat down beside her. Tears stung his eyes, turned his precious baby into a blur. "Oh, Izzy," he whispered, unable to find any other words.

"I love you, Daddy," she said, and now she was crying, too.

He pulled her into a bear hug, hiding his face in the crook of her neck so she wouldn't see him crying. "Oh,

Izzy-bear, I love you, too," he whispered over and over again, stroking her hair, feeling her tears mingle with his on the softness of her cheek. He held her tightly, wondering if he'd ever have the strength to let her go.

She fell asleep in his arms, and still he held her. Finally, he laid her head gently on the pillow and tucked the covers up to her small, pointed chin. When he looked down at his sleeping child, he felt a rush of emotion so pure and sweet and all-consuming that no single word—not even *love*—could possibly be big enough.

Triumph was a trembling, high-pitched aria in his bloodstream. And all because of something as simple, and as infinitely complex, as a child's *I love you*. Three little words he'd never take for granted again.

He couldn't contain the enormity of his emotions; they were spilling over, breaking one after another in waves. He felt the most incredible urge to laugh out loud. He wanted to share this moment with someone he cared for.

Annie.

He knew it was dangerous, this sudden desire to talk to her, be with her, tell her what he was feeling. Knew it, and didn't care. Couldn't care.

He went into his room and picked up the phone.

Monday was a magical day, filled with laughter. Once again the sun banished the clouds from the sky. Nick and Annie and Izzy rode bicycles and collected wildflowers and made crowns from the dainty purple and white flowers that had opened during the night.

Annie couldn't remember when she'd had so much fun. Blake had never spent a day like this with his girls, just the three of them; even when he'd had a rare day at home, he'd spent it on the phone or the fax or the computer. Annie was only now beginning to realize how lonely her life had been.

As she pedaled her bike down the National Park trail, she found herself recalling bits and pieces of her phone conversation with Nick last night. *She talked to me, Annie. She told me she loved me.* The awe in his voice had brought tears to Annie's eyes, and when he went on, telling her about their day at the beach, she'd envied them the easy perfection of it all.

Though neither one of them had mentioned the conversation today, it hung in the air between them, like dust motes that were occasionally thickened by a flash of sunlight. They'd woven a new strand of intimacy during their conversation. The distance of the telephone had made it easier somehow.

In the middle of it all, Annie had begun to remember the old Nick—the young Nick—and how she'd loved him. And when she closed her eyes while he was talking, she saw the boy who'd first kissed her beneath a starry night sky. The boy whose gentle, tentative kiss had made her cry.

She could feel herself drifting into dangerous waters. So many things about Nick touched her, but it was the depth of his love for Izzy that tangled her up inside and left her aching. No matter how hard she tried to forget the life she'd lived in California and the choices she'd made, Nick brought it all up again. Annie had raised a daughter who would never truly know the comforting embrace of a father's adoration.

And she had been a wife in love alone for too many years.

She had felt pathetic and small as she crossed the rickety bridge to that realization. For years, she'd mistaken habit and affection for true love. She had assumed that the love she gave her husband was a reflection of the love he felt for her, and now, because of her blindness, she was alone, a thirty-nine-year-old woman who faced her "golden" years without a child at home or a husband in her bed.

At that moment, she and Nick were separated by miles, and she was glad because if he'd been beside her, she would have reached for him, would have begged him to hold her and kiss her and tell her she was beautiful . . . even if the words were a lie.

Now, as they drove home after their bike ride, Annie prayed that Nick hadn't heard all that loneliness and pain in her voice. Every time he looked at her today, she'd looked away, fast.

By the time they returned to the house, she was a wreck. She sat quietly at the table, her eyes focused on her food, her right foot tapping nervously on the floor.

As soon as dinner was over, she bolted from the table and hustled Izzy up to bed, leaving Nick to wash and dry the dishes.

"Good night, Izzy," she said, tucking the child into bed. "Your daddy will be up in a minute."

" 'Night, Annie," Izzy muttered, rolling onto her side.

Annie closed the bedroom door and headed downstairs. She found Nick in the living room, staring out at the lake. Even from this distance, she could see that his hands were shaking. There was a damp dishrag lying at his feet.

The last step creaked beneath her foot and she froze.

He spun toward her. His skin was pale in the lamplight, and sweat sheened his forehead.

"You want a drink," she said.

"Want?" His laugh was low and rough. "That doesn't even begin to cover it."

Annie didn't know what to do. It was dangerous to touch him, but she couldn't turn away. Cautiously, she moved toward him. He reached for her hand, his sweaty fingers coiling around hers with a desperate squeeze.

After a long minute, she said, "How 'bout a bowl of Chocolate Chip Mint instead?"

"Great. I'll just go say good night to Izzy, then . . . I'll meet you by the fire." He gave her a relieved smile before turning and bolting up the stairs.

Annie went to the kitchen and scooped out two bowls of ice cream. The whole time she told herself that it was nothing, just a bowl of ice cream between friends. By the time she was finished, Nick was back downstairs. Together, they sat on the sofa.

In silence, they ate. The tinny clang of spoons on porcelain seemed absurdly loud. She was sharply aware of everything about him, the uneven way he tapped his foot anxiously on the floor, the way he kept tucking a flyaway lock of hair behind his right ear.

All at once, he turned to her. "How long will you be here?"

So that was it. She sighed. "About another month and a half. Natalie gets home on the fifteenth of June."

His gaze caught hers, and she felt as if she were falling into his blue eyes.

Annie's breath caught in her chest. She found herself waiting to hear what he would say next, though she couldn't imagine what it would be.

"What do you think of Mystic?" he asked slowly, watching her. "You sure couldn't wait to leave after high school."

"It wasn't Mystic that sent me running."

It was a long minute before he answered softly, "I never meant to hurt you."

"I know."

"You scared me."

She felt it blossom again at his words, that delicate bud of intimacy that had drawn them together last night. It scared her, especially now when she was so close to him. She tried to brush it away with a laugh. "You're kidding, right?"

He leaned forward and set the bowl down on the coffee table. Then, slowly, he turned toward her. One arm snaked down the back of the sofa toward her, and she had to fight the urge to lean back into it. "I think our lives are mapped out long before we know enough to ask the right questions. Mine was cast in stone the day my dad abandoned my mom. She had . . . trouble handling life. Before I even knew what was happening, I was her caretaker. I learned what every child of a drunk learns: don't talk, don't trust, don't care. Hell, I was an adult before I was ten years old. I shopped, I cooked, I cleaned . . . wherever we lived. I loved her, so I took care of her, and when she turned on me or became violent, I believed what she said—that I was worthless and stupid and lucky she stayed with me." He leaned back into the sofa.

Annie felt his fingertips brush her shoulders. She gazed at him, remembering how handsome he had been, how when she'd looked at him for the first time, she hadn't been able to breathe.

"Living here with Joe was like a dream for me. Clean sheets, clean clothes, lots to eat. I got to go to school every day and no one ever hit me." He smiled at her, and the heat of it sent shivers through her blood. "Then I met you and Kath. Remember?"

"At the A and W, after a football game. We invited you to sit with us. There was a K-Tel album playing in the background."

"*You* invited me. I couldn't believe it when you did that . . . and then, when we all became friends, it stunned me. Everything about that year was a first." He smiled, but his smile was sad and tired around the edges and didn't reach his eyes. "You were the first girl I ever kissed. Did you know that?"

Annie's throat felt dangerously tight. "I cried."

He nodded. "I thought it was because you *knew*. Like you could taste it in me somehow, that I wasn't good enough."

She wanted to touch him so badly her fingers tingled. She forced her hand into a fist. "I never knew why I cried. Still don't."

He smiled at her. "See? The paths are set before we're aware. Kathy was so much simpler. I *understood* her. She needed me, even then she needed me, and to me that was the same as love. I just plopped into the role I knew. I mean, what was I supposed to do? Ask you to give up Stanford? Or wait for you, even though you hadn't asked me to?"

Annie had never once considered being bold enough to talk to Nick about how she felt. Like him, she'd fallen easily—tumbled—into the role she knew. She did what was expected of her; Annie the good girl. She went away to college and married a nice boy with a bright future . . . and lost herself along the way.

"I always figured you'd be famous," he said at last, "you were so damned smart. The only kid from Mystic ever to get an academic scholarship to Stanford."

She snorted. "Me, famous? Doing what?"

"Don't do that, Annie." His voice was as soft as a touch, and she couldn't help looking at him. The sadness in his eyes coiled around her throat and squeezed. "That's a bad road to go down. Believe me, I know. You could succeed at anything you tried. And screw anyone who tells you different."

His encouragement was a draught of water to her parched, thirsty soul. "I *did* think of something the other day. . . ."

"What?"

She drew back. "You'll laugh."

"Never."

Dangerously, she believed him. "I'd like to run a small bookstore. You know the kind, with overstuffed chairs and latte machines and employees who actually *read*."

He touched her cheekbone, a fleeting caress that made her shiver. It was the first time he'd deliberately touched her since that night by the lake. "You should see yourself right now, Annie."

Heat climbed up her cheeks. "You probably think I'm being ridiculous."

"No. Never. I was just noticing how your eyes lit up when you said 'bookstore.' I think it's a great idea. In fact, there's an old Victorian house on Main Street. It used to be a gift shop until a few months ago. When the owner died, they closed it up. They've been trying to find a renter. With a little elbow grease, it could make a great location." He paused and looked at her. "If you wanted to open that bookstore in Mystic."

The fantasy broke apart. They both knew that her life wasn't in Mystic. She belonged in another state, beneath another sun, in a white house by the sea. She stared down at her diamond ring, trying to think of something to say, a way to brush off the silly daydream and pretend she'd never voiced it.

He said suddenly, "Have you seen *Same Time, Next Year*?"

She frowned. "The Alan Alda movie—the one about the couple who have an affair for one weekend every year?"

"Yeah."

She found it difficult to breathe evenly. The air seemed electrified by the simple word: *affair.* "I-I always loved it."

"It's starting in ten minutes. You want to watch?"

Her breath expelled in a rush. She felt like a fool for reading something into a simple little question about a movie.

"Sure."

They settled onto the sofa and watched the movie, but all the while, Annie had the strangest sensation that she was falling. She kept glancing at Nick, whom she often caught staring at her in return. She didn't want to consider how much he had begun to matter, but there was no way to avoid the obvious.

Last night, she'd learned that he liked chocolate chip ice cream and hated beets . . . that blue was his favorite color and professional sports bored him to tears . . . that he liked his baked potatoes with butter and bacon bits, but no salt or pepper, and that sometimes a kiss from Izzy, given as she snuggled close to him, had the power to make him cry.

She knew that often the need for a drink rose in him with such sudden ferocity that it left him winded and glassy-eyed. In those moments, he would push away from Annie and Izzy and run into the forest alone. Later, he would return, his hair dampened by sweat, his skin pale and his hands trembling, but he would smile at her, a sad, desperate smile that didn't reach his eyes, and she would know that he had beaten it again. And sometimes, in that moment, when their gazes locked across the clearing, she could feel the danger, simmering beneath the surface.

She didn't want to care too deeply about Nick Delacroix, and yet she could feel each day bringing them closer and closer.

When the movie ended, she couldn't look at him, afraid of what she'd see in his eyes . . . afraid of what he'd see in hers. So, she grabbed her box of tissues and her purse and ran for the door. She hardly even mumbled a good-bye.

Chapter 17

Izzy woke up scared. She'd been dreaming about her mommy . . . that was all she could remember. Her mommy had been down by the lake, calling out to her . . . crying.

She threw back the covers and climbed out of bed. Without bothering to put on her robe and slippers, she crept out of her bedroom and hurried down the hall. She paused at her daddy's bedroom, then moved past. Down the stairs and out the front doors, into the darkest part of the night.

She stared at the lake. At first it was nothing but a charcoal-gray shadow in the vee of the mountains, but after a while, she could see the glistening waves and hear the murmuring voice of the water against the gravelly shore. The mist had thickened into a gray fog spiked with black toothpick trees.

Izzy-bear, is that you?

She flinched. The screen door jumped out of her hand and banged back into place. "Mommy?"

Something white flashed beside the shore.

She glanced back at the house and saw that her daddy's

bedroom was dark. She knew she should tell her daddy where she was going, but then she saw the flash of white again and heard the sound of a woman crying, and she forgot all about it. She picked up the hem of her nightgown and hurried across the wet grass, her toes squishing in muddy ground.

There were sounds everywhere—the cawing of crows, the hooting of a lonely owl, the ribbiting of bullfrogs—and though the sounds scared her, she didn't stop until she reached the lake.

"Mommy?" she whispered.

A fine mist rose from the water. It was in the mist that she saw her mommy. Clear as day, she was standing on the water, her hands clasped at her waist, her golden-blond hair a halo around her face. Izzy got a flashing glimpse of white wings, and she heard a rhythmic sound, like the blurring start of a lawn mower, but she couldn't be sure of what she was seeing. There was a brightness to her mommy that hurt Izzy's eyes, like looking right at the sun. She blinked and tried to focus, but she kept seeing a spray of black dots and stars and her mommy went in and out of focus.

Izzy-bear, why did you call me?

Izzy blinked and tried to see her mommy's pretty blue eyes. "I didn't call you this time."

I heard you calling in your sleep.

Izzy tried to remember her dream, but it was just pictures and feelings and panic and it didn't seem to mean anything at all right now. "I don't know what I wanted."

She felt her mother's touch, a breeze on her forehead, brushing the hair away, a kiss that smelled of mist and rain and her mommy's favorite perfume. "I miss you, Mommy."

Your daddy's back now.

"What if he goes away again?"

Another touch, softer. *He won't, Izzy-bear.*

This time, when Izzy looked up, her mother was closer, and she was certain she saw dove-white wings. "I can't follow you, can I?"

For a split second, the mist was gone, and Izzy saw her mom. There were no wings, no white brightness, no mist. There was just a sad-eyed, blond-haired woman in a pink-flowered flannel nightgown, looking down at her little girl. *I'll always be inside you, Izzy. You don't have to disappear or follow me or reach for me. All you have to do is close your eyes and think of me and I'll be there. You think about the time we went to the circus and I was laughing so hard at the clowns that I fell off the bench. And when you smile at that, you'll find me.*

Tears streaked down Izzy's face, plopped on her hands. She stared, blinking, into her mommy's blue, blue eyes. "I love you, Mommy . . ."

And then suddenly her mommy was gone.

"Izzy!"

Her father's panicked voice sliced through Izzy's thoughts. She twisted around and saw him running toward her. "Daddy?"

He pulled her into his arms and held her tightly. "Izzy." He said her name in a weird way, as if he'd been running for miles. "Oh, Izzy . . . you scared me. I didn't know where you were. . . ."

"I di'n't go anywhere bad, Daddy."

He gave her a wobbly smile. "I know, honey."

He carried her back into the house and put her gently in bed. She scooted under the covers, but she wasn't ready to be by herself yet. She grabbed a book off the table by the bed. It was her treasured copy of *Cinderella*, the one that had been handed down from Grandma Myrtle, to Mommy, to Izzy. "Could you read me a story, Daddy?"

He climbed into bed beside her. Very gently, he opened the book to the first page. He read as he'd always read to her, with vigor and gusto and lots of funny voices.

Only Izzy didn't laugh. She couldn't; instead, she sat propped against the bright yellow Big Bird pillow, staring at the vibrant paintings on the page. When he finished the story, she was very quiet. "What happened to Cinderella's mommy?"

It was a minute before he said softly, "I think Cinderella's mommy went to heaven."

"Oh."

"And you know what I think?"

She shook her head. "No."

"I think she and Mommy are friends now, and they're looking down on us, making sure we're okay."

Izzy thought about that. It was sort of what she thought, too. "Annie says that when it rains, it's Mommy and the angels crying."

He brushed the tangle of hair from her face. "Annie knows an awful lot."

She turned away from him, trying to hide the tears that burned her eyes. "I'm startin' to forget her, Daddy."

He slipped an arm around her and drew her close, gently stroking her moist cheek. "Mommy had the prettiest eyes in the world, and when she looked at you, it felt as if the rain had stopped and the sunlight was on your face. And she had a crooked front tooth—it sort of slanted sideways, and a tiny mole right next to her ear. She loved you, Izzy . . . she loved you more than her own life."

"She loved both of us, Daddy."

He didn't say anything. He just kissed her, right on the tip of her nose, and it reminded her of when she was a baby; he used to do that all the time. For the first time since her mommy died, Izzy wasn't scared. The scream that had been inside her for months shriveled up like an old raisin and rolled away. She knew, finally, that everything was going to be okay.

Her daddy loved her again.

She squeezed her eyes shut, really hard so she wouldn't cry like a baby. When she could breathe again, she slowly opened her eyes.

She couldn't believe what she saw. "Daddy?" she said softly.

"Yeah, Sunshine?"

She slowly lifted her left hand. Clear as day, she could see the little black glove that grew out of her sleeve. She bit down on her trembling lower lip, afraid it was a mistake. Slowly, she took off the glove, and there was her hand. "Do you see it, Daddy?"

He looked right at her hand—she was sure he saw it—but he didn't smile. Instead, he looked at her. "What *should* I see?"

She swallowed thickly. "I see my hand . . . and my arm. Do you see 'em?"

Her daddy made a raggedy sound. "Yeah. I see your hand." Very slowly, like he was afraid she was going to stop him, he took the glove from her.

She giggled, wriggling her fingers. "I guess I'm stayin' here with you, Daddy."

"Yeah, Izzy-bear. I guess you are."

He made a sniffing sound. Izzy looked up and saw the strangest thing: her big, strong daddy was crying.

She loved both of us.

Much later, when Nick was in bed, with his arms wishboned behind his head, he finally allowed himself to think about what Izzy had said to him.

She loved both of us.

It was the sentence he'd been unable to believe in for so long, spoken with such certainty in the voice of a child.

The tears he'd hidden away for over a year came spilling down his cheeks. He had loved his wife, loved her from the time he first saw her, and somehow in the last few years he'd forgotten; he'd seen all that darkness and forgotten the light. She had loved him, too, with all her broken heart; she had loved him.

"I loved you, Kath," he whispered into the quiet solitude of his bedroom. "I loved you . . ."

The Mystic Rain Festival started on schedule, on the first Saturday in May, just as it had for each of the last hundred years. A low-slung gray sky hung over downtown. Rain fell in a stuttering curtain on the storefront awnings. Fresh green leaves floated in murky gutter water, swirling alongside the sidewalks.

Annie wore a slick yellow raincoat, with her Levi's tucked into high-topped black rubber boots, and a Seattle Mariners baseball cap. Hank stood beside her, munching on a homemade scone he'd purchased at the Rotary Club booth.

The parade moved slowly down Main Street, splashing on the wet pavement. There were fire trucks, police cars,

Boy Scout troops, and six little girls in pink tutus from Esmeralda's Dance Barn.

Annie was enchanted by the schmaltzy, small-town production. She knew from experience that the parade would clatter down the six blocks and then turn around and come back.

She had missed this. How was it that she hadn't known that? She'd gone to California and raised her daughter behind iron gates and in air-conditioned rooms, in a city where hometown parades had celebrity marshals and corporate sponsors.

She didn't want to go back there.

It surprised her, the sudden certainty of her decision. It was the first time in her life she'd come to a conclusion without thinking of other people's feelings, and it felt good.

She didn't want to live in California anymore, and she didn't have to. After the divorce, when Natalie went away to college, Annie could return to Mystic, maybe even open that bookstore. . . .

Dreams. They were such precious commodities, and she'd given so many of hers away without a fight. Never again.

She turned to her dad. "Let me ask you something, Dad. Do you think this town could use a bookstore?"

He smiled. "Hell, yes. We've needed one for years. Your mom used to dream of opening one."

Annie shivered. For a strange, disorienting second, she felt as if her mom were beside her. "Really? I was thinking the same thing."

He turned to her, looked at her long and hard. "You're hurting right now, Annie, and you're running, but don't forget where your real life is. You're never going to live in

Mystic again, and besides, you're not a businessperson. You're a housewife." He slipped an arm around her, drawing her close.

His lack of faith stung. For the first time, she wondered how long her father had been spoon-feeding her a diet of self-doubt. When had it begun? When she was a child? The first time he told her not to worry her pretty head about something? Or all the times he'd told her that Blake would take care of her?

If she were a different kind of woman, Annie might feel angry right now, but as it was, all she felt was the vague residue of sadness. Her father was from another generation, and he'd done the best he could with his only child. If his wife had lived, everything would have been different. . . .

But she hadn't, and with her death, Hank had been thrown into a role he couldn't handle. All he knew of womanhood came from his own mother, a tired, washed-out woman who died at forty-seven, driven to an early grave by hard work. Like his father, Hank had grown up in Mystic, and never seen much of the world beyond. He'd thought the best he could do for Annie was to get her educated, so that she could find a husband who could give her a better life than the one to which she'd been raised.

Unfortunately, Annie had followed his lead. She'd gone all the way to Stanford—where the world had been open to her if only she'd known where to look—and she'd kept her gaze on the straight and narrow. She'd asked too little of herself . . . and gotten exactly what she'd sought. It was funny how that worked in life.

It wasn't her father's fault, any more than it was Blake's or Annie's fault. It simply was. She was lucky to have seen the truth at all, she supposed. If not for Blake, she would have walked down the road of the ordinary for the whole of her life, a middle-aged woman, and then at last an old woman, wearing the blinders that had been passed down from generation to generation.

She slipped her hand into her dad's and gave him a gentle squeeze. The last entry in the parade, the Bits and Spurs 4-H club, clattered past on horseback, and as it rounded the corner and disappeared, everyone clapped and cheered. When the applause died down, the crowd began to disperse, slipping off the sidewalk and onto the street.

Annie and Hank strolled arm in arm down the sidewalk, past the artisans' booths and hot-dog stands, past the Victorian house with a FOR RENT sign in the window.

Hank stopped at the Lutheran church stand and bought two mocha lattes, handing one to Annie. The pungent aroma of the coffee swirled between them, and the heat of it soothed her scratchy throat. Neither of them noticed the gentle patter of the rain; it had never bothered Annie. It was funny how she'd forgotten that. In California, she used to race for an umbrella at the first hint of precipitation. Here, the only people who used umbrellas were tourists.

"So, Natalie gets home in six weeks."

Annie took a sip of coffee, then nodded. "June fifteenth. I can't wait."

"What will you say to Blake when you see him?"

The question surprised Annie. It wasn't something she wanted to think about, and it was unlike her father to ask. She shrugged. "I don't know. For weeks, all I wanted was to see him again, to make him remember what we had together, but now I can't seem to grab hold of what we had."

"Is it because of him?"

She started to ask what he meant, but when she looked up, she saw Nick. He was standing across the street, with Izzy on his shoulders. They were both eating ice cream cones. He turned, and across the crowded street, their eyes met and held for a heartbeat. He flashed her a smile, waved, then moved on. She tried to frame an answer for her dad, but she honestly didn't know how Nick fit into the picture. "Who knows what causes anything? All I know is that I'm not the same woman I was before."

"You be careful, Annie."

She glanced across the street again, but Nick was gone. She felt a pang of disappointment. "You know what, Dad? I'm tired of being careful."

"When you play with fire, you get burned."

She laughed. "More bumper stickers, Dad?"

He laughed with her. "How do you think people come up with bumper stickers? Some things are just plain true."

Chapter 18

On Monday Annie, Nick, and Izzy drove to Sol Duc Hot Springs and hiked deep into the Olympic National Forest. Afterward, they swam in the lodge's huge swimming pool and relaxed in the steaming, sulphuric hot springs. When dusk started to fall, they piled back into the car and headed home.

By the time they unpacked the car and got everything put away, it was almost midnight. Nick offered Annie his room, and she took him up on the offer. She called her dad, who was waiting up for her again, and told him that she'd be home first thing in the morning.

Is that wise, Annie Virginia? he asked in a quiet voice.

She told him not to worry, and hung up the phone. Afterward, she wasn't so sure she'd made a smart decision, but the truth was that she didn't feel well. She wanted to collapse in a convenient bed and sleep for ten hours. Her back hurt, her head hurt, and she'd felt nauseous for most of the drive home. She was definitely not cut out for hiking.

She was careful to avoid Nick as she hurried upstairs, brushed her teeth, and fell into a deep sleep.

The next morning, she woke up feeling even worse. A headache pounded behind her eyes, and she had to lie very still in bed, concentrating on each breath, or she was certain she was going to throw up.

She counted slowly to ten, then angled up to her elbows. Sunlight slanted through her bedroom window. The glare hurt her eyes and intensified her headache. A beautiful morning in May, and she couldn't enjoy it.

Swallowing thickly, she threw back the comforter and stumbled into the small adjoining bathroom. She didn't bother turning on the light—she could see the shadowy pockets under her eyes perfectly well. She moved like a hundred-year-old woman, taking forever to brush her teeth and wash her face. When she was finished, she felt even worse.

She went back to bed and snuggled under the covers. A chill racked her body, and she closed her eyes.

Some time later—an hour? a minute?—a knock sounded at her door. Annie forced herself to sit up. "Come in."

Izzy poked her head through the open door. "Annie? I'm hungry."

Annie manufactured a wan smile. "Hi, honey. Come on in—but don't get too close, I think I have the flu."

Izzy slipped into the room, closing the door behind her. "I was waitin' for you to show up. I thought maybe you'd left us . . . but then Daddy tole me you'd spent the night."

Annie's heart went out to the girl, whose brown eyes looked so big and worried. "I wouldn't do that, Izzy. I wouldn't disappear without saying good-bye."

"Grown-ups do that sometimes."

"Oh, Izzy . . ." Annie shifted her position, trying to ignore a sudden wave of dizziness. "I know they do." She started to say something else, preferably something blindingly insightful, when she sneezed hard. She barely had time to get her hand in front of her mouth before she sneezed again. She sagged in bed, trying to remember when she'd felt this rotten.

Izzy's eyes widened. "Are you sick?"

Annie gave her a weak smile of understanding. "Not *really* sick," she answered quietly. "It's just a cold. I bet you get them all the time."

Izzy visibly relaxed. "Yeah. That's when green snot comes out of your nose."

"A lovely image, to be sure. I think I'm going to go to sleep for a while, but we'll talk later. Okay?"

Izzy nodded slowly. "Okay. See yah."

Annie smiled weakly. "See you, pumpkin." When Izzy was gone, she leaned toward the bedside table and picked up the phone. After asking for the number from directory assistance, she called Dr. Burton's office.

The receptionist answered on the first ring. "Mystic Family Clinic. This is Madge, how can I help you?"

"Hi, Madge. This is Annie Colwater. I'd like to make an appointment to see Dr. Burton."

"Is it an emergency, sweetie?"

Only if green snot constituted an emergency. "No."

"Well, the doctor's out of town right now, on vacation at Orcas Island. He was afraid you might call. He wanted me to refer you to Dr. Hawkins in Port Angeles." Her voice lowered to a stage whisper. "He's a *psychiatrist.*"

Even in her weakened state, Annie smiled. "Oh, that's not necessary."

"Oh, good. Now, you're still booked for June first. Is that appointment okay?"

Annie had forgotten all about it. The depression she'd felt in March had faded into a dull, sepia-toned memory. She probably didn't need the appointment, but it would reassure Doc Burton. He'd be proud of how well she'd recovered. "Yeah, that appointment's fine. Thanks, Madge."

"Okay. Ten-thirty in the morning. Don't forget."

Before she even hung up the phone, Annie had closed her eyes.

Annie dreamed she was in a cool, dark place. She could hear the cascading fall of water and the buzzing drone of a dragonfly. There was someone waiting for her in the forest's darkness. She could hear the even cant of his breathing in the shadows. She wanted to reach for him, but she was afraid. Where she was felt familiar, safe, and he was waiting for her in a strange world where she didn't know the rules. She was afraid that if she followed, she'd lose her way.

"Annie?"

She woke up suddenly and found Nick sitting on the end of her bed. Trying to smile, she struggled to sit up half way. "Hi."

"Izzy tells me you're sick." He leaned toward her, touched her forehead. "You're warm."

"I am?"

He slid closer to her and produced a thermometer. "Open up."

Like an obedient child, she opened her mouth. The slick, cool thermometer slid under her tongue and settled in place. She closed her lips, but she couldn't take her eyes away from Nick.

"I've brought you some orange juice and a couple of scrambled eggs. Oh, and Tylenol and a pitcher of ice water."

Annie watched in surprise as he went into the bathroom. Then he came back to her, carefully folding a wet cloth in thirds as he walked. He sat back on the chair beside the bed and placed the cool rag on her forehead. Then he handed her two Tylenols. "Here."

She stared down at the two little pills in his hand.

He frowned. "Annie? You're crying."

She blinked hard. *Damn.* "Am I? Don't worry about me. It's probably allergies. Or menopause. I've been feeling hormonal all week. And I think I'm gearing up for a howler of a—" She bit back the word *period.* This wasn't her husband she was talking to, and her periods weren't exactly an acceptable topic for conversation. The realization isolated her. With that one tiny word she couldn't say, she understood how adrift she was, how unconnected. It was something she'd always taken for granted in her marriage, the way you could say anything at any time, reveal any secret thing about yourself. There was no one now with whom she could be so free.

"What is it, Annie?"

The gentleness in his voice only made her cry harder, and though it was humiliating to sit here crying for no reason, she couldn't seem to stop herself.

"Annie?"

She couldn't meet his eyes. "You'll think I'm an idiot."

He laughed, a quiet, tender sound. "You're worried about what the town drunk thinks?"

She sniffed hard. "Don't talk about yourself that way."

"Is that how the rich people in California do it—am I just supposed to pretend you're not crying? Now, tell me what's the matter."

Annie closed her eyes. It seemed to take forever to find her voice. "No one has ever given me an aspirin before— I mean, without me asking for it." God, it sounded as pathetic as she'd thought it would. She felt ashamed and horribly exposed. She tried to tack an explanation on, so it sounded better. "I've been a wife and mother for so long. I've always been the one who took care of people when they were sick."

"But no one took care of you." He said it as a simple statement, and though she wanted to reject it as being silly, she couldn't.

It was all there, in that simple, simple sentence, everything that had been wrong with her marriage. She'd done everything to make Blake's life safe and perfect; she'd loved him and cared for him and protected him. All those years she'd made excuses for his selfishness: he was tired, or busy, or distracted by business. They were just layers of pretty wrapping paper on a dark and ugly truth.

No one took care of you.

Suddenly she was crying for all of it, every missed moment, every dream she'd ever had. The marriage she'd had wasn't good enough. She'd never really, truly been loved . . . not the way she deserved to be loved.

With a deep, ragged sigh, she wiped her eyes and smiled up at Nick. "I'm sorry for being such a baby."

She glanced at the things he'd placed on her nightstand. Orange juice, water, cold tablets, Tylenol, a plate of scrambled eggs, and a piece of cinnamon toast. And it made her want to cry all over again. She didn't know what to say to him, this man who'd accidentally opened a door on her old life and shown her the truth.

"You should drink something."

She wiped her runny nose and gave him a crooked grin. "Well, you should know."

He looked stunned for a second, then he burst out laughing.

The cold hung on for two days, and when it was over, Annie was left feeling tired and weak. Her stomach stayed queasy afterward, but she refused to pay any attention to it.

On Friday, she and Nick and Izzy drove to Kalaloch and spent the day beachcombing. Izzy squealed with delight every time she found a sand dollar or a crab. They raced down the beach together, all three of them, turning over rocks and sticks in their search for hidden treasures, and when the sun was high in the sky, they had a picnic lunch in a secret cave. Afterward, they waded and splashed in the icy cold water until their cheeks and hands and feet turned a stinging red. Finally, when the sun began its slow descent, they returned to the car and headed home.

Annie sat in the passenger seat of her Mustang, with a plastic bucket of shells and rocks in her lap.

"Daddy, can we stop and get ice cream, Daddy?"

Nick answered easily, laughing. "Sure, Izzy-bear."

Annie glanced at him, mesmerized. In the past few weeks, he'd become a new man entirely. He smiled all the time, and laughed easily, and spent hours playing with his little girl. Sometimes, like now, when the sunlight hit his profile and cast him in golden light, he was so handsome, he took Annie's breath away.

But there was more to Nick; his vulnerability and his strength moved her, and the tenderness of his care had almost undone her. She'd never known anyone who loved as deeply, as completely as Nick. That was why life had been able to pummel him so brutally. Nothing was easier to shatter than the fragile shield of an idealist.

She was still watching him hours later, after she'd put away the last dinner dish and picked up the last of Izzy's crayons. He was standing down at the lake again, his body a shadow within shadows, but Annie was well aware of the subtle differences of light and dark, the pale outline of his hair, the broad shelf of his shoulders, the moonlight that glimmered every now and then off the metal rivets on his jeans.

She threw the damp dishrag on the kitchen counter and headed outside. She wanted to be with him, and though the realization frightened her, it also set her heart racing with anticipation. When she was with Nick, she was a different woman. Some of his glitter fell onto her and made her feel beautiful and sparkly and more alive.

There were stars everywhere. Frogs and crickets sang in a staccato chorus that died at her approach. The grass was cold and wet on her bare feet.

Nick stood motionless, his shoulders rounded, his head dropped forward.

"Hi, Nick," she said softly.

He spun around, and she saw the pain in his eyes.

"Hi, Annie." His voice was low, and as rough as old bricks. A cool night breeze caressed her face and slid between the buttons of her cotton shirt, like a man's cold fingers, inching tenderly along her flesh. She had come to know him so well in the past weeks that his longings were obvious to her. "You want a drink."

He laughed, but it was a sharp, bitter sound, not his laugh at all. He reached out and held her hand, squeezing hard.

She knew from experience that he needed the sound of her voice now. It didn't matter what she said, anything would do; he simply needed an anchor to hold him steady. "Remember the senior party, when Kath disappeared for a half hour or so?" she said quietly. "We were at Lake Crescent. You and I sat by the lake, right in front of the lodge, and talked and talked. You said you wanted to be a cop."

"You said you wanted to be a writer."

She was surprised that he remembered, and though she didn't want to, she found herself remembering the girl who'd wanted to be a writer. The old dream was heavy now. "That was before I'd learned . . ." Her voice faded into the breeze and fell silent.

He turned, gazed down at her. "Learned what?"

She shrugged, unable suddenly to meet his gaze. "I don't know. How life slips away from you while you're standing in a grocery line, waiting to pay for a quart of milk . . . how time passes and takes everything in its path—youth, hopes, dreams. Dreams—it takes those most of all."

She felt his gaze on her again, and she was afraid to meet it, afraid of what she'd see in his eyes.

"Sometimes I don't even recognize you," he said, gently tilting her chin up. "You say things like that and I don't know the woman who is speaking at all."

She released a laugh that fluttered like a moth into the darkness. "You're not alone."

"What happened to you, Annie?"

The question was startling in its intimacy. The night fell silent, awaiting her answer, so quiet that she could hear her own rapid intake of breath. She pushed the poisonous words out in a rush. "My husband is in love with another woman. He wants a divorce."

"Annie—"

"I'm fine, really." She tried to think of something to say that would make them both laugh, but when she looked in his eyes, she saw a terrible, harrowing compassion, and it was her undoing. The strength she'd been gathering and hoarding for the past weeks fell away from her. A single tear streaked down her cheek. "How does it happen? I loved Blake with all my heart and soul and it wasn't enough. . . ."

He sighed, and the sadness of the sound bound them together. She watched as he tried to find the words to answer her, saw his frustration when he came up empty.

"The worst thing is you don't see it coming," she said. "You don't even suspect that Monday will be the last time you'll ever come up behind him and kiss the back of his neck . . . or the last time you'll sit watching television and rub the soft skin just below his ankle. And you think you'd remember something like the last time you made love, but you can't. It's gone."

She gazed up at him, surprised at how easily the words had come to her. In the weeks since Blake's confession, she'd trapped the pain inside her heart and kept it there, fanning the hot coal with dreams and nightmares and memories. But now, all at once, the fire of it was gone. In its place was a dull, thudding ache.

She still had the hurt; probably that would never completely heal. Like a broken bone that was badly reset, the wound would always be a place of weakness within her. When the cold weather hit, or she remembered a special time, she would recall the love she had had for Blake, and she would ache. But the raging fire of it had burned down to a cold, gray ember.

Nick didn't know when it happened exactly, or who moved first. All he knew was that he needed Annie. He reached for her. His hand slipped underneath her flannel collar and curled around the back of her neck, anchoring her in place. Slowly, watching her, he bent down and kissed her. It was gentle at first, a soft mingling of lips and breath. But then she moved toward him, settled into his embrace. He felt her hands, so small and pliant, moving across his back in a soothing, circular motion.

He deepened the kiss. His tongue explored her mouth, tasting, caressing. He kissed her until he was light-headed with longing, and then slowly he drew back.

She stared up at him. He saw sadness in her eyes, but something else, perhaps the same quiet wonder he had felt. "I'm sorry," he said softly, even though it wasn't true. "I had no right—"

"Don't be," she whispered. "Please . . . don't be sorry. I wanted you to kiss me. I . . . I've wanted it for a long time, I think."

She opened the door to intimacy, and he couldn't walk away. He didn't care if he was being stupid or careless or asking for trouble. He only knew that he wanted her, heart, body, and soul. He curled a hand around her neck and urged her closer, so close he could feel her rapid breathing against his mouth. "I want you, Annie Bourne. It feels like I've wanted you all my life."

A tear slipped down her cheek, and in that glittering bead of moisture, he saw reflections of all the distance that separated them. She still looked amazingly like the sixteen-year-old girl he'd first fallen in love with, but like him, the life she'd led and the choices she'd made lay collected in the tiny network of lines around her beautiful face.

"I know" was all she said in answer, but in the two simple, sadly softened words, he heard the truth: that sometimes, the wanting wasn't enough.

He reached down and took hold of her hand, lifting it. In the glittering silver moonlight, the diamond ring seemed to be made of cold fire. He stared at the ring a long time, saying nothing. Then he turned from her. "Good night, Annie," he said softly, walking away from her before he made a fool of himself.

Back in his room, Nick peeled off his clothes and crawled into his unmade bed. He was surprised to realize that he was shaking. And for once, it wasn't an absence of alcohol that was playing hell with his body. It was a woman.

Don't think about her . . . think about AA and their advice. No new relationships when you're getting sober. . . .

Thinking about the Twelve Steps didn't help. He closed his eyes and pictured Annie. She was probably to town by now. He wondered what song was playing on the Mustang's radio, what she was thinking.

It had taken every bit of strength and honor he possessed to walk away after that kiss. He'd wanted to pull her into his arms and ravish her on the spot. Lose himself and his past in the sweet darkness of her body. But it wasn't right, and he didn't dare . . . for so many reasons. And so here he lay, alone.

It occurred to Annie that if she were smart, she would leave right then. But all she could think about was Nick, and the way he'd kissed her. The way he'd touched and held her had swept her away. And when it was over, when he'd said, *I want you, Annie Bourne,* she'd known that she was lost.

She glanced up at his bedroom. A shadow passed in front of the glass, then disappeared. He thought she'd gone home—and she knew that she should.

Instead, she glanced down at the wedding ring on her left hand. The diamond glittered with color in the lamp's glow. The ring she'd worn for years. Blake had placed it on her hand beneath a shower of romantic words on their tenth anniversary.

Gently, she pulled the ring from her finger. "Good-bye, Blake." It hurt to say the words, even to think them, but there was a surprising freedom in it, too. She felt unfettered, on her own for perhaps the first time in her life. There was no one to guide her choices or determine her path. No one but her.

Before she could talk herself out of it, she hurried back into the house and up the stairs. Outside Nick's door, she paused. In the time it took to draw a breath, she lost her nerve. All the reasons for being here scurried away, cowards leaving a sinking ship. Suddenly she didn't feel sexy; she felt vulnerable and alone. A middle-aged woman begging for sex from an old friend . . .

She was just about to turn away when she heard the

music. Beyond the door, a radio was playing, a scratchy old rendition of Nat King Cole's "Unforgettable."

It soothed her ragged nerves, that song, and even more the fact that he was listening to it. Nick wasn't some inexperienced teenager; he was a man, her age, and as ravaged by life and love as she was. He would understand why she was here. He would ask nothing of her except the simple, uncomplicated act of sharing.

She rapped sharply on the door.

There was a pause. The music snapped off. "Come on in, Izzy."

Annie cleared her throat. "It's me . . . Annie."

Another pause, a scuffling sound. "Come in."

She pushed on the door; it opened with a slow, creaking noise.

Nick was in bed.

She swallowed hard and moved toward him. Anxiety was a rattling jangle inside her; she felt as gawky and awkward as a teenager. She thought about the weight she'd gained in the past weeks, and wondered if he'd find her attractive. Blake had always made such cutting remarks when Annie gained a pound. . . .

He looked at her and the intensity of his gaze caused a heat to flutter through her. She shivered.

"Are you sure?" He asked it simply, the only question that mattered.

And she was. Utterly, absolutely, positively sure. She felt herself moving toward him, reaching out. Later, she would never be able to remember who had touched first, or how they had come to be naked together on that massive, four-poster bed . . . but she would never forget the soft, singsongy way he whispered her name while he kissed her . . . or the way his arms wrapped around her body, holding her so close that sometimes she couldn't breathe . . . or the shattering intensity of their lovemaking. All she could remember was that at the jagged peak of her pleasure, it was *his* name she cried out. Not Blake's.

Chapter 19

Beside the bed, an oil lamp flickered gently; a ribbon of black smoke curled lazily up from the glass mouth.

Annie lay cuddled alongside Nick, her naked leg thrown across his thigh. They had been together for hours now, talking softly and laughing, and making love. About midnight, she'd reluctantly called her father and told him that she wouldn't be home tonight—that Izzy was fighting a cold and needed Annie; but her father hadn't been fooled. He'd listened to her rambling excuse, then asked the now familiar question: "Are you sure that's wise, Annie Virginia?"

She'd brushed him off with a schoolgirl's giggle and told him not to worry. She didn't want to think about whether this was wise. For the first time in her life, she felt wicked and wild, and wonderfully alive. She'd been a good girl for so damned long. . . .

So much had changed for her tonight. The simple act of removing her wedding ring had transformed her. She'd become younger, braver, more adventurous. She had never known that sex could be so . . . fun. Tonight, in the hours she'd spent in Nick's arms, she'd discovered a whole new woman.

When it was over—the first time—she'd expected to feel guilty and ashamed. She'd tensed herself for it, quickly devising rationalizations for her wanton behavior; but all it had taken was a word from Nick, a smile, a kiss, and all her explanations had taken flight.

Don't pull away, he'd said, and that was all it took.

Now, they were tangled in the sheets together. About an hour ago, they'd gone scouting in the kitchen and come up with a plate of cheese and crackers and fruit, which they'd taken back into bed with them. Neither of them wanted to leave the bed and reenter the world that lurked outside this room.

Nick slid an arm around Annie and drew her close. For the first time, there was sadness in his blue eyes. "June fifteenth, huh?"

Annie caught her breath. Their gazes locked, and she felt her smile weaken.

In less than a month, Annie would be going home— such as it was. She would be leaving Nick and Izzy and Mystic, and returning to the brown world of her real life . . . or whatever was left of it.

He touched her face with a tenderness that made her heart ache. "I shouldn't have said that."

"We have what we have, Nicky. Let's not ruin it by looking ahead. The future isn't something I like to think about."

His hand slid down her bare arm and settled possessively on her left hand. She knew that he was thinking about the ring she no longer wore—and about the tiny white tan line that remained to mark its place. When he

finally looked at her, he was smiling again. "I'll take whatever you have to give, and . . ."

"And what?"

It took him a long time to answer, so long that she
thought he'd changed his mind. Then, in a quiet voice, he
said, "And hope it's enough."

Every day brought them closer together. In the last week
of May, summer threw its multicolored net across the rain
forest. Entire days passed without a drop of rain. Tempera-
tures hovered around the low seventies. It was an unsea-
sonal heat wave, and everyone in Mystic treasured the
newfound warmth. Kids dug out last year's cutoffs and
pulled their bicycles out of storage. Birds clustered on telephone wires and swooped down, chattering and cawing, in
search of plump, juicy worms.

Annie spent less and less time at her father's house, and
more and more in Nick's bed. She knew she was playing
with fire, but she couldn't help herself. She was like a
teenager again, consumed by her first lover. Every time she
looked at Nick—which was about every fifteen seconds—
she remembered their lovemaking. She couldn't believe
how uninhibited she'd become.

During the day, they were careful not to touch each other,
but the forced abstinence only increased their desire. All
day, Annie waited for the night to begin, so that she could
creep into his bed again.

Today they'd had a wonderful time at Lake Crescent.
They'd played volleyball on the beach, and rented paddle-
boats, and on the long ride home, they had sung along with
the radio. At home, Annie made a big pot of spaghetti, and

after dinner, they sat around the big kitchen table and worked on Izzy's reading skills.

Later, when they went upstairs, they all climbed into Izzy's bed for story time.

Annie refused to think about how *right* all of this felt, how much she was beginning to belong here. She reached behind Izzy's head and touched Nick's shoulder, squeezing so hard for a moment that he looked up at her. At first he smiled, then slowly, that smile fell, and she knew he was seeing it in her eyes, the sudden fear, the desire that was going to hurt them all.

She turned away, focused instead on the open book.

Nick had read only the first page when the sound of a ringing telephone interrupted them. "I'd better go answer that," he said.

"We'll wait for you, Daddy," Izzy said, snuggling up to Annie.

Nick pressed the book into Izzy's hands and hurried out of the room. He came back a few minutes later, looking solemn.

Annie felt a prickling of fear. She sat up straighter, leaning forward. "Nick?"

He eased back into the bed, on the other side of Izzy. "That was your teacher, Izzy-bear. She said they're having a class party on Friday—and all the kids want you to come."

Izzy looked scared. "Oh."

Nick smiled at her, a soft, gentle smile that seemed to reach right into Annie's heart. "She said something about cupcakes."

Izzy frowned. "I *do* like cupcakes."

"I know you do, Sunshine." He pulled her against him with one strong arm. "There's nothing wrong with being scared, Izzy. It happens to all of us. What's wrong is if we don't try things because we're afraid. We can't hide away from the things that scare us."

Annie heard so much in his voice, all the remnants of the lessons he'd learned the hard way. She felt a warm rush of pride for him, and she wondered again how she was going to leave this man, how she was going to return to her cold, sterile life, where she would end up searching in mirrors once again for evidence of her own existence.

Izzy sighed. "I guess a party would be okay. Will you'n Annie take me?"

"Of course we will."

"Okay." She looked up, gave Nick a tentative smile. "Daddy, will you read me another story, Daddy?"

He grinned. Reaching down to the floor beside the bed, he produced another book. "I thought you might ask that."

He read like an actor, using deep, bass monster voices and high-pitched little-boy roars. Izzy sat perfectly still, her adoring eyes focused on her daddy's face. When he smiled, she smiled; when he frowned, she frowned.

As he turned a page, he glanced at Annie. Over the child's dark head, their gazes locked. There was nothing sexual in his eyes at all; there was just the simple pleasure of a man reading his daughter a bedtime story. The way he looked, as if this moment were the culmination of his every hope and dream, tore a ragged bite from Annie's heart and left her with the strangest urge to cry.

After story time was over, Nick went back to his room and waited. Twice, he poked his head out and looked down the hallway. Twice it was empty, save for the feeble glow of a few poorly placed wall lights.

He paced the tiny room, bumping his head on the slanted roof almost every time he turned to the right.

Then he heard a knock.

He surged to the door and yanked it open. Annie stood in the doorway, wearing an oversized T-shirt and a pair of navy-blue kneesocks.

They barely made it to the bed. Kissing, groping, laughing, they fell onto the pile of wrinkled sheets. The tired old mattress creaked and groaned beneath them.

Nick had never wanted a woman so badly in his life, and Annie seemed to share his urgency. He held her, stroked and fondled and caressed her. She rolled with him, kissing him with a greediness that left him breathless, pulling his tongue deep into her mouth. They did anything and everything, made love and slept and made love again.

When it was over, Nick lay exhausted on his bed, one arm flung out against the wall, the other curled protectively around Annie's naked hip. She lay tucked against him, her bare leg thrown casually over his, her nipple pressed against his rib cage.

He could feel the aftermath of their lovemaking in the fine sheen of sweat that clung to her skin, smell it in the sweetness of the air. Her head was resting on the ball of his shoulder, her breath caressed his skin.

He was afraid suddenly that she would pull away now, draw out of his arms and scurry back to her father's house, and that he'd be left with nothing but her lingering scent and the cold chill of her absence along his side. "Talk to me, Annie," he said softly, stroking the velvety skin in the small of her back.

"That's always dangerous," she said with a laugh. "Most people who know me want me to shut up."

"I'm not Blake."

"Sorry." She snuggled closer to him. One pale finger coiled in his chest hair, then absently caressed his skin. "You . . . bring out something in me. Something I wouldn't have believed was there."

"Oh yeah? What is it?"

She rolled half on top of him, her crotch settled intimately against his thigh. Her beautiful breasts swung enticingly in front of his face, and it was damned hard to keep his concentration on her words. "I used to be . . . organized. Efficient. I fed everyone and dressed everyone and went shopping and made lists and kept appointments. Blake and I had sex, if we were lucky, on Friday nights at eleven forty-five, between Jay Leno's first and second guests. It was always . . . nice sex, comfortable. It felt good and I had orgasms. But it wasn't like it is with you. I never felt as if I were going to leap out of my skin." She laughed, that broad, infectious laugh that seemed to come from someplace deep inside her. Kathy had never made him feel this way, as if the whole world was open to him and all he had to do was reach for his dreams.

Dreams. He closed his eyes. They came to him so often now, the dreams he'd long ago put aside. He remembered again how important a family had always been to him, how he'd imagined his life would chug along on a bright and easy road, crowded with laughing children all around him.

If he'd chosen Annie, all those years ago, maybe everything would have been different. . . .

"How come you and Kathy never had more children?" Annie asked suddenly.

Her question disconcerted Nick for a second, made him wonder if she could read his mind. "I always wanted to. Hell, I wanted six kids, but after Izzy, it was obvious that Kathy couldn't handle any more. When Izzy was about two, I had a vasectomy." He glanced down at her, cuddled so close to him. "How about you? You're such a wonderful mother."

It was a long time before she answered. "Adrian would have been fourteen this year. He was my son."

"Annie . . ."

She didn't look at him. "He came prematurely and only lived for four days. After that, we tried everything, but I couldn't get pregnant again. Usually he's just a little smile I get, or a tear that stings my eyes, but sometimes . . . it's harder. I always wanted more children."

He didn't want to say he was sorry; he knew firsthand how plastic the words could sound, a Band-Aid on an arterial wound. Instead, he pulled her into his arms and held her as close as he could, so close he could feel her heartbeat against his skin.

He knew he was losing himself in the moment, in Annie, but right now he didn't care. It was too late to be safe, too late to keep from loving her.

Jefferson R. Smithwood Elementary School sat on a grassy hill surrounded by hundred-year-old fir trees. A long cement walkway started at the double black doors and slid down to the parking lot, where cars were lined along a tall chain-link fence.

Nick stood close to the curb, with Izzy beside him. Annie stood on Izzy's other side.

His little girl was scared, and it was up to him to make

her feel confident; but he had no idea how to do that. Over Izzy's dark head, he gave Annie a helpless look.

You can do it, she mouthed with a smile.

Swallowing hard, he bent to his knees and looked at Izzy. She tried to smile, but it was a quick, jerking little tilt of the mouth that didn't reach her eyes. He reached out and plucked up the satiny yellow ribbon that hung at the bottom of her braid.

Her lower lip quivered. "They'll make fun o' me."

"Then I'll beat the sh—"

Annie squeezed his shoulder and Nick bit back the words. "They won't make fun of you," he said instead.

"I'm . . . different."

He shook his head. "No. You've had some . . . sadness. And sometimes that makes a person go a little . . . crazy. But you're going to be okay this time. I promise."

"Will you be here to pick me up after the party?"

"Yep."

"*Right* after?"

"Right after."

"Okay," she said at last.

He smiled. "That's my girl."

Slowly, knees popping, he got back to his feet. He glanced at Annie, who was grinning at him, although her eyes were suspiciously moist.

Together, the three of them started up the cement sidewalk toward the school.

"Lions and tigers and bears, oh my!" Annie said suddenly.

Nick almost burst out laughing. It was a ridiculous thing to do, but at that moment it felt exactly right. He joined in. "Lions and tigers and bears, oh my!"

At first, Izzy's voice was hesitant, but with each chorus

it gained strength, until all three of them were singing at the top of their lungs as they strode up the sidewalk, up the steps, and right to the front door.

Nick pushed through the double black doors, and the three of them entered the quiet hallways of the elementary school. To the left there was a long Formica table, piled high with all the jackets and lunch boxes and sweaters that the children left behind.

Izzy stopped. "I wanna go in by myself," she said quietly. "That way they won't think I'm a baby." She gave Nick and Annie one last, frightened look, then started down the hallway.

Nick fought the urge to run after her.

Annie slipped her hand in his. Nick sighed, watching his little girl walk down the hallway. He saw the hesitation in each of her footsteps and knew how hard she was trying to be brave. He knew how that felt, going forward when all you wanted to do was crawl into a warm darkness and hide. Finally, he had to look away. He'd never known it would be so damned hard to watch your child face fear.

"She'll be fine," Annie said. "Trust me."

He looked at her, and at the soft certainty in her gaze, something in his chest felt swollen and tender. "I do, Annie," he said softly. "I do."

At the end of the hall, a door opened. A feminine voice said, "Izzy! We've missed you." A bubble of applause floated through the open door. Izzy glanced back, gave Nick and Annie a huge grin, then raced into the classroom.

Chapter 20

"Well, that certainly took my mind off Izzy," Nick said, panting, when finally he could speak. He rolled off of Annie but kept an arm around her. Gathering her against him, he settled comfortably with his back against the wall and propped his sweaty cheek in his hand, gazing down at her.

She looked incredibly beautiful, with the sunlight from the half-open window on her face and her hair all spiky in a dozen different directions. Her breathing was shallow, and it reminded him with every tiny, wheezing sound that, for now at least, she was his. Beneath the flimsy cotton blanket, his hand found her breast and held it.

He wanted to lie with her for hours, talking about nothing and everything, sharing more than just their bodies. It was a dangerous desire, he knew, wanting more from Annie than the body she shared so willingly. No matter how hard he tried to forget it, he remembered that she was leaving June fifteenth—now less than three weeks away. She was going back to her real life.

He held her tightly, knowing he should just keep his

mouth shut. But he couldn't. "What was your marriage like?"

"From whose perspective? I thought it was nineteen great years with the only man I ever loved. Then one day he pulled our car into the driveway and said, 'I love another woman; please don't make me say it again.' " She released a laugh that was short and bitter. "Like I wanted to hear it twice."

"Are you still in love with him?"

"*In* love? How would that be possible?" She sighed, and he felt the gentle swell and fall of her chest. "But love . . . ah, now that's a harder thing. He is . . . was my best friend, my lover, my *family* for almost twenty years. How do you stop loving your family?"

"What . . . what if he wanted you back?"

"Blake's not that kind of man. It would mean admitting that he'd been wrong in the first place. In all our years together, I've never once heard him say he was sorry. To anyone."

He heard sorrow in the quietly spoken words.

She smiled weakly and looked away from him, staring beyond his shoulder to a spot on the wall.

He gathered her into his arms, turning her so that he could lose himself in the green of her eyes. "I remember a story you wrote in Senior English. It was about a dog who helped a lost boy find his home. I always thought you'd be a famous writer."

"That was 'Finding Joey.' I can't believe you remembered it."

"It was a good story."

She was silent for a long time, and when finally she spoke, her voice was thick. "I should have trusted myself, but Blake . . . he thought writing was a silly little hobby, and so I put it away. It's not his fault, it's mine. I gave in too easily. After that I tried everything—calligraphy, judo, painting, sculpting, floral arranging, interior design." She snorted derisively. "No wonder Blake made fun of me. I was a poster child for a missing soul."

"I can't imagine that."

"It's true. I wrapped up my two unfinished novels in pretty pink boxes and tucked them under my lingerie chest. I let Blake's acid comments about 'Mom's current hobby' derail me. After a few years, I forgot I'd even had a dream in the first place. I became Mrs. Blake Colwater, and without him, I felt like nobody. Until now. You and Izzy gave me my self back."

He touched her face. "No, Annie. You took it back yourself. Hell, you *fought* for it."

She stared at him. "I lost myself once, Nick. I'm terrified of doing it again."

There was no point in asking what she meant. He knew. Somehow, she'd seen the secret he was trying so hard to keep from her. He'd fallen in love with her, and they didn't have much time together; that was the truth he'd understood at the outset, the truth that came from sleeping with a married woman, even if she was headed for divorce. She still had Natalie, and a whole life that didn't include Nick. "Okay, Annie," he said quietly. "Okay for now."

But it wasn't okay. He knew it, and now she was beginning to know it as well.

Annie stood on the porch of her father's house, staring out at the sinuous silver ribbon of the salmon stream. Bright blue harebells danced nimbly through the high grass at the river's edge. Somewhere, a woodpecker was drilling through a tree trunk; the ra-ta-ta-tat echoed through the forest.

She heard the door squeak open behind her, then the banging of the screen door.

"Okay, what's going on, Annie Virginia?"

She knew by the quiet tone of his voice that it was the question he'd followed her out here to ask. "What do you mean?" She played dumb.

"You know what I mean. You blush like a teenager every time you say Nick's name, and I've hardly seen you in the past two weeks. You're doing a hell of a lot more than baby-sitting up there. Last night I heard you talking on the phone. You were telling Terri that Nick was just a friend. So, I guess I'm not the only one who has noticed."

"It isn't love," she answered quietly, but even as she spoke the words, she wondered. When she was with Nick, she felt young, full to bursting with adrenaline. Dreams seemed tangible to her again, as close as tomorrow; it wasn't how she'd felt in her marriage. Then, she'd thought dreams were the toys of childhood, to be put away when real life came to call.

"Are you doing it to get back at Blake?"

"No. For once, I'm not thinking about Blake or Natalie. I'm doing this for me."

"Is that fair?"

She turned to him. "Why is it that only women have to be fair?"

"It's Nick I'm thinking of. I've known that boy for a long time. Even as a kid, he had eyes that had seen a dozen miles of bad road. When he started dating Kathy, I thanked God it wasn't you. But then he settled down and became the best cop this town has ever had. We all saw how he loved Kathy; and that little daughter of his was the apple of his eye. Then, that . . . thing happened with Kathy, and he . . . disintegrated. His hair turned that weird color, and every time I saw him, I remembered what had happened. It was like a physical badge of sorrow. No one blamed him, of course; but he blamed himself, you could tell. It was damned hard to watch."

"Why are you telling me this?"

"You're a fighter, Annie, and—"

"Ha! Come on, Dad, I'm a doormat of the first order."

"No. You never have seen yourself clearly. You've got a steel core inside you, Annie—you always did. And you see the world in positive terms. Your glass is always half full."

"When Blake left me, I fell apart," she reminded him.

"For what—a month?" He made a tsking sound. "That's nothing. When your mom died, I didn't hide out for a couple of weeks and then emerge stronger than I'd started." He paused, shaking his head. "I'm not good at saying what I mean. What I'm trying to say, honey, is that you don't understand despair or weakness, not really. You can't get your mind wrapped around hopelessness."

She stared out at the river. "I guess that's true."

"You're still a married woman, and if you think Blake is really going to leave you for a bimbo, you're crazy. He'll be back. When he comes to his senses, Blake will come home to you."

"I don't feel married."

"Yes, you do."

She had no answer to that; it was true and it wasn't. As much as she'd grown and changed in the last months, Hank was right: Annie *did* still feel married to Blake. She'd been his wife for almost twenty years . . . that kind of emotional commitment didn't evaporate on account of a few hastily thrown words, even if those words were *I want a divorce*.

Hank came up beside her, touched her cheek. "You're going to hurt Nick. And he's not a man who rolls easily with life's punches. I don't mean to tell you what to do. I never have and I'm sure as hell not going to start now. But . . . this thing . . . it's going to end badly, Annie. For all of you."

The next night, long after the dinner dishes were washed and put away and Izzy had gone to bed, Annie sat in the rocker on the front porch. She watched a tiny black spider spin an iridescent web on a rhododendron bush. The scratchy creak-creak-creak of the rocker kept her company in the quiet. She knew she should go inside; Nick would be waiting for her upstairs. But it was so quiet and peaceful out here, and the lingering echo of her father's words seemed softer and more distant when she was alone. When she actually went inside and looked into Nick's blue, blue eyes, she knew her dad's advice would return, louder and too insistent to ignore.

Nick and Izzy had already been hurt so badly. She didn't want to do anything that would cause them more pain, and yet she knew, as certainly as she was sitting here, that she was going to do just that. She had another life in another town, another child that was going to need a mother as desperately as Izzy had only a few months ago. Her real life was out there, waiting for Annie, circling in the hot, smoggy air of Southern California, readying itself for the confrontation that was only a few short weeks away. It would test Annie, that reunion; test everything that she was and everything she'd decided up here that she wanted to be.

Behind her, the screen door creaked open. "Annie?"

She closed her eyes for a second, gathering strength. "Hey, Nick," she said softly, staring down at the hands clasped in her lap.

The door banged shut and he came up beside her. Placing a hand gently on her shoulder, he crouched down. "What are you doing out here all by yourself?"

She looked at him and, for a second, felt a flash of panic. The thought of giving him up was terrifying.

But it was Nick she had to think of, not herself. She gazed at him. "I don't want to hurt you, Nick."

He took hold of her left hand, tracing the white tan line with the tip of his finger. "Give me some credit, Annie. I know it's not as simple as taking off a ring."

She stared at him for a long time. The urge rose in her to make impossible promises, to tell him she loved him, but she couldn't be that cruel. She would be leaving in two weeks. It would be infinitely better to take the words with her.

"We don't have forever, Annie. I know that."

She heard something in his voice, a little crack in the word *forever*, but he was smiling at her, and she didn't want to think about what he was feeling. "Yes," she whispered.

He swept her into his arms and carried her up to his bed. And as always, once she was in his arms, she stopped thinking about the future and let the present consume her.

On Tuesday morning, they planned a trip to the beach. Annie glanced down at the picnic basket beside her, checking the food supplies for the tenth time, then she checked her watch. It was already ten-thirty. She went to the bottom of the stairs and yelled up at Nick and Izzy to get a move on. Then, humming to herself, she headed back toward the kitchen.

The phone rang as she walked past it. She bent down and picked it up on the second ring. "Hello?"

"Hold for Blake Colwater, please."

For a disorienting moment, Annie couldn't connect the name to her own life. Nick came down the stairs. She threw him a confused look. "It's Blake."

Nick froze in mid-step. "I'll . . . leave you your privacy."

"No. Come here. Please."

Nick crossed the room and came up beside her. Turning slightly, she took hold of his hand.

Blake's authoritative voice came on at last. "Annie—is that you?"

At the sound of his voice, it all came rushing back. She stood perfectly still. "Hello, Blake."

"How are you, Annalise?"

"I'm fine." She paused, trolling for what came next. "And you?"

"I'm . . . okay. I got your number from Hank. You know Natalie will be getting home soon."

"The fifteenth of June. She wants us to meet her at the airport." She put the slightest emphasis on *us*.

"Of course. Her plane lands at . . ."

She hated that he didn't know. "Five-ten in the afternoon."

"I knew that."

An uncomfortable silence followed the apparent lie. Blake laughed easily, as if it had been three hours since they'd spoken instead of almost three months. "We need to talk, obviously, before we meet Natalie. I want you to come down to Los Angeles this weekend."

"Do you?" It was so like Blake. He wanted to talk, so she had to get on an airplane.

"I'll FedEx a ticket."

She drew in a sharp breath. "I'm not ready to see you yet."

"*What?* I thought—"

"I doubt it. We don't have anything to talk about now."

"I do."

"Funny words, coming from you."

"Annalise." He sighed. "I want you to come home this weekend. We need to talk."

"I'm sorry, Blake. I have no intention of coming home this weekend. I know we agreed to discuss our separation in June. Let's leave it at that, okay? I'll come home on the thirteenth."

"Goddamn it, Annalise. I want—"

"Good-bye, Blake. See you in two weeks." She hung up the phone and stared down at it.

"Are you okay, Annie?"

Nick's voice pulled her back from the dark edge gathering on her horizon. Forcing a smile, she turned into his arms. "I'm fine."

He stared down at her a long, long time. For a second, she thought he was going to kiss her, and she pushed onto her toes to meet his lips. But he just stood there, gazing down at her face as if he were memorizing everything about this moment. "It's not going to be long enough."

Chapter 21

As Blake drove down the rutted pavement of Mystic's main street, he remembered how much he'd always disliked this shabby little logging town. It reminded him of the town he'd grown up in, a dingy, forgotten farming community in Iowa—a place he'd worked hard to forget.

He pulled the rented Cadillac into a gas station and parked. Flipping up the collar of his overcoat—who in the hell wanted to live in a place where you needed an overcoat in late May?—he strode through the pouring rain toward the phone booth. Rain thumped overhead, so loud he could barely hear himself think.

It took him a minute to remember Hank's number. He hadn't dialed his own calls in years. Dropping a quarter in the slot, he punched out the number and listened to the ring.

On the third ring, Hank answered. "Hello?"

"Hi, Hank. It's me, Blake . . . again. I wanted to speak to my wi—to Annie."

"Did you? That wasn't my understanding."

Blake sighed. "Just put her on the line, Hank."

"She isn't here. She's *never* here during the day."

"What do you mean?"

"I gave you a number the other day. You can reach her there."

"Where is she, Hank?"

"She's out visiting . . . friends at the old Beauregard place."

"The old Beauregard place. Now, that certainly pinpoints it for me."

"You remember the old house at the end of the lake road? An old friend of hers lives out there now."

Blake got a strange feeling in the pit of his stomach. "What's going on, Hank?"

There was a pause, then Hank said, "You'll have to figure things out for yourself, Blake. Good luck."

Good luck. What the hell did that mean?

By the time Blake had asked directions to the lake road and got back in his car, he was irritated as hell. Something was not right here.

But then, things hadn't been right in a long time.

He'd first realized that something was wrong about a month ago; he'd stopped being able to concentrate. His work had begun to suffer.

And it was little things, nothing really. Like the tie he was wearing today. It was wrong.

It was a stupid, nonsensical thing, and certainly no one would notice, but *he* knew. When Annie had bought him the two-thousand-dollar black Armani suit, she'd chosen a monogrammed white shirt and a silk tie of tiny gray and white and red stripes to go with it. It was a set, and he always wore them together. He'd realized a few weeks ago that he couldn't find the tie. He'd torn the bedroom apart looking for it.

"I hope you're going to pick all that shit up" was what Suzannah had said when she'd seen the mess.

"I can't find the tie that goes with this suit."

She'd eyed him over the rim of her coffee cup. "I'll alert the press corps."

She thought it was funny that the tie was missing, and that he needed it so much. It had occurred to him that maybe it was at the cleaner's somewhere, his favorite tie, his *necessary* tie.

Annie would know where it is.

That had been the beginning.

He flicked on the car's Bose stereo, wincing as some hick country song blasted through the speakers. He flipped through the channels, but nothing else came through clearly. Disgusted, he turned off the radio.

The road unfurled in front of him, steeped in shadows in the middle of the day and battered by silver rain. After a few miles, he began to see flashes of the lake through the trees. The pavement gave out to a gravel road that turned and twisted and finally led him to a huge clearing. A bright yellow house sat primly amid a front yard awash in brightly colored flowers. A red Mustang and a police car were parked beneath an old maple tree.

He parked the car and got out. Flipping his collar up again, he strode across the yard and bounded up the stairs, knocking hard on the front door. It opened almost instantly, and a little girl stood in the opening. She was wearing a pair of Gortex overalls and a baseball cap. In her arms, she held a raggedy old doll.

Blake smiled down at her. "Hello. I'm—"

A man appeared suddenly behind the child. His hands

rested protectively on the girl's shoulders and drew her back slightly into the house. "Hello?"

Blake stared at the tall, silver-haired man, then craned his neck to look inside the house. "Hi. I'm sorry to bother you, but I'm looking for Annalise Colwater. Her father, Hank, told me she'd be here."

The man tensed visibly. His eerie blue eyes narrowed and swept Blake from head to toe in a single glance. Blake was somehow certain that the man's eyes missed nothing, not the expense of his Armani suit nor even the oddness of his tie. "You're Blake."

Blake frowned. "Yes, and you are . . ."

From somewhere inside the house, Blake heard the clattering of someone running down stairs. "I'm ready, you guys."

Blake recognized Annie's voice. He sidled past the silent man and child and slipped into the house.

Annie saw him and skidded to a stop.

He almost didn't recognize her. She was wearing yellow rain gear and a big floppy hat that covered most of her face. The boots on her feet had to be four sizes too big. He forced a big smile and opened his arms. "Surprise."

She threw an odd glance at the silver-haired man, then slowly her gaze returned to Blake. "What are you doing here?"

He looked at the two strangers; both were watching him. Slowly, he let his arms fall to his sides. "I'd rather not discuss it in public."

Annie bit on her lower lip, then sighed heavily. "Okay, Blake. We can talk. But not here."

The girl whined and stomped her foot. "But Annie—we were gonna get ice cream."

Annie smiled at the child. "I'm sorry, Izzy. I need to talk to this man for a while. I'll make it up to you, okay?"

This man. Blake's stomach tightened. What in the hell was going on here?

"Don't make this hard on Annie, okay, Sunshine? She has to go for a minute." It was the man's voice.

"But she'll be comin' back . . . won't she, Daddy?"

The question fell into an awkward silence. No one answered.

Annie moved past the little girl and came up beside Blake. "I'll meet you at Ted's Diner and Barber shop in about ten minutes. It's right downtown. You can't miss it."

Blake felt as if the world had tilted. He looked down at her, this woman he barely recognized. "Okay. See you in ten minutes."

He stood there for an interminable moment, feeling awkward and ill at ease. Then he forced a smile. All they needed was a few minutes alone, and everything would be fine. That's what he told himself as he turned and left the house. He was still telling himself that ten minutes later as he parked in front of the cheesiest, sleaziest diner he'd ever seen. Inside, he slipped into a yellow Naugahyde booth and ordered a cup of coffee. When it came, he checked his Rolex: 11:15.

He was actually nervous. Beneath the Formica woodgrain table, he surreptitiously wiped his damp palms on his pants.

He glanced at his watch again—11:25—and wondered if Annie was going to show. It was a crazy thought and he dismissed it almost instantly. Annie was the most dependable person he'd ever known. If Annie said she'd be someplace, she'd be there. Late, maybe; harried, often. But she'd be there.

"Hello, Blake."

He snapped his head away from the window at the sound of her voice. She was standing beside the table with one hip cocked out and her arms crossed. She was wearing a pair of faded blue jeans and a sleeveless white turtle-neck, and her hair . . . it looked as if someone had hacked it off with a weed-eater.

"What did you do to your hair?"

"I think the answer is obvious."

"Oh." He frowned, disconcerted by the sight of her and by her answer. It was flip and unlike her. He'd imagined this moment—dreaded and looked forward to it in equal measure—for weeks. But whenever he'd imagined their meeting, it was with the old Annie, impeccably dressed, smiling wanly, a little nervous. This woman standing in front of him was someone he didn't recognize. "Well, it'll grow back." Belatedly, he got to his feet. "It's good to see you, Annie."

The smile she gave him was reserved and didn't reach her eyes. She sidled into the booth and sat across from him.

With a quick wave of his hand, he signaled a polyester-clad waitress, who hurried to the table. Blake looked at Annie. "Coffee?"

"No." She drummed her fingernails on the table, and he noticed that she was wearing no polish and that her nails were blunt, almost bitten-off short. And on her left hand, in the place where his ring belonged, there was only a thin band of pale, untanned skin. She smiled up at the waitress. "I'll have a Budweiser."

He stared at her in shock. "You don't drink beer." It was

a stupid thing to say, but he couldn't think of anything else. All he could focus on was the ring she wasn't wearing.

Another false smile. "Don't I?"

The waitress nodded and left.

Annie turned her attention back to Blake. Her gaze swept him in a second, and he wondered what this new woman saw when she looked at the old Blake. He waited for her to say something, but she just sat there with her new haircut and her no makeup and her terrifyingly ring-less finger and stared at him.

"I thought we should talk . . ." he said—rather stupidly, he thought afterward.

"Uh-huh."

Another silence fell, and into the quiet, the waitress came to the table. She placed a frosted mug of beer on a small, square napkin, and Annie gave her a bright smile. "Thanks, Sophie."

"You bet, Miss Bourne."

Miss Bourne? The address left him winded.

"So," she said at last, sipping her beer. "How's Suzannah?"

Blake winced at the coldness in her voice. He knew he had it coming, but still he hadn't expected anger. Annie never got angry. "I'm not living with her anymore."

"Really?"

"Yes. That's what I wanted to talk to you about."

She stared at him across the rim of her glass. "Really?"

He wished he'd rehearsed this more, but he hadn't ex-pected her to make it so difficult. In his mind, it always went the same way: He swept into a room and she hesi-tated, then smiled and cried and told him how much she missed him. He opened his arms and she hurled herself at him . . . and that was that. They were back together.

He tried to gauge her emotions, but the eyes he knew so well were shuttered and unwelcoming. He tripped through the words uncharacteristically. "I made a mistake." He slid his hand across the table.

"A mistake." She drew her hand back.

He heard the censure in her voice and knew what she meant. It was a mistake to be late on your Visa payment; what he'd done was something else entirely. The way she looked at him, the soft, reserved sound of her voice—not Annie at all—punched a hole in his confidence, and he began to feel as if something vital were leaking away from him. "I want to come home, Annie," he said softly, pleading with her in a way he'd never pleaded in his life. "I love you, Annalise. I know that now. I was a stupid, stupid fool. Can you forgive me?"

She sat there, staring at him, her mouth drawn in a tight, hard line.

In the silence, he felt a spark of hope ignite. He scooted around the vinyl booth and came up beside her, staring at her, knowing that all his heart and soul was in his eyes and hoping to hell that she still cared. Memories of their life together swelled inside him, refueled his confidence. He remembered a dozen times he'd hurt her, birthdays he'd missed, nights he hadn't come home, dinners that had been ruined by his absence. She had always forgiven him; it was who she was. She couldn't have changed that much.

She stared straight ahead, her eyes wary and filled with a pain he knew he'd put there. He gazed at her profile, willing her to look at him. If she did, if she looked at him for even a second, he'd see the answer in her eyes. "Annie?" He took her hand in his, and it was cold. "I love you, Annie," he said again, his voice choked. "Look at me."

Slowly, slowly, she turned, and he saw then that her eyes were flooded with tears. "You think you can say you're sorry and it's all over, Blake? Like it never happened?"

He clutched her hand, feeling the delicacy of her bones and the softness of her skin. "I'll spend the rest of my life making it up to you."

She closed her eyes for a second, and a tear streaked down her cheek. Then she opened her eyes and looked at him. "You did me a favor, Blake. The woman I was . . ." She drew her hand away from his and swiped the moisture from her cheek. "I let myself become a nothing. I'm not that woman anymore."

"You're still my Annie."

"No. I'm *my* Annie."

"Come back to me, Annie. Please. Give us another chance. You can't throw it all—"

"Don't you *dare* finish that sentence. *I* didn't throw anything away. You did, with your selfishness and your lies and your wandering dick. And now you've figured out that little Suzannah wants to be your lover, not your wife and your mother and your doormat and you come running back to me. The woman who'll take your shit with a smile and give you a safe place where nothing is expected of you and everything goes your way."

He was stunned by her language and her vehemence. "Annie—"

"I've met someone."

His mouth dropped open. "A man?"

"Yes, Blake. A man."

He slid back over to his seat. He took a long gulp of his lukewarm coffee, trying to get over the shock of her statement. *A man? Annie with another man?*

The silver-haired man with the sad blue eyes.

Why was it that in the months they'd been apart, he had never considered such a thing? He'd always pictured her as quiet, dependable Annie, mothering everyone, smiling and laughing and trying her hand at some god-awful craft or another. He'd pictured her sewing and decorating and pining. Goddamn it—mostly, he'd pictured her pining away for him, inconsolable. He looked up at her. "Did you . . . sleep with him?"

"Oh, for God's sake, Blake."

She had. Annie—his Annie, his *wife*—had slept with another man. Blake felt a surge of raw, animal anger, a fury he'd never known before in his life. He wanted to throw his head back and scream out his rage, but instead, he sat very still, his hands fisted in tight, painful blocks beneath the table. Now things were different, very different, and he had to proceed with the greatest caution.

"An affair," he said quietly, wincing at the sound of the word and the images it brought to mind. Annie, writhing in pleasure, kissing another pair of lips, touching another man's body. He pushed the horrible thoughts away. "I guess you did it to get back at me."

She laughed. "Not everything revolves around you."

"So . . ." What in the hell did you say at a time like this? He wanted to put his fist through a plate-glass window, and instead he had to sit here like a gentleman, pretending it didn't hurt like hell, pretending she hadn't just ripped his heart out and stomped on it. "I guess . . ." He shrugged. "I guess we can forgive each other."

"I don't want your forgiveness."

He flinched. They were the same words he'd thrown at her a few months ago, and they hurt. Sweet Jesus, they hurt.

"I'm sorry, Annie," he said quietly, looking up at her. For the first time, he truly understood what he'd done to her. In his arrogant selfishness, he hadn't really thought about what he'd put her through. He'd sugar-coated his behavior in the vocabulary of the nineties: *I need my space; there's no reason to stay together if you're not happy; you'll be better off without me; we've grown apart.* And he'd believed all of it. Now, he saw his mistake. The words were meaningless excuses for a man who didn't think the rules applied to him. He'd acted as if their marriage were an inconvenient encumbrance, an irritating lien on property you wanted to develop. The words that truly mattered—*love, honor, and cherish, till death do us part*—he'd slapped aside as if they meant nothing.

He felt the first wave of honest-to-God shame he'd ever experienced. "I never knew how it could hurt. But Annie, I love you—you can believe that. And I'm going to go on loving you for the rest of my life. No matter what you do or where you go or what you say, I'll always be here, waiting for your forgiveness. Loving you."

He saw a flash of pain in her eyes, and saw the way her mouth relaxed. For a heartbeat, she weakened, and like any great lawyer, he knew how to pounce on opportunity. He touched her cheek gently, forcing her to look at him. "You think I don't really love you, that I'm just the same selfish prick I always was, and that I want you because you make my life easier . . . but that's not it, Annie. You make my life complete."

"Blake—"

"Remember the old days? When we lived in that beach house in Laguna Niguel? I couldn't wait to get home from work to see you. And you always met me at the door—remember that?—you'd yank the door open and throw yourself into my arms. And how about when Natalie was born, when I crawled into that narrow hospital bed with you and spent the night—until that bony old nurse came and threw me out? And how about that time on the beach, when you and I made sand castles at midnight and drank champagne and dreamed of the house we would someday own. You said you wanted a blue and white bedroom, and I said you could paint it purple if you wanted, as long as you promised to be in my bed forever. . . ."

She was crying now. "Don't, Blake, please . . ."

"Don't what? Don't remind you of who we are and how long we've been together?" He pulled a handkerchief from his breast pocket and wiped the tears from her face. "We're a *family*. I should have seen that before, but I was blind and stupid and selfish, and I took so much for granted." His voice fell to a throaty whisper and he stared at her through a blur of his own tears. "I love you, Annie. You have to believe me."

She rubbed her eyes and looked away from him, sniffling quietly. "I believed you for twenty years, Blake. It's not so easy anymore."

"I never thought it would be."

"Yes, you did."

He smiled ruefully. "You're right. I thought you'd hear my apology and launch yourself into my arms and we'd ride off into the sunset together." He sighed. "So, where do we go from here?"

"I don't know."

It was an opening, something at least. "You have to give me—give *us* another chance. When you asked for one, I agreed, and I thought about where we'd gone wrong and here I am. You owe me the same consideration, Annie. You owe it to our family."

"Oh, good. A lecture on family values from *you*." She pulled a compact from her purse and flipped the mirror open. "Perfect. I look like the Pillsbury Dough Girl."

"You look beautiful."

She looked up at him sharply. "But my hair will grow out."

"I shouldn't have said that."

She clicked the compact shut. "No, you shouldn't have."

Her gaze was uncomfortably direct, and he was reminded that in some ways, after almost twenty years of marriage, he didn't know the woman sitting across from him at all. "On June fourteenth, I'll meet you at the house. We can discuss . . . this . . . then." She got to her feet, and he saw that she was a little unsteady. She was obviously holding herself together with incredible effort.

He took hope from that. "I won't give up, Annie. I'll do whatever it takes to get you back."

She sighed. "Winning was always very important to you, Blake." On that final, cutting remark, she turned and walked out of the diner.

Chapter 22

Nick waited for Annie to return. For the first hour, he told himself he was being an idiot. He knew she couldn't possibly meet with her husband and be back here in less than two hours.

But then two hours had stretched into three, and then four, and then five.

Forcing a smile, he'd made a big production out of dinner, for Izzy's sake. He'd stumbled through one of Annie's recipes: chicken breasts breaded with cornflakes and potato chips. He'd forgotten to start the rice in time, and so he served the oven-fried chicken with sliced bananas and chunks of cheese. He'd tried his best to keep a conversation going, but he and Izzy were both keenly aware of the empty chair at the table.

Everything had gone well enough until Izzy had looked at him, her upper lip mustachioed with a thin band of milk. "Daddy, she's comin' back, isn't she, Daddy?"

Nick's fork had hit the edge of his plate with a *ping*. He hadn't known how in the hell to answer, and so he'd fallen back on standard parenting. Avoidance. "Don't talk with your mouth full," he'd said, looking quickly away.

By the time they'd done the dishes and he'd given Izzy her bath and put her to bed, he was as jittery as a bird. He couldn't even concentrate enough to read her a bedtime story. Instead, he'd kissed her forehead and run from the room.

Blake had been exactly what Nick had expected—and precisely what he'd feared. When he'd seen the handsome, confident, obviously successful man in his expensive black suit, Nick had felt as if he were nothing. He saw his own flaws in sharp relief: the cheap, small-town jeans that needed hemming, the T-shirt that had once been blue but after countless washings had been rendered a dull and lifeless gray, the ripped belt loop he'd never bothered to sew. And he didn't even want to *think* about his looks—the deeply etched lines around his eyes that were Kathy's legacy, and the unnatural color of his hair.

Blake was everything that Nick could never be.

He wished he could push his worry aside, think about something else—anything else. But the more he tried to clear his thoughts, the more she was there, inside him. Annie held his heart and soul in the palm of her hand, and she didn't even know it.

He'd never felt as much a part of a family as he did now.

With another man's wife.

Annie saw him standing out at the lake. She got out of her Mustang and eased the door shut quietly, walking slowly across the grass.

Wordlessly, she came up beside him. She waited for him to touch her, move close enough that she could feel the comforting heat of his presence, but he didn't. Instead, he stood stiffly in place. "How did it go?"

There was no point in lying to him. "He made a terrible mistake and he loves me."

"He *did* make a terrible mistake."

There was a crack in his voice, and in it, she heard his pain.

"What are you going to do?" he asked softly.

"I don't know. I spent two and a half months trying to fall out of love with him, and now when I've almost succeeded, he wants to take it all back. I can't adapt this quickly."

He fell silent, and she realized what she'd said. *Almost succeeded.* Almost fallen out of love with her husband. She wanted to place a Band-Aid on the wound of her words, but *almost* was the sad truth of her feelings for Blake. Anything else would be a lie.

On the shore, the water lapped quietly against the gravel. Breezes whispered through the leaves of a huge old maple tree.

The thought of leaving here terrified her. She thought of her big, empty house in California, and all the time she'd have alone. "What if—"

He turned to her. "What if what?"

She took a deep breath. "What if I . . . came back here? After . . . everything is settled? I've been thinking more and more about a bookstore. You were right, that house on Main Street would be perfect. And God knows, this town needs one . . ."

He went very still. "What are you saying?"

"After the divorce . . . and after Natalie leaves for college, I'll be down in Southern California all by myself—"

"Don't do that to me, Annie. Don't throw me hope like it was a bone to bury in my backyard. I can't spend the rest of my life waiting for you, watching the driveway, thinking *today, maybe today.* It'd break what's left of my heart. Don't make me any promises if you can't keep them. It's . . . easier for me that way."

The wind seemed to leak out of her lungs. She sagged. He was right; she knew he was right. Her future was a mystery, impenetrable and uncertain. She had no idea what would happen when she returned home. She wasn't even sure what she wanted to happen. "I'm sorry," she whispered. She wanted to tack on some kind of excuse, to remind him that she'd known Blake forever, that Natalie was her daughter, that she had always been a married woman, but none of the words mattered.

He didn't say anything. He just stood there, swaying slightly, gazing down at her as if he had already lost her.

The next morning, Annie was so depressed she didn't even go to Nick's. Instead, she lay in bed and alternately cried and stared.

Her mind was too full; it was making her crazy, all the things she had to think about. Her husband—the man she'd loved since she was nineteen years old—wanted another chance to make their marriage work. He was sorry. He'd made a mistake.

Hadn't she *begged* him to give their marriage a chance just a few months ago?

Beside her bed, the phone rang. She leaned over and picked it up. "Hello?"

"Annie Colwater? This is Madge at Dr. Burton's office.

I'm calling to remind you of your ten-thirty appointment this morning."

She'd forgotten all about it. "Oh, I don't know—"

"Doc Burton told me not to take no for an answer."

Annie sighed. Last week she'd thought she'd beaten the depression, but now she was there again, slogging through the bleak confusion, unable to break through to the surface. Maybe it would be good to talk to the doctor. If nothing else, it gave her somewhere to go and something to do. She would probably feel better just getting out of bed. "Thanks, Madge," she said softly. "I'll be there."

With a tired sigh, she rolled out of bed and headed for the shower. By ten-fifteen, she was dressed in a pair of jeans and a worn sweatshirt. Without bothering to comb her hair—what was the point?—she grabbed her handbag and car keys and left her room.

Hank was on the porch, sitting in his rocker, reading a book. At her hurried exit, he looked up. "You're running late this morning."

"I have a doctor's appointment."

His smile faded. "Are you okay?"

"Other than the fact that I'm depressed and retaining more water than a Sea World seal tank, I'm fine. Doc Burton made the appointment when I saw him. He wanted to make sure I wasn't still feeling blue before I . . . went home."

Blue. Such a nothing little word for the emptiness seeping through her bloodstream.

Forcing a smile, she leaned down and kissed his forehead. " 'Bye, Dad."

" 'Bye."

She hurried down the steps and jumped into her Mustang.

Downtown, she parked in the shade of an elm tree and left her car without bothering to lock the door. She hurried up the concrete steps and into the brick building she'd visited so often in her youth.

Madge grinned up at her. "Hello, sweetie. The doctor's waiting for you. Go on back to exam room two."

Annie nodded and headed down the white-walled hallway. She found a door with a huge black *2* stenciled on it, and she went inside. Taking a seat on the paper-covered table, she flipped through the current issue of *Fishing News*.

About five minutes later, Dr. Burton knocked on the door and pushed it open. "Hi, Annie. Are you still feeling blue?"

How in the hell could she answer that? One minute she was pink, and the next—especially since Blake's call—the blue was so bad it was a dark, violent purple. She tossed the magazine onto the vacant chair. "Sometimes," she answered.

"Marge tells me you tried to make an appointment while I was gone. What was that about?"

"A bout with the flu. I won, but . . . in the last day or two, the nausea has come back a bit."

"I told you that this was a time to take extra good care of yourself. When the depression bites, your system has a hard time with bugs. How about if we draw a little blood and see what's what. Then, if everything's okay, we can talk about how you really feel."

Three hours later, Annie stood in front of her father's house. Shivering, she moved forward. Her legs didn't seem to work; it felt as if she were walking through a dense gray fog that resisted her movements.

Slowly, she climbed the steps and went inside.

Hank was sitting by the fireplace, doing a crossword puzzle. At her entrance, he looked up. "I didn't expect you until—"

She burst into tears. He was beside her in an instant. He scooped her into his big arms and held her, stroking her hair. Holding her close, he guided her onto the sofa, sitting beside her. Behind her, the door slammed shut, closing out the world.

"What is it, Annie?"

She sniffed hard and wiped her runny nose on her sleeve. She turned to him, but the words wouldn't come.

"Annie?"

"I'm pregnant," she whispered, and at the words, she started to cry again. She wanted to be filled with joy over the news; she was three months pregnant. After endless years of taking her temperature, religiously charting her ovulation cycles, and standing on her head after sex, she had effortlessly conceived a child.

Blake's child.

She'd never been so confused and shaken in her whole life, not even when Blake had asked for a divorce. At first when Dr. Burton had given her the results of the blood test, she'd assumed it was a mistake. When she realized it was no mistake, she'd had a moment of paralyzing, gut-wrenching fear. She wondered whose baby it was.

Then she remembered what Nick had told her. He'd had a vasectomy when Izzy was two. And then there'd been the pelvic exam, which showed that Annie was three months along.

It was definitely Blake's child.

Hank touched her cheek, gently turned her to face him. "It's a miracle," he said, and she knew it was true. She *felt* it, the small seed of a baby growing inside her. She placed her hand on her stomach. It thrilled her and terrified her.

"It changes everything," she said softly.

That's what scared her most. She didn't want to step back into the cold, sterile life she'd had in California. She wanted to stay here, in Mystic, to let the cool green darkness become her world. She wanted to keep on loving Nick. She wanted suddenly, ferociously to watch Izzy get braces and cut her hair and learn to dance. She wanted to open her own bookstore and live in her own house and be accountable to no one but herself.

But mostly, she wanted to be in love for the rest of her life, to wake up every morning with Nick beside her and go to sleep each night in his arms. But she couldn't do that. There wasn't a good enough perinatologist within a hundred miles of Mystic, and no hospital with a neonatal ICU. She'd called her obstetrician in Beverly Hills and been told to get home. Bed rest was the order of the day. Just like it had been with Adrian. Only this time Annie was almost forty years old; they weren't going to take any chances. The doctor was expecting Annie in three days—and not one day more, she'd said sternly.

"Have you told Blake?"

This time, she wanted to cry, but she couldn't. She stared at her dad, feeling already as if everything she wanted was moving away, receding just beyond her touch. "Oh, Dad, Blake will want—"

"What do *you* want?"

"Nick," she whispered.

Hank gave her a sad smile. "So, you think you're in love with him now. Annie, you've been with him for a few months. You've loved Blake since you were a teenager. Just a couple of months ago, you were so devastated by the breakup of your marriage that you couldn't get out of bed. Now you're willing to toss it out like yesterday's garbage?"

She knew her father was right. What she had with Nick was special and magical, but it didn't have the foundation that was her marriage. "Blake and I tried for so long to have more children. After Adrian, I was desperate to conceive again, but years went by and . . . nothing. When he finds out about the baby . . ."

"You'll go back to him," Hank said, and the quiet certainty in his voice tore her apart.

It was the right thing to do, the only thing to do, and Annie knew it. She couldn't take Blake's child from him and move up here on her own. A baby deserved its father.

There it was, the truth that stripped her soul and left her with nothing but a handful of broken dreams and soon-to-be-broken promises.

She was crying again; she couldn't help herself. She kept picturing what was to come—the moment when she would tell Nick about the baby—and it hurt so badly she couldn't breathe. She didn't want to be strong, didn't want to be honorable, didn't want to do the right thing.

She thought about all their time together, all the moments he'd held her and touched her and kissed her lips with a gentleness she'd never imagined. She thought about Izzy, and how much she'd lost, and then she thought about going back to California, to Blake's bed, to a place where the air was brown and the earth was dry. But most of all, she thought about how desperately lonely her world would be without Nick. . . .

Annie drove and drove, until she couldn't drive anymore. Finally, she made her way back to Nick's house. When she got there, he was in the garden with Izzy.

It would all go on without her, this place, this family. Izzy would grow up and learn to dance and go on her first date, but Annie wouldn't be there to see it.

She looked at Nick and was horrified to realize that tears were blurring her vision.

"Annie?"

She took a deep, shaking breath. More than anything, she wanted to throw herself into his big, strong arms. She ached suddenly to say the precious words, *I love you,* but she didn't dare. She knew that if Nick could, he'd promise that the sun would shine on them forever. But neither of them was so naive anymore; both had learned that everything could change in an instant, and that the heartfelt vows of people in love were fragile words that, once shattered, could cut so deeply you'd bleed forever.

He stood up, moved toward her. With one dirty finger, he touched her chin, so gently it was like the brush of a butterfly's wing. "Honey, what is it?"

She forced a bright smile, too bright, she knew, but there was no help for that. "I got something in my eye. It's nothing. Let me change my clothes, then I'll come out and help you guys."

Before he could answer—or ask another painful, loving question—she ran into the house.

Nick and Annie lay in bed, barely touching, the sheets thrown back from their naked legs. A big old oak fan turned lazily overhead, swooshing through the air, stirring it with a quiet *thwop-thwop-thwop*.

After Izzy had been put to bed, they'd circled each other, he and Annie, saying none of the things that seemed to be collecting in the air between them. Now, he held her tightly, stroking the soft, damp flesh of her breast. She'd been quiet all evening, and every so often he'd looked at her and seen a faraway sadness in her eyes. It scared him, her sudden and unexpected quiet. He kept starting to ask her what was wrong, but every time the words floated up to his tongue, he bit them back. He was afraid of whatever it was that lay curled in all that silence.

"We need to talk," she said softly, rolling toward him.

"God, if those aren't the worst four words a woman can say." He waited for her to laugh with him.

"It's serious."

He sighed. "I know it is."

She angled her body until she was almost lying on top of him. Her eyes looked huge in the pale oval of her face, huge and filled with sadness. "I went to see a doctor today."

His heart stopped. "Are you okay?"

The smile she gave him was worn and ragged at the edges. "I'm healthy."

His breath expelled in a rush. "Thank God."

"I'm also three months pregnant."

"Oh, Christ . . ." He couldn't seem to breathe right.

"We tried for years and years to get pregnant."

Blake's baby. Her husband's baby, the man who'd said

he'd made a terrible mistake and wanted her back. Nick felt as if he were melting into the hot, rumpled sheets that smelled of her perfume and their spent passion.

I always wanted more children. Those had been her exact words, and in them, he'd heard the residue of a lifetime's pain. He'd known then it was the one thing he couldn't give her. Now it didn't matter.

He knew Annie too well; she was a loving, honorable person, and a ferocious mother. It was one of the things he loved about her, her unwavering sense of honor. She would know that Blake deserved a chance to know his child.

There would be no future for them now, no years that slid one into the next as they sat on those big rockers on the porch.

He wanted to say something that would magically transform this moment into something it wasn't, to forge a memory that wouldn't hurt for the rest of his life. But he couldn't.

Before their love song had really begun, it was coming to an end.

Chapter 23

Nick knew that Annie was making her arrangements to return home, but she was careful around him. She hung up the phone when he came into the room.

He tried to erect a shield between them, something that would soften his fall when she left, but it was impossible. Yesterday, he and Annie had driven to Seattle to see a specialist in high-risk pregnancies. He couldn't stay detached. He was there for her every minute, encouraging her to keep drinking water when she thought she couldn't take another sip, holding her hand during the ultrasound. When he saw the baby—that tiny, squiggly gray line in a sea of fuzzy black, he'd had to turn quickly away and mumble something about having to go to the bathroom.

Each day, he tried not to think about what was to come, but he felt the silent, insistent march of every hour, ticking away what he wanted most in his life.

Sometimes, in the middle of the day, when a strand of sunlight slid through an open window and highlighted Annie's cropped hair, he was stunned by her beauty; and then she'd smile at him, that soft, sad, knowing smile, and it would all come crashing back. He'd hear that ticking in his head again.

She had changed him so much, his Annie. She'd given him a family and made him believe that love was a heavy winter coat that kept you warm all year. She'd shown him that he could pull himself out of the destructive patterns of his life; he could quit drinking and take care of his daughter. She'd given him everything he'd dreamed of.

Except a future.

When they were together, they didn't talk about the baby or the future.

Now she was standing in the living room, staring at the pictures on the fireplace mantel. Absently, she stroked her still-flat abdomen.

As he walked down the stairs, he wondered what she was thinking. The steps creaked beneath his weight, and at the sound, she looked up, giving him a tired smile. "Hey ya, Nicky," she said.

He went to her, slipped his arms around her, and pulled her against him. She leaned her head back against his shoulder. Tentatively, he reached a hand out, let it settle on her stomach. For a single heartbeat, he allowed himself to dream that the child was his, that *she* was his, and this moment was the beginning instead of the end.

"What are you thinking?" he asked quietly, hating the fear that came with the simple question of lovers everywhere.

"I was thinking about your job." She twisted in his arms and looked up at him. "I . . . want to know that you'll be going back to it."

It hurt, that quiet statement of caring. He knew what she needed from him right now, a smile, a joke, a gesture that reassured her that he would be all right without her. But he didn't have that kind of strength; he wished he did. "I don't know, Annie . . ."

"I know you were a good cop, Nick. I've never known anyone with such a capacity for caring."

"It almost broke me . . . the caring." The words held two meanings, and he knew that she understood.

"But would you give it all up . . . the caring and the love and trying . . . would you give it up because in the end there is pain?"

He touched her face gently. "You're not asking about my job. . . ."

"It's all the same, Nick. All we have is the time, the effort. The end . . . the pain . . . that's out of our control."

"Is it?"

A single tear streaked down her face, and though he longed to wipe it away, he was afraid that the tiny bead of moisture would scald his flesh. He knew that this moment would stay with him forever, even after he wanted to forget. "I'll never forget us, Annie."

This time he didn't care how much it hurt; he let himself dream that the baby she carried was his.

Annie showed up at her dad's house bright and early. For a moment after she got out of the car, she simply stood there, staring at her childhood home as if she'd never seen it before. The windows glowed with golden light, and a riot of colorful flowers hugged the latticework below the wrap-around porch. She wouldn't be here to see the chrysanthemums bloom this year, and though she hadn't seen them flower for many, many years, now it saddened her.

She would miss seeing her dad. It was funny; in California she had gone for long stretches of time without seeing him—sometimes as much as a whole year would slip by without a visit—and she hadn't had the ache of longing that now sat on her chest like a stone. She felt almost like a girl again, afraid to leave home for the first time.

With a sigh, she slammed her car door shut and walked up to the house.

She hadn't even reached the porch when Hank flung the door open. "Well, it's about time, I haven't seen you in days. I was—"

"It's time, Dad."

"Already?"

She nodded. "I'm leaving tomorrow morning."

"Oh." He slipped through the door, closing it behind him. He sidestepped around her and sat down on the wicker love seat. Then he motioned for her to sit beside him.

She sat down in her mom's rocking chair and leaned back. Memories of her childhood were close out here; they came encoded in the sound of the rocker on the wooden porch. She could almost *hear* her mother's voice, calling Annie to come into the house.

Hank stared out at the green darkness of the forest. "I'm sorry, Annie. About all of it."

Annie felt her throat tighten. "I know, Dad."

Hank turned to her at last. "I made you something." He went into the house and came out a moment later, carrying a present.

She took the thin box, wrapped in beautiful blue foil, and opened it. Inside was a thick, leatherbound photograph album. She flipped the cover open. The first page held a small black-and-white Kodak print that had seen better days; the edges were dog-eared, and tiny white creases covered the print in maplike patterns.

It was a rare photo of Annie and her mom, one she'd never seen before. Her mother was wearing a pair of white pedal pushers and a sleeveless shirt, with her hair pulled back into a ponytail. She was smiling. Beside her, a spindly Annie was standing next to a brand-new bike.

Annie remembered that bicycle. She'd gotten it for her birthday, amid a shower of balloons and cake and laughter. She remembered how proud her mother had been when she first rode it. *There you go, Annie, honey, you're on your way now.*

Slowly, she turned the pages, savoring each and every photograph. Here she was at last, Annie . . . from the early, toothless days of kindergarten through the midriff-baring teenage years.

It was her life spread out before her, one frozen moment at a time, and each one brought a bittersweet remembrance. Lady, the puppy they'd brought home from the grocery store . . . the Christmas tree ornament she'd made in Mr. Quisdorff's woodshop class . . . the white satin sleeveless dress she'd worn to the junior prom.

The memories crowded in on her, clamoring to be held and savored, and she wondered how it was that she'd forgotten so much. In every photograph, she saw herself, saw the woman emerging through the freckled, gap-toothed features of the girl in these pictures. The final page of the book was reserved for the family photograph she and Blake and Natalie had posed for only two years ago.

There I am, she thought, gazing at the smiling, bright-eyed woman in the black St. John sweater . . . *and there I'm not.*

"I couldn't find very many pictures of your mom," Hank said softly. "I went through a dozen boxes up in the attic. That's pretty much what there is. I'm sorry."

Annie was surprised to hear his voice. She'd fallen so deeply into her own thoughts, she'd forgotten that her dad was beside her. She gave him a small smile. "We're like that, we moms. We take the pictures, but we don't record our own lives very well. It's a mistake we never realize until it's too late. . . ."

She flipped back to the beginning of the album, to a five-by-seven black-and-white copy of her mom's graduation picture. She looked so heartbreakingly young. Though you couldn't tell, Annie could recall perfectly the hazel hue of her mother's eyes. She caressed the photograph. *Did you ever look for yourself in mirrors, Mom? Were you like the rest of us? Is that why you dreamed of opening a bookstore?*

She wondered now, for the first time in years, what her mom would be like today. Would she be dying her hair, or would she have allowed her beautiful blond to fade into gray? Would she still be wearing that electric-blue eye shadow from the seventies, and those fuzzy hot-pink bits of yarn to tie up her layered ponytails? Or would she have gracefully turned to a conservative shoulder-length cut by now?

"She was beautiful," Hank said quietly, "and she loved you very much." He touched Annie's cheek with his papery, old man's hand. "I should have told you that—and given you these pictures—a long time ago. But I was young and stupid and I didn't know. . . ."

There was an emotional thickness in Hank's voice. It

surprised Annie, his unexpected journey into intimacy. "What didn't you know?"

He shrugged. "I thought you grieved for a few respectable months and then got on with your life. I didn't know how . . . *deep* love ran, how it was in your blood, not your heart, and how that same blood pumped through your veins your whole life. I thought you'd be better off if you could forget her. I should have known that wasn't possible."

Annie's heart constricted painfully. Never had her father shown his grief and his love in such sharp relief. It moved her to touch his velvety cheek. "She was lucky to be so loved, Dad. By both of us."

"She's still loved—and still missed. No one can ever take her place for me, except you, Annie. You're the best of Sarah and me, and sometimes, when you smile, I see your mama sitting right beside me."

She knew then that she would remember this day forever. She would buy a wicker love seat for her deck, and she would sit there with her new baby and remember what she had once allowed herself to forget.

"I'll visit more often this time," she said. "I promise. And I want you to come down for Thanksgiving or Christmas this year. No excuses. I'll send a ticket."

"It better be coach."

She smiled. It was exactly what she would have expected him to say. "Hell, Dad, I'll put you on a bus if it'll get you down there."

"Are you going to be okay, Annie Virginia?"

"Don't worry about me, Dad. That's the one thing I learned up here in Mystic. I'm stronger than I thought. I'm always going to be okay."

* * *

It rained on the day Annie left. All the night before, she and Nick had lain awake in bed, talking, touching, trying in every way they could to mark the memory on their souls. They had watched in silence as the sun crept over the dome of Mount Olympus, turning the glaciers into spun pink glass on the jagged granite peaks; they'd watched as the clouds rolled in and wiped the sunlight away, and as the rain tiptoed along the surface of the lake, turning from a gentle patter to a roaring onslaught, and then back to a patter again. They'd stared at each other, their gazes full of pent-up longing and fear, and still they'd said nothing.

When finally Annie rose from the passion-scented warmth of his bed, he reached out and clasped her hand. She waited for him to speak, but he didn't. Slowly, hating every motion, she slipped out of her T-shirt and dressed in a pair of leggings and a long sweatshirt.

"My bags are in the car," she said at last. "I'll . . . say good-bye to Izzy and then . . . go."

"I guess we've said our good-byes," he said softly. Then he smiled, a tender, poignant smile that crinkled his eyes and made her want to cry. "Hell, I guess we've been saying them from the moment we met."

"I know . . ."

They stood for a long time, gazing at each other. If it were possible, she fell in love with him even more. Finally, she couldn't stand how much it hurt to look at him.

She pulled away from his hand and went to the window. He came up behind her. She wanted him to take her in his arms, but he just stood there, distant and apart.

"I've been married for almost twenty years," she said quietly, watching her own reflection in the glass. She saw

her mouth move, heard the words come out of her lips, but
it felt as if it were another woman talking.

And it was. Annalise Colwater.

Slowly, slowly, she turned to face him.

"I love you, Annie." He said it like he said everything,
with a quiet seriousness. "It feels like I've loved you forever." His voice was gravelly and low. "I never knew it
could be this way . . . that love could catch you when you
fell. . . ."

The words made her feel fragile, as if she were crafted
of hundred-year-old glass and could be shattered by the
touch of the wind. "Oh, Nick . . ."

He moved closer, close enough to kiss, but he didn't
touch her. He just stared down at her through those sad
blue eyes and gave her a smile that contained all his joy
and sadness, his hope and fear.

And his knowing. His knowing that love wasn't
everything it was cracked up to be. That sometimes it
could break your heart. "I need to know, Annie . . . am I in
love alone?"

Annie closed her eyes. "I don't want to say it, Nick.
Please . . ."

"I'm going to be alone, Annie, we both know that. As
the months pass, I'm going to start forgetting you—the
way your eyes crinkle in the corner when you smile,
the way you bite down on your lower lip when you're nervous, the way you chew on your thumbnail when you
watch the news."

He touched her face with a tenderness that broke her
heart. "I don't want to make you cry. I just want to know
that I'm not crazy. I love you. And if I have to let you go to

make you happy, I'll do it, and you'll never hear from me again. But, God, Annie, I have to know how you feel—"

"I love you, Nick." She smiled sadly. "I'm crazy in love with you. Over the moon in love with you. But it doesn't matter. We both know that."

"You're wrong, Annie. Love matters. Maybe it's the only thing that does."

Without waiting for her to answer, he leaned down and gave her one last tender kiss—a kiss that tasted of tears and regret, a last kiss that said good-bye.

As Annie walked through the house, it occurred to her that she should have left something behind, a sweater hanging in the closet or a pair of shoes tucked under the bed. There was nothing of her here now, no token that recalled the times she'd laughed in this room or the nights she'd slept in Nick's arms.

Biting down on her lower lip, she went to Izzy's room and found the little girl sitting on the end of her bed, her feet swinging just above the floor. She was wearing Annie's white sweater, the cashmere cardigan with the pearl buttons. A pretty lacquered box lay open on her lap.

"Hey, Izzy-bear," Annie said softly, "can I come in?"

Izzy looked up. She tried to smile, but already her brown eyes held a sheen of tears. "You wanna look through my collection again?"

Annie went to the bed and sat down beside Izzy. She pointed to a pretty purple ring. "That one is awfully pretty."

"It was my grandma Myrtle's . . . and these buttons were my mommy's." Izzy picked out a big cream-colored one with four holes in the middle. She handed it to Annie. "Smell it."

Annie took the button and lifted it to her nose.

"That one smells like my mommy's bedroom."

Slowly, Annie put the button down. Then she reached into her pocket and pulled out a folded-up handkerchief. It was a pretty pink thing with a big red *AVC* sewn across the bottom. "Why don't you put this in your collection?"

Izzy pressed it to her nose. "It smells like you."

Annie was afraid she was going to cry. "Does it?"

Izzy pulled a faded pink ribbon from her box. "Here. This is one o' my hair ribbons. You can have it."

Annie took the satin ribbon. "Thanks, pumpkin."

Izzy closed her box and clambered into Annie's lap. Annie held her tightly, savoring the feel of her, the smell of her hair.

Finally, Izzy drew back, and her brown eyes were huge in her pale face. Annie could tell that she was doing her best not to cry. "Today's the day, isn't it? You're leavin' us."

"Yes, Izzy, today's the day."

Izzy swallowed hard. "But, Annie, who's gonna braid my hair now? Who's gonna paint my toenails and make me look pretty?"

Annie couldn't meet Izzy's earnest, overbright eyes. Forcing a wan smile, she took the child's hand. "Come with me." She led Izzy outside. They walked through the soggy grass, and Annie eased open the new white gate to the garden. They picked their way down the stone path toward the park bench that sat in the midst of the flowers.

They stared in silence at the blooming flowers, and Annie knew that, like her, Izzy was remembering the day they'd planted them. Afterward, when the first flower had bloomed, she and Izzy and Nick had sat in the garden in a darkening night and shared their memories of Kathy. They'd laughed and cried and talked. And since then, Izzy said that every new blossom reminded her of her mommy.

Izzy scooted closer. Annie tried to shore up her courage for what was to come. With a sigh, she reached into her pocket and pulled out the antique coin. Closing her damp fingers around the slim metal disk, she stared blindly at the colorful wash of blooming flowers. "I'm going to miss you something fierce, Izzy."

"I know, but you gotta go be with your daughter now."

It was a heartbeat before Annie could find her voice. "Yes."

"I wish . . . I wish I was your daughter."

"Oh, Izzy . . . your mommy loved you very, very much. And your daddy loves you with all his heart and soul."

Izzy turned to her. "Natalie could come here, couldn't she? I'd let her have my room. And when the baby comes, he could sleep with me. I'd . . . I'd share Miss Jemmie with him. Honest, I would. I'll be a good girl, I promise. I'll brush my teeth and make my bed and eat my vegetables."

"You already are a good girl, Izzy." She touched the child's small, tear-streaked face. "Natalie and I have a home in California. And the baby has a daddy who misses me."

Izzy sighed. "I know. By Disneyland."

"Um-hmm." She squeezed Izzy's tiny hand. "But it doesn't mean I don't love you, Izzy. I'll be thinking about you, and I'll call you lots and lots. . . ." Her voice cracked, and for a minute the pain was so intense, Annie was afraid she was going to spoil everything by bursting into tears. "I'll always love you, Izzy-bear."

"Yeah." It was a quiet sigh, barely audible.

She twisted around to face Izzy. "I need you to do something for me while I'm gone."

"What's that?"

"You have to take care of your daddy for me. He's big and strong, but he's going to need you sometimes."

"He's gonna be sad."

The words stung. "Yes." She handed Izzy the coin they'd found at the abandoned ranger's station, the one Izzy had asked Annie to protect. "You'd better give this to your daddy. He's a safe place now, Izzy. You can trust him with everything."

Izzy stared at the coin in Annie's hand; then, slowly, she looked up. Tears magnified her brown eyes. "You keep it."

"I can't."

Izzy's tears started to fall. "You keep it, Annie. Then I know you'll be back."

The next thing she knew, Annie was crying. She pulled Izzy into her lap and hugged her. It started to rain softly; droplets slid down the white pickets and hit the marshy grass, their fall as quiet as the sound of a woman's tears or of a soul breaking softly in two.

"I love you, Izzy," she whispered, stroking the child's hair. Then, very softly, she said, "Good-bye."

Nick left Izzy with Lurlene and followed Annie out of town, keeping the squad car a safe distance behind. He felt like one of those crazy stalkers, but he couldn't help himself. He followed her all the way to the Hood Canal Bridge.

There, he pulled over and got out, watching her red

Mustang speed across the bridge, becoming smaller and smaller and smaller.

And finally, just as suddenly as she'd come into his life, she was gone.

Out of the corner of his eye, he saw a bank of beautiful delicate yellow flowers along the edge of the road.

Look, Annie, the glacier lilies are blooming. The thought came out of nowhere, cutting deep. He could no longer turn to her and say whatever came to mind. Besides, she was going to a place where flowers bloomed all year.

The urge for a drink came on him, hard and fast.

He closed his eyes. *Please, God, help me hold on . . .*

But the prayer was useless. He felt himself starting to fall, and there was no one to catch him. He lurched for his car and jumped in. The car spun away from the bridge turnout, fishtailing back onto the highway, speeding back toward Mystic.

At Zoe's, he found his favorite chair empty, waiting for him in the darkened corner. It was middle-of-the-day quiet, with just the occasional clinking of a heavy glass on the bar and the low buzz of a television.

It looked like it always had, and for no good reason, that surprised him. The same oak bar, flanked by empty stools. The same cheap fans, circling tiredly overhead, barely disturbing the smoky air. There weren't more than a handful of people in the place, the old faithfuls who'd staked out their usual spots and sat, glassy-eyed and smoking, clutching drinks.

"Jesus, Nick, where yah been?"

Nick looked up and saw Zoe standing by him. She plunked a drink down in front of him. Then, with a slow nod, she turned and headed back to her place at the bar.

Nick took the glass in his hand. It felt cool and smooth and comforting. He swirled it around, watching the booze shimmer in the dull light from an overhead fixture.

He brought the drink to his lips, inhaling the sweet, familiar fragrance of the scotch. *Drink . . . drink,* said a tiny voice deep inside. *You know it will take the pain away. . . .*

It was seductive, that voice, luring him into the fragrance of the scotch, promising a solution to the pain in his heart, a blurring filter through which to remember Annie.

He wanted to guzzle this drink and then order another and another and another, until he could barely remember that he'd loved her in the first place.

But then he thought of Izzy.

Can I come home, Izzy? When he'd said those words to her, he'd wanted her trust more than anything else in the world. And he wanted it still.

The booze wouldn't help; the rational part of his brain knew that. He'd get drunk—be a drunk again—and then what? Annie wouldn't be any closer to coming back to him, and he would have failed his little girl again.

He slammed the drink down, threw a ten-dollar bill onto the table, and lurched to his feet, backing away. At the bar, he waved at Zoe. "I'm outta here."

She grabbed a wet towel from underneath the bar and wiped the wood down, eyeing him. "You okay, Nick?"

He tried to smile, but couldn't quite manage it. "Good as always, Zoe."

He raced out of the bar. His hands were shaking and his throat felt uncomfortably dry, but he was glad to be out of there.

He ran until his side ached and his breathing was ragged, until the need for a drink didn't consume him.

Then he sat for two hours on a park bench, watching the sun slowly set on Main Street. Breath by breath, the panic and fear passed. The pain was still there, throbbing on his heart like an open wound, and he recognized that it would be there for a long, long time, but Annie had changed him, helped him to see himself in a different and kinder light. That's what he had to focus on now. He had a life that mattered, a daughter who loved and needed him. Falling apart was a luxury he couldn't afford.

By the time the AA meeting started, Nick had pushed the need for a drink to a small, dark corner of his soul. He filed into the smoke-filled room behind a string of friends.

Joe was right behind him. He felt Joe's hand on his shoulder, heard his rough, sandpapery voice, "How are you doing, Nicholas?"

Nick was able to smile. "I'm doing okay, Joe. Thanks." He took a seat on a folding metal chair, and Joe sat down beside him.

Joe eyed him. "Are you sure you're all right?"

Nick knew he must look pale and tired. "I'm okay, Joe," he said, settling onto the hard plastic seat.

Joe grinned and clapped him gently on the shoulder. "I'm proud of you, Nicholas."

Nick closed his eyes and leaned back, sighing deeply. At first, he didn't notice the tap on his back. When he did, he snapped upright. His heart pounded with anticipation. Annie had changed her mind, she had turned around and come back. He spun around in his metal chair—

And saw Gina Piccolo standing behind him. Her unmade-up eyes looked tired against the chalky pallor of her face. He noticed that the nose ring was gone, as was the black lipstick. She looked as young and innocent as when he'd first seen her, riding her bike to the World-of-Wonders putt-putt golf course all those years ago.

He got slowly to his feet. "Gina," he said. "What are you doing here?"

"Drew died this week. O.D." Her voice was quiet and shaky. Tears washed her eyes, slid slowly down her gaunt cheeks. "You said if I ever needed help . . . I mean . . . I couldn't think of anybody else . . . at the station they told me you might be here. . . ."

"It's okay, Gina. . . ."

"I don't want to die, Mr. Delacroix."

Before this spring, Nick would have been afraid of this moment; he would have seen another tragedy in the making, another failure nipping at his heels. But now, he felt Annie beside him, as strong and warm as sunlight. He heard her voice whispering inside him: *Would you give it all up, Nick . . . the caring . . . would you give it all up because at the end there is pain?*

Maybe he would fail—probably he would fail—but he wouldn't let that stop him now. It was in the trying that he could save himself, and possibly this one desperate girl beside him.

He took her hand. "You've come to the right place, Gina. It's scary and hard to give up the crutches, but I'll be here for you. I won't give up on you if you won't."

A smile broke across her face, making her look impossibly innocent and hopeful. "I'll just get a Coke, and then I'll sit with you."

"Okay." He watched her walk through the crowded room, and then he sat down.

"So, Nicholas," said Joe. "What's that all about?"

Nick turned to his mentor, smiling broadly. "I guess it's just another cop trying to save another kid from ruin."

Joe grinned. "Welcome back, Nicholas. We missed you."

The words settled through Nick, sifting gently, finding a comfortable perch. "I missed me, too," he said quietly. "I guess you can put me back on the schedule. Say, Monday morning?"

"Ah, Nicholas. I never took you off."

Smiling, Nick leaned back in his seat. In a moment, Gina sat in the chair beside him.

The meeting got under way. Nick listened to the stories, and with each one, each tale that was so like his own, he felt himself grow stronger. When at last the meeting was coming to a close, he motioned to the chairman. "I'd like to speak," he said quietly.

There was a flutter of surprise around the room. Chairs squeaked as people turned in their seats to look at Nick.

"My name is Nick," he said into the quiet. The next part stuck in his throat, so he tried again. "My name is Nick, and I'm an alcoholic."

"Hi, Nick," they answered in unison, smiling proudly at him.

He saw the understanding in their eyes, in the way they nodded or looked at him or leaned forward. *It's okay,* they said wordlessly, *we know.* "I think I was an alcoholic long before I took my first drink. But everything started getting out of control about a year ago, when my wife died. . . ."

Word by tender word, he relived it all, picked through the rubble of his life and exposed all his vulnerabilities and failures and triumphs and heartbreaks. He gave everything inside him to the nodding, understanding faces in this cheap, smoke-filled room, knowing that they would hold his pain in careful hands and transform it into something else, a new awareness that would get him through the long, lonely nights without Annie. As he spoke, he felt the weight of the past year begin to lift. It wasn't until he spoke of Izzy, sweet Izzy, and the memory of the day she'd said, *I love you, Daddy,* that he finally broke down.

Part Three

God gave us memories
so that we might have
roses in December.
—James M. Barrie

Chapter 24

Heat rose in shimmering waves from the black ribbon of asphalt and melted into the brown, smog-filled air. Annie leaned deeper into the smelly velour upholstery of the taxicab and sighed, resting her hand on her stomach.

Already, she couldn't stand being away from Nick and Izzy; it felt as if a vital part of her had been hacked off and left to wither in some other place.

This concrete-encrusted land didn't hold her life anymore. It seemed to her to be an apocalyptic vision of the future in which green trees and blue skies and white clouds had been replaced by a million shades of man-made gray.

The cab veered off the Pacific Coast Highway and turned onto her road—funny, she still thought of it as her road. Beyond the Colony's guarded gate, they drove past the carefully hidden beach houses, each cut from the same contemporary designer's cloth; huge, multilayered homes built practically on top of each other, most with less than eight feet of ground between them. Each one a tiny kingdom that wanted to keep the rest of the world at bay.

They turned into her driveway, and the white angles of the house soared toward the blue sky. The yard was in full bloom, a riot of pink and red hibiscus and glossy green leaves. Its beauty was so . . . false. If they stopped watering, this contrived garden would shrivel and die.

The cab pulled up to the garage and stopped. The driver got out of the car and went to the trunk, popping it open.

Slowly, Annie got out. She stared down at the driveway, remembering how she had watched over the placement of the bricks, each and every one. *That one's not right, it's crooked. Could you please do it again before the cement hardens?*

"Ma'am? Is that everything?" The cabdriver was standing beside her Louis Vuitton luggage.

"Yes, thank you." She flipped her purse open and retrieved the fare from her wallet, plus a healthy tip. "Here you go."

He snatched the money and pocketed it. "You call me if you need to go to the airport again," he said.

The airport.

"Thanks. I will."

When he was gone, she turned back to the house. For a second, she thought she couldn't do it, couldn't walk down to the hand-carved mahogany door, push it open, and go inside. But then, she was moving, walking beneath the arched entrance that smelled of jasmine, pulling the jangle of keys from her pocketbook.

The key slid in; what had she expected? That it would no longer fit here because she didn't? The door whooshed open, and the smell of stale air greeted her.

She walked through the house, room by room, waiting to feel something . . . sad, happy, depressed . . . something. The floor-to-ceiling windows framed the brilliant blues of the sea and sky.

She felt as if she were walking through a stranger's house. Thoughts of Nick and Izzy crowded in on her, begging to be replayed and picked over, but she didn't dare. Instead she focused on the little things: the grand piano she'd purchased at a Sotheby's auction, the chandelier she'd rescued from an old San Francisco hotel, the Lladró statue collection she'd begun when Natalie started junior high.

Things.

She went up to her bedroom. Their bedroom.

There, certainly she would feel *something*. But again, there was only that odd sensation that she was viewing the remains of a long-dead civilization. This was Annie *Colwater's* room, and it was all that remained of her.

Her closet was full of expensive silks and woolens and cashmeres, skirts in every color and length, shoes in boxes still marked with exorbitant price tags.

At the bedside table, she picked up the phone and listened for a long time to the dial tone. She wanted to call Nick and Izzy, but she didn't. Instead, she carefully dialed Blake's office number. Without waiting to speak to him, she left a message that she was home.

Then she replaced the receiver and sat heavily on the end of her bed.

Soon, she'd see Blake again. In the old days, she would have obsessed over what to wear, but now, she couldn't have cared less. There was nothing in that vast, expensive closet that mattered to her anymore, nothing that felt like hers. It was nothing but acres and acres of another woman's clothes.

*   *   *

The office was like the man, understated, expensive, and seething with power. Years before Blake could afford this corner office in Century City, with its expansive views of glass and concrete skyscrapers, he'd imagined it. He always knew it would be stark and unrelieved, that there would be nothing in the room that said, *Come on in, sit down, tell me your troubles.* He'd never wanted to be that kind of lawyer, and he wasn't. It was the kind of office that made a client squirm and reminded him with every silent tick of the desk clock how much it was costing to sit here.

In truth, of course, it was Annie who'd given him this office. She'd spent hours choosing the drapes and the upholstery. She had designed and commissioned the ornate African mahogany desk and each hand-stained leather accessory.

Everywhere he looked now, he saw her.

He sighed and leaned back in his chair. The pile of paperwork on his desk blurred in front of him. He shoved the papers aside, watched as the Beaman deposition fluttered to the marble floor.

He felt odd and out of sorts, and he'd felt this way since his impromptu trip to that shithole diner in Mystic.

He'd thought he could apologize to Annie and step back into the comfortable shoes of his old life. Except that Annie wasn't Annie anymore, and he didn't know what to say or do to get her back.

On his desk, the intercom buzzed. He flicked the button impatiently. "Yes, Mildred?"

"Your wife called—"

"Put her through."

"She left a message, sir. She wanted you to know that she was home."

Blake couldn't believe it. "Clear my schedule, Mildred. I'm gone for the rest of the day."

He sprinted out of the building and jumped into his Ferrari, speeding out of the parking lot and onto the freeway.

At home, he raced up the front steps and jammed the key in the lock, swinging the door open. There was a pile of luggage at the base of the stairs. "Annie?"

She was standing at the edge of the archway that separated the living room from the formal dining room.

She was home again. *Now,* at last, everything would be all right.

He moved cautiously toward her. "Annie?"

She turned away from him and walked into the living room, standing alone at the windows. "I have something to tell you, Blake."

It unnerved him, the way she wouldn't look at him. The sight of her, so stiff and unyielding, was a sharp reminder that she was not the same woman he'd left only a few months before. His throat was dry. "What is it?"

"I'm pregnant."

His first thought was *no,* not again. He couldn't go through that again. Then he remembered the other man, the man Annie had slept with, and he could hardly breathe. It was as if someone had just run an ice cube down his spine. "Is it mine?"

She sighed, and it was a sad little sound that didn't reassure him. "Yes. I'm three months along."

He couldn't seem to think straight. He shook his head, sighing. "A baby . . . Christ, after all these years."

She turned and gave him a quirking smile, and there she

was at last. His Annie. He realized then what he hadn't before. It was the baby that had brought her back to him. "A baby." This time he could smile. "*Our* baby . . ."

"All those years I thought God wasn't listening. It turns out He's got a mean sense of humor. He obviously wanted me to go through menopause and potty training at the same time."

"We'll make it work this time," he said softly.

She flinched at the words, and he wondered if he should have phrased it as a question. "Blake—"

He didn't want to hear what she was going to say. "Whatever happened in Mystic is over, Annie. This is our child you're carrying. *Our* child. We have to become a family again. Please give me another chance."

She didn't answer, just stared for a long time at his hand on her stomach. Then, unsmiling, she looked away.

Please give me another chance.

Annie closed her eyes. God, how many nights had she lain in her lonely bed, aching to hear those words from him? Yet now they fell against her heart like stones down an empty well. Clattering, bouncing, signifying nothing.

And what had she said to him, all those months ago? *I can't believe you'd throw it all away. We're a family, Blake, a family.*

"Annie—"

"Not now, Blake," she said in a fragile voice. "Not now."

She heard him sigh, a tired, disappointed sound that she knew well. He was confused and more than a little angry; he didn't know how to lose or how to be patient or how to hold his tongue.

"I'll have to be bedridden, just like with . . . Adrian." She gazed up at him. "It's going to take some work on your part. I won't be able to be good old Annie, taking care of everyone else. For once, you'll have to put me first."

"I can do that."

She wished she could believe it.

"I know it won't be easy for you to trust me again. I screwed up. . . ."

"A mammoth understatement."

His voice dropped to a plaintive whisper. "I can't believe you don't love me anymore. . . ."

"Neither can I," she said softly, and it was true. Somewhere, deep inside of her, a shadow of their love had to remain. She'd loved him for twenty years. Certainly that kind of emotion didn't simply disappear. "I'm trying to believe in what we had, and I pray we can find our way back to love, but I'm not in love with you now. Hell, I don't even *like* you much."

"You will," he answered with a confidence that set her teeth on edge. He leaned toward her. "Let's go to bed."

"Hel-*lo* Blake. Have you been listening to me? I'm not ready to sleep with you yet . . . besides, Dr. North said it was risky. Remember? Early contractions."

He looked ridiculously deflated. "Oh, yeah. I just thought, if this is a reconciliation, you should—"

"No more telling me what I should and shouldn't do, Blake. I'm not the same woman I was before. And I'm scared to death you're the same damn man."

"I'm not. Really, I'm not. I've grown, too. I know how precious our life was. I won't make the same mistakes again."

"I hope not."

He moved toward her. "You always used to say that the longest journey begins with a single step." ·

He was right; it used to be one of her favorite sayings. Now, that kind of optimism felt far, far away.

He was obviously waiting for her to respond, and when she didn't, he glanced around. "Well, do you want to watch television for a while? I could make some popcorn and hot chocolate—like the old days."

The old days.

With those simple words, she saw her whole life flash before her eyes. This spring she'd worked to unearth the real Annie, and now Blake wanted to bury her once again beneath the sand of their old patterns. Tomorrow, she knew she would have to make an effort, an *honest* effort to find her way back to Blake, but tonight, she was too damned tired to start. "No, thanks," she said quietly. "I think I'll just go to bed. It's been a long day. You can sleep in the green guest room. I put fresh sheets on the bed today."

"Oh. I thought—"

"I know what you thought. It isn't going to happen."

She might have laughed at his expression—so confused and crestfallen—but it wasn't funny. He was her husband, the father of her children, the man she'd vowed to love, honor, and cherish until death parted them, and right now, standing in the living room of the house they'd shared for so many years, she couldn't think of a single thing to say to him.

Blake met Natalie at Customs.

She gave him a big hug, then drew back, looking around. "Where's Mom?"

"She couldn't make it. I'll tell you all about it in the car on the way home."

"Do you have the Ferrari?"

"What else?"

"Can I drive?"

Blake frowned. "Did someone tell you I'd suffered recent brain damage? I never let—"

"Oh, *please,* Dad. I haven't driven in months."

"This is hardly an argument that helps your cause."

"Come on, Dad. *Pleeeeease.*"

He imagined the look on Annie's face if she heard he'd let Natalie drive. Slowly, he pulled the keys out of his pocket and tossed them in the air. Natalie snagged them in one hand. "Come on, Dad!" She grabbed his hand and dragged him through the terminal. Within moments, they were strapped into the sports car and heading down the freeway for home.

As always, Blake was uneasy around his daughter. He tried to think of something to say to her now, something to break the uncomfortable silence that always stood between them.

She changed his radio station. A hard-edged rock-and-roll song blasted through the speakers.

"Turn that thing down," he said automatically.

She clicked the music off, then signaled for a turn and jerked into the fast lane, sucking up behind a black Mercedes convertible. Before he had time to tell her what to do, she slowed down and backed off.

"So, Dad, how's Grandpa Hank?"

"How should I know?"

She glanced at him. "You *did* go up to Mystic?"

He shifted uncomfortably, thankful when her gaze turned

back to the road. He wasn't good at handling this stuff. It was Annie's job to put the right spin on their separation. "I . . . was really busy. There was this big case between a rock star and—"

"So, you were really busy," she said quietly, her hands curled tightly around the wheel, her eyes staring straight ahead.

"Consumed."

"That must be why you never called me."

He heard the hurt in her voice and he didn't know what to say. He'd never heard that tone before, but he wondered suddenly if it had been there all along. "I sent flowers to you every Friday."

"Yeah. You thought of me long enough to ask your secretary to send flowers every week."

Blake sighed. He was way out in left field with this one. How could he tell his teenage daughter he'd thrown their family away—and all for a few months of hot sex with a woman who hadn't been alive when Kennedy was shot.

What was he supposed to tell her? The truth, a lie, or something in between?

Annie would know what to do and say. She'd always guided his relationship with Natalie. She told him subtly, with a look or a touch or a whisper, when to reach out to Natalie and when to pull back.

But he had to say *something*. Natalie was obviously waiting to hear his explanation. "Your mother's . . . angry with me. I made a few mistakes, and . . . well . . ."

"You two were separated this spring." She said it in a dull, monotonous voice, without looking at him.

He winced. "Just a little break, is all. Everything will be fine now."

"Really? Did you have surgery while I was gone—a personality transplant maybe? Or did you retire? Come on, Dad, how is everything going to get better? You hate being at home."

He frowned, staring at her stern profile. It was an odd thing for her to say. "That's not true."

"Yeah, right. That's why I have no memories of you until high school."

He sank deeper into his seat. Maybe this was *why* he stayed away so much. Annie and Natalie were masters at piling on the guilt. "Everything will be fine, Natalie. You'll see. Your mom's . . . going to have a baby."

"A *baby*? Oh, my God, how could she not tell me that?" She laughed. "I can't believe it . . ."

"It's true. She's back in bed with this one—just like with Adrian. And she's going to need our help."

"*Our* help?" It was all she said, and he was glad she'd dropped the subject of the separation, but after a while, the silence began to gnaw at him. He kept thinking about that ridiculous little sentence, *I have no memories of you.* It kept coming back even as he tried to push it away.

He stared out the window at his whole life. Years ago, when Natalie was a pudgy-faced child who talked incessantly, it hadn't been like this between them. She'd looked at him through adoring eyes.

But somewhere along the way, she'd stopped thinking he'd hung the moon, and for no reason that he could remember now, he'd let it go. He was always so damned busy.

He'd never had much time for her; that was certainly true. But that was Annie's job, motherhood, and she'd done it so effortlessly that Blake had told himself he wasn't necessary. His job was to bring home money. And by the time he realized that his daughter had stopped coming to him with her problems—a wiggly tooth, a lost teddy bear—it was too late. By then he barely knew her. One day she was a toothless toddler, and the next, she was off to the mall with a group of girls he didn't recognize.

Sadly, when he thought about it, he had damn few memories of her, either. Moments, yes; pictures in his mind, certainly. But memories, recollections of time spent together, were almost totally absent.

Annie heard the scream first.

"Mommmm!"

She sat up in bed, fluffing the pillows behind her. "I'm in here, Nana!"

Natalie burst into Annie's bedroom. Grinning, laughing, she dove onto the big king-size bed and threw her arms around Annie. Blake came in a few moments later and stood beside the bed.

Finally, Natalie drew back. Her beautiful blue eyes were filled with tears, but she was smiling from ear to ear.

Annie drank in the sight of her daughter. "I missed you, Nana," she whispered.

Natalie cocked her head, eyeing Annie critically. "What happened to your hair?"

"I got it cut."

"It looks *great*. We could be sisters." A look of mock horror crossed her face. "I hope this doesn't mean you're going to college with me. . . ."

Annie feigned a hurt look. "I didn't think you'd mind. I signed up to be your dorm mother."

Natalie rolled her eyes. "From anyone else's mother it

would be a joke." She looked at Blake. "You're not letting her go, are you, Dad?"

Annie looked up at Blake, who was staring down at her. He moved in closer and laid a possessive hand on her shoulder. "I'm trying like hell to keep her at home," he said evenly.

"Dad tells me you're pregnant." A tiny bit of hurt flashed through Natalie's blue eyes and then was gone. "I can't believe you didn't tell me."

Annie gently touched her daughter's cheek. "I just found out, honey."

Natalie grinned. "I ask for a sister for sixteen years, and you get pregnant just before I leave for college. Thanks a lot."

"This definitely falls into the 'accident' category. Believe me, I always wanted to fill this house with children—but not just before I cashed my first Social Security check."

"You're not that old. I read about a sixty-year-old woman who had a kid."

"How comforting. You understand, of course, that the rules have changed now. You aren't allowed to have a child until your sister or brother graduates from high school. And you will have to introduce me as your stepmother."

Natalie laughed. "I've been lying about you for years, Mom. Ever since you sobbed at my dance recital and had to be escorted from the building."

"That was an allergy attack."

"Yeah, right." She laughed. "Hey, guess what, Mom. Dad let me drive the Ferrari home."

"You're kidding."

"It's a good thing you weren't there. You'd have made

me wear a crash helmet and drive on the side of the road— preferably with my emergency blinkers flashing."

Annie laughed, and she couldn't escape how *right* this all felt—the teasing, the joking, the familiarity. How natural.

They were a family. A *family.*

Blake bent closer to Annie. He whispered in a voice so soft that only she could hear, "People change, Annalise."

It scared her, that deceptively simple sentence that seemed to promise the sun and the moon and the stars.

That's when she knew she was at risk. This man she'd loved for so long knew what to say, always, what to do. He could push her onto the edge again. If she wasn't careful, she'd slide without a ripple into the gently flowing stream of her old life, pulled back under the current without a whimper of protest. Another housewife lost in the flow.

Chapter 25

The shattered pieces of their family fell back together with a surprising ease. Like a glass vase that had been broken and carefully mended, the tiny fissures could be seen only on close examination, when Blake and Annie were alone. They were soldiers, the two of them, warily circling each other, negotiating an awkward and unfelt peace.

But Annie had spent twenty years wearing a groove into her life, and she now slipped smoothly back into it. She awakened early, dressed in an expensive silk robe with a pretty bow tied at her expanding waist. She carefully accentuated her features with makeup, layering putty color beneath her eyes to erase the dark circles that came from restless nights.

On Mondays, she made out the weekly grocery lists and sent Natalie to the gourmet shop on the corner. On Tuesdays, she paid the household bills. On Wednesdays, she conferred with the housekeeper and gardener, and on Thursdays she sent Natalie on errands, using her daughter to collect all the various and sundry pieces of their lives. Once again, the house was a well-run unit.

She helped Blake choose his suits and ties, and reminded him when to pick up his dry cleaning. Every morning, she kissed him good-bye—a chaste, dry little kiss planted on his cheek—and every night she welcomed him home from work with a smile. He sat on her bed and talked stiltedly about his day.

In truth, she was glad to spend her days in bed, hidden away from the reality of the marriage. Most days, while Blake was at work, she and Natalie spent long hours talking and laughing and sharing memories.

Annie learned that Blake hadn't called Natalie in London. She heard the hurt and disappointment in her daughter's voice when she spoke, but there wasn't a damn thing Annie could do to fix it. "I'm sorry" was all she could say. Again and again.

Increasingly, Annie noticed changes in Natalie, a maturity that hadn't been there before. Every now and then, she zinged Annie with an unexpected observation. Like yesterday.

All you think about is making us happy. What makes you *happy, Mom?*

Or: *This spring . . . you sounded so different. So happy.*

And the most surprising of all: *Do you love Dad?*

Annie had meant to respond reflexively, to say, *Yes, of course I love your dad.* But then she'd looked in Natalie's eyes and seen a grown-up understanding. And so, Annie had spoken to the woman her daughter had become.

I've loved your dad since I was a teenager. We're just going through a hard time, that's all.

He loves you, Natalie had said. *Just like he loves me,*

*but . . . his love . . . it isn't very warm . . . I mean . . . it's
not like being loved by you, Mom.*

It had brought tears to Annie's eyes, that quiet observation. She was saddened to realize that Natalie would never really understand what a father's love could be. It would be a loss in Natalie's life forever. . . .

Unlike Izzy.

She closed her eyes and leaned back in bed, remembering Nick and Izzy when they'd played Candy Land, Nick hunched over the board . . . or when the two of them had played Barbies on the living room floor, Nick saying in a falsetto voice, *Have you seen my blue dancing shoes?*

Yesterday, when she and Natalie had gone into the doctor's, Annie had been unable to stave off the memories. It was simply too painful. There had been no husband there to hold her hand and laugh at how badly she had to pee. No husband to watch the fuzzy black screen and marvel at the miracle.

No Nick.

How long would it be this way? she wondered. Would she spend the rest of her life feeling that she'd left an essential part of herself in another place and time?

The first letter, when it arrived, was small and crinkled. A blue, faded postmark read *Mystic, WA.*

Annie stared down at the pink envelope. Very gently, she eased the back open and pulled out the paper. It was a penand-ink drawing of Mount Olympus. Inside was a letter from Izzy.

Dear Annie:
How are you? I am fin.
The flwrs are pritty. Today I learnd to ride a bike.

> *It was fun.*
> *I miss you. When are you cuming home?*
> *Love, Izzy.*
> *P.s. My Dadde helped me rite this lettr.*

Annie clutched the note in her hand. Everything about it, every misspelled word, tugged at her heartstrings. She sat stiffly in bed, staring out at the blue, blue sky beyond her room, wishing it would rain. She knew she would write back to Izzy, but what would she say? A few hopeless words that held no promises? Or a string of pointless banalities that pretended they'd all be friends. Nothing but friends, and sometimes friends moved on. . . .

There were only a few words that mattered, and they were the truest of them all. "I miss you, too, Izzy. . . ."

She opened the nightstand drawer and pulled out Izzy's hair ribbon, stroking the satin strip. She knew that tomorrow she would answer the letter, and she would fill a sheet of paper with words and more words, but it wouldn't say what mattered. It wouldn't say what Izzy wanted to hear.

She picked up the cordless phone from the table and listened to the dial tone for a long time, then slowly she hung up. It was unfair to call Nick and Izzy, unfair to let the sound of their voices soothe her loneliness. *Don't do that to me, Annie,* Nick had said, *don't throw me hope like it was a bone to be buried in my backyard. . . .*

"Mom?" Natalie poked her head into the bedroom. "Are you all right?"

Annie sniffled and turned away.

Natalie hurried over to the bed and crawled up beside Annie. "Mom? Are you okay?"

No, she wanted to say, *no, I'm not okay.* I miss the man I love and his daughter, and I miss a place where rainfall is measured in feet and your hair is never dry and where grown-ups play Chutes and Ladders in the middle of the afternoon with a six-year-old girl. . . .

But none of that was the sort of thing you said to your teenage daughter, no matter how grown up she looked. "I'm fine, honey. Just fine."

No matter how hard she tried to be her old self, Annie couldn't quite manage it. No matter how many of the old routines she pushed herself through, she felt herself slipping away. With each day, she saw the future approaching in a low-rolling fog of lost chances and missed opportunities.

Summer blasted through Southern California on a tide of unseasonable heat. The Malibu hills dried up and turned brown. Leaves began, one by one, to curl up and die, dropping like bits of charred paper on artificially green lawns.

Blake stood on the deck outside his room, sipping a scotch and soda. The wood was warm beneath his bare feet, the last reminder of a surprisingly hot day.

He hadn't slept well last night. Hadn't, in fact, slept well in weeks. Not since he'd apologized to Annie and discovered that she didn't care.

She was trying to make their marriage work. He could see the effort, in the way she put on makeup every morning and wore the colors she knew he liked. She even touched him occasionally—brief, flitting gestures that were designed to make him feel better, but that had the opposite effect. Every time she touched him, he felt a tiny, niggling ache in his chest, and he remembered the way it used to be, the way she used to touch him all the time and smile at his jokes and brush the hair away from his face, and when he remembered he hurt.

She wasn't herself anymore, that was obvious. She lay in their big bed like a silent, pregnant ghost, and when she smiled, it was a brittle, fleeting thing, and not Annie at all.

She was . . . disappearing, for lack of a better word.

She used to talk and laugh all the time. She used to find joy in the craziness of life, but nothing intrigued her anymore. Her moods were a flat line, even and smooth. So smooth, there was no hint of Annie inside the quiet woman who sat with him in the evening, watching television.

Last week, when it rained, she had sat up in bed, staring through the silver-streaked window. When he called out to her, she'd turned, and he hadn't missed the tears in her eyes. She'd been holding some ragged scrap of a hair ribbon as if it were the Holy Grail.

He couldn't stand this much longer. He wasn't the kind of man who liked to work this hard for what he wanted. Enough was enough.

He set down his drink on the table and strode back into the house. He knocked on Annie's door—quickly, before he lost his nerve.

"Come in," she called out.

He opened the door and went inside. The room was as comforting as ever, with its sea-blue walls and carpet and white bedding.

Annie was in bed, reading a book called *How to Run Your Own Small Business*. Beside her, there was a pile of similarly titled self-help books.

Jesus, was she thinking of getting a *job*?

It would humiliate him if she sought employment; she knew how he felt about his wife working. Especially with her lack of skills. What would she do—pour lattes and pick croissants from a glass case?

He had no idea who this woman was who sat in bed and read how-to books. He felt unconnected to Annie; he had to do something to get them back together.

She looked up, and he noticed the dark circles under her eyes and gray cast to her skin. In the past month, she'd gained a lot of weight, but somehow her face looked thinner. Her hair had grown out some, and the tips were beginning to curl wildly. Again, she looked like a woman he didn't know. "Hi, Blake," she said softly, closing the book. "Is it time for the movie to start? I thought—"

He went to the bed and sat beside her, gazing down into her beautiful green eyes. "I love you, Annie. I know we can work all this out if we're . . . together."

"We are together."

"Where's your wedding ring?"

She cocked her head toward the mahogany highboy. "In my jewelry box."

He got up and went to the highboy, carefully opening the hand-painted box that held all the treasures he'd given her over the years. There, among the black velvet rolls, was the three-carat diamond he'd given her on their tenth wedding anniversary. Beside it was the plain gold band they'd originally bought. He picked up the two rings and returned to the bed, sitting down beside his wife.

He stared down at the fiery diamond. "Remember that vacation we took, years ago, at the Del Coronado Hotel? Natalie wasn't more than a year old—"

"Six months," she said softly.

He looked at her. "We brought that big old blue and red blanket—the one I had on my bed in college—and laid it out on the beach. We were the only people out there, just the three of us."

Annie almost smiled. "We went swimming, even though it was freezing cold."

"You were holding Natalie, with the waves splashing across your thighs. Your lips were practically blue and your skin was nothing but goose bumps, but you were laughing, and I remember how much I loved you. My heart hurt every time I looked at you."

She looked down at her hands, folded on her lap. "That was a long time ago."

"I found a sand dollar, remember? I handed it to you with our baby wobbling on the blanket between us, rocking her little butt back and forth. I think she was trying to learn to crawl."

Annie closed her eyes, and he wondered what she was thinking. Could she remember the rest of that day? How often he'd touched her . . . or when he'd leaned over and grazed the back of her neck with a kiss. *Hey, Godiva,* he'd whispered. *They rent horses down the road. . . .*

And her laughing answer, *Babies can't ride.*

"When did we stop having fun together, Annie? When?" He was seducing her with their memories, and he could see that it was working; he could see it in the way she stared at her hands intently, in the sheen of moisture that filled her eyes.

Slowly, he reached down and placed the two rings back on her finger. "Forgive me, Annie," he said quietly.

She looked up. A tear streaked down her cheek and dropped onto her nightgown, leaving a gray-wet blotch. "I want to."

"Let me sleep with you tonight. . . ."

She sighed. It was a long time before she answered, time

enough for him to feel hope sliding away. "Yes," she said at last.

He told himself that nothing mattered but the answer. He ignored the uncertainty in her voice and the tears in her eyes and the way she wouldn't quite look at him. It would all be okay again after they slept together. Finally, the bits of their broken lives would fuse together again.

He wanted to crush her against him, but he forced himself to move slowly. He got up, went into the closet, and changed into his pajamas. Then, very slowly, he went to the bed and peeled back the coverlet, slipping beneath the cool, white cotton sheets.

It was soothing to hold her again, like easing into a favorite pair of slippers after a long day at the office. He kissed her lightly, and as always, she was quiet and undemanding in her response. Finally, he turned over—the regular beginning of their nightly ritual. After a long moment, she snuggled up behind him.

Her body spooned against his, her belly pressed into his back. It was the way they'd always slept, only this time she didn't curl her arms around him.

They lay there, touching but not touching in the bed that had held their passion for so many years. She didn't speak, other than to say good night, and he couldn't think of anything else.

It was a long time before he fell asleep.

Natalie set a big metal bowl full of popcorn at the foot of Annie's bed, then she climbed up and snuggled close to her mom. It was Friday afternoon: girls' day. Annie and Natalie and Terri had spent every Friday together since

Annie returned home. They laughed and talked and played cribbage and watched movies.

"I left the front door open for Terri," Natalie said, pulling the bowl of popcorn onto her lap.

Annie grinned. "You know what your dad would say. He thinks criminals spend all day in the rosebushes, just *waiting* for us to leave the door open."

Natalie laughed. They talked about this and that and everything. Their conversation followed the river of their years, flowing from one topic to the next. They laughed about antics that were as old as Natalie and as new as yesterday. Through it all, Annie was amazed at Natalie's maturity; the teenager who had gone off to London had come home a young woman. It seemed light years ago that Natalie had rebelled, that she'd shorn her hair and dyed it platinum and pierced her earlobes with three holes.

"How come Dad never talks about the baby?"

The question came out of the blue, smacking Annie hard. She tried not to compare Nick and Blake, but it was impossible at a moment like this. Nick would have been with Annie every step of the way, sharing in the miracle, watching her belly swell. She would have clung to his hand during the amniocentesis, letting his jokes distract her from the needle . . . and she would have laughed with him later, when they found out it was a girl, skipping through name books and spinning dreams. . . .

She sighed. "Your dad is uncomfortable with pregnancy; he always has been. Lots of men are like that. He'll be better after the baby is born."

"Get real, Mom. Dad's good at doing his own thing. I mean, you guys are supposedly getting over your 'bad patch,' but he's never here. He still works seventy hours a week, he still plays basketball on Tuesday nights, and he still goes out for drinks with *the boys* every Friday night. When are you guys working out your problems? During Letterman?"

Annie gave her a sad smile. "When you get older, you'll understand. There's a certain . . . comfort in the familiar."

Natalie stared at her. "I have almost no memories of Dad—did you know that? All I remember about him are a few hurried good-bye kisses and the sound of a slamming door. When I hear a car engine start or a garage door close, I think of my dad." She turned to Annie. "What about after this summer . . . when I'm gone?"

Annie shivered, though the room was warm. She looked away from Natalie, unable to bear the sad certainty in her daughter's eyes. "When you're gone, I'll be worried about potty training and what to do with the Baccarat on the living room table. I'll consider plastic surgery to pull my breasts back up from my navel. You know, the usual stuff."

"And you'll be lonely."

Annie wanted to deny it. She wanted to be grown up and a good parent and say just the right thing that would alleviate Natalie's worry. But for once, no parental lies came to her. "Maybe a little. Life can be like that, Nana. We don't always get what we want."

Natalie glanced down at her own hands. "When I was little, you told me that life *did* give you what you wanted, if you were willing to fight for it and believe in it. You told me that every cloud had a silver lining."

"Those were a mother's words to a little girl. These are a mother's words to a nearly grown woman."

Natalie looked at her, long and hard. Then she turned away.

Annie felt suddenly distant from her daughter. She was

reminded of four years ago, when Natalie had turned into someone else. It had seemed that overnight, their tastes had diverged: whatever Annie liked, Natalie hated. Christmas that year had been a tense, horrible affair, with Natalie dully opening each carefully wrapped package and then muttering a caustic *gee thanks*. "Nana? What is it?"

Slowly, Natalie turned to face Annie. "You don't have to be this way, you know."

"What do you mean?"

Natalie shook her head and looked away. "Never mind."

Understanding dawned slowly, and with it, pain. It all fell into place: Natalie's desire to study biochemisty at Stanford, her sudden trip to London, her unwillingness to date the same boy for more than a few months. Behind it all was a sad message: I don't want to be like you, Mom. I don't want to be dependent on a man for everything.

"I see," Annie said.

Natalie turned to her at last, and this time there were tears in her eyes. "What do you see?"

"It doesn't matter."

"It *does*. What are you thinking?"

"I'm thinking you don't want to grow up to be like your old mom, and . . . as much as that hurts, it makes me proud. I want you to count on yourself in life. I guess, in the end, it's all we have."

Natalie sighed. "You never would have said that before he broke your heart."

"I think I've grown up a little bit lately. Life isn't all sunny days and blue skies."

"But you always taught me to look for the silver lining to every cloud. Are you doing that, Mom? Are you looking to be happy?"

"Of course I am," she answered quickly, but they both knew it was a lie. Annie couldn't meet her daughter's penetrating gaze. "I'm glad you don't want to be like me, Nana."

Sadness suffused Natalie's face. "I don't want to have a marriage like yours, and I don't understand why you stay with him—I never have. That doesn't mean I don't want to be like you. There are only two people in the world who don't respect you . . . as far as I know, anyway."

She looked at Natalie, shaking her head slightly, as if she could stop her daughter's words.

"Just two," Natalie said. A single tear streaked down her cheek and she impatiently brushed it away. "Dad . . . and you."

You. Annie felt a sudden urge to disappear, to simply melt into the expensive bed linens and vanish. She knew that Natalie was waiting for her to say something, but she didn't know what was the right answer. She felt as if she were the child, and Natalie the mother, and as the child, she'd let her parent down.

She opened her mouth to say something—she had no idea what—when suddenly Terri charged into the bedroom like a multicolored bull, her body draped in layers of red and gold lamé.

She came to a breathless stop beside the bed. Planting her fists on her meaty hips, she surveyed the bowl of popcorn. "So, where's *my* popcorn? I mean, that's enough for two skinny chicks like you, but we real women like our popcorn to come in bowls that could double as lifeboats. And I certainly want it coated in butter."

Natalie grinned. "Hey, Terri."

Terri smiled back, her heavily mascaraed lashes almost obscuring her twinkling eyes. "Hiya, princess."

"I'll go make another batch of popcorn."

"You do that, sweetie," Terri said, uncoiling the gold turban from her head.

When Natalie scurried from the room, Terri sat down on the end of the bed and leaned back against the footboard, sighing. "Christ, what a day. Sorry I'm late."

Annie smiled wanly at the theatrics. "What happened?"

"My character is running from the law—again—only this time they put her on a plane." Terri shook her head. "Bad news."

"What's wrong with that?"

"In the soaps, there's only one thing worse than getting on a plane, and that's getting in a car. The next thing you hear is sirens . . . and funeral music. If they actually *name* the flight tomorrow, I'm dead meat."

"You'll bounce back."

"Oh, perfect, make fat jokes." Terri scooted up the bed and twisted around to sit beside Annie. "So, kiddo, how's the ever-growing Goodyear blimp?"

Annie glanced down at her stomach. "We're doing okay."

"Well, I've been coming every Friday for weeks now, and we talk on the phone constantly. I think I've been patient as hell."

"About what?"

Terri looked at her, hard. "About *what*? Come on."

Annie sighed. "Nick."

"What else? I've been waiting patiently—and we both know that patience is not one of my virtues—for you to bring his name up, but obviously, you're not going to. I'm sick of respecting your privacy. Now, spill the beans. Have you called him?"

"Of course not."

"Why not?"

Annie turned to her best friend. "Come on, Terr."

"Ah . . . that honor thing. I've read about it. We don't see much of it in Southern California. And *none* on the soaps. But you *are* in love with him?"

"I don't think I want to talk about this."

"There's no point lying to an old slut like me. Hell, Annie, I've been in love more times than Liz Taylor and I've slept with enough men to protect this country in time of war. Now, do you love him?"

"Yes," she whispered, crossing her arms. It hurt to say the word aloud, and instantly she regretted it. "But I'll get over it. I *have* to. Blake is doing his best to put our family back together. Things are . . . rough right now, but they'll get better."

Terri gave her a sad smile. "I hope it works that way for you, Annie. But for most of us, when love is gone, it's gone, and all the pretending and wishing in the world can't bring it back."

"Can't bring what back?" It was Natalie, standing in the doorway with another bowl of popcorn and a bottle of spring water.

"Nothing, honey," Annie said softly.

Natalie produced a videotape from behind her back. "I rented us a movie." She popped it in the VCR, then climbed up onto the bed beside Terri.

Terri grabbed a handful of popcorn. "What's the movie?"

"Same Time, Next Year."

"That Alan Alda movie?" Terri gave Annie a sharp,

knowing look. "I always thought that was a hell of an idea. An affair once a year, I mean. Ellen Burstyn's husband is probably a real shithead—a workaholic with the moral integrity of an alley cat. He probably fucked around on Ellen and then came crawling back like the worm he is. And because Ellen's a grade-A sweetie pie, she took him back and tried to pretend that everything was okay. Still, she meets her secret lover for one weekend a year on the wild Oregon coast. Yep, sounds like heaven to me."

"Shhh," Natalie said. "It's starting."

Annie looked away from Terri. She tried not to feel anything at all, but when the music came on and the credits began to roll, she sank deeper and deeper into the pillows, as if distance could soften the sharp edges of her memories.

Chapter 26

Nick made it through the summer one day at a time. The last thing he did every night was stand by the lake, where Annie's memory was strongest. Sometimes, the missing of her was so acute, he felt it as a pain in his chest. Those were the nights when he heard the call of the booze, the soothing purr of his own weakness.

But he was making it. For the first time in years, he was actually living life on his own terms. Annie had been right in so many of the things she said to him. He'd gone back to work, and the job had given him a purpose. He was the best policeman he'd ever been. He gave everything to the people under his protection, but when his shift was over, he left the worries behind. He had learned, finally, to accept that there would be failures, and that it was okay. All he could do was try.

Like with Gina. She was still fighting the pull of old patterns and comforting, self-destructive routines. The other kids were often blatantly cruel to her. The "good" kids didn't want to hang around with a loser, and the "bad" kids spent all their time trying to lure her back into their circle of drugs and truancy, but, like Nick, Gina was holding her own. She'd moved back into her old bedroom and was reforging the bonds of the family she'd so carelessly torn apart. Last month she'd registered for school.

And there was always Izzy, waiting for Nick at the end of the day with a smile and a picture she'd drawn or a song she had learned. They'd become inseparable. Best buddies. He never took a moment or a word for granted.

During the week, he worked from nine to five; the second his shift was over, he picked up Izzy from the Raintree Day Care, and they were off. They spent all their free time together.

Today, he'd gotten off work three hours ago and their nightly ritual had begun. First, dinner on the porch (lasagna and green salads from Vittorio's), then they quickly washed the dishes together.

Now, Nick sat cross-legged on the cold plank floor, staring down at the multicolored Candy Land game board. There were three little pieces at the starting box, a red, a green, and a blue.

But there are only two of us, Izzy, he'd said when Izzy put the third man down.

That's Annie, Daddy.

Nick watched with a growing sadness as Izzy stoically rolled for Annie and moved her tiny blue piece from square to square.

"Come here, Izzy," he said at last, pushing the game away. She crawled across the floor and settled into his lap, hooking her spindly legs around him. He stared down at her. The words congealed in his throat; how could you tell a little girl to stop believing?

"She's comin' back, Daddy," Izzy said in the high-pitched, certain voice of an innocent.

He stroked her hair. "It's okay to miss her, Sunshine, but you can't keep thinking that she's going to come back. She has another life . . . she always did. We were lucky to have her for as long as we did."

Izzy leaned back into his laced fingers. "You're wrong, Daddy. She's comin' back. So, don't be so sad."

Sad. Such a little word, no more than a breath; it didn't begin to describe the ocean of loss he felt at Annie's absence.

"I love you, Izzy-bear," he whispered.

She planted a kiss on his cheek. "I love you, too, Daddy."

He stared down at her, lying in his arms in her pink flannel jammies with the bunny feet, with her black hair still damp and squiggly around her face, and her big brown eyes blinking up at him with expectation.

He knew then, as he'd known so many times before, that no matter what, he'd always love Annie for what she'd given him.

The air was crisp the next morning, chilly with the promise of fall. The flowers were fading now at the end of summer, and autumn colors—orange and green and scarlet—had replaced the bright hues of August. A cloudy sky cast shadows across the cemetery, where acres of grass rolled gently toward a curtain of evergreen trees. It was well cared for, this final resting place for most of Mystic's citizens.

Nick walked slowly toward the easternmost corner of the cemetery. Izzy was beside him, holding his hand. With each step, he felt his insides tighten, and by the time he reached his destination, his throat was dry and he needed a drink desperately.

He gazed down at the headstone. *Kathleen Marie Delacroix. Beloved Wife and Mother.*

He sighed. Four words to sum up her life. They were the wrong four words; he'd known it at the time, but then he'd been so twisted with grief that he'd let the small, round-faced funeral director handle everything. And in truth, Nick didn't know what other words he would have chosen, even now. How could you possibly express the sum of a person's life in a few words cut into smooth gray stone?

He glanced down at Izzy. "I should have brought you here a long time ago."

Izzy let go of his hand. She reached into her pocket and pulled out a wrinkled sheet of paper. Last night, when he'd told her they were going to come here, Izzy had picked up a piece of paper and her crayons, then she'd gone into her room alone. When she emerged, she held a picture of her mom's favorite flower. *Daddy, I'll give her this. That way she'll know I was visitin' her.*

He had nodded solemnly.

She walked over to the wrought-iron bench and sat down. Smoothing the paper on her lap, she stared at the headstone. "Daddy said I could talk to you, Mommy. Can you hear me?" She drew in a ragged breath. "I miss you, Mommy."

Nick bowed his head, thinking of a dozen things at once, and thinking nothing at all. "Heya, Kath." He waited for her to answer, but, of course, there was nothing except the swaying of the evergreen boughs and the trilling call of a bird.

This place had so little to do with his Kathy. It was why

he hadn't come here before, not since the day they placed her gleaming mahogany casket in a gaping hole in the earth. He couldn't stand to look at the evenly clipped carpet of grass and know that she was below it, his wife who'd always been afraid of the dark and afraid of being alone. . . .

He reached out, touched the cold headstone with the tip of a finger, tracing the etched canal of her name.

"I came to say good-bye, Kath," he said softly, closing his eyes against the sudden sting of tears. His voice broke, and he couldn't speak out loud. *I loved you for most of my life, and I know you loved me, too. What . . . what you did was about something else, something I never could understand. I wanted you to know that I forgive us. We did the best we could. . . .*

He touched the stone again, felt it warm beneath his fingertips, and for a moment—a heartbeat that winged into eternity—he imagined her beside him, her golden hair streaming in the sunlight, her black eyes crinkled in a smile. It was the day Izzy was born, that was the memory that came to him. Kathy sitting up in the hospital bed, her hair all askew, her skin left pale by exhaustion, her pink flannel nightgown buttoned improperly. She had never looked so lovely, and when she looked down at the sleeping infant in her arms, she'd begun softly to cry. "Isabella," she'd said, trying the name on her tongue before she looked up at Nick. "Can we call her Isabella?"

As if Nick could deny her anything. "It's perfect."

Kathy had continued to look at him, while tears streaked down her cheeks. "You'll always take care of her, won't you, Nicky?"

She had known even then the darkness that was coming for her.

But did she know that he loved her, that he had always loved her, and that he always would? She was a part of him, perhaps the biggest part, and sometimes even now, he heard her laughter in the whisper of the wind. Last week, when he'd seen those beautiful white swans across the lake, he stopped and stared and thought, *there they are, Kath . . . they've come back again. . . .*

Izzy slipped her hand in his. "It's okay, Daddy. She knows."

He pulled her into his arms and held her, looking up at the sky through hot, stinging tears. *I have her, Kath—the best part of us—and I'll always be here for her.*

They placed a wicker basket full of blooming chrysanthemums on the grass, then drove home.

"I'm gonna check the garden," Izzy said when they pulled into the driveway.

"Don't be long. It looks like it's going to rain."

Nodding, she got out of the car and made a beeline to the white picket fence. Nick slammed the door shut and headed for the house. Sure enough, it started to rain before he reached the porch.

"Daddy, Daddy, come here, Daddy!"

He turned. She was standing in front of the cherry tree they'd planted last year. She was hopping up and down like an agitated bird, flapping her arms.

He raced across the yard. When he reached her, she looked up at him, grinning, her face washed by rain. "Look, Daddy."

Nick saw what she was pointing at, and slowly he dropped to his knees in the already moist grass.

The cherry tree had produced a single, perfect pink bud.

* * *

Autumn brought color back to Southern California. Brown grass began to turn green. The gray air, swept clean by September breezes, regained its springtime blue. The local radio stations started an endless stream of football chatter. The distant whine of leaf blowers filled the air.

It was the season of sharp, sudden changes: days of bright lemon heat followed by cold, starlit nights. Sleeveless summer shirts were packed away in boxes and replaced by crew-neck sweaters. The birds began one by one to disappear, leaving their nests untended. To the Californians, who spent most of their days in clothes as thin as tissue and smaller than washrags, it began to feel cold. They shivered as the wind kicked up, plucking the last dying red leaves from the trees along the road. Sometimes whole minutes went by without a single car turning toward the beach. The crossroads were empty of tourists, and only the stoutest of spirit ventured into the cool Pacific Ocean at this time of year. The stream of surfers at the state beach had dwindled to a few hardy souls a day.

It was time now to let go. But how did you do that, really? Annie had spent seventeen years trying to protect her daughter from the world, and now all of that protection lay in the love she'd given Natalie, in the words she'd used in their talks, and in the examples she'd provided.

The examples.

Annie sighed, remembering the talk she'd had with Natalie and the disappointment she'd felt in realizing that she hadn't been a good role model. Now it was too late to change all that she'd been and done as a mother. Annie's time was over.

"Mom?" Natalie poked her head into Annie's bedroom.

"Hey, Nana," she answered, trying to inject cheerfulness into her voice. "Come on in."

Natalie climbed onto the bed and stretched out alongside Annie. "I can't believe I'm really going."

Annie put an arm around her daughter. Surely this beautiful creature couldn't be the child who'd once licked the metal ski-chair pole at Mammoth Mountain . . . or the girl who'd climbed into her parents' bed after a nightmare when she was only a year away from being a teenager.

Seventeen years had passed in the blink of an eye. It was too fast. Not long enough . . .

Idly, Annie finger-combed her daughter's long blond hair. She'd been preparing for this day for ages, almost since she'd first dropped Nana off at kindergarten, and still she wasn't ready. "Have I told you today how proud I am of you?"

"Only a billion times."

"Make it a billion and one."

Natalie snuggled closer and pressed a hand to Annie's stomach. "How were the latest stress tests and ultrasounds?"

"Everything shows a healthy baby girl. There's nothing for you to worry about."

"She's lucky to have you for a mom."

Annie laid her hand on Natalie's. There were so many things she wanted to say, on this day when her daughter was embarking on the adventure of her own life, but she knew that she had had her time. Everything of magnitude that was hers to say had been said, and if it hadn't, it was too late now. Still, she wished she could think of one single, flawless bit of advice to hand down like an heirloom to her child.

Natalie leaned against her. "What are you going to do while I'm gone?"

Gone. Such a hard, cold, uncompromising word. It was like *death*, or *divorce*. Annie swallowed. "Miss you?"

Natalie turned to her. "Remember when I was little . . . you always used to ask me what I wanted to be when I grew up?"

"I remember."

"What about you, Mom? What did you used to tell Grandpa Hank when he asked you the same question?"

Annie sighed. How could she make Natalie understand what Annie herself had only figured out this year, after almost forty years of living? Hank had never asked his only daughter that question. He'd been a lonely, lost single father, caught between the decades of Donna Reed and Gloria Steinem, and he had taught his daughter that a woman was defined by the men around her. He had been taught, and so he believed, that girls didn't need dreams for the future—those were for little boys, who would grow up to run businesses and make money.

Annie had made so many mistakes, and most of them had been because she'd planted herself firmly in the middle of the road. But now she knew that life without risk was impossible, and if by chance you stumbled across a safe, serene existence, it was because you'd never really reached for anything in the first place.

At last, Annie had something she wanted to reach for, a risk she wanted to take. She turned to her daughter. "When I was in Mystic, I started thinking about opening my own bookstore. There was a wonderful old Victorian house at the end of Main Street, and the downstairs was vacant."

"That's why you've been reading all those business books."

Annie bit down on her smile and nodded. She felt like a child again, who'd just shown a friend her most precious possession and found that it was as beautiful as she'd imagined. "Yes."

Natalie gave her a slow-building grin. "Way to go, Mom. You'd be *excellent* at that. You could give the Malibu bookstore a run for its money. Maybe I could even work for you in the summers."

Annie looked away. That wasn't part of her dream at all, doing it here, under the watchful, critical eye of her husband. She could just *hear* his comments. . . .

Not like Nick's response.

There was a knock at the door.

Annie tensed. *It's time.* "Come in," she called out.

Blake strode into the room, wearing a black silk suit and a bright smile. "Hey guys. Is Natalie ready? Mrs. Peterson and Sally are here to pick her up."

Annie manufactured a brittle laugh. "I always pictured myself lugging your suitcases up the dorm stairs and unpacking your clothes for you. I wanted you to at least *start* school with your things organized."

"I would have had to call security to get rid of you." Natalie started out laughing and ended up crying.

Annie pulled Natalie into her arms. "I'll miss you, baby."

Natalie clung to her, whispering, "Don't you forget that bookstore while I'm gone."

Annie was the first to draw back, knowing she had to be the one to do it. She touched Natalie's soft cheek, gazed into her precious blue eyes, remembering for the first time in years how they used to be the color of slate. So long ago . . .

"Good-bye, Nana-banana," she whispered.

"I love you, Mom." It wasn't a child's wobbly voice that said the words. It was a young woman, ready at last to be on her own. Sniffling, her smile trembling, Natalie pulled away.

She gave her dad a weak grin. "Okay, Dad. Walk me out."

After they'd turned and walked away, Annie kept watching, as the door slowly clicked shut. She surprised herself by not crying.

Oh, she knew that later, in the long darkness of the night, and in the many days that lay ahead, a new kind of loneliness would creep toward her, loose its silent voice in the echo of this emptier house, but she knew, too, that she would survive. She was stronger than she'd been in March. She was ready to let her eldest daughter go into the world.

"Good-bye, Nana," she whispered.

Annie went into labor in the first week of November. She woke in the middle of the night, with her stomach on fire. The second cramp hit so hard, she couldn't breathe.

She doubled forward. "Oh . . . God . . ." She focused on her own hands, until the pain released her. Clutching her belly, she flung the covers back and clambered out of bed. She started to scream, but another cramp sliced her voice into a pathetic hiss. "Blake—"

He sat upright in bed. "Annie?"

"It's too . . . early," she wheezed, clutching his pajama sleeve. She thought of Adrian and panicked. "Oh, God, it's too early. . . ."

"Jesus." He lurched out of bed and raced for the clothes

that lay heaped over a chair. In a matter of minutes, he had Annie in the car and they were speeding toward the hospital.

"Hang on, Annie. I'll get you to the hospital." He shot her a nervous look. "Just hang on."

She squeezed her eyes shut. *Imagine you're on a white sand beach.*

Another cramp.

"Shit," she hissed. It was impossible. All she could think about was the pain, the red-hot pain that was chewing across her belly, and the life inside her. *Her baby.* She clutched her stomach. "Hold on, baby girl . . . hold on."

But all she saw was Adrian, tiny Adrian, hooked up to a dozen machines, being lowered into the ground in a casket the size of a bread box. . . .

Not again, she prayed silently over and over. *Please God . . . not again.*

The sterile white walls of the hospital's waiting room pressed in on Blake. He paced back and forth, one minute watching the clock, then skimming through some idiotic magazine about celebrities and their infantile problems.

He kept reliving it in his mind. Annie being rushed into the delivery room, her eyes wide with fear, and her voice, broken and braying, saying over and over again, *It's too early.*

Everything had flashed before his eyes in that single, horrifying moment when they'd put her on a gurney and wheeled her away from him. He'd seen his whole marriage in an instant, all the good times and the bad times and the in-between times; he'd seen Annie go from a fresh-faced college sophomore to a pregnant thirty-nine-year-old.

"Mr. Colwater?"

He spun away from the window and saw Annie's obstetrician, Dr. North, standing in the doorway. She wore a crisp white coat and a tired smile. "The baby—"

"How's Annie?"

Dr. North frowned for a second, then said, "Your wife is sleeping peacefully. You may see her now."

He sagged in relief. "Thank God. Let's go." He followed Dr. North down the quiet white hallway to a private room.

Inside, the curtains were drawn and the room lay steeped in bluish shadows. The bed was a narrow, steel-railed thing tucked neatly inside an L-shaped privacy curtain. A bedside table held a telephone and a blue plastic water pitcher with the room number scrawled across the side—as if someone would steal it. Metal IV racks stood alongside the bed like tall, thin vultures, their plastic bags and see-through veins connected to Annie's pale wrists.

She looked young and frail in the strange bed. It brought back a dozen painful memories of his son.

"When will she wake up?" he asked the doctor.

"It shouldn't be long."

Blake couldn't seem to move. He stood in the center of the room, staring at his wife. He'd almost lost her. It was the thought that kept spinning through his head. He'd almost lost her.

He went to the bed and pulled up a chair. He sat there, staring at the woman who'd been his wife for almost twenty years. Dr. North said something—he didn't know what—and then left the room.

After forever—he'd lost track of time—she opened her eyes. "Blake?"

His head snapped up. He saw her sitting up, looking at

him. She looked scared and broken. "Annie," he whispered, reaching for her hand.

"My baby," she said. "How's our little girl?"

Shit. He hadn't even asked. "I'll go find out." He rushed away from her and hurried down the hall. He found Dr. North at the nurses' station, and he dragged her back to Annie's room.

At the doctor's entrance, Annie straightened. She was trying desperately not to cry; Blake could see the effort she was making. "Hi, doctor," she said, swallowing hard.

Dr. North went to Annie, touched her hand. "Your daughter is alive, Annie. She's in neonatal intensive care. There were some complications; she was barely five pounds and developmentally that's a problem. We're worried about—"

"She's alive?"

Dr. North nodded. "She still has a lot of hurdles to overcome, Annie, but she's alive. Would you like to see her?"

Annie clamped a hand over her mouth and nodded. She was crying too hard to answer any other way.

Blake stood aside as the doctor helped Annie into the wheelchair stationed in the corner. Then, feeling left out, he followed them down the hallway and into the neonatal ICU.

Annie sat huddled beside the incubator. Inside the clear plastic sides, the baby lay as still as death, a dozen tubes and needles connected to her thin red arms.

Blake came up beside her and laid a hand on her shoulder.

She looked up at him. "I'd like to call her Kathleen Sarah. Is that okay?"

"Sure." He glanced around—up, down, sideways, anywhere except at the incubator. "I'm going to get us something to eat."

"Don't you want to sit with us?"

He didn't look at the baby. "I . . . can't."

Annie didn't know why she was surprised, or why it hurt so deeply. Blake was no good with tragedy or fear; he never had been. If the emotions couldn't fit in a neat little box, he pretended they didn't exist. She would have to handle this in the way she'd handled every upset in her life: alone. Dully, she nodded. "Fine. Get yourself something. I'm not hungry. Oh, and call Natalie. She'll want to know what's happening."

"Okay."

After he left, she reached through the bagged opening in the incubator's side and held her baby's hand. Though she couldn't feel the skin, she could still remember the velvety softness. She tried not to think about Adrian, and the four futile days she'd sat beside him in a room exactly like this one, mouthing the same useless prayers, crying the same wasted tears.

Katie's hand was so damned small and fragile. Annie tucked her fingers around the minuscule wrist. For the next hour, she talked, hoping that the familiar sound of her voice would soothe her daughter, make her know that even in this brightly lit new world full of needles and breathing machines and strangers, she wasn't alone.

She couldn't have said later what she talked about, what she dredged up from her frightened soul to spill onto that austere, frightening plastic box.

But it didn't take long for the words to dry up, taking the false optimism with them.

Finally, the nurses came and took her away. They

reminded Annie that she needed to keep her strength up, that she needed to sleep and eat. Annie had tried to argue with them—didn't they know that she couldn't? Not while her precious newborn was struggling for every breath of life.

But of course, she went back to her room, climbed back into her narrow, uncomfortable bed, and stared at the blank walls. She called Stanford and talked to Natalie, who had booked a flight for Friday evening—right after her big Oceanography test. Then she'd called both Hank and Terri.

When the calls were done, Annie lost her strength. She kept thinking about those tiny red fists and the legs that looked like strands of spaghetti, and she closed her eyes. The pain in her chest was so great, she wondered if she could withstand it, or if this old heart of hers would simply seize up and die.

Somewhere, a phone rang. The sudden, blaring sound jarred her from her thoughts. Blinking, she glanced around, realized it was the phone beside her bed.

She picked up the phone and answered dully. "Hello?"

"Annie? It's Nick. Your friend Terri called me . . ."

"Nick?" That's all she said—just his name—and the floodgates opened. She couldn't hold it in anymore. "Duh-did Terri tell you about the baby? My beautiful little girl . . . oh, Nick . . ." She sobbed into the telephone. "She only weighs five pounds. Her lungs aren't fully developed. You should see all the needles and . . ." She cried until there were no more tears inside her, until she felt exhausted and drained and inexpressibly old.

"Where are you?"

"Beverly Hills Memorial, but—"

"I'll come right down."

She closed her eyes. "You don't have to do that. I'll be fine, really . . . Blake's here."

There was a long, scratchy silence between them, then finally, Nick said, "You're stronger than you think you are. You can get through this, whatever happens, you can get through it. Just don't forget."

She wiped her eyes. "Forget what?"

"The rain," he said softly. "It's an angel's tears. And every glass you've ever seen is half full. Don't let yourself forget that. I know what it does to a person . . . forgetting that hope is out there."

She almost said, *I love you, Nick,* but she held the words back just in time. "Thanks."

"I love you, Annie Bourne."

It made her want to cry all over again, that soft, quiet reminder of something that was already leaking away. *Colwater,* she wanted to say. *I'm Annie Colwater, and you love a woman who is fading every second.* Instead, she forced a wan, tired smile, thankful that he couldn't see it. "Thank you, Nick," she whispered. "Thank you so much. Tell Izzy I'll call her in a few days, when . . . when I know what's happening."

"We'll be praying for . . . all of you," he said finally.

She sighed, feeling the useless tears start all over again. "Good-bye, Nick."

Chapter 27

It was the middle of the night, but Annie couldn't sleep. Though she was no longer technically a patient, the hospital had given her a room so she could be near Katie. She'd tried reading and eating and writing, anything to take her mind off of Katie, but nothing worked.

She'd spent hours hunched alongside the incubator, reading, singing, praying. She'd expressed milk into a bottle, but when she looked at the creamy-colored liquid, she wondered if her baby would ever get a chance to drink it. Or a chance to grow strong and move out of this sterile world, a chance to grow and start school and snuggle with her mommy. . . .

We'll get through this, she said to herself, straightening her spine, but every time a machine buzzed, Annie thought *this is it, she's stopped breathing.*

Blake had tried to help, in his own way, but it hadn't worked. He'd said, *She'll be okay,* in a quiet voice, over and over again, but when he spoke, his eyes were blank and afraid.

In truth, Annie had been glad when he left the hospital.

I just can't stay here, he'd said.

Okay. That was her answer, and even then, in the quiet darkness, the single word seemed coiled in sorrow and regret.

He'd tried to laugh it off. *I don't have to sleep in a chair to prove my love—do I?*

Of course not, she'd answered, knowing that it was a lie. *Go get Natalie. Her plane lands at nine o'clock.*

He'd jumped on the opportunity, just as she'd known he would. He'd rather be anywhere than in this cold, unfamiliar world where his wife cried all day.

She climbed out of bed and moved slowly to the window. Her stitches hurt, but she welcomed the pain. She leaned forward and pressed her forehead against the window's cold glass. Below, the parking lot was a huge gray square, dotted with a few shadowy black cars.

Finally, she turned away. She'd just gotten back into bed when the phone rang. She picked it up. "Hello?"

"Annie? It's me, Nick."

"Nick." His name came out on a whisper of longing.

"I thought you might need me."

It sounded so simple, those few little words, but they wound around her heart and squeezed. She'd spent a lifetime going through crises alone, always being the strong one, always being in control, and she hadn't realized until just now how much she yearned to be comforted.

"How is she doing?" he asked.

She ran a shaking hand through her short hair. "She's holding on. The neonatologist says she'll be okay if she can just . . . hold on another few weeks. . . ." Quietly, she began to cry again. "I'm sorry, Nick. I'm tired and scared. All I seem to do is cry."

"You want to hear a story?"

She wanted desperately to be whisked away from reality on the wings of his voice. "Yes, please . . ."

"It's about a man who started life as poor white trash, a kid who ate out of Dumpsters and lived in the backseat of an old Impala. After his mom died, the world gave this young boy a singular chance, and he moved to a soggy little town he'd never heard of, where they didn't know about his ugly past. He went to high school there, and he fell in love with two girls. One was the sun and the other was the moon. He was young, and he reached for the moon, figuring it was a safe, quiet place—and he knew that if you reached for the sun it could burn you away to nothing. When his wife died, he lost his soul. He turned his back on his child and his dreams and he crawled into a bottle of booze. All he wanted was to die, but he didn't have the guts."

"Nick, don't . . ."

"So this drunk waited for someone to end his life for him. He waited for someone to take his child away. *Then,* he thought, then he'd have the guts to kill himself. Only none of that happened, because a fairy princess came into his life. He still remembers what it was like that day, the way the rain was just starting to fall and the lake was as still as glass. He remembers everything about the day she came into his life."

"Nick, please . . ." She wanted him to stop, now, before the story spun its gossamer strands around her heart and romanced her beyond repair.

"She changed his world, this woman who wandered uninvited into his life and demanded the very best of him. Before he knew it, he had stopped drinking and he'd taken the first steps toward becoming a parent again, and he'd fallen in love—for the second and last time in his life."

"You're drowning me, Nick," she whispered brokenly.

"I don't mean to. I just wanted to let you know that you aren't alone. Love can rise above tragedy and give us a way home. You taught me that, and now you need me to remind you."

Annie's days bled one into the next in a monotonous flow of hours spent huddled alongside the incubator in a helpless, hopeless confusion. The hospital had given her a new room, so she was always close to Katie, but at night, when she lay alone on her narrow bed, she felt miles away from the people she loved.

She counted the passing of time in little things: Natalie was here on the weekends and at school during the week; Hank showed up unannounced and came daily to the hospital. Terri and Blake both visited each day after work. The clock ticked. Every day, Rosie O'Donnell showed up on the television screen in the corner of the room, and with each new segment, Annie knew that a day had passed. Thanksgiving came and went; they ate pressed turkey and canned gravy off yellow plastic trays in the frighteningly empty cafeteria.

But Annie barely noticed any of it. Sometimes, when she sat beside the incubator, Natalie became Adrian and Adrian became Katie, and in those moments, when Annie closed her eyes, she couldn't see anything except that tiny coffin draped in flowers. But then an alarm would go off, or a nurse would come in, and Annie would remember. With Katie, there was hope.

She talked to her baby constantly. *(I am sitting beside*

you now. Can you feel me? Can you hear my breathing? Can you feel me touching you?)

"Mom?"

Annie wiped her eyes and glanced at the door. Natalie and Hank stood there. Her dad looked ten years older than he was.

"We brought Yahtzee," he said.

Annie smiled tiredly. It must be another week gone by; Natalie was home again. "Hey guys. How did the Psych test go, Nana?"

Natalie pulled up a chair. "That was two weeks ago, Mom, and I already told you I aced it. Remember?"

Annie sighed. She had no memory of that conversation at all. "Oh. Sorry."

Natalie and Hank sat beside the bed and started unpacking the game. They kept up a steady stream of chatter, but Annie couldn't concentrate.

All she could do was stare at the side of her bed. It was where the bassinet belonged, where they put it when the tiny, pink-swaddled baby inside of it was healthy. She remembered that the bassinet had been there with Natalie— and never with Adrian.

Hank leaned toward her, touched her cheek. "She's going to be fine, Annie. You've got to believe that."

"She's gaining weight steadily, Mom. I talked to Mona— you know, the ICU night charge nurse—and she said Katie's a champ."

Annie didn't look at either of them. "She hasn't been held yet . . . does anyone realize that but me?" It plagued her, that thought, kept her up at night. Her baby, stuck full of needles and tubes, had never felt the comfort of her mommy's arms, had never been soothed to sleep by a lullaby. . . .

"She will, Mom," Natalie said, squeezing her wrist. "She's going to be fine. Maybe—"

There was a knock at the door, and Dr. North pushed through the opening. Dr. Overton, the neonatologist, was standing beside her, wearing green surgical scrubs.

Annie's heart stopped at the sight of them. Blindly, she reached out for Natalie's hand, squeezing the slim fingers until she could feel the birdlike bones shift. Hank shot to his feet and squeezed Annie's shoulder.

"Oh, God," she whispered.

The door opened again and a stout, white-clad nurse named Helena swept into the room on a tide of rustling polyester. In her arms she held a small pink-swaddled bundle.

Dr. North came to the end of the bed. "Would you like to hold your daughter?"

"Would I—" Annie couldn't seem to draw a solid breath. She hadn't believed in this moment; hoped, yes, but she hadn't really believed. She'd been afraid to believe; afraid that if she believed and lost, she would never find the surface again.

Unable to say anything, she reached out.

The nurse moved toward her and placed her daughter in Annie's arms.

The newborn smell filled her nostrils, at once familiar and exotic. She peeled back the pink blanket and stroked her daughter's forehead, marveling at the softness of the skin.

Katie's rosebud mouth puckered and yawned, and a little pink fist shot out from the blanket. Smiling, cooing, Annie peeled back the cotton fabric and stared down at her little girl, dressed in a tiny doll's diaper. A network of blue veins crisscrossed her pale chest and dappled her thin arms and legs.

Katie opened her mouth and made an angry squeaking sound.

Annie's breasts tingled; moisture seeped through her nightgown. Quickly, she untied her gown and eased Katie toward the nipple. There was a moment of fumbling around, a few repositionings, and then Katie latched on.

"Oh, Katie," she whispered, stroking her daughter's soft, soft head, laughing quietly at the miracle of it all. "Welcome home."

The first days home were crazy. Hank and Terri hovered beside Annie, demanding to help, refusing to take no for an answer. They decorated the house for Christmas, dragging box after box from the attic and squealing as each new treasure was found. They put up a ten-foot tree in the living room and proceeded to add an obsessive number of gifts beneath it. Natalie called home between every class and asked how Katie was doing. Annie couldn't handle it all, not when all she wanted to do was stare at the miracle of her child. At last, Hank went home—but only after he vowed to return at Christmas.

Alone again, Blake and Annie tried to find their way back to the familiar routine, but it wasn't as easy as before. Annie spent all her time huddled on the sofa with Katie, and Blake spent more and more time at the office.

In the third week of December, Hank met Natalie at the San Francisco airport, and they flew down to LAX together. The family shared a tense, quiet holiday dinner that only reminded Annie of how shredded their relationships had become. Even opening the presents on Christmas morning had been a subdued affair.

Hank watched Blake every minute. Annie had heard the questions he jabbed at her husband: *Where are you going? Why won't you be home tonight? Have you spoken to Annie about that?*

Annie had known that Blake felt like a stranger in his own home. Natalie watched him warily, waiting for him to pick up Katie, but he never did. Annie understood; she'd been through it before. Blake simply wasn't one who fell head-over-heels in love with newborns. They frightened and confused him, and he was not a man who liked either emotion. But Natalie didn't understand that, and Annie saw her daughter's disappointment again and again as she handed her baby sister to their father, only to watch Blake shake his head and turn away.

Now, Annie lay huddled along the mattress's edge. Beside her, Blake was stretched out, one arm flung her way, one knee cocked against her hip, hogging the bed in his characteristic fashion. She could hear his breathing; the rhythmic score had accompanied her own sleep for so many years.

She gently peeled out of the bed and went to the French doors, opening them. Sheer white silk curtains billowed with night's breath along her bare leg.

She woke so often, alone, desperate to reach out for comfort in the darkness, but there was no comfort in her marriage. Oh, they'd tried, each of them in their own way. Him, with gifts and promises and quiet conversations about things that mattered to Annie; her, with brittle smiles and rented movies and elegant dinners for two. But it wasn't working. They were like butterflies caught on separate sides of a window, each trying with fluttered desperation to break through the glass.

With a tired sigh, Blake pushed the Dictaphone aside and shoved the depositions back into their folder. He was having trouble concentrating lately, and his work was beginning to suffer. Katie only slept a few hours at a time, and whenever she woke up, crying or whimpering, Blake couldn't get back to sleep.

He got to his feet and poured himself a scotch. Swirling the amber liquid around in the Waterford tumbler, he walked to the window and stared outside. The city was a blurry wash of January gray. A few ragged New Year's decorations swung forgotten from the streetlights.

He didn't want to go home to his strangely unfamiliar wife and his squalling newborn daughter. As he'd expected, Annie's whole existence revolved around the baby's needs. There was no time left for Blake, and when she did finally get the child to sleep, Annie stumbled blindly to bed, too exhausted for anything beyond a quick peck on the cheek and a mumbled *good night*.

He was too damned old to be a father again. He'd been no good at it when he was young, and he had even less interest now.

There was a knock at the door.

Blake set the glass down. "Come in."

The door swung open and Tom Abramson and Ted Swain, two of Blake's partners, stood in the opening. "Hey, bud—it's six-thirty," Ted said with a wicked grin. "What do you say we head on down to the bar and celebrate the Martinson decision?"

Blake knew he should say no. In the back of his mind

was the thought that he had something to do at home, but he couldn't for the life of him remember what it was.

"Sure," he said, reaching for his coat. "But just one. I have to get home."

"No problem," Tommy said. "We've all got families."

It was true, of course. All three of them had wives and children at home, waiting for them. But somehow they were still at the bar at eleven o'clock that night, laughing and shouting and clanking toasts.

Ted went home at eleven-thirty, and Tom followed him out. That left Blake, sitting alone on the bar stool. He'd told his friends that he wanted to finish his drink, but the truth was, he'd been nursing the same cocktail for about an hour. He kept looking at the door, thinking, *I should go;* then he'd think of that big bed at home, and the way his wife slept huddled along the mattress's edge, and he stayed where he was.

Annie had set the table beautifully. Candlelight flickered above the Battenberg lace cloth, casting slippery shadows on the sterling silver dishes that held all of Natalie's favorite dishes: homemade macaroni and cheese, hot crescent rolls with honey and butter, and corn on the cob. There was a small stack of multicolored, foil-wrapped presents at one end of the table, and bright, helium-filled balloons were tied above each chair.

Tonight was Natalie's eighteenth birthday party, and they were all coming together to celebrate. Annie was determined to fit this family back into its groove, at least for these few hours.

Annie glanced once again at the table, her critical eye missing no detail. Hank came up beside her, put an arm around her shoulder and drew her close. Through the open archway to the kitchen, they could hear Natalie and Terri laughing. Annie leaned against her dad. "I'm glad you could come down for the holidays, Dad. It means a lot to Natalie and me."

"I wouldn't miss it for the world." He glanced around. "So, where's that busy husband of yours? We're ready to party."

"He's only fifteen minutes late. For Blake, that's nothing. I told him six-thirty so he'd be here by seven."

Slowly, Hank withdrew his arm. Turning slightly, he went to the window that overlooked the driveway.

She followed him. "Dad?"

It was a full minute before he spoke, and then his voice was softer than she'd ever heard it. "When you first brought Blake home, I was impressed. Sure, he was young and skinny and poor, but I could see the man emerging inside him. He was what every father dreams of for his daughter, intelligent and ambitious. Not like the boys I knew in Mystic. I thought to myself, now here's a boy who will take care of my little girl—"

"I know the story, Dad. . . ."

He turned to her. "I was wrong, wasn't I?"

She frowned. "What do you mean?"

"What you'd brought home was just someone else for you to take care of." He frowned. "I should have worried about your heart instead of your financial comfort. If your mother had been alive . . . she would have known what to look for. It's just that I wanted you to have better than I could give you."

"I know, Dad."

"It . . ." His voice trembled and he wouldn't meet her

gaze. "It hurts me to see how you are now. Last spring you were so happy. I miss hearing you laugh. I think . . . when you were in Mystic, I gave you some bad advice. Hell, I gave you bad advice your whole life. I should have told you that you'd make a wonderful bookseller. I should have been telling you that kind of thing for years." He turned to her at last. "I should have told you that you were the smartest, most talented, most incredibly gifted person I've ever known . . . and that I was proud of you. That's what your mama would have said."

"Oh, Daddy . . ." Annie knew that if she tried to say anything more, she'd start to cry.

"A dad . . . he teaches responsibility and accountability, but a mom . . . ah, a mom teaches her child to dream, to reach for the stars and to believe in fairy tales. At least, that's what Sarah would have given you. But me? What does an uneducated old millworker like me know about fairy tales and possibilities and dreams?" He sighed, and when he looked at her there were tears in his eyes. "I wish I had it to do over again, Annie Virginia. . . ."

She stepped into her father's big, strong arms and clung to him. "I love you, Dad," she whispered against his warm neck.

When she finally drew back, her mascara was running down her face. She grinned. "I must look like something out of the *Rocky Horror Picture Show.* I'd better run to the bathroom and freshen up."

She spun away and hurried through the kitchen. She passed Terri and Natalie, who were busy arranging candles on the cake.

Natalie looked up. "Are you okay?"

Annie nodded. "Fine. My mascara is bothering me."

"Is Dad home yet?"

"I'm going to try his car phone right now. He's probably pulling up the driveway."

Above Natalie's head, Terri shot Annie an irritated look. Annie shrugged helplessly and went to the phone, punching in Blake's cellular number. It didn't even ring; it just patched her through to his voice mail.

Annie turned, faced their expectant looks. "He's not in the car."

They waited another forty minutes for Blake, and then by tacit consent, they started the party without him. They came together at the table, the adults talking furiously to cover the awkwardness and disappointment. Still, the empty chair at the head of the table couldn't be ignored.

Annie forced a bright smile all through the meal. Terri regaled them with funny anecdotes about life on the soaps—and death in the air—until everyone was laughing. After dinner, they sat around the fireplace and opened gifts.

At ten o'clock, Terri reluctantly went home. She hugged Natalie tightly, then held Annie's hand as they walked to the front door. "He's a real shithead," she whispered furiously.

There was no point in answering. Annie hugged her friend and said good-bye, and then walked slowly back to the living room.

Hank rose immediately. "I think I'll go to bed. Us old guys need our beauty sleep." He squeezed Natalie's shoulder and bent to kiss her cheek. "Happy birthday, honey." Straightening, he threw Annie a frustrated look and strode from the room.

Silence fell.

Natalie went to the window. Annie came up beside her. "I'm sorry, Nana. I wish I could change it."

"I don't know why I keep expecting him to be different. . . ."

"He loves you. It's just . . ." Words failed Annie. She'd said the same tired thing too many times and she couldn't even pretend tonight that it made a difference.

She turned to Annie. "What good does his love do me?"

The softly spoken question raised a red, stinging welt on Annie's heart. "It's his loss, Natalie."

Natalie's eyes filled slowly, heartbreakingly, with tears. "When I was a little girl, I used to pretend that he wasn't my real dad. Did you know that?"

"Oh, Nana . . ."

"Why do you stay with him?"

Annie sighed. She wasn't up to this conversation. Not tonight. "You're young and passionate, honey. Some day you'll understand. Obligations and commitments build up around you—sort of like plaque. You have to do the right thing. I have other people to think about."

Natalie snorted. "I may be young and passionate, but you're naive, Mom. You always have been. Sometimes *I* feel like the grown-up around you. You always think everything will work out for the best."

"I used to think that. Not so much anymore."

Natalie's gaze was solemn. "You should have heard yourself last spring, Mom. You sounded so . . . happy. Now, I know why. He wasn't around, making you jump every time he came into the room and scurry around to do his bidding."

It took Annie a second to find her voice, and when she did it was soft and hurting. "Is that how you see me?"

"I see you for who you are, Mom. Someone who loves with all her heart and will do anything to make us happy. But last spring, something made *you* happy."

Annie swallowed past the lump in her throat. She turned away, before Natalie could see the moisture gathering in her eyes.

"Tell me about Izzy. I bet you fixed her right up."

"Izzy." Although Annie knew it was opening the door on her pain, she let herself remember. Her thoughts scrolled back to the garden, to a handful of straggling shasta daisies, and a small, black-gloved hand. "She was something, Natalie. You would have loved her."

"And what about him?"

Annie turned slowly back to Natalie. "Who?"

"Izzy's dad."

"He's an old friend of mine from high school." Annie could hear the way her voice softened, and though she knew it was dangerous, she couldn't change it. She smiled at a memory. "He was the first boy I ever kissed."

"There it is again, Mom."

Annie frowned. "There's what?"

"That voice. It's the way you sounded while I was in London. Is he part of what made you happy, Mom?"

Annie felt vulnerable and exposed, a woman walking out on a thin, rickety bridge. She couldn't tell her daughter the truth. Perhaps someday, when the bridge of their years had brought Natalie to full womanhood, when she'd seen something more of life and love. When she could understand. "A lot of things made me happy in Mystic."

It was a long minute before Natalie spoke. "Maybe he and Izzy can come down here some time. Or maybe you and I can visit them."

"No," Annie said softly. She wanted to say something more, tack an excuse onto the simple word that seemed to make no sense. But she couldn't manage it. Instead, she pulled Natalie into her arms and squeezed tightly. "I'm sorry your dad forgot your birthday."

Natalie sniffled. "You're the one I feel sorry for."

"How come?"

"In eighteen years you'll be saying the same thing to Katie."

Chapter 28

Some time around midnight, a woman walked up to Blake. She was wearing a skintight black catsuit with a huge silver belt and black stiletto heels. With an easy smile, she sat down next to him. She tapped a long finger-nail on the bar. "Vodka martini—two olives," she said to the bartender.

In the background, a throaty Dwight Yoakam song came on, something about the pocket of a clown.

The woman turned to him. Nibbling on her olive, she asked him to dance.

Blake pushed off the bar stool and stumbled back from her, putting as much distance as he could between them. "Sorry," he mumbled. "I'm married."

But he didn't turn away; he couldn't. He stood there like a man possessed, staring at the woman. He couldn't help wondering how those breasts would feel in his hands—the young, solid breasts of a woman who'd never had children, the small, pink nipples that had never nursed a baby.

At that, Blake felt something inside him shift and give way. He realized the truth, the one he'd been denying for

ON MYSTIC LAKE 387

months. He loved Annie, but it wasn't enough. He'd cheat on her. Maybe not tonight, maybe not even this year; but sooner or later, he'd slide back into his old routine. It was only a matter of time.

And when he did, he would be lost again. There was nothing on earth lonelier than a man who betrayed his wife on a regular basis. Blake knew how seductive it was—the temptation to possess a stranger, make love in the middle of the night with a nameless woman. But afterward, it left him broken somehow, ashamed of himself and unable to meet his wife's gaze.

Shaken, he turned away from the woman in the catsuit and left the bar. He drove home and parked in the garage. Tiredly, he went into the dark, cool house. Without bothering to flick on any lights, he headed through the kitchen.

He found Annie waiting for him in the living room. She was sitting on the sofa, with her feet tucked up underneath her. "Hello, Blake," she said in a soft, tired voice that seemed to cut through his heart.

He stopped dead. For no reason at all, he thought she'd seen him tonight, that she knew what he'd almost done. "Hey, Annie," he said, forcing a smile.

"You're late."

"A bunch of us went to the sports bar on Fourth. We won a big settle—"

"It was Natalie's birthday party tonight."

Blake winced. "Oh. *Shit*. I forgot to mark it on my office calendar."

"I'm sure she'll love that answer."

"You should have called to remind me."

"Don't turn it on me, Blake. You're the one who screwed up. You can remember when a client owes an alimony

check, but you forget your daughter's eighteenth birthday."
She sighed. "You should go see her now—I'll bet she's still
awake."

"She's probably tired. . . ."

"She deserves an explanation."

He turned and moved to the elegant stone table that
hugged the wall, staring at his own reflection in a gilt-
framed mirror. "Natalie's angry with me," he said softly.
"When she was in London, I didn't call her. I sent flowers
every week. A girl loves to get flowers, that's what Suz . . ."
He realized what he was going to say and clamped his
mouth shut.

"Suzannah was wrong," Annie said tiredly, reading his
thoughts. "A seventeen-year-old girl needs a lot more than
flowers from her father's secretary every Friday."

He ran a hand through his hair. "Without you, I was . . .
lost with Natalie. I kept thinking I should call, and then a
deposition or a court date would come up, and I'd forget.
I'll make it all up to her, though, even tonight."

He turned back to Annie. Now she was on her feet. She
stood a few feet away, her arms crossed. In a pair of ratty
sweats and a UW sweatshirt that had seen better days, she
looked more like a runaway teen than his wife. "I'll get her
a laptop."

"She'll be leaving for school on Sunday. We won't see
her again until spring break, and soon . . . we won't be
seeing much of her at all. She'll find her own place in the
world and she won't be coming home to us as much."

Us. He tried to take courage from that single, simple word,
but he couldn't quite manage it. "So, what do I say to her?"

"I don't know."

"Of course you do. You always—"

"No more. If you're going to forge a relationship with your daughter, it's up to you. No more Cliffs Notes on the situation from me."

"Come on—"

"Who's her boyfriend, Blake?"

"She doesn't have one."

"Really? That will come as something of a surprise to Brian. And what does she want to study in school?"

It was hard to think with her looking at him that way. "Law, like me. She wants to be a partner in the firm some day."

"Really? When did you last discuss it?"

"Last year?" It came out as a question, and at her look, he knew it was wrong. "Two years ago?"

"Really?"

She kept throwing that word at him like a dart. He felt like a man reaching for a lifeline that was just beyond his grasp. At last he gave up trying to lie and told the truth. "I don't know."

Annie's face softened at the admission. "You have to talk to her, Blake. But mostly you have to listen." She gave him a smile that was as sad as it was familiar. "And we both know you're listening-impaired."

"Okay. I'll go talk to her."

He said the words, softly and in exactly the right tone of voice, but they both knew the truth. They'd had this same discussion a hundred times before, with Annie begging him to spend time with Natalie.

They both knew he'd never quite get around to doing it.

On the last day of January, Terri showed up bright and early, holding a bottle of Moët & Chandon and a bag of croissants. "When a woman turns forty," she said brightly, "she should begin drinking early in the day. And before you start whining about nursing and alcohol in the breast milk, let me reassure you that the champagne is for me and the croissants are for you."

They sat together on the big wooden deck. The hot tub bubbled gently beside them.

"So," Terri said, sipping her champagne. "You look like shit, you know."

"Thanks a lot. I hope you'll come by to celebrate my fiftieth birthday—when I *really* need cheering up."

"You're not sleeping."

Annie winced. It was true. She hadn't slept well in weeks. "Katie's been fighting a cold."

"Ah," Terri said knowingly, "so Katie's the problem."

"No . . . not really, Dr. Freud." Annie glanced out at the glittering surface of the sea, watching the white-tipped waves lick gently at the sand. She didn't have to close her eyes to see another place, a place where winters were real. There, nature would have reclaimed its rain forest. The tourists would be long gone, driven away by the swift and sudden darkness that came with winter. There would be alpine mountainsides where the snow was five feet deep, where tiny purple flowers would still bloom amid the whiteness, against all the laws of nature. Deep in the woods, where the land had never been damaged by human hands, the trees would seem to draw closer together, creating a curtain of black tinged only occasionally with the faintest hint of green. In the middle of the day, it would be dark, and not even the brightest winter sun would make it to the cold, frosted forest floor. Anyone crazy enough, or desperate enough, to venture into that gray and black wilderness this time of year would be lost forever.

Annie longed to see it now, to feel the crisp winter air on her cheeks. She wanted to bundle up in layers and layers of clothing and lie in the snow, to make angels with her arms and legs while she watched her breath puff into the silver air.

"Why do you stay with him?"

Annie sighed. She had known the question was coming; she'd expected it every day since the fiasco of Natalie's birthday party. It was the same thing she asked herself at night, as she lay in her bed, beside her husband, unable to sleep.

She thought so often about Natalie, grown now and on her own, and Katie, with so many years before her. At those times, achingly lonely, she would stare into the darkness of her own life, searching for some dim reflection of herself. And when she looked back, she saw a skinny, brown-haired girl who'd done what was expected of her, always.

She missed the woman she'd become on the shores of Mystic Lake, the one who dared to dream of her own bookstore, and learned to wager her heart on a game as risky as love. She missed Nick and Izzy and the family they'd quilted together from the scraps of their separate lives.

It was the kind of family Annie had always dreamed of . . . the kind of family Katie deserved. . . .

Did you know I have no memories of Dad?

Terri touched her shoulder. "Annie? You're crying. . . ."

She'd been holding it in for too long, pretending that

everything was okay, pretending that everyone mattered but her. She couldn't hold it in anymore.

"I matter," she said quietly.

"Well, praise God," Terri whispered and pulled Annie into her arms. Annie let herself be held and rocked by her best friend.

"I can't live this way anymore."

"Of course you can't."

Annie eased back, shakily pushing the grown-out hair away from her eyes. "I don't want some day to hear Katie tell me that she has no memories of her dad, either."

"And what about *you,* Annie?"

"I deserve more than this . . . Blake and I don't share anything anymore. Not even the miracle of our two children."

It was the truth she'd been avoiding all these months. Their love was gone, simply gone, extinguished as cleanly as candlelight, with the sooty scent of smoke the only reminder that it had ever burned at all. She couldn't even remember those days, long ago, when they had been in love.

She couldn't help grieving for the loss of that fire, and she was as much to blame as he. She'd spent a lifetime in the shadows, too afraid of failure or abandonment to reach for even the light of a single candle. Their marriage was what they together had created—and that was the saddest truth of all.

Blake wasn't happy, either. Of that she had no doubt. He wasn't ready to let go of Annie quite yet, but the Annie he wanted was Annalise Bourne Colwater, the woman she'd become after years and years of living in a rut of their combined creation.

He wanted back what couldn't be had.

* * *

Faint strains of music came from the bedroom speakers. Blake stood in front of the baby's bassinet, staring down at the tiny infant swaddled in pink.

He reached into his pocket and withdrew a slim black velvet box. His finger traced the soft fabric as he remembered a dozen gifts he'd given Annie in the past, presents on Christmas mornings, on anniversaries, on birthdays.

Always, he'd given her what he thought she should have. Like her wedding ring. On their tenth anniversary he'd bought her the three-carat diamond solitaire, not because she wanted it—Annie was perfectly happy with the gold band they'd bought when it was all they could afford—but because it made Blake look good. Everyone who saw his wife's ring knew that Blake was a successful, wealthy man.

He'd never given her what she needed, what she wanted. He'd never given her himself.

"Blake?"

At the sound of her voice, soft and tentative, he turned around. She stood in the open archway, wearing a beautiful blue silk robe he'd given her years ago, and she looked incredibly lovely.

"We need to talk," she said.

Steeling himself, he moved toward her. "I know."

She stared up at him, and for a second, all he wanted to do was hold her so tightly that she could never leave him again. But he'd learned that holding too tightly was as harmful as never reaching out at all. "I have something for you. A birthday present." He held the box out to her. It lay in his palm like a black wound.

Tentatively, still staring up at him, she took the box and

opened it. On a bed of ice-blue silk lay a glittering gold bracelet. The name *Annie* was engraved across the top.

"Oh, Blake," she whispered, biting down on her lower lip.

"Turn it over," he said.

She eased the bracelet from the box, and he saw that her hands were trembling as she turned it over and read the inscription on the underside.

I will always love you.

She looked up at him, her eyes moist. "It's not going to work, Blake. It's too late."

"I know," he whispered, hearing the unmanly catch in his voice and not caring. Maybe if he'd cared less about things like that in the past, he wouldn't be standing here, saying good-bye to the only woman who'd ever truly loved him. "I wish . . ." He didn't even know what he wished for. That she had been different? That he had? That they'd seen this truth a long time ago?

"Me, too," she answered.

"Will you . . . remember the words on that bracelet?"

"Oh, Blake, I don't need a bracelet to remember how much I loved you. You were my life for more than twenty years. Whenever I look back, I'll think of you." Tears streaked in silvery lines down her cheeks. "What about Katie?"

"I'll support her, of course. . . ."

He could tell that she was hurt by his answer. "I don't mean money."

He moved toward her, touched her cheek. He knew what she wanted from him right now, but it wasn't really in his power to give. It never had been, that was part of their problem. He wouldn't be there for Katie, any more than he'd been there for Natalie. Suddenly, he grieved for all of it. For the good times and the bad, for the roads not taken and the lives that had carelessly grown apart. Sadly, he gazed down at her. "Do you want me to lie to you?"

She shook her head. "No."

Slowly, he pulled her into his arms. He held her close, knowing he'd carry this image in his heart for as long as he lived. "I guess it's really over," he whispered into her sweet-smelling hair. After a long moment, he heard her answer, a quiet, shuddering little "Yes."

Natalie's dorm room was cluttered with memorabilia from London. Pictures of new friends dotted her desk, mingled with family photos and piles of homework. The metal-framed twin bed was heaped with expensive Laura Ashley bedding, and at the center was the pink pillow Annie had embroidered a lifetime ago, the one that read: A PRINCESS SLEEPS HERE.

Natalie sat cross-legged on the bed, her long, unbound hair flowing around her shoulders. Already she looked nervous and worried—a normal teenage response to *both* parents flying up to see you at college.

Annie wished there were some way to break the news of their divorce without words, a way to silently communicate the sad and wrenching truth.

Blake stood in the corner of the room. He looked calm and at ease—his courtroom face—but Annie could see nervousness in the jittery way he kept glancing at his watch.

Annie knew this was up to her; there was no use putting it off any longer. She went to the bed and sat down beside Natalie. Blake took a few hesitant steps toward them and then stopped in the middle of the room.

Natalie looked at Annie. "What is it, Mom?"

"Your dad and I have something to tell you." She took Natalie's hand in hers, stared down at the slender fingers, at the tiny red birthstone ring they'd given her on her sixteenth birthday. It took an effort to sit straight-backed and still. She took a deep breath and plunged ahead. "Your dad and I are getting a divorce."

Natalie went very still. "I guess I'm not surprised." Her voice was tender, and in it, Annie heard the echo of both the child Natalie had once been and the woman she was becoming.

Annie stroked her daughter's hair, untangling it with her fingers like she used to when Natalie was little. "I'm sorry, honey."

When Natalie looked up, there were tears in her eyes. "Are you okay, Mom?"

Annie felt a warm rush of pride for her daughter. "I'm fine, and I don't want you to worry about anything. We haven't worked out all the details yet. We don't know where we'll each be living. Things like addresses and vacations and holidays are all up in the air. But I know one thing. We'll always be a family—just a different kind. I guess now you'll have two places in the world where you belong, instead of only one."

Natalie nodded slowly, then turned to her father.

Blake moved closer, kneeling in front of Natalie. For once, he didn't look like a three-hundred-fifty-dollar-an-hour lawyer. He looked like a scared, vulnerable man. "I've made some mistakes. . . ." He glanced at Annie and gave her a hesitant smile, then turned back to Natalie. "With your mom and with you. I'm sorry, Sweet Pea." He touched her cheek.

Tears leaked from Natalie's eyes. "You haven't called me that since I fell off the jungle gym in third grade."

"There are a lot of things I haven't said—or done—in years. But I want to make up for lost time. I want to do things together—if that's okay with you."

"*Phantom of the Opera* is coming to town in May. Maybe we could go?"

He smiled. "I'd love to."

"You mean it this time? I should buy two tickets?"

"I mean it," he said, and the way he said it, Annie believed him. Of course, she always believed him.

Slowly, Blake got to his feet and drew back.

"We're still going to be a family," Annie said, tucking a flyaway strand of hair behind Natalie's ear. "We'll always be a family." She looked at Blake and smiled.

It was true. Blake would always be a part of her, always be her youth. They'd grown up together, fallen in love and built a family together; nothing would ever erase that connection. A piece of paper and a court of law couldn't take it all away—it could only take what they were willing to give up, and Annie was going to hold on to all of it, the good, the bad, the in-between. It was part of them. It made them who they were.

She reached out. He took her hand in his, and together they drew around Natalie, enfolding her in their arms. When Natalie was little, they'd called this a "family hug," and Annie couldn't help wondering why they'd ever stopped.

She heard the soft, muffled sound of her daughter's crying and knew it was one of the regrets that would be with her always.

*   *   *

It was like going back in time. Once again, Annie and Blake were strolling through the Stanford campus. Of course, this time Annie was forty years old and as much of her life lay behind her as lay ahead . . . and she was pushing a stroller.

"It's weird to be back here," Blake said.

"Yeah," she said softly.

They'd spent the whole day with Natalie, being more of a family in one afternoon than they'd been in many of the previous years, but now it was time to go their separate ways. Annie had driven the Cadillac up here, and Blake had flown in, renting a car to get to the campus.

At Annie's car, they stopped. Annie bent down and unstrapped Katie from the stroller.

"What will you do now?" he asked.

Annie paused. It was the same question he'd asked her when Natalie had left home last spring. Then, it had terrified her. Now, these many months later, the same words opened a door, through which Annie glimpsed a world of possibilities. "I don't know. I still have tons to do at the house. Twenty years has to be sorted and catalogued and packed away. I know I want to sell the house. It's not . . . me anymore." She straightened, looking at him. "Unless you want it?"

"Without you? No."

Annie glanced around, a little uncertain as to what to say. This was the fork in the road of their lives; after all these years, he would go one way and she another. She had no idea when she would see him again. Probably at the lawyer's office, where they'd become a cliché—a cordial, once-married couple coming in as separate individuals to sign papers. . . .

Blake stared down at her. There was a faraway sadness in his eyes that made her move closer to him. In a soft voice, he asked, "What will you tell Katie about me?"

Annie heard the pain in his voice, and it moved her to touch his cheek. "I don't know. The old me would have fabricated an elaborate fiction to avoid hurting her feelings." She laughed. "Maybe I'd have told her you were a spy for the government and contacting us would endanger your life. But now . . . I don't know. I guess I'll cross that bridge when I come to it. But I won't lie to her."

He turned his head and looked away. She wondered what he was thinking, whether it was about lying, and how much it had cost him over the years. Or if it was about the daughter he had lived with for eighteen years and didn't know, or the daughter he'd hardly lived with at all, and now would never know. Or if it was the future, all the days that lay ahead for a man alone, the quiet of a life that included no child's laughter. She wondered if he'd realized yet that when he was an old, old man, when his hair had turned white and his eyes had grown coated with cataracts, that he would have no grandchildren to bounce on his knee, no daughter to kneel in the grass beside his wheelchair and reminisce about the time-worn antics of the past. Unless he reached out now, in the days that mattered, he would learn that some roads could not be refound and that true love took time and effort . . . that a life lived in the glare of summer sunlight never produced a rainbow.

"Will you miss me?" he asked, finally looking at her again.

Annie gave him a sad smile. "I'll miss who we used to be—I already do. And I'll miss who we could have been."

His eyes filled slowly with tears. "I love you, Annie."

"I'll always love the boy I fell in love with, Blake. Always . . ."

She moved toward him, pressing up on her toes to kiss him. It was the kind of kiss they hadn't shared in years; slow, and tender, and heartfelt. There was no undercurrent of sexuality in it. It was everything a kiss was supposed to be, an expression of pure emotion—and they had let it go so easily in their life together. She couldn't remember when kisses had become something perfunctory and meaningless. Maybe if they had kissed this way every day, they wouldn't be here now, standing together in the middle of the Stanford campus, saying good-bye to a commitment that had been designed to last forever.

When Blake drew back, he looked sad and tired. "I guess I screwed up pretty badly."

"You'll get another chance, Blake. Men like you always do. You're handsome and rich; women will stand in line to give you another chance. What you do with that chance is up to you."

He ran a hand through his hair and looked away. "Hell, Annie. We both know I'll screw that up, too."

She laughed. "Probably."

They stared at each other for a long minute, and in that time, Annie saw the arc of their love; the bright and shining beginning of it, all those years ago, and the way it had eroded, one lonely night at a time for years.

Finally, Blake checked his watch. "I have to go. My plane leaves at six o'clock." He bent down to the stroller and gave Katie a last, fleeting kiss. When he drew back up, he gave Annie a weak smile. "This is hard. . . ."

She hugged him, one last time, then slowly she drew back. "Have a safe flight."

He nodded and turned away from her. He got into his rented car and drove away.

She stood there watching him until the car disappeared. She had expected to feel weighed down by sadness at this moment, but instead she felt almost buoyant. Last week she had done what she'd never thought she could do: she'd traveled alone. Just for fun. She'd given Katie to Terri for the day—complete with two sheets of instructions and a shelf full of expressed milk—and then Annie had just started to drive. Before she'd even realized where she was going, she'd arrived at the Mexican border. A flash of fear had almost stopped her as the rickety red bus pulled up to the curb, but she hadn't let it own her. She'd boarded the bus with all the other tourists and ridden into Mexico. All by herself.

The day had been wonderful, magical. She'd walked down the dingy, overcrowded streets, eating *churros* from the stands along the way. At lunchtime, she'd found a seat at a restaurant and eaten unrecognizable food and loved every bite, and as night had begun to fall and the neon sputtered to life, she'd understood why she'd always been afraid of traveling alone. It changed a person somehow— wasn't that the point, after all? To go to a wildly different place and learn that you could negotiate for a silly trinket in a foreign language, and then to hold that item a little closer to your heart because it represented something of your self. Each peso she'd saved had somehow become an expression of how far she'd come. And when she finally had returned home that night, dragging her tired body up the stairs, snuggling up with her cranky daughter in her big king-size bed, she'd known that finally, at forty years of age, she had begun.

"Come on, Katie Sarah. Let's go." She picked up her almost-sleeping daughter and strapped her into the car seat in the back of the Cadillac. Then, throwing her clunky diaper bag onto the passenger seat, she climbed into the car and started the engine. Before she even pulled out, she flicked on the radio and found a station she liked. Humming along with Mick Jagger, she maneuvered onto the highway and nudged the engine to seventy miles per hour.

What will you do now?

She still had months of responsibilities in Southern California. Closing and selling the house, packing everything up, deciding where she wanted to live and what she wanted to do. She didn't have to work, of course, but she didn't want to fall into that life-of-leisure trap again. She *needed* to work.

She thought again about the bookstore in Mystic. She certainly had the capital to give it a try—and that Victorian house on Main Street had plenty of room for living upstairs. She and Katie could be very comfortable up there, just the two of them.

Mystic.

Nick. Izzy.

The love she felt for them was as sharp as broken glass. Sometimes, when she woke in the middle of the night, she reached out for Nick—only he wasn't there, and in those quiet moments the missing of him was an actual pain in her chest.

She knew she would go to him again when her life was

in order; she had planned it endlessly in the past few weeks.

She would buy herself a convertible and drive up Highway 101 along the wild beaches, with her hair whipping about her face. She would play show tunes and sing at the top of her lungs, free at last to do as she pleased. She would drive when the sun was high in the sky and keep going as the stars began to shimmer overhead. She would show up without warning and hope it was not too late.

It would be springtime when she went to him, in that magical week when change was in the air, when everything smelled fresh and new.

She would show up on his porch one day, wearing a bright yellow rain slicker that covered most of her face. It would take her a minute to reach for the doorbell; the memories would be so strong, she'd want to wallow in them. In her arms would be Katie, almost crawling by now, wearing a fuzzy blue snowsuit—one they'd bought just for Mystic.

And when he opened the door, she would tell him that in all the long months they'd been apart, she'd found herself falling, and falling, and there'd been no one there to catch her. . . .

Ahead, the road merged onto the interstate. Two green highway signs slashed against the steel-gray sky. There were two choices: I-5 South. I-5 North.

No.

It was crazy, what she was thinking. She wasn't ready. She had oceans of commitments in California, and not even a toothbrush in her diaper bag. It was winter in Mystic, cold and gray and wet, and she was wearing silk. . . .

South was Los Angeles—and a beautiful white house by the sea that held the stale leftovers of her old life.

North was Mystic—and in Mystic was a man and a child who loved her. Once, she had taken love for granted. Never again. Love was the sun and the moon and the stars in a world that was otherwise cold and dark.

Nick had known that. It was one of the last things he'd said to her: *You're wrong, Annie. Love matters. Maybe it's the only thing that does.*

She glanced in the rearview mirror at her daughter, who was almost asleep. "Listen to me, Kathleen Sarah. I'm going to give you lesson number one in the Annalise Bourne Colwater book of life. I may not know everything, but I'm forty years old and I know plenty, so pay attention. Sometimes you have to do everything right and follow the rules. You have to wait until all your ducks are in a row before you make a move." She grinned. "And other times . . . like now . . . you have to say 'what the hell' and go for it."

Laughing out loud, Annie flicked on her turn signal, changed lanes—

And headed north.

Summer Island

In memory of my mother,
Sharon Goodno John

Acknowledgments

Thanks to Gina Centrello, Shauna Summers, George Fisher, and the whole Ballantine team for making 2000 so memorable.

Thanks to Chip Gibson, Steve Ross, Andrew Martin, Joan De Mayo, Barbara Marks, Whitney Cookman, Alison Gross, and everyone at Crown Publishers.

Thanks to Kim Fisk for keeping me (as much as possible) on track.

Thanks to Ann Patty and Megan Chance again, for everything.

Last but not least, thanks to my family. I was blessed to be born into a great clan. So, here's to Kent and Laura and Dad. We're lucky to be friends as well as family.

And to the "Canadian contingent"—Uncle Frank, Aunt Toni, Leslie, Jacqui, Dana, and, of course, to Johnsie, the first storyteller.

And most important, to Tucker and Benjamin, who teach me a little more about love every day.

Part One

*"There is only the fight to recover what has been lost
And found and lost again and again: and now under conditions
That seem unpropitious. But perhaps neither gain nor loss.
For us, there is only the trying. The rest is not our business."*

—T. S. ELIOT, FROM "EAST COKER"

Chapter One

An early evening rain had fallen. In the encroaching darkness, the streets of Seattle lay like mirrored strips between the glittering gray high-rises.

The dot-com revolution had changed this once quiet city, and even after the sun had set, the clattering, hammering sounds of construction beat a constant rhythm. Buildings sprouted overnight, it seemed, reaching higher and higher into the soggy sky. Purple-haired kids with nose rings and ragged clothes zipped through downtown in brand-new, bright-red Ferraris.

On a corner lot in the newly fashionable neighborhood of Belltown, there was a squat, wooden-sided structure that used to sit alone. It had been built almost one hundred years earlier, when few people had wanted to live so far from the heart of the city.

The owners of radio station KJZZ didn't care that they no longer fit in this trendy area. For fifty years they had broadcast from this lot. They had grown from a scrappy local station to Washington's largest.

Part of the reason for their current wave of success was Nora Bridge, the newest sensation in talk radio.

Although her show, *Spiritual Healing with Nora,* had been in syndication for less than a year, it was already a bona fide hit. Advertisers and affiliates couldn't write checks fast enough, and her weekly newspaper advice column, "Nora Knows Best," had never been more popular. It appeared in more than 2,600 papers nationwide.

Nora had started her career as a household hints adviser for a small-town newspaper, but hard work and a strong vision had moved her up the food chain. The women of Seattle had been the first to discover her unique blend of passion and morality; the rest of the country had soon followed.

Reviewers claimed that she could see a way through any emotional conflict; more often than not, they mentioned the purity of her heart.

But they were wrong. It was the *impurity* in her heart that made her successful. She was an ordinary woman who'd made extraordinary mistakes. She understood every nuance of need and loss.

There was never a time in her life, barely even a moment, when she didn't remember what she'd lost. What she'd thrown away. Each night she brought her own regrets to the microphone, and from that wellspring of sorrow, she found compassion.

She had managed her career with laserlike focus, carefully feeding the press a palatable past. Even the previous week when *People* magazine had featured her on the cover, there had been no investigative story on her life. She had covered her tracks well. Her fans knew she'd been divorced and that she had grown daughters. The hows and whys of her family's destruction remained—thankfully—private.

Tonight, Nora was on the air. She scooted her wheeled chair closer to the microphone and adjusted her headphones. A computer screen showed her the list of callers on hold. She pushed line two, which read: *Marge/mother–daughter probs.*

"Hello and welcome, Marge, you're on the air with Nora Bridge. What's on your mind this evening?"

"Hello . . . Nora?" The caller sounded hesitant, a little startled at actually hearing her voice on the air after waiting on hold for nearly an hour.

Nora smiled, although only her producer could see it. Her fans, she'd learned, were often anxious. She lowered her voice, gentled it. "How can I help you, my friend?"

"I'm having a little trouble with my daughter, Suki." The caller's flattened vowels identified her as a midwesterner.

"How old is Suki, Marge?"

"Sixty-seven this November."

Nora laughed. "I guess some things never change, eh, Marge?"

"Not between mothers and daughters. Suki gave me my first gray hair when I was thirty years old. Now I look like Colonel Sanders."

Nora's laugh was quieter this time. At forty-nine, she no longer found gray hair a laughing matter. "So, Marge, what's the problem with Suki?"

"Well." Marge made a snorting sound. "Last week she went on one of those singles cruises—you know the ones, where they all wear Hawaiian shirts and drink purple cocktails? Anyway, today, she told me she's getting married again to a man she met on the boat. At *her* age." She snorted again, then paused. "I know she wanted me to be happy for her, but how could I? Suki's a flibbertigibbet. My Tommy and I were married for seventy years."

Nora considered how to answer. Obviously, Marge knew that she and Suki weren't young anymore, and that time had a way of pulverizing your best intentions. There was no point in being maudlin and mentioning it. Instead, she asked gently, "Do you love your daughter?"

"I've always loved her." Marge's voice caught on a little sob. "You can't know what it's like, Nora, to love your daughter so much . . . and watch her stop needing you. What if she marries this man and forgets all about me?"

Nora closed her eyes and cleared her mind. She'd learned that skill long ago; callers were constantly saying things that struck at the heart of her own pain. She'd had to learn to let it go. "Every mother is afraid of that, Marge. The only way to really hold on to our children is to let them go. Let Suki take your love with her, let it be like a light that's always on in the house where she grew up. If she has that for strength, she'll never be too far away."

Marge wept softly. "Maybe I could call her . . . ask her to bring her boyfriend around for supper."

"That would be a wonderful start. Good luck to you, Marge, and be sure and let us know how it all works out." She cleared her throat and disconnected the call. "Come on, everybody," she said into the microphone, "let's help Marge out. I know there are plenty of you who have mended families. Call in. Marge and I want to be reminded that love isn't as fragile as it sometimes feels."

She leaned back in the chair, watching as the phone lines lit up. Parenting issues were always a popular topic—especially mother–daughter problems. On the monitor by her elbow, she saw the words: *line four/trouble with stepdaughter/Ginny.*

She picked up line four. "Hello and welcome, Ginny. You're on the air with Nora Bridge."

"Uh. Hi. I love your show."

"Thanks, Ginny. How are things in your family?"

For the next two hours and thirteen minutes, Nora gave her heart and soul to her listeners. She never pretended to have all the answers, or to be a substitute for doctors or family therapy. Instead, she tried to give her friendship to these troubled, ordinary people she'd never met.

As was her custom, when the show was finally over, she returned to her office. There, she took the time to write personal thank-you notes to any of those callers who'd been willing to leave an address with the show's producer. She always did this herself; no secretary ever copied Nora's signature. It was a little thing, but Nora firmly believed in it. Anyone who'd been courageous enough to publicly ask for advice from Nora deserved a private thank-you.

By the time she finished, she was running late.

She grabbed her Fendi briefcase and hurried to her car. Fortunately, it was only a few miles to the hospital. She parked in the underground lot and emerged into the lobby's artificial brightness.

It was past visiting hours, but this was a small, privately run hospital, and Nora had become such a regular visitor—every Saturday and Tuesday for the past month—that certain rules had been bent to accommodate her busy schedule. It didn't hurt that she was a local celebrity, or that the nurses loved her radio show.

She smiled and waved to the familiar faces as she walked down the corridor toward Eric's room. Outside his closed door, she paused, collecting herself.

Although she saw him often, it was never easy. Eric Sloan was as close to a son as she would ever have, and watching him battle cancer was unbearable. But Nora was all he had. His mother and father had written Eric off long ago, unable to accept his life's choices, and his beloved younger brother, Dean, rarely made time to visit.

She pushed open the door to his room and saw that he was sleeping. He lay in bed, with his head turned toward the window. A multicolored afghan, knitted by Nora's own hands, was wrapped around his too-thin body.

With his hair almost gone and his cheeks hollowed and his mouth open, he looked as old and beaten as a man could be. And he hadn't yet celebrated his thirty-first birthday.

For a moment, it was as if she hadn't seen him before. As if . . . although she'd watched his daily deterioration, she hadn't actually *seen* it, and now it had sneaked up on her, stolen her friend's face while she was foolishly pretending that everything would be all right.

But it wouldn't be. Just now, this second, she understood what he'd been trying to tell her, and the
grieving—which she'd managed to box into tiny,
consumable squares—threatened to overwhelm her.
In that one quiet heartbeat of time, she went from
hopeful to . . . not. And if it hurt her this terribly, the
lack of hope, how could he bear it?

She went to him, gently caressed the bare top of his
head. The few thin strands of his hair, delicate as spiderwebs, brushed across her knuckles.

He blinked up at her sleepily, trying for a boyish
grin and almost succeeding. "I have good news and
bad news," he said.

She touched his shoulder, and felt how fragile he
was. So unlike the tall, strapping black-haired boy
who'd carried her groceries into the house . . .

There was a tiny catch in her voice as she said cheer-
fully, "What's the good news?"

"No more treatments."

She clutched his shoulder too hard; his bones
shifted, birdlike, and immediately she let go. "And the
bad news?"

His gaze was steady. "No more treatments." He
paused. "It was Dr. Calomel's idea."

She nodded dully, wishing she could think of something profound to say, but everything had already been
said between them in the eleven months since his diag-
nosis. They'd spent dozens of nights talking about and
around this moment. She'd even thought she was ready
for it—this beginning of the end—but now she saw her
naïveté. There was no "ready" for death, especially not
when it came for a young man you loved.

And yet, she understood. She'd seen lately that the cancer was taking him away.

He closed his eyes, and she wondered if he was remembering the healthy, vibrant man he'd once been, the boy with the booming laugh . . . the teacher so beloved by his students . . . or if he was recalling the time, a few years before, when his partner, Charlie, had been in a hospital bed like this one, fighting a losing battle with AIDS . . .

Finally, he looked up at her; his attempt at a smile brought tears to her eyes. In that second, she saw pieces from the whole of his life. She pictured him at eight, sitting at her kitchen table, eating Lucky Charms, a shaggy-haired, freckle-faced boy with banged-up knees and soup-ladle ears.

"I'm going home," he said quietly. "Hospice will help out . . ."

"That's great," she said thickly, smiling too brightly, trying to pretend they were talking about where he was going to live . . . instead of where he'd chosen to die. "I'm way ahead on my newspaper columns. I'll take the week off, visit you during the day. I'll still have to work the show at night, but—"

"I mean the island. I'm going *home*."

"Are you finally going to call your family?" She hated his decision to handle his cancer privately, but he'd been adamant. He'd forbidden Nora to tell anyone, and as much as she'd disagreed, she'd had no choice but to honor his wishes.

"Oh, yeah. They've been so supportive in the past."

"This is different than coming out of the closet, and you know it. It's time to call Dean. And your parents."

The look he gave her was so hopeless that she wanted to turn away. "What if I told my mother I was dying and she still wouldn't come to see me?"

Nora understood. Even a thin blade of that hope could cut him to pieces now. "At least call your brother. Give him the chance."

"I'll think about it."

"That's all I ask." She forced a smile. "If you can wait until Tuesday, I'll drive you—"

He touched her hand gently. "I haven't got much time. I've arranged to be flown up. Lottie's already up at the house, getting it ready."

Haven't got much time. It was infinitely worse, somehow, to hear the words spoken aloud. She swallowed hard. "I don't think you should be alone."

"Enough." His voice was soft, his gaze even softer, but she heard the barest echo of his former strength. He was reminding her, as he sometimes had to, that he was an adult, a grown man. "Now," he said, clapping his hands together, "we sound like a goddamn Ibsen play. Let's talk about something else. I listened to your show tonight. Mothers and daughters. That's always tough on you."

Just like that, he put them back on solid ground. As always, she was amazed by his resilience. When life seemed too big to swallow, she knew he made it through by cutting it into bites. Normal things . . . ordinary conversations were his salvation.

She pulled up a chair and sat down. "I never really know what to say, and when I do offer advice, I feel like the biggest hypocrite on the planet. How would Marge feel if she knew I hadn't spoken to my own daughter in eleven years?"

Eric didn't answer the rhetorical question. It was one of the things she loved best about him. He never tried to comfort her with lies. But it helped her that someone recognized how painful it was for Nora to think about her younger daughter. "I wonder what she's doing now."

It was a common question between them, one they speculated about endlessly.

Eric managed a laugh. "With Ruby it could be anything from having lunch with Steven Spielberg to piercing her tongue."

"The last time I talked to Caroline, she said that Ruby had dyed her hair blue." Nora laughed, then fell abruptly silent. It wasn't funny. "Ruby always had such pretty hair . . ."

Eric leaned forward. There was a sudden earnestness in his eyes. "She's not dead, Nora."

She nodded. "I know. I try to squeeze hope from that thought all the time."

He grinned. "Now, get out the backgammon board. I feel like whooping your ass."

It was only the second week of June, and already the temperature hovered around one hundred degrees. A freak heat wave they called it on the local news, the kind of weather that usually came to southern California later in the year.

The heat made people crazy. They woke from their damp bedsheets and went in search of a glass of water, surprised to find that when their vision cleared, they were holding instead the gun they kept hidden in the bookcase. Children cried out in their sleep, and even doses of liquid Tylenol couldn't cool their fevered skin. All over town, birds fell from phone wires and landed in pathetic, crumpled heaps on the thirsty lawns.

No one could sleep in weather like this, and Ruby Bridge was no exception. She lay sprawled in her bed, the sheets shoved down to the floor, a cold-pack pressed across her forehead.

The minutes ticked by, each one a moaning sound caught in the window air-conditioning unit, a *whooshping* that did little but stir the hot air around.

She was lonely. Only a few days earlier, her boyfriend, Max, had left her. After five years of living together, he'd simply walked out of her life like a plumber who'd finished an unpleasant job.

All he'd left behind was a few pieces of crappy furniture and a note.

Dear Ruby:
I never meant to fall out of love with you (or into love with Angie) but shit happens. You know how it is. I need to be free. Hell, we both know you never really loved me anyway.
Be cool.
Max.

The funny thing was (and it definitely wasn't ha-ha funny), she hardly missed him. In fact, she didn't miss *him* at all. She missed the idea of him. She missed a second plate at the dinner table, another body in this bed that seemed to have enlarged in his absence. Mostly, she missed the pretense that she was in love.

Max had been . . . hope. A physical embodiment of the belief that she could love, and be loved in return.

At seven A.M., the alarm clock sounded. Ruby slid out of bed on a sluglike trail of perspiration. The wobbly pressboard headboard banged against the wall. Her bra and panties stuck to her damp body. She reached for the glass of water by the bed, pressed it to the valley between her breasts, and went to the bathroom, where she took a lukewarm shower.

She was sweating again before she was finished drying off. With a tired sigh, she headed into the kitchen and made a pot of coffee. She poured herself a cup, then added a generous splash of cream. White chunks immediately floated to the surface and formed a cross.

Another woman might have thought simply that the cream had gone bad, but Ruby knew better: it was a sign.

As if she needed magic to tell her that she was stuck in the spin cycle of her life.

She tossed the mess down the sink and headed back into her bedroom, grabbing the grease-stained black polyester pants and white cotton blouse that lay tangled on the floor. Sweating, headachy, and in desperate need of caffeine, she got dressed and went out into the stifling heat.

She walked downstairs to her battered 1970 Volkswagen Bug. After a few tries, the engine turned over, and Ruby drove toward Irma's Hash House, the trendy Venice Beach diner where she'd worked for almost three years.

She'd never meant to *stay* a waitress; the job was supposed to be temporary, something to pay the bills until she got on her feet, caused a sensation at one of the local comedy clubs, did a guest spot on Leno, and—finally—was offered her own sitcom, aptly titled *Ruby*! She always pictured it with an exclamation mark, like one of those Vegas revues her grandmother had loved.

But at twenty-seven, she wasn't young anymore. After almost a decade spent trying to break into comedy, she was brushing up against "too old." Everyone knew that if you didn't make it by thirty, you were toast. And Ruby was beginning to think that she should start collecting jam.

Finally, she maneuvered between the old station wagons and Volkswagen buses that filled the 1950s-style diner's crowded parking lot. Surfboards were lashed to every surface; most of the cars had more bumper stickers than paint. The sun-bleached "hey dude" set came from miles away for Irma's famous six-egg omelette. She parked alongside a bus that could have come from *Fast Times at Ridgemont High*.

She forced a smile onto her face and headed for the diner. When she opened the front door, the bell tinkled gaily overhead.

Irma bustled toward her, her three-story beehive hairdo leading the way. As always, she moved fast, keeled forward like the prow of a sinking ship, then came to an abrupt halt in front of Ruby. Her heavily mascaraed eyes narrowed, and Ruby wondered—again—if human beings could be carbon-dated by makeup. "You were scheduled for last night."

Ruby winced. "Oh, shit."

Irma crossed her bony arms. "I'm letting you go. We can't count on you. Debbie had to work a double shift last night. Your final paycheck is at the register. I'll expect the uniform back tomorrow. Cleaned."

Ruby's lips trembled mutinously. The thought of pleading for this shitty job made her sick. "Come on, Irma, I *need* this job."

"I'm sorry, Ruby. Really." Irma turned and walked away.

Ruby stood there a minute, breathing in the familiar mixture of maple syrup and grease, then she snagged her paycheck from the counter and walked out of the restaurant.

She got in her car and drove away aimlessly, up one street and down the other. Finally, when it felt as if her face were melting off her skull, she parked alongside the street in a shopping district. In the trendy, air-conditioned boutiques, she saw dozens of beautiful things she couldn't afford, sold by girls who were half her age. She realized she was close to hitting rock bottom when a HELP WANTED sign on a pet-store window actually caught her attention.

No way. It was bad enough serving beef sludge to the Butt family. She'd be damned if she'd sell them a ferret, too.

She got back into her car and drove away, this time speeding recklessly toward her destination. When she reached Wilshire Boulevard, she pulled up in front of a high-rise building and parked.

Before she had time to talk herself out of it, she went to the elevator and rode it up to the top floor. When the doors opened, sweet, cooled air greeted her, drying the sweat on her cheeks.

She walked briskly down the hallway toward her

agent's office and pushed through the frosted-glass double doors.

The receptionist, Maudeen Wachsmith, had her nose buried in a romance novel. Barely looking up, she smiled. "Hi, Ruby," she said. "He's busy today. You'll have to make an appointment."

Ruby rushed past Maudeen and yanked the door open.

Her agent, Valentine Lightner, was there, seated behind the glassy expanse of his desk. He looked up. When he saw Ruby, his smile faded into a frown. "Ruby . . . I wasn't expecting you . . . was I?"

Maudeen rushed in behind Ruby. "I'm sorry, Mr. Lightner . . ."

He raised a slim hand. "Don't worry about it, Maudeen." He leaned back in his chair. "So, Ruby, what's going on?"

She waited for Maudeen to leave, then moved toward the desk. She was humiliatingly aware that she was still wearing her uniform, and that her underarms were outlined in perspiration. "Is that cruise ship job still available?" She'd laughed at it three months before—cruise ships were floating morgues for talent—but now it didn't seem beneath her. Hell, it seemed above her.

"I've *tried* for you, Ruby. You write funny stuff, but the truth is, your delivery sucks. And that's no ordinary chip on your shoulder, it's a section of the Hoover Dam. You've burned too many bridges in this business. No one wants to hire you."

"Someone—"

"No one. Remember the job I got you on that

sitcom? You slowed down the first week's production and made everyone insane with rewrites."

"My character was an idiot. She didn't have one funny line."

Val looked at her, his ice-blue eyes narrowed slowly. "Shall I remind you that the show's still on the air and another—less talented—comedian is making thirty thousand dollars an episode saying what she's told to say?"

"It's a shitty show." Ruby collapsed into the plush leather chair in front of his desk. It took her a moment to squeeze her ego into a tiny box. "I'm broke. Irma fired me from the diner."

"Why don't you call your mother?"

She closed her eyes for a second, drawing in a deep breath. "Don't go there, Val," she said quietly.

"I know, I know, she's the bitch from hell. But come on, Ruby, I saw that article in *People*. She's rich and famous. Maybe she could help you."

"You're rich and famous and you can't help me. Besides, she's *helped* me enough. Any more motherly attention and I could end up strapped to a table in Ward B singing 'I Gotta Be Me.'" Ruby got to her feet. It took a supreme effort, considering that she wanted to curl into a ball and sleep. "Well, thanks for nothing, Val."

"It's that sparkling personality that makes helping you so damned easy." He sighed. "I'll try Asia. They love U.S. comedians overseas. Maybe you can do the nightclub circuit."

It made her feel sick, just thinking about it. "Telling jokes to a translator." She winced, imagining herself in one of those men's bars, with naked women writhing up and down polished silver poles behind her. She'd already put in her time in joints like that. Her whole youth had been spent in the shadows behind another performer's light. "Maybe it's time for me to give up. Cash in. Throw in the towel."

Val looked at her. "What would you do?"

Not, *don't do that, Ruby; you're too talented to give up*. That's what he'd said six years earlier.

"I've got half an English lit degree from UCLA. Maybe it would get me a supervisor spot at Burger King."

"You certainly have the right personality for serving the public."

She couldn't help laughing. She'd been with Val a long time, since her first days at the Comedy Store. Val had always been her champion, her biggest fan, but in the past few years, she'd disappointed him, and some-how that was worse than disappointing herself. She'd become hard to work with, temperamental, difficult to place, and, worst of all, unfunny. Val could over-come anything except that. She didn't know what was wrong with her, either. Except that she seemed to be angry all the time. She should be standing on a ledge somewhere. "I appreciate everything you've done for me, Val. Really, I know it's hard to get work for a prima donna with no talent."

The moment the words were out, Ruby heard what lay beneath them. Hesitant, afraid, but there nonethe-less. A good-bye. And the worst part was that she knew Val heard the same thing, and he didn't say *no, don't do that, we're a long way from over*.

Instead, he said, "You have as much raw talent as

anyone I've ever seen. You light up a goddamn room with your smile, and your wit is as sharp as a blade." He leaned toward her. "Let me ask you a question. When did you stop smiling, Ruby?"

She knew the answer, of course. It had happened in her junior year of high school, but she wouldn't think about that time—not even to give Val an answer.

Objects in a mirror are closer than they appear. That was true of memories as well; it was best not to look.

"I don't know." She spoke softly, refusing to meet his gaze. She wished she could let Val see how frightened she was, how alone she felt. She thought that if she could do that, if she could for once show a friend her vulnerability, she would perhaps be saved.

But she couldn't do it. No matter how hard she tried, Ruby couldn't let down her guard. Her emotions were packed tightly inside her, hermetically sealed so that every wound and memory stayed fresh.

"Well," she said at last, straightening her shoulders, puffing out her unimpressive chest. She had the fleeting sense that she looked absurd, a wounded sparrow trying to impress a peregrine falcon. "I guess I'd better go. I'll need to pick up some fishnet hose and a can of Mace if I'm going to start hooking."

Val smiled wanly. "I'll make the calls about Asia. We'll talk in a few days."

"I'm grateful." She would have added more, maybe even groveled a little, but her throat seemed swollen shut.

Val came around the desk and closed the distance between them. She saw the sadness in his eyes, and the regret. "You lost yourself," he said quietly.

"I know."

"Listen to me, Ruby. I know about getting lost. You need to start over."

She swallowed hard. This sort of honesty was more at home in other parts of the country, where time was measured in seasons or tides. Here in L.A., time elapsed in thirty-second spots; true emotion didn't thrive under that kind of pressure. "Don't worry about me, Val. I'm a survivor. Now, I'm going to go home and learn to speak Japanese."

He squeezed her shoulder. "That's my girl."

"Sayonara." She wiggled her fingers in an oh-so-California-darling wave and did her best to sashay out of the office. It was tough to pull off, sashaying in a sweat-stained waitress uniform, and the minute she was out of his office, she let go of her fake smile. She walked dully into the elevator and rode it down to the lobby, then headed for her car. The Volkswagen looked like a half-dead june bug, huddled alongside the parking meter. When she got inside, she immediately winced. The seat was scorchingly hot.

There was a parking ticket on her windshield.

She rolled down her window and reached out, yanking the paper from beneath the rusted windshield wiper. She wadded it into a ball and tossed it out the window. To her mind, ticketing this rattrap and expecting to get paid was like leaving a bill on the pillow at a homeless shelter.

Before the ticket even hit the street, she'd started the engine and pulled out onto Wilshire Boulevard, where she was immediately swallowed into the stream of traffic.

In Studio City, the streets were quieter. A few neighborhood kids played lethargically in their small front yards. With the risk of fire so high, there was no wasting water for things like slip-n-slides or sprinklers.

Ruby maneuvered past a big, drooling Saint Bernard who lay sleeping in the middle of the street, and pulled up to the curb in front of her apartment complex.

Sopping her forehead, she headed up the stairs. No one came out to say hello; it was too damned hot. Her neighbors were probably huddled in family pods around the window-unit air conditioners in their apartments—the modern L.A. equivalent of cavemen camped around the marvel of fire.

By the time she reached her floor, Ruby was wheezing so badly she sounded like Shelley Winters after her swim in *The Poseidon Adventure*, and she was practically that wet. Sweat slid down her forehead and caught on her eyelashes, blurring everything.

It took her a moment to open her door; it always did. The shag carpeting had pulled up along the threshold. She finally crammed the door open and stumbled through the opening.

She stood there, breathing hard, staring at the wretched furniture in her dismal little apartment, and felt the hot sting of tears.

Absurdly, she thought: If only it would rain.

Her whole day might have been different if the damned weather had changed.

Chapter Two

June was a hard month in Seattle. It was in this season, when the school bells rang for the last time and the peonies and delphiniums bloomed, that the locals began to complain that they'd been cheated. The rains had started in October (invariably Seattleites swore it had come early this year); by the last week in May, even the meteorologically challenged denizens of Seattle had had enough. They watched the news religiously, seeing the first tantalizing shots of people swimming in the warm waters farther south. Relatives began to call, talking on cell phones as they stood outside to barbecue. Summer had come to every other corner of America.

The locals saw it as a matter of fairness. They *deserved* summer. They'd put up with nine solid months of dismal weather and it was past time for the sun to deliver.

So, it was hardly surprising that it rained on the day Nora Bridge celebrated her fiftieth birthday. She didn't take the weather as an omen or a portent of bad luck.

In retrospect, she should have.

Instead, she simply thought: Rain. Of course. It almost always rained on her birthday.

She stood at the window in her office, sipping her favorite drink—Mumm's champagne with a slice of fresh peach—and stared out at the traffic on Broad Street. It was four-thirty. Rush hour in a city that had outgrown its highway system ten years ago.

On her windowsill, dozens of birthday cards fanned along the gleaming strip of bird's-eye maple.

She'd received cards and gifts from everyone who worked on her radio show. Each one was appropriate and lovely, but the most treasured card had come from her elder daughter, Caroline.

Of course, the joy of that card was tempered by the fact that, again this year, there had been no card from Ruby.

"You'll be fine tomorrow," she spoke softly to her own reflection, captured in the rainy window.

She gave herself a little time to wallow in regret—ache for the card that wasn't there—and then she rallied. Fifteen years of therapy had granted her this skill; she could compartmentalize.

In the past few years, she'd finally gotten a grip on her tumultuous emotions. The breakdowns and depressions that had once plagued her life were now a distant, painful memory.

She turned away from the window and glanced at the crystal clock on her desk. It was four-thirty-eight.

They were down in the conference room now, setting out food, bottles of champagne, plates filled with peach slices. Assistants, publicists, staff writers, producers, they were all preparing to spend an hour of their valuable personal time to put together a "surprise" party for the newest star of talk radio.

She set her champagne flute down on her desk and opened one of her drawers, pulling out a small black Chanel makeup case. She touched up her face, then headed out of the office.

The hallways were unusually quiet. Probably everyone was helping out with the party. At precisely four forty-five, Nora walked into the conference room.

It was empty.

The long table was bare; no food was spread out, no tiny bits of colored confetti lay scattered on the floor. A happy-birthday banner hung from the overhead lights. It looked as if someone had started to decorate for a party and then suddenly stopped.

It was a moment before she noticed the two men standing to her left: Bob Wharton, the station's owner and manager, and Jason Close, the lead in-house attorney.

Nora smiled warmly. "Hello, Bob. Jason," she said, moving toward them. "It's good to see you."

The men exchanged a quick glance.

She felt a prickling of unease. "Bob?"

Bob's fleshy face, aged by two-martini lunches and twenty-cigarette days, creased into a frown. "We have some bad news."

"Bad news?"

Jason eased past Bob and came up to Nora. His steel-gray hair was perfectly combed. A black Armani suit made him look like a forty-year-old mafia don.

"Earlier today, Bob took a call from a man named Vince Corell."

Nora felt as if she'd been smacked in the face. The air rushed out of her lungs.

"He claimed he'd had an affair with you while you were married. He wanted us to pay him to keep quiet."

"Jesus, Nora," Bob sputtered angrily. "A goddamn *affair*. While your kids were at home. You should have told us."

She'd told her readers and listeners a thousand times to be strong. *Never let them see you're afraid. Believe in yourself and people will believe in you.* But now that she needed that strength, it was gone. "I could say he was lying," she said, wincing when she heard the breathy, desperate tone of her voice.

Jason opened his briefcase and pulled out a manila envelope. "Here."

Nora's hands were shaking as she took the envelope and opened it.

There were black-and-white photographs inside. She pulled out the top sheet. It wasn't more than halfway out when she saw what it was.

"Oh, God," she whispered. She reached out for the chair nearest her and clutched the metal back. Only pure willpower kept her from sinking to her knees. She crammed the pictures back into the envelope.

"There must be a way to stop this." She looked at Jason. "An injunction. Those are private photographs."

"Yes, they are. His. It's obvious that you . . . knew the camera was there. You're posing. He's probably been waiting all this time for you to become famous. That piece in *People* must have done it."

She drew in a deep breath and looked at them. "How much does he want?"

There was a pregnant pause, after which Jason stepped closer. "A half million dollars."

"I can get that amount—"

"Money never kills this kind of thing, Nora. You know that. Sooner or later it'll come out."

She understood immediately. "You told him no," she said woodenly. "And now he's going to the tabloids."

Jason nodded. "I'm sorry, Nora."

"I can explain this to my fans," she said. "Bob? They'll underst—"

"You give *moral* advice, Nora." Bob shook his head. "This is going to be a hell of a scandal. Jesus, we've been promoting you as a modern version of Mother Teresa. Now it turns out you're Debbie Does Dallas."

Nora flinched. "Not fair, Bob."

"Believe us," Jason said. "The trailer-park set in Small-town U.S.A. will *not* understand that their idol just had to be free."

Bob nodded. "When these photos hit the air, we'll lose advertisers instantly."

Nora clasped her trembling hands and tried to appear calm. She knew it wasn't working. "What do we do?"

A pause. A look. Then Jason said, "We want you to take some time off."

It was all coming at her too fast. She couldn't think straight. All she knew was that she couldn't give up. This career was all she had. "I can't—"

Jason moved closer, touched her shoulder gently. "You've spent the better part of the past decade telling people to honor their commitments and put their families first. How long do you think it will take the press to uncover that you haven't spoken to your own daughter since the divorce? Your advice is going to ring a little hollow after that."

Bob nodded. "The press is going to rip you limb from limb, Nora. Not because you deserve it, but because they can. The tabloids love a celebrity in trouble . . . and with sexy pictures. Hell, they'll be jumpin' up and down over this."

And just like that, Nora's life slipped beyond her grasp.

"It'll blow over," she whispered, knowing in her heart that it wasn't true, or if it was true, it wouldn't matter, not in the end. Some winds were hurricane force and they demolished everything in their path. "I'll take a few weeks off. See what happens. Spend some time coming up with a statement."

"For the record," Jason said, "this is a scheduled vacation. We won't admit that it has anything to do with the scandal."

"Thank you."

"I hope you make it through this," Jason said. "We all do."

Jason and Bob both spoke at once, then an awkward silence descended. Nora heard them walk past her. The door clicked shut behind them.

She stood there, alone now, her gaze blurred by tears she couldn't hold back anymore. After eleven years of working seventy-hour weeks, it was over.

Poof. Her life was gone, blown apart by a few naked photographs taken a lifetime ago. The world would see her hypocrisy, and so too—oh, God— would her daughters.

They would know at last, without question, that their mother had had an affair—and that she'd lied to all of them when she walked out of her marriage.

Ruby had a pounding headache. She'd slept on and off all day.

Finally, she stumbled into the kitchen and went to the fridge. When she opened it, the fluorescent lighting stabbed her aching eyes. Squinting, she grabbed the quart of orange juice and drank it from the container. Liquid trickled down her chin. She backhanded it away.

In the living room—what a joke; if you were living in this empty room, you were either dying or too stupid to keep breathing—she leaned against the rough wall and slid down to a sit, stretching her legs out. She knew she needed to walk down to Chang's Mini-Mart and pick up a newspaper, but the thought of turning to the want ads was more than she could bear. The job at Irma's hadn't been much—had been godawful, in fact—but at least it had been hers. She hadn't had to stand in a hot line, begging for a chance, saying *I'm really a comedian* again. As if she were special, instead of just another loser in the string of men and women who came to Hollywood with a cheap one-way ticket and a dream of someday.

The phone rang.

Ruby didn't want to answer. It could hardly be

good news. At best, it would be Caroline, her *über*-yuppie, Junior League sister who had two perfect kids and a hunk of a husband.

It was *possible* that Dad had finally remembered her, but Ruby doubted it. Since he'd remarried and started a second family, her father was more interested in midnight baby feedings than in the goings-on of his adult daughter's life. Frankly, she couldn't even remember the last time he'd called.

The ringing went on and on.

Finally, she crawled across the shag carpet and answered on the fourth ring. "Hello?" She heard the snarl in her voice, but who gave a shit? She was in a bad mood and she didn't care who knew it.

"Whoa, don't bite my head off."

Ruby couldn't believe it. "Val?"

"It's me, darlin', your favorite agent."

She frowned. "You sound pretty goddamn happy, considering that my career is circling the hole in the toilet bowl."

"I am happy. Here's the scoop. Yesterday I called everyone I could think of to hire you. And baby, I hate to say it, but no one wanted you. The only nibble was from that shit-ass, low-rent cruise line. They said they'd take you for the summer if you promised no foul language . . . and agreed to wear an orange sequined miniskirt so you could help out the magician after your set."

Ruby's head throbbed harder. She rubbed her temples. "Let me guess, you're calling to tell me there's a man named Big Dick who has a night job for me on Hollywood and Vine."

Val laughed. It was a great, booming sound, with none of the strained undertones she was used to hearing. A client got to know the subtle shades of enthusiasm—it was a skill that came with being at rock bottom on the earning-potential food chain. "You won't believe it. Hell, *I* don't believe it, and I took the call. I'm going to make you guess who called me today."

"Heidi Fleiss."

There was a palpable pause; in it, Ruby heard Val's exhalation of breath—he was smoking. "Joe Cochran."

"From *Uproar*? Don't screw with me, Val. I'm a little—"

"Joe Cochran called me. No shit. He had a sudden cancellation. He wants to book you for tomorrow's show."

How could a world spin around so quickly? Yesterday, Ruby had been pond scum; today, Joe Cochran wanted her. The host of the hottest, hippest talk show in the country. It had been patterned after *Politically Incorrect*, but because *Uproar* was broadcast on cable, the show explored racier issues—and foul language was encouraged. It was a young comedian's dream gig. Even if she wasn't so young anymore.

"He's giving you two minutes to do stand-up. So, kiddo, this is it. You'd better spend the time between then and now practicing. I'll send a car around to pick you up at eleven tomorrow morning."

"Thanks, Val."

"I didn't do anything, darlin'. Really. This is all you. Good luck."

Before she hung up, Ruby remembered to ask, "Hey, what's the topic of the show?"

"Oh, yeah." She heard the rustle of papers. "It's called 'Crime and Punishment: Are Mommy and Daddy to Blame for Everything?' "

Ruby should have known. "They want me because I'm *her* daughter."

"Do you care why?"

"No." It was true. She didn't care why Joe Cochran had called her. This was her shot. Finally, after years of crappy play dates in smoke-infested barrooms in towns whose names she couldn't remember, she was getting national exposure.

She thanked Val again, then hung up the phone. Her heart was racing so hard she felt dizzy. Even the empty room looked better. She wouldn't be here much longer, anyway. She would be brilliant on the show, a shining star.

She ran to her bedroom and flung open the louvered doors of her closet. Everything she owned was black.

She couldn't afford anything new . . .

Then she remembered the black cashmere sweater. It had come from her mother, disguised in a box from Caroline two Christmases earlier. Although Ruby routinely sent back her mother's guilty gifts unopened, this one had seduced her. Once she'd touched that beautiful fabric, she couldn't mail it back.

She grabbed the black V-necked sweater off its hanger and tossed it on the bed.

Tomorrow she'd jazz it up with necklaces and wear it over a black leather miniskirt with black tights. Very Janeane Garofalo.

When Ruby had picked out her clothes, she kicked the bedroom door shut. A thin full-length mirror on the back of the door caught her image, framed it in strips of gold plastic.

It was hard to take herself seriously, dressed as she was in her dad's old football jersey and a pair of fuzzy red knee socks. Her short black hair had been molded by last night's sweatfest into a perfect imitation of Johnny Rotten. Pink sleep wrinkles still creased her pale face. Remnants of last night's makeup circled her eyes.

"I'm Ruby Bridge," she said, grabbing a hairbrush off the dresser to use as a mike. "And yes, you're right if you recognize the last name. I'm *her* daughter, Nora Bridge's, spiritual guru to Middle America." She flung her hip out, picturing herself as she would look tomorrow—hair tipped in temporary blue dye, a dozen tacky necklaces, tight black clothes, and heavy black makeup. "Look at me. Should that woman be telling you how to raise kids? It's like those commercials on television where celebrities come on and tell you to be a mentor to a kid. And who does Hollywood pick to give out advice?

"A bunch of anorexics, alcoholics, drug addicts, and serial marriers. People who haven't spent ten minutes with a kid in years. And *they're* telling you how to parent. It's like—"

The phone rang.

"Damn." Ruby raced into the living room and yanked the cord out of the wall. She couldn't be bothered for the next twenty-four hours. Nothing mattered except getting ready for the show.

* * *

Like all big cities, San Francisco looked beautiful at night. Multicolored lights glittered throughout downtown, creating a neon sculpture garden tucked along the black bay.

Dean Sloan glanced at the wall of windows that framed the panoramic view. Unfortunately, he couldn't leave his seat. He was—as always—trapped by the flypaper of good manners.

Scattered through the ornately gilded ballroom of this Russian Hill mansion were a dozen or so tables, each one draped in shimmering gold fabric and topped by a layer of opalescent silk. The china at each place setting was white with platinum trim. Four or five couples sat at each table, making idle conversation. The women were expensively, beautifully gowned and the men wore tuxedos. The party's hostess, a local socialite, had hand-chosen the guest list from among the wealthiest of San Francisco's families. Tonight's charity was the opera, and it would benefit mightily, although Dean wondered how many of the guests actually cared about music. What they really cared about was being seen, and even more important, being seen doing the *right* thing.

His date, a pale, exquisite woman named Sarah Brightman-Edgington, slid a hand along his thigh, and Dean knew that he'd been silent too long. With practiced ease, he turned to her, giving her the smile so well documented by the local society media.

"That was a lovely sentiment, don't you think?" she said softly, taking a small sip of champagne.

Dean had no idea what she was talking about, but a

quick look around the room enlightened him. An elderly, well-preserved woman in a deceptively simple
blue dress was standing alongside the ebony Steinway.
No doubt she'd been waxing poetic about the opera
and thanking her guests in advance for their unselfish
contributions. There was nothing the wealthy liked
quite so much as pretending to be generous.

It was, he knew, the official beginning of the end of
the evening. There would be dancing yet, some serious
schmoozing and even more serious gossiping, but
soon it would be polite to leave.

There was a smattering of quiet applause, then the
sound of chairs being scooted back.

Dean took hold of Sarah's hand. Together they
slipped into the whispering crowd. The band was
playing something soft and romantic, a song that was
almost familiar.

On the dance floor, he pulled Sarah close, slid his
hand down the bare expanse of her back, felt her
shiver at his touch.

The crowd eddied and swirled around them. Overhead, thousands of tiny lights twinkled like stars.
There was a faint, sweet smell of roses in the air.

Or maybe that was the scent of money . . .

He gazed down at Sarah's upturned face, noticing
for the first time how lovely her gray eyes were. Without thinking about it, he bent slightly and kissed her,
tasting the champagne she'd drunk. He could tell by
this kiss where the night could go. She would want
him. If he cared to, he could take her hand, lead her
out of this crush, and take her to his bed. She would
offer no objections. After that, he would call her, and

they would probably sleep together a few times. Then, somehow, he would forget her. Last year, a local magazine had named him San Francisco's most *in*eligible bachelor because of his reputation for nanosecond affairs. It was true; he'd certainly slept with dozens of the cities' most gorgeous women.

But what the reporter hadn't known, hadn't even imagined, was how tired Dean was of it all. He wasn't even twenty-nine years old and already he felt aged. Money. Power. Disposable women who seemed to hear his family name and become as malleable as wet clay. For more than a year now, Dean had felt that something was wrong with his life. Missing.

At first, he'd assumed it was a business problem, and he'd rededicated himself to work, logging upwards of eighty hours a week at Harcourt and Sons. But all he'd managed to do was make more money, and the ache in his gut had steadily sharpened.

He'd tried to speak to his father about it. As usual, that had proven pointless. Edward Sloan was now— and always had been—a charming, frivolous playboy who jumped at his wife's every command. It was Mother who held all of the ambition, and she'd never been one to care overly about things like fulfillment or satisfaction. Her comment had been as he'd expected: *I ran this company for thirty years; now it's your turn. No whining will be allowed.*

He supposed that she'd earned that right. Under his mother's iron fist, the family business, begun by her grandfather and expanded by her father, had become a hundred-million-dollar enterprise. That had always been enough for her. All she ever wanted. But that same success felt vaguely hollow to Dean.

He'd even tried to talk to his friends about it, and though they'd wanted to help, it was clear that none of them understood his feelings. It wasn't so surprising, after all. Although they were all from the same background, Dean had grown up in a slightly different world than his peers.

Lopez Island. Summer Island.

He'd spent ten perfect years in the San Juan Islands. There, he and his brother, Eric, had been—for a short time—ordinary boys. Those remote islands had formed and defined Dean somehow, provided a place where he felt whole.

Of course, Ruby had been there. And before she went crazy and ruined everything, she'd taught him how love felt.

Then she'd shown him how easily it was broken.

Dean sighed, wishing he hadn't thought about Ruby now, when he had a beautiful, willing woman in his arms . . .

Suddenly he was tired. He simply didn't have the energy to spend tonight with another woman he didn't care about.

"I'm not feeling well," he said, wondering briefly whether it was a lie, or not quite one.

She smiled up at him, revealing a set of perfect white teeth. Her hand moved up his arm, curled possessively around the back of his neck. They were always possessive, he thought tiredly. Or perhaps that was merely his sense of it.

"Me, too," she purred. "My place is just around the corner."

He reached up and took her hand, kissing the back of her knuckles gently. "No, I'm *really* not feeling well, and I've got a crack-of-dawn conference call coming from Tokyo. I think I'll take you home, if you don't mind."

She pouted prettily, and he wondered if that was one of the things they taught wealthy young girls at schools like Miss Porter's. If not, it had been passed down from one generation to another as carefully as the secret of fire.

"I'll call you tomorrow," he said, although he didn't mean it. There were only two choices available to a man at a time like this: hurt her by not saying it, or hurt her by not doing it. One—lying now—was easier.

Once he'd made his decision, Dean couldn't get out of the room fast enough. He maneuvered through the crowd like a Tour-de-France cyclist, saying good night to the few people who really mattered, getting Sarah's wrap (fur in June???), and hurried out to stand beneath the portico.

Sarah made idle chitchat as they stood there together, and he listened politely, answered at what he assumed were the appropriate places. Finally, he heard his car drive up. The black Aston-Martin roared up the driveway and screeched to a halt. A uniformed valet jumped out of the driver's seat and rushed around to open Sarah's door, then helped her into her seat.

Dean nodded at the man as he walked past. "Thanks,

Ramon," he said, getting into his car. He slammed the door shut and drove off, hitting the gas too hard.

It was a full minute before Sarah asked, "How did you know his name was Ramon?"

"I asked him when we arrived."

"Oh."

Dean glanced at her, saw her perfect profile cameoed against the blackened window glass. "What? Is there something wrong with knowing his name?"

A frown darted across her face. She lifted a hand, pointed idly. "Here's my house."

Dean pulled up the circular driveway and parked beneath an antique street lamp.

She turned to him, frowning slightly. "You're not what I expected. The girls . . . they talk about you."

He ran a hand through his too-long blond hair. "I hope it's a good thing, not being what you expected."

"It is," she said quietly. "I won't see you again, will I?"

"Sarah, I—"

"*Will* I?" she interrupted forcibly.

Dean took a deep breath, released it. "It's not you. It's me. I'm restless lately. It doesn't make for good company."

She laughed; it was a practiced, silvery sound that only held traces of mirth. "You're young and rich and sheltered. Of course you're restless. Poor people are driven and hungry. Rich people are restless and bored. I've been bored since grade school, for God's sake."

It was such a sad thing to say. Dean didn't know how to respond. He got out of the car and went around to her door, helping her out. Slipping a hand along the small of her back, he walked her to the door of her father's hilltop mansion. Quietly, he said, "You're too beautiful to be bored."

She looked sadly up at him. "So are you."

Dean kissed her good night, then returned to his car and raced home.

In less than fifteen minutes, he was standing in his living room, staring out at the night-clad city, sipping warmed brandy from a bowl-size snifter. On the walls all around him were framed photographs—his hobby. Once, the sight of them had pleased him. Now, all he saw when he looked at his photographs was how wrong his life had gone.

Behind him, the phone rang. He waited a few rings for Hester, his housekeeper, to answer it. Then he remembered that Hester had gone to see her kids tonight. He strode to the *latte*-colored suede sofa, collapsed onto the down-filled cushion, and answered the phone. "Dean Sloan." It was, he knew, an impersonal greeting, but he didn't care.

"Dino? Is that you?"

"Uh . . . Eric? How in the hell are you?" Dean was stunned. He hadn't heard from his brother in what . . . a year? Eighteen months?

"Are you sitting down?"

"That doesn't sound good."

"It isn't. I'm dying."

Dean felt as if he'd been punched in the gut. A cold chill moved through him. "AIDS?" he whispered.

Eric laughed. "We *do* get other diseases, you know. My personal favorite is cancer."

"We'll get you the best treatment. I can make some calls right now. Mark Foster is still on the board at—"

"I've *had* the best treatments. I've seen the best specialists, and they," Eric said softly, "have seen me." He took a deep breath. "I don't have much time left."

Dean couldn't seem to draw a decent breath. "You're thirty years old," he said helplessly, as if *age* were relevant.

"I should have told you when I was first diagnosed, but . . . I kept thinking I'd tell you when it was over, and we'd laugh about it . . ."

"Is there *any* chance we'll someday laugh about it?"

It took Eric a moment to answer. "No."

"What can I do?"

"I'm going back to the island. Lottie's already there, waiting for me."

"The island," Dean repeated slowly. A strange sense of inevitability drifted into the room. It was as if Dean had always known that someday they'd end up back there, where everything had begun. Where everything had gone so wrong. Maybe a part of him had even been waiting for it.

"Will you come up?"

"Of course."

"I want us to be brothers again."

"We've always been brothers," Dean answered uncomfortably.

"No," Eric said softly, "we've been members of the same family. We haven't been brothers in years."

Chapter Three

The scandal broke with gale force. Those humiliating photographs were everywhere, and the newspapers and television stations that didn't own the pictures described them in excruciating detail.

Nora sat huddled in her own living room, refusing to go anywhere. The thought of being seen terrified her.

Her assistant, Dee Langhor, had shown up bright and early in the morning—*I came the minute I heard*—and Nora had felt pathetically grateful. Now Dee was in Nora's home office, fielding phone calls.

With everything on Nora's mind, one thing kept rising to the surface; she should have called Caroline the day before, to warn her about the coming media storm.

But how did you tell your child something like this? *Oh, honey, and don't mind about the pictures of your naked mother that are front-page news?*

In the end, Nora had chosen to handle the impending disaster as she handled all difficult things: she'd taken two sleeping pills and turned off her phone. In the morning, she'd had a short respite . . . then she'd turned on the television. The story had been picked up by every morning show.

Now she had no choice. She had to call.

She reached for the phone, accessed the second line, and pushed number one on the speed-dial list. Her heart was pounding so hard she couldn't hear the ringing on the other end.

"Hello?"

It took Nora a moment to respond—God, she wanted to hang up the phone. "Caro? It's me. Mom."

There was a pause that seemed to strip away a layer of Nora's tender flesh. "Well. Well. I hope you're going to tell me you were kidnapped yesterday and the FBI just freed you from your prison in the back of some psycho fan's trunk."

"I wasn't kidnapped."

"I found out this morning when I dropped Jenny off at preschool." She laughed sharply. "Mona Carlson asked me how it felt to see pictures of my mother like that. How it *felt*."

Nora didn't know how to respond. Defending herself was pointless; worse, it was offensive. "I'm sorry. I couldn't . . . call."

"Of course you couldn't." Caroline was quiet for a moment, then she said, "I can't believe I let it hurt my feelings, either. I should have known better. It's just that in the last few years . . . I thought . . . oh, hell, forget it."

"I know. We've been getting closer . . ."

"No. Apparently *I've* been getting closer. You, obviously, haven't changed at all. You've been like some Stepford mom, pretending, saying the right things, but never really feeling connected to me at all. I don't know when I got stupid enough to expect honesty from you. And I'm not even going to get into the content of those photographs, what they mean to our family."

"Please," Nora pleaded, "I know I screwed up. Don't shut me out of your life again . . ."

"You're priceless. You really don't get it, do you? I'm not the one who shuts people out, not in this family. Maybe Ruby was the smart one—she hasn't let you hurt her in years. Now, I've got to go."

"I love you, Caroline," Nora said in a rush, desperate to say the words before it was too late.

"You know what's sad about that?" Caroline's voice broke. A little sob sounded in her throat. "I believe you." She hung up.

The dial tone buzzed in Nora's ears.

Dee rushed into the living room, her eyes wide. "Mr. Adams is on the phone."

"Oh, God—"

"I told him you weren't here, but he screamed at me. He said to tell you to pick up the *f*-ing phone or he was going to call his lawyers."

Nora sighed. Of course. Tom Adams hadn't become a newspaper mogul by playing nice. He was a good ole boy who had fought his way to the top by never giving an inch to anyone.

She rubbed her suddenly throbbing temples. "Put him through."

"Thanks," Dee said. Turning, she hurried out of the living room and went back into Nora's office.

Nora answered the phone. "Hello, Tom."

"Jee-zuz Kee-riste, Nora, what in the Sam Hill were

you thinking? I heard about this godawful mess when I was on the crapper this A.M. If I hadn't had the television on, I don't know when I'da found out. My little woman said to me, 'Gee, Tommy, your little gal has herself in a pickle, don't she?' "

Nora winced. "Sorry, Tom. I was caught off guard by the whole thing myself."

"Well, you're on guard now, little lady. Tamara tells me that you haven't gotten any letters yet, but you will. My guess is they'll start comin' in tomorrow."

"You've got two months' worth of columns from me on file. That'll give me some time to figure out how I want to handle this."

He made a barking sound. "I pay you a wagonload of money to answer readers' letters, and now that they finally got something interesting to ask about, you sure as hell aren't going to play possum. Scandals sell newspapers and I mean to cash in on your heartache. Sorry, Nora—and I do mean that; I've always liked you—but business is business. Your agent sure understood business when he bled me for that million-dollar contract."

Nora felt sick to her stomach. "The radio station is giving me some time off—"

"Don't you confuse me with those tie-wearin' pantywaists. I haven't backed down from a fight in my life, and my people aren't going to, either."

The headache blossomed into a full-blown migraine. "Okay, Tom," she said softly. She'd say anything to end this conversation. "Give me a few days. Use what you have for now, and then I'll start to answer the hate mail."

He chuckled. "I knew you'd see the light, Nora. Bye now."

She hung up. The silence that came after all that yelling was strangely heavy.

Tom actually expected her to sit down and read angry, disappointed letters from the very people who used to love her.

Impossible.

Ruby stood in her steam-clouded bathroom, staring through the mist at her watery reflection. The lines beneath her puffy eyes looked like they'd been stitched in place by an industrial sewing machine.

It wouldn't do to look this old, not in Hollywood. She wanted people to think of her as young and hip and defiant, not as a woman who'd wasted her youth in nightclubs and had nothing to show for it except early-onset wrinkles.

She used makeup to take off the years. Enough "heroin-chic" black eyeliner and people would assume she was young and stupid. Sort of the way gorgeous celebrities wore godawful hairdos to the Academy Awards; their message had to be *looks don't matter to me*.

As if.

Only a beautiful woman would even consider making that ridiculous statement.

Ruby dressed carefully—V-necked cashmere sweater, black leather miniskirt, and black tights. She hadn't had time to run to the store for temporary hair dye, but a lot of gel had made her hair poke out everywhere instead. She layered fourteen cheap plastic Mardi Gras necklaces around her neck and painted her stubby, bitten-off fingernails a glittery shade of midnight blue. Finally, she put on a pair of clunky black sunglasses—Rite Aid knockoffs of the newest designer fashion.

Then she took a deep breath, grabbed her handbag, and headed outside.

The sleek black limousine was already parked at the curb. Ruby couldn't help wishing that Max were here right now. She'd just love to shove past him and drive away.

A uniformed driver stood beside the car. "Miss Bridge?"

She grinned. No one ever called her that. "That's me. I'm going to—"

"I know, miss. The Paramount lot. I'll be waiting to take you home after the taping."

The driver came around and opened the door for her. Ruby peered into the dark interior and saw a dozen white roses in a sheath of opalescent tissue paper lying on the backseat. An ice bucket held a bottle of chilled Dom Pérignon.

Ruby slid into the seat, heard the satisfying thud of the closing door, and plucked the card from the flowers.

People as talented as you don't need luck. They need a chance, and this is yours. Love, Val.

God, it felt good. As if those tarnished dreams of hers were finally coming true.

She had never meant to need it all so much. It had begun as a lark—something she did well without a lot of effort. Ruby the class clown, always making people laugh. But after her mother abandoned them, everything had changed. *Ruby* had changed. From that moment on, nothing and no one had been quite enough for her. She'd come to need the unconditional acceptance that only fame could provide.

She scooted closer to the window, grinning as the limo pulled up to the security booth at the entrance to Paramount. The twin white arches, trimmed in golden metallic scrollwork, announced to the world that through these gates was a special world, open only to a lucky few.

Ruby hit the button to lower the privacy shield just in time to hear the driver say, "I have Miss Bridge for *Uproar*."

The guard stepped back into his booth, consulted a clipboard, then waved them through. Ruby plastered herself close to the window, looking for celebrities, but all she saw were regular people milling about. The closest she came to seeing a movie star was a red sportscar parked in a stall marked JULIA ROBERTS.

At the visitors' lot, the driver parked the car and came around, opening Ruby's door. "There's your ride," he said, pointing to a vehicle that looked like a stretched-out golf cart. A man in tan-colored shorts and a matching polo shirt was standing beside it. "They'll zip you up to the studio. I'll be right here whenever you get back."

Ruby tried to look blasé, as if she did this all the time. To tell the truth, if her blood pressure bumped up another notch, she was probably going to stroke out.

She took a deep breath and headed toward the cart. Once she got in, the driver settled behind the wheel and started the soundless engine. The cart moved jerkily between the huge soundstages. There were people everywhere, walking, riding bicycles. They passed a battalion of aliens—was that Patrick Stewart?—and veered around a gathering of cowboys. Finally, they pulled up to soundstage nine, a hulking, flesh-colored building. Above the door was a neon sign that read UPROAR! A NEW KIND OF TALK SHOW WITH JOE COCHRAN.

Ruby jumped off the cart and crossed the street. She paused a minute, then opened the door. Inside was a kaleidoscope of colored lights, darkened seating, and people. That's what she noticed most of all—there were people everywhere, scurrying around like ants with clipboards, checking and rechecking, nodding and cursing and laughing.

"You're Ruby Bridge?"

Ruby jumped. She hadn't even noticed the small, platinum blonde who now stood beside her, peering up at Ruby through the ugliest pair of brown-framed glasses she'd ever seen. "I'm Ruby."

"Good." The woman grabbed Ruby's arm and led her through the swarming people, down a quieter hallway and into a small waiting room. On the table beside a brown sofa were a bowl of fruit and a bottle of Perrier on ice. "Do you need makeup?"

Ruby laughed. "Are you thinking of an intervention?"

The woman frowned, cocked her head, birdlike. "Excuse me?"

Ruby nodded stiffly. "My makeup's fine. Thanks."

"Good. Sit here. Someone will come and get you when it's time to go on." The woman consulted her papers. "You get two minutes up front. You were a last-minute guest, so there's no time for an interview; we'll just have to make do. Be fast and be funny." With a quick sniff, the woman was gone.

Ruby collapsed on the sofa. Suddenly she was more than nervous. She was terrified. *Be funny.*

What had she been thinking? She wasn't funny. Her material might be funny, but *she* wasn't. It usually took her three minutes into a routine before she calmed down enough to make people laugh.

So, a minute after she was finished, she'd be a riot.

She shot to her feet. Her heart was pounding so hard she thought for a second that someone was at the door.

"Calm down, Ruby," she said, forcing her fingers to uncurl. She focused on her breathing. In and out, in and out. "You are funny. You are."

There was a knock at the door. "They're ready for you, Miss Bridge."

"Oh, my God." Ruby glanced at the wall clock. She'd been standing here, hyperventilating, for thirty minutes, and now she couldn't remember one goddamn line of material.

The door swung open.

Bird lady stood there, pointy face tilted to the left. "Miss Bridge?"

Ruby exhaled slowly, slowly. "I'm ready," she said, and though she was facing the woman, she was really talking to herself. She *was* ready; she'd been ready all her life.

She followed the woman toward the stage. As she got closer, she could hear the familiar strains of the opening music. Then came Joe's voice; the audience laughed in response to something he said.

"Remember," the woman said in a stage whisper, "we want *opinions*, the more outrageous and controversial the better."

Ruby nodded in understanding, although truthfully, she didn't think she had an opinion on anything right now except her own shortcomings. And as an added bonus, she was sweating like a geyser. Mascara was probably running down her cheeks.

She'd look like something out of *Alien* by the time—

"Ruby Bridge!" Her name roared through the sound system, chased by the sound of applause.

Ruby pushed through the curtains, smiling to the best of her ability. She forced herself not to squint, although the lights were so bright she couldn't see anything. She just hoped she didn't walk off the end of the stage.

She went to the microphone. It made a fuzzy, crackling sound as she pulled it off its stand. "Well," she said with a bright smile, "it's nice to know I'm not the only person who can come to a talk show in the middle of the day. Of course, it's easy for me. I was fired yesterday. *Fired,* from a trendy, shit-ass restaurant that I won't name—but it sounds like Irma's Hash House. I won't even *tell* you what I thought we'd be selling . . ."

A smattering of laughter.

"Actually, if they were going to fire me, I'm glad it happened on Thursday. Friday is all-you-can-eat night. And trust me, people take that literally. Irma's is the only restaurant in L.A. where they have defibrillators on the table. Ketchup? Mustard? Restart your heart?" She let silence have a beat of her time. "I mean, this is the new millennium. I kept saying to people, for the love of God, *eat fruit.*"

More laughter, deeper this time. It gave her confidence.

She grinned, then launched into the rest of her

routine, saving the best jokes—about her mother—
for last.

At the end of her abbreviated routine, Ruby stepped
back from the mike. Amid the beautiful sound of applause, Joe Cochran crossed the stage toward her. He
was smiling, which was definitely a good sign.

He placed a hand warmly on her shoulder and turned
to face the crowd. "You've all met the very funny
Ruby Bridge. Now, let's meet the rest of our players
for tonight. There's family therapist Elsa Pine, author
of the bestselling book *Poisonous Parents*, and the honorable Sanford Tyrell, congressman from Alabama."

Elsa and Sanford walked onstage, looking like a
pencil and a softball. They were careful not to make
eye contact with each other.

Joe clapped his hands together. "Let's get started."

The three guests followed Joe to the artfully arranged leather chairs on the stage. Joe sat down in the
center seat, then looked up at the audience and smiled.
"I don't know about you all, but I'm sick and tired of
the way our judicial system handles criminals. Every
time I open the paper, I read about some psychopath
who killed a little girl and got off because the jury felt
sorry for him. I mean, sorry for *him*. Who's looking
out for the victims here?"

"Now, Joe." Elsa leaned forward, her eyes narrowed
and hard beneath the sensible, round glasses. She was
so thin, Ruby wondered how her lungs could fill with
air without knocking her over. "Criminals aren't born,
they're made. It makes perfect sense to understand that
some people have been so abused by their parents that
they no longer know right from wrong."

"Little lady," the good congressman said, his florid face creasing into a good-ole-boy grin, "that's about as wrong-headed as a filly can be."

Ruby frowned at the audience. "Did he call her a filly? Tell me I heard wrong . . ."

Laughter.

Elsa ignored it. "You heard right. Congressman—"

"Call me Sanford." He pulled almost four syllables out of his name.

"The measure of a society is its compassion."

"What about compassion for the victim's family," Joe said, "or do you bleeding-heart liberals just want us to be compassionate toward the murderer?" He looked at Ruby. "You know something about toxic parents, Ruby. Is everything wrong in your life your mother's fault?"

Elsa nodded. "Yes, Ruby, you of all people should understand how deeply a parent can wound a child. I mean, your mother is a huge proponent of marriage. She positively waxes poetic about the sanctity of the vows—"

Ruby laughed. "So does Bill Clinton."

Elsa wouldn't be sidetracked by the audience's laughter. "You were probably the only person in America who wasn't surprised by the *Tattler* today."

"I don't read the tabloids," Ruby answered.

A whisper moved through the audience, chairs squeaked. Joe's enthusiastic smile dimmed. He shot a quick look at bird woman, who was standing just off-stage. Then he leaned forward. "You haven't read today's *Tattler*?"

Ruby's frown deepened. "Is that a crime now?"

Joe reached down, and for the first time Ruby noticed the newspaper folded beneath his chair. He picked it up, handed it to her. "I'm sorry. You were supposed to have known."

Ruby felt a sudden tension in the room, the kind of hush that fell just before a bar fight started. She took the newspaper from him, opened it. At first, all she noticed was the headline: RAISING MORE THAN SPIRITS. It made her smile. How did they come up with this stuff?

Then she saw the photograph.

It was a blurry, grainy shot of two naked people entwined. The editors had carefully placed black "privacy strips" across the pertinent body parts, but there was no denying what was going on. Or who the woman was.

Ruby looked helplessly at the faces around her. Joe appeared focused, a dog poised on the scent. The therapist frowned thoughtfully. They were imagining her pain.

She tossed the newspaper down in disgust. It landed on the floor with a muffled thwack. "There's a lesson to women everywhere in this. When your lover says, 'One little photo, honey, just for us,' you better cover your naked ass and run."

Elsa leaned forward. "How does it make you feel to see—"

Joe raised his hands. "We're getting off the topic here. The question is, how much of our screw ups are our fault? Does a bad parent give someone a free ride to commit crime?"

"This country's gone excuse crazy," the congressman said, not meeting Ruby's gaze. "Every time some loony bin goes crazy, we put his mother on trial. It ain't right."

"Exactly!" Joe said. "Too damn bad if you were abused. If you do the crime, you do the time."

Ruby sat perfectly still. There was no reason for her to speak, and truthfully, she couldn't think of a thing to say. She knew she'd given *Uproar* what it had wanted—a reaction. Her surprise was icing on the cake. By tomorrow, she knew her blank-eyed, dim-witted reaction to the scandal would lead every report. She'd look like an idiot from coast to coast.

She should have known it would be like this . . . her big break. What a joke. How could she have been so naive?

Finally, she heard Joe wrapping up. She blinked, trying to look normal.

"That's all the time we have for today, folks. Tune in next week, when our subject will be communicating with the dead—possible? Or just plain fraud? Thank you."

The applause sign lit up and the audience responded immediately, clapping thunderously.

Ruby rose from her chair and moved blindly across the stage. People were talking to her, but she couldn't hear anything they were saying.

Someone touched her shoulder. She jumped and spun around.

"Ruby?" It was Joe. He was standing beside her, his handsome face drawn into a tight frown. "I'm really sorry about ambushing you. The story broke yesterday. It never occurred to us that you'd miss it. Every station covered it, and since so much of your material is about your relationship with your mother . . ." He let the explanation founder.

"I turned off my phone and television," she answered, then added, "I was getting ready for the show."

He sighed. "You thought this was your big break. And it turned out—"

"Not to be." She cut him off. The pity in his eyes was more than she could bear. She knew he used to be a stand-up comic himself; he knew exactly what had happened. She didn't want her disappointment cemented into words she'd remember forever.

"You know, Ruby," he said, "I've seen your act a few times. The Comedy Store, I think. Your material's good."

"Thanks."

"Maybe you should think about writing, like for a sitcom. They could use your talent at the networks."

Ruby stood there with a fake smile pasted on her face. He was telling her to give up. Try something else.

It felt to Ruby as if she were fading away, but like the Cheshire cat, she'd smile to the end. "Thanks, Joe. I have to go now."

She ran back to her chair and grabbed her handbag. At the last second, she plucked up the *Tattler* and crammed it under her armpit. Without glancing at anyone, she raced out of the studio.

In her apartment, Ruby closed all the blinds and turned off the lights.

She slumped onto her worn sofa and thumped her feet onto the cheap, wood-grain coffee table. A half-full water glass rattled at the movement. The tabloid lay beside her, barely seen in the darkness.

Mommie Dearest had an affair, after all.

It didn't surprise her, that realization, not truly. Any woman who would leave her children to go in search of fame and fortune wouldn't think twice about having an affair. What surprised Ruby was how much it still hurt.

Her fingers shook as she reached for the phone and dialed her sister's number. It was rare that Ruby called Caroline—too expensive—but it wasn't every day you saw naked pictures of your mother having sex with a stranger.

Caroline answered on the second ring. "Hello?"

"Hey, sis," Ruby said, feeling a sudden tide of loneliness.

"So, you finally plugged your phone in. I've been going crazy trying to reach you."

"Sorry," she said softly. Her throat felt embarrassingly tight. "I saw the pictures."

"Yeah. You and everyone else in America. I was always afraid something like this would happen."

Ruby was stunned. She had *never* imagined it. "Did you know about the affair?"

"I suspected."

"Why didn't you ever tell me?"

"Come on, Rube. You've never once mentioned her name to me, not in all these years. You didn't want to know anything about her."

Ruby hated it when Caroline acted like she knew everything. "I suppose you've already forgiven her, Caroline-the-saint."

"No," Caro said softly. "I'm having a hard time with this one. It's so . . . public."

"Ah. Appearances. I forgot about that."

"Don't make me sound so shallow. There's more to it than that and you know it."

Ruby was instantly contrite. She hated how easy it was for her to say hurtful things—even to the people she loved. When Mom had left them, Caroline had been the one who held the family together, even though she'd been no more than a teenager herself. She'd stepped up and been everything Ruby needed. Without Caroline, Ruby honestly believed she wouldn't have made it through that awful year. "I'm sorry. You know how goodness brings out the worst in me."

"I'm not so good. Yesterday, I said some really nasty things to her. I couldn't seem to help myself. I was so mad."

"You talked to her? What did she say?"

"She's sorry. She loves me."

Ruby snorted. "Yeah, just imagine if she hated us."

Caroline laughed. "I'm going to call her when I calm down. Maybe we can finally talk about some of the things . . . you know, the stuff that matters."

"Nothing she has to say matters, Caro. I've been telling you that for years."

"You're wrong about that, Rube. Someday you'll see that, but for now, all I know is that this thing is going to get a heck of a lot worse before it gets better."

"Only for you, Glenda. I'm not the one who keeps trying to forgive her."

Before Caroline could respond, the doorbell rang. It played a stanza of *I just met a girl named Maria* . . .

Ruby made a mental note to change the damned bell. Max had thought it was funny; Ruby disagreed. "I gotta run, Caroline. There's someone here to see me. With my luck, it's probably the landlord, looking for my rent check."

"Take care of yourself."

"You, too. And kiss my niece and nephew for me." She hung up, then decided not to answer the door anyway. It probably *was* the landlord.

She went into the kitchen. Flipping through the mostly empty cabinets, she found a half-full fifth of gin and a bottle of vermouth, both of which Max had obviously forgotten. She made herself a martini in a Rubbermaid container, then poured the drink into a plastic tumbler.

By the third repeat of "Maria," she gave up. Taking a quick sip of the martini, she padded across the shag carpeting and peered through the peephole.

It was Val, standing beside a woman so thin she looked like a windshield wiper.

"Oh, *perfect*."

She wrenched the door open. Val grinned at her. He looked acutely out of place in the dim, ugly corridor.

Val leaned forward and kissed Ruby's cheek. "How's my newest star?"

"Fuck you," she whispered, smiling brightly at the strange woman. "I never saw it coming."

Val drew back, frowning. "I tried to call you. I even sent a messenger over. You didn't answer the door."

Ruby would have said more, but the way the lady was watching them made her uncomfortable. She turned to her, noticing the woman's severe haircut and expensive black dress. An unlit cigarette dangled from her bony fingers.

New Yorker. Definitely. Maybe a mortician.

"I'm Ruby Bridge," she said, extending her hand.

The woman shook her hand. Firm grip. Clammy skin. "Joan Pinon."

"Come on in." Ruby backed away from the door, made a sweeping gesture with her hand. She tried not to see the apartment through their eyes, but it was impossible. Tacky furniture, dusty shag carpeting, garage-sale decor.

Val went right to Max's old velour Barcalounger and sat down. Joan perched birdlike on the end of the sofa.

Ruby flopped down on the sofa's other cushion. She took a sip of her drink. A big gulp, actually. "I know it's early for drinks, but it's not every day you see nude pictures of your mother *and* lose your career. I'll probably get hit by a bus later today."

Val leaned forward. "Joan is an editor from New York."

"Really?"

"She's here because of your mother."

Ruby took a long, stinging swallow. "Of course she is." She wished she had an olive to nibble on; she needed something to do with her hands. She turned to Joan. "What do you want?"

"I work for *Caché* magazine. We'd like you to write an exposé on your mother." Joan smiled, showing a mouthful of smoker's teeth. "We could hire a ghostwriter if you'd like, but Val tells me you're a first-rate writer."

A compliment. That felt good. Ruby settled back in her seat, eyeing Joan. "You want a daughter's betrayal."

"Who betrayed whom?" Joan said. "Your mother has been telling America to honor commitments and put their children first. These photographs prove that she's a liar and a hypocrite, plain and simple. We checked the records. Nora was married to your father when those pictures were taken. People have a right to know who they're taking advice from."

"Ah, the people's right," Ruby said, taking another sip of her martini.

"It's just an article, Ruby, not a book. No more than fifteen thousand words, and . . ." Val said, "it could make you famous."

"*Rich* and famous," Joan added.

Now *that* got Ruby's attention. She set the glass down and looked at Joan. "How rich?"

"Fifty thousand dollars. I'm prepared to pay you half of that amount right now, and the other half when you deliver the article. The only catch is: you can't do any interviews until we publish."

"Fifty thousand *dollars*?" Ruby reached for her drink again, but she was too wound up to take a sip. For a few measly words . . .

And all she had to do was serve up her mother's life for public consumption.

She set her drink down. This wasn't something to take lightly. She wished she had someone to ask about it, but Ruby had always had problems trusting people, and that made close friendships impossible. There was her dad, but he was so busy with his new family that he and Ruby weren't as close as they'd once been. And her sister had spent the past decade trying to forgive their mother; there was no doubt she'd tell Ruby to turn down the deal. Caro would despise the idea of airing their family's dirty laundry in public.

"I don't know my mother that well," she said

slowly, trying to think through it. "The last time I saw her was at my sister's wedding nine years ago. We didn't speak."

That wasn't entirely true. Ruby had spoken to her mother. She'd said, "And I thought the worst part of this day would be wearing pink polyester." Then she'd walked away.

"We don't want cold facts and figures. We want your opinions, your thoughts on what kind of a person she is . . . what kind of a mother she was."

"That's easy. She'd step on your grandmother's throat to get ahead. Nothing—and no one—matters to her, except herself."

"You see?" Joan said, eyes shining. "That's exactly the perspective we want. Now, I'm sure you'll understand that we need to go to press fast. While the scandal's still hot. I brought the contract with me— Val has already had a literary agent look it over—and a check for twenty-five thousand dollars." She reached into her black snakeskin (appropriate, Ruby thought) briefcase and pulled out a stack of papers and a check. She slapped the papers down on the table, with the check on top.

Ruby stared down at all those zeros and swallowed hard. She'd never had that much money at one time. Hell, it was more than her salary for all of last year.

Joan smiled, a shark's grin. "Let me ask you this, Ruby. Would your mother turn down this offer if *you* were the subject of the article?"

The answer to that question came easily. Her mother had once had to make a choice like this. She could have chosen her husband and her daughters . . .

or her career. Without a backward glance, Nora Bridge had chosen herself.

"This is your chance, Ruby," Val said. "Think of the exposure. The networks will be fighting over you."

She felt flushed. There was this strange sensation that she was removed from her body, watching the scene unfurl from a distance. Slowly, she heard herself answer, "I'm a good writer . . ." That was one thing she'd always believed. Now she knew that Val believed it, too. She bit her lower lip, worrying it. If the article made her famous, maybe she could parlay notoriety into a sitcom. "I certainly know the beginning of her career—who she may have fucked to get to the top and who she just plain screwed."

Joan was smiling now. "We've tentatively booked you on *The Sarah Purcell Show* for a week from now . . . to promote the article."

The Sarah Purcell Show . . .

Ruby closed her eyes, wanting it so much her head hurt. She'd clawed and scratched through life for so long, been a nobody, a nothing . . .

She thought of all the reasons she should say no— the moral, ethical reasons—but none of them found a place to stick. Instead, she thought about those damned photos . . .

And all of her mother's lies.

She took a deep breath, then exhaled. Slowly, she reached down for the check and picked it up. The numbers swam before her eyes. "Okay," she said. "I'll do it."

Chapter Four

Ruby cranked the Volkswagen's radio to full blast. A raucous Metallica song blared through the small black speakers. Her whole body was moving to the beat.

Fifty thousand dollars.

She wanted so badly to share this day with someone. If only she had Max's new number; she'd call him and tell him what he'd missed out on. She would have spent a lot of this money on him . . . on them . . .

The thought brought a quick thrust of sadness, and the feeling pissed her off. Max didn't deserve one cent of this fortune.

She drove into Beverly Hills. Usually, she didn't even drive past this area; it was too depressing to see all the luxuries she couldn't afford. But today, she was flying high. She felt invincible.

When she saw an open spot on Rodeo Drive, she pulled over and parked. Grabbing her purse (with the yellow deposit slip for twenty-five thousand dollars inside), she got out of the car and slammed the door shut behind her. For once, she didn't bother locking the car; if someone was desperate enough for transportation to steal *this* one, they were welcome to it.

She strolled around for a while, passing pods of women dressed in expensive, beautiful clothing. No one made eye contact with her. In this part of the world, a twenty-seven-year-old woman dressed in what could only be called "grunge" simply didn't exist. And fifty thousand dollars wasn't nearly enough to get these women's attention.

Then she looked into a store window and saw a sheer, beaded, silvery blue dress with a plunging V neckline and a split in the side that came up to midthigh. It was the most perfect dress she'd ever seen, the kind of thing she'd never imagined she could own.

She held her handbag close and pushed through the glass doors. A bell tinkled over her head.

Over in the corner, across an ocean of white marble flooring and chrome-topped rounders of clothing, a woman looked up. "I'll be right with you, dear," she said in one of those cultured, sorority-girl voices.

Ruby felt uncomfortable. She wished she could tape the deposit slip to her forehead.

Finally the saleswoman came over. She was tall and reed-thin, dressed in black from head to foot. Not a hair was out of place. She gave a little sniff when she saw Ruby, but her voice was kind. "May I help you?"

Ruby pointed helplessly toward the window. "I saw a blue dress in the window."

"You have excellent taste. Would you like to try it on?"

She nodded.

"Wonderful."

The woman led Ruby to a dressing room that was bigger than the average bedroom. "Would you like a glass of champagne?"

Ruby laughed. Now, *this* was shopping. "I'd love some."

The saleswoman raised her hand; just that, and within a minute, a man in a black tuxedo was handing Ruby a sparkling glass of champagne.

"Thanks," she said, collapsing onto the cushy seat in the dressing room. The champagne's bubbles seemed to float through her blood, making her instantly giddy. For the first time in years, she felt like somebody.

Someone knocked at the door.

"Come in."

The saleslady peeked her head in. "Here you go. I'm Demona. Just holler if you need me."

Ruby trailed her fingers down the beaded, sheer-as-tissue fabric, then quickly undressed and slipped into the dress.

It was like stepping into another personality . . . a different life. Self-consciously, she peeked out of the dressing room. The coast was clear. She walked over to the wall-size mirrors in the corner.

Her breath caught. Even with her hair too short and her makeup too heavy, and her feet wedged into scuffed old Reeboks, she looked . . . beautiful. The plunging neckline accentuated her small breasts; her waist appeared tiny, and the slit slimmed her fleshy thighs.

This was the woman she had hoped someday to become. How had she veered so far off the path?

"Oh, my," Demona said wistfully, "it's perfect. And

you don't need a stitch of alterations. I've never seen anything fit so well right off the rack."

"I'll take it," Ruby said in a thick voice.

At least she could have this moment, she thought, this memory of a perfect day. The dress would hang in her closet forever, a pristine reminder of the woman Ruby wanted to be.

She wrote a check—almost thirty-five hundred dollars, including the tax and shoes—and hung the dress carefully in the backseat of the Volkswagen.

Then, cranking the music back up—Steppenwolf this time—she sped toward the freeway. She was almost home when she passed the Porsche dealer.

Ruby laughed and slammed on the brakes.

Nora lay curled on the elegant sofa in her darkened living room. Hours ago, she'd sent Dee home and disconnected the phones.

Then she'd watched the news.

Big mistake. Huge.

Every station had the story; they played and replayed the same footage, showed the lurid blacked-out photographs again and again, usually followed with sound bites of Nora expounding on the importance of fidelity and the sanctity of the marriage vows. What hurt the most were the "man in the street" interviews. Her fans had turned on her; some women even cried at the betrayal they felt. "I trusted her" was the most common refrain.

She was finished. Never again would someone write her a letter and ask for advice; never again would people stand in line in the pouring rain outside the station for a chance to meet her in person.

She knew, too, what was happening in the lobby downstairs. She'd called her doorman several times today, and the report was always the same. The press was outside, cameras at the ready. One sighting of Nora Bridge and they would spring on her like wild dogs. Her doorman claimed that the garage was safe— they weren't allowed in there—but she was afraid to chance it.

She sat up. Huge glass windows reflected the town's bright lights, turned them into a smear of color. The Space Needle hung suspended in the misty sky, an alien ship hovering above the city.

She walked toward the window. Her reflection, caught in the glass, looked bleary and small.

Small.

That's how she felt. It was a familiar feeling, one that had defined her life long ago. It was this sense of being . . . nothing . . . that had set her on the path to ruin in the first place, and she didn't miss the irony that she was here again.

If her father were alive, he'd be laughing. *Not so big a star now, are you, missy?*

She walked into the kitchen and stood in front of the makeshift "bar" she kept for company. Nora hadn't taken a drink in more years than she could count.

But now she needed *something* to help her out of this hole. She felt as if she were drowning . . .

She poured herself a tumbler full of gin. It tasted awful at first—like isopropyl alcohol—but after a few gulps, her tongue went dead and the booze slid down easily, pooling firelike in her cold stomach.

On her way back into the living room, she paused at the grand piano, her attention arrested by the collection of gilt-framed photographs on the gleaming ebony surface. She almost never looked at them, not closely. It was like closing her hand around a shard of broken glass.

Still, one caught her eye. It was a picture of her and her ex-husband, Rand, and their two daughters. They'd been standing in front of the family beach house, their arms entwined, their smiles honest and bright.

She tipped the glass back and finished the drink, then went back for another. By the time she finished that one, she could barely walk straight; there seemed to be a sheet of wax paper between her and the world.

That was fine. She didn't want to think too clearly right now. When her mind was clear, she knew that she'd been on the run for all of her life, and—at last—she'd hit a brick wall. The world knew the truth about her now, and so did her children.

She swayed drunkenly, staring at the photographs. On one side of the piano were family pictures—Christmas mornings, little girls in pink tutus at dance recitals, family vacations taken in that old tent trailer they'd hauled around behind the station wagon.

On the other side were photographs of a woman who was always alone, even in the biggest of crowds. She looked beautiful—makeup artists and hairdressers and personal trainers saw to that. She was flawlessly dressed in expensive clothes, often surrounded by fans and employees.

Adored by strangers.

She stumbled away from the piano and plugged the phone into the wall. Bleary-eyed, she dialed her psychiatrist.

A moment later, a woman answered. "Dr. Allbright's office."

"Hi, Midge. It's Nora Bridge." She hoped she wasn't slurring her words. "Is the doctor in?"

A sniff. That was the only sound, but Nora knew. "He's not in, Ms. Bridge. Shall I take a message?"

Ms. Bridge. Only days ago it had been Nora.

"Is he at home?"

"No, he's unreachable, but I can put you through to his service. Or he left Dr. Hornby's number for emergency referrals . . ."

Nora struggled to remain steady. Call waiting beeped. "Thanks, Midge. There's no need for that." She waited an endless second for Midge to respond, and when the silence began to ache, Nora hung up. Then she ripped the cord out of the wall again.

In some distant part of her mind, she knew that she was sinking into a pool of self-pity, and that she could drown in it, but she didn't know how to crawl out.

Eric.

He would be on the island by now. If she hurried, maybe she could still make the last ferry . . .

She grabbed her car keys off the kitchen counter and staggered into her bedroom. After cramming a blond wig over her cropped auburn hair, she put on a pair of Jackie O sunglasses. On the bedside table, she found her sleeping pills. Of course it would be bad—wrong—to take one now; even in her drunken state, she knew she couldn't mix booze and pills. But she wanted to.

God, she wanted to . . .

She tossed the brown plastic bottle in her purse.

The only thing she took from her condominium was an old photograph of their family, one taken at Disneyland when the girls were small. She shoved it in her handbag and left without bothering to check the lock.

She banged along the wall, using it as a guardrail as she tottered toward the elevator. Once inside, she clung to the slick wooden handrail, praying there wouldn't be a stop in the lobby. She got lucky; the mirrored elevator went all the way down to the parking garage, where it stopped with a clang.

The doors opened.

She peered out; the garage was empty. She careened unsteadily toward her car, collapsing against the jet-black side of her Mercedes. It took her several tries to get the key in the lock, but she finally managed.

She slid awkwardly into the soft leather seat. The engine started easily, a roar of sound in the darkness. The radio came on instantly. Bette Midler singing about the wind beneath her wings.

Nora caught sight of herself in the rearview mirror. Her face was pale, her cheeks tear-streaked. She'd chewed at her lower lip until it was misshapen.

"What are you doing?" she asked the woman in the sunglasses. She heard the slurring, drunken sound of her voice, and it made her cry. Hot tears blurred her vision.

"Please, God," she whispered, "let Eric still be there."

She slammed the car into reverse and backed out of the spot. Then she headed forward and hit the gas. Tires squealed as she rounded the corner and hurtled up the ramp. She didn't even glance left for traffic as she sped out onto Second Avenue.

Dean stood on the slatted wooden dock. The seaplane taxied across the choppy blue waves and lifted skyward, its engine chattering as it banked left and headed back to Seattle.

He'd forgotten how beautiful this place was, how peaceful.

The tide was out now, and this stretch of beach, as familiar to him once as his own hand, smelled of sand that had baked in the hot sun, of kelp that was slowly curling into leathery strips. He knew that if he jumped down onto that sand, it would swallow his expensive loafers and reclaim him, turn him into a child again.

It was the smell that pulled him back in time, that and the slapping sound of the waves against barnacled pilings. A dozen memories came at him, gift-wrapped in the scent of his parents' beach at low tide.

Here, he and Eric had built their forts and buried treasures made of foil-wrapped poker chips; they'd gone from rock to rock, squatting down, scraping their knees on driftwood in search of the tiny black crabs that lived beneath the slick gray stones.

They had been the best of friends in those days, inseparable brothers who seemed so often to think with a single mind.

Of the two of them, Eric had been the strong one, the golden boy who did everything well and fought for his heart's desires. At seven, Eric had demanded to be taken to Granddad's island house on Lopez, the one they'd seen pictures of. And it was Eric who'd first convinced Mother to let them stay.

Dean could still remember the arguments. They were hushed, of course, as all Sloan disagreements were required to be, full of sibilant sounds and pregnant pauses. He remembered sitting at the top of the stairs, his scrawny body pressed so tightly against the railing that he'd worn the marks later on his flesh, listening to his older brother plead for the chance to go to the island school.

Absurd, Mother had declared at first, but Eric had worked on her relentlessly, wearing her down. As a child, Eric had been every bit as formidable as their mother, and in the end, he'd won. At the time, it had seemed a monumental victory; with age came wisdom, however. The truth was, Mother was so busy running Harcourt and Sons that she didn't care where her children were. Oh, occasionally she tried to do the "right" thing, as she called it—make them transfer to Choate— but in the end, she simply let them be.

Dean closed his eyes, then opened them quickly, startled by the sound of laughter.

But it was only an echo in his mind, an auditory memory. He hated what had brought him home at last, hated that it had taken a disease to bring him back to his brother. Even more, he hated the way he felt about Eric now; they'd grown so far apart. And all of it was Dean's fault. He saw that, knew it, hated it, and couldn't seem to change it.

It had happened on a seemingly ordinary Sunday. Dean had moved off of the island by then, gone to prep school; he'd been a senior, nursing a heart so broken that sometimes he'd forgotten to breathe. Eric had been at Princeton. They were still brothers then, separated only by miles, and they'd spoken on the phone every Sunday. One phone call had changed everything.

I've fallen in love, little bro . . . get ready for a shock . . . his name is Charlie and he's . . .

Dean had never been able to remember more than that. Somehow, in that weird, disorienting moment, his mind had shut down. He'd felt suddenly betrayed, as if the brother he'd known and loved was a stranger.

Dean had said all the right things to Eric. Even in his shocked confusion, he'd known what was expected of him, and he'd complied. But they'd both heard the lie beneath the words. Dean didn't know how to be honest, what words he could mold into an acceptable truth. He'd felt—ridiculously—as if he'd lost his brother that day.

If they'd gotten together back then, talked it through, they might have been okay. But they'd been young men, both of them, poised at the start of their lives, each one faced in a different direction. It had been easy to drift apart. By the time Dean graduated from Stanford and went to work for the family business, too much time had passed to start again. Eric had moved to Seattle and begun teaching high-school English. He'd lived with Charlie for a long time; only a few years before, Dean had received a note from Eric about Charlie's lost battle with AIDS.

Dean had sent flowers and a nice little card. He'd meant to pick up the phone, but every time he reached for it, he wondered what in the world he could say.

He turned away from the water and walked down the dock, then climbed the split-log stairs set into the sandy cliff. He was out of breath when he finally emerged on top of the bluff.

The sprawling Victorian house was exactly as he remembered it—salmony pink siding, steeply pitched roof, elegant white cutwork trim. Clematis vines curled around the porch rails and hung in frothy loops from along the eaves. The lawn was still as flat and green as a patch of Christmas felt. Roses bloomed riotously, perfectly trimmed and fertilized from year to year.

It was something his mother never forgot: home maintenance fees. Every house she owned was precisely cared for, but this one more than most. She knew—or imagined, which to her was the same as certainty—that Eric occasionally visited the summer house with *that man*. She didn't want to hear any complaints from them about the property.

Dean headed toward the house, ducking beneath the outstretched branches of an old madrona tree. As he bent, a glint of silver caught his eye. He turned, realizing a moment too late what he'd seen.

The swing set, rusted now and forgotten. A whispery breeze tapped one of the red seats, made the chains jangle. The sight of it dragged out an unwelcome memory . . .

Ruby. She'd been right there, leaning against the slanted metal support pole, with her arms crossed.

It was the moment—the exact second—he'd realized his best friend was a *girl*.

He'd moved toward her.

What? she'd said, laughing. *Am I drooling or something?*

All at once, he'd realized that he loved her. He'd wanted to say the words to her, but it was the year his voice betrayed him. He'd been so afraid of sounding like a girl when he spoke, and so he'd kissed her.

It had been the first kiss for both of them, and to this day, when Dean kissed a woman, he longed for the smell of the sea.

He spun away from the swing set and strode purposefully toward the house. At the front door, he paused, gathering courage and molding it into a smile. Then he knocked on the door.

From inside came the pattering sound of footsteps.

The door burst open and Lottie was there. His old nanny flung open her pudgy arms. "Dean!"

He stepped over the threshold and walked into the arms that had held him in his youth. He breathed in her familiar scent—Ivory soap and lemons.

He drew back, smiling. "Hey, Lottie. It's good to see you."

She gave him "the look"—one thick gray eyebrow arched. "I'm surprised you could still find your way here."

Though he hadn't seen her in more than a decade, she had barely aged. Oh, her hair was grayer, but she still wore it drawn back into a cookie-size bun at the base of her skull. Her ruddy skin was still amazingly wrinkle-free, and her bright green eyes were those of a woman who'd enjoyed her life.

He realized suddenly how much he'd missed her. Lottie had come into their family as a cook for the summer and gradually had become their full-time nanny. She'd never had any children of her own, and Eric and Dean had become her surrogate sons. She'd raised them for the ten years they'd lived on Lopez.

"I wish I were here for an ordinary visit," he said.

She blinked up at him. "It seems like only yesterday I was wiping chocolate off his little-boy face. I can't believe it. Just can't believe it." She stepped back into the well-lit entryway, wringing her hands.

Dean followed her into the living room, where a fire crackled in the huge hearth. The furniture he remembered from childhood still cluttered the big space. Cream-colored sofas on carved wooden legs faced each other. A large, oval-shaped rosewood coffee table stood between them, a beautiful Lalique bowl on its gleaming surface.

The room was gorgeously decorated in a timeless style. Not a thing was trendy or cheaply made. Every item reflected his mother's impeccable taste and boundless bank account.

The only thing missing from the room was life. No child had ever been allowed to sit on those perfect sofas, no drink had ever been spilled on that Aubusson carpet.

Dean glanced toward the stairway. "How is he?"

Lottie's green eyes filled with sadness. "Not so good, I'm sorry to say. The trip up here was hard on him. The hospice nurse was here today. She says that the new medication—something called a pain cocktail—will help him feel better."

Pain.

That was something Dean hadn't thought about, although he should have. "Jesus," he said softly, running a hand through his hair. He'd thought he was ready. He'd been mentally preparing himself, and yet now that he was here, he saw what an idiot he'd been. You couldn't prepare to watch your brother die. "Did Eric call our parents?"

"He did. They're in Greece. Athens."

"I know. Did he speak to Mother?"

Lottie glanced down at her hands; he braced himself. "Your mother's assistant spoke to him. It seems your mother was shopping when he called."

Dean's voice was purposely soft. He was afraid that if he raised it, even a bit, he'd be yelling. "Did Eric tell her about the cancer?"

"Of course. He wanted to tell your mother himself, but . . . he decided he'd better just leave a message."

"And has she returned his call?"

"No."

Dean released his breath in a tired sigh.

Lottie moved toward him. "I remember how you boys used to be. You'd walk through fire for one another."

"Yeah. I'm here for him now."

"Go on up." She smiled gently. "He's a bit the worse for wear, but he's still our boy."

Dean nodded stiffly, resettled the garment bag over his shoulder, and headed upstairs. The oak steps creaked beneath his feet. His hand slid up the oak banister, polished to sleek perfection by the comings and goings of three generations.

At the top of the stairs, the landing forked into two separate hallways. On the right was his parents' old wing; his-and-hers bedrooms that hadn't been occupied in more than fourteen years.

To the left were two doors, one closed, one partially open. The closed door led to Dean's old room. He didn't need to enter the room to picture it clearly: blue wool carpeting, maple bed with a plaid flannel bedspread, a dusty poster of Farrah Fawcett in her famous red bathing suit. He'd dreamed a million dreams in that room, imagined his unfolding life in a thousand ways . . . and none had presaged a moment like this.

Tired suddenly, he rounded the corner, passed his old bedroom, and came to Eric's door.

There he paused and drew in a deep breath, as if more air in his lungs would somehow make things better.

Then he walked into his brother's room.

The first thing he noticed was the hospital bed. It had replaced the bunk bed that once had hugged the wall. The new bed—big and metal-railed and tilted up like a lounging chair—dominated the small room. Lottie had positioned it to look out the window.

Eric was asleep.

Dean seemed to see everything at once—the way Eric's black hair had thinned to show patches of skin . . . the yellowed pallor of his sunken cheeks . . . the smudged black circles beneath his eyes . . . the veiny thinness of the arm that lay atop the stark white sheets. His lips were pale and slack, a colorless imitation of the mouth that had once smiled almost continually. Only the palest shadow of his brother lay here . . .

Dean grabbed the bed rail for support; the metal rattled beneath his grasp.

Eric's eyes slowly opened.

And there he was. The boy he'd known and loved. "Eric," he said, wishing his voice weren't so thick. He struggled to find a smile.

"Don't bother, baby brother. Not for me."

"Don't bother what?"

"Pretending not to be shocked at the way I look." Eric reached for the small pink plastic cup on his bedside tray. His long, thin fingers trembled as he guided the straw to his mouth. He sipped slowly, swallowed. When he looked up at Dean, his rheumy eyes were filled with a terrible, harrowing honesty. "I didn't think you'd come."

"Of course I came. You should have told me . . . before."

"Like when I told you I was gay? Believe me, I learned a long time ago that my family didn't handle bad news well."

Dean fought to hold back tears, and then gave up. They were the kind of tears that hurt deep in your heart. He felt a stinging sense of shame.

Remorse, regret, boredom, anticipation, ambition . . . these were the emotions that had taken Dean through life. Those, he knew how to handle, how to manipulate and compensate for. But this new emotion . . . this feeling in the pit of his stomach that he'd been a bad person, that he'd hurt his brother deeply and known it and never bothered to make it right . . .

Eric smiled weakly. "You're here now. That's enough."

"No. You've been sick for a long time . . . by yourself."

"It doesn't matter."

Dean wanted to smooth the thin strands of hair from Eric's damp forehead, to offer a comforting touch, but when he reached out, his hands were trembling, and he drew back.

It had been years since he'd comforted another human being; he didn't remember how.

"It matters," he said, hearing the thickness in his voice. He would give anything right now to erase the past, to be able to go back to that Sunday afternoon, listen to that same confession of love from his brother, and simply be happy.

But how did you do that? How did two people move backward through time and untie a knot that had tangled through every moment of their lives?

"Just talk to me," Eric said sleepily, smiling again. "Just talk, little brother. Like we used to."

Chapter Five

The phone rang in the middle of the night. Ruby groaned and glanced bleary-eyed at the bedside clock. One-fifteen.

"Shit," she mumbled. It had to be one of those idiot reporters.

She reached across Max's empty half of the bed and yanked the phone off the hook. Rolling onto her back, she brought it to her ear. "Bite me."

"I gave that up in kindergarten."

Ruby laughed sleepily. "Caro? Oh, sorry. I thought you were one of those bottom feeders from the *Tattler*."

"They aren't calling me. Of course, I haven't made a career out of dissing Mom."

"It isn't much of a career." Ruby scooted backward and leaned against the rough stucco wall. Through the phone lines, she could hear a baby crying. It was a high-pitched wailing sound, one only dogs should be able to hear. "Jesus, Caro, you must be chewing Excedrin. Does the baby Jesus always wail like that?"

"Mom's been in a car accident."

Ruby gasped. "What happened?"

"I don't know. All I know is that she's at Bayview. Apparently she'd been drinking."

"She never drinks . . . I mean, she never used to." Ruby threw back the covers and stood up. She wasn't sure why she did it, except that she had a sudden need to be moving. She held the cordless phone to her ear, walking toward the darkened kitchen. There, she stared out the slit in the tattered curtains at the black street below. The pink neon vacancy sign flickered and buzzed. She ran a hand through her sweaty hair. "How bad is it?"

"I don't know. I'm going to drop the kids off with Jere's mom first thing in the morning and go to the hospital. But I don't want to do this alone. Will you come?"

"I don't know, Car—"

"She could be dying. Think of someone besides yourself for a change," Caroline said sharply.

Ruby sighed heavily. "Okay, I'll come."

"I'll call Alaska Airlines and put a ticket on my card. There's a flight at five forty-five. You can pick it up at the counter."

"Uh . . . you don't have to do that. I have money now."

"*You?* Oh . . . well, that's great."

"I'll be there by noon." Ruby hung up the phone. Crossing her arms tightly, she paced her apartment, back and forth, back and forth, unable to stop.

She had been angry at her so-called mother forever. She couldn't really remember *not* hating her . . . and the past few days had only added fuel to the fire.

But now . . . an accident. Horrible images slammed through her mind. Paralysis . . . brain damage . . . death.

She closed her eyes. (It took her a moment to realize that she was praying.) "Take care of her," she whispered, then added a single, unfamiliar word, "Please?"

When Nora woke up the next morning, she had a moment of pure, heart-pumping fear. She was in a strange bed, in an austere room she didn't recognize.

Then she remembered.

She'd been in a car accident. She recalled the ambulance ride . . . the flashing red lights . . . the metallic taste of her own blood . . . the surprise on the young paramedic's face when he'd realized who he was treating.

And the doctors. The orthopedist who'd spoken to her just before and after the X rays. *A severe break above the ankle; another, small fracture below the knee . . . a sprained wrist.* He'd said she was lucky.

When he'd said that, she'd cried.

Now, her leg was in a cast. She couldn't see it beneath the blankets, but she could feel it. The flesh tingled and itched and her bone ached.

She sighed, feeling sorry for herself and deeply ashamed. Drinking and driving.

As if the *Tattler*'s photographs weren't enough to ruin her career, she'd added a crime to the list.

It wouldn't be long before the media picked up her scent. Someone would figure out that there was a buck to be made in telling the world that Nora Bridge was in Bayview. The accident report was probably worth thousands.

There was a knock at the door, short and sharp, and

then Caroline swept into the room. Her back was
ramrod straight, her pale hands clasped at her waist.
She wore a pair of camel-colored cashmere pants and
a matching sweater set. Her silvery blond hair was cut
in a perfect bob, one side tucked discreetly behind her
ear. Huge diamond studs glittered in her earlobes.
"Hello, Mother."

"Hi, honey. It's nice of you to come." Nora recognized instantly how distant she sounded, and it shamed
her. She and Caroline had worked hard in the past few
years, trying to come back together in an honest way.
Nora had treated her elder daughter with infinite care,
always letting Caro make the first move. Now, all that
progress had been blown to hell; she could see how far
apart they'd fallen again. There was a coldness in Caroline's eyes that Nora hadn't seen in years.

Caroline glanced at her quickly, smiled—or winced.
She looked vulnerable suddenly.

Nora couldn't stand the awkward silence that fell
between them. She said the first thing that popped
into her mind. "The doctors say I'll need to be in a
wheelchair for a few days—just until my wrist gets
strong enough to make crutches possible."

"Who is going to take care of you?"

"Oh . . . I hadn't thought about that. I guess I'll hire
someone. Shouldn't be difficult." She kept talking—
anything was better than that silence. "The big question is, *where* will I go? I can't go back to my condo.
The press has the place staked out. But I need to stay
close to my doctors."

Caroline took a step toward the bed. "You could
use the summer house. Jere and I never find time to

make it up there, and Ruby won't set foot on the island. The old house is just sitting there . . ."

The house on Summer Island. A stone's throw from Eric. It would be perfect. Nora looked up at her daughter. "You'd do that for me?"

Caroline gave her a look of infinite sadness. "I wish you knew me."

Nora sagged back into the pillows. She'd said the wrong thing again. "I'm sorry."

"God, I've heard that from you so often, I feel like it's tattooed on my forehead. Quit saying you're sorry and start acting like it. Start acting like my mother." She reached into her purse and fished out a set of keys. Pulling a single key from the ring, she set it down on the bedside table.

Nora could see that her daughter was close to breaking. "Caro—"

"Call me when you've settled in." Caroline stepped back, putting distance between them.

Nora didn't know what to say. Caroline was right; Nora hadn't had the courage to act like a mother in years.

"I have to go now."

Nora nodded stiffly, trying to smile. "Of course. Thanks for coming." She wanted to reach out for Caroline, hold her daughter's hand, and never let go.

"Good-bye, Mom."

And she was gone.

Ruby stepped out of the main terminal at SeaTac International Airport. Rain thumped on the skybridge and studded the street, creating a pewter curtain between the terminal and the multilayered parking garage across the street.

The early morning air smelled of evergreen trees and fertile black earth. Like a dash of spice in a complex recipe, there was the barest tang of the sea; a scent only a local would recognize.

As she stood beneath this bloated gray sky, smelling the moist, pine-scented air, she realized that memories were more than misty recollections. They stayed rooted in the soil in which they'd grown. There were places up north, in the San Juan Island archipelago, where bits and pieces of Ruby's life had been left scattered about like seashells on the shore. Somewhere up there sat the shadow of a thin, bold-eyed girl on a pebbly beach, tearing the petals off a daisy, chanting *He loves me; he loves me not*. She knew that if she looked hard enough, she would be able to find the invisible trail she'd left behind, the pieces of her that led from the present back to the past.

She wasn't surprised at how fresh the memories were. Nothing could ever dry up and turn to dust in the moist Seattle air. Everything thrived.

Ruby hailed a cab and climbed into the backseat, tossing her carry-on bag in beside her. She glanced at the cabbie's registration (a habit she'd formed during visits to New York) and saw that his name was Avi Avivivi.

There was a joke in that, but she was too tired to go digging around for it. "Bayview," she said, thumping back into the smelly brown velour seat.

Avi hit the gas and rocketed into the next lane.

Ruby closed her eyes, trying not to think of anything

at all. It seemed like only a few minutes later, Avi was tapping her on the shoulder.

"Mrs.? Ma'am? You are well, yes?"

Ruby jerked awake, rubbing her eyes. "I'm fine, thanks." Fishing thirty rumpled dollars out of her pocket, she handed Avi the fare and tip. Then she grabbed her purse and bag, slung both straps over her shoulder, and headed toward the hospital's double glass doors, where a few people were milling about.

Ruby was almost in their midst when she realized they were reporters.

"It's her daughter!"

The reporters turned to her all at once, yelling above one another, elbowing for position.

"Ruby, look here!"

"Was your mother drunk at the time of—"

"What did you think of the photographs—"

Ruby heard every shutter click, every picture frame advance. She noticed the strand of hair that was stuck to her lower lip, the tiny paper cut on her index finger.

It was as if she were standing miles apart from the crowd, even though she could have reached out and touched the woman from CNN.

"Ruby! Ruby! Ruby!"

For a dizzying moment, she let herself pretend that this was for her, that she had earned this attention.

"Did you know about your mother's affair?"

At that, Ruby turned. She locked eyes with a small, beak-nosed man wearing a KOMO 4 hat. "No." She flashed a bright, fake smile. "I'd make a joke about it, but it's not very funny."

She pushed through the crowd, holding her head

up, looking straight ahead. Their questions followed her, rocks thrown at her back, some hitting hard.

She strode through the pneumatic doors. They whooshed shut behind her.

Inside, it was quiet. The air smelled of disinfectant. Boldly patterned chairs dotted the vast white lobby. There were cheery, generic paintings on the walls, placed awkwardly between gilt-framed portraits of sour-looking men and women who'd obviously donated millions to the hospital.

"Ruby!"

Caroline rushed forward. Her hug almost knocked Ruby off her feet. As she held her sister, Ruby could feel how thin Caro had become, could feel the tremble in her sister's body.

At last, Caro drew back. Her mascara had run, ruining the impossible perfection of her face. "I'm sorry," she said, snapping her purse open, fishing for a lace handkerchief, which she found and dabbed at her eyes. Ruby could sense that Caroline was embarrassed by her uncharacteristic display of emotion. If old patterns ran true, Caro would pull back now, distance herself while she whittled her feelings down to an acceptable size.

Caroline closed her eyes for a moment. When she reopened them, she looked at Ruby with a kind of quiet desperation. Ruby recognized that look. Her sister was wondering why everything in life couldn't be easier, why they all couldn't simply love each other.

Silence fell between them, soft and cold as an early morning rain. In that quiet, Ruby heard the echo of a broken family; they were individual pieces, now separate, wanting a wholeness that had been shattered.

"So, how is Nora?" Ruby asked at last.

Caroline gave her a sharp look. "She still hates it when we call her Nora."

"Really? I'd forgotten that."

"I'll bet you did. Anyway, she drove her car into a tree. Her leg is broken; her wrist is sprained. She'll be in a wheelchair for a few days. That makes it pretty tough to do the ordinary bits and pieces of life. She'll need help."

"I pity the poor nurse who takes *that* job."

Caroline looked at her. "Would *you* want to be cared for by a stranger?"

It took Ruby a minute to get her sister's drift. When she did, she burst out laughing. "You're delusional."

"This isn't funny. You saw the reporters out front. They're ready to tear Mom apart, and she's always been fragile."

"Yeah, in that pit-bull kind of way."

"Ruby," Caroline said in her we're-a-team-and-you're-not-playing-fair voice. "A stranger could sell her out to the tabloids. She needs someone she can trust."

"Then you'd better do it. She can't trust me."

"I have kids. A husband."

A life. The implication was clear, and the truth of it stung. "Doesn't she have any friends?"

"It should be you, Ruby." Caroline looked disgusted. "Jesus. You're going to be thirty in a few years. Mom's fifty. When are you going to get to know her?"

"Who says I'm *ever* going to?"

Caro moved closer. "Tell me you didn't think about it last night."

Ruby couldn't swallow. Her sister was so close . . . she smelled of expensive perfume, gardenias, maybe. "About what?"

"Losing her."

The words hit dangerously near their mark. Ruby stared down at the speckled linoleum floor. There was no doubt in her mind what she should do—go out those front doors and fly home. But it wasn't quite so easy this time, especially with the *Caché* article out there to write. A little time with Nora Bridge would certainly make the piece better. A *lot* better.

She took a deep breath, then turned to face her sister. "One week," she said evenly. "I'll stay with her for one week."

Caroline pulled Ruby into a fierce hug. "I knew you'd do the right thing."

Ruby felt like a fraud. She couldn't meet her sister's gaze. Weakly, she said, "A week with Nora. You'd better start a defense fund."

Caroline laughed. "Go tell her. She's in six twelve west. I'll wait for you here."

"Coward." Ruby flashed her a nervous smile, then headed for the elevators. On the sixth floor, she began a room-to-room search until she found 612.

The door was ajar.

She took another deep breath and stepped inside.

Her mother was asleep.

Ruby exhaled in relief. The tension in her shoulders eased a little, she unclenched her fists.

She stared down at her mother's pale, beautiful face

and felt an unexpected tug of longing. She had to forcibly remind herself that this lovely, red-haired woman who looked like Susan Sarandon wasn't really her mother. Ruby's mother—the woman who'd played Scrabble and made chocolate-chip pancakes every Sunday morning—had died eleven years ago. This was the woman who'd killed her.

Nora opened her eyes.

Ruby felt an almost overwhelming urge to run away.

Nora gasped and scooted up to a sit, self-consciously smoothing the tangled hair from her face. "You came," she said softly, a note of wonder in her voice.

Ruby forced her hands to stay bolted to her sides. It was an old stand-up rule. No fidgeting. The audience could smell a set of nerves. "How are you?"

Stupid question, but Ruby was off-balance, afraid of pitching headfirst.

"I'm fine." Nora smiled, but it was an odd, uncertain smile.

Ruby crossed her arms—another antifidget technique. "So, I guess you've lost your good-driver discount."

"That's my Ruby. Quick with a joke."

"I wouldn't say 'your' Ruby."

Nora's smile faded. "I'm sure you wouldn't." She closed her eyes and rubbed the bridge of her nose, exhaling softly. "I see you still think you know everything . . . and you still don't take any prisoners."

Ruby could feel the shale of old habits sliding beneath her feet. A few more well-chosen words and there would be a full-scale war going on between them.

"I don't know everything," Ruby said evenly. "I don't think I ever knew my mother."

Nora laughed, a fluttery, tired sound. "That makes two of us."

They stared at each other. Ruby felt a mounting urge to escape; she knew it was a survival instinct. Already she knew she couldn't spend a week with this woman and feel nothing . . . the anger was so sharp right now it overwhelmed her.

But she had no choice.

"I thought . . . I'd stay with you for a while. Help you get settled."

Nora's surprise was almost comical. "Why?"

Ruby shrugged. There were so many answers to that question. "You could have died. Maybe I thought of what it would be like to lose you." She smiled woodenly. "Or maybe this is your darkest hour, the loss of everything you left your family for, and I don't want to miss a minute of your misery. Or maybe I got a contract to write a magazine article about you and I need to be close to get the inside scoop. Or maybe I—"

"I get it. Who cares why. I need help and you obviously have nothing better to do."

"How do you do it—slam me in the middle of a thank-you? Jesus, it's a gift."

"I didn't mean to slam you."

"No, you just thought you'd point out that I have no life. It wouldn't occur to you that I've rearranged my life to spend some time with you, would it?"

"Let's not start, okay?"

"You started it."

Nora's hand moved to the bed rail, her fingers slid close to touch Ruby. She looked up. "You know I'm going to the summer house, right?"

Ruby couldn't have heard right. *"What?"*

"Reporters are camped outside my condo. I can't face them." Nora's gaze lowered, and Ruby saw how hard it was for her mother to face *her*, too. The past was between them again, a sticky web that caught old hurts and held them. "Your sister offered me use of the summer house. If you want to change your mind, I'll understand."

Ruby went to the window and stared out at the gray, rainy streets of Capitol Hill.

It had seemed doable a few moments ago; go to this woman's house—Nora's house, not really her mother at all—sit with her for a few days, make a few meals, look through a few old photo albums, ask a few questions. Get enough information to write the "where Nora Bridge came from" section of the article.

But . . . at the summer house.

It was where so many of the memories were buried, both good and bad. She would rather see Nora in some glass-walled high-rise that success had purchased. Not in the clapboard farmhouse where Ruby would remember gardening and painting and the sound of laughter that had long since faded.

Fifty thousand dollars.

That's what she had to think about. She could handle a week at the summer house.

"I guess it doesn't matter where we are . . ."

"You mean it?" There was a disturbing wistfulness in her mother's voice.

Finally, Ruby turned. She meant to close the distance between them, but her feet wouldn't move. "Sure. Why not?"

Nora was looking at her thoughtfully. She said, "You'll need to rent me a wheelchair—just until my wrist is strong enough for crutches. And I'll need a few things from my apartment."

"I can do that."

"I'll talk to my doctor and get checked out of here. We'll have to leave quietly, through the back way, maybe. We don't want to be followed."

"I'll rent a car and pick you up in—what—three hours?"

"Okay. My purse is in the closet. Get my credit cards. Use the platinum Visa for anything you need. I'll draw you a map to my apartment and call Ken— he's the doorman. He'll let you in. And Ruby . . . get a nice car, okay?"

Ruby tried to smile. This was going to be bad. Her mother was already making demands—and judgments. "Only the best for you, Nora." She went to the closet, saw the expensive black handbag, and grabbed it. The wide strap settled comfortably on her shoulder. Without a backward glance, she headed out.

Her mother's voice stopped her. "Ruby? Thank you."

Ruby shut the door behind her.

Chapter Six

Ruby walked into her mother's penthouse condominium and closed the door behind her. The place was
eerily silent and smelled faintly of flowers.

She dropped her jacket onto the gleaming marble
floor, beside an ornate wrought-iron and stone table
that held a huge urn full of roses.

She turned the corner and literally had to catch her
breath. It was the most incredible room she'd ever seen.

A wall of floor-to-ceiling windows wrapped around
the whole apartment, showcasing a panoramic view
of Elliot Bay.

The floors were polished marble, a color somewhere between white and gold, with twisting black and
green threads running through each square. Brocade-
covered furniture, perched on gilded legs, sat in a
cluster in the living room around a beautiful gold and
glass coffee table. In one corner stood an ebony Steinway, its lacquered top cluttered with photographs in
gilt-edged frames.

A dimly lit hallway led past several more rooms—

formal dining room, gourmet kitchen, home office—
and ended at the master bedroom. Here, the windows
were dressed in steel-gray silk curtains that matched
the woven cashmere bedspread. There were two huge
walk-in closets. She opened the first one, and a light
came on automatically, revealing two rows of clothes,
organized by color.

Ruby's fingers drifted through the clothing. Silks,
cashmeres, expensive woolens. She saw the labels:
St. John, Armani, Donna Karan, Escada.

She released her breath in an envious sigh. The
thought *This is what she left us for* winged through her
mind, hurting more than she would have expected.

She pulled the list out of her pocket.

Hairdryer
Curling iron
Shorts
Sundresses
Socks

They were ordinary items, but nothing in this closet
cost less than three hundred dollars.

She backed out, closing the door behind her. At
the rosewood, gilt-trimmed bombé chest, she opened
the top drawer. Little piles of perfectly folded lingerie
lay there. She picked out a few pieces, then gathered
up some shorts and cap-sleeved tops from the second
drawer. She set the pile on the bed and moved to the
second closet.

Again, the light came on automatically, but the
clothing in this closet looked as if it belonged to

another woman. Worn gray sweatpants; baggy, stained sweatshirts; jeans so old they were out of date. A few brightly colored sundresses.

Her mother had expensive designer clothes, and lie-around-the-house clothes, but nothing in between. No clothes for going out to lunch with a friend or stopping by to catch a matinee.

No clothes for a real life.

Weird . . .

She reached for a sundress. As she pulled it toward her, the lacy hem caught on something. Ruby gently pushed the other clothes out of the way and saw what had snagged the dress.

It was the upraised flap of a cardboard box. On the beige side, written in red ink, was the word *Ruby*.

Her heart skipped a beat. She had a quick, almost desperate urge to back out of the closet and slam it shut. Whatever was in that box, whatever her mother had saved and marked with Ruby's name, couldn't matter . . .

But she couldn't seem to make herself move. She dropped the dress, let it clatter to the floor, hanger and all, and fell to her knees. Scooting forward, she dragged the box toward her. Her fingers were trembling as she opened it.

Inside, there were dozens of tiny wrapped packages, some in the reds and greens of Christmas, some in bright silvery paper with balloons and candles.

Birthdays and Christmases.

She counted the packages. Twenty-one. Two each year for the eleven Nora had been gone from them, less the black cashmere sweater that Caroline had sneaked past Ruby's guard.

These were the gifts that Nora had bought every year and sent to Ruby, the same ones Ruby had ruthlessly returned, unopened.

"Oh, man." She let out her breath in a sigh and reached for one of the boxes. It was small, like many of the others, the size of a credit card and about a half inch deep. The one she'd chosen was wrapped in birthday paper.

The paper felt slick in her hands and as she lifted it toward her, she heard a tiny clinking from inside, and the sound filled her with a terrible longing. It made her angry, this welling up of useless emotion, but she couldn't make it go away.

Carefully, she peeled the paper away and was left with a small white box imprinted with a jewelry store logo. She lifted the lid.

Inside, on a bed of opalescent tissue, lay a silver charm. It was a birthday cake, complete with candles.

Ruby knew she shouldn't pick up the charm, but she couldn't help herself. She reached down and picked it up, feeling the steady weight of it in her palm, then turned it over. On the back, it was inscribed.

HAPPY 21ST. LOVE, MOM.

The silver charm blurred.

She refused to open any more; she didn't need to. She knew that somewhere in these boxes were a bracelet and more carefully chosen charms—many representing the years they'd been apart.

She could imagine her mother, dressed perfectly, makeup flawless, going from store to store for the ideal gift. She would be chatting pleasantly with the sales-people, saying things like, *My daughter is twenty-one today. I need something extra special.*

Pretending that everything was normal . . . that she hadn't abandoned her children when they needed her most.

At that, Ruby felt a rush of cold anger, and control returned. A few trinkets didn't mean anything.

What mattered was not what Nora had tried to *give* Ruby, but rather what she'd taken away.

There had been no seventeenth birthday party for Ruby. On that day, there had only been more silence. No family had gathered around a big kitchen table strewn with gifts. Those times . . . those precious moments had died when their family died.

A few nicely wrapped gifts found stuffed in a cardboard box in a closet couldn't change that.

Ruby wouldn't let it.

As Ruby neared her mother's hospital room, she slowed. A man was standing by the door. He was tall and effete, a man who dressed for women—gray slacks, pink shirt, and vibrant navy blue suspenders. His hair was snowy white and thinning. She noticed that he kept running his hand through it, as if to assure himself that it was still there.

At her approach, he looked up. Narrowed, penetrating black eyes fixed on her. "Are you Ruby Bridge?"

She came to a stop. She'd misjudged the distance, and taken one step too close to him. He exuded a sweet, musky scent. Expensive cologne, used too liberally. She could see that he was disturbed by her invasion of his personal space.

He took a step backward and cleared his throat—a gentle reminder that he'd asked if she was Ruby Bridge.

"Who wants to know?"

Smiling—as if that was precisely what he would have expected Ruby Bridge to say—he extended his hand. "I'm Dr. Leonard Allbright, your mother's doctor."

"Where's your white coat?"

"I'm her psychiatrist."

That surprised Ruby. She couldn't imagine her mother spilling her guts to anyone. "Really?"

"I've just spoken to her, and she told me all about your . . . arrangement." He said the final word as if it tasted bitter. "I'm aware of your past history, so I thought I'd caution you to keep in mind that your mother is fragile."

"Uh-huh. Are you married, Dr. Allbright?"

A pained expression slipped into the grooves of his face. "No. Why do you ask?"

"My mother collects men who believe she's fragile. She's a real Tennessee Williams kind of gal."

Dr. Allbright did not look pleased by that observation. "Why have you offered to care for her?"

"Look, Doc, when it's all over, you can ask Nora all the questions you want. She'll pay you a huge fee to listen to her moan about the bitch daughter who betrayed her. But *I'm* not going to talk to you."

" 'Betrayed' is an interesting word choice."

Ruby flinched. "If that's all . . ."

He reached into his pocket and withdrew a slim silver case with the initials LOA etched in gold. Inside lay a neat stack of expensive business cards. He handed her one. "I don't know if it is a good idea for you to take care of Nora. Especially not in her current state of mind."

Ruby took the card, tucked it into the elastic waistband of her leggings. "Yeah? Why not?"

He studied her, and she could see by the deepening frown that he wasn't pleased. "You haven't seen or spoken to your mother in years, and you're obviously very angry at her. Considering . . . what happened to her, it could be a bad mix. Maybe even dangerous."

"Dangerous how?"

"You don't know her. And as I said, she's fragile now—"

"I lived with her for sixteen years, Doc. You've talked to her once a week for . . . what, a year or two?"

"Fifteen years."

Ruby's chin snapped up. "*Fifteen* years? But everything was fine back then."

"Was it?"

His question threw her into confusion. Fifteen years ago, Ruby had been barely out of braces, singing along to Madonna and wearing a dozen crucifixes and imagining that her future would follow the course of her childhood, that her family would always be together.

"Your mother keeps a lot to herself," Dr. Allbright went on, "and as I said, she's fragile. I believe she always has been. You obviously disagree." He took a step toward her. This time it was Ruby who felt encroached upon. She steeled herself to stand her ground. "Your mother was doing almost seventy miles per hour when she hit that tree. And on the same day she lost her career. Pretty coincidental."

Ruby couldn't believe she hadn't made that connection. A chill moved through her. "Are you telling me she tried to kill herself?"

"I'm saying it's coincidental. Dangerously so."

Ruby released a heavy breath. Suddenly, it didn't seem like a good idea to be responsible for her mother, not even for a few days. No one emotionally unstable should be entrusted to Ruby—hell, *goldfish* couldn't survive her care.

"You don't know your mother. Remember that."

That observation put Ruby back on solid ground. "And who's fault is that? I'm not the one who walked out."

He stared down at her, gave her the kind of look she'd seen time and time again in her life.

Oh, good, she thought, *now I'm disappointing total strangers.*

"No, you're not," he said evenly, "and you're not sixteen anymore, either."

Ruby should have rented a bigger car. Like maybe a Hummer or a Winnebago.

This minivan was too small for her and Nora. They were trapped in side-by-side front seats. With the windows rolled up, there seemed to be no air left to breathe, and nothing to do but talk.

Ruby cranked up the radio.

Celine Dion's pure, vibrant voice filled the car, something about love coming to those who believed.

"Do you think you could turn that down?" Nora said. "I'm getting a headache."

Ruby's gaze flicked sideways. Nora looked tired; her skin, normally pale, now appeared to have the translucence of bone china. Tiny blue veins webbed the sunken flesh at her temples. She turned to Ruby and attempted a smile, but in truth, her mouth barely trembled before she closed her eyes and leaned against the window.

Fragile.

Ruby couldn't wrap her arms around that thought. It was too alien from her own experience. Her mother had always been made of steel. Even as a young girl, Ruby had known her mother's strength. The other kids in her class were afraid of their fathers when report cards came out. Not the Bridge girls. They lived in fear of disappointing their mother.

Not that she ever punished them particularly, or yelled or screamed. No, it was worse than that.

I'm disappointed in you, Ruby Elizabeth . . . life isn't kind to women who take the easy road.

Ruby had never known what the easy road was, exactly, or where it led, but she knew it was a bad thing. Almost as bad as "fooling yourself"—another thing Nora wouldn't abide.

The truth doesn't go away just because you shut your eyes had been another of her mother's favorite sayings.

Of course, those had been the "before" days. Afterward, no one in the family cared much about disappointing Nora Bridge. In fact, Ruby had gone out of her way to do just that.

"Ruby? The music?"

Ruby snapped the radio off. The metronomic *whoosh-thump, whoosh-thump* of the windshield wipers filled the sudden silence.

Only a few miles from downtown Seattle, the gray city gave way to a sprawling collection of squat, flat-topped strip malls. A few miles more and they were in farming land. Rolling, tree-shrouded hills and lush green pastures fanned out on either side of the freeway. The white ice-cream dome of Mount Baker sat on a layer of fog above the flat farmland.

Ruby actually sped up as they drove through the sleepy town of Mount Vernon; she was afraid her mother would say something intimate, like *Remember how we used to bicycle through the tulip fields at festival time?*

But when she glanced sideways, she saw that Nora was asleep.

Ruby breathed a sigh of relief and eased off the accelerator. It felt good to drive the rest of the way without wondering if she was being watched.

At Anacortes, the tiny seaside town perched at the water's edge, she bought a one-way ferry ticket and pulled into line. It was still early in the tourist season; two weeks from now the wait for this ferry could well be five hours.

Less than a half hour later, a ferry docked, sounded its mournful horn, and unloaded its cargo of cars and bikes and walk-on passengers. Then, an orange-vested attendant directed Ruby's car to the bow, where she parked and set the emergency brake. First car in lane two, a primo spot. The gaping, oval mouth of the ferry was a giant, glassless window that framed the view.

The Sound was rainy-day flat, studded by the ceaseless rain into a sheet of hammered tin. Watery gray skies melted into the sea, the line between them a smudge of charcoal, thin as eyeliner. Puppy-faced gray seals crawled over one another to find a comfortable perch on the swaying red harbor buoy.

Ruby got out of the car and went upstairs. After buying a latte at the lunch counter, she walked out onto the deck.

No one was out here now. The rain had diminished to little more than a heavy mist. Moisture beaded the handrails and slickened the decks.

A long, single blast of the boat's horn announced their departure.

Ruby slid her fingers along the wet handrail, holding on, shivering at a sudden burst of cold. A few brave seagulls hung in the air in front of her, wings outstretched, motionless, riding a current of air. They cawed loudly, begging for scraps.

Lush green islands dotted the tinfoil sea, their carved granite coastlines a stark contrast to the flat silver water. Polished red madrona trees slanted out from the shore, their roots clinging tenaciously to a thin layer of topsoil. Houses were scattered here and there but, for the most part, the islands looked empty.

She closed her eyes, breathing in the salty, familiar sea air. In eighth grade, she'd started taking the ferry to school at Friday Harbor on San Juan Island; memories of high school were inextricably linked with this boat . . .

She and Dean had always stood together at just this spot, right at the bow, even when it was raining.

Dean.

It was strange that she hadn't thought of him right away.

Well, perhaps not so strange. It had been more than a decade since she'd seen him, and still it hurt to remember him.

After her mother had left, Ruby hadn't thought it was possible to hurt more. Dean had taught her that the human heart always made room for pain.

She still thought of him now and then. Sometimes, when she woke in the middle of a hot, lonely night and found that her cheeks were slicked and wet, she knew she'd been dreaming of him. She knew from Caroline (who knew from Nora) that he'd followed in his mother's footsteps after all, that he was running the empire now. Ruby had always known that he would.

At last, the ferry turned toward Summer Island. The horn sounded, and the captain came on the loud-speaker, urging passengers to return to their vehicles.

Ruby raced downstairs and jumped into the minivan.

The captain cut the engine and the boat drifted toward the rickety black dock. A weatherbeaten sign— it had been old when Ruby was a child—hung at a cockeyed angle from the nearest piling. It read SUMMER ISLAND WELCOMES YOU.

A woman walked out of the closet-size terminal building and stood watching the ferry float toward her. She was wearing a floor-length brown dress with neither collar nor cuffs. An ornate silver crucifix hung from a thick chain around her neck. Waving at the few walk-on passengers clustered at the bow's railing, she dragged a tattered, wrist-thick length of rope across the dock and tied the boat down.

"Oh, Lord," Nora said, blinking awake, "is that Sister Helen?"

Ruby couldn't believe it herself. The nuns had always run the ferry traffic on Summer Island, but it was still a shock to see that nothing had changed. "Amazing, isn't it?"

Nora sighed. It was a tired sound, as if maybe she wondered if changelessness were a good thing. Or maybe, like Ruby, she had just realized how it would *feel* to be here again, at the site of so much heartache.

Ruby drove off the ferry, past the post office and general store. What struck her first was the total lack of meaningful change. She felt as if she'd just taken a boat ride back in time. Here, on Summer Island, it was still 1985. If she turned on the radio, it would probably be Cyndi Lauper or Rick Springfield . . .

This was why she'd stayed away.

The road turned, climbed up a short hill, then flowed down into a rolling green valley.

To her left, the land was a Monet painting, all golden grass and green trees and washed-out silvery skies. To her right lay Bottleneck Bay, and beyond that was the forested green hump of Shaw Island. Weathered gray fishing boats sat keeled on the pebbly beach, forgotten by their owners more than a generation ago. A few sleek sailboats—mostly owned by the few Californians brave enough to purchase a summer home on this too-quiet island where drinking water was never

guaranteed and power came and went with the wind—
bobbed idly in the gently swelling sea.

There were only a few farmhouses visible from the
road. The island boasted five thousand acres, but only
one hundred year-round residents. Even in the summer,
when mainlanders swarmed to their island vacation
homes, Summer Island had fewer than three hundred
residents.

It was as different from California as a place could
be. Here, hip-hop was the way a rabbit moved, and a
drive-by meant stopping to say hello to your neighbor
on your way to town.

Nora looked out the rain-dappled window. Her
head made a thumping sound as she rested it against
the glass. The lines around her mouth were deeply
etched, heavy enough to weigh her lips into a frown.
"When I first came here . . . no, that doesn't matter
now . . ."

Ruby approached the beach road. Instead of turning, she eased her foot off the gas and coasted to a stop.
Her mother's half sentence had implied . . . secrets . . .
things unspoken, and Ruby didn't like it.

Fifteen years, Dr. Allbright had said. He'd been
treating Nora for fifteen years . . . yet none of them
had known it.

"What were you going to say?"

Nora's laughter was a fluttery thing, a bit of spun
sugar. "Nothing."

Ruby rolled her eyes. Why had she even bothered?
"Whatever."

She eased her foot back onto the accelerator, flicked
the signal on, and turned toward the beach. The narrow,

one-lane road wound snakelike through the towering trees. Though it was afternoon, you wouldn't have known it. The tree limbs were heavy with rain; their drooping branches darkened the road. Here and there, small turnouts, overgrown with weeds, made space for parking when another car was coming from the opposite direction.

At last, they came to the driveway. A pair of dogwood trees stood guard on either side of the needle-strewn lane. Any gravel that had once been dumped here had long ago burrowed into the dirt.

Ruby turned down the driveway. The knee-high grass that grew in a wild strip down the center of the road thumped and scraped the undercarriage.

At the end of the tree-lined road, Ruby hit the brakes.

And stared through the rain-beaded windshield at her childhood.

The farmhouse was layered in thick white clapboards with red trim around the casement windows. One side jutted out like an old woman's bad hip—that was the addition her grandparents had built for their grandchildren. A porch wrapped around three sides of the house. It sat in the midst of a pie-shaped clearing that jutted toward the sea. In this, the middle of June, the lawn was lush and lime green; in the dog days of summer, Ruby knew it would grow tall and take on the rich hue of burnished gold. Madrona trees marked the perimeter.

"Oh, God," she whispered, soaking it all in.

A white picket fence created a nicely squared yard

around the farmhouse. Inside it, the garden was in full, riotous bloom.

Obviously Caroline had paid a gardener to keep the place up. It looked as if the Bridge family had been gone a season instead of more than a decade.

With a tired sigh, Ruby got out of the car.

The tide made a low, snoring sound. Birds chattered overhead, surprised and dismayed by their unexpected guests. But no city sounds lived this far north, no horns or squealing tires or jets flying overhead.

There was now, as there had always been, a quiet otherworldliness to Summer Island, and as much as she hated to admit it, Ruby felt the island's familiar welcome. Time here was measured in eons, not lifetimes. In how long it took the sea to smooth the rough edges off a bit of broken glass, in how long it took the tide to shape and reshape the shoreline.

She went around to the back of the van and pulled out the wheelchair, then wheeled it around to the passenger side and helped Nora into the seat.

Taking hold of the rubber-coated grips, she cautiously pushed her mother down the path. At the gate, Ruby stopped and walked ahead, unlatching it. The metal piece clanked, the gate swung creakily open.

When Ruby turned back around, she noticed how pale her mother was. Nora touched the fence's sagging slat. A heart-shaped patch of paint fell away at the contact, lay in the grass like a bit of confetti.

Nora looked up, her eyes shiny and moist. "Remember the summer you and Caro painted every slat a different color? You guys looked like a pair of rainbow Popsicles when you were finished."

"I don't remember that," Ruby said, but for a split second, when she looked down, her tennis shoes were Keds, speckled with a dozen different colors of paint. It pissed her off, how easy it was to remember things in this place, to *feel* them. Nothing seemed to have changed here except Ruby, and the new Ruby sure as hell didn't belong in this fairy-tale house.

She walked back up the slope and took her place behind the wheelchair. She cautiously moved down the rutted path, guiding the chair in front of her. They had just reached the edge of the porch when her mother suddenly spoke.

"Let me sit here for a minute, will you? Go on in." Nora fished the key out of her pocket and handed it to Ruby. "You can come back and tell me how it looks."

"You'd rather sit in the rain than go into the house?"

"That pretty much sums up my feelings right now."

Ruby stepped around her and walked onto the porch. The wide-planked floor wobbled beneath her feet like piano keys, releasing a melody of creaks and groans.

At the front door, she slipped the key into the lock. *Click.*

"Wait!" her mother cried out.

Ruby turned. Nora was smiling, but it was grim, that smile. More like gritted teeth.

"I . . . think we should go in together."

"Jesus, let's not make an opera out of it. We're going into an old house. That's all." Ruby shoved the door open, caught a fleeting glimpse of shadows stacked on top of each other, then she went back for Nora.

She maneuvered the wheelchair up onto the porch, bumped it over the wooden threshold, and wheeled her mother inside.

The furniture huddled ghostlike in the middle of the room, draped in old sheets. Ruby could remember spreading those sheets every autumn, snapping them in the air above furniture. It had been a family ritual, closing up this house for winter.

The house may not have been lived in in a while, but it had been well cared for. There couldn't have been more than a few weeks' worth of dust on those white sheets.

"Caroline has taken good care of the place . . . I'm surprised she left everything exactly as it was." There was a note of wonder in Nora's voice, and maybe a touch of regret. As if, like Ruby, she'd hoped that Caroline had painted over the past.

"You know Caro," Ruby said, "she likes to keep everything pretty on the surface."

"That's not fair. Caro—"

Ruby spun around. "*Tell* me you aren't going to explain my sister to me."

Nora's mouth snapped shut. Then she sneezed. And again. Her eyes were watering as she said, "I'm allergic to dust. I know there's not much, but I'm really sensitive. You'll need to dust right away."

Ruby looked at her. "Your leg's broken; not your hand."

"I can't handle it. Allergies."

It was the best reason for not cleaning Ruby had ever heard. "Fine. I'll dust."

"And vacuum—remember, there's dust in the carpets."

"Oh, really? That comes as a complete surprise to me."

Nora had the grace to blush. "I'm sorry. I forgot for a minute that you're not . . . never mind."

Ruby gazed down at her. "I'm not a kid anymore, and dusting was one of the many things Caroline and I had to learn to do after you left us." She saw the pain move into Nora's green eyes; it made her look old suddenly, and fragile.

That word again. It was not something Ruby particularly wanted to see. She grabbed the wheelchair and pushed her mother into the center of the room, where the ancient Oriental carpet sucked up the metallic thump of the chair's wheels and plunged them into silence again.

"I guess I'll have to sleep in your old room. There's no way we can get me upstairs."

Ruby dutifully wheeled Nora into the downstairs bedroom, where two twin beds lay beneath a layer of sheeting. Between them was a gingham-curtained window. A painted wooden toy box held most of Ruby's childhood.

The wallpaper was still the pale pink cabbage roses that she and Caroline had picked out when they were children.

Ruby refused to feel anything. She yanked the sheets away. A fine layer of dust billowed into the air. She heard her mother coughing behind her, so Ruby leaned forward and wrenched the window open, letting in the sound of the waves slapping on the shore.

"I think I'll lie down for a minute," Nora said when the dust had settled. "I'm still fighting a headache."

Ruby nodded. "Can you get out of the chair by yourself?"

"I guess I'd better learn."

"I guess so." Ruby turned for the door.

She was almost free when her mother's voice hooked her back again. "Thanks. I really appreciate this."

Ruby knew she should say something nice, but she couldn't think of anything. She was too damned tired, and the memories in this room were like gnats, buzzing around her head. She nodded and kept walking, slamming the door shut behind her.

Chapter Seven

Dean tossed his garment bag on the floor of his old bedroom and sat down on the end of the bed.

Everything was exactly as he'd left it. Dusty baseball and soccer trophies cluttered the bureau's top; posters covered the cream-colored walls, their edges yellowed and curled. If he opened the toy chest, he'd find all the mementos of his past—G.I. Joe with the kung-fu grip, Rock 'Em–Sock 'Em Robots, maybe even his old Erector set. An autographed GO SEA-HAWKS pennant hung above the desk, a reminder of the year Jim Zorn had visited the grade school.

Dean hadn't taken anything with him when he left here, not even a photograph of Ruby. *Especially* not a picture of her. He got to his feet and crossed the room. At the bureau, he bent down and pulled at the bottom drawer; it screeched and wobbled, then slid open.

And there they were, still stacked and scattered exactly as he'd left them: reminders of Ruby. There were framed pictures and unframed ones, shells they'd collected together on the beach, and a couple of dried boutonnieres. He reached randomly inside, drawing out a small strip of black-and-white pictures—a series that had been taken in one of those booths at the Island County Fair. In them, she was sitting on Dean's lap, with her arms curled tightly around him and her head angled against his. She was smiling, then frowning, then sticking her tongue out at the unseen camera. In the last frame, they were kissing.

It was bad enough to remember Ruby in the abstract; to follow this photographic trail of their childhood would be like swallowing glass bits. They'd started together as kids, he and Ruby, kindergarten best friends. Then they'd fallen into the sweet, aching pool of first love, and ultimately washed up on that emotion's rocky, isolated shore. He remembered the ending, and that was enough.

He dropped the photos back into the drawer and kicked it shut.

Someone knocked at the door, and Dean opened it.

Lottie stood there, clutching her big vinyl purse. "I'm off to the store," she said. "The fridge isn't making ice; we need a bag."

"I'll go—"

"Of course you won't. You'll be needing time with Eric." Smiling, she thrust a champagne glass at him. Inside was a thick pink liquid. "This is your brother's medicine. He needs it now. Bye."

She left him standing there, a grown man in a boy's room, holding pain medication in a fluted champagne glass.

He walked slowly to Eric's bedroom. The door was closed.

Dean stared at it for a long time, remembering the days when these doors had never been closed. They'd always come bursting into each other's room whenever they wanted.

He turned the knob and went inside. The room felt stuffy and too warm. The curtains were drawn.

Eric was asleep.

Dean moved quietly toward the bedside table and set down the glass, then he started to leave.

"I *hope* that's my Viagra," Eric said sleepily. In a second, the bed whirred to life, eased him to a near sitting position.

"Actually, it's a double shot of Cuervo Gold. I added the Pepto-Bismol to save you time."

Eric laughed. "You'll never let me forget Mary-Anne's going-away party."

"A night that will live in infamy." Dean opened the windows and flung back the curtains. The windows boxed a gray and rainy day and let a little watery light into the room.

"Thanks. Bless Lottie, but she thinks I need peace and quiet. I haven't the nerve to tell her that I'm getting a little scared of the dark. Too damn coffinlike for me." He grinned. "I'll be there soon enough."

Dean turned to him. "Don't talk about that."

"Death? Why not? I *am* dying, and I'm not afraid of it. Hell, another week like this one and I'll be looking forward to it." He gave Dean a gentle look. "What am I supposed to talk about—the Mariners' next season? The next Olympic Games? Or maybe we could discuss the long-term effects of global warming." Eric eased back into the pillows with a heavy sigh. "We used to be so close," he said quietly.

"I know," Dean answered, moving toward the bed. He saw Eric move, try to turn slightly to look up at him; he saw, too, when the sudden pain sucked the color from his brother's cheeks. "Here," Dean said quickly.

Eric's hands were shaking as he reached for the glass and brought it back to his colorless lips. Wincing, he swallowed the whole amount, then wiped his mouth with the back of his bony wrist.

Eric tried to smile. "I'd kill for a margarita from Ray's Boathouse right about now . . . and a platter of Penn Cove mussels . . ."

"Tequila and shellfish—with your tolerance for booze? Sorry, pal, but I'll have to pass on that little fantasy."

"I'm not seventeen anymore," Eric said. "I don't slam alcohol until I puke."

There it was, the sharpened reminder of how they'd drifted apart. They'd known each other as boys; the men were strangers to each other.

"Will that medication help?" Dean asked.

"Sure. In ten minutes I'll be able to leap tall buildings in a single bound." Eric frowned. "What is a single bound, exactly? And why have I never wondered about that before?"

"Whatever it is, it's better than flying. Even first class has gone to hell. My flight up here was godawful."

Eric smiled. "Even first class is bad? You're talking to a high-school English teacher who was disinherited, remember?"

"Sorry. I was just trying to make conversation."

"Don't. I'm dying. I don't need time-filler. Jesus, Dean, you and I have spent our whole adulthood talking around anything that mattered. I know it's genetic, but I don't have time for it anymore."

"If you remind me that you're dying again, I swear to God, I'll kill you myself. It's not like I'm going to *forget*."

Eric laughed. "Praise Jesus! That's the first hint of my brother I've seen in a decade. I'm glad to know he survived."

Dean relaxed a little. "It's good to hear you laugh. It's been a long time." He moved idly to the chest of drawers beside the bed, where a collection of pictures sat clustered together. Most of them were photographs of Dean and Eric as boys.

But there was one—a shot of the brothers and another boy from the football team—all standing with their arms around one another, grinning.

It looked ordinary enough, but when he turned back to Eric, Dean couldn't help wondering. Had it been there all along, the difference between him and his brother? Had Dean simply *missed* the obvious?

"I wish I'd never told you I was gay," Eric said.

It was as if Eric had read his mind. Slowly, Dean turned. He wasn't ready for this conversation yet, but he had no choice. Eric had thrown him into cold water, now he had to swim. "It's kind of hard to keep a secret like that when you're living with a man."

"People do it all the time, keep that secret, I mean. I was so naive, I *wanted* to tell you." Eric lifted his head off the pillows and stared at Dean. "I knew our folks wouldn't accept it. But you . . ." His voice cracked a little. "You, I didn't expect. You broke my heart."

"I never meant to."

"You stopped calling me."

Dean sighed, wondering how to say it all. "You were away at college, so you didn't know what it was like back here. The technicolor meltdown of the Bridge family. It was front-burner news. And then . . . Ruby and I broke up."

"I always wondered what happened between you two. I thought—"

"It was fucking awful," Dean said quickly, unwilling to delve into that particular heartache. "I called Mother and demanded to be transferred to Choate—where, I might add, I met a bunch of snotty elitist rich kids. I hated it there. I couldn't seem to make friends. But every Sunday night, my brother called, and that one hour made the rest of the week bearable. You weren't just my best friend, you were my only friend. Then one Sunday, you forgot to call." Dean remembered how he'd waited by the phone that day, and the next Sunday and the next. "When you finally did call again, you told me about Charlie."

"You felt abandoned," Eric said softly.

"More than that. I felt like I didn't know you at all, like everything you'd ever said to me was a lie. And then all you wanted to talk about was Charlie." Dean shrugged. "I was seventeen years old and nursing a broken heart. I didn't want to hear about your love life. And yeah, the fact that it was with another man was hard for me to handle."

Eric leaned deeper into the pillows. "When you

stopped returning my calls, I assumed it was because you hated me. Then you went to work for the family biz, and I wrote you off. I never thought about what it was like for you. I'm sorry."

"Yeah. I'm sorry, too."

"Where do these apologies take us?"

"Who the hell knows? I'm here. Isn't that enough?"

"No."

Suddenly Dean understood what Eric wanted. "You want me to remember who we used to be, to remember *you*, and then . . . watch you die. It doesn't sound like a real kick-ass plan from where I'm standing."

Eric reached up, placed a cold, trembling hand on top of Dean's. "I want *someone* in my family to love me while I'm alive. Is that so much to ask?" He closed his eyes, as if the conversation had exhausted him. "Ah, hell . . . I'm going too fast. I need *time* damn it. Just stay here until I fall asleep—can you do that for me?"

Dean's throat felt tight. "Sure."

He stayed at his brother's bedside until long after Eric's breathing had become regular and his mouth had slipped open. And still he didn't know what to say.

He would have given his fortune—hell, he'd have given everything he had or owned or could borrow— in exchange for the one thing he'd always taken for granted. The one thing Eric needed.

Time.

By the time Nora hopped to the bathroom and back into the bedroom, she was dizzy and out of breath. She shifted onto the bed and leaned back against the wobbly wooden headboard.

She knew she needed to handle Ruby with kid gloves, to treat her daughter's pain (which Nora never forgot that *she* had caused) respectfully, to let Ruby make all the first moves toward a reconciliation. No matter how much it hurt, how deeply the ache went, Nora didn't want to bulldoze the situation.

But Ruby had always brought out the worst in her. Even in the good times, her younger daughter had had a way of saying things that rubbed Nora the wrong way. More often than not, they both ended up saying something they regretted.

And Ruby knew that every coldly spoken "Nora" would break her heart just a little. It was, she knew, Ruby's way of reminding Nora that they were strangers.

You have to keep your cool.

And for God's sake, don't tell her what to do . . . or pretend you know her.

If they'd gone somewhere else, maybe this would have been easier, but nothing new could grow here, not in this soil contaminated by the past.

It was in this house that Nora had made her biggest mistake—and given the life she'd led, that was saying a lot. This was where she'd come when she left Rand. She had meant for it to be temporary. At the time she'd simply thought: *Space; if I don't get some space I'll start screaming and never stop.*

All she'd wanted was a little room, some time to herself. She'd been overwhelmed by her life. A twenty-minute ferry ride had seemed perfect. She hadn't known that two miles could stretch into more than a decade.

She remembered that whole summer, and the bad years that had preceded it, in excruciating detail.

She remembered how it had felt and tasted, that slowly descending depression, like a thick glass jar that closed around you, sucking away the air you needed to breathe, creating a barrier between you and the world. The hell of it was that she'd been able to see all that she was missing, but when she'd reached out, all she touched was cold, hard glass.

It had started with a few dark days, a few nightmares, but as the winter had turned into spring, and then into summer, she had simply . . . fallen. All these years later, she'd never found a better word for it. She'd felt then—as she did now—as brittle as a winter leaf. It had always taken so damned little to break her.

If she hadn't left Rand then, she believed she would have died. Her pain had been that great. Still . . .

She'd thought she could come home again, that women were granted the same latitude in marriage that men were. How naive she had been.

She reached for the bedside phone and picked it up, thankful to find a dial tone. She wouldn't have expected any less from Caroline.

She dialed Eric's number, but no one answered. He was probably exhausted from the trip. He tired so easily these days.

She didn't want to think about that now, about how the cancer was erasing him. If she thought about that now she'd fall apart, and with Ruby on the other side of that door, Nora didn't dare fall apart.

She dialed another number. Dr. Allbright answered on the second ring. There was a moment of silence at the other end, the sound of a match flaring. "Hello?"

"Hi, Leo. It's me, Nora."

He inhaled, blew the smoke from his cigarette into the phone. It came through in a whooshing sound. "How are you?"

"I'm fine," she said, wondering if he could *hear* the lies in the same way that he could see them on her face. "You asked me to call when we arrived, so . . ."

"You don't sound fine."

"Well . . . Ruby and I are crowded in with a lot of old ghosts." She tried to laugh. "This house . . ."

"I don't think you should be there. We talked about this. With all that's happening, you should be in the city."

It was nice to have someone care about her—even if she paid him to do so. "And let the vultures pick at me?" She smiled ruefully. "Of course, it appears to be open season on Nora Bridge wherever I go."

"Ruby," he said.

"I knew it wouldn't be easy." That much was true, at least. She'd known how much it would hurt to see her daughter's bitterness in such sharp, close detail; and it did.

"We talked about this, Nora. If she hates you, it's because she was too young to understand."

"I'm fifty, Leo, and I don't understand it all."

"You owe it to yourself—and to Ruby—to tell her the truth."

She sighed wearily. The thought of opening herself like a rotting flower to her beloved daughter was more than she could bear. "I just want to see her smile at me. That's all. Just once and I could carry that image forever. I don't expect her to like me . . . let alone love me."

"Ah, Nora," he said, and she heard the familiar disappointment in his tone.

"You ask too much of me, Leo."

"And you ask too little, Nora. You're so afraid of your past that—"

"Tell me something useful, Leo. You're a parent, give me some advice."

"Talk to her."

"About what? How do we get past what happened eleven years ago?"

"One step at a time, that's how. Try this: tell her one personal thing about you every day. Just one, and try to find out one thing about her. That would be a start."

"One personal thing." Nora considered it.

Yes, she could do that. She'd just have to find a way to share one honest moment a day with her daughter. It wasn't much, and it wouldn't change everything, but it felt . . . possible. For now, that was all she could hope for.

Ruby strode through the house, going from window to window, yanking the gingham cotton curtains open, letting what little sunlight was possible into every room. By now it was nearly three o'clock. Soon there would be no daylight through the clouds at all. She wanted to catch what she could.

She was desperately tired all of a sudden. The middle-of-the-night phone call, the predawn flight, the drive to the islands . . . suddenly it all caught up with her and sapped her strength. If she wasn't careful, she could lose a fight with her own emotions and start crying at the sight of this old house.

At last, she found herself in the kitchen/dining room. Nothing had changed.

A round maple table sat tucked beneath the kitchen window, its four ladder-back chairs pulled in close. A centerpiece of dirty pink plastic dahlias was flanked by a set of porcelain salt and pepper shakers shaped like tiny lighthouses. A cookbook was in its rack on the kitchen counter, its pages open to a recipe for lemon squares. Four hand-embroidered dishcloths hung in a row across the front of the oven.

She passed beneath the archway that separated the kitchen from the living room, noticing the brass mariner's clock that hung in the center of the arch's plaster curl. That clock was silent now, its chimes— two quick *ding-dings* every half hour—had been a constant punctuation to their family's noisy sound-track. But it had probably been years since anyone had remembered to change the batteries.

In the living room, an overstuffed sofa and two leather chairs faced a big, river-rock fireplace. On the back wall were bookcases filled with two generations' worth of Reader's Digest editions, and an RCA stereo. A red plastic milk box held all of the family's favorite albums. From here, Ruby could see the upper half of the top album: "Venus" by Bananarama.

That one was hers.

Next, the photographs on the mantel caught her eye. They were different frames than she remembered. Frowning, she walked toward the fireplace.

All the pictures were of Caroline's children.

There was not a single shot of Ruby. Not even one of Ruby and Caroline.

"Nice, Caro," she said, turning away. She headed for the stairs, but as she walked up the creaking, narrow steps to the second floor, she felt . . . forgotten.

Her fingers trailed through the dust on the oak banister, leaving two squiggly lines. The second floor was small, barely big enough for a full-size bedroom. The bathroom—added by Grandpa Bridge in the early 1970s—had once been a closet. It was barely big enough to bend over at the sink to brush your teeth. Ugly, avocado-green shag carpeting covered every inch of the floor.

She pushed the door open to her parents' old bedroom and flicked the light switch.

A big brass bed filled the room, flanked by two French Provincial end tables. The bedside lamps were yellow, their green shades draped in golden plastic beads.

A touch of Las Vegas class, her grandmother had often said, and with that unexpected memory, Ruby remembered her grandma, sitting in that corner rocker, her veiny hands making knitting needles work like pistons. *You can never have too many afghans,* she'd said every time she started a new one. There had always been an Elvis album playing on the turntable when Grandma knitted . . .

It had been a long time since she'd had so clear a memory of her Nana.

Maybe all she'd needed to remember the good times was to see this place again. The room was exactly as Nana had made it; Nora had never bothered to redecorate. When Nana and Pop had died, Dad had moved their family into the bigger house on Lopez Island, and left this house for summer use.

Ruby crossed the room and went to the French doors, opening them wide. Sweet, rain-scented air made the lacy curtains tremble and dance. The bloated gray sky and steel-blue water were perfectly framed by twin Douglas firs, as thin and straight as pipe cleaners.

She stepped out onto the tiny second-floor balcony. A pair of white deck chairs sat on either side of her, their slatted backs beaded with rain.

For a split second, she couldn't imagine that she'd ever lived in a valley so hot and airless that boiling water sometimes squirted out of ordinary green garden hoses.

She backed off the balcony and turned into the room. Out of the corner of her eye, she noticed the new photographs on the bedside table.

"God *damn* it," she muttered, looking through them.

Caroline had done it again. They were all pictures of Caroline's new life. It was as if her sister were trying to exorcise Ruby from the family.

Frowning, she marched back downstairs and went outside. She grabbed their two suitcases from the car and carried them inside, dropping her mother's in front of the closed bedroom door.

Upstairs, she opened the closet's louvered doors, then yanked down on the beaded light chain. A bare lightbulb in the ceiling came on in the empty closet.

She tossed her suitcase inside. It hit a cardboard box, rattling it.

She knelt onto the dusty shag carpet and pulled the

box toward her. In bold, black marker pen, someone had written BEFORE across the top flap.

Ruby opened the box . . . and found herself.

Photographs. Dozens of them. These were the pictures that used to sit on every flat surface in this house—tables, mantels, windowsills. Pictures of two littles girls in matching pink dresses . . . of Dean and Eric in Little League uniforms . . . of Dad waving from the stern of the *Captain Hook*. And one of Nora.

She slowly withdrew that one.

This was the mother she'd forgotten, the woman she'd grieved for. A tall, thin woman, with auburn hair cut in the layered Farrah Fawcett style, wearing crisp white walking shorts and a celery-green T-shirt. The photograph was old and creased, but even the maplike fissures couldn't dim her mother's smile. In the background was the peaked white tip of the Matterhorn.

Their trip to Disneyland.

In a bittersweet rush, Ruby remembered all of that day; the screams of older kids on scarier rides, the sudden, plunging darkness of Mr. Toad's Wild Ride, the rollicking music of Country Bear Jamboree, the sugary residue of churros, eaten while you walked, the magic of the Electrical Light Parade. Ruby had watched it from the best seat in the house—on her daddy's shoulders.

And she understood what Caroline had done. Caro, who couldn't stand conflict or confrontation . . . Caro, who just wanted everything to be *normal.*

It had hurt her sister to look back on these years.

Better to simply . . . go on. Start over. Pretend that

there had never been happy summers spent on these shores, in these rooms.

Ruby released her breath in a heavy sigh and boxed the photographs back up. Her sister was right. It was too damned hard to see the past in Kodachrome.

God . . . she'd already lost her equilibrium in this house, and it had only been a day. Suddenly she was wound tightly, full of nervous energy. She had to get back on track. Remember why she was here.

The magazine article. *That* would keep her focused.

She unzipped the side pocket of her suitcase and withdrew a yellow legal pad and a blue pen. Then she crawled up onto the dusty bed, drew her knees in . . .

. . . and stared down at all those blue lines.

We want your thoughts, your memories, what kind of mother you thought she was.

"Okay, Ruby," she said aloud. "Just start. You can always change the beginning later."

It was the first rule of comedy writing; it should work here, too.

She took a deep breath, released it slowly, and wrote the first thing that came to mind.

In the interest of full disclosure, I must tell you (she decided to talk directly to the *Caché* readers) *that I was paid to write this article. Paid handsomely, as they say in the kind of restaurants where a person like me can't afford to order a dinner salad. Enough so that I could trade in my beat-up Volkswagen Bug for a slightly less beat-up Porsche.*

I should also tell you that I dislike my mother.

No, that's not true. I dislike the snotty salesclerk who works the night shift at my local video store.

I hate my mother.

That seems like a pretty harsh statement, I know. We're taught in childhood not to use the word "hate" because it represents a blight on our own soul, perhaps even a karmic misalignment. But silencing a word doesn't eliminate its meaning.

It's not like I hate her for no reason, or even for a stupid, petty reason. She's earned my contempt. To explain, I have to open the door to my mother's and my life, and welcome you in as friends.

The story of us starts eleven years ago, in a place few of you have ever seen: the San Juan Islands up in Washington State. I grew up in a small farm-house on a patch of land that had been home-steaded by my great-grandfather. The island . . . the town . . . my house . . . they all belong on Hallmark cards. I went to school with the same kids for thir-teen years; the only crime I can recall happened in 1979, when Jimmy Smithson broke into the local pharmacy, ripped open all the condom packages, and wrote "Peggy Jean likes sex" in Dial soap on the front window.

And then there was my family.

My dad was—is—a commercial fisherman who repairs boat engines in the winter months to make ends meet. He was born and raised on Lopez Is-land; he is as fixed in that place as one of the ancient trees that line the main road.

Although my mother was born off-island, she

was a local by the time I came along. She volunteered for every town charity event and was a fixture around school.

In other words, we were a perfect family in a quiet little town where nothing ever happened. In all my growing-up years, I never heard my parents argue.

Then, in the summer before my seventeenth birthday, everything changed.

My mother left us. Walked out the door, got into her car, and drove away. She didn't call or write all that summer, she just . . . vanished.

I can't remember now how long I waited for her to return, but I know that somewhere along the way, in the pool of a thousand tears, she became my Mother, and then, finally, Nora. My mom was gone. I accepted the fact that whatever she wanted out of life, it wasn't me.

I could describe what it was like, the waiting, but I won't. Not even for the money. The worst of it was my father. For my last two years of high school, I watched him . . . disintegrate. He drank, he sat in his darkened bedroom, he wept.

And so, when Caché came to me, asking for my story, I said yes. Hell yes.

I figured it was time that America knew who they were listening to, who was giving them moral advice.

Like the rest of you, I heard her message stream over the airwaves: Commit to your family and make it work. Be honest. Hold fast to the vows you made before God.

This from a woman who walked out on her marriage and abandoned her children, and—

"Ruby!"

She tossed down the pen and paper and went to the doorway, poking her head out. "Yeah?"

"Can you breathe okay, with all this dust?"

Ruby rolled her eyes. As always, her mother was as subtle as an exclamation mark. "I see you found enough air in your lungs to scream at me," she muttered, hurrying downstairs.

As she passed her mother's bedroom, she heard a sneeze.

Ruby smiled; she couldn't help it.

In the kitchen, she knelt in front of the cabinet beneath the sink and opened the doors. Everything she needed to clean the house, and in quantities large enough to clean *any* house, stood in four straight rows. When she realized that the supplies were organized in alphabetical order, she burst out laughing.

"Poor Caro," she whispered, realizing how badly her sister wanted everything to be tidy. "You were *definitely* born into the wrong family."

Then, as tired as she was, she started to clean.

Chapter Eight

Nora tried not to watch her daughter clean the house. It was simply too irritating.

Ruby dusted without moving anything, and she clearly thought a dry rag would do the job. Oh, she'd brought out the industrial-size can of Pledge, but she'd left it sitting on the tile counter in the kitchen. When she started mopping the floor with soapless water, Nora couldn't help herself.

"Aren't you going to sweep first?" she asked from her wheelchair, tucked into the open doorway of her bedroom.

Ruby slowly turned around. Her face was flushed—from what exertion, Nora couldn't imagine. "Excuse me?"

Nora wished she'd kept silent, but now there was nowhere to go except forward. "You need to sweep the floor before you mop . . . and soap in the water is a big help."

Ruby let go of the mop. The wooden handle clattered to the floor. "You're criticizing my cleaning technique?"

"I wouldn't call it a technique. It's just common sense to—"

"So, I have no common sense, either."

Nora sighed. "Come on, Ruby. You know better than that. I taught you—"

Ruby was in front of Nora before she could finish the sentence. "*You* do not want to bring up the things you taught me. Because if I do as I've been *taught,* I'll walk out that door, climb into the minivan, and drive away. I won't even bother to wave good-bye."

Nora's irritation vanished; regret swooped in to take its place. She sagged like a rag doll in her chair. "I'm sorry."

Ruby took a step back. "According to Caro, those are your favorite words. Maybe you should think about what it really means to apologize before you bother." She stomped back to the kitchen sink, grabbed some liquid soap, and squirted a stream into the white plastic bucket. Then she began mopping again; her strokes were positively vicious.

Nora sat there, watching. The *thwop-squish-clack* of the mop moving across the floor (streaking clumps of dirt, Nora noticed but obviously didn't mention) was the only sound in the room.

Finally, Nora wound up the nerve for a different approach. "Maybe I could help?"

Ruby didn't look at her. "I stripped the bed upstairs. The sheets are piled on the washing machine. You could take care of your bed and start a load of laundry."

Nora nodded. It took her almost an hour of maneuvering in her chair to strip the sheets off her bed, roll into the cubicle-size laundry room, and start the first load. By the time she finished, she was wheezing like a dying crow.

She rolled back into the kitchen and found that the room was sparkling clean. Ruby had even replaced the horrid plastic flowers on the table with a fragrant bouquet of roses.

"Oh," Nora said, taking her first decent breath since coming into the house. "It looks beautiful. Just like—"

"Thanks."

Nora understood that Ruby didn't want the past mentioned. It didn't surprise Nora, that reaction. Ruby had always been an expert at denial. Even as a child, she'd had the ability to compartmentalize and forget. She could box up whatever she didn't want to face and store it away. It had been this very trait that had allowed her to shut Nora out of her life so completely.

Out of sight for Ruby had always meant out of mind. Nora decided not to let it be so easy this time. "I thought I'd help you make dinner."

Ruby turned to look at her. There was a look of genuine horror on her face.

Nora smiled. "You look like John Hurt, just before the alien popped out of his chest. Close your mouth."

"There's no food. We—I—have to go shopping."

"We both know Caroline better than that. In these cupboards, I guarantee you, are the makings for several emergency dinners. Probably labeled as such. All we have to do is look around."

"You don't need my help, then. I'll just run upstairs—"

"Not so fast. I can't reach everything. We'll need to work together."

Ruby looked like she'd just bitten down on a lemon. "I don't know how to cook."

Nora wasn't surprised. "You were never too interested in it."

"I got interested in it when I was seventeen. Not that you would know this."

Direct hit. "I could teach you now."

"Lucky me."

Nora refused to be hurt by that comment. She wheeled into the kitchen. With her back to Ruby, she scavenged through the cupboards, finding several cans of tomatoes, a bag of angel-hair pasta, an unopened bottle of olive oil, jars of marinated artichoke hearts and capers, and a container of dried Parmesan cheese. She pulled out everything she needed and set the supplies beside the stove. Then she waited patiently.

Her patience didn't last as long as she would have liked. "Ruby?" she said at last.

Ruby walked over to the stove. "Okay, what do you want me to do?"

"See that big frying pan hanging on the rack—no, the bigger one. Yes. Take that and put it on the front burner."

It hit with a clang.

Nora winced. "Now put about a tablespoon of olive oil in it and turn on the gas."

Ruby opened the oil and poured in at least a half cup.

Nora could practically *feel* her hips expanding, but she bit back a comment as she reached for the can opener. She was proud of herself for saying simply,

"The measuring spoons are in the top drawer, to your left." Then she opened the canned tomatoes. "Here, add these. And turn the flame to low."

When Ruby had done that, Nora went on. "Cut up the marinated artichoke hearts and add them. Maybe a half cup of that canned chicken broth would be good, too."

Ruby went to the counter, turned her back to Nora, and began chopping.

"Ow. *Shit!*"

Nora spun the wheelchair toward her daughter. "Are you okay?"

Ruby stepped back. Blood was dripping in a steady red stream from her index finger; it plopped onto the tile counter.

Nora yanked a clean towel off the oven door. "Come here, honey. Get on your knees in front of me. Keep your hand up."

Ruby dropped to her knees. She seemed unable to look away from her finger. Her face was pale.

Nora gently took hold of her daughter's hand. Seeing that blood—her child's—made Nora's own hand throb. Just like old times; Nora had always experienced a phantom pain whenever one of her kids was hurt. She carefully coiled the towel around the wound, and without thinking, wrapped her own hands around Ruby's.

When she looked up, Nora saw the emotion on Ruby's face, and knew that her daughter remembered this simple routine. The only thing missing was a kiss to make it all better. She saw the longing flash through

Ruby's eyes. It was only there for an instant, but Nora had waited so long to see it . . .

Ruby yanked her hand back. "It's just a cut, for God's sake. We don't have to go looking for my finger on the floor or anything."

That gap yawned between them again, and Nora wondered suddenly if she'd imagined the longing in her daughter's eyes. If she'd seen only what she wanted so desperately to see.

Her voice was shaky when she said, "Put the artichoke hearts and two tablespoons of capers into the sauce." She turned quickly to the spice drawer, yanking it open. But when she stared down into the drawer, all she saw was Ruby's face as it had been for that one second, that instant that had somehow been both then and now.

Nora grabbed the herbs she needed and wheeled back around, adding them to the sauce. "Put a big pot of water on to boil, won't you?"

For the next thirty minutes, Ruby did as she was told without uttering a word. She was vigilant in her refusal to make eye contact.

But finally, the meal was ready, and they were seated across from each other at the round wooden kitchen table. Ruby picked up her fork and rammed it into the pasta, twirling it.

"Don't you want to say grace?" Nora asked.

Ruby looked up. "No."

"But we—"

"There is no *we*. Dinnertime prayers are one of those family traditions that went the way of our family. God and I have an understanding. When He stopped listening, I stopped talking."

Nora sighed. "Oh, Ruby . . ."

"Don't give me that wounded-deer look." Ruby turned her attention back to the plate and started eating. "This is good."

"Thanks." Nora closed her eyes. "Thank you, God," she said softly, her voice barely loud enough for Ruby to hear. "For this food . . . and this time that Ruby and I have together."

Ruby kept eating.

Nora tried to eat, but the silence tore at her nerves. It was hard enough to be estranged from your child when thousands of miles separated you . . . but estrangement at the same table was brutal.

One personal thing.

Leo's advice came back to her. It had seemed easy enough when she was on the phone with her doctor; now, sitting beneath this cone of silence, it felt like a herculean undertaking.

She was still trolling for an icebreaker when Ruby said, "Excuse me," got up from the table, and went across the kitchen. She started filling the sink with water.

Nora hadn't realized that eating was a timed event. Fortunately, she kept this observation to herself. She cleared the table, stacked the dishes on the counter at Ruby's elbow. In an unnerving silence, Ruby washed and Nora dried. When they were finished, Nora wheeled herself into the living room.

She mentally prepared for round two.

Ruby swept past her—practically running—and headed for the stairs.

Nora had to think fast. "Why don't you make us a fire? June nights are always chilly."

Ruby stumbled to a halt. Without answering, she went to the hearth and knelt down to build a fire.

She did it exactly as she'd been taught by Grandpa Bridge.

"I guess some things you never forget," Nora said.

Ruby sat back on her heels and held her hands out toward the fire. It was a full minute before she turned to Nora and said, "Except how it feels to have a mother."

Nora sucked in a sharp breath. "That's not fair. I was with you every day until . . ."

"Until the day you weren't."

Nora clasped her hands together and slid them between her legs. She didn't want Ruby to see how badly she was trembling. "You and Caroline were my whole world."

Ruby laughed drily and got to her feet, moving toward Nora. "We weren't your whole world the summer I was sixteen; that *was* the year you walked into the living room, dropped your suitcase on the floor, and announced that you were leaving, wasn't it? And what was it you said to us—'Who wants to come with me?' Yes, that was it. 'Who wants to come with me?' As if Caroline and I would set down our forks, clear the table, and move away from our dad and our home just because you decided you didn't want to be here."

"I didn't decide . . . I left because—"

"I don't care *why* you left. That's what you care about."

Nora longed to make Ruby understand, even if it was only the merest bit. Just enough so that they could simply talk. "You don't know everything about me."

Ruby looked down at her. Nora thought she saw a war going on inside her daughter, as if Ruby wanted both to keep fighting and to stop. It surprised Nora. She understood why her daughter would want to keep distance between them. What she couldn't imagine was why Ruby was still standing here. It was, in truth, a little disconcerting. She got the unsettling feeling that Ruby—honest-to-a-fault Ruby—was hiding something.

"Tell me something about you, then," Ruby said at last.

This was Nora's chance. She knew she needed to tread carefully. "Okay, let's go sit on the porch—like we used to, remember? We'll each share one piece of information about ourselves."

Ruby laughed. "I asked you to tell me about *you*. I didn't offer to reciprocate."

Nora stood her ground. "I need to know about you, too. Besides, if we're both talking, we can pretend it's a conversation."

Ruby wasn't laughing now. "Very *Silence of the Lambs* of you, Nora. Quid pro quo. For every secret you tell me, I tell you one."

"I suppose I'm Hannibal Lecter in your little comparison. A cannibal . . . and a psychopath, how lovely."

Ruby studied her a minute longer. "This should be interesting. I'm twenty-seven; you were fifty . . . when, the day before yesterday? I guess it's time we talked. Come on."

She watched her daughter walk through the kitchen and disappear onto the porch. The screen door banged shut behind her. Nora finally allowed herself to smile.

Ruby had remembered her birthday.

Finally, she wheeled out onto the porch, thankful to see that the rain had stopped. Cool night air breezed across her cheeks, carrying with it the smells of a life gone by—the sea, the sand, the roses climbing along the railings. They had bloomed early this year, as they always did after a mild winter. In another two weeks there would be saucer-size blossoms crawling up the trellises and along the picket fence.

Shadows crept along the ground like slowly seeping India ink, moved up the sides of the house, and slipped through the slats on the picket fence. Sunset tinted the sky purple and pink.

The porch light cast Ruby's back in an orangey glow. She looked young and vulnerable, with her black hair so poorly cut, and her clothes all tattered and torn. The urge to reach out, to brush the hair off Ruby's face, and say softly—

"Don't say it, Nora."

Nora frowned. "Say what?"

" 'Ah, Ruby, you could be so beautiful if you'd just try a little.' "

It startled Nora, that bit of mind reading. Sure, she'd said that often to Ruby, had thought in fact to say it a second ago, but it meant nothing. To Nora, the comment had simply been grains of sand in the desert of a mother's advice. Obviously, Ruby had felt otherwise, and she'd carried the words with her into womanhood.

Nora saw how heavy they had become, and she was ashamed. "I'm sorry, Ruby. What I should have said is: you're beautiful, just the way you are."

Ruby turned, stared down at her.

Silence settled between them, broken only by the sounds of the sea and the occasional caw of a lone crow hidden in the trees.

"Okay, Nora," Ruby said, crossing her arms, leaning with feigned nonchalance against the porch rail. "Tell me something I don't know."

Nora gazed up at her daughter, saw the wary expectation in those dark eyes, and took a deep breath. "You think I don't understand you," she began softly, "but I know how it feels to turn your back on a parent."

Ruby pulled away from the railing. Frowning, she sat down on the white wicker chair beside Nora. "You loved your parents. You told us all about them."

"The stories I told you girls were true," she answered slowly, "and they were lies. I was never good at making stuff up, so my bedtime stories were always bits and pieces of my life . . . cleaned up. I wanted you and Caro to have a sense of where you'd come from."

"What do you mean, cleaned up?"

Nora's gaze was steady. "No matter how dark a place is, there are always moments of light. That's what I passed on to you and Caroline, my moments of light." She took a deep breath. "On the day I graduated from high school, I left home, and I never went back again."

"Did you run away?"

"From my father, yes. I loved my mother."

"How long was it before you saw them again?"

Nora couldn't help it; she closed her eyes. "I saw my father once—at my mother's funeral. Before you and Caroline were born."

"And never again?"

"Never again." Nora wished those two little words didn't hurt. The emotion was so old it ought to have decomposed by now. She leaned toward Ruby. "I never saw him again, didn't even attend his funeral, and all my life I've had to live with that decision. It's not regret I feel so much, but more of . . . a sad longing. I wish he had been a different man. Most of all, I wish I could have loved him."

"Did you *ever* love him?"

"Perhaps . . . when I was young. If so, I don't remember it."

Ruby got up, walked to the railing, and stared out at the sea. Without turning around, she said, "I read the *People* magazine article about you. It said—and I quote: 'The cornerstones of Nora Bridge's message are forgiveness and commitment.' " Ruby turned around at last. "Did you try to forgive him?"

Nora wanted to lie. It was easy to see that Ruby was asking as much about *their* relationship as she was about Nora and her father's. But there was little enough chance for Nora and Ruby; with deception, there would be none at all. "Years later, after I'd had my own children—and lost their love—I began to regret how I'd treated him. As a young woman, I didn't—couldn't—understand how hard life can be. I think that's how he felt. It's no excuse, but it gives me a way to see him that turns the hatred into pity. Of course, that understanding came too late. He was already gone."

"So, I should forgive you now, while I still have the time. Is that your none-too-subtle message?"

Nora looked up sharply. "Not everything is about you, Ruby. I told you something painful about me tonight, painful and private. I expect you to handle my life with respect, if you can't manage care."

Ruby looked abashed. "I'm sorry."

"Apology accepted. Now, tell me something about you."

Ruby stared at Nora through unreadable eyes.

Nora steeled herself. This was going to be bad . . .

"That summer—you remember it, that time you left—I thought you'd come back."

"That's no secret."

"I waited and waited. By the next June, Caroline had left, and it was just Dad and me at home. One night I just . . . snapped." She swallowed hard and looked away for a moment, then collected herself and began again. "I drove down to Seattle and went to that dance club, the Monastery, all by myself. I picked up some kid—I can't even remember his name. He had blue hair and pierced ears and dead eyes. I went back to his apartment and let him fuck me." She paused for effect. "It was my first time."

It hurt as much as Ruby had intended. Nora thought: *There it is. My legacy.* She didn't dare to say she was sorry. Ruby would only toss those ridiculously inadequate words right back at her.

"I did it to hurt you. I thought you'd come home

eventually and then I'd tell you. I used to imagine the look on your face when I described it."

"You wanted to see me cry."

"At the very least."

Nora sighed. "I would have, if that makes you feel better."

"It's too late for any of us to be feeling better." She sighed. "Dean didn't take it very well, either."

Dean. For a moment Nora hurt so much she couldn't breathe evenly.

That's how the grief hit her lately. Like a rogue wave rising from a flat sea, it came out of nowhere and hit with hurricane force. Sometimes she went whole hours without thinking about Eric, and then she would suddenly remember.

Now, it had been Dean's name that reminded her, but it could have been anything—the sound of a school bell ringing, a man's laughter coming from another room. Anything.

She knew she should say something—the pain in Ruby's eyes when she said Dean's name was unmistakable—but Nora's throat was blocked too tightly to speak.

"That's enough quid pro quo for one night," Ruby said sharply. "I'm going to go upstairs and take a bath."

Nora watched her daughter leave. Then, quietly, she said, "Good night, Ruby."

Wheeling back into her bedroom, Nora elbowed the door shut behind her and crawled up onto the bed. Then she reached for the phone and dialed Eric's number.

He answered on the third ring, and she could tell that he was heavily medicated. "Hullo?"

"Hey, Eric," she said, leaning back against the head-board. "You sound like you've been shooting heroin."

"Thass how I feel." It seemed to take a long time for him to speak, and the words came out mangled and elongated.

"Are you okay?" she asked softly.

"Ssshure. Jesst a little doped up. New meds . . ."

Nora had seen him go through this before. It was al-ways hell to get the pain prescription just right. She knew it wasn't a good time for them to speak. "I'll let you sleep now, okay? I'll call back tomorrow."

"Ssleep," he murmured. "Yeah. Morrow."

"Good night, Eric."

"Goo' night."

Nora listened to the dial tone so long the recording came on, then, finally, she hung up.

Ruby went upstairs, where she grabbed her yellow legal pad and crawled up onto the bed.

This place, Summer Island, is killing me. When I left Los Angeles, I was strong and funny—not suc-cessful, perhaps, but at least I was me. Here, things are different. I smell the roses my grandmother planted and dry my hands on towels she embroi-dered . . . I sit at the table where I grew up, remem-bering when I couldn't reach the floor with my feet. I stare at the beach, and in the movement of the waves, I hear my sister's laughter.

And then there is my mother.

We have battles to fight; there is no doubt about it, but I'm afraid to ask the questions, and she, I can tell, is afraid to answer them. So we dance out of time to different pieces of music.

Quid pro quo. My secret for one of yours; this is the game we have begun to play. With it, I know I won't be able to stand on the edge of intimacy. Sooner or later, I will have to dive into those cold, deep waters, and there is no end to the ripples my entrance will make.

I will learn things about my mother that I don't want to know. Hell, I already have. I know, for instance, that she ran away from home right after high school and never spoke to her father again.

Even yesterday, I wouldn't have been surprised by that. I would have said, "Of course. Running away is what Nora Bridge does best."

But I watched her eyes as she spoke of her father. I saw the pain . . .

It hurt her to run away. Part of me wishes I hadn't seen that because, as I stood there, listening to my mother's heartache, I wondered for the first time if it hurt her to leave her children.

Chapter Nine

Dean sat cross-legged on the end of the dock, watching the sun rise.

The Sound was rough now at the changing of the tides. Waves slapped against the old sailboat that bobbed alongside the dock. The lines creaked and moaned.

He heard the sound of motors in the distance, and he smiled.

The fishing boats were going out. They were too far away to see clearly—they were, as always, hugging the coast of Shaw Island on their way to Haro Strait—but Dean had seen it all a thousand times, the battered, rat-trap boats, made of painted wood or aluminum, setting out for the day. How many times had he and Ruby stood on a dock somewhere, watching Rand's boat chug out to sea? She'd always squeezed Dean's hand at the last moment, when the *Captain Hook* rounded the point and disappeared. He had known, without her ever having to tell him, that she lived with a tiny bit of fear that one day her father wouldn't return.

Dean had taken his watch off when he arrived on Lopez Island, so he wasn't sure how long he sat there. All he knew was that by the time the sun gained strength and heated his cheeks, he'd been there long enough.

Tiredly, he got to his feet and turned around. To his right, the old family sailboat bobbed wearily in the tide.

The mast—once a bright white—had been discolored by the endless rain and pitted by the wind. Red sides had been scraped down to bare wood in a dozen places, and the deck around the big metal steering wheel was hidden beneath a layer of blackened, slimy leaves and green-gray mold.

Of course, that was when he heard her voice: *Let's take out the* Wind Lass, *Dino, come on!*

He closed his eyes, remembering Ruby. In the beginning, he'd flinched at every memory, held his breath, and waited for the images to pass, but then the memories had started to fade, and he'd gone in search of them, reaching out like a blind man.

Now he understood how precious were his memories of first love, and he treasured both their pleasure and their pain.

He grabbed the line and pulled the boat closer to the dock, then stepped aboard. The boat undulated unsteadily, as if surprised to be boarded after so many lonely years.

He had always felt free on this boat. The flapping sound of sails catching wind had buoyed his spirits like nothing else. He and Eric had spent so much of their youth on the *Wind Lass*. On these teak decks, they'd spun dreams for a future that stretched out years and years. Though neither of them had ever said it aloud, they'd both imagined growing old on this boat, bringing wives and children and grandchildren aboard.

Dean loved to sail, and yet he'd walked away from it, let sailing be part of the life he'd left behind . . .

Obviously Eric had done the same. The *Wind Lass* could have been docked in Seattle, a stone's throw from Eric's house, and yet here she sat, untended and untouched.

And suddenly Dean knew what he needed to do.

He would restore the *Wind Lass*. Scrape the old paint away, strip the wood and re-oil it, scrub its every inch. He'd take this forgotten, once-loved boat and return it to its past glory.

If he could get Eric out here for an afternoon—just that, a single afternoon—maybe the wind and the sea could take them back in time . . .

Ruby woke to the smell of frying bacon and brewing coffee. Snagging yesterday's leggings off the floor, she pulled them on underneath her long nightshirt and hurried through her morning bathroom routine, then padded downstairs.

Nora was in the kitchen, maneuvering the wheelchair like General Patton along the front. There were two cast-iron skillets on the stove, one with steam climbing out. A yellow crockery mixing bowl sat by the empty skillet; a metal-handled spoon rested against its side. She smiled up at Ruby. "Good morning. Did you sleep well?"

"Fine." She stumbled past the wheelchair and poured herself a cup of coffee, adding sugar and cream.

After a sip, she felt more human. Leaning back against the cupboards, she saw that her mother had made bacon and pancakes. "I haven't eaten a breakfast like this since you left us."

It was obviously an effort for her mother to keep smiling. "Do you want me to put an M-and-M face on your pancakes like I used to?"

"No, thanks. I try to avoid carbohydrates layered with chocolate."

Ruby set the table, then dished up two plates and sat down.

Nora sat down across from her. "Did you sleep well last night?" she asked, pouring syrup in a tiny puddle by her pancakes.

Ruby had forgotten that her mother dipped each bite of pancake into syrup. The quirk reminded her of all the bits and pieces of their common life; the things that inextricably bound a mother and daughter, whether Ruby wanted those ties or not. "You already asked me that."

Nora's fork clanged on the plate edge. "Tomorrow I'll remember to wear a Kevlar vest under my nightgown."

"What am I supposed to do? Be like Caroline— pretend everything is fine between us?"

"My relationship with Caroline is not for you to judge," Nora said sharply, looking up at her. "You've always thought you knew everything. I used to think it was a good trait for a girl to have, but there's a dark side to all that certainty, Ruby. You . . . hurt people." Ruby saw her mother swell up with anger, and then as quickly fade into a tired thinness. "But I suppose it's not entirely your fault."

"Not *entirely*? How about not at all my fault?"

"I left Caroline, too. It didn't make her cold and hard and unable to love people."

Now *that* pissed Ruby off. "Who said I couldn't love people? I lived with Max for five years."

"And where is he now?"

Ruby pushed back from the table and stood up. Suddenly she wanted distance between them.

Nora looked up. There was a gentle understanding in her gaze that didn't sit well with Ruby. "Sit down. We won't talk about anything that matters. I'll comment on the weather, if you like."

Ruby felt like a fool standing there, breathing too hard, showing exactly how deeply she'd been wounded by her mother's remark.

"Ruby Elizabeth, sit down and eat your breakfast." Her mother spoke in one of those voices that immediately turned a grown woman into a child. Ruby did as she was told.

Nora took a bite of bacon. Her chewing was a loud *crunch-crunch-crunch*. "We need to go grocery shopping."

"Fine."

"How about this morning?"

Ruby nodded. Finishing her last bite, she stood up and began cleaning the table. "I'll do the dishes. We'll leave in about thirty minutes?"

"Make it an hour. I have to figure out how in the hell to do a sponge bath."

"I could lasso your leg and lower you into the bath like an anchor."

Nora laughed. "No, thanks. I don't want to drown naked with my leg stuck up in the air. The tabloids would have a field day with that."

The remark took a moment to sink in. When it did, Ruby turned back to the table. "I wouldn't let you drown."

"I know. But would you rescue me?" Without waiting for an answer, Nora spun around and rolled into her bedroom, shutting the door behind her.

Ruby stood there, staring at the closed door.

Would you rescue me?

The Benevolent Order of the Sisters of St. Francis had first come to Summer Island during World War One. A generous donor (who had no doubt lived a life that imperiled his immortal soul) had granted them more than one hundred waterfront acres. The sisters, who were equally high-minded in spiritual and business matters, had opened a general store next to the dock that would become the ferry terminal. On the rolling acreage behind the store, they'd built a sanctuary that tourists never saw. They raised cattle and owned the most profitable apple orchard on the island. They wove their own cloth, dyed it with extracts from their own gardens, and hand-stitched it into brown robes. Their sanctuary was open to any of their order, as well as to any woman who sought refuge from an unhappy life. Such women were welcomed into the fold and given that precious commodity so missing from the hectic, violent outside world: time. Here, they could don the clothing of their grandmothers, do the simple chores required of subsistence living, and commune with the God they felt they'd lost.

On Sundays, the sisters opened their small wooden chapel to their friends and neighbors. A priest from the monastery on a nearby island conducted quiet services in Latin. It was a humble church, where no one minded the cries of bored babies or the emptiness of a collection plate when times turned hard.

Theirs was still the only store on the island. Ruby pulled the minivan into the gravel parking lot behind the "He Will Provide" grocery store and parked beside a rusty pickup truck.

She helped Nora into the chair. Together they made their way down the rickety wooden boardwalk that connected the town's three buildings. Wisteria grew along the posts that supported the roof's overhang and festooned the upper timbers with fragrant white flowers. Here and there along the boardwalk were benches, handmade by the sisters. Later in the tourist season, those seats would be filled by people waiting for a ferry.

Ruby came to the store's screen door and pulled it open. A bell tinkled gaily overhead as they wheeled inside. The murky store was long and narrow, built like a shoe box.

Light pushed through the twin windows and illuminated a small desk with a cash register on it. Beyond that, layered wooden bookcases held carefully arranged dried goods. A small freezer offered all manner of island-raised meat—beef, chicken, pork, lamb—and a refrigerated case held vegetables grown on the sisters' own land.

The nun at the cash register looked up at their entrance.

"Nora Bridge? Ruby? I don't believe it!" Sister Helen waddled around the desk, her skirt hiked up to reveal heavy white calves sheathed in nubby woolen socks. Her green rubber clogs thumped with every step. Her fleshy face was scrunched into a welcoming grin that turned her bespectacled eyes into slits. She looked—as always—like a sprightly old gnome. "Praise God," Sister said. Her thick German accent turned the words into *prais Gott*. "It has been so long . . ." She turned to Ruby. "And how is the funny one?"

Ruby smiled. "I'm still a stitch, Sister. How 'bout you—got any good Heaven jokes for me?"

"I will think on it, that is for sure. It is *wunderbar* to see you both." She elbowed Ruby. "Mother Ruth still talks about the day your rabbit ran through services, *ja?* She will be happy to see you again."

Ruby stepped away from the wheelchair. "I . . . uh . . . haven't been to services in a while. I'm only on the island a week, anyway."

Helen gave her "the look"—every Catholic recognized it. "There is a Sunday in every week, *ja?*"

"Uh . . . maybe."

Nora smiled up at the nun. "Some things never change."

Helen nodded. Her habit slipped down on her forehead and she gave it a quick shove back. "Most things never change. That is what I have learned in seventy-three years of life." She leaned back on her heels and crossed her beefy arms. "It is good to see you two together again, that much is for sure. You have stayed away from this island for too long." She turned to Ruby. "You have babies, *ja,* like your sister?"

"No babies—and before you ask, no husband. I'm either footloose and fancy free or lonely and unlovable. Take your pick."

Helen laughed. "Always you were this way, Ruby. Making a joke out of everything. However—just for the record—my guess would be . . . fancy free and lonely." She clapped her hands together. "Anyway, the store is set up as it always was. Get what you need. Shall I begin a new account for you?"

"No," Ruby answered.

"Yes," Nora said at the same time, shooting her a dark look. "*I* may be here a while."

Ruby grabbed one of the small red baskets stacked by the desk and handed it to Nora. "Let's get started."

They moved past the tourist supply section—postcards, pens with ferries on them, little brown and white candlesticks made from Mount Saint Helens ash, Christmas ornaments. Ruby went on ahead; Nora rolled slowly behind her.

They came to the cereal first. Ruby grabbed a box of Cap'n Crunch and tossed it into the basket in her mother's lap.

"There's nothing good for you in that cereal."

Ruby turned, saw her mother's frown. "Should I get the kind with crunchberries? It adds fruit."

"Very funny. Will you grab one of those granolas for me—the sisters make it, if I remember correctly."

Ruby reached for the beribboned bag of cereal and

plopped it into the basket. If *she* remembered correctly, it tasted like carpet fibers.

"We'll need several cans of tomatoes," Nora said. "No, not those; the ones in the green cans."

Ruby put back the unacceptable canned tomatoes and chose the "right" brand.

"Spaghetti and penne, please. God, no, not that cheap brand; get the good stuff . . . from Italy."

Like it was actually made in Italy. Ruby gritted her teeth and kept moving, but with every word her mother spoke, she felt her anger rise. When Ruby reached for the Twinkies, her mother practically shrieked.

"You cannot eat that."

That was it. Very slowly, Ruby turned around. "I'm sorry, do you *hear* me asking for dietary advice?"

"No, but—"

"That's the point. It's *my* butt that's going to swell to the size of Nebraska, not yours. So please . . . shut . . . up."

Nora snapped her teeth together. "Fine."

Ruby could hear Sister Helen chuckling.

Miraculously, she and her mother made it all the way to the end of the aisle without another argument.

Apparently, Nora was saving her strength for the battle over vegetables.

"That ear of corn is gross. Get one of the white ones . . . not *that* onion, for God's sake, get a Walla Walla Sweet . . . come on, Ruby, that broccoli is half dead. What on earth do you eat in California?"

Ruby dropped the broccoli into the basket and walked away. It was safer that way. She poked her head around the end of the aisle and called out to Sister Helen, "Where are the aspirin?"

Sister Helen chuckled. "Along the back wall, honey, by the Pepto-Bismol . . . which you might want to consider, too."

Ruby snagged an industrial-size container of Excedrin and tossed it into the basket. It hit a tomato with a juicy *thwack!*

"Lovely," Nora said, wiping her cheek. Then she glanced toward the left corner, where the nuns offered a few T-shirts and shorts for sale. "I could get you some clothes, if you'd like—"

"That's it. We're done." Ruby grabbed the handles on the wheelchair and spun it around, then strode up to the cash register. She stopped so suddenly her mother was thrown forward like a rag doll.

Sister Helen was doing her level best not to smile. "It's just like old times, seeing you two together."

Nora gave her a tight smile. "Yes, Sister, we've always enjoyed these mother–daughter outings."

Ruby nodded. "Just remember what she was like to shop with . . . when the police come to question you."

Sister Helen laughed at that and started ringing up the groceries. She chattered nonstop about this and that—who was running for mayor come autumn, whose horse had recently foundered, whose well had gone dry—as her fingers flew across the keys.

Ruby left the store and stared at the cars in line for the next ferry. She was just about to turn around when the row of newspaper machines caught her eye.

She glanced back into the store, then hurried down to the box that held *USA Today.*

And there, in the upper-right-hand corner, was a picture of her mother beneath the headline: WHERE IS NORA BRIDGE HIDING?

Ruby dug into her fanny pack, found two quarters, and slipped them into the machine.

"Ruby, honey?" came her mother's voice from inside the store.

Ruby yanked the paper out, rolled it up, and shoved it into her waistband, pulling her shirt down in front of it. "Just a second," she hollered, running past the store. At the minivan, she opened the back door and shoved the paper in underneath the backseat. By the time she got back into the store, she was breathless.

Nora was staring up at her. "The bags are on the counter. I can carry two of them if you can manage the third."

Ruby was certain that the patented mother's X-ray vision had somehow seen what she'd bought.

"Sure. Bye, Sister Helen." She snatched the bag off the counter, settled it under one arm, and wheeled her mother toward the car.

As soon as they got home, Ruby helped her mother into the house, carried the groceries in, and put them away. Then she turned to Nora, who was watching her closely.

"I . . . uh . . . I'm going to walk on the beach. It's such a nice day." Flashing a fake smile, Ruby went back outside. At the minivan, she retrieved her paper and tucked it under her shirt—just in case—then walked down to the beach.

She sat down on a flat granite rock and pulled out the lifestyle section, using a big chunk of silvery driftwood to pin the rest of the paper into the sand. The wind flapped at the edges of the paper and tried to rip it from her hands.

WHERE IS NORA BRIDGE HIDING?

In the wake of an ugly scandal, Nora Bridge has disappeared. Executives at KJZZ, which broadcasts her popular talk show, "Spiritual Healing with Nora," are closing ranks, saying only that Ms. Bridge is on a previously scheduled vacation.

Tom Adams, the controversial and outspoken owner of Adams News Organization, reports that nothing has changed with Ms. Bridge's daily advice column, "Nora Knows Best."

Yesterday, Adams talked to Katie Couric. He encouraged viewers to write to Nora, promising that "she wants to hear from her faithful readers and she will answer their questions. Even the tough ones."

Sources close to Ms. Bridge, however, seem unconvinced that she will return. As one employee, who asked to have her name withheld, put it, "I guess she was a big talker. All that advice about the sanctity of marriage . . . well, it's a real disappointment to find out what a liar she is."

There was obviously a full-scale media frenzy going on out there—*Today . . . Larry King Live.* Reporters were probably scouring the country, talking to anyone and everyone who ever knew Nora Bridge; they'd tear her apart if they could.

And Ruby's article would make it worse . . .

* * *

Ruby sat on the bed in her parents' old bedroom, with her knees drawn up and her yellow pad in her lap. The *USA Today* lay beside her; that grainy, unflattering photograph of her mother stared up at her.

> *My mother is being destroyed in the press. It's only fitting, I suppose. She ruined her family in pursuit of a career, and now that career is detonating.*
>
> *It's what I wanted to happen. I'm sure it's part of what made me accept the money for an article. A need for some kind of ... if not vengeance, then fairness.*
>
> *And yet ... something about it doesn't sit well with me—*

"Ruby! Come help me make dinner."

For a weird, disorienting second, Ruby was fourteen again, hiding in her bedroom, reading *The Lord of the Rings* when she was supposed to be doing homework. Shaking her head to clear it, she rolled over on her stomach and yanked open the top drawer in her mother's nightstand. Pens and junk clattered forward. As she started to put her pad away, she saw a brown prescription bottle.

She picked it up and read the label. VALIUM. NORA BRIDGE. 1985. The doctor listed was Allbright.

Ruby frowned. Her mother was on Valium in 1985?

Chapter Ten

Valium.

That discovery opened a door, hinted at a woman Ruby had never known, never even imagined.

In 1985, everything had been fine. Great.

Or so Ruby had thought.

She wished she hadn't found the bottle. It was the sort of thing she didn't want to know. Like accidentally finding your mother's vibrator. Some things were supposed to remain hidden.

Finally, Ruby couldn't stand being in the bedroom anymore. She went downstairs and found Nora already in the kitchen.

"We're going to make chicken divan. How does that sound?"

Ruby groaned. "Cooking together."

"I want you to chop that broccoli. The cutting board is right there."

Ruby did as she was told.

"Smaller, please. Each piece needs to fit in a human mouth."

Ruby took a deep breath and started over.

For the next half hour, they worked side by side. Ruby boiled and cut up the chicken—in human-size bites—while Nora did everything else. Finally, the casserole was in the oven.

"I have a surprise for you," Nora said, putting the cutting board away. "There's a big cardboard box in my closet. Will you get it?"

Ruby shook her head. "I don't think so." A surprise from her mother just couldn't be a good thing.

Nora gave her "the look," and Ruby caved. Some things were bigger than willpower, and a mother's raised eyebrow was one of them. She went into the bedroom, opened the closet's louvered doors, and found the box. As she hefted it into her arms, it made a rattling, clanking sound like auto parts crammed together.

She took it into the living room and set it down on the glossy wormwood coffee table. It hit with a clatter.

Nora had followed her into the living room. "Open it."

Ruby pulled the cardboard flaps apart and peered inside the box. "Oh, *shit*."

It was their sixteen-millimeter movie projector and a reel of film. She turned to her mother.

"Home movies," Nora said with a forced smile.

"Don't tell me you want us to bond over old times?"

"*I* want to watch them, that's all. You can join me . . . or you can set it up and leave me . . . alone."

Ruby was trapped. Whether she watched the movies or not, she'd know that the film was here, in the house, waiting like a monster beneath a child's bed. She reached deeper into the box and found a folded white sheet and a set of thumbtacks. Their old "screen."

She set up the projector on a table in the living room, clicked the reel into place, and plugged the cord in. Then she tacked the sheet onto the wall.

She refused to dwell upon how big a deal it used to be to watch family movies. Every Christmas Eve, they'd sat together in their pajamas, with their unopened gifts glittering seductively beneath the tree, and watched the highlights of their year. It was an essential tradition in a family that had only a few.

Ruby turned off the lights. With a dull, clacking sound, the film started as a gray and black square in the center of the sheet.

Ruby lowered herself to the sofa's arm.

The words LOPEZ ISLAND TALENT REVUE stuttered understood across the makeshift screen. There was a buzz of people talking, then her mother's voice, clear as day, *There! Rand; she's coming.*

Ruby couldn't have been more than five years old, a scrawny, puffy-cheeked kindergartner dressed in a ragged pink tutu. She twirled and swirled drunkenly across the stage, her toothpick arms finding all kinds of awkward angles.

—*Oh, Rand, she's perfect*—

—*Hush, I'm trying to concentrate*—

Onstage, Ruby executed an uneven spin and sank into a curtsy. Applause thundered.

The picture went dark, then stuttered back to life. This time they were down at the beach. Caroline, in a skirted one-piece bathing suit, was splashing in the ankle-deep water, laughing. Ruby was wearing a bikini; her belly poked out above banged-up stick legs. Her mother was sitting in the sand, looking through a plastic bucket full of shells and rocks. Ruby ran over to her and stamped a foot down beside the bucket. Mom leaned over and fixed a strap on her saltwater sandals, then pulled a wiggly, laughing Ruby into her arms for a kiss.

Mom . . .

There she was.

Ruby slid off the arm of the sofa and landed on the soft, threadbare cushion. Her whole childhood played out in front of her in staccato, black-and-white images accompanied by the sounds of children laughing.

How was it she'd forgotten how much they'd laughed . . . or how regularly her mother had hugged and kissed her? She'd remembered the feel of riding on her dad's strong shoulders, of seeing the world from way up high, but not the gentle pressure of her mother's kiss.

But she remembered it now. She was *seeing* it.

There was no way to keep her distance from this.

There was Dad, twirling Ruby around and around in a circle . . . and Mom, teaching Ruby how to tie her shoe . . . a rainy Halloween with two princesses skipping hand in hand up to the Smithsons' front door, carrying pumpkin-headed flashlights . . . the snowy Christmas morning when Ruby had gotten a guinea pig from Santa . . . Mom and Dad, dancing in the living room of this very house, the picture blurry and bouncing from a camera held in a child's hands . . .

By the time the final bit of film flapped out of the reel and the screen went blank, Ruby felt as if she'd run a ten-mile race. She was unsteady as she turned off the camera and hit the lights.

Her mother (*Nora,* she reminded herself) sat hunched in her wheelchair, hands drawn into a tight-fisted ball in her lap. Tears glistened on her cheeks and lashes. She caught Ruby's gaze and tried to smile.

At the sight of her mother's tears, Ruby felt something inside of her break away. "You and Dad looked so happy together."

Nora smiled unevenly. "We were happy for a lot of years. And then . . . we weren't."

"You mean *you* weren't. I saw what it did to him when you walked out. Believe me, he loved you."

"Rand would have stayed with me forever; you're right about that. Just as he'd vowed to do."

Ruby frowned. "He would have stayed because he loved you, not just because he'd promised to."

"Ah, Ruby . . . there's so much you don't know. Your dad and I have a . . . history that's ours alone. No child can judge her parents' marriage."

"You mean you won't tell me why you left him."

"Beyond saying that we were unhappy? No, I won't."

Ruby wanted to be angry, but in truth, she was too battered. The movies had hurt so much she couldn't think straight. For the first time in years, she'd seen *Mom.*

"I had forgotten you," Ruby said softly, closing her eyes. "I've never dreamt of you or had a single childhood memory with you in it." When Ruby opened her eyes, she saw that her mother was crying, and it made Ruby uncomfortable, as if she'd done something wrong. It was crazy to feel that way, but there it was. Strangely, she didn't want to make her mother cry. "But tonight I remembered the locket you gave me on my eleventh birthday. The silver oval that opened up. I kept a picture of you on one side and Dad and Caro on the other side."

Nora wiped her eyes and nodded. "Do you still have it?"

Ruby got up, went to the fireplace. She stared at the pictures of Caroline's family. When she reached up and touched her own bare throat, she felt the phantom locket. She'd been sixteen the last day she'd worn it.

It had been a hot, humid day in the second week of August. Ruby and Caroline had refused to go school shopping. It had been the rock-bottom basement of their faith, the thing they'd said to each other for weeks: *Mom would be home in time for school . . .*

But she wasn't, and August had bled into September, and their lives couldn't be kept on hold anymore.

In that season, when all their friends and neighbors had been gathered together for picnics and barbecues and parties at Trout Lake, the Bridge family had stayed huddled in their too-quiet house. Ruby and Caro had learned to move soundlessly that summer. They did their best to disappear. Girls who were invisible didn't have to answer people's questions or make painful explanations.

It had been easy to do. Dad had seen to that. He'd started drinking and smoking when Nora left in

June. By August, he never came out of his room. The *Captain Hook* sat idle all summer, and by the fall, Dad had had to sell off another chunk of land to pay their bills.

Finally, on the first day of school, Ruby had taken the locket off and thrown it to the ground . . .

"Ruby? I asked about the locket."

She turned and looked at her mother. "I threw it away."

"I see."

"No, you don't. I didn't throw it away because I hated you." She drew in a deep breath. For a split second, she almost lost her nerve; she had to force the confession out. "I threw it because it hurt too much to remember you."

"Oh, Ruby . . ."

In the kitchen, the oven's timer went off.

Ruby lurched to her feet. "Thank God. Let's eat."

Nora wrestled through a long and sleepless night. Finally, around dawn, she gave up and went out onto the porch to watch the sunrise. As soon as the sun was up, she called Eric, but there was no answer, and somehow, that made her feel even lonelier. She wheeled herself back out to the porch.

It was low tide now. The shy water had drawn back, revealing a wide swatch of glistening, pebbled shoreline.

She remembered so many times on that beach, gathering oysters, clams, and geoducks with Rand's father for a Sunday barbecue.

I had forgotten you.

Nora had known that Ruby blamed her, hated her. But to have *forgotten* her?

Nora didn't know how to combat that.

Do you want me to be like Caroline? Ruby had asked. *Pretend that everything is fine between us?*

Nora leaned back in her chair, sighing tiredly. Ruby was right. Ruby, with her fire, her anger, her chipped shoulder . . . at least she was honest. All or nothing. Black or white. She couldn't live in the shades of gray that comforted her sister.

"I miss you, Ruby," she whispered, daring to say the words to this silent world; words she couldn't imagine being able to say to her younger daughter. Sadness welled up inside her. Instead of pushing it away or pretending it didn't exist, she allowed herself to wallow in it. *I miss you, baby girl . . .*

She thought of all the years that had passed her by—Ruby leaving for college . . . quitting college . . . moving to Los Angeles (had she taken Rand's ratty old Volkswagen or had she found a way to buy a new car?) . . . renting her first apartment . . .

So much time gone.

"Enough," she said at last. Straightening her spine, she opened her eyes.

What she needed was a plan. She needed to attack the problem with Ruby aggressively—there was no other way to deal with her.

There would be no second chance; she knew that. Nora had one week—six days, now—to crack through the hard shell of the past.

But how?

"Okay," she counseled herself. "Pretend this is a reader letter."

Dear Nora:

Years ago, I walked out on my marriage and left my children. My younger daughter has never forgiven me. Now she tells me that she's forgotten all memories of me. How do I make amends?

She took a deep breath, thinking it through. If Nora had received a letter like this, she would have taken the woman to task for her unpardonable behavior, would have told her it was no surprise that her daughter hated her.

"Hypocrite," she hissed. No wonder she'd lost her career.

Anyway, after moralizing for a few sentences, she would have said . . .

Force her to remember you.

The answer came easily when offered to a stranger.

Nora smiled. If she forced Ruby to remember the past, they could possibly find their way into the present . . . maybe even peek at a different future.

It wouldn't be easy, she knew. Or particularly pleasant.

Probably excruciating, in fact.

But it was the only way. Right now, it was easy for Ruby to hate Nora—she only remembered the horrible choices made that summer. Would it be so easy if Ruby remembered the good times?

Behind her, the screen door squeaked open. "Nora?"

Nora wheeled around, smiling brightly. "Hi, honey."

Ruby frowned. "You're awfully chipper for eight in the morning. Do you want a cup of coffee?"

"No, thanks. I've got some. Why don't you get a cup and join me out here? It's beautiful."

Ruby ran a hand through her spiky, sleep-molded hair and nodded. Wordlessly, she went back inside, then came out a few minutes later and sat down in the rocker.

Nora stared down at the beach. The silence between them was strangely companionable, not unlike a thousand other mornings, long ago, when they'd sat together out here.

She took a sip of her coffee and glanced out at the point. "Remember the Fourth of July barbecues we used to have out here? Your dad was always gone fishing and the three of us girls would load up on firecrackers."

Ruby smiled. "Sparklers were my favorite. I couldn't wait for it to get dark."

"We wrote things in the light, remember?" Nora said, watching Ruby. "I always wrote: I love my girls."

Ruby curled her hands around her coffee cup, as if she needed a sudden infusion of warmth. "Caroline always scrawled the name of whatever boy she was in love with at the time. Remember when it was Alexander Jorgenson? It took two sparklers to spell his whole name—she was in a panic."

Nora smiled. She pictured Eric and Dean, standing around the grill, laughing. They'd had impeccable timing, those boys. They never missed a meal. There was a sudden lump in her throat, and so her voice was soft when she said, "You only wrote Dean's name. Year after year."

Ruby sighed. "Yeah . . . He and Eric always showed up right when you put the salmon on the barbecue—remember?" She looked up. "Caroline tells me you've stayed in touch with Eric. How is he?"

Nora had known this moment was coming; she'd thought she was prepared for it, but she wasn't. She released her breath in a slow sigh. There was no way to honor Eric's wish for privacy, not with Nora unable to drive. Sooner or later, she would have to elicit Ruby's help, and when she did, Ruby would learn about Eric. But how did you tell your daughter that one of her best childhood friends was dying?

"Mom?"

Nora casually wiped her eyes and met Ruby's expectant gaze. "Eric has cancer."

Ruby paled. "Oh, my God . . ."

Nora watched the memories move through Ruby's eyes. She knew her daughter was thinking back to lazy summer days spent down at the lake with Dean and Eric. It was a long time before Ruby found her voice. "How bad is it?"

"Bad."

"Is he going to die?"

It hurt to answer. "Yes, honey, he is."

Ruby slumped forward, burying her head in her hands. "I should have stayed in contact with him. God . . ." She fell silent, shaking her head, and Nora knew her daughter was crying. "It seems like yesterday we were all together. I can't imagine him . . . sick."

"I know. I keep thinking about those Fourth of July barbecues. I used to watch you and Dean on the beach. You'd hold hands and duel with your sparklers. I could hear your laughter all the way up here, and when you got older, and started whispering . . . then I worried."

Ruby looked up. Tears spiked her eyelashes, made her look about ten years old. "I never knew that."

"Motherhood is full of secret worries." Nora realized a second too late that she'd made herself vulnerable. She should never have used the word *secret*. But, thankfully, Ruby had bigger things on her mind.

"Can we visit Eric?"

"Of course. He's staying at the old house on Lopez. I know he'd love to see you." Nora leaned back in her chair and stared out at the Sound. "Sometimes, when I close my eyes, I can picture all of us. You, me, Caroline . . . Eric and Dean. What I remember most are days out on the *Wind Lass*. Dino and Eric loved that boat . . ."

"I know what you're doing," Ruby said after a long pause; her voice was thick and low. "You want me to remember."

"Yes."

"Remembering stuff like that hurts."

"I know, honey. But—"

Inside the house, the phone rang. Ruby got slowly to her feet and went inside. The screen door banged shut behind her. "Hello?"

Nora could hear Ruby's half of the conversation.

"Who is this? Oh, I'm her daughter, Ruby . . . Yes,

she is . . . just a minute, I'll get her. Nora?" Ruby yelled. "It's your personal assistant, Dee."

"Tell her I'm not here."

Ruby opened the screen door and poked her head out. "I already told her you were here. Come on. She's waiting."

Nora wheeled into the kitchen and took the phone. "Hello, Dee."

"Oh, Nora, thank God. A box of letters just landed on your desk. There was nothing I could do about it. Tom Adams called—he threatened to get me fired if I didn't forward them to you. Today." Dee made a sniffling sound. "I *need* this job, Nora. I know you'd never fire me, but what if . . . you know . . ."

"I lose my job." Nora sighed. "I understand completely. Go ahead and mail the stuff to me at the address I gave you."

"Tom wants me to send Lake Union Air up for today's delivery."

Of course. With Tom, everything had to happen instantly. "Did you read the letters, Dee?"

"Uh . . . a few."

Nora's stomach turned sour. "How bad is it?"

"It's ugly, Nora. People around here are starting to talk to the tabloids . . . they're not saying nice things . . . and some lady in Iowa went on television last night and said she was going to file a lawsuit against you. Fraudulent advice or some stupid thing."

Nora glanced over at Ruby, who was shamelessly eavesdropping. "Okay, Dee. Send me the letters."

"I thought I'd send your 'best of' file, too. In case

you wanted to sneak some old letters in. Tom wouldn't know."

"Good thinking."

Dee sighed heavily. "I *knew* you were going to do the column. People are saying—"

"I'll make sure that you're taken care of. Don't you worry about that. Thanks for everything, Dee. Really. Good-bye." She leaned forward and hung up the phone. She wanted to make a joke for Ruby's benefit, but she hadn't the strength.

"Nora?"

Slowly, she lifted her head.

Ruby stood by the refrigerator, her arms crossed. Her cup of coffee sat on the counter, forgotten. "What was that all about?"

"My boss at the newspaper expects me to answer some . . . rather unflattering letters from my readers."

"Well, it *is* your job."

Nora didn't bother answering. Ruby couldn't possibly understand. She didn't know how it felt to *need* acceptance; and how, without it, you could feel invisible. Worse than invisible.

Some lady in Iowa . . . a lawsuit . . . fraudulent advice . . .

She closed her eyes and rubbed the bridge of her nose. "David Letterman is probably having a field day with this . . ."

For two days, she'd been able to forget that her life was unraveling, that she was a national scandal. No more.

She heard Ruby run upstairs.

Thank God.

But in a minute, Ruby was back, tapping her on the shoulder. "Nora?"

Nora opened her eyes.

Ruby was standing beside her, holding a section of newspaper. "I bought this yesterday at the store. Maybe you should . . . read what they're writing about you."

Nora stared at the newspaper. She could see a big, grainy picture of herself.

It had been taken at the Emmys last year—God, she hated that shot. It made her look all puffy-cheeked and squinty-eyed.

She took the paper from Ruby and glanced through the article. "It's over," she said dully, letting the newspaper fall to the floor.

Ruby frowned. "Don't be stupid. You'll get through this. Look at Monica Lewinsky—she's selling expensive handbags now. She went to the Oscars last year. And that idiot who married the millionaire got a fortune from *Playboy*."

"Thank you for those comforting comparisons."

"I just meant—"

"You're too young to understand, Ruby. My career is over. I have no intention of answering a single letter. I'm going to hide out until this . . . shit . . . is over. Another story will come along and they'll forget about me. Then I'll just fade away."

"You're kidding me, right?"

"No."

"But you're *famous*."

"I'm infamous. Believe me, there's a difference."

"With the right spin, you can—"

"You don't understand my career, Ruby. I've never put a wall between me and my readers. Everything I think and feel and believe is found in my words to strangers. That's why they believed in me, they sensed my honesty."

Ruby's eyebrow arched upward. "According to the press, your columns said you believed in marriage. Is that the kind of honesty they got from you?"

"I *do* believe in marriage. And love, and family, and commitments. I just . . . failed at it."

Ruby looked surprised by that answer. "That's an interesting word choice. Failed."

"I don't suppose either one of us would characterize my wife-and-motherhood as successful."

"No. But I wouldn't have expected you to see it that way. As a failure, I mean."

They were finally circling something that mattered. Nora's voice was gentle. "How did you imagine I'd feel?"

Ruby frowned. "I would have thought you'd see leaving us as . . . a success. You did it so well. Like leaving a job you hate. You might miss the income, but you're proud of yourself for finding the guts to quit."

"I wasn't proud of myself."

"Why?" Ruby asked the question in a whispered voice. "Why did you do it? Couldn't you have a career *and* raise children?"

Nora sighed. There were so many ways to answer that, and she was too damned depressed to pick the right one. So, she said the first thing that came to mind. "What happened to us isn't some event, like the sinking of the *Titanic*. It's little things, strung together over decades. To really understand it all, you'd have to grow up and see the way things really were in our family, but you don't want to do that, Ruby. You want to forget I ever existed . . . forget *we* ever existed."

"It's easier that way," Ruby said quietly.

"Yes. And it's easier for me to walk away from my career. I can't fight these charges . . . not with the life I've led and the choices I've made. The press will uncover what I did to my children . . . to you, Ruby . . . and it'll get even worse."

"I never saw you as a quitter."

Nora gave her a sad, knowing smile. "Ah, Ruby . . . you, of all people . . . you should have."

Chapter Eleven

It was early afternoon, the peak of a surprisingly hot June day. The sea and sky were a solid sheet of sparkling blue. Sunlight glinted along the surface of the water. At the edge of the property, just before it dipped down to meet the sand, trees reached out to one another, their leaves whispering in the wind. Starlings banked and dove along the eaves, chirping loudly, flying low above the grass.

Ruby sat in the white Adirondack chair on the second-floor balcony. She couldn't seem to stop crying.

She kept thinking about Eric, about all the times they'd spent together, how he'd been the big brother she'd never had—and the thought of losing him was unbearable . . . but no worse than the realization that she'd lost him years earlier, thoughtlessly, by walking away and never bothering to call.

Never bothering to call.

It was the story of her life. Ruby the half-wit girl who exits stage right.

She had loved Eric. Not in the searing, heartbreaking

way she'd loved his brother, but in a solid, dependable way. For all the years of her youth, he'd been there. It was Eric who'd taught her to set up a pup tent when the Girl Scout jamboree was coming . . . Eric who'd shown her how to stand on the bow pulpit of the *Wind Lass* on a windy day.

And yet she'd walked away, let him become a faded snapshot in the drawer of her life.

"I'm sorry," she whispered aloud, hearing the pathetic edge to her voice. It wasn't good enough, her apology into thin air. She acknowledged that. But the thought of *seeing* him terrified her. How could she stand by his bed and talk to him . . . smile as if they'd stayed friends . . . and say good-bye?

How could she watch him die?

Closing her eyes, she leaned back into the chair. In the bedroom behind her, the phone rang, but when she picked it up, there was no answer.

When the *briiiiing* sounded again, she realized it was her cellular phone. She dove over the bed and reached for the phone on the floor. She'd plugged it in less than an hour earlier.

"Hello?"

"Jesus, Rube, I've been trying this number endlessly. How's life in the outback?"

It was Val. She could hear his exhalation of cigarette smoke into the receiver. "It's Summer Island, Val, not Siberia. And things are fine."

"I thought you might need to be airlifted out."

Ruby laughed. "No, just keep that alibi handy in case I need it."

"How's the article coming?"

"Okay, I think. Maybe even good."

"Excellent news. I talked to Joan this morning. Things are really heating up on this story. The press is crucifying your mother."

Ruby was caught off guard by her reaction to that. It made her mad. "She doesn't care. She's walking away from her career. Quitting."

"No shit?"

"Amazing, huh? Anyway, I'm working hard."

"Joan'll be glad to hear that. Remember, you're booked on *Sarah Purcell* for next week. See you then, babe."

Babe. Ruby couldn't help rolling her eyes. He'd never called her that before; it must be a term reserved for clients who actually made him money. "Okay, Val. Talk to you soon."

After she hung up, she retrieved her paper and pen, then went back out onto the balcony and sat in the oversize chair her grandfather had made by hand.

She forced herself to stop thinking about Eric. For now, she needed to work on the article.

She looked down at her yellow pad, then slowly picked up her pen and began to write.

I have spent most of my adult life pretending I was motherless. At first, it took effort. When a memory of my mother came to me, I ruthlessly squelched it and forced other images into my mind—a slamming door; the sound of tires sputtering through gravel; my father, sitting on the edge of his bed, weeping into his hands.

In time, I taught myself to forget, and in that

state of suspended amnesia, things were easy. Time moved on.

But last night, my mother and I watched some old home movies. There, in a darkened living room, the doors I'd tried to keep closed slowly opened.

Now I am left with a disturbing and disorienting question: In forgetting my mother, how much have I forgotten about myself?

It seems I don't know either one of us. My mother tells me now that she is going to walk away from her career. I don't know what to make of that. She traded our family for fame and fortune; how could it mean so little to her?

Ruby set the pen and pad down on the rusty, frosted glass table beside her chair, unable to think of anything to add.

She couldn't forget her mother's face when she'd said, *I'll just fade away.*

Her mother had looked . . . broken, resigned, and more than a little afraid. Just like another time.

I'm leaving. Who wants to come with me?

For eleven years, Ruby had remembered only the words, the harsh, ugly sound of them in the silence of that morning.

Now, she remembered the rest.

Her mother's eyes had been filled with that same agonizing pain, and when she spoke, her voice had been strained . . . not her voice at all.

Then, Ruby had heard nothing beyond the good-bye. She'd understood that her mother was leaving . . . but what if Nora had been running away?

I never saw you as a quitter, Ruby had said today.

And her mother's answer: *You, of all people . . . you should have.*

But what could her mother have been running away from? And what had kept her away?

The package arrived from Seattle in the late afternoon, while her mother was taking a nap. Ruby knew what it was. She debated with herself for a few moments—after all, she'd purposely chosen never to read her mother's newspaper columns—but the *Caché* article changed things. Now, Ruby needed to know what "Nora Knows Best" had been about.

Quietly, she opened the box and pulled out a manila envelope marked BEST OF. In the living room, she plopped onto the sofa, tucked her feet up underneath her, and withdrew the pile of clippings. The one on top was dated December 1989, from the *Anacortes Bee.*

> *Dear Nora:*
> *Do you have any tips for getting red wine out of white silk? At my sister's wedding, I got a little drunk and spilled a glassful on her gown. Now she's not talking to me, and I feel just awful about it.*
> *Wedding Dress Blues.*

Nora's answer was short and sweet.

> *Dear Wedding Dress Blues:*
> *Only your dry cleaner can get the stain out. If it can't be done, you must offer to replace the gown. Because you were drunk, even a little, this is more*

than an ordinary accident, and your sister deserves a perfect reminder of her special day, a dress she can pass down to her daughter. It may take you a while to save the money, but in the end, you'll feel better. Nothing is more important than family. I'm sure you know that; it's what made you write to me. It's so easy to do the wrong thing in life, don't you think? When we see a clear road to being a better person, we ought to take it.

As Ruby continued to read the columns, she noticed that her mother's mail changed gradually from household-hint questions to earnest, heartfelt questions about life. Ruby had to admit that her mother was good at this. Her answers were concise, wise, and compassionate.

Ruby began to hear her mother in the column. Not the sophisticated, greedy, selfish Nora Bridge, but her *mother*, the woman who'd told Ruby to wear her coat, or brush her teeth, or clean her room.

As she read a column about a sixteen-year-old girl who was having a problem with drugs, Ruby remembered a time from her own life . . .

It had been in that terrible year that Ruby had almost "gone bad." She'd been fourteen, and Lopez Island—and her own family—had seemed hopelessly small and uncool. For a time, skipping school and smoking pot had offered Ruby a better way. She'd even turned away from Dean.

Dad had gone ballistic when Ruby got suspended from school for smoking, but not Nora.

Her mother had picked Ruby up from the principal's office and driven her to the state park at the tip of the island. She'd dragged Ruby down to the secluded patch of beach that overlooked Haro Strait and the distant glitter of downtown Victoria. It had been exactly three in the afternoon, and the gray whales had been migrating past them in a spouting, splashing row. Nora had been wearing her good dress, the one she saved for parent–teacher conferences, but she had plopped down cross-legged on the sand.

Ruby had stood there, waiting to be bawled out, her chin stuck out, her arms crossed.

Instead, Nora had reached into her pocket and pulled out the joint that had been found in Ruby's locker. Amazingly, she had put it in her mouth and lit up, taking a deep toke, then she had held it out to Ruby.

Stunned, Ruby had sat down by her mother and taken the joint. They'd smoked the whole damn thing together, and all the while, neither of them had spoken.

Gradually, night had fallen; across the water, the sparkling white city lights had come on.

Her mother had chosen that minute to say what she'd come to say. "Do you notice anything different about Victoria?"

Ruby had found it difficult to focus. "It looks farther away," she had said, giggling.

"It *is* farther away. That's the thing about drugs. When you use them, everything you want in life is farther away." Nora had turned to her. "How cool is it to do something that anyone with a match can do? Cool is becoming an astronaut . . . or a comedian . . . or a scientist who cures cancer. Lopez Island is exactly what you think it is—a tiny blip on a map. But the world is out there, Ruby, even if you haven't seen it. Don't throw your chances away. We don't get as many of them as we need. Right now you can go anywhere, be anyone, do anything. You can become so damned famous that they'll have a parade for you when you come home for your high-school reunion . . . or you can keep screwing up and failing your classes and you can snip away the ends of your choices until finally you end up with that crowd who hangs out at Zeke's Diner, smoking cigarettes and talking about high-school football games that ended twenty years ago." She had stood up and brushed off her dress, then looked down at Ruby. "It's your choice. Your life. I'm your mother, not your warden."

Ruby remembered that she'd been shaking as she'd stood up. That's how deeply her mother's words had reached. Very softly, she'd said, "I love you, Mom."

That was Ruby's last specific memory of saying those words to her mother . . .

She turned her attention back to the columns. She noticed that this last set was paper-clipped together. The very first sentence pulled her in.

Dear Nora:

Do you ever feel so alone in the world that everything normal looks out of focus? It's as if you're the only black-and-white human being in a technicolor city.

I have married the wrong woman. I knew it when the day came to walk down the aisle. I knew when I lifted the veil and looked down into her eyes. But sometimes you do the right thing for the wrong reasons, and you pray that love will grow.

When it doesn't, a piece of you dies, and day by day, it keeps dying until finally you realize there's nothing of you left.

You tell yourself that only your child matters—the reason you got married in the first place—and you can almost believe it. When you hold your baby in your arms, you finally learn what true love really is.

And yet still you wonder, even as you're holding your daughter's hand or brushing her hair or reading her a bedtime story . . . you wonder if it can really be enough.

I don't know what to do. My wife and I have drifted so terribly far apart. . . . Please, can you help me?

Lost and Lonely.

Dear Lost and Lonely:

My heart goes out to you. I think all of us know how it feels to be lonely, especially within the supposedly warm circle of a family.

I can tell that you're an honorable man, and you obviously know that breaking up a family is the kind of act that irrevocably destroys lives. Believe me, the loneliness you feel within your family is a pale shadow of the torment you'll feel if you walk away.

I pray that if you look hard enough, you will unearth some remnant of the love you once felt for your wife, and that with care, a seed of that emotion can grow again. Seek counseling; talk to professionals and to each other. Take a vacation to-

gether. Touch, and not only sexually. Little touches along the way can mean a lot. Get involved in activities—community events, church events, that kind of thing.

Go see a marriage counselor. You don't want to end a marriage and break your children's hearts until and unless there is no possible chance for reconciliation.

Trust me on this.

Nora.

The last item was a handwritten letter; there was no column attached to it. Obviously, it had been submitted for publication and rejected. Yet Nora had saved it.

Dear Nora:

My daughter—my precious baby girl—was killed by a drunk driver this year. I understand tragedy now; its taste, its texture . . . the imprint it leaves on you.

I find that I can't talk to people anymore, not even my wife, who needs me more than ever. I see her, sitting on the end of the bed, her hair unwashed, her eyes rimmed in red, and I can't reach out to her, can't offer comfort. If left alone, I'm certain I could go through the rest of my life without ever speaking again.

I want to gather my belongings, put them in a shopping cart, and disappear into the faceless crowd of vagrants in Pioneer Square. But I haven't the strength even for that. So I sit in my house,

*seeing the endless reminders of what I once had . . .
and I ask myself why I bother to breathe at all . . .
    Lost and Lonely.*

Across the top of that letter, someone had written: *FedEx the attached letter to this man's return address immediately.* Paper-clipped to the letter was a photocopy of a handwritten note.

Dear Lost and Lonely:

I will not waste time with the pretty words we wrap around grief. You are in danger; you are not so far gone that you don't know this. I am going to do what I have never done before—what I imagine I'll never do again.

You will come and talk to me. I will not take no for an answer. Your letter mentioned Pioneer Square; I see that your return address is in Laurelhurst.

My secretary at the newspaper will be expecting your call tomorrow and she will set up an appointment. Please, please, do not disappoint me. I know how life can wound even the strongest heart, and sometimes all it takes to save us is the touch of a single stranger's hand.

Reach out for me . . . I'll be there.

It was signed *Nora*.

Ruby's hands were trembling. No wonder these readers loved her mother. She carefully put the columns and letters back in the manila folder and left the whole package on the kitchen table for her mother to find, then she went upstairs.

She hadn't even realized that she was going to call Caroline until she'd picked up the phone. But it made sense. Ruby felt unsteady . . . and Caroline had always been her solid ground.

Caro answered on the third ring. "Hello?"

Ruby couldn't help noticing how tired her sister sounded. "Hey, sis. You sound like you need a nap."

Caroline laughed. "I always need a nap. Of course, what I do that makes me so darned tired is a complete mystery."

"What *do* you do all day?"

"Only a single woman would ask that question of a mother. So, what's going on up there? How are you and Mom doing?"

"She's not who I thought she was," Ruby admitted softly.

"How could she be? You haven't spoken to her since *Moonlighting* was on television."

"I know, I know . . . but it's more than that. Like, did you know she was seeing a shrink when she was married to Dad . . . or that she took Valium in nineteen eighty-five?"

"Wow," Caroline said. "I wonder if her doctor told her to leave Dad?"

"Why would he do that?"

Caroline laughed softly. "That's what they do, Ruby. They tell unhappy women to find happiness. If I had a buck for every time my therapist told me to leave Jere, I'd live on Hunt's Point."

"You see a shrink, too?"

"Come on, Ruby. It's like getting a manicure. Good grooming for the mind."

"But I thought you and Mr. Quarterback had a perfect life."

"We have our problems, just like anyone else, but I'd rather talk about—aah! Darn it, Jenny! That's not okay. I gotta run, Ruby. Your niece just poured a cup of grape juice on her brother's head."

Before Ruby could answer, Caroline hung up.

Everything was ready.

Dean knocked on Eric's door, heard the muffled "Come in," and went inside.

Eric was sitting up in bed, reading a dog-eared paperback copy of Richard Bach's book *Illusions*. When he saw Dean, he smiled. "Hey, bro. It's almost dinnertime. Where have you been?" He reached for the cup on his bedside tray. His thin fingers trembled; he groaned tiredly and gave up.

Dean hurried to the bed and grabbed the cup, carefully placing it in Eric's quavering hand. He guided the straw to his brother's mouth.

Eric sipped slowly, swallowed. Dean helped him replace the cup on the tray, then Eric turned his head, let it settle into the pile of pillows. "Thanks, I was dying of thirst." He grinned. "No mention of death was intentional."

Dean wanted to smile; honestly, he did. But all he could think about was his big brother, up here all alone, thirsty and too weak to reach for his glass of water. He crossed his arms and stared out the window. He didn't dare make eye contact with Eric. He needed just a minute to collect himself. "I've been working on something," he said.

"A surprise?"

Dean looked down at his brother then and saw a glimpse of the old Eric—the young Eric—and his throat tightened even more. It was all he could do to nod. Slowly, he lowered the metal bed rail. When it clanged into place, he said, "Are you up for a little trip?"

"Are you kidding? I'm so sick of this bed I could cry. Hell, I *do* cry . . . all the time."

Dean leaned forward, scooped his brother into his arms and lifted him up from the bed.

God, he weighed nothing at all.

It was like holding a fragile child; only it was his brother. His strong, outspoken big brother, who'd once led the island football team in touchdown passes . . .

Dean shut the memories off. If he remembered who Eric used to be—now, while this frail, hollowed man was in his arms—he would stumble and fall.

He carried his brother downstairs and through the house, past Lottie in the kitchen, who waved, her eyes overbright . . . across the manicured green lawn and down the bank to the beach. On the slanted, wooden dock, he'd already set up an oversize Adirondack chair and piled pillows onto it.

"The *Wind Lass,*" Eric said softly.

Dean carefully placed his brother into the chair, then tucked the cashmere blanket tightly around his thin body.

It was nearing sunset. The sky was low enough to touch. The last rays of the setting sun turned everything pink—the waves, the clouds, the pebbled beach that curled protectively along the fish-hook shape of the shoreline. The sailboat was still in bad shape, but at least she was clean.

Dean sat down beside Eric. Stretching out his legs, he leaned back against one of the wooden pilings. "I still have some more work to do on her. Jeff Brein, down at the Crow's Nest, is repairing the sail, and it should be done tomorrow. Wendy Johnson is cleaning the cushions. I thought . . . maybe if we could take her out . . ." Dean let the sentence trail off. He didn't know quite how to sculpt his amorphous hope into something as ordinary as words.

"We could remember how it used to be," Eric said. "How *we* used to be."

Of course Eric had understood. "Yeah."

Eric drew the blanket tighter against his chin. "So, what's it like, being the favored son?"

"Lonely."

Eric sighed and leaned back into the pillows. "Remember when she loved me? When I was a star athlete with awesome grades and a promising future. I was her trophy boy."

Dean remembered. Their mother had adored Eric, her dark-haired angel, she called him. The only time Mom and Dad came to the island was football season. Every homecoming game, Mom had dressed in her best "casual" clothes and gone to the game, where she cheered on her quarterback son. When the season ended, they were gone again.

Eric had lived in the warm glow of his parents' affection for so long, he'd mistaken pride for love, but when he'd told them about Charles, he'd learned the depth of his naïveté. Mother hadn't spoken to him since.

So it had been Dean, the younger, less perfect son, who'd taken over the family business. It had never been something he wanted to do, but family expectations—especially in a wealthy family—were a sticky web. "I remember," he said quietly.

"I heard the phone ring last night about eleven o'clock," Eric said.

Dean looked away; eye contact was impossible. "Yeah. Some phone company rep who—"

"Don't bother, bro. It was her, wasn't it?"

"Yeah."

"Still in Athens?"

"Florence. Mother had the nerve to tell me that the shopping was great." She'd also said, *Come on over, Dean—we've got plenty of room at the villa.* As if it didn't matter at all that her elder son lay dying.

Eric's gaze was pathetically hopeful as he turned to Dean. "Are they coming to see me?"

There was no point in lying. "No."

"Did you tell them this is it? I'm not going to be around much longer?"

Dean reached out, touched his brother's hand. It surprised both of them, that sudden bit of intimacy. "I'm sorry."

Eric released a thready sigh. "What good is an agonizing death by cancer if your own family won't weep by your bedside?"

"I'm here," Dean said softly. "You're not alone."

Tears came to Eric's eyes. "I know, baby brother. I know . . ."

Dean swallowed hard. "You can't let her get to you."

Eric closed his eyes. "Someday she'll be sorry. It'll be too late, though." By the end of the sentence, his words were garbled and he was asleep.

Dean leaned closer. Carefully, he tugged up the blanket, tucked it beneath his brother's chin.

Eric blinked awake and smiled sleepily. "Tell me about your life."

"There's not much to tell. I work."

"Very funny. I get the San Francisco newspapers, you know—just to read about you and the folks. You seem to be quite the bachelor-about-town. If I didn't know better, I'd say you were a man who had everything."

Dean wanted to laugh and say, *I do; I do have everything a man could want,* but it was a lie, and he'd never been able to lie to his brother. And more than that, Dean wanted to talk to Eric the way he once had. Brother to brother, from the heart. "There's something . . . missing in my life. I don't know what it is."

"Do you like your job?"

Dean was surprised by the question. No one had ever asked him that, and he'd never bothered to ask himself. Still, the answer came quickly. "No."

"Are you in love with anyone?"

"No. It's been a long time since I was in love."

"And you can't figure out what's *missing* in your life? Come on, Dino. The question isn't, what's missing? The question is, what the hell *is* your life?" Eric yawned and closed his eyes again. Already he was tiring. "God, I wanted you to be happy all these years . . . " He fell asleep for a second, then blinked awake. "Remember Camp Orkila?" he said suddenly. "I was thinking about that yesterday, about the first time we went up there."

"When we met Ruby." Dean found an honest smile inside of him, drew it out. "She climbed up into that big tree by the beach, remember? She said arts and crafts were for babies and she was a big girl."

"She wouldn't come down until you asked her to."

"Yeah. That was the beginning, wasn't it? We'd never seen a real family before . . ." Dean let the words string out, find one another, and connect. Like threads, he wove them together, sewed a quilt from the strands of their life, and tucked it around his brother's thin body.

Chapter Twelve

Nora woke up groggy from her nap. She lay in bed for a minute, listening to the gentle, whooshing sound of the sea through her open window. It was almost nighttime; she'd been asleep for hours.

Eric.

She pulled the phone onto her lap and dialed the number.

She spoke to Lottie for a few minutes, then waited patiently for Eric to come on the line.

"Nora? Well, it's about damn time."

She laughed. God, it felt good to smile, even better to hear his voice. He sounded almost like his old self. "I've had an . . . interesting last few days. I'm on Summer Island. Caroline is letting me relax here for a while."

"Ah, the lifestyles of the rich and famous. I suppose it's tough to make time for a dear old friend who is facing the Grim Reaper with quiet dignity." He laughed at his own joke, but the laughter dwindled into a cough.

Nora closed her eyes, trying to picture him as he'd been only a few years ago . . . like on the afternoon his team had won the league championships and the kids had poured Gatorade on his head and chanted his name . . .

"Nora? Did you lapse into a coma?"

"I'm here." She made an instant decision: she wouldn't tell him about the scandal. He didn't need to worry about her. But she had to tell him *something*—she couldn't just show up at his house in a wheelchair. "I had an accident and wound up in Bayview."

"Oh, my God, are you okay?"

"For a fifty-year-old woman who drove into a tree, I'm great. And you told me that Mercedes was a waste of money—ha! It saved my life. I came out of it with a broken leg and a sprained wrist. Nothing to worry about. But that's why I haven't been to see you."

"There's something you're not telling me."

She forced a laugh. "Your intuition is wrong this time."

"Nora?" He said her name with infinite tenderness, and in it, she heard the gentle, chiding reminder of all they'd been through together. For the first time since this mess had begun, she felt truly cared for. "No, really, I—" She pinched the bridge of her nose and concentrated on taking shallow breaths.

"Nora. You know you can talk to me about anything."

"You don't need to hear about my troubles."

"Who was it who sat by me in the hospital every night while Charlie was dying? Who was it who held my hand at the gravesite . . . who was there when I started chemotherapy?"

Nora swallowed hard. "Me."

"So, talk."

All the emotions she'd bottled up in the past few days came spilling out. She didn't cry; she was almost preternaturally calm, in fact. But as she spoke, it felt as if the very fabric of her soul was ripping. "The *Tattler* just published naked pictures of me in bed with a man."

"Jesus . . ." His voice was a whisper.

"That's not even the worst of it." Amazingly, she laughed. "I was actually *posing* with this guy. And fortunately for me, the photos were dated—proving that I was married to Rand at the time they were taken. The press is crucifying me. Apparently people are crawling out of the woodwork to call me a hypocrite."

"That's why you're at the summer house? You're hiding out?"

"My career is over. I couldn't get a job counseling toddlers about potty training."

"Come on, this is *America*. Celebrities screw up all the time. It just makes us love them more. Jack Nicholson beats up a car with a baseball bat . . . and we give him another Oscar. Hugh Grant shows us not only moral flexibility but outright *stupidity*, and after a quick apology on Leno, he's in a movie with Julia Roberts. So, you flashed your ass. Big deal. It's not like the photographs showed you giving a blow job to a drug dealer. Hold your head up, cry when you admit your mistake, and beg for a second chance. Your fans will love you more for being one of them. Human."

"That's why I love you, Eric. The glass is always half full. Honest to God, if you were my son I'd be so proud." She heard a sound—a clearing of his throat—

and she knew. She could have slapped herself for her insensitivity. "You called your mother."

"She's in Europe. The shopping is great." He sighed, made a sound that was nearly a groan. "She hasn't called me. But it's only been a couple of days."

A couple of days since she found out her son had cancer, and she hadn't found time to call. The woman should be shot. "How about if I come to see you tomorrow? Between the wheelchair and the hospital bed, we'll look like a scene from *Cuckoo's Nest*."

"That'd be great. And you won't believe who's here."

Nora laughed. "Believe me, you won't believe who is *here*, either."

"Dean—"

"Ruby—"

They spoke at the same time.

Nora was the first to recover. "Dean is on the island?"

"He came up to see me."

"I knew he'd come if you called. How is it between you two?"

"Awkward. A little unsure. We're like best friends from high school who meet at the twenty-year reunion and don't quite know what to say. But we'll find our way back. And Ruby?"

"Angry. Truthfully, she hates me."

"But she's there. That means something. Remember, there's a thin line between love and hate."

"Thank you, Yoda." She paused. "I had to tell her about your cancer."

"That's okay. Hell, I don't care who knows anymore." She could hear the smile in Eric's voice. "Hey, do you know what happened between Dean and Ruby? He won't talk about it."

"She won't, either."

"I was at Princeton when they broke up, but it must have been bad. Dean went all the way to boarding school to get away from her. But it's interesting that neither of them ever married."

"Are you thinking what I'm thinking?"

"How do we get them together?"

Nora grinned. It felt great to talk about something besides Eric's illness or her own scandal. And this made her feel like a *mother* for the first time in years. "Carefully, my boy. Very carefully."

By the time Nora hung up, her ankle was throbbing; the pain was only marginally worse than the itching that came with it. She wheeled into the bathroom, washed her face and brushed her teeth, then left the room.

"Ruby?" she called out. There was no answer.

She was halfway into the kitchen when she saw the package on the table.

Slowly, she wheeled closer.

It had been opened.

No wonder Ruby was hiding.

With a sigh, she pulled the slim box onto her lap and went into the living room, where she settled herself onto the sofa, plopping her foot on a pillow on the coffee table. All thoughts of Ruby and Dean and true love vanished.

Her fingers were shaking as she opened the manila envelope marked NEW LETTERS and pulled out the stack of mail. On the top was a small, wrinkled, stationery-size envelope postmarked GREAT FALLS, MONTANA. She carefully opened it, unfolded the letter, and began to read.

Nora:

I can't bring myself to write "Dear" anymore. I've written to you a dozen times over the last few years. Twice you have published my letters, and once you wrote me a private letter, saying that you hoped things were getting better.

You can't imagine what that meant to me. I was drowning in a bad marriage, and you were always there.

Can you imagine how it feels to know the kind of person I've been taking advice from?

I looked up to you. Believed in you. My husband only broke my heart. You have broken my spirit.

If only you had been honest, I might have continued to admire you.

Now, I see that you're just another hack celebrity selling a product you don't use.

Don't bother answering this letter, or even printing it in Nora Knows Best. I don't care about your opinion, and I certainly won't be reading your columns anymore. I don't suppose I'm alone in that decision. If I want to read fiction, I'll go to the library. You have no right to offer anyone advice on anything anymore.

May God forgive you, Nora Bridge. Your fans will not.

Nora folded the letter and slid it back into the envelope. She needed something to get her mind off of this. She reached for the television remote, not surprised at all to see that Caroline had upgraded the television here at the summer house. With small kids in this media age, it was probably essential.

She pressed the "on" button—and heard her own name being spoken.

It was *The Sarah Purcell Show*—one of those talk-fests where women came together to chat. The coffee klatch of the new millennium.

Nora wanted to change the channel or look away, but she was like a fish caught on the hook of her own name.

On-screen, a heavyset woman was standing in the audience. Sarah was beside her, holding a microphone to the woman's mouth. "I *trusted* Nora Bridge," the lady said. "Now, I feel like an idiot."

Another woman in a nearby row stood up. "How could you be stupid enough to trust a celebrity? They all lie and cheat to get ahead. That's how public life is."

The heavyset woman flushed. She looked ready to cry. "I didn't think she was like those other ones . . ."

Sarah took the microphone back. "That brings up a good point, Dr. Harrison," she said, speaking to the gentleman sitting on the stage. "People are angry at Nora Bridge because she lied to them, but is it really a lie? Do you have to tell people *everything* about your life, just because you're in the public eye?"

The doctor smiled coolly for the camera. "Certainly a public figure has a right to his or her secrets . . . unless and until those secrets become germane. In this case, Nora had no right to hold herself out as an expert on love and family and commitments. But of course, it's ludicrous for people to trust her anyway . . . an uneducated woman whose only claim to fame is a daily newspaper column. Trust should be reserved for professionals who are trained to help people."

Sarah stopped. "Now, wait a minute, Doctor. I don't think education—"

"Nora Bridge pretended to have answers, but no one bothered to wonder where those answers came from. Hopefully, Americans have learned that it takes more than an open microphone to solve people's problems. It takes education, and empathy, and integrity— areas in which Ms. Bridge is sorely lacking."

"And she's a coward," someone said from the crowd. "I mean . . . where is she? She owes us—"

Nora snapped off the television.

She couldn't seem to move, not even to wheel herself out of the room. A tremor was spreading through her, chilling her from the inside out, and her throat was so tight it was hard to breathe.

"Nora?"

She froze, her heart pounding. She hadn't even heard footsteps on the stairs.

God, she didn't want her daughter to see her like this . . .

Ruby came into the room, walked slowly around the wheelchair, then sat down on the leather chair across from Nora. "Did you sleep well?"

Nora stared down at her own hands, and thought, Oh, please, just go away . . . don't talk to me now. . . . "Yes," she managed, "thank you."

"I read your columns," Ruby said when the silence had gone on too long.

"Really?" It was a tiny word, barely spoken.

"You're good at it."

Nora's relief was so profound, she gasped. Only *I love you* could have meant more to her in that moment. And yet even as the relief buoyed her, it dragged her down again, too, reminded her of all that she'd lost this week.

"Thank you," she said softly. Finally, she looked up, and found Ruby watching her through narrowed eyes.

"I take it you read a few of your new letters," Ruby said, leaning forward, resting her elbows on her knees. She seemed to see it all—the shaking hands, the television remote that had been thrown onto the floor.

Nora wanted to say something casual and flip, to show how meaningless a few ugly letters were, but she couldn't. "They hate me now."

"They're strangers. They don't even know you. They can't love you or hate you, not really." Ruby flashed a smile. "Leave the big, ugly emotions to your family."

Who also hated her.

That only made it worse. "What family?" Nora moaned quietly. "Really, Ruby . . . what family have I left myself?"

Ruby looked at her for a long minute, then said, "After I read your columns, you know what I remembered?"

Nora wiped her eyes. "What?"

"When I was twelve years old—seventh grade—and my class elected me to run the first tolo. Remember? It was a big deal on Lopez, a dance where the girls asked the boys. Mr. Lundberg, down at the hardware store, said it meant that the world was going to hell in a leaky rowboat."

Nora sniffled again. "Yeah . . . I remember that."

"I wanted the local newspaper to cover the event. You were the only one who didn't laugh at me." Ruby smiled. "I watched you charm that fat old editor from the *Island Times*. I remember being surprised by how easily you got him to agree to what you wanted . . . what I wanted."

Nora remembered that day for the first time in years. "The minute I walked into that cheesy, airless office, I loved it. The smell of the paper, the clacking of typewriters. I envied the reporters, with their ink-stained fingertips, and for the first time in my life, I felt as if I *belonged* somewhere. I'd always known I had words banging around in my chest, but I'd never known what to do with them." She looked up.

Ruby's gaze was solemn. "I realized . . . later . . . that I'd shown you the way out of our lives."

Nora took a deep breath. "I didn't leave my family for a career, Ruby. That had nothing to do with my decision. Less than nothing."

"Yeah, right."

"Ah, Ruby," she said, "you want answers, but you don't even know what the questions are. You have to look at the beginning of a thing, not the end. For me, leaving your dad started before I met him."

"I don't understand."

Nora wanted to ask her daughter if all this talking would actually lead them anywhere, or if it was just a way to pass the hours before they each moved on. A part of her—the cowardly part—wanted to change the subject, maybe talk about Dean or Eric, but she wouldn't let herself take the easy way. She and Ruby were finally approaching something that mattered.

She stared out the window. Night was falling, drizzling dark syrup down the evergreen trees. "My dad was an alcoholic. When he was sober, he was almost human, but when he was drunk—which was most of the time—he was pit-bull mean. It was a secret I learned to keep from everyone. It's what children of alcoholics do. They keep secrets. Hell, it took me fifteen years of therapy to even say the word *alcoholic*."

Ruby's mouth fell open a little. "Huh? You never told us that."

"On a farm like ours, the neighbors couldn't hear a woman's scream. Or a young girl's. And you learn fast that it doesn't help to cry out . . . to reach out. Instead, you try to get smaller and smaller, hoping that if you can become tiny enough, and still enough, he'll pass you by."

"He abused you?"

Such a thin word, *abuse*. "He didn't do the worst thing a father can do to his daughter, but he . . . molded me. I grew up trying to be invisible, flinching all the time. I don't think I stood up straight until I left your father." She leaned forward, making direct eye contact with her daughter. "For years, I thought that if I didn't talk about my dad, he'd float out of my life . . . out of my nightmares. I thought I could forget him."

Ruby drew in a sharp breath. "Did it work?"

Nora knew her daughter was making the connection: *I'd forgotten you.* "No. All it did was give him more power . . . and turn me into a woman who couldn't imagine being loved."

"Because your own father didn't love you."

"Not unlike how a girl would feel if her own mother abandoned her." Nora wouldn't let herself look away. "Did you ever fall in love . . . after Dean?"

"I lived with a guy—Max Bloom—for almost five years."

"Did you love him?"

"I . . . wanted to."

"Did he love you?"

Ruby got to her feet and went to the bookcase, where she started thumbing through their old record collection. "I think he did. In the beginning."

"How did it end between you?"

Ruby shrugged. "I came home from work one day and he'd moved out. He took everything from the kitchen except our coffeemaker. In the bathroom, he left a razor full of his hair and an almost empty bottle of Prell, but no towels."

Nora longed to empathize with her daughter, tell her how much she understood that kind of pain, but that was the easy way—understanding. What mattered now, in this moment when they were actually *talking,* was not Nora's understanding. It was Ruby herself. Like Nora, Ruby liked to run away from her problems, and sometimes she ran so far and so fast that she never bothered to really look at why she'd left. "Did you ever tell him you loved him?"

"Almost. Practically."

"Ah."

Ruby frowned at her. "What does that mean—'ah'?"

"Did he say he loved you?"

"Yeah, but Max was like that. He told the checker at Safeway he loved her."

Nora could see that she'd have to be more direct. "Let me ask you this, Ruby. How long do you think it takes to fall in love?"

Ruby sighed raggedly. "So your point is this: I never really loved Max, so why did I cry when he left me?"

"No. You lived and slept with a man for almost five years and never told him you loved him, even after he'd said those precious words to you. The question isn't why he left. It's why he stayed so long."

Ruby's mouth dropped open. "Oh, my *God*. I never thought about it like that." She looked helplessly at Nora.

"I told your father I loved him the first time we made love. I'd never said the words before, not to anyone. It wasn't the sort of thing my family did. I'd been hoarding *I love you*'s all my life. And do you know when Rand told me he loved me?"

"When?"

"Never. I waited for it like a child waits for Christmas morning. Every time I said it, I waited, and every second of his silence was a little death."

Ruby closed her eyes and shook her head. "No more. Please . . ."

"I wanted to raise you to be strong and sure of yourself, and instead I turned you into me. I made you afraid to love and certain you'd be left behind. I was a bad mother and you paid the price. I'm so, so sorry for that."

"You weren't a bad mother," Ruby said quietly, "until you left."

Nora was pathetically grateful for that. "Thank you."

She knew she was following a dangerous path, sitting here, falling in love with her daughter all over again . . . but she couldn't help herself. "I still remember the little girl who cried every time a baby bird fell out of its nest."

"That girl has been gone a long time."

"You'll find her again," Nora said softly, "probably about the same time you fall in love. And when it's real, Ruby, you'll know it . . . and you'll stop being afraid."

After dinner, Ruby stayed in the bathtub until the water turned cold.

The world—her world—had changed, but she couldn't put her finger on precisely how. It was like walking into a perfectly decorated room and knowing instinctively that somewhere a picture was crooked.

She climbed out of the clawfoot tub and stood on the fuzzy pink bath mat, dripping. By the time she dried off and slipped into a pair of sweats and an oversized UCLA Bruins sweatshirt, she could smell dinner cooking.

She finger-combed her hair and lay down on the bed with her yellow pad open in front of her.

Today I talked to my mother. This is a remarkably ordinary sentence for a truly revolutionary act.

I talked to her. She talked to me. By the end of it, we had both wept, although not, I'm sure, for the same reasons.

What I don't know is where we go from here. How can I walk downstairs and pretend that nothing has changed? And yet, it was simply a conversation, words passed back and forth between women who are strangers to each other even though they share a past. I want to believe I'm wrong in feeling that things are different now.

Why then did I cry? Why did I look at her and feel like a child again and think—even for a moment—"What if?"

Chapter Thirteen

Dean carried the breakfast tray up to his brother's bedroom. It wasn't much—a glass of juice, a soft-boiled egg, and a piece of wheat toast. He knew Eric wouldn't eat more than a few small bites, but it made life seem normal, this offering of food.

When Dean stepped into the room, he found his brother already awake, sitting up in bed.

"Heya, Dino," Eric said.

Dean set the tray down, helped his brother sit up higher in the bed, then carefully placed the tray across Eric's lap.

"I'll bet this smells great," Eric said as Dean went to the window and flipped the curtains open.

Dean opened the casement window just enough to let in the sound of the sea. When he turned back around, he noticed how wan and wasted his brother looked this morning. The shadows beneath his eyes were as dark as bruises. He seemed to have grown sicker since yesterday. "Bad night?"

Eric nodded. His head lolled back into the pillows,

as if the pretense of eating breakfast had exhausted him. "I can't seem to sleep anymore, which is pretty damned ironic since it's all I do. The pain cocktail knocks me out but it's not the same as a good night's sleep." He smiled tiredly. "It's funny the things you miss. I don't dream anymore."

Dean pulled his chair up to the bed and sat down.

"I wanted to talk to you last night, but I couldn't seem to stay focused."

Dean reached out and held his brother's cold, thin hand.

Eric turned to him, smiling. "I always thought we'd come back to this house as old men. I pictured us sitting on the porch. We'd have white hair by then . . . or maybe only I would have hair, and you'd be bald as Grandpa. We'd play Chinese checkers and watch your kids run up and down the dock, looking for shrimp."

Dean let himself be carried away by the dream. "They'd have nets . . . just like we used to."

Eric's eyes fluttered shut. "I wonder whatever happened to those nets we bought every year? You and Ruby used to play down on that dock for hours . . ."

Dean swallowed hard. He thought about changing the subject, but suddenly he wanted to remember her, to reminisce with someone who'd known her. "Sometimes when I close my eyes at night, I hear her laughing, yelling at me to hurry up. She was always running off ahead."

"I thought I'd be the best man at your wedding. It's crazy, isn't it, you and Ruby were sixteen years old, but I thought it was true love."

"I thought so, too."

Eric looked at him. "And now?"

Dean wanted to smile, pretend it was just a silly question between grown men about something that had happened long ago and didn't matter. But what was the point? He knew now how precious this time with Eric was. It was obvious that it was running out, leaking away like the color in his brother's cheeks. "Now I know it was."

"She's on Summer Island."

Dean frowned; it took a moment for the full impact of those words to hit him. "Ruby's at the summer house?"

Eric grinned. "Yep."

Dean leaned back. "What . . . with her husband and kids?"

"She's never been married, baby brother. I wonder why that is?"

Dean stood up and strode toward the window. He stared through the glass, trying to see Summer Island through the trees. His heart was beating so fast he felt faint. *Ruby is here.*

"Go see her," Eric said softly.

Dean changed into a pair of Levi's and a T-shirt. At the front door, he slipped on his boat shoes and grabbed his ten-speed from its resting place beneath the eaves. There was no doubt that in this week of June, with the sun shining brightly on the islands, the ferry lines would be endless. Bikes always got on first.

He pedaled down the short, winding hill to the dock and got lucky. A boat was loading. He got right on.

He didn't go up top. Instead, he stood with his bike at

the bow of the boat, barely noticing the cars streaming into lines behind him.

On Summer Island, he didn't even wave to Sister Helen as he bicycled past. By the time he swooped onto the Bridges' heavily shaded driveway, he was sweating and out of breath. At the top of the yard, he jumped off the bike and let it clatter to the ground.

Then he stopped. For the first time, he wondered what in the hell he was doing, running toward his first love as if eleven years hadn't passed, as if he'd seen her yesterday . . .

But they'd been apart for all of their adulthood; he had no way of knowing whether she'd thought of him at all.

Their last day together came at him in a rush of images and phrases.

The sky had been robin's-egg blue. Strangely, he remembered looking up, seeing the white trail from a passing jet. He'd been about to point it out to Ruby, to start their familiar "if I were on that plane, where would I be going?" daydream.

But when he'd turned to her, he'd seen what he should have noticed before.

She'd been crying.

That was not so unusual, of course; those were the days when Ruby had cried all the time.

The difference was, this time, she wouldn't let him get near her. He couldn't remember precisely what he'd said, how he'd tried uselessly to comfort her. What he did recall was how she finally stilled, and the sight of Ruby, his Ruby, looking pale and cold had scared him.

I had sex with a boy last night. She'd said it without

preamble, as if she'd wanted to wound him with her confession.

He had pulled the whole, sordid story out of her, one painful syllable at a time, and when she was finished, he knew all the facts, but they hadn't added up to a whole truth he could understand.

If he'd been older, more sexually experienced, he would have known the question to ask, the only one that mattered: Why? But he'd been seventeen and a virgin himself. All he'd cared about was the promise he and Ruby had made . . . to wait for each other until marriage.

Anger and hurt had overwhelmed him. She'd lied to him, and she hadn't loved him as much as he'd loved her. He'd felt foolish and used. He'd waited desperately for her to throw herself at his feet, to beg for forgiveness, but she'd just stood there, close enough to touch and yet so far away he couldn't see her clearly. Or maybe it was his tears that were blurring the world, turning her into a girl he'd never seen before.

Go ahead, she'd said, staring dully up at him. *Go. It's over.*

He'd had to leave fast—before she could see that he was crying. He'd turned away from her and run back to his bike. He'd pedaled hard, trying to outdistance the pain, but it had raged inside of him, thumping with every beat of his heart. Everywhere he'd looked, he'd seen her . . . in the shade of Miss McGinty's oak tree, where he'd read Shakespeare's sonnets to Ruby the previous week . . . in the tree-lined darkness of the state park's driveway, where they'd once set up their lemonade stand. And finally, on his parents' land, where he'd kissed her for the first time.

At home, he'd picked up the phone and called his mother. Within hours, he'd been on a seaplane, heading for Seattle. By the next day, he'd been on his way to boarding school back east.

Whatever should have been said or done between them had been lost.

Dean released his breath in a steady, even stream. There was no turning back now.

He walked down the path and stepped up onto the porch. After another quick breath, he knocked.

And she answered.

The minute he saw her, he understood what had been missing from his life. It was hokey, he knew, and sentimental and sappy, but that didn't make it any less true. What he'd been longing for, without even realizing it, had been that elusive, magical mixture of friendship and passion that he'd only ever found with her.

"Ruby," he whispered. It actually hurt to say her name. She was so beautiful that for a second he couldn't breathe.

"Dean," she said, her eyes widening.

He didn't know what to say. He felt like a seventeen-year-old kid again, tongue-tied in front of the prom queen. He was trying like hell to appear casual, but it was difficult. He was sweating suddenly and his throat was painfully dry. All he could think was, *Ruby's home,* and she was standing in front of him and he didn't want to say the wrong thing, but he couldn't imagine what the right thing was. He'd dreamed of seeing her for so long, but now . . . the moment felt spun from sugar, so fragile a soft breeze could shatter it. "I . . . uh . . . I came home to see Eric . . . you probably heard about that."

"How is he?" Her voice was barely audible.

"Not good."

She closed her eyes for a second, then looked up at him again. "I'm here with my mother. She had a car accident and I'm taking care of her."

"*You?*" It had slipped out, an intimate observation from a man who'd once known the girl. He was instantly afraid he'd offended her.

A smile hitched one side of her mouth. "I know. I should call Ripley's Believe It or Not."

"So, you've forgiven her, then."

Sadness darkened her eyes. "Forgiveness doesn't matter, does it, Dean? When a thing is done, it's done. You can't unring a bell." She smiled, but it wasn't the smile he remembered, the one that crinkled her whole face and sparkled in her eyes. She seemed to be waiting for him to say something, but he couldn't think fast enough, and as usual, she didn't wait long. "Well, it was good seeing you again. Nora is in my old room. Say hello before you leave. She'd hate to miss you."

And with that, she walked past him and headed down to the beach.

Ruby thought she was going to be sick. That was why she'd left Dean so quickly. She couldn't stand there, making polite conversation, not when it felt as if carbonated water had replaced her blood.

She ran down the path toward the beach and sat

down on her favorite moss-covered rock, just as she'd done a thousand times in her life.

"Ruby?"

She heard her name, spoken softly in the voice that had filled her dreams since adolescence, and she froze. Her heart picked up a wild, thumping beat. She hadn't heard his footsteps, hadn't prepared to see him again so quickly.

"Can I sit with you?"

She tried not to remember all the hours they'd spent here, huddled out on this rock, staring first out to sea, then gradually at each other. She sidled to the right—it had always been her side.

Dean sat down beside her.

She felt his thigh along hers, and she ached to scoot closer . . . to lay her hand on his the way she'd done so many times before. But she'd lost that right. In her angry, confused youth, she'd thrown it away.

She had always known that she still carried a torch for Dean, but obviously she hadn't understood what that meant. It was more than fond memories or adolescent longings. A torch was hot; it would sear your flesh if you weren't careful.

"This brings back memories," he said softly.

She didn't mean to turn to him, but she couldn't help herself. She wanted to say something witty, but when she gazed into his blue eyes, she was sixteen again. Except he had become a man. Lines bracketed his mouth and crow's-feet fanned out from the corners of his eyes. If it were possible, he was even more handsome now.

She felt a rush of shame. If only she'd worn better clothes today than torn black shorts and a ragged

T-shirt, or cut her hair recently. He was probably disgusted that she'd let herself get so . . . ugly.

She reached deep inside for a casual voice. "It's good to see you again," she said, staring back out at the sea. "I hear from Caro that you're a corporate bigwig now."

"It doesn't mean much."

"Spoken like a rich man." She tried to smile. "So, how's life treated you?" God, she wished he'd take the reins of this awkward conversation and ride away . . .

"I saw your act once. At the Comedy Store."

She turned to him, and immediately regretted it. She was close enough to see the green flecks in his blue eyes. She remembered suddenly how his eyes used to seem to change color, to take on the hue of the sea or the sky. "Really?"

"I thought you were funny as hell."

Her smile softened into the real thing. "Really?"

"I was going to talk to you after the show, but there were so many people around you. A man . . ."

"Max." She felt the sting of that missed opportunity, and wondered how often that happened in life. Chances lost and won on a turn of fate so small they couldn't be seen by the naked eye. "We broke up a while ago. And what about you? Are you married?" The moment she asked the question, she flinched, feeling completely exposed. If she could have sucked it back into her mouth, she would have.

"No. Never."

She felt a sudden euphoria, then it fell away, left her even more confused. He could ruin her with a word, this boy she'd loved who'd become a man she didn't know. She'd loved him so much, and yet she'd broken his heart. She still barely knew why. "That summer . . . I found out from Lottie that you'd moved away," she said, her voice unsteady.

"I couldn't face you," he answered, looking at her. "You didn't just hurt me, Ruby. You ruined me."

"I know." She almost reached for him then, placed her hand on his thigh as if she had every right to touch him. And the stinging realization that she *couldn't* touch him, that she didn't even know him, brought her up short.

She lurched to her feet, terrified that if he looked at her again, she would burst into tears. "I have to get back to Nora."

Slowly, he got to his feet and reached for her.

She stumbled back so fast she almost fell over the bank. His hand dropped back to his side, and she had a sudden, overwhelming fear that he wouldn't try to touch her again.

She could see the disappointment in his eyes. "Time is precious," he said. "If I didn't know that before this week, I know it now. So I'm just going to say it: I missed you."

She couldn't imagine what to say next, how to answer. She had missed him, too—missed him so much—and it hurt to know that she would go on missing him until she was an old woman. A more bendable, trusting person could have changed the future in this very moment, but Ruby couldn't imagine that kind of strength.

He waited, and the silence stretched out between them. Then, slowly, he turned and walked away.

Chapter Fourteen

Nora sat on the porch. She could see Dean and Ruby sitting out on that old rock of theirs.

Ruby was the first to stand. Slowly, Dean followed. They stood frozen, close enough to kiss.

Then Dean turned and headed back up toward the house, leaving Ruby behind. He strode up the path, saw Nora on the porch, and came toward her. At the railing he stopped, hung his arms over the wisteria-covered edge, and smiled tiredly. "Hey, Miz Bridge."

She smiled. "Call me Nora. It's good to see you again, Dean. I'm glad you finally made it back to the island."

"It's good to see you, too." He looked at her, and in his eyes, she saw pain. "Thank you, Nora," he said softly. "You're everything to him."

She nodded, knowing she didn't need to say anything. Everything that mattered had passed between them in silence.

Dean turned back, stared down at the beach. Nora knew that they both wanted to talk about Ruby, but neither of them knew what to say. Finally, he pulled away from the porch. "Will you guys come over on Saturday? I've got the *Wind Lass* working. I'm going to take Eric sailing."

"That would be great."

Dean shot a last, lingering look at Ruby, then walked away.

Nora waited, knowing that Ruby wouldn't stay down there for long. Sure enough, a few minutes later, she headed up the path. When she saw Nora on the porch, she paused.

Nora noticed that her daughter's eyes were red. A thin tracing of tears streaked her cheeks.

Nora's heart went out to her. "Come," she said, "sit with me."

Ruby looked torn. She probably couldn't decide which was worse—being alone right now or being with Nora. Finally, she walked up onto the porch, hitched her butt up onto the railing.

Nora longed to touch her daughter, to simply lay a hand on Ruby's head the way she used to. But such intimacy was impossible between them now. The only way she could touch her daughter was with words, with memories. "You know what I was remembering just now? The winter I was pregnant with you. A freak weather pattern moved through the islands."

Ruby looked up. "Yeah?"

"The snow came earlier that year than anyone could remember. Just after Thanksgiving. At first people tried to drive, but by evening, there were more cars in the ditches than on the roads, and we all gave up. By nightfall, the clouds were gone, and we'd never seen such a starry sky." She smiled at the memory. "Your dad and I were on the porch when we heard the laughter. We put on every piece of winter clothing we owned and followed the sound, walking through snow that came up to our knees. I remember having the strangest feeling that I could *see* our words; they seemed to be written in the steam of our breath. The snow didn't crunch beneath our boots. It sort of . . . sighed. We followed the laughter all the way to the McGintys' place. That ugly old swamp on their property— remember it?—well, it had frozen solid. Every kid on the island was there, skating or sliding or inner-tubing. I never knew how it was that everyone knew to be there at just that moment. . . . At midnight, stars started falling. Hundreds of them. The next day on the news, they had all kinds of scientific explanations for it, but we believed it was magic."

Nora closed her eyes, and for a moment, she could almost smell the newly fallen snow, almost feel that stinging cold on her cheeks. "After that, for almost a month, things on the island went a little crazy. Roses bloomed on prickly bushes that had been brown and dead for weeks. Rain fell from cloudless skies. But what I remember most of all were the sunsets. From then until the new year came and chased the magic away, the night sky was always red. We called it the ruby season."

Ruby said softly, "Is that where my name came from?"

"Your dad and I used to sit out here, wrapped in blankets, and watch that ruby sky. We never talked about naming you after it, but when you came, we knew. You'd be our Ruby. Our own bit of magic."

Ruby smiled. "Thanks."

Nora looked at her and paused. "Dean invited us to go sailing on Saturday."

"What will I say to Eric?"

"Oh, Ruby," she said gently, "you start with hello."

Ruby barely slept that night. At first, she tried to tell herself it was the heat. Even with the windows open, summer had always been sweltering on the second floor.

I missed you.

If there was one thing Ruby knew, it was that she hurt people, and she didn't want to hurt Dean again. He deserved a woman who could return his love as fully and freely as he gave it. That was the one thing she'd known even as a teenager.

Finally, at about three-thirty, she went out onto the balcony and sat in the chair her grandfather had made. In the dark before the rising sun, she tried to pull peace from the familiar sounds and smells. The whoosh of the waves . . . the hoot of a barn owl, not too far away . . . the scent of her grandmother's roses, climbing up trellises on the side of the house.

Write. That'll get your mind off everything.

She reached for the pad beside her. Then she stopped. Frowning, she drew her hand back.

For the first time, she considered the impact of her article. She'd agreed to write it because she'd *wanted* to hurt her mother, to strike back for all the pain she'd suffered as a young girl.

But she wasn't a child anymore.

Before, she hadn't wanted to know why Nora left them. Or maybe she'd been so damned certain that she'd seen everything that mattered.

But marriages broke up for *reasons;* women like her mother didn't just up and leave their husbands on a sunny summer's day.

Ruby had glimpsed moments in the past days, images that didn't fit with the picture she'd drawn of her mother. And there was the "best of" file she'd read. The first "Nora Knows Best" column appeared months after her mother had left . . . and in a cheesy local newspaper that couldn't have paid her more than gas money.

It didn't fit, and that bothered Ruby.

She closed her eyes . . . and remembered a cold, crisp October day that smelled of ripening apples and dying black leaves. Dad had been in the living room, sitting in that leather chair of his, drinking and smoking cigarettes he'd rolled himself. The whole house had smelled of smoke. Caroline had been gone on a field trip to the Museum of Flight in Seattle and they'd missed the ferry back. Ruby had been in the bedroom, reading *Misery* by Stephen King. "Groovy Kind of Love" was on the turntable . . .

There was a knock at the door. Ruby sat up in bed, waiting to hear her dad's footsteps, and when he went past her open door, she recognized the stumbling drunkenness of his gait. Please, she thought, don't let it be one of my friends . . .

She heard him say, "Nora," in a voice that was too loud, belligerent.

Ruby froze; then she heard the scratching whine of the record player's needle being scraped across vinyl. Everything went quiet. Chair springs creaked.

Ruby slipped out of bed and crept to the door of her room, pushing it farther open.

Dad was in his chair, Mom was kneeling in front of him.

"Rand," Mom said quietly, "we need to talk."

He stared down at her, his hair was too long, and dirty. "It's too late for talking."

Mom reached for him; he lurched to his feet, swaying unsteadily above her.

Ruby couldn't stand it another minute, seeing her father's pain in such sharp relief. "Get out," she yelled, surprised at the strength in her voice.

Mom got to her feet, turned around. "Oh, Ruby," she said, holding her arms out.

As Mom came toward her, Ruby saw the changes in her mother, the gray pallor in her cheeks . . . the weight she'd lost . . . the way her hands, always so strong and sure, were blue-veined and trembling as she reached out.

Ruby sprang backward. "G-go away. We don't want you anymore."

Mom stopped; her hands fell uselessly to her sides. "Don't say that, honey." She gazed at Ruby. "There are things you don't understand. You're so young . . ."

Ruby ignored her mother's tears. It was easy; she'd cried so many of them herself they'd lost their

currency. "I understand how it feels to be left be-
hind, as if you were . . . nothing." Her traitorous
voice broke, and the sudden rawness of her pain
made it difficult to breathe. Ruby fisted her hands
and drew in a deep, shuddering breath. "Go away,
Mother. No one here loves you anymore."

Mom glanced back at Dad, who'd slumped into
his chair again. He was holding his head in his
hands.

Ruby wanted to put her arms around him and tell
him she loved him, just as she'd done so often in the
past few months, but she didn't have the heart for it
now. It was all she could do to keep from wailing.
She stepped back into her bedroom and slammed
the door shut.

She didn't know how long she stood there, per-
fectly still, her hands balled into cold fists, but after
a while, she heard footsteps crossing the kitchen,
then the quiet opening and closing of the front door.
Outside, a car engine started; tires crunched through
gravel. And quiet fell once again, broken only by
the sound of a grown man crying . . .

Ruby lurched to her feet, and found herself unsteady. She couldn't have *forgotten* that day . . . she
must have blocked it out, buried it beneath the cold,
hard stones of denial.

The world, once so firm, felt as if it had given way
beneath her.

Things you don't understand.

Even then, her mother had had a story to tell . . .
but no one had wanted to hear it.

Now Ruby was ready. She wanted to learn what had happened more than a decade earlier, under her own roof, within her own family.

And if her mother wouldn't answer those questions, there was always an alternative.

She would ask her father.

Part Two

"We shall not cease from exploration
And the end of all our exploring
Will be to arrive where we started
And know the place for the first time."

—T. S. ELIOT, FROM "LITTLE GIDDING"

Chapter Fifteen

It had been easy to get out of the house. Ruby had simply left a note—*Gone to Dad's*—on the kitchen table.

Now she was in the minivan, driving up the tree-lined road that led away from the Lopez Island ferry dock.

She was a fourth-generation islander, and at this moment, seeing all the new houses and bed-and-breakfasts that had sprouted on Lopez, the full impact of that heritage hit her. She had *roots* here, a past that grew deep into the rich black island soil. Lopez had grown up, and she didn't like the changes. She couldn't help wondering if there were still places where grass grew up to a young girl's knees and apple trees blossomed by the side of the road, where wild brown rabbits came out beneath a full moon and munched their way through summer gardens.

Her great-great-grandfather had come to this remote part of the world from a dreary, industrialized section of England. He'd brought his beautiful, black-eyed Irish wife and seventeen dollars, and together they'd homesteaded two hundred acres on Lopez. His brother had come along a few years later and staked his own claim on Summer Island. Both had become successful apple and sheep farmers.

Now, more than one hundred years later, there were only ten acres on Lopez that belonged to her father. The house on Summer Island had been willed to Ruby and Caroline; their grandparents had feared that their son would lose this land, one acre at a time. And they'd been right.

Randall Bridge now lived on what had once been the farm's highest point, a rounded thumbprint of land that stuck out high above the bay.

He was an island man, through and through. He'd grown up on this tiny, floating world and he'd raised his children here. He had a closet full of plaid flannel shirts for winter and locally made tourist T-shirts for summer.

He lived on a financial shoestring, from one fishing season to the next. Money had always been tight and "next summer" was always going to change things. He made it through the lean months doing local boat repairs. Most years, it was the repairs—not the fishing—that kept food on the table and paid the steadily rising property taxes.

Ruby came to the crest of the hill and had to slam on the brakes to avoid hitting a trio of deer. A doe and her two spotted fawns stood in the middle of the road, their ears pricked forward. Suddenly they leapt over the ditch and disappeared into the tall, golden grass.

She eased forward again, going more slowly now. She'd forgotten how it was to share the road with animals. In Los Angeles, there had been a different kind of wildlife on the freeways.

She turned off the main road. A gravel road wound through acres of apple trees, their limbs propped up by slanted, graying slats of wood.

At last, she was home. The yellow clapboard house, built in the late twenties, sat wedged between two huge willow trees. The original house—a squat, broken-down log cabin with a moss-furred roof—could still be seen amid the tumbling blackberry brambles at the edge of the property.

She parked alongside her dad's battered Ford truck, got out of the car, and stood there, looking around. It was exactly as she remembered. She walked down the gravel path, past the now empty rabbit hutches she'd built with her dad, toward the back porch. The yard was still a riot of runaway weeds and untended flowers. Shasta daisies grew in huge, hip-high mounds, drawing every bee on the place. A tattered screen door hung slanted, a set of screws missing.

She paused on the porch, steeling herself for the sight of her dad's new family, walking as they did across the floorboards of his old one.

She knew she'd be entering another woman's house . . . a woman she barely knew, who was less than ten years older than Ruby herself . . . seeing a baby brother for the first time. A baby who had no idea that his father had started over in his life, had left his other children stranded in the gray hinterlands of a broken family.

Taking a deep breath, she knocked on the door and

waited. When there was no answer, she eased the
screen door open and stepped into the kitchen.

The changes were everywhere.

Frilly pink gingham curtains. Lacy white table-
cloths. Walls papered in a creamy white pattern with
cabbage roses twining on prickly vines.

If she'd needed evidence that Dad had gone on with
his life (and she hadn't), it was right here. Their old
life had been painted over.

"Dad?" she said, not surprised to find that her voice
was weak. She stepped past the table—the chairs had
been painted a vibrant green—and poked her head
into the living room.

He was there, kneeling in front of the small black
woodstove, loading logs into the fire. When he looked
up and saw her, his eyes widened in surprise, then a
great smile swept across his lined face. "I don't believe
it. . . . You're here." He clanged the stove's door shut
and got to his feet.

Moving toward her, he started to hold his arms out,
then he paused, uncertain. At the last minute, he
pulled her into an awkward hug. "Caroline told me
you were home. I wondered if you'd come to see me."

She clung to him, fighting a sudden urge to cry. He
smelled of wood smoke and varnish and salt air.

"Of course I'd come," she said shakily, drawing
back. Although both of them knew it was a half-truth,
a wished-for belief. She hadn't even called him, and
the realization of her own selfishness tasted black and
bitter.

He touched her cheek. His rough, callused skin reminded her of hours spent sanding boat decks at the

marina, a girl and her dad, huddled together in the dying red sunlight, saying nothing that mattered. "I missed you," he said.

"I missed you, too." It was true. She had missed him, every day and all the time. Now, standing here, seeing in his eyes how much he loved her, she wished she'd been more forgiving when he remarried, more accepting of his new life.

It was the sort of thought that winged through Ruby's mind all the time, regrets, hoped-for improvements; in the end, she never changed. She said whatever popped into her head and hurt whoever hurt her first. She couldn't seem to help it.

She collected grudges and heartaches the way she'd once collected Barbies, never sharing, never abandoning. Her dad, in the end, had hurt Ruby deeply; it was the sort of thing she had no idea how to overcome. It was always between them, a sliver embedded just below the skin.

She glanced uneasily up the stairs, wondering where Marilyn was. "I don't want to intrude—"

"Mari took Ethan off island for a doctor's appointment." He grinned. "And don't even *pretend* you aren't happy about that."

She smiled sheepishly. "Well . . . I wanted to see the kid. My brother," she added, when she saw the way he was looking at her. She winced, wishing she'd said it right the first time.

"Don't worry about it." But he turned away quickly and headed back into the living room. She knew she'd hurt his feelings. He sat down on the threadbare floral

sofa, cocked one leg over his knee. "How's it going between you and your mom?"

She flopped down onto the big overstuffed chair
near the fire. "Picture Laverne and Shirley on crack."

"I don't see any visible bruising. I have to admit, I
was shocked when Caro told me you'd volunteered to
take care of Nora. Shocked and proud."

Ruby ached suddenly for what had been lost between them, and the hell of it was, they hadn't fought
or argued. When he'd found Marilyn, he'd simply
drifted away from his daughters. He'd stopped calling
as much.

"I meant to come visit you this week," he said,
giving her that *you-know-how-it-is* smile of his. The
one that always reminded you that he had other
things—other people—on his mind.

She refused to be stung by his laid-back attitude.
"So, how is the fishing this season?"

Something passed through his eyes, so quickly it
would have been easy to overlook. But Ruby saw it.
"Dad? What is it? What's wrong?"

"Last summer was terrible. I might . . . have to sell
off another chunk of land."

"Oh, Dad . . ." Ruby remembered the last time
they'd had this talk. It had been the year after her
mother left, when her father hadn't fished all season.
Then there had been forty acres left. They'd sold the
last waterfront piece. She'd wanted desperately to
help, but all she'd had was her berry-picking money.
"How much do you need?"

"Three thousand. Don't worry about it. Let's talk
about—"

"I could lend you the money."

"*You?*"

She reached for her purse and pulled out her check-book. Over her father's protests, she wrote out a check and set it on the table. "There," she said, grinning. "It's done."

"I can't take that, Ruby."

But they both knew he *would* take it. "It means a lot to me to be able to help you."

Slowly, he said, "Okay." Then softly, "Thank you."

An unfamiliar silence settled between them, broken only by the popping of the fire. She wondered if he was thinking about his father; Grandpa Bridge had been deeply disappointed in his only son's lack of ambition. He wouldn't have been proud of Rand at a moment like this.

Suddenly Dad stood up. "Come on, let's take a walk."

She followed him into the bright sunshine. As they'd done a thousand times, they strolled down the gravel path to the marina, where a few fishing boats bobbed along the docks, their green nets wound on huge drums.

Dad headed to his slip—8A—where the *Captain Hook* bobbed lazily against the dock. He climbed aboard, then turned around and helped Ruby on.

He tossed her a tangle of new white line. "Splice that, would you? Ned and I are heading out tomorrow. I told him I'd have everything ready."

Ruby sat cross-legged on the boat's aft deck and brought the slithering heap of rope onto her lap. She had a moment's hesitation, when her mind couldn't access the memory, but then her fingers started moving.

She worked the rope, twined the triple strands into a new, stronger whole and began building the eye. "Nora isn't quite what I expected," she said, trying to sound casual.

"That's hardly surprising."

Ruby experienced a momentary lapse in courage. *Shut up,* she thought, *don't ask.* She drew in a deep breath and looked at her father. "What happened between you two?"

He looked up sharply, eyeing her, then he got to his feet and walked past her to the stern. Every footfall upset the balance and made a soft, creaking sound. All at once, he turned back to face her, but she had the weird sensation that he wasn't really seeing her. He seemed . . . frozen, or trapped maybe, and she wondered what images were running through his mind. "Dad?"

Now she felt as if he were seeing too much of her. Beyond the skin and the hair, to the very bones. Maybe even deeper. "Are you in for the long haul this time, Ruby?"

"What do you mean?"

"Ah, Rube . . ." He sighed. "You have a way of moving on. I've never seen anyone who could shut herself off so easily from the people around her."

"It isn't easy."

He smiled grimly. "You made it look easy. You went off to California and started a new life without any of us . . . but after a while, it was *our* fault, Caroline's and mine. We didn't call enough . . . or not on the right days . . . or we didn't say the right things when we did call. And you moved farther and farther away. You didn't come to my wedding or even call when your brother was born or come to see Caroline when she suffered through that terrible labor. But somehow that was our fault, too. We abandoned *you*. Now, you want to stir up an old pot. Will you be here tomorrow or next month or next Christmas to see what comes of it?"

Ruby wanted to say he was *wrong*. But she couldn't. "I don't know, Dad." It was all she could manage now; a quiet, simple honesty.

He stared down at her for a long minute, then dropped the rope. "Follow me," he said at the same time he jumped off the boat and headed up the rickety dock.

He was walking so fast that Ruby had to run to catch up. They hurried down the docks and up the hill. He pushed through the screen door so fast it almost banged Ruby in the face. He didn't seem to notice.

Ruby stumbled over the threshold. "Jesus, Dad—"
When she looked up, she lost the sentence.

Her father was standing at the kitchen table with a bottle of tequila. He thumped it down hard, then yanked out a chair and sat down.

It was a move that brought back *way* too many memories. She was surprised by the depth of her reaction. The sight of him holding a bottle of booze shook her to the core. She grabbed the ladderback of the chair. "I thought you'd quit drinking."

"I did."

"You're scaring me."

"Honey, I haven't begun to scare you. Sit down,

snap on your seat belt, and lock your seat in the up-right position."

Ruby pulled the chair out and perched nervously on its edge. Her foot started tapping so hard it sounded like gunfire.

Her dad looked . . . different. She couldn't have put her finger on exactly how, but the man sitting across from her, with the graying hair and well-worn sweater with its threadbare elbows, wasn't the man she'd expected.

This man, hunched over, staring at a full bottle of Cuervo Gold, looked as if he hadn't smiled in years. He looked up suddenly. "I love you. I want you to remember that."

She heard the tender underbelly of his voice, saw the emotion in his eyes, and it reminded her of exactly how far apart they'd drifted. "I could never forget that."

"I don't know. You're good at forgetting the people who love you. The story starts in nineteen sixty-seven, just a few years before the whole damn world exploded. I was at the University of Washington; I'd just finished my senior year, and I was certain I'd get drafted into the NFL. So certain I never bothered to get a degree. I barely studied. Hell, they paid someone to take tests for me. Things were crazy back then. The world was off its axis. Everyone I knew had been bent or mangled by it.

"And then I met Nora. She was scrawny and scared and looked like she hadn't slept in a week. Still, she was the most beautiful girl I'd ever seen. She believed absolutely that I'd play pro football . . ." Dad slumped forward a little, thumped his elbows on the table. "But it didn't happen. No one called. I walked around in a daze; I couldn't believe it. I had no backup plan, no second choice. Then my draft number came up. I probably could have gotten out of it—said they needed me to run the farm—but I hated this island and I couldn't imagine how I'd survive here." He sighed and leaned back. "But I wanted someone to wait for me, to write me letters. So I went back to Nora, my pretty little waitress at Beth's Diner in Greenlake, and I asked her to marry me."

Ruby frowned. She'd heard this story a thousand times in her childhood and this was definitely not the way it went. "You didn't love her?"

"Not when I married her. No, that's not true. I'd just loved other women more. Anyway, we got married, spent a wonderful honeymoon at Lake Quinalt Lodge, and I shipped out. Your mom moved into this house with my folks. By the end of the first week, they were both in love with her. She was the daughter my parents never had, and she loved this land in a way I never could.

"Her letters kept me alive over there. It's funny. I fell in love with your mother when she wasn't even on the same continent. I meant to *stay* in love with her, but I didn't come home the same cocky, confident kid who'd left. Vietnam . . . war . . . it did something to us." He smiled sadly. "Or maybe not. Maybe the bad seeds were always in me, and war gave them a dark place in which to grow. Anyway, I turned . . . cynical and hard. Your mom tried so hard to put me back together, and for a few years, we were happy. Caroline was born, then you . . ."

Ruby had this bizarre sensation that her whole existence had turned into sand and was streaming through her fingers.

"When I came home, your mom and I moved into the house on Summer. I went to work at the feed store on Orcas. Everyone thought I was a failure. 'So much promise wasted,' they whispered to my dad over drinks at Herb's Tavern. God, I hated my life." He looked up suddenly. "I didn't mean for it to happen."

Ruby swallowed convulsively, as if something bitter was backing up in her throat. "Don't say—"

"I slept with other women."

"*No.*"

"Your mom didn't know at first. I was careful—at least as careful as a drowning man can be. I was drinking a lot by then—God knows *that* didn't help—and I knew when she started to suspect. But she always gave me the benefit of the doubt."

"Oh, God," Ruby whispered.

"Finally, that summer, someone told her the truth. She confronted me. Unfortunately, I was drunk at the time. I said . . . things . . . it was ugly. The next day, she left."

Ruby felt as if she were drowning, or falling, and she was desperate for something to cling to. "Oh, my *God*," she said again. It was too much; she felt as if she might explode from trying to hold it all inside her.

He leaned toward her, reached for her across the table.

She got up so fast her chair skidded out from underneath her.

He pulled back and slowly got to his feet. "We've all been carrying this baggage for too long. Some of us have tried to go on." He looked at her. "And some of us have refused to. But all of us are hurting. I'm your father; she's your mother—whatever she's done or hasn't done, or said or hasn't said—she's a part of you and you're a part of her. Don't you see that you can't be whole without her?"

Ruby's past seemed to be crumbling around her. There was nothing solid to hold on to, no single thing to point to and say *There, that's my truth.* "I'm leaving."

He smiled sadly. "Of course you are."

"Call Nora. Tell her I'm going to Caroline's. I'll be home . . . whenever."

"I love you, Ruby," he said. "Please don't forget that."

She knew he was waiting for her to say the words back to him, but she couldn't do it.

Chapter Sixteen

Ruby had never been to her sister's house, but the address was imprinted on her brain. Caroline was the only person on earth who regularly received a Christmas card from Ruby. It was simply required. Ruby had long ago discovered that it wasn't worth the eleven months of sarcastic jabs. Better to mail off a damn card.

The traffic was stop-and-go as she exited Interstate 5 and crept toward the sprawling suburb of Redmond.

Not so many years earlier, this had been the sticks; hundreds of acres of unspoiled farmland nestled between two rivers. Now it was MicrosoftLand, the *über* suburbia of the geek set. The developments had tried to keep the rural flavor—lots were big; subdivisions had names like Evergreen Valley and Rainshadow Vista, and trees were preserved at all cost. Unfortunately, the houses all looked disturbingly similar. Stepford in a coat of Ralph Lauren paint.

Ruby checked the handy rental car map and turned down Emerald Lane. One big, brick-faced house followed another, each built to the edge of its lot. New landscaping gave the neighborhood an unsettled look.

At last she found it: 12712 Emerald Lane.

She drove up the stamped blue concrete driveway and parked next to a silver Mercedes station wagon, then grabbed her purse from the passenger seat and headed up the path to a pair of oak doors trimmed in beaded brass.

She knocked. From inside came a rustle of movement, then a muffled "Just a minute."

Suddenly the door sprang open and Caroline stood there, looking flawless at one o'clock in the afternoon in a pair of ice-blue linen pants and a matching boatneck cashmere sweater.

"Ruby!" Caroline pulled Ruby into her arms, holding her tightly.

Ruby closed her eyes; for the first time in hours, she was able to draw a decent breath.

Finally, Caro drew back. "I'm so glad you came."

"I didn't have a chance to go shopping. I meant to get the kids something—"

"Forget about that." Caroline yanked Ruby into the house.

Of course, it was perfect. Uncluttered and flawlessly decorated. Not a thing was out of place.

It didn't look as if a child had ever *been* in here let alone lived here.

They passed through a pristine kitchen, all gleaming metallic surfaces and black granite countertops. Here was the first hint of the family. Pictures covered the Sub-Zero refrigerator. Above the double sinks, a bay window held on to a view of rolling, green lawn. A golf course.

Caro led her through the formal dining room, where Grandma's silver tea service glittered on a massive oak sideboard, and into the living room. Walls painted in a lovely faux marble finish dropped down to a wide-planked oak floor. Two wing chairs, upholstered in an elegant brandy-colored silk weave, flanked a gold-and-bronze tapestried sofa. A pair of crystal lamps sat on gilded rosewood end tables, pouring golden light onto the plush antique Chinese rug.

"Where are the kids?"

Caroline brought a finger to her lips and said harshly, "*Sshh*. We don't want to wake them up."

"Could I tiptoe upstairs and just—"

"Trust me on this. You can see them when they wake up."

Ruby got a glimpse of something—someone—behind Caro's perfect, smiling face, but it was there and gone so fast, it left no imprint behind.

She felt a little prickle of unease. Nothing was ever wrong with Caroline. She was the most balanced, well-adjusted person Ruby had ever known. Even during that horrible summer, Caro had moved along on an even keel, accepting what Ruby never would, smiling, forgetting, going on . . .

And yet now, impossibly, Caroline looked unhappy. "Something's going on with you," Ruby said, "what is it?"

Caro sat like a parakeet on the edge of the chair. Her perfectly manicured hands were clasped so tightly together the skin had gone pale. A Julia Roberts smile flashed across her serene face. "It's nothing, really. Just a bad week. The kids have been acting up. It's nothing."

Ruby couldn't put her finger on it, exactly, but *something* was wrong here. Suddenly she knew. "You're having an affair!"

This time there was no mistaking the genuineness of Caro's smile. It showed how false the others had been. "Since Fred was born, I'd rather hit myself in the head with a jackhammer than have sex."

"Maybe that's your problem. I try to have sex at least twice a week—sometimes even with someone else."

Caro laughed. "Oh, Ruby . . . God, I missed you . . ." She sounded normal now.

"I missed you, too."

"So," Caro said, leaning back now. "What brought you racing to my door?"

"What makes you think I raced?"

Caro gave her "the look." "Nice outfit. I haven't seen so much black since Jenny went to the Halloween party as a licorice whip."

"Good point." They both knew that Ruby usually dressed defensively for Caro. It was easier that way.

"So what is it? You left Mom strapped to the wheel-chair and ran screaming out of the house." Caro grinned at her own black humor. "Or maybe you left her at a rest area a few miles back and now she's thumbing it."

Ruby couldn't even smile. "I went to Dad's house this morning."

"Yeah, so?"

She had no idea how to put a pretty spin on such ug-liness, so she just said it. "When Nora left . . . Dad was having an affair."

Caroline sat back. "Oh, *that*."

"You *knew*?"

"Everyone on the island knew."

"Not me."

Caroline's smile was soft and tender. "You didn't want to know."

Ruby had trouble finding her voice. "She's not who I thought she was, Caro. We're trapped in that house together, and whether I like it or not, I'm getting to know her. We . . . talk."

"*You're* getting to know her?" Something passed through Caroline's eyes at that. If Ruby hadn't known better, she would have called it envy. Suddenly Caro walked out of the room. A few minutes later, she re-turned with two glasses of wine and a pack of cigarettes.

Ruby laughed. "*Smoking*—you're kidding, right? A cig in your hand would be like—"

"No jokes, Ruby. Please."

Ruby saw how fragile her sister looked. "Point the way to cancer. That doesn't count—it wasn't funny."

Caro opened the French doors and led Ruby to a seat at an umbrellaed table. The golf course stretched alongside the flowered yard, dipped to a valley, and rose on the other side to a row of houses remarkably similar to this one.

Caroline pulled a cigarette from the pack and lit up.

Ruby followed suit. She hadn't smoked in years, and she had to admit, the novelty of it was fun.

Her sister took a drag, exhaled, and stared out across

the green. A stream of smoke clouded her face. "I've been talking to Mom for years, meeting her now and then for lunch, calling her on Sunday mornings, being the daughter she expects, and we're polite strangers. And *you*—" She shot Ruby a narrowed gaze. "You, who treats her like Typhoid Mary, she talks to."

An awkward silence fell between them, and Ruby couldn't think of how to step over it. "We're stuck together."

Caroline took a drag and exhaled slowly, staring out at the green lawn. "That's not it. What's she like?"

"The worst part is, she's smarter than I am. She keeps making me remember who she used to be. Who *we* used to be. And you know, it hurts. When I was on the ferry this morning, before Dad dropped his A-bomb, I was thinking about our visits to the county fair. How we used to walk through the midway with her, eating cotton candy, tossing pennies at ugly china dishes, and I . . . missed her."

"I know how that feels."

Ruby noticed that her sister's hands were trembling. "Have you forgiven her?" she asked. "I mean, *really?*"

Caro looked up. "I tried to forget it, you know? Most of the time, I do, too. It's like it happened to another family, not mine."

"So, you haven't forgiven her any more than I have. You're just nicer about it."

Caroline tried to smile, though there was a bleakness in her eyes that was unsettling. "Your honesty is a gift, Rube, even if it hurts people. You're . . . real. I can't seem to—"

A scream blared through the open window behind them.

Ruby jumped. "Good God. Has someone been shot?"

Caroline deflated. Her shoulders caved downward, and the color seemed to seep out of her cheeks. "The princess is up."

Ruby moved closer to her sister. "Are you okay, Caro?"

The smile was too fleeting to be real. "I'll be fine," she said, and Ruby saw that her sister was pretending again. She got up from her seat and walked woodenly back into the house.

Ruby followed her.

"AAAGH . . ." This time there were two screams.

A jack-in-the-box came crashing and jangling down the stairs and skidded across the kitchen floor.

"Go," Caro said with a tired smile. "Save yourself."

A naked Barbie doll cartwheeled down the stairs and thumped into the table leg.

The screams were getting louder. Ruby fought the urge to cover her ears. "Let's go upstairs. I want to at least *see* my niece and nephew."

"Not when Jenny's in this kind of a mood. Trust me."

Another toy came crashing down the stairs, followed by a shrieking cry. "MO-MMY NOW!"

Caroline turned to her. "Please? Another time?"

"Well . . . next week I'm going to come down here and baby-sit. You and Jere can go out dancing or something."

"Dancing." Caroline smiled wistfully. "That would be nice."

Ruby remembered suddenly that she wouldn't be here next week. She'd be back in California on *The Sarah Purcell Show,* telling the world about her mother. Suddenly she felt sick.

"You'd better get going. The ferry lines are hell this time of day."

Ruby checked her watch. "Shit. You're right."

Caroline looped an arm around Ruby, drew her close, and guided her toward the door. There she paused. "I'm sorry you had to find out about Dad, but maybe it'll help. We're human, Ruby. All of us. Just human."

Ruby hugged her sister, holding her so tightly that neither of them could breathe. "I love you, Caro."

"I love you, too, Rubik's Cube. Now, get going."

Ruby drew back. She had the strange thought that if she said anything except good-bye, Caro would simply shatter.

So good-bye was all she said.

Nora sat at the kitchen table, staring down at the package of letters. Earlier, she'd spoken to Eric, but afterward, the silence had tackled her again.

Idly, she rubbed her throbbing wrist. She'd spent an hour in the morning practicing with her crutches, and she was improving. She could go short distances. By the end of the week, she hoped to be out of the damned chair completely.

But the practice hadn't fulfilled all of its purpose. She couldn't clear her mind completely. The letters were always there.

She'd tried giving herself a little pep talk. They were

just words, she told herself, scribblings on paper, and they were from *strangers*. Certainly she could find the strength to pick up a pen and fashion some kind of response. A good-bye and a thanks-for-the-good-times, at the very least.

Not true. Every letter she'd attempted began the same: *Dear readers*.

Sometimes she came up with a sad, pathetic beginning—*I'm more sorry than you can know. . . .* or *How can I begin to say what's in my heart. . . .* or *By now you all know who I really am.*

But there was never a second sentence. And if all that wasn't bad enough, she was worried about Ruby.

Her gaze landed on the note she'd found sitting on the kitchen table. *Dear Nora—Gone to see Dad.*

It looked innocuous enough, but appearances were often deceiving. Ruby wasn't coming back.

It was Nora's own fault. She'd pushed her daughter too hard in the past few days, and that was dangerous. Ruby *always* shoved back; she had from infancy. Unlike Caroline, who smiled coolly and held your hand and stepped aside when reality got too close.

Nora had recognized her mistake the second she saw the good-bye note. Her daughter had had enough.

She slumped forward, dropping her head onto her crossed arms. A good cry would probably help, but she couldn't find even that easy road to relief. She was wrung dry.

Then she heard a car drive up . . . footsteps on the porch . . .

The door opened, and Rand stepped into the kitchen.

Nora understood instantly: Ruby had sent her father to deliver the bad news.

"Hey, Randall," she said, pulling her casted leg off the second chair. "Have a seat."

He glanced around. "I've got a better idea."

Before he'd even finished the sentence, he'd crossed the room and scooped her into his arms. She made a garbled, whooping sound of surprise and put her arms around his neck, hanging on. "What the—"

"Just hang on."

She clung to him as he carried her over the threshold and out onto the porch. There, he pulled an old mohair blanket off of the rocker and wedged it under his arm. He walked down the steps, across the shaggy lawn, out to the edge of the bank.

Beneath a huge madrona tree, he laid the blanket over the rocky ground, then gingerly set her down. Her bare toes stuck out from the end of her cast, and he leaned over and tucked the fringed end of the blanket around her foot.

He sat down beside her, propped up on his elbows, and stretched out his long legs.

"Still can't stand to be inside on a sunny day?" she said.

"Some things never change." He turned to her, his face solemn. "I'm sorry, Nora."

"About what?"

His gaze shifted to a point just beyond her left shoulder. "I should have said it a long time ago."

She drew in a breath. Time seemed to hang suspended

between them. She felt the hot summer sunlight on her face, smelled the familiar fragrance of the sea at low tide.

He looked at her finally, and in his eyes, she saw the sad reflection of their life together. "I'm sorry," he said again, knowing that this time she understood.

"Oh" was all she could say.

He leaned closer, touched her face with a gentleness that sapped her strength. "It was *my* fault. All mine. We both know that. I was young and stupid and cocky. I didn't know how special we were."

Nora was surprised by how easy it was suddenly for her to smile. She'd spent twenty years loving this man, eleven more vaguely missing him, and yet now, with him beside her on an old blanket that held their youth in its rough weave, she finally felt at peace. Maybe that was all she'd needed, all these years. Just those few, simple words.

She laid her hand against his, and a peacefulness settled around her, as if everything in their lives had led to this moment. He was her youth, she realized sadly, a youth that was neither well spent nor quite misspent. Just . . . spent. In his eyes, and his alone, was the woman she'd once been. "We were both at fault, Rand. We tried. We just didn't make it."

He leaned closer. She thought for a breathless moment that he was going to kiss her. He wanted to—she could see the desire in his eyes. But at the last second, he drew back, gave her a smile so soft and tender it was better than a kiss. "When I look back—and believe me, I try not to—you know what I remember?"

"What?"

"That day you came back. Jesus . . ." He closed his eyes. "I should have dropped to my knees and begged you to stay. In my heart, I knew it was what I wanted, but I'd heard about you and that guy, and all I could think of was *me*. How would it look if I took you back after that?" He laughed, a bitter, harsh sound. "*Me,* worrying about that, after the way I'd treated you. It makes me sick. And I paid for it, Nora. For eight long years, I went to sleep every night alone. And I missed you."

Nora wanted to weep at what they'd thrown away. "You should have called. I was alone, too." She paused, then said, "It's too bad."

"Yeah."

She reached out, brushed the hair from his eyes in a gesture as natural to her as breathing. "But you've gone on now. Married. I'm happy for that." She realized how true it was. Those few small words—*I'm sorry*—had released her, turned Rand into what he truly was: her first love. Her great love, perhaps, but there would be another one for her someday. She smiled and arched one eyebrow. "And are you being a good boy, Randall?"

He laughed, easy with her now. "Even a stupid dog doesn't get hit by the same bus twice."

"Good. You deserve to be happy."

"So do you."

She flinched, unable to help it. "You screwed around on your wife. I abandoned my children. It's not the same thing."

He gazed at her. She saw the heavy lines around his

mouth and eyes, grooves worn by years in the sun and wind. "I told Ruby the truth."

"About what?"

"*The* truth. About us."

Nora felt sick. "That was a foolish thing to do."

"I thought you'd be pleased. It's something I should have done a long time ago."

"Perhaps, but when you didn't—when I didn't—we buried that little piece of family history. You shouldn't have dug it up. It won't make a difference now."

"You deserved it, Nora," he said. "After all these years, you deserved it."

"Oh, Rand. She believed in you. This will break her heart."

"You know what I learned from us, Nora?" He touched her face, smiled tenuously. "Love doesn't die. Not real love. And that's what Ruby's going to discover. She's always loved you. I just gave her a reason to admit it."

Nora couldn't help thinking that, for a grown man, he was incredibly naive.

Chapter Seventeen

After two hours of waiting in the line for the ferry with two hundred eager tourists and a few beleaguered locals, Ruby remembered why she'd been so eager to move off island. Timing your life around a state-operated transportation system was miserable.

The last thing she needed was time to think. The conversation with Caroline repeated relentlessly through her mind. Even when she turned on the minivan's cheesy radio, she heard the singers' voices moaning the words *Everyone knew.*

"Except me," she said bitterly.

She still couldn't get over that.

Finally, the ferry pulled in—late, as usual—and she drove aboard, following the orange-vested woman's directions to a spot at the very back of the lane. As the ferry pulled out, she adjusted her seat to a more comfortable position and closed her eyes. Maybe sleep would help.

Everyone knew.

She opened her eyes and stared up at the van's puffy,

velourlike ceiling. She still felt shaky, as if the foundation of her life had turned to warm Jell-O and was
slowly letting her sink.

I slept with other women.

It changed everything.

Didn't it?

That was the sheer hell of it. Ruby couldn't hold the
ramifications of the day in her hands and study them.

One thing she knew: her novelization of the past,
with Dad cast as hero and her mother as villain,
wouldn't work anymore.

The world wasn't as she'd thought it was. Perhaps
she was late in making that elemental and yet monumental discovery. She felt as if she'd been a child all
these years, walking through a land that she alone had
devised.

And now something was changing inside of her,
growing. It was nothing as cliché or readily definable
as her heart. Rather, it was the bones themselves; they
were shifting, pressing against her sinew and muscles,
and deep down inside, there was a new ache.

She reached under the seat and pulled out the pen
and legal pad she'd packed in the morning. After only
a moment's hesitation, she started to write.

*I was sixteen years old when my mother left us. It
was an ordinary June day; the sun rode high in a
robin's-egg-blue sky. It's funny the things you remember. The Sound was as flat and calm as a
brand-new cookie sheet, and a gaggle of baby geese
were learning to swim on the McGuffins' pond.*

We were an average family. My father, Rand, was

an islander through and through, a commercial fisherman who repaired boats in the off season. He went bowling with his friends every Saturday night and helped us girls with our math and science homework. He wore plaid flannel shirts in the winter and Lacoste golf shirts in the summer. It never occurred to any of us, or to me anyway, that he was anything less than the perfect father.

There was no yelling in our family, no raging arguments, no nights where my sister and I lay in our side-by-side twin beds and worried feverishly that our parents would divorce.

After we'd all gone our separate ways, I often looked back on those quiet years. I was obsessive in my search for an inciting incident, a moment where I could say, Aha! There it is, the beginning of the end.

But I never found one. Until now.

Today, my parents pulled back the curtain, and the Great Oz—my dad—was revealed to be an ordinary man.

I didn't know that then, of course. All I knew was that on a beautiful day, my mother dragged a suitcase into the living room.

"I'm leaving. Is anyone coming with me?"

That's what she said to my sister and me. I heard my father in the kitchen. He dropped a glass into the sink, and the shatter sounded like bones breaking.

That was the day I learned the concept of before and after. Her leaving sliced through our family with the bloody precision of a surgeon's scalpel.

At the time, we assumed it was temporary. A

vacation getaway that should have been with "the girls," only my mother had no girlfriends. Maybe all kids think things like that.

It's hard to say when my feelings about my mother changed from guilt to anger to disgust to hatred, but that was the arc of it.

I saw what her absence did to my father. In the span of a few short days, he became hardly recognizable. He drank, he smoked, he spent the day in his pajamas. He ate only when Caroline or I cooked for him. He let the marina business go to hell and by the next spring, he had to sell land to pay the taxes and keep food on the table.

I formed an image of my mother that summer. From the hard stone of everything that happened, I carved the image of a woman and called it mother. For all these years, I've kept it on my bedside table; it was no less real for being visible only in my own mind. The statue was a collection of hard edges— selfishness, lies, and abandonment.

But now I know the truth: My father was unfaithful to my mother.

Unfaithful. A cold, detached word that gives no hint of the heat involved in passion. He wore a wedding ring and fucked women other than the one he'd sworn to love, honor, and protect.

That says it better for me. The vulgarity of the sentence matches the obscenity of the act.

I know it changes everything, but I can't seem to follow where it leads. My childhood, I thought naively, was mine alone, those memories painted in vibrant oil strokes on the canvas of my years. Now, it

seems that Barbra Streisand was right. Memories are
watercolor, and a heavy rain can wash them away.

My father is not the man I thought he was.

Even as I look down on this sentence I have just
written, I see the childishness of it, but I can't think
of another way to say it. I don't know how to look
at him now, this father who has proven to be a
stranger.

My mother didn't leave him—and us—for fame
and fortune, but simply because she was human,
and the man she loved had broken her heart.

I know how it feels when someone you love stops
loving you back. It's a kind of mini-death that
breaks something inside of you.

This knowing, this understanding . . . it should
make me want to forgive my mother, shouldn't it?

I think I'm afraid to love her, even the tiniest bit.
The hurt she caused me is so deep that my bones
have grown around it. I wonder perhaps who I am
without it—

Before she could finish her sentence, the ferry honked
its horn. They were docking on Lopez. Ruby looked
up. She knew that as soon as it had unloaded a few
cars, it would turn to Orcas Island. Summer was the
last stop before the boat turned back to the mainland.

Ruby made a snap decision. She didn't want to see
her mother yet. They would have to talk about this
new information, and Ruby wasn't ready.

She started the car and pulled out of line, speeding
down the empty lane. Ferry workers shouted at her,
waving their hands. No doubt they thought she was a

tourist, getting off on the wrong island. She didn't care. She sped forward, bumped over the ramp, and drove off.

The Sloan house was only a few blocks from the ferry terminal. It was a big, gingerbread-cute Victorian mansion placed on a breathtaking promontory overlooking the bay.

She pulled the minivan into the driveway and parked. It was twilight now; a purple haze fell across the garden, still impeccably tended. A newly painted white picket fence kept everything neatly contained. Just the way Mrs. Sloan liked it, although she probably hadn't set foot on this island in years.

Ruby walked up the crushed seashell pathway that led to the front door. There she paused, gathered her courage, and knocked.

Lottie opened the door. She looked just as Ruby remembered her—puffy cheeks, eyes that disappeared when she smiled. "Ruby Elizabeth!" she said, clapping her plump hands together. "Lordy, it's good to see you."

Ruby grinned. "Hello, Lottie. It's been a long time."

"Not so long that you can't give me a hug, you upstart." She reached out and grabbed Ruby, pulling her against her ample breast. Ruby noticed that Lottie still smelled of the lemon hard candies she kept tucked in her apron pockets.

Ruby drew back, trying to maintain her smile when she said, "I came to see Eric."

"He's upstairs. Dean had to fly to Seattle—something about business."

Ruby was relieved. Now that she was here, she

wasn't ready to talk to Dean, either. She glanced past Lottie, into the living room. "Can I go up?"

"Why, I'd beat you with a stick if you didn't. I'll make you some tea if—"

"No, thanks. I'm fine."

"Ah. Run along with you, then." As Ruby passed her, Lottie reached out, touched her shoulder. "Don't be afraid, Ruby. He's still our boy."

Ruby took a deep breath and released it, then slowly mounted the stairs. At the upper landing, she turned toward Eric's old room. The door was closed. She gave it the tiniest push to open it. "Eric?"

"Ruby? Is that you?"

She heard how weak his voice was, how different from the melodious baritone of old, and she swallowed hard. "It's me, buddy." She pushed past the door and walked into his room.

Only sheer willpower kept her from gasping. He looked thin and tired. His beautiful black hair was practically gone, there was only the barest film of it left. Bruise-dark shadows circled his eyes; his cheekbones stood out in pathetic relief above the pale, sunken flesh.

He gave her a smile that broke her heart. "I must be dead if Ruby Bridge is back on the island."

"I'm home," she said, looking away quickly so he couldn't see her shock. She strode over to the window and opened the curtains—anything to get her composure back.

"It's okay, Ruby," he said softly, "I know how I look."

She turned back around. "I missed you, Eric," she

said, meaning it, hating herself once again for how easily she'd been able to leave this place, these people.

"It feels like old times with you here," he said, pushing a button and maneuvering his bed to a more upright position.

She smiled. "Yeah. All we need is—"

He reached into the bedside drawer and held out a fat joint. He gave her that same tilted, crooked-toothed grin she remembered so well. "Cancer makes pot easy to come by." He brought the joint to his lips and lit it.

Ruby laughed. "So, you've been getting all our old friends high, huh?"

He took a toke and handed it to her. When he finally exhaled, he said, "There are no old friends around here. Not for me, anyway."

Ruby took a hit. The smoke scalded her throat and made her cough. She handed the joint back to him. "I haven't smoked pot in years."

"That's good news. So, how's the comedy biz?"

She took a smaller drag this time, breathed in, held the smoke in her lungs, then released it. After that, they passed it back and forth. "I'm not funny enough to make it big."

"You're a riot. You always cracked me up."

"Thanks, but that's like being the prettiest girl in Paducah. It doesn't make you Miss America. The funniest girl on Lopez Island isn't going to knock 'em dead on *Leno*. Sad truth."

"Are you giving up on it?"

"I guess so. I think I'll try my hand at writing." She giggled. "Get it—try my *hand* at writing."

Eric laughed with her. "It's not like you can try your foot," he said between bursts of laughter. They both knew it wasn't funny, but just now, with the sweet smell of pot clouded between them, it seemed hilarious. "What kind of book will you write?"

"Well, it won't be on the joys of sex."

"And it won't be on fashion."

Ruby shot him a look. "Very funny. I have my mother to rag about my appearance, if you don't mind. Hey! That's what I'll write about. Dear Old Mom."

Eric laughed more quietly this time. Snuffing the joint out, he leaned back on his elbows. "Somebody *should* do a book on her. She's a saint."

"I must be so high I've lost my hearing. I thought you said she was a saint."

He turned to her. "She is."

His face seemed to loom in front of her, two sizes too big. His pale blue eyes were watery, rimmed in nearly invisible strands of red. His full, almost feminine lips were colorless. And suddenly she couldn't pretend, couldn't make small talk. "How are you, Eric . . . really?"

"It's what the docs call end stage." He smiled weakly. "Funny, they come up with a euphemism for every step of the illness, but then, when you really need a little lip gloss to cover everything, they call it end stage. As if you need another reminder that you're dying."

Ruby brushed the fine, limp strands of hair from his face. "I should have stayed in better touch with you.

What happened between Dean and me, I shouldn't have let that extend to you, too."

"You broke his heart," Eric said softly.

"All of our hearts got broken that year, I guess, and the king's horsemen couldn't put us back together."

He touched her cheek. "What your mother did . . . it was really fucked. But you're not sixteen anymore. You ought to be able to see things more clearly."

"Like what?"

"Come on, Ruby. The whole island knew your dad was screwing other women. Don't you think that makes just a little bit of difference?"

So it was true: Everyone did know. "Caroline and I didn't do anything and she left us, too."

There it was, the thing she still couldn't get past.

"I've gotten to know your mom pretty well in the past few years, and let me tell you, she's great. I'd give *anything* to have a mom like her."

"Jet-set Lady had troubles with your lifestyle, I take it?"

"No. No trouble. When I told my mother I was gay, she said she never wanted to see me again."

"How long did that last?"

"She's not like your mom. When my mom said 'Get out of my house,' she meant it. I haven't seen her since."

"Even now?"

"Even now."

"God . . . I'm sorry," she said, knowing how utterly inadequate the words were.

"You know who got me through those tough

times . . . when I first realized I was gay and my parents disowned me?"

"Dean?"

"Your mother. She had just moved her 'Nora Knows Best' column to the *Seattle Times*. I wrote to her, anonymously at first. She wrote back, praising my bravery, telling me to keep my chin up, that my mom was sure to come around. It gave me hope. But after a few more years, I knew she was wrong. My mom had drawn her line in the sand. She wouldn't have a faggot son. Period." He grabbed his wallet from the top of the bedside table. Opening it, he withdrew an often-folded piece of paper and carefully unfolded it. "Here. Read this."

Ruby took the piece of paper from him. It was yellowed from age and veined with tiny fold lines. A brown stain blotched the upper-right corner. She focused on the small, neat lettering. It took her a moment to recognize the handwriting. Her mother's.

Dear Eric,

I can't express the depth of my sympathy for your pain. That you would choose to share it with me is an honor I do not take lightly.

For me, you will always be Eric, the rope swing king. When I close my eyes, I see you hanging monkeylike from that old rope at Anderson Lake, yelling Bonsai! as you let go. I see a boy who came by our house when I was sick, who sat on the porch crushing mint in a bowl to spice up my tea. I remember a sixth-grade boy, his face reddened by new pimples, his voice sliding down the scale, who was never afraid to hold Mrs. Bridge's hand as they walked down the school corridor.

This is who you are, Eric. Whom you choose to love is a part of you, but not the biggest part. You are still that boy who couldn't bear to eat anything that had once had parents. I hope and pray that someday your mother will wake up and remember the very special boy she gave birth to. I hope she will look up then, and smile at the man he has become.

But if she does not, please, please don't let it tear your heart apart. Some people simply can't find it in themselves to bend, to accept. If this terrible thing happens, Eric, you must go on. There's no other word for it. Life is full of people who are different, broken, hurting, who simply put one foot in front of the other and keep moving.

It is your mother I fear for. You will grow up and fall in love, and find yourself. When I come to visit you, and we are both old, we will sit on your porch and laugh about the golden days that almost killed us. But not so your mother. If she continues on this path, it will eat her up from the inside. She will find that certain pains are endless.

So, forgive her. It is the only way to lighten this ache in your heart. Forgive her and love her and go on.

I love you, Eric Sloan. You and your brother are the sons I never had, and had I given birth to you, I would have been proud of who you've become.

XXOO

Nora

Ruby folded the letter back into a small triangle that fit in his wallet. "That's a beautiful letter. I can see why you carry it around."

"It saved me. Literally. It took some work—lots of work—but I forgave my mom, and when I did that, my chest stopped hurting all the time."

"I don't know how you could forgive her. What she did—"

"Was human, that's all."

"What about now?"

He sighed, pushed a hand through his hair. "It's harder now. I realize how precious time is. I want just one moment with her to tell her I love her. To hear—" His voice broke, dropped to a whisper. "To hear her say she loves me."

Ruby turned to him, touched his face.

He smiled, pressed his hand on top of hers. "Forgive your mother, Ruby."

"I'm afraid," she said, using the words she rarely allowed herself to speak aloud.

He let go of her arm. "*Christ.* Time is short, don't you understand that? We bump along, blindly assuming we have forever to do things, say things . . . but we don't. You can feel perfectly fine, and go to your annual checkup on a sunny Wednesday afternoon, and discover that your time's up. Game over."

She looked down at him. "How do you forgive someone?"

He smiled tenderly. "You just . . . let go. Unclench."

"If I let go . . . I'm afraid I'll fall."

"There's nothing wrong with falling." He kissed the

tips of his own fingers, then pressed the kiss to her cheek. "I love you, Ruby. Don't forget that."

"Never," she whispered. "Never."

When Ruby finally got home, it was past midnight. She crept past her mother's closed bedroom door and went upstairs. Crawling into bed, she reached for her pad of paper and began to write.

One of my best friends from childhood is dying. I stood at his bedside today and talked to him as if life were normal, and yet all the while, I couldn't breathe.

Until a few hours ago, I had not seen him in more than a decade, and in all that time, I had barely thought of him.

Barely remembered him.

This boy, now a man, who had walked hand in hand with me through childhood, I had forgotten. I kept the Saint Christopher's medal he gave me for my thirteenth birthday, but the boy, I lost.

Maybe he never noticed or cared. We did, after all, go on with our separate lives as childhood friends tend to do, but now I see the sadness in that ordinary course of things. I walked away too easily; I didn't think enough about what—and who—I left behind. Now, I can't think about anything else.

I left a boy with black hair and a booming, heartfelt laugh, and I returned to a man so thin I was afraid to touch him for fear that I would see my own bones through his papery flesh.

And this dying man welcomed me home as if I'd

never left. Did he know, I wonder, how much it hurt me to look in his watery eyes and see the reflection of my own emptiness? My own lack.

I want to gather the broken pieces of my heart together, pull them into my lap, and study them. Maybe then I could find the hole, the missing piece, that allows me to forget those I love.

I am tired of my solitary life, weary to the bone. I have been running for years, so fast and hard, I am breathless. And here, at the end of it, I see that I've gone nowhere at all.

I want my mother. Isn't that amazing? I would— if I could—go to her now, walk into the circle of her arms and say, "Eric is dying and I can't imagine living in a world without him."

How would that feel? I wonder. Letting her comfort and soothe me? When I close my eyes, I can imagine it, but when I waken, all I see are the doors closed between us. And the ache that is spreading through my chest hurts more and more.

I recognize what it is now, this pain that has been a part of me for so many years.

It is longing, pure and simple. I miss my mom.

Chapter Eighteen

The next morning was one of those perfect June days that convinced out-of-towners to buy land in the San Juan Islands.

Ruby woke late, which wasn't surprising, given that she'd tossed and turned all night.

She knew, of course, that she and Nora would have to talk about her father's confession. Hopefully, they could put it off for a while—like, until Britney Spears's boobs started to sag.

She pushed the covers back and stumbled out of bed. A shower made her feel almost human, and she stayed in it until the water turned lukewarm. Even then, she was reluctant to get out. At least in the shower, she had a purpose.

She stepped out of the shower and stood, dripping, on the fuzzy pink patch of carpet. The old pipes pinged and clanged as water gurgled down the drain.

Through the mist, she saw herself in the mirror. She swiped the moisture away and stared at a blurry reflection of her face.

She experienced one of those rare moments when, for a split second, you see yourself through a stranger's eyes. Her hair was too short, and raggedly cut, as if that stupid, gum-chewing, purple-haired girl at the beauty school had used pinking shears instead of scissors. What in God's name had made Ruby choose to dye it Elvira Mistress-of-the-Night black?

It made her skin look vampire-pale in comparison.

No wonder she'd been unable to attract a decent guy. Laura Palmer looked better in *Twin Peaks*—and she'd washed up dead on the shore.

Ruby realized she'd been *trying* to make herself unattractive. The truth of that realization was so stunning she literally watched her mouth drop open.

All that mascara, the black eyeliner, the haircut and color . . . all of it was a camouflage.

She dropped her makeup bag in the metal trash can. It hit with a satisfying clang. No more heroin-chic makeup or refugee clothing. Hell, she'd even quit dying her hair and find out what color it really was. Her last memory was of a nice, ordinary chestnut brown.

The decision made her feel better. She went into her bedroom, dressed in jeans and a jade-green V-neck T-shirt, and then hurried downstairs.

Nora was standing by the counter, leaning on her crutches. The *plop-drip-plop* of the coffeemaker filled the kitchen with steady sound. She looked up as Ruby entered the room.

An almost comical look of surprise crossed her face. "You look . . . beautiful." Immediately, she flushed. "I'm sorry. I shouldn't have sounded surprised."

"It's okay. I guess I didn't look so great with all that makeup on."

"I'm not touching *that* one with a ten-foot pole."

Ruby laughed, and it felt good. "I need a haircut. Badly. Is there still a beauty salon in Friday Harbor?"

"I used to cut your hair."

Ruby hadn't remembered until that moment, but suddenly it came rushing back: Sunday evenings in the kitchen, a dishrag pinned around her neck with a clothespin, the soothing *clip-clip-clip* of the scissors, Dad's steady turning of the newspaper pages in the living room. Ruby stood there a moment, strangely uncertain of what to do. She had a nagging sense that if she said the right thing now—in this heartbeat of time which felt steeped in sudden possibility—she could change things. She felt vulnerable suddenly, a child wearing her emotions like a kindergarten name tag. "Could you cut it again?"

"Of course. Get the towel, and a clothespin. The scissors should be here . . ." Nora reached for her crutches and limped toward the utility drawer, where the scissors had always been kept.

Ruby was momentarily nonplussed, though she wasn't sure why.

It seemed as if Nora were as eager as Ruby to avoid a breakfast conversation.

"Get the stool from the laundry room and take it outside. It's such a pretty morning."

Ruby gathered up the necessary supplies and carried everything outside. She set the stool on a nice flat patch of grass overlooking the bay and sat down on it. She heard Nora coming toward her. *Thump-step-*

thump-step. Down the porch steps and across the grass, her mother moved awkwardly, a woman clearly afraid of stepping into a hole and twisting her good ankle.

"Are you sure about this?" Ruby asked, watching her. "I'm suddenly hearing you say *oops!* behind me, and I wind up with one of those horrible asymmetrical cuts from when I was in grade school."

Nora moved around behind Ruby. "Remember your sophomore year? You didn't use hairspray—you used boat lacquer. I was scared to death I'd accidentally pat your head and shatter my wrist." Laughing, she wrapped the towel around Ruby's neck and pinned it in place, then began running her fingers through Ruby's still-damp hair.

Ruby released her breath in a sigh. It wasn't until she heard the sound—air hissing through her teeth—that she realized what she was feeling.

Longing, again.

"I'm just going to give it some shape, okay?"

Ruby blinked, came stumbling out of the past. "Yeah," she said. Her voice was barely audible. She cleared her throat and said again, louder, "Okay."

"Sit up straight. Quit fidgeting."

The steady *snip-snip-snip* of the scissors seemed to hypnotize Ruby, that and the comforting familiarity of her mother's touch.

Nora touched Ruby's chin, tenderly forcing her to look straight ahead. *Snip-snip-snip*. "Eric called me last night. He said you'd visited him."

Ruby closed her eyes. "I'm not ready to talk about Eric," she said quietly.

"Okay. Why don't you tell me about your life in Hollywood?"

Ruby's first thought was: *the article.* "There's not much to say. It's like living on the third floor of hell. I don't want to talk about that, either."

Nora paused; the scissors stilled. "I don't mean to pry. I just wonder who you have become."

"Oh." It wasn't something she thought much about—who she was. She usually concerned herself with who she wanted to be. Better to look ahead than behind, and all that. "I don't know."

"I remember when Doc Morane first put you in my arms." Nora paused in her cutting. "From the very beginning, you were fire and ice. You'd scream for what you wanted, but a hurt animal could reduce you to tears. You were walking by eight months and talking by two. And boy, did you have a lot to say. It was like living with a Chatty Cathy doll who could pull her own string. You never shut up."

Ruby realized suddenly that she *missed* herself, missed who she used to be. In forgetting her mother, she'd misplaced herself. "What was I like?"

"You wanted a tattoo at twelve—the infinity symbol, I believe. You never pierced your ears, because everyone else *did.* You wanted to go to an ashram the summer you turned thirteen. You were afraid of the dark for a long, long time, and whenever there was a windstorm, I rolled closer to your dad in bed, because I knew you'd come bolting into our room and crawl into bed with us." Nora turned to her, gently pushing the wet hair out of Ruby's eyes. "Is every part of that girl gone?"

Ruby felt shaky suddenly, uncertain. "I never got my ears pierced."

"Thank you."

"For what?"

"It would break my heart to think that you had changed so much." She reached out, touched Ruby's cheek in a fleeting, tender caress. "You could always light up a room like no one I've ever known. Remember that day we went to the island newspaper to get them to cover the eighth-grade dance?" She smiled. "I sat there, watching you make your argument, and thought, She could run the country, this girl of mine. I was so damned proud of you."

Ruby swallowed hard.

Nora went back to cutting Ruby's hair. A few minutes later, she said, "Ah, there we are. All done." She stepped aside and handed Ruby a mirror.

Ruby looked at her reflection, captured as it was in the silvered oval. She looked young again. A woman with most of her life ahead of her, instead of a bitter, struggling comic who'd left her youth sitting on barstools. "It looks great," she said, turning to her mother.

Their eyes met, locked. Understanding passed between them, quick as an electric shock.

"I went to see Dad yesterday."

"I know. He came to see me."

Ruby should have guessed. "We have to talk about it."

Nora sighed. It was a sound like the slow leaking of air from a punctured tire. "Yes." She bent down and retrieved her crutches. "I don't know about you, but I'll need a cup of coffee for this . . . and a chair. I'll *definitely* need to sit down." Without waiting, she hobbled toward the porch.

Ruby put the stool away, then grabbed two cups of coffee and went out onto the porch. Nora was seated on the loveseat; Ruby chose the rocker.

Nora took a cup of coffee from her. "Thanks."

"Dad told me he'd been unfaithful to you," Ruby said it in a rush.

"What else?"

"Does anything else matter?"

Nora frowned. "Of course other things matter."

Ruby didn't know what to say to that. "He sort of blamed it on Vietnam . . . well . . . maybe not. I wasn't sure what he blamed it on. He said the war changed him, but I got the feeling he thought he would have fooled around anyway."

Nora leaned back in her chair. "I loved your dad from the moment I first saw him, but we were young, and we got married for childish reasons. I wanted a family and a place where I could feel safe. He wanted . . ." She smiled. "I'm still not sure what he wanted. A woman to come home to, maybe. A woman who thought he was perfect. For a while we were an ideal couple. We both thought he was God."

"It was easy to see him that way. He acted so . . . loving and nice."

"Don't judge him too harshly, Ruby. His infidelity was only part of what broke us up. It was just as much my fault."

"Did you screw other men, too?"

"No, but I loved him too much, and that can be as bad as not loving someone enough. I needed so much reassurance and love, I sucked him dry. No man can fill up all the dark places in a woman's soul. I knew he'd be unfaithful sooner or later. I think I made him crazy with my questions and my suspicions."

Ruby didn't understand. "You *knew* he'd be unfaithful? How?"

"You said you lived with a man. Max was his name, right?"

Ruby nodded. "Yeah. But what—"

"Was he faithful?"

"No. Well . . . for a while, maybe."

"Did you expect him to be?"

"Of course." Ruby said it quickly. Too quickly. Then she sighed and sat back. "No. I didn't expect him to want only me."

"Of course not. If a girl's mother doesn't love her enough to stick around, why should a man?" Nora gazed at her; the smile she gave Ruby was sad. "That's the gift my father gave me, the one I passed on to you."

"Jesus," Ruby said softly. Her mother was right. Ruby had spent a lifetime being so afraid of heartbreak that she hadn't let herself be loved. That's why she'd stayed with Max all those years. She knew she'd never fall in love with him, and her heart would be safe. All that loneliness . . . because she couldn't believe in being loved.

Ruby walked toward the railing and stared out at the Sound. She couldn't figure out what she was feeling . . . or what she should be feeling. "I remembered the day you came back." She heard her mother's sharp intake of breath and waited for an answer. When none came, she turned around.

Nora was sitting there, hunched over, as if waiting for a blow. "I don't like thinking about that day."

"I'm sorry . . . Mom," Ruby said quietly. "I said some horrible things to you."

Her mother looked up sharply. Tears filled her eyes. "You called me *Mom*." She stood up, hobbled toward Ruby. "Don't you dare feel guilty over what you said to me. You were a child, and I'd broken your heart."

"Why did you come home that day?"

"I missed you girls so much. But when I saw what I'd done to you, I was ashamed. You looked at me the way I'd once looked at my father. It . . . broke me."

Ruby couldn't avoid the question any longer. "Okay, so I know why you left Dad, but why did you stay away?"

Nora gazed at her steadily. "The leaving . . . the staying away . . . to you, these were the beginning of the story. To me, it was deep into the middle . . ."

Nora took a deep breath and dove in. The waters of the past were as cold as she'd expected, even in the heat of this gorgeous summer morning. "Everyone thought Rand and I were the perfect couple." She curled her hands around the porcelain of her coffee cup and let it warm her. "I was young then, and I cared about appearances more than substance. Living with an alcoholic will do that to you. You grow up hiding, flinching, protecting the very man you should expose. You make sure that none of the ugliness that goes on inside your house ever spills into the streets. That was a lesson my mother taught me before I was old enough to brush my teeth. Pretend and smile . . . and cry behind closed doors. I suspected your dad of having affairs long before I got hard proof." She glanced at Ruby. "No pun intended."

Ruby almost spit up her coffee. "How can you make a joke about it?"

"What is it they say about comedy—it only hurts when you laugh?" She smiled and went on. "It . . . hurt me to suspect him, but that wasn't the worst of it. The worst was his drinking. He started drinking after dinner—on the nights he came home. You girls probably didn't even notice. A few beers, a scotch and soda here and there. By ten o'clock he was wobbly, and by eleven he was stumbling drunk. And he got . . . mean. All his insecurities—you remember how hard Grandpa was on him—and his disappointments came tumbling out, and everything was my fault. Every time he yelled at me, I heard my dad's voice, and though Rand never hit me, I started expecting it, flinching away from him, and that only made him madder. How could I think he'd *hit* me, he'd scream, stomping out of the house." She looked up at Ruby. "So, you see, I was at least half of the problem. I couldn't separate my past from my present, and the harder I tried, the more the two braided together. I was terrified I'd become like my mother—a woman who never spoke more than two words at a time and died too young. But I was handling everything okay until Emmaline Fergusson told me about Shirley Comstock—"

"My soccer coach?"

Nora nodded. "You remember how much your dad suddenly started liking soccer?"

Ruby gasped. "He didn't . . . not with my coach."

"It's a small island," Nora said ruefully, "there

weren't a lot of women to choose from. I told myself it didn't matter. I was his *wife*, and there was honor in that. But he started drinking more and coming home less, and I fell apart.

"It started with insomnia. I simply stopped sleeping. Then the panic attacks hit. I got a prescription for Valium, but it didn't help enough. I would lie awake at night with my heart pounding and sweat pouring off me. Every time I picked you up from soccer, I went home and threw up. Finally, I started to black out. I'd wake up lying on the kitchen floor, and I couldn't remember huge chunks of my day."

"Jesus," Ruby said softly. "Did you tell Dad?"

Nora gave a shaky smile. "Of course not. I thought I was losing my mind. All I had to hold on to was the pretense of a marriage. You and Caro were the center of a world that kept shrinking around me."

Nora looked up, wondering if it was possible to make a single twenty-seven-year-old woman understand how stifling marriage and motherhood could sometimes be. "I couldn't handle it all—your dad's drinking, his screwing around, my insomnia, my sense of being overwhelmed and trapped. It was a combustible mix. And then . . ."

Nora closed her eyes. The day she'd worked so hard to keep at bay welled up inside her. It had been a gorgeous early summer day, not unlike today. She'd gone to the soccer field early to drop off cookies . . . and she'd seen them. Rand and Shirley, kissing, right out in the open as if they had every right. "I took too many sleeping pills. I don't remember if I meant to or if it was an accident, but when I woke up in the hospital, I knew that if I didn't do something quickly, I was going to die. I don't know if you can understand that kind of depression; its debilitating, overwhelming. So, I held my breath, packed my bag, and ran. I only meant to stay away for a few days, maybe a week. I thought I'd come here, stay a few days, get some rest, and be healthy."

"And?"

Nora drew in a deep breath. She wanted to look up, but she couldn't. Instead, she stared down at the cup in her hands. "And I met Vince Corell."

"The guy who sold the pictures to the *Tattler*."

"He was a photographer, taking pictures of the islands for a calendar. Or so he said; I didn't care about that. All that mattered was the way he looked at me. He told me I was the most beautiful woman in the world. By then, your father and I hadn't been intimate in a long time, and I *wasn't* beautiful. I was rail-thin and I trembled all the time. When Vince touched me . . . I let him. We had a wonderful week together— photographs and all. For the first time, I found someone I could talk to about my dreams—and once I'd said them aloud, I couldn't go back to the way I'd been living. And then . . . he was gone.

"I was devastated. I knew your father would have heard about what I'd done; Vince and I made no secret of our relationship. Maybe I even *wanted* Rand to find out. I don't know, but when the affair was over, and I realized I'd thrown my marriage away and lost my girls, I took too many sleeping pills again. This time it was serious. I ended up in a mental institution in Everett."

"How long were you there?" Ruby's voice was whisper soft.

"Three months."

"*What?*"

"Time wasn't real there. In those days, in that place, they were still doing electric shock therapy. We all lined up at eight forty-five in the morning for medications. After a week, I'd forgotten most of the outside world. It was Dr. Allbright who saved me. He came every day and talked to me . . . just talked until I could breathe again. I worked so hard to get better, so I could come home. But when I did . . ."

"Oh, God," Ruby said softly. "That was the day."

Nora felt tears sting her eyes and it surprised her. She thought she'd spent all her tears for that day long ago. "It's not your fault," she said, and she meant it.

"But Dad should have let you come home. After what he'd done to you—"

"I didn't ask Rand to take me back," Nora answered. "I was too screwed up to take care of my children, and I knew it. I didn't want my marriage back. I wanted . . . me. It's a horrible thing to say, a horrible thing to have done. But it's the only truth I can give you." She longed to reach out, to take her daughter into her arms, but she was afraid. They were moving toward each other now, stepping over the hurts that had accumulated like boulders on the road between them. "The world is full of regrets and times where you think *if only*. We have to move past that. Your dad was angry and arrogant. I was frightened and fragile. You were heartbroken. And on that one day, we came together, and we hurt each other. Mistakes," she said.

"Just ordinary human mistakes. But I want you to know this, Ruby, and it's the only part that matters. I never stopped loving you or thinking about you. I never stopped missing you."

Ruby stared at her a long time. Then, softly, she said, "I believe you."

And Nora knew the healing had finally begun.

Chapter Nineteen

Ruby retreated to her bedroom.

I'd wake up, lying on the kitchen floor, with huge chunks of my day gone. I don't know if you can understand that kind of depression.

Mom must have been so afraid, so alone . . .

Ruby knew how it felt. It was the worst, she knew, in the middle of a long, dark night, when the man you lived with was in bed beside you. If he smelled of another woman's perfume, that hand-span between you could feel like the North Atlantic.

She opened the nightstand drawer and pulled out her legal pad. She'd learned that it calmed her to write down her thoughts, and God knew she needed to relax.

She sat down on the bed and drew her knees up, angling the pad against her thighs, and began to write.

I'd always believed that the truth of a person was easily spotted, a line drawn in dark ink on white paper. Now, I wonder. Maybe the truth of who we are lies hidden in all those shades of gray that everyone talks about.

My mother was in a mental institution. This is her newest revelation. One of them, anyway; in truth, there have been too many to count.

Tonight, Mom painted a portrait of our family, and through her eyes I saw people I'd never imagined—a drunken, unfaithful husband and a depressed, overwhelmingly unhappy wife.

How is it that I saw none of this? Are children so sublimely oblivious to their own world?

She was right to hide this truth from me. Even now, I wish I didn't know it.

Sometimes, knowing where we come from hurts more than we can stand.

The phone rang.

Ruby was startled by the sound. Tossing the pad aside, she leaned over and answered. "Hello?"

"Ruby?"

It was Caroline's voice, soft and thready. Ruby immediately felt the hairs on the back of her neck stand up. "What's wrong?"

"Wrong? Nothing. Can't a girl just call her little sister?"

Ruby leaned back against the headboard. Caro sounded better now; still, that feeling of wrongness lingered. "Of course. You just sounded . . ."

"What?"

"I don't know. Tired."

Caro laughed. "I have two small children and a cat

that pukes up ten thousand hairballs a day. I'm *always* tired."

"Is it really like that, Caro? Does motherhood suck something out of you?"

Caroline was quiet for a minute. "I used to dream of going to Paris. Now I just want privacy when I use the toilet."

"Jesus, Caro. How come we never talk about things like that?"

"There's nothing to say."

Ruby tried to sculpt an amorphous realization into words. "That's not true. When we talk on the phone, it's always about me. My career. My worthless excuse for a boyfriend. My thoughts on comedy. It's always about me."

"I like to live vicariously."

Ruby knew that was a lie. The truth was, Ruby had always been selfish. She didn't form relationships; she collected photographs of people and then cropped away the edges of anything that didn't fit with what she wanted to see. But those edges mattered. "Are you happy, Caro?"

"Happy? Of course I'm—" Caro started to cry.

The soft, heartbreaking sound tore at Ruby's heart. "Caro?"

"Sorry. Bad day in suburbia."

"Just one?"

"I can't talk about this now."

"What's wrong with our family that we can't talk about anything that matters?"

"Talking doesn't change things. Believe me. It's better to just go on."

"I used to think that, but I'm learning so much up here—"

"Ruby!" It was Mom's voice. She must be standing at the bottom of the stairs, yelling up.

Ruby held the phone to her chest. "I'll be right down. Hey, Caro," she said, coming back to the line. "Why don't you come up here? Spend the night."

"Oh, I can't. The kids—"

"Leave them with the stud muffin. It's not like you're stapled to the house."

Caroline's laughter was sharp. "Actually, that's exactly what it's like."

"She's not who we thought, Caro," she said softly, realizing that she'd said the words before, but without truly knowing their power. "She's the . . . gatekeeper of our memories. Who we are. You should come."

Caroline paused, drew in a breath. "I'm afraid."

Ruby understood. She wouldn't have a week ago, but now she did. "You won't break." She halted, thinking. It was important that she phrase it well, that she pass on something of what she'd learned about this family of theirs. "You think you have to hold it all in, and if you let any of it go, you'll shatter into tiny pieces and you won't know who you are. But it doesn't work that way. It's more like . . . opening your eyes in a room you'd expected to be dark. You can *see* things, and it makes you feel stronger." She laughed. "God, I sound like Obi-Wan on heroin."

"Jeez, Rube," Caroline said, sniffling a little. "My baby sister has finally grown up."

"And only a moment before menopause. But then, I've always been gifted. Top of my class, don't forget."

"There were ten people in your class."

"And three of them flunked out. Come on, Caro, come up and visit us. Run on the beach with me like we used to . . . slam tequila and dance with me. Let's see—finally—who we are."

"RUBY! Can you hear me?"

It was Mom's voice again. This time she was yelling at the top of her lungs.

Ruby accepted defeat. "I gotta go. I love you, big sis."

"You sound like the big sister now," Caroline answered, "and I'm proud of you, Rube. And jealous. God . . . Bye."

Ruby hung up, then hurried downstairs. "Good God, is there a fire in the—"

She skidded to a stop in the kitchen.

Dean was standing there, holding a bouquet of Shasta daisies wrapped in tinfoil.

"Oh," Ruby said, feeling heat climb into her face.

Mom stood beside the table, grinning. "You have a visitor," she said in a perfect sorority-housemother voice.

Ruby took stock of herself: She hadn't brushed her teeth yet and she was still in her pajamas—an old Megadeath T-shirt and fuzzy pink kneesocks. If she were lucky—and she couldn't be—the oak floorboards would simply open up and swallow her.

Dean stepped forward and handed her the flowers. "Do you still like daisies?"

She nodded.

He closed the gap between them. "We need to

talk." His voice dropped; its quiet timbre matched the soft pleading in his eyes. "Please."

The way he said it made her shiver. "Okay."

They stood there, staring at each other. Finally, Mom thumped toward them and gently tugged the flowers out of Ruby's hand.

"I'll put them in water," she said.

Ruby turned to her. It felt as if she'd just stumbled into a weird Bradys-gone-wild episode. Then she realized that moms were *supposed* to say things like that.

"Thanks, Mom." Ruby turned to Dean. "So, where are we going?"

He grinned. "Just wear a bathing suit under your clothes. Oh . . . and tennis shoes. I'll meet you outside." He gave her another quick smile, then kissed her mother on the cheek and headed outside.

Ruby could hear his footsteps crunching through the gravel behind the house. She looked at her mother. "Did you organize this?"

"Of course not."

"This is not a good idea."

"Ruby Elizabeth Bridge, you don't have the sense God gave a banana slug. Now get upstairs and get dressed. If you're too damned scared to go out with your first love, then try remembering that he used to be your best friend, too."

She couldn't think of anything brilliant to say, so she left the room. Upstairs, she stood in front of her opened suitcase, staring down at the clothing she'd brought.

A bathing suit. Yeah, right.

Had she noticed when she packed that everything

was black? Or did she always dress this way? Every T-shirt said something—MEGADEATH, UCLA BRUINS, PLANET HOLLYWOOD. Her personal favorite was a white T-shirt with a cartoon drawing of a plumber bent over a broken toilet. His low-slung pants revealed a huge part of his ass. The punch line was: *Say no to crack*.

Hardly the right choice for a visit with your first love . . .

Finally, at the very bottom of the suitcase, she found a plain, peach-colored tank top and a pair of frayed cutoffs.

She didn't bother with socks, just brushed her teeth, slicked her hair back (thank God Mom had cut it), grabbed her sunglasses, and raced back downstairs.

Her mother was sitting at the kitchen table, doing a crossword puzzle and sipping tea as if this were an ordinary morning. "Have a nice time," she said, not looking up.

"Bye." Ruby went outside. The first thing she noticed was the sweet scent of the roses and the salty tang of the sea. Baking kelp and hot rocks gave the air a faintly scorched, metallic smell.

She headed down the porch and skipped around to the side of the house.

There stood Dean, just outside the picket fence, with a bicycle on either side of him.

She stopped. "You've obviously confused me with a woman who likes to sweat."

He handed her a bike helmet. It was pink and had a Barbie decal on the forehead. She crossed her arms. "That is definitely not gonna happen."

He smiled. "Too old to ride a bike, Rube? Or too out of shape?"

Damn him. He *knew* she couldn't refuse a challenge. She grabbed the handlebars and yanked the bike around. "I haven't ridden a bike since . . ." She stumbled over the memories. "In a long time."

His smile faded. He was remembering it, too, the day she'd asked him out for a bike ride . . . and broken his heart.

She stared at him for a minute more, trying to read his mind. It was closed to her. "Okay," she said at last. "Lead on."

He jumped on his bike and pedaled on ahead of her. She wanted to watch him, maybe ride alongside, but frankly, she was terrified that she was going to do a face-plant on the gravel driveway and end up as a medical episode on the Discovery channel.

He turned at the end of the driveway and headed uphill.

Ruby tried to keep up. By the top of the street, her pores had turned into geysers. Her vision was blurred by sweat; she could have been pedaling underwater for all she could see.

And it was hot.

Really, really hot.

She would have complained—was, in fact, *dying* to complain—but there wasn't enough breath in her lungs to form the word *stop*, let alone, *you asshole*.

Just when she felt her heart start to stutter, they turned a corner.

Levinger Hill.

They were flying now, racing side by side down the

long, two-lane road. Golden pastures studded with apple trees rushed past them.

Dean leaned back, held his arms out . . .

And Ruby sailed into the past. They were fourteen again, that summer they learned to ride without using their hands, when every scraped knee was a badge of courage . . . when they'd whooshed down this very hill, arms outflung, together, the radio strapped to the handlebars blaring out Starship's "Nothing's Gonna Stop Us Now."

The hill slowed down into a long, even S curve, then wound into the entrance of Trout Lake State Park.

Ruby should have known he'd bring her here. "No fair, Dino," she said softly, wondering if he even heard her.

He heard. "What's that they say about love and war?"

"Which one is this?"

"That's up to you. Come on, race you to the park." Without waiting for an answer, he pedaled away from her, down the long, winding, tree-lined street.

It was dark on this road, even on this hot summer morning. Shadows fell across the thin layer of pavement in serrated strips. The air was cold.

She sped up to Dean, then pulled ahead. She heard him laughing quietly behind her, and she knew they were both thinking of the girl she'd been—the one who couldn't stand to lose at anything, even a popcorn dare like "race you to the park."

The road curled around a huge Douglas fir tree and spilled out into the sunshine. Ruby jumped off her bike and set it against the wooden bike rack. There was no need to lock it.

She heard Dean's bike land against the rack with a clatter, but she was already walking toward the lake. She had forgotten how beautiful it was here. The heart-shaped sapphire-blue lake was surrounded by lush green trees and rimmed in granite. A ribbon of water cascaded over the "giant's lip"—a flat, jutting rock at the top of the cliffs—and splashed onto the placid surface of the lake.

There were children everywhere, locals and tourists, playing on the grass, shrieking, swimming along the shore.

Dean came up beside her. "Are you up for a climb?"

She laughed. "I'm an *adult* now. Waterfall Trail is for mountain goats and kids who are desperate to smoke pot or get laid."

"*I* can make it," he said, letting the challenge in his words hang there.

She sighed. "Lead on."

Side by side, not talking, they walked around to the western side of the lake, wound through the horde of picnickers, Frisbee-catching dogs, and screaming children. When they reached the heavy fringe of trees, they left the people behind. Gradually, the sound of human voices faded away. The gurgling, splashing sound of falling water grew louder and louder.

Once again, Ruby was sweating.

The trail was rocky and narrow. It corkscrewed straight up through the trees, salal, and blackberries (which scratched her exposed arms and legs, thank you very much).

Finally, they reached the top. The giant's lip.

It was a slab of gray granite as big as a swimming pool and as flat as a quarter. A thick green moss furred the stone; dainty yellow wildflowers grew impossibly from the moss. A stream of water no wider than the length of a man's arm flowed across the rock in a groove worn long ago, then spilled over the edge and fell twenty feet to the lake below.

Ruby stepped into the clearing and saw the picnic basket. It was sitting on a familiar red-and-black plaid blanket.

Dean touched her shoulder. "Come on." He led her to the blanket, which he'd carefully spread out on a spot where the moss was several inches thick.

They sat down. He reached into the basket, pulled out a thermos, and poured two glasses of lemonade.

Ruby drank hers greedily. When she was finished, she set the glass aside and leaned back on her elbows. The hot sun beat down on her cheeks. "We used to come up here all the time."

"This is where you first told me you were going to be a comedian."

"Really?" She smiled. "I don't remember that."

"You said you wanted to be famous."

"I still do. And you wanted to be a prize-winning photographer." She didn't look at him. It was better to stay separate and talk about the past, as if they were just two old high-school friends who'd bumped into each other. "That's a long way from junior executive."

"Yeah . . . but I still wish for it. If I could, I'd throw everything away and start over. Money sure as hell doesn't make you happy."

It bothered her to think of him as unhappy. "Spoken like a man whose family business is on the Fortune Five Hundred."

He laughed softly. "Yeah, I guess."

A quiet settled in between them, and she was vaguely afraid of what he would say, so she said, "I saw Eric yesterday."

"He told me. It really meant a lot to him."

Ruby wishboned her arms behind her head. A single, gauzy cloud drifted above the trees. "I wish I'd stayed in better touch with him."

"*You?*" Dean laughed bitterly. "I'm his brother and I hadn't seen him in years."

That surprised Ruby. She rolled onto her side and faced Dean, but he didn't look at her. "You guys were always so close."

"Things change, don't they?"

"What happened?"

He stared up at the sky. "I seem to have a problem with really knowing the people I love. I get blindsided."

"You're talking about his being gay?"

Finally, he looked at her. "That's part of what I'm talking about."

She understood, and knew that it was time. For more than ten years, she'd sworn to herself that if she ever got the chance with Dean, she would say the thing that mattered. "I'm sorry, Dean," she said. "I didn't want to hurt you."

He rolled onto his side, facing her. "You didn't want to hurt me? Jesus, Ruby, you were my whole world."

"I knew that. I just . . . couldn't be someone's world then."

"I tried to take care of you after your mom left, but it was hard. You were constantly picking a fight with me. But I kept telling myself it would be okay, that you'd get past it and come back to me. And I kept loving you."

Ruby didn't know how to explain it to him. How could she? She'd only barely begun to understand it herself. "You believed in something I didn't. Every time I closed my eyes at night, I dreamed about you leaving me. In my nightmares, I heard your voice, but I could never find you. I couldn't stand waiting for you to stop loving me. To leave me."

"What made you so damned sure I would leave you?"

"Come on, Dean . . . we were kids, but we weren't stupid. I knew you'd go off to some college I couldn't afford and forget about me."

Their faces were close together, and if she'd let herself, she could have lost her way in the blue sea of his eyes. "So, you dumped me before I had a chance to dump you."

She smiled sadly. "Pretty much. Now, let's change the subject. This is old news, and we both know it doesn't matter anymore. Tell me about your life. How is it to be a jet-setting superbachelor?"

"What if I said I still love you?"

Ruby gasped. "Don't say that . . . please—"

He took her face in his hands, gently forced her to look up at him. "Did you stop loving me, Ruby?"

She felt the soft exhalation of his breath against her lips. A second later, she heard his question. She wanted to say *Of course; we were just kids,* but when she opened her mouth to answer, the only sound she made was a quiet sigh that tasted of surrender.

His lips brushed against her, and it was a sensation at once familiar and new. She melted against him, moaning his name as his hand curled around the back of her neck.

It was the kind of kiss they'd never shared before. The kind of achingly lonely kiss a pair of teenagers couldn't imagine, the kiss of two adults who'd been alone for too long and knew that God had given them this moment, and that it was a gift too precious to ignore. And for a few brief, heart-stopping seconds, their past faded like a photograph left in the hot sun.

When he drew back, she opened her eyes and saw the missing years drawn in lines on his face. Sun . . . time . . . heartache . . . they had all left imprints on his skin.

"I've waited a long time for a second chance with you, Ruby."

If he said he loved her, she would believe him, and she would love him back. She closed her eyes, battling a wave of helplessness. She wished desperately to have grown up, to have been profoundly changed by all that she'd seen and learned in the past days. But it wasn't that easy.

Her fear of abandonment was so deep it had calcified in her bones. She couldn't get past it. She'd discovered a long time ago why the poets called it *falling* in love. It was a plunging, eye-watering descent, and she'd lost her ability to believe that anyone would catch her.

She pushed him away. "I can't do this. It's too

much . . . too fast. You've always wanted too much from me."

"Damn it, Ruby," he said, and she heard the disappointment in his voice. "Have you grown up at all?"

"I won't hurt you again," she said.

He touched her face. "Ah, Rube . . . just looking at you hurts me."

She had never felt so alone. When he'd kissed her, she'd glimpsed a world she'd never imagined. A world where passion was part of love, but not the biggest part. Where a kiss from the right man, at the right time, could make a grown woman weep. "I can't give you what you want. It's not in me."

He brushed the hair away from her eyes, let his fingertips linger at her temple. "You ran me off when I was a boy. I'm not seventeen anymore, and we both know, this thing between us isn't over. I don't think it ever was."

Chapter Twenty

Dean followed Ruby back down the trail. Though they didn't talk, the forest was alive with sounds. Birds squawked and chirped in the trees overhead, squirrels chattered, water splashed.

At the park, he tossed the picnic basket—still filled with a lunch unpacked and uneaten—in the trash can. Curling the heavy blanket around his shoulders, he climbed tiredly onto his bike.

When they reached the summer house, he pulled off to the side of the road and got off his bike.

Ruby stopped a few feet ahead, then set her kickstand and turned to him, frowning. "I guess this is where I say good-bye."

He heard the crack in her voice and it gave him hope. Ruby could push him away from now until forever, and he would still know the truth. He could see it in her eyes, hear it in her tremulous voice. He'd felt it in her kiss. "For now."

"It was just a kiss," she said. "Don't turn it into *Gone with the Wind.*"

He took a step toward her. "You must have confused me with one of your Hollywood idiot-boys."

She wanted to move backward; he could tell. "Wh-what do you mean?"

Now he was close enough to touch her, to kiss her, but he stood perfectly still. "I know you, Ruby. You can pretend all you want, but that kiss meant something. Tonight we'll both lie in bed and think about it."

Ruby flushed. "You knew a teenager a decade ago. That doesn't mean you know *me*."

He smiled. It was so precisely the sort of thing she would have said at sixteen. "You might have built a wall around your heart, but you haven't exchanged it. Somewhere, deep inside, you're still the girl I fell in love with." At last he touched her cheek, a fleeting caress.

He wanted to do more, to pull her into his arms, hold her close and whisper, *I love you,* but he knew he couldn't push her that far. Not yet.

"For years after you were gone, I thought I saw you," he said quietly. "Every time I rounded a corner or came up to a stoplight or got off an airplane, I'd think for a split second, *There she is.* I'd run up to the person, tap her shoulder, and find myself smiling awkwardly at a stranger. I still walk on the right side of the sidewalk, because you like the left."

Her mouth trembled. "I'm afraid."

"The girl I knew wasn't afraid of anything—"

"That girl's been gone for years."

"Isn't there some part of her left?"

She stood there a long time, staring up at him, then finally she turned away.

He knew she wasn't going to answer. "Okay," he

said with a sigh. "I'll concede this round." He climbed onto his bike and started to go.

"Wait."

He stumbled off his bike so fast he almost fell. It clattered to the ground as he spun back to face her. The way she was looking at him reminded him of when she was nine years old and she fell out of the oak tree on Finnegans' farm . . . or when she was twelve and broke her arm skateboarding down Front Street.

She took a step closer and looked up at him. He couldn't be certain, but she looked ready to cry. "You sound so sure."

He smiled. "You taught me love, Ruby. Every time you held my hand when I was scared, or came to one of my ball games or left a note in my locker, I learned a little more about it. Maybe when we were kids, I took that for granted, but I'm not a kid anymore. I've spent a lot of years alone and every date I went on only proved again how special we were."

"My parents were special," she said slowly. "You and Eric were special."

"So, your point is, love dies."

"An ugly, painful death."

It saddened him, knowing how her heart, once so open and pure, had been trampled by the very people who should have protected it. "Okay. Love hurts. I can't deny that. But what about loneliness?"

"I'm not lonely."

"Liar."

She stepped away from him. Without a backward look or a wave or anything, she jumped on her bike and rode away.

"Go ahead," he called after her. "Run away. You can only go so far."

Ruby knew her mother would be waiting for her. She'd probably be sitting at the kitchen table, or in the rocker on the porch, pretending to be occupied by some small task. Maybe knitting; she'd always loved to knit.

Ruby stopped pedaling. The bike slowed down, rattling and bumping over the uneven road. When she reached the minivan, she dumped the bike at the side of the gardening shed and headed down to the house. The gate creaked loudly at her touch.

She stepped into the kitchen and found her mother at the stove, stirring something in an old iron pot. She was wearing her old apron—the one that said A WOMAN'S PLACE IS IN THE HOUSE . . . AND THE SENATE.

"Ruby," she said, looking up in surprise. "I didn't expect you back so soon." She glanced at the door, now closed behind Ruby. "Where's Dino?"

Ruby stood there. God help her, she couldn't talk. The kitchen smelled of pot roast, slow-cooking all day with baby carrots and oven-browned potatoes. A cookie sheet sat on the counter. On it, homemade biscuits were rising. And unless Ruby missed her guess, that was vanilla custard Mom was stirring.

She'd made Ruby's all-time favorite dinner.

Just then, Ruby didn't know which hurt more—the effort her mother had made to please her, or the fact that Dean wasn't here to share it. All she knew was that if she didn't get out of this room soon, she was going to burst into tears.

"Dean went home," she said.

A frown darted across her mother's face. She turned off the burner, carefully placed the wooden spoon across the top of the pot, and grabbed her crutches, then limped toward Ruby. *Step-thump-step-thump.* The uneven footsteps matched the beat of Ruby's heart. "What happened?"

"I don't know. I guess we started something we couldn't finish. Or maybe we finished something we'd started a long time ago." She shrugged and looked away.

"This won't be like Max," her mother said.

"I love Dean," Ruby admitted. "But that's not enough. It wouldn't last, anyway."

"Love is nothing without faith."

"I lost that faith a long time ago."

"Of course you did. And you're right to blame your dad and me for it, but that doesn't matter anymore— whose fault it is. What matters is *you*. Can you let yourself jump without a net? Because that's what love is, what faith is. You're looking for a guarantee, and those come with auto parts. Not love."

"Yeah, right. Love put you in a mental institution."

Mom laughed. "I think it makes lunatics of us all."

It felt good to talk to her mother this way. As friends. It was something Ruby had never even imagined.

It was true; love made everybody crazy. All those years Ruby had spent angry with her mother, sending back presents unopened and refusing all contact—it wasn't because she'd felt betrayed.

Those years, those feelings and actions, had been about . . . longing. Simple longing.

She'd *missed* her mother so much that the only way

she'd been able to go on in the world was to pretend she was alone.

I'm not alone anymore.

That one sentence, once thought, formed a road that led Ruby to herself. She didn't say it aloud. Instinctively, she knew that if she spoke, her voice would be a child's, full of awe and bewilderment. And she would cry.

I can't write the article.

"I've got to go upstairs," she said suddenly, seeing the surprise on her mother's face. Ruby didn't care. She ran upstairs and went to the phone, dialing Val's number.

Maudeen answered on the second ring. "Lightner and Associates, may I help you?"

"Hi, Maudeen," Ruby said, sitting on the bed, drawing her knees up. "It's Ruby Bridge. Is the Great Oz in?"

Maudeen laughed. "He and Julian went to a premiere in New York. He'll be back on Monday, and he's calling in for messages."

"Okay. Tell him I won't be delivering my article."

"You mean it's going to be late?"

"I'm not going to turn it in at all."

"Oh, my. You'd better give me your address and phone number again. He'll want to talk to you."

Ruby gave out the information, then hung up. She hadn't even realized that she was reaching for her writing pad, but there it was, sitting on her lap. It was time now to finish what she'd begun. Slowly, she began to write.

I have just called my agent. When he calls back, I will tell him that I can't turn in this article. I never thought about what it meant to write an exposé on my own mother.

Can you believe I was so blind? I took the money that was given to me—my thirty pieces of silver—and I spent it like a teenager would, on a fast car and expensive clothes.

But I didn't think.

I dreamed. I imagined. I saw myself on Letterman and Leno, a witty, charming guest plugging her own skyrocketing career. I never noticed that I'd be standing on my mother's broken back to reach the microphone.

My dreams, as usual, were all about me.

Now, I see the people around me, and I know what the price of my selfish actions will be.

As I write, I am reminded of that passage from the Bible—the one that is read at every wedding: "When I was a child, I spake as a child, I understood as a child, I thought as a child."

Now, I understand as an adult. Maybe for the first time in my life. This article would break my mother's heart, and perhaps even worse, her spirit. That didn't matter to me a week ago; in fact, I wanted to hurt her then.

My only excuse: then I was a child.

I can't do it anymore; not to her and not to me. For the first time, I have drawn back the dark curtain of anger and seen the bright day beyond.

I can be my mother's daughter again.

Even as I write that sentence, I feel its powerful

seduction. I can't fully express to you—strangers— how it feels to be motherless. The ache . . . the longing.

She is the keeper of my past. She knows the secret moments that have formed me, and even with all that I have done to her, I can feel that still she is able to love me.

Will anyone else ever love me so unconditionally? I doubt it.

I can't give that up. Caché *will have to find someone else to betray Nora Bridge. I am going home.*

Ruby felt better now. Her decision was down in print, formed and solid in bright blue letters.

She would not turn in the article.

In Friday Harbor, the marina was a hive of activity; boats coming in and going out, kids racing along the cement docks, nets in hand, boaters bringing groceries down to their moored boats in creaky wooden carts.

This town was the center of the American section of this archipelago. For more than one hundred years, islanders had come to this port for groceries, boat repairs, and companionship. The town was an enchanting mix of old, decrepit buildings and newer ones, built with a reverence for the past in mind. It was a place where pedestrians and bikers were as liable to be in the middle of Main Street as an automobile, and the honk of a car horn was almost never heard. Like all of the islands, San Juan had learned long ago to depend on the tourist trade. The downtown area was an eclectic mix of art galleries, souvenir shops, gift emporiums, and restaurants—with prices that forced the locals to drive off island for their daily needs, and encouraged the Californian tourists to buy two of everything.

Dean walked aimlessly up and down the streets. Today had depressed the hell out of him, and he knew it shouldn't have. Nothing had ever been easy with Ruby. Love would be the most difficult of all.

He came to a camera shop and went inside. On a whim, he bought a kick-ass camera and enough film to record the tearing down of the Berlin Wall. Finally, he heard the ferry's horn, and knew it was time to get down to the dock. He jumped on his bike and raced downhill. He was late, so he followed the last car onto the boat.

On Lopez, he stopped by the grocery store and bought a few things, then pedaled home as fast as he could. By the time he reached the house, the sun was just beginning to set. In the kitchen, Lottie was busy chopping up vegetables for stir-fry. He gave her a quick wave hello and hurried up to Eric's room.

"Hey, bro," Eric said, smiling tiredly, sitting up. "How was your bike ride?"

Dean went to him. "Guess what I bought?" He opened the small blue insulated bag and withdrew a melting Popsicle.

Eric's eyes widened. "A Rainbow Rocket. I didn't think they still made them."

Dean unwrapped the soggy white wrapper and handed his brother the dripping, multicolored Popsicle. He had to help Eric hold it—his hands were weak and unresponsive—but the smile on Eric's face was straight from the old days.

Eric closed his eyes and made groaning sounds of pleasure as he licked the Popsicle. When he finished, he set the gooey stick on the bedside tray and sighed. The bed whirred to a more upright position. "That was great," he said, leaning deeper into the pillows. He slowly turned his head. "I'd forgotten how much I loved those things."

"I remembered," Dean said. "I've been remembering a lot of things lately."

"Like?"

"Remember the fort we made inside that dead log on Mrs. Nutter's land? When she discovered us, she chased us all the way down her driveway with a broom—"

"Screaming that we were rich-kid hooligans."

"She threatened to call our parents—"

"And we told her Mom was in Barbados and the call would cost her a fortune." Eric's laughter faded into a hacking cough, then disappeared altogether.

"There's something else, too," Dean said. He went to his own bedroom, then returned with a comic book.

Eric blinked up at him. "My missing *Batman*. The only issue I ever lost."

Dean smiled. "You didn't lose it. Your little brother was mad at you one day for not sharing your Wacky Wallwalker, and he took your *Batman*. He could never figure out how to give it back."

Smiling, Eric took the comic, thumbed through it. "I always knew you took it. Shithead."

"Do you want me to read it to you?"

Eric set it on his lap. "Ah . . . I guess not. I'm too tired. Just talk to me."

Dean leaned over the bed rail and gazed down at his brother. "I went to see Ruby today."

"And?"

"Let's just say the door hit me in the ass on the way out."

Eric laughed. "That's our Ruby. Never gives an inch. Did you tell her you loved her?"

"I asked her what she would say if I did."

Eric rolled his eyes. "How Cary Grant of you. It's hard to sweep a girl off her feet with a line like that."

"How would you know?"

"Girl. Boy. It's all the same, kiddo. Romance. And frankly, you'd better get a move on. I want to be around for your happily-ever-after."

"I know, I know. You're dying."

"Damn right, I am. So, when is round two?"

Dean sighed. "I don't know. I'll need to stock up on defensive weapons. Maybe something will happen tomorrow, when we all go sailing."

"You *do* love her, though?"

"I don't think I ever stopped loving her. I wanted to, I tried to, but she was always in my dreams, the girl I measured every other woman against. But that doesn't mean she still loves me. Or that, if she did love me, she'd believe in it."

"Don't let her push you away again."

"It's not that easy. I can't do all the work. I *won't* do all the work. If she wants a future, she's gonna have to put out a little effort."

"Well, I hope it works out fast. I wanted to be the best man at your wedding."

"You will be." Dean struggled to keep his voice even. Their eyes met, and in his brother's gaze, he saw the sad truth. They both knew it was dream-spinning, this conversation of theirs. Eric would not be putting on a tuxedo and standing in shiny shoes beside Dean at the altar.

"I'm glad you came home, Dino. I couldn't have done this without you."

Home. The simple, complex word found purchase in his heart. He'd known it would be hard to stand by and watch his brother die, but until this moment, he hadn't realized that it would end. This good-bye, strung out as it was over the briefest of time spans, was all that was left to them, and Dean would have to cling to these memories in the dark days that were sure to follow.

If Ruby did miraculously admit to loving Dean, who would he tell? Who would laugh at him and say, *You must have done something to piss God off if He chose Ruby as your one true love.*

There were so many things left to say between him and Eric, but how—where—did you begin? How could you experience a lifetime in a few short days? And what about the things that floated past them, accidentally unsaid? What if Dean ended up moving through a colorless, Eric-less world in which he couldn't think of anything except what should have been said?

"Don't," Eric said.

Dean blinked, realizing he'd been silent too long.

Tears stung his eyes. He tried to casually wipe them away. "Don't what?"

"You're imagining the world without me."

"I don't know how to get through this."

Eric reached out. His pale, blue-veined hand covered Dean's and pressed firmly. "When I start feeling overwhelmed, I go back in time instead of ahead. I remember how we used to play red rover at Camp Orkila. Or how you used to sit cross-legged in your room, with your eyes closed, trying to levitate your toys when Lottie made you clean your room." He smiled tiredly and closed his eyes, and Dean could see that he was losing his brother to sleep once again. "I remember the first time I saw Charlie. He was making a sandwich at the college lunch hangout. Mostly, I just remember what I've had and not what I'm leaving behind."

Dean's throat was so tight he couldn't answer.

"The best part is you." Eric's voice was barely above a whisper now. His words were starting to sound garbled, as if he were more than half asleep. "Since you're back, I dream again. It's nice . . ."

"Dream," Dean said softly, placing his brother's limp hand on top of the blanket, then stroking his warm forehead. "Dream of who you would have been, and who you were. The bravest, smartest, best brother a kid ever had."

After dinner, Nora went out to the porch and sat in her favorite rocking chair. In this magical hour, poised between day and night, the sky was the soft hue of a girl's ballet slipper.

The screen door squeaked open and banged shut. "I

brought you some tea," Ruby said, stepping into the porchlight's glow. "Constant Comment with cream and sugar, right?"

"Thanks," Nora said. "Join me."

Ruby sat down in the rocker. Leaning back, she crossed her legs at the ankle and rested her feet on the small, frosted glass table beside the loveseat. "I've been thinking."

"There's aspirin in the bathroom cabinet."

"Very funny. It didn't give me a headache. It gave me . . . a heartache."

Nora turned to her.

"I think I was easy to leave."

"Don't say that. You were an innocent victim."

"I'm tired of that answer." Ruby smiled, but it was a sad, curving of the lips that lasted no time at all. "I was a bitch to Dean after you left."

"That's understandable."

"I know. I had every right to be a bitch. I was lost and in pain. But was he supposed to love me when I wasn't lovable, when I wouldn't let him get close? I expected love from him when I gave none, and then I fucked another guy just to see if Dean would love me no matter what. Big surprise: He didn't." She leaned forward again, rested her forearms on her thighs, and studied Nora. "And I was worse to you. All those years, you sent letters and gifts and left phone messages. I knew you cared about me. I knew you were sorry, and I was *proud* of hurting you. I thought it was the least you deserved. So, don't disagree with me when I say that I have been the architect of some of my own pain."

Nora smiled. "We all are. Growing up is when we finally understand that. Remember those strawberry hard candies that used to show up in your Easter basket every year?"

"Yes."

"That's you, Ruby. You've built a hard shell to protect your soft heart. Only it doesn't work. I know you don't have faith in love, and I know I made you that way, but it's a half life, kiddo. Maybe you see that now. Without love, the loneliness just goes on and on."

Ruby looked down at her clasped hands. "I was lonely when I lived with Max."

"Of course you were. You didn't love him."

"I wanted to. Maybe I could have if I'd let myself."

"I don't think love is like that. It just . . . strikes. Like lightning."

"And fries you to a crisp."

"And turns your hair white."

"And stops your heart."

Nora's smile faded. "You should give Dean a chance. Stick around a while longer, see what happens. Unless you need to get back to your career . . ."

"What career?" The moment she said it, Ruby looked up sharply, as if she hadn't meant to say that.

"What do you mean?"

"I'm not funny."

The words seemed to take something away from Ruby; she looked young and vulnerable.

Nora didn't know how to respond. Did her daughter want honesty, empathy, or contradiction?

There was no way to know. All Nora could do was speak to the girl she'd once known. That girl, the young Ruby, had been honest to a fault and able to look life square in the eye.

"We both know you *are* funny. You've always had a great sense of humor. But are you funny enough, and often enough, to make a living at it? Have you taken classes, analyzed people like Robin Williams and Richard Pryor and Jerry Seinfeld? Do you know *how* they make their material sound funny?"

Ruby looked stunned. "You sound like my agent. He's always trying to get me to take classes. At least, he used to. He's kind of given up on me now."

"Why didn't you take his advice?"

"I thought it was about talent." The word seemed to make her uncomfortable. She gave Nora a little half smile as if to acknowledge it.

"Most things take more discipline than talent." Nora studied her daughter. "Is your material funny?"

"Most of the time. It's my delivery that sucks. And I'm not comfortable onstage."

Nora smiled. She couldn't help remembering—

"Mom? You're spacing out on me."

"I'm sorry. I heard your act once. One of my readers sent me a tape of it."

Ruby turned pale. "Really?"

"I have to admit it hurt like hell. You compared me to a rabbit—soft and pretty on the outside, and capable of eating her young." She laughed. "Anyway, I thought your stuff was funny, and I wasn't surprised by that. I always thought you'd be a writer."

"Really?"

"Your stories were wonderful. You had a way of looking at the world that amazed me."

Ruby swallowed hard. "I like writing. I . . . think I'm good at it. Lately, I've been thinking about writing a book."

"You should give it a try."

Ruby bit her lower lip, worrying it, and Nora knew she'd overstepped. "I'm sorry. I didn't mean to suggest—"

"It's okay, Mom. It's just that I almost did write something, but it was too personal. About us, our family. I didn't want to hurt . . . anyone."

Ruby looked heartbreakingly young and earnest right then. "Sometimes people get hurt, Ruby. It's never something you should seek out, or do on purpose, but you can't live a life that hurts no one. If you try, you'll end up touching no one."

"I wouldn't want to hurt you," Ruby said quietly.

Before Nora could respond, she heard the sound of a car driving up. It parked, and the engine fell silent. A door slammed shut.

Ruby glanced toward the garden. "Are we expecting someone?"

"No."

Footsteps rattled on gravel. A rusty gate creaked open and clattered shut.

Someone thumped up the sagging porch steps and walked into the light.

Chapter Twenty-one

Nora stared up at her elder daughter in shock. "Caroline?" she whispered, setting her tea down on the table beside her.

"I don't *believe* it!" Ruby ran across the porch and pulled her sister into a fierce hug.

Nora drank in the sight of it, her girls, back together on Summer Island. In the old days, she would have joined them, thrown her arms around both girls for a "family hug." But now a lifetime's worth of poor choices left her on the outside, looking at her own daughters through a pane of glass as thick as a child's broken heart.

Nora got awkwardly to her feet and limped forward. "Hey, Caro. It's good to see you."

Caroline drew back from Ruby's embrace. "Hello, Mother." Her smile seemed forced; it wasn't surprising. Even as a child, she'd been able to smile when her heart was breaking.

"This is *great*," Ruby said. "My big sis is home for

a slumber party. We haven't done that since Miranda Moore's birthday party."

In the soft, orange light, Nora studied her elder daughter. Caroline was flawlessly dressed in a pair of creased white linen pants and a rose-colored silk blouse with ruffles that fell around her thin wrists. Not a strand of silvery-blond hair was out of place, not a fleck of mascara marred the pale flesh beneath her eyes. Nora had the feeling it wouldn't dare.

And yet, in all that perfection, there was a strange undercurrent of fragility. As if she were hiding some tiny, hairline crack. Her gray eyes seemed suffused with a silent sadness.

Nora wondered suddenly what had brought Caroline here. It was unlike her daughter to do anything spontaneously—she planned her grocery-shopping days and marked them down on a planner. An unannounced trip to the island was startlingly out of character.

Ruby peered past her sister's shoulder. "Where are the kids?"

"I left them with Jere's mom for the night." She glanced nervously at Nora. "It's just me. I hope that's okay. I know I should have called."

"Are you *kidding*? I begged you to come," Ruby said, laughing.

Ruby looped an arm around her sister's narrow shoulders. The two women moved into the house, their heads tilted together.

As she limped along behind them, Nora heard Ruby say softly, "Is everything okay at home?" but Caroline's answer was too hushed to be overheard.

Nora felt like a third wheel. She stopped at the

kitchen table and cleared her throat. "Maybe I should leave you two alone for a while. You know, for a sisterly chat."

Caro and Ruby were almost to the living room. Together they turned around.

It was Ruby who spoke. "That's what got us into this pathetic mess, don't you think?"

"I just thought—"

"I know what you thought," Ruby said with a tenderness that squeezed Nora's heart.

Caroline moved forward, her left arm clamped tightly down on her designer overnight bag, her heels clacking on the hardwood floor. Nora could see her daughter's fear; it was close to the surface now.

Poor Caro. She actually thought it was possible—if you were careful—to skate on ice too thin to hold your weight.

"So," Caro said, offering a quick smile that didn't reach her eyes, "would you like to see the newest photos of your grandchildren?"

"We could start there," Nora said, knowing it wasn't her line. She was supposed to be desperately thankful for even the pretense of normalcy. "But if we really want to get to know each other, it will take more than pictures."

Caroline paled—if that were possible—then went on seamlessly. "Good." She unzipped her bag and took out two flat photo albums. "Let's go sit in the living room," she said, already moving. She went to the sofa and sat down, her knees pressed demurely together, her fingers splayed on top of the albums on her lap.

Ruby rushed over and sat beside her.

Nora ignored her crutches and hopped on one foot after her daughters. She sat down beside Caroline.

Caroline glanced down at the album. Her long, manicured fingers stroked the tooled leather.

Nora noticed that those hands, so perfectly cared for and heavy with gold and diamond jewelry, were trembling.

Slowly, Caroline opened the book. The first photograph was an eight-by-ten color shot of her wedding. In it, Caroline stood tall and stiffly erect (not nearly as thin as she was now), sheathed in an elegant, beaded-silk off-the-shoulder gown. Jere was beside her, breathtakingly handsome in a black Prada tuxedo.

"Sorry," Caro said quickly, "the new photos are in the back." She started to turn the page.

Nora boldly laid her hand on top of Caroline's. "Wait."

Who gives this woman to be married to this man?

When the priest had asked that special question, it had been Rand alone who'd answered. *I do.* Nora had been in the back of the church, doing her best not to weep. It should have been: *We do; her mother and I.*

But Nora had given up that precious moment.

She had been there for Caroline's wedding, but she hadn't *been* there. Caroline had invited her, placed her at a close-yet-distant table, one reserved for special guests, but not family. Nora had known that she was a detail to her daughter on that day, no more or less important than the floral arrangements. And Nora, lost in the desert of her own guilt, had thanked God for even that. She'd gone through the receiving line and kissed her elder daughter's cheek, whispered "Best wishes," and moved on. There were endless questions she hadn't allowed herself to even ask then, but now, as she stared at the beautiful photograph of her daughter, Nora couldn't remain detached.

Who had acted as Caroline's mother on that day? Who had sewn the last-minute beads on Caro's dress . . . or taken her shopping for ridiculously expensive lingerie that she would never wear again . . . who had held her, one last time, as an unmarried young woman and whispered, *I love you?*

Nora drew her hand back. She heard the sound of a turning page and forced her eyes open again.

Ruby laughed, pointing to a shot of the whole wedding party. "I want you to know, I never wore that dress again."

"Yeah, and you never came home again, either," Caroline shot back.

Ruby's smile faded. "I meant to."

Caroline smiled sadly. "Words that could be our family motto."

She quickly turned another page. "This is our honeymoon. We went to Kauai."

Nora noticed that Caroline's fingers were trembling again. She kept gently touching the photographs.

"You look so happy," Nora said softly.

Caroline turned, and Nora saw the sadness stamped on her daughter's face. "We were."

And Nora knew. "Oh, Caro . . ."

"Enough honeymoon shots," Ruby said loudly. "Where are the kids?"

Caroline turned back to the album, flipped through

a few more sand-and-surf photographs, and came to a stop.

This one was in a hospital room festooned with balloons and flower bouquets. Caroline was in bed, wearing a frilly white nightgown and an exhausted smile. For once, her hair was a mess. She held a tiny baby in her arms; the red-faced infant was wrapped in a pink blanket.

Here, at last, was a genuine smile, the kind that shone like sunlight.

Nora should have seen that smile in person, but she hadn't. Oh, she'd visited Caroline in the hospital, of course. She had come, bearing an armload of expensive gifts. She'd talked to her daughter, commiserated about labor, then commented on how pretty the baby was . . . and then she'd left. Even then, with the miracle of a new generation between them, they hadn't really talked.

Nora hadn't been there when Caroline realized how terrifying motherhood was. Who had said to her, *It's okay, Caro; God made you for this?*

No one.

Nora clamped a hand over her mouth, but it was too late. A small, noise escaped. She felt the tears burn her eyes and streak down her cheek. She tried to hold her breath but it broke into little gasps.

"Mom?" Caroline said, looking at her.

Nora couldn't meet her daughter's gaze. "I'm sorry . . . " She meant to add *for crying*, but the apology cracked in half.

Caroline was quiet.

Nora didn't realize that her daughter was crying

until a tear splashed onto the album, landed in a gray blotch beside a picture of Jenny in a bassinet.

Nora reached out, placed her hand on Caroline's cold, still fingers. "I'm so sorry," she whispered again.

Caroline bent her head. A curtain of hair fell forward, hid her face. "That was the day I missed you most." She laughed unevenly. "Jere's mom was a take-charge kind of gal. She whipped in and packed me up and sent me on my way with a list of instructions." Another tear fell. "I remember the first night. Jenny was in a bed beside me. I kept reaching out for her, touching her little fingers, stroking her little cheek. I dreamed you were standing beside my bed, telling me it would be okay, not to be afraid." She turned, looked at Nora through mascara-ruined eyes. "But I always woke up alone."

Nora swallowed hard. "Oh, Caroline . . ."

"I tried to remember that prayer you used to say when I was scared at night. I know it was stupid, but I just kept thinking that everything would be fine if I could only remember those words."

" 'Starlight, star bright, protect this baby girl against the night.' " Nora smiled uncertainly. "Caro, there aren't enough words in this galaxy to say how sorry I am for what I did to you and Ruby."

Caroline leaned toward her and let Nora take her in her arms.

Nora's heart cracked open like an egg. She was crying so hard she started to hiccup. When Nora drew back, she saw Ruby, sitting on Caroline's other side. Her face was pale, her lips drawn into a thin line. Only her eyes revealed emotion; they were shimmering with unshed tears.

Ruby stood up. "We need to drink."

Caroline wiped her eyes self-consciously and frowned. "I don't drink."

"Since when? At the junior prom, you—"

"It's a dozen lovely memories like that one that keep me sober. In college, Jere used to call me E.D. for easy drunk. Two drinks and I start thinking strip-and-go-naked is a perfect game."

"E.D? *E.D.?* Oh, this is too good. I'm twenty-seven years old and I haven't gotten drunk with my sister since before it was legal. Tonight we're changing all that."

Nora laughed. "The last time I drank, I drove into a tree."

"Don't worry—I won't let you drive," Ruby promised.

Caroline laughed. "Okay. One drink. *One.*"

Ruby did a little cha-cha-cha toward the kitchen, then threw back her head and said, "Margaritas!" Before Nora had figured out how to start another conversation with Caroline, Ruby was back, dancing into the living room with glasses that could have doubled as Easter baskets.

Nora took her drink, then laughed out loud when Ruby went to the record player, picked an album, and put it on.

We will . . . we will . . . rock you blared through the old speakers. Ruby had the volume so high the windows rattled and knickknacks seemed to dance spasmodically across the mantel.

Ruby took a laughing gulp of her drink, wiped her mouth with the back of her hand, and slammed the drink down onto the coffee table. Then she snapped a hand toward Caroline. "Come on, Miss America, dance with Hollywood's worst comic."

Caroline frowned. "That's not true."

"Dance with me."

Shaking her head, Caroline grabbed Ruby's hand and let herself be pulled into a twirl.

Nora cautiously sipped her cocktail and leaned forward, mesmerized by the interplay between her daughters. They were standing side by side, both sweaty from dancing, and they looked so happy and carefree it actually hurt Nora's heart. These were the adult versions of the girls Nora had borne, the women she'd imagined her daughters would have become if their mother had never left.

The girls danced and drank and laughed together, bumping hips and holding hands, until Caroline held up her hands and said breathlessly, "No more, Ruby. I'm getting dizzy."

"Ha! You're not dizzy enough, that's your problem," and with that proclamation, she handed her sister her margarita. "Bottoms up."

Caroline wiped the damp hair off her face. It looked for a moment as if she were going to decline.

"Oh, what the hell." Caroline drank the rest of her margarita without stopping, then held out the empty glass. "Another one, please."

"Yee ha!" Ruby danced into the kitchen and started up the blender.

On the stereo, the next album dropped down,

clicked on top of the first one. With a whining screech, the arm moved to the beginning and lowered.

It was an old album by the Eurythmics. *Sweet dreams are made of these* pulsed through the speakers.

Caroline stumbled unsteadily to one side and held her hand out. "Dance with me, Mom."

Mom. It was the first time Caroline had called her that in years.

"If I step on your foot, I'll break every bone."

Caroline laughed. "Don't worry, I'm anesthetized." The last word came out hopelessly mangled, and Caroline laughed again. "Drunk," she said sternly, *"drunk."*

Nora grabbed her fallen crutch and limped over to Caroline. She slipped one arm around her daughter's tiny (too tiny; frighteningly tiny) waist and used the crutch for support.

Caroline pressed her hands against Nora's shoulders. Slowly, they began to sway from side to side.

"This is the last song they played at the senior prom. I had them play it at my wedding, remember?"

Nora nodded. She was going to say something impersonal, but then she noticed the way Caroline was looking at her. "Do you want to talk about it?" she asked gently, tightening her hold on Caro's fragile waist.

"Talk about what?"

Nora couldn't help herself. She stopped dancing and released Caroline's hand, then touched her daughter's cheek. "Your marriage."

Caroline's beautiful face crumpled. Her mouth quavered as she released a heavy sigh. "Oh, Mom . . . I wouldn't know where to start."

"There's no—"

Ruby spun into the room, singing, "Margaritas for the señoras." She saw Nora and Caro standing there, and she stopped in her tracks. "Jesus, I leave you two for five minutes and the waterworks start again."

Nora shot her a pleading look. "Ruby, please."

Ruby frowned. "Caro? What is it?"

Caroline took an unsteady step backward. She looked from Nora to Ruby and back to Nora. She was weeping silently, and it was a heart-wrenching sight. It was the way a woman wept in the middle of a dark night with her husband beside her in bed and her children sleeping down the hall.

"I wasn't going to tell you," Caro said to both of them in a breathy, broken voice.

Ruby stepped toward her, hand outstretched.

"Don't touch me!" Caro said. At the shrill desperation in her voice, she laughed. "I'll fall apart if you touch me, and I'm so goddamn sick of falling apart I could scream."

Caroline sank slowly to her knees on the floor. Ruby sat down beside her, and Nora followed awkwardly, landing on her fallen crutch.

Caroline took a big gulp of her margarita, then looked up. Her eyes were dry now, but somehow that only made her look more wounded. A little girl looking out through a woman's disillusioned eyes, wondering how she'd stumbled into such heartache.

"Are you sleeping?" Nora asked.

Caroline looked shocked. "No."

"Eating?"

"No."

"Medications?"

"No."

Nora nodded. "Well, that's a good thing." She held Caroline's hand. "Have you and Jere talked about this?"

Caroline shook her head. "I can't tell him. We're always going in different directions. I feel like a single parent most of the time. And I'm lonely. God, I'm so damned lonely sometimes I can't stand it."

"You haven't even *talked* to him about it?" Ruby said, leaning toward her sister.

Caroline turned to her. "You don't know what it's like, Ruby. You can say anything to anyone. It's harder for me."

"Yeah, but—"

Nora touched Ruby's thigh. "She doesn't need that now, Ruby. There's a time for the real world and consequences, Caroline knows that. This is a time for letting her know that whatever happens, we'll always be there for her." Nora gazed lovingly at Caroline. "I know what you're going through, believe me. You're at that place where your own life overwhelms you and you can't see a way to break free. And you're suffocating."

Caroline drew in a gulping, hiccuping breath. Her eyes rounded. "How did you know that?"

Nora touched her cheek. "I know" was all she said for now. There would be more to come, she knew, but now they had to lay all the cards on the table. "Is Jere seeing another woman?"

Caroline made a desperate, moaning sound. Tears rolled down her cheeks. "Everyone always said Jere was just like Daddy. I guess I should have been afraid." She sniffled and wiped her eyes. "I'm going to leave him, though."

"Do you love him?" Nora asked gently.

Caroline went pale. Her lower lip trembled; the hands in her lap tightened into a bloodless knot. "So much . . ."

Nora's heart felt as if it were breaking. Here was another legacy of her motherhood: she'd taught her children that marriages were disposable.

"Let me tell you what it's like, this decision you think you've made," she said to Caroline. "When you leave a man you love, you feel like your heart is splitting in half. You lie in your lonely bed and you miss him, you drink your coffee in the morning and you miss him, you get a haircut and all you can think is that no one will notice but you. And you go on with a broken heart, you go on." She took a deep, unsteady breath. "But that's not the worst of it. The worst is what you do to your children. You tell yourself it's okay; divorces happen all the time and your children will get over it. Maybe that's true if the love is really gone from your marriage. But if you still love him, and you leave him without trying to save your family, you will . . . break. You don't just cry in the middle of the night, you cry forever, all the time, until your insides are so dry there are no tears left, and then you learn what real pain is."

Nora knew that what she was saying wasn't true for all marriages, all divorces. But she was certain that Caroline hadn't tried hard enough, not yet, not if she loved Jere. She closed her eyes, trying to think of Caroline . . . but then she was thinking about her own life, her own mistakes, and before she knew it, she was talking again. "You walk around and get dressed and maybe you even find a career that makes you rich and famous. You think that was what you wanted all along, but you find out it doesn't matter. You don't know how to feel anymore. You're dead. Somewhere, your daughters are growing up without you. . . . You know that somewhere they're out there, holding someone else's hand, crying on someone else's shoulder. And every single day, you live with what you did to them. Don't make my mistake," Nora said fiercely. "*Fight.* Fight for your love and your family. In the end, it's all there is, Caroline. All there is."

Caroline didn't look up as she whispered, "What if I lose him anyway?"

"Ah, Caro," Nora said, stroking her daughter's hair, "what if you find him again?"

Chapter Twenty-two

Ruby felt as if someone were pounding a drum inside her head. Though she was exhausted, she couldn't sleep. She'd tried turning the light on, hoping Caroline would wake up, but no such luck. Her sister had obviously lapsed into a tequila coma.

After their evening of margaritas and tears, she and Caro had finally stumbled up to bed. They'd lain in the darkness for hours, talking, laughing; sometimes they'd even cried. They'd said all the things they'd gathered up in the years between then and now, but finally, Caroline had fallen asleep.

Ruby closed her eyes and pictured Mom as she'd been a few hours earlier . . . sitting on the dirty rag rug like a kindergartner, with her casted leg sprawled out to the side, a half-finished margarita beside her thigh. In profile, with the firelight haloing her face, she'd looked like an angel carved from the purest ivory.

She had been talking quietly to Caroline.

They'd held hands, Mom and Caro, and whispered about marriage, about how it wasn't what you expected. Their two voices had blended into a music that Ruby couldn't quite comprehend. At first, she'd felt left out, a child eavesdropping at her parents' closed bedroom door.

She had been right there, sitting beside them, and yet she'd felt isolated and alone. Unconnected. Never in her life had Ruby felt such an intense sense of her own shortcomings.

She'd been unable to join in the conversation because she'd never made a commitment to another human being; she'd never tried to love someone through good times and bad. In fact, she'd purposely chosen men she *couldn't* love. In that way, her heart had always seemed safe. And always, it had been empty.

She'd had the realization before, but this time it struck deep.

Caroline and Mom had been talking about love and loss, and most of all, commitment; about how love was more than an emotion. In the end, Mom had said, sometimes love was a choice. Like the tide, it could ebb and flow, and there were slack-tide times when a woman had nothing to believe in except a memory, nothing to cling to except the choice she'd made a long time ago.

Mom had looked at Caroline and said softly, "I let the bad times overwhelm me, and I ran. It wasn't until I'd gone too far to turn back that I remembered how much I loved your father, and by then it was too late. For all these years, I've been left wondering, 'What if?'"

What if?

Ruby closed her eyes. The darkness pressed in on

her. She heard the whispering of the sea through the open window.

Do you believe in second chances?

Dean's question came back to her, filled her longing.

"I do," she said out loud, hoping that tomorrow, when they went sailing, she would find the courage to say the same words to Dean.

Before tonight, it would have seemed impossible to expose her heart so openly, so boldly. To admit she wanted to love and be loved. But tonight, life seemed different.

As if anything were possible.

The next morning, Nora woke feeling refreshed and rejuvenated. Almost young again. She thanked God that she'd sipped a single margarita all night.

She pushed back the coverlet and limped into the bathroom. When she was finished with her morning routine, she dressed quickly in a pair of khaki walking shorts and a white linen shirt.

In the living room, she saw the relics of last night's blowout—three glasses, each with at least an inch of slime-green liquid in the bottom; an ashtray filled with the cigarettes Caroline had furtively smoked; a pile of discarded record albums.

For the first time this summer, the house looked lived in. This was a mess made by Nora and her daughters, and she'd waited a lifetime to see it.

She put a pot of coffee on, then limped upstairs. The bedroom door was closed. She pushed it open. Caroline and Ruby were still sleeping.

In sleep, they looked young and vulnerable, and at

the sight of them, she remembered her own nights in this room, nights she'd slept in this bed with her husband, more often than not with two small, warm bodies tucked in between them.

And now those babies were women full grown, sleeping together in the bed that had once held their parents. Caroline slept curled in a ball, her body pressed close to the mattress's edge. Ruby, on the other hand, lay spread-eagle, her arms and legs flung out above the bedding.

Nora walked to the bed. Slowly, she reached down and caressed Ruby's pink, sleep-lined cheek. Her skin was soft, so soft . . .

"Wake up, sleepyheads."

Ruby groaned and blinked awake, smacking her lips together as if she could still taste the last margarita. "Hi, Mom."

Caro blinked awake beside her, stretching her arms. She saw Nora and tried to sit up. Halfway there, she groaned and flopped backward. "Oh, my God, my head is swollen."

Ruby didn't look a whole lot better, but at least she could sit upright. "Obviously E.D. here should have done a little alcohol training before last night." She squeezed her eyes shut and rubbed her temples. "Do we have any aspirin?"

"Aspirin?" Caroline moaned. "That's an over-the-counter medication. I have prescription-level pain." She scooted slowly to a seated position, and slumped against Ruby. "I'm never listening to you again. Oh, shit, I'm gonna puke."

Ruby slipped an arm around her sister. "Aim at Mom. She looks way too happy this morning."

Ruby's laughter rang out, and Nora felt a sharp tug of nostalgia. *My girls,* she thought. Suddenly it seemed like only yesterday they'd begged for Disco Barbies for Christmas.

Nora clapped her hands. "Get a move on, girls. We're going sailing today with Dean and Eric—remember, Ruby? Lottie has dinner planned for us around seven."

Caroline turned green. "Sailing?" She rolled out of Ruby's arms and dropped onto the floor, landing on all fours. She crouched there a minute, breathing shallowly, then she crawled toward the bathroom. At the door, she grabbed onto the knob and hauled herself upright. She turned and gave Ruby a pained smile. "First in the shower!"

"Shit." Ruby sagged forward, buried her face in her hands. "Don't use all the hot water."

Nora smiled. "It's like old times around here."

Ruby angled a look at her, gave her a pathetically sloppy smile. "I don't remember tequila in grade school, or all of us dancing to 'Footloose,' singing at the tops of our lungs, but . . . yeah."

" 'You and Me Against the World,' " Nora said, her smile fading at the suddenness of the memory. "That was our song."

"I remember."

Nora wanted to move toward her, but she remained still. Last night, Caro had come back to Nora completely, but even in the midst of their laughter-and-sob-fest, Ruby had held herself back. "Well, I'm going to start breakfast and pack us a light lunch. Dean's supposed to bring the boat around eleven." She waited for Ruby to say something, but when the silence stretched out, Nora turned and headed downstairs, thumping down each step.

She was halfway down when she heard a car drive up. A quick glance at her watch told her it was nine-thirty. Not dawn, certainly, but pretty early for the local islanders to be visiting.

Nora tried to hurry down the stairs, but with her cast, it was difficult. She felt like Quasimodo hurrying down the bell tower.

She made it into the kitchen just as a rattling knock struck the front door. She finger-combed her hair and opened the door.

Standing on her porch was one of the best-looking young men she'd ever seen. He had the kind of beauty that made old women long for youth. Though she hadn't seen him since the wedding, she'd recognize her son-in-law anywhere.

"Hi, Jeremy," she said, smiling.

He looked surprised. "Nora?"

"I guess it's a shock to realize you have a mother-in-law." She took a step backward, motioning for him to come inside.

He smiled tiredly. "Given my other shocks in the past twenty-four hours, that's nothing."

Nora nodded, unsure of how to respond. "Caroline is upstairs. She's not feeling real well."

He looked instantly concerned. "Is something wrong? Is that why she left?"

"Tequila. That's what's wrong."

He relaxed, even grinned. "So, you met Ed."

"It wasn't a pretty sight. Can I get you a cup of coffee?"

"That would be great. I missed the final ferry last night, so I slept in my car on the dock. My body feels like it's been canned."

Nora went into the kitchen and poured him a cup of coffee. "Cream? Sugar?"

"Yeah, thanks."

She returned with the coffee, and handed him a cup.

"Thanks." He glanced toward the stairs. "Is she awake?"

The look he gave Nora was so utterly helpless that she said, "I'll get her. You wait here."

"I'm here."

Nora and Jere both spun around. Caroline stood in the living room. She was wearing the same silk and linen clothes from last night, only now they were wrinkled beyond recognition. Her hair was a tangled mess. Flecks of caked mascara turned her eyes into twin bruises. "Hi, Jere," she said softly. "I heard your voice."

Ruby came stumbling down the stairs and rammed into her sister. "Sorry, Caro, I—" She saw Jeremy and stopped. Her laughter dwindled into an uncomfortable silence.

Jere walked over to Caroline. "Care?"

The tenderness in his voice told Nora all she needed to know. There might be trouble between Caro and Jere—maybe big trouble—but underneath all that there was love, and with love, they had a chance.

"You shouldn't have come," Caro said, crossing her

arms. She took a step backward, and Nora knew her daughter was afraid of getting too close to this man she loved so deeply.

"No," he said softly, "you shouldn't have left. Not without talking to me first. Can you imagine how—" His voice cracked. "—how I felt when I got your letter?"

"I thought—"

"Your *letter*, Care. All these years and you leave me a *letter* that says you'll be back when you feel like it?"

Caro looked up at him. "I thought you'd be glad I left, and I couldn't stand to see that."

"You thought." He sighed, ran a hand through his hair. "Come home," he whispered. "Mom's watching the kids for the rest of the weekend."

Caroline smiled. "She'll be bleeding from her ears before tomorrow morning."

"That's *her* problem. We need some time alone."

"Okay." Caroline turned and went upstairs. She came down a minute later with her overnight bag. She enfolded Ruby in a fierce hug, whispering something that Nora couldn't hear, and then both girls laughed.

Finally, Caroline walked across the kitchen to Nora. "Thanks," she said quietly.

"Oh, honey, I've waited a lifetime for last night."

Caroline's eyes were bright. "I won't miss you anymore."

"No way. You can't get rid of me now. I love you, Caro."

"And I love you, Mom." Nora pulled her daughter into her arms and held her tightly, then slowly released her.

Jeremy took the overnight bag from his wife, then held on to her hand. Together, they left the house.

Ruby and Nora followed them as far as the porch, watching as the gray Mercedes followed the white Range Rover out of the driveway.

"She's gone," Ruby said.

"She'll be back." Nora stared out at the beautiful blue sky and choppy green sea. It was going to be a great day for sailing; no clouds, a little breeze shivering through the trees, sunlight on the water.

Ruby sidled up to Nora, stood so close their shoulders were touching. "I'm sorry, Mom."

Nora turned. "For what?"

Ruby looked different somehow. Serious. "For all the presents I sent back and all the years I stayed away. But mostly I'm sorry for being so damned unforgiving."

Nora wasn't sure how it happened—who moved first—but suddenly they were clinging to each other, laughing and crying at the same time.

At exactly eleven, a boat horn blared. A loud *ah-oo-gah, ah-oo-gah*. The *Wind Lass* pulled up to the dock.

Ruby glanced down at the water, watching Dean tie the boat down. "They're here." There was a strand of worry in her voice.

Nora understood. "Are you afraid to see Dean?"

Ruby nodded.

Nora laid a hand against Ruby's cheek. "You could travel the world and you wouldn't find a better man than Dean Sloan."

"He's not the problem. I am."

"Your whole life has been tangled up with Dean.

When someone pinched him, you got a welt in the same place. He's a part of you, Ruby, like it or not. Being afraid of him is like being afraid of your own arm. Just let go. Have fun. Let yourself remember the good times, not only the bad."

Ruby looked up at her. "I want that, Mom. I want it so much . . ."

The sailboat honked its horn again.

"Grab the picnic basket," Nora said, pointing to the pile of supplies on the kitchen table.

Within minutes, they were headed down the path to the beach. Nora moved as fast as her crutches would allow.

The sailboat was tied down. Dean was on the bow, holding the two ropes that held the boat against the dock. "Welcome aboard."

Nora handed her crutches to Ruby and stepped carefully onto the boat, trying to ensure that her cast didn't leave a mark on the teak decking. When her balance was steady, she took her crutches and tossed them onto the settee belowdecks. Limping awkwardly, she sidled around the giant silver wheel and sat down beside Eric. A pillow rested behind his stocking-capped head and a thick woolen Navajo blanket covered his body. Although he was smiling, he looked terribly pale and weak. The shadows were purple beneath his eyes. His lips were chapped and colorless.

Nora was shocked by his appearance. He looked so much worse than the last time she'd seen him. It wasn't Eric; this gaunt, too-fragile man was a whittled-down version of him, perhaps, but when she looked into his huge, sad eyes, she saw the spirit that cancer couldn't touch. With exquisite gentleness, she curled an arm around him and drew him close.

He rested his head against her shoulder, shivering a little. "You feel good," he murmured.

Dean started the engine. Ruby untied the boat and jumped aboard; they motored out of the bay, and when they passed the tip of the island, Dean rigged up the mainsail.

The boat immediately heeled starboard and caught a gust of wind, slicing through the water.

Eric pressed his face into the wind, smiling brightly.

Nora tilted her head against his and stared out at the lush, green islands. Ruby was up on the bow of the boat, standing in the wind. Nora didn't have to see her daughter's face to know that she was grinning.

Dean hurried belowdecks. When he came back up, Robert Palmer's "Addicted to Love" blared through the speakers.

On the bow, Ruby moved her hips to the beat. Nora imagined that she was singing—off key—at the top of her lungs.

There was a pause between songs, and the silence seemed endless and perfect, a moment trapped in a time that was somehow both then and now: Dean at the wheel, Eric and Nora sitting on the aft deck, Ruby poised at the bow, always eager to see where they were going.

Nora felt the hot sun on her cheeks and heard the loose flapping of the ties against the mast.

"I'm glad you're here," Eric said.

She smiled at him. "Where else could I be? You and Dean and Ruby . . . you're the best parts of my life. I'll always remember my dark-haired boy. Every time I turned around, you were there, grinning up at me, saying, 'What are we gonna do next, Miz Bridge?' It seems like only yesterday you were sitting at my kitchen table with your banged-up elbows on the pink placemat. God, the time goes so fast . . ."

"Too fast." Eric's gaze was steady.

Nora's throat closed up, but she refused to let him see her cry. Gently, she touched his face.

Eric turned away; she could tell that he was collecting himself again, distancing himself from the truth they'd dared to touch upon.

He looked at Ruby, standing on the bow, then at Dean. They were the full boat-length apart, each trying not to get caught staring at the other. "You think they'll figure it out?"

"I hope so. They need each other."

"Take care of him for me," Eric said in a throaty voice, wiping his eyes with the edge of the blanket. "I thought I'd always be there for him . . . my baby brother."

"You will be."

Eric laughed and wiped his eyes. "God, we're out sailing and we look like we just watched *Brian's Song.*"

Nora laughed and wiped her eyes.

A swift breeze rose suddenly, filling the canvas sail with a *tharumping* noise. The boat keeled over and cut through the sunlit, glistening water.

Dean looked down at his brother. "Do you want to take the wheel?"

Eric's face lit up. "Oh, yeah."

Dean slipped an arm around his brother's frail body and helped him hobble toward the big, silver wheel. Eric took hold; Dean stood behind and beside him, resting a hand on his brother's shoulder, to keep him steady.

Wind-tears streaked across Eric's temples, his thinning hair flapped against the sides of his face, his T-shirt billowed against his sunken chest.

"Orcas!" Ruby said suddenly, pointing starboard.

At first, Nora didn't see anything. She stood up and tented a hand across her eyes.

She saw the first black fin rise slowly, slowly from the water. Then there were six of them—black fins moving through the sea like the upended teeth of a comb, impossibly close together.

"I'm the queen of the world!" Eric yelled, flinging his arms out. He laughed out loud, and for the first time in weeks, it was *his* laughter, not the weak, watered-down version that cancer had left him with.

Nora knew that when she looked back on Eric's life, and the ugliness of the past few weeks and months seemed overwhelming, she would picture him now. Standing tall, squinting into the sun, laughing.

And she would remember her boy. Her Eric.

Chapter Twenty-three

It was early evening by the time they got back to the house. Lottie served them a delicious dinner of Dungeness crabs, Caesar salad, and French bread. She'd laughed as she set the meal on the table, saying that she hadn't figured too much had changed over the years—the Sloans and the Bridges loved crab, but were too softhearted to boil one.

Even though they'd eaten a big lunch on the boat, they'd descended on dinner like *Survivor* contestants. Eric had even managed to eat a few tender, buttery bites.

While "the girls" washed and dried the dishes, Dean had carried Eric up to bed. Finally, Nora and Ruby went upstairs, and they all stood around Eric's bed, talking softly until he fell asleep.

Now, the three of them were back on the *Wind Lass*, headed for Summer Island. The trip, being undertaken at night, without radar, took twice the usual amount of time. And still Ruby hadn't found the courage to hand Dean her heart.

All day she'd waited for The Moment, the one when she could turn to him and touch his arm and say she wasn't afraid anymore. But every time she'd started for him, she'd seized up. The shale of old habits collected beneath her feet and made it dangerous to move.

There had always been a roadblock between them, something Ruby couldn't climb over—a crowd of people (okay, so Eric and Mom weren't *really* a crowd, but when you were eating crow, one extraneous witness was too many), a set of chores, a whooshing wind.

So Ruby had waited. And waited.

She was still waiting when the *Wind Lass* glided up to the Bridges' dock.

"Get the lines, Ruby," Dean yelled.

She grabbed the lines and jumped onto the dock, tying the boat down. She was still figure-eighting the line around the midship cleat when she saw her mother step down onto the dock.

"Thanks, Dean," she heard her mother say. She felt, rather than saw, Mom turn toward her. "Ruby? Honey, I'll need some help up to the house. The bank is slippery."

Ruby shot a glance to the boat; it was all shadows up close, strips of white and gray that bobbed up and down. She couldn't see a flash of Dean's blond hair. He was probably down below. What if he left before she could get back?

"Ruby?"

She dropped the excess coil of line and headed toward her mother. Mom turned and waved. "Bye, Dean. Thanks for a great day."

And there he was, standing beside the wheel. She

could make out his golden hair and yellow sweater, and even a flash of white teeth as he smiled, but that was all. "Bye," he said in a subdued voice.

"Uh . . . If you need help leaving—you know, untying or something—I could come right back down," Ruby said.

There was a moment's pause before he answered. She wished she could see his face. "I can always use help."

Ruby felt a rush of relief. She tightened her hold on her mother's shoulders, and together they walked up the slightly angled bank and across the lawn.

At the front door, Mom smiled. "Go ahead. And Ruby?"

Ruby reached down for the afghan on the rocker and slung it around her shoulders. It was getting chilly out here. "Yeah?"

"He loves you."

"That would be a miracle. I've done everything but stab him in the eye."

Mom grinned. "All love is a miracle. Now, go to him. Don't be afraid. And try not to be your usual obnoxious self."

Ruby couldn't help laughing. "Thanks, Mom."

As she hurried across the yard, a cloud scudded across the sky and revealed a nearly full moon. It lit up the sky, tinged the world in eerie blue.

At the edge of the bank, Ruby paused, tightening the blanket around her shoulders. She knew what she needed to do, but knowing didn't grant her courage. She was afraid that she'd taken too long to grow up and had lost her chance.

He was standing at the end of the dock, with his back to her. She moved soundlessly down the bank and stepped onto the dock. Her footsteps were indistinguishable from the ordinary creaks and moans of old wood. "I remember when we used to jump off of that dock at high tide," she said softly. "Only Washington kids would swim in that water."

He spun around.

Ruby moved toward him.

She was afraid suddenly to speak. She wanted to simply put her arms around him and kiss him until she couldn't think, couldn't move, couldn't remember everything that was between them. But she couldn't do it. For once, she had to do the right thing. She owed Dean a few words—small, simple words—and she couldn't be too cowardly to speak.

She couldn't turn back now.

The silence between them felt loaded, dangerous. In it, she heard the slap of the waves on the pilings below.

She closed the last, small space between them and took hold of his left hand, caressing his fingers. Then, slowly, she drew her hand away. "I remember the first time you kissed me. I got so dizzy, I couldn't breathe. I was glad we were sitting down, because I would have fallen. But I fell anyway, didn't I? I fell in love with my best friend. When most kids were planning how to sneak out of their parents' house on a Saturday night, you and I were dreaming about our wedding . . . the children we would have." She swallowed hard and smiled. "When we were fifteen, you said we'd live in a penthouse on Central Park . . . that we'd honeymoon in Paris. When we were seven, you promised that someday we'd own a boat as big as a ferry, with a bathtub in the master stateroom, and that Elvis would sing at our wedding." She gave him a smile. "The dreams of children playing at adulthood. We should have known we were in trouble when Elvis died."

Dean closed his eyes for a moment, only that, and she wondered if it hurt him to hear the old dreams. "Yeah," he said woodenly, "we were young."

"I tried to forget those things we said, but mostly, I tried to forget how it felt when you kissed me," she said. "I kept telling myself it was a crush . . . that I'd grow up and go on and feel that way again. But I didn't." She heard the rawness in her voice, the desperate tenor of hope, and she knew he heard it, too. She was exposed now, vulnerable.

"You never fell in love again?"

"How could I . . . when I never fell out of love the first time?"

"Say it."

She stepped closer and tilted her face up to his. "I love you, Dean Sloan."

He didn't respond for a heartbeat, just stared down at her. Then he pulled her into his arms and kissed her the way she'd always dreamed of being kissed. And suddenly she wanted more. More . . .

She fumbled with his T-shirt, shoved it over his head, and let her fingers explore the coarse, wiry hair on his chest. She touched him everywhere, moved her hands across the hardness of his shoulders, down the small of his back, down into his underwear.

He yanked the afghan down, letting it puddle on the dock around their feet. With a groan, he slipped his hands beneath her shirt, scooping it off her, and tossed it away. She kicked it aside and grappled with the buttons on her cutoffs.

Naked, kissing, groping, they knelt on the blanket, smoothed it out, then collapsed on top of it, laughing at the awkwardness of their movements.

Ruby heard the hiss of paper ripping. She blinked, feeling drugged by the intensity of her desire, and saw that he was opening a small foil packet.

It stunned her. "You *planned* this?"

He gave her a crooked, boyish grin. "Let's just say I prayed for it."

And he was laughing again, kissing her, and she couldn't think. Her body was on fire. His hands were everywhere—her breasts, her nipples, between her legs—stroking, rubbing, pulling. His mouth followed the path of his magical fingers, and when he leaned over her and took a nipple in his searching mouth, she gave in to sex in a way she never had before. She relinquished control over her body and let him bring her to the throbbing, desperate edge of pain. Finally, she couldn't stand it anymore; her whole body was aching, needing . . .

"Please," she moaned beneath his touch, "now . . ."

He flipped onto his back and pulled her on top of him, entering her with a thrust. His hands were on her bottom, holding her against his grinding hips, teaching her to match his movements.

She threw her head back and closed her eyes.

He arched forward, capturing her nipple in his mouth, and she cried out. Her release was so intense it felt as if she were breaking apart. "Oh, God," she said, breathing heavily, feeling his own climax inside her.

She collapsed on top of him, buried her face in his sweaty chest.

He held on to her tightly, as if he expected her to pull away, and stroked her damp back.

"Oh, my God," she whispered, finally rolling off of him. She remained tucked against him, one leg thrown across his thighs.

"We should have done that a long time ago."

"Believe me, it wouldn't have been as good." She sighed, flopping back, staring up at the moonlit sky.

So simple. It had always been like this between them. Just a touch, a gentle brushing of his skin against hers, and she'd known a kind of peace that could be found nowhere else. She rolled onto her side and stared down at him. "Let's live together."

He gave her a strange look. "In Hollyweird?"

"God, no." It was an instinctive answer. She hadn't even thought about it, but as she heard her voice, she knew it was true. She didn't want to live there anymore. "I could live in San Francisco."

He laughed. "No, thanks." He reached up, touched her hair. "We've had those lives, Ruby. I don't know about you, but I don't want to go back to anything that came before. I want to start over. And I'm *not* going to live with you."

"Oh." She tried to sound casual, as if he hadn't just stomped on her heart.

"We're getting married, Ruby Elizabeth. No more excuses or running away or lost time. We are *going* to get married. My vote is that we move back here and try like hell to find out what we want to do with the rest of our lives. I'm going to give photography a try; it's what I've always wanted to do. Most importantly, we're going to promise to grow old together. And we're going to do it. We'll sit on our own porch until we're blind and hairless and I can't remember what the hell my own name is. And the last thing you're going to feel in this world is me kissing you good night."

"We'll have children," she said, dreaming of it for the very first time.

"At least two, so they'll each have a best friend."

"And our son. We'll name him Eric . . ."

Ruby would have slept on the dock all night, wrapped in Dean's arms and that old blanket, but he'd wanted to get back to Eric, and so they'd kissed—and kissed and kissed—good-bye.

Then she helped Dean untie the boat and walked up to the top of the bank to watch him leave. Moonlight shimmered on all the white surfaces of the boat, turned everything silvery blue. He started the engine; the boat pulled away from the dock. The *chug-chug-chug* of the motor broke the silence of the night.

Moment by moment, he lost coloring. It started with the tip of the mast; it turned black suddenly, then the rest of the boat followed. In the last slice of moonlight, a dark hand lifted, raised, waved good-bye. Though Dean couldn't see her, he knew somehow that Ruby was still there, watching him leave.

It was what she'd always done.

She stood there until the boat disappeared into the

choppy silver-tipped sea, then turned and went to the house.

The kitchen light was on, and Mom's bedroom door was closed.

Ruby walked—okay, skipped—over to the closed door. There was no doubt in her mind that her mother would want to be wakened. After all, it wasn't every day your daughter got engaged.

She was just about to knock when the phone rang.

She ran for the kitchen and answered the phone on the second ring, hoping it wasn't about Eric. "Hello?"

"Ruby—where in the goddamn hell have you been? I've been calling all night. And what kind of podunk, backwater, double-wide house doesn't have an answering machine?"

Ruby immediately relaxed. "Val?" She glanced at the clock. It was one in the morning. "Can we have this discussion in the morning? I—"

His voice was muffled. "Yeah, another Stoly martini, babe . . . three olives. Sorry, Ruby. Anyway, what is this *shit* about you not turning in the article? Tell me Maudeen wasn't listening well."

"Oh, that. I'm not going to deliver, that's all."

"That's all. That's *all*? Look comedy princess, this isn't some low-rent vanity-press publisher we're talking about. This is *Caché* magazine. They've reserved the space in the issue, printed the cover—with *your* picture on it, I might add—and leaked the story." He paused; she heard the exhalation of smoke into the receiver. "And I've gotten some interest in you from the networks; NBC wants to talk to you about writing a pilot."

"A . . . pilot? My own sitcom?" Ruby felt sick. That had always been a pie-in-the-sky dream of hers. Every comedian dreamed about her own show.

"Yeah, your own sitcom. So, no dicking around. You're supposed to deliver the article tomorrow. I FedExed your plane tickets yesterday. They're probably on your front door now. You're scheduled for *Sarah Purcell* on Monday morning."

"I can't do it, Val." Ruby closed her eyes. In that minute, she could *feel* the warm imprint of her mother's hand on her head, the gentleness of that touch. Panic rushed through her.

Val drew in a deep breath, then exhaled slowly. "Christ. I knew you were a pain in the ass, but I promised them you were professional. I gave them my word, Ruby."

"I am a professional." Even to her own ears, her voice sounded small. Afraid.

"Professionals don't take money from national magazines and then break the contract. Can you pay them back?"

Ruby flinched, thinking of the Porsche in her parking spot, the designer dress in her closet, the money she gave her dad. "If they'll give me some time—" *Like, twenty years.*

"It doesn't work that way. The only chance of getting out of this deal is to pay them back, and even then they have to agree. And baby doll, they won't."

"You mean they can *force* me—"

Val laughed. "Where have you been living . . . Potatoville, USA? This is big business. You can't just change your mind. Is it written?"

She hated the weakness that made her answer. "Yes."

"And the problem is . . ."

Ruby felt like crying. "I like her." She swallowed thickly. "No. I love her."

Val was quiet for a moment, then he said, "I'm sorry, Ruby."

His concern was harder to take than the yelling. "I am, too," she answered dully.

"You'll be on the plane then, right? I'll have Bertram pick you up."

Ruby hung up the phone in a daze. She wandered out onto the porch, found the FedEx envelope. Inside, there was a first-class ticket and a short itinerary. They were taking her to Spago to celebrate after the taping of *Sarah Purcell* . . .

A week ago that would have thrilled her.

She walked dully past her mother's door. At the last minute, she stopped, pressed her fingertips to the wood.

"I'm sorry," Ruby breathed. But she knew those two little words wouldn't be enough. Not nearly enough.

With a sigh, she turned and went upstairs. She flopped onto the bed and tried to sleep, but she couldn't keep her eyes closed. At last, she flicked on the light and reached for her pad of paper.

I just got off the phone with my agent.

The joke is on me, it seems. I can't get out of this deal. I have to deliver the article as promised or some corporate Mr. Big will sue me until I bleed.

And I will lose my mother, this woman whom

I've waited and longed for all of my life, whom I've alternately deified and vilified. Whatever we could have become will be gone. And this time it will be all my fault. The whole world will see the bank-ruptcy of my soul.

I finally learned that life is not made up of BIG moments and sudden epiphanies, but rather of tiny bits of time, some so small they pass by unnoticed.

All this I can see now . . . and it is too late.

Monday, I will appear on The Sarah Purcell Show, *and after that, what I see will matter only to me. My mother won't care.*

But I want to say this—for the record, although I'm aware it comes too late and at too great a price—I love my mother.

I love my mother.

Ruby released her hold on the pen. It rolled away from her, plopped over the edge of the bed and onto the floor, where it landed with a little click.

It was too much, all of this, and on the day she'd finally believed in a happy-ever-after future for herself. She couldn't write anymore, couldn't think.

"I love you, Mom," she whispered, staring up at the spidery crack in the ceiling.

Chapter Twenty-four

Nora sat at the kitchen table, reading a fifteen-year-old newspaper that she'd found in the broom closet and sipping a cup of lukewarm coffee. The front-page story was an outraged report that Washington State officials had set off underwater firecrackers to scare away sea lions at the Ballard Locks. The sea lions were eating the salmon and the steelhead. Beside that story was a smaller column—complete with photograph. President Reagan's dog had received a tonsillectomy.

Mostly, she was waiting for Ruby to come downstairs. Nora had tried to wait up for her daughter the previous night, but at about twelve-thirty, she'd given up. It had to be a good sign that Ruby hadn't come home early.

At least, that's what Nora told herself.

She was about to turn the page when the phone rang. Ignoring the crutches leaning against the wall, she hobbled to the counter and answered. "Hello?"

"It's me. Dee."

Nora sagged against the cold, pebbled surface of

the refrigerator. "Hi, Dee. What excellent news do you have for me today?"

"You're not going to like it."

"That's hardly surprising."

"I just got off the phone with Tom Adams. He called me at *home*. On *Sunday*, to tell me to tell you that if you didn't get those blankety-blank columns on his blankety-blank desk by Wednesday morning, he was going to slap a ten-million-dollar lawsuit on you. He said the paperwork was already done on it, he was just giving you a last chance." She made a little coughing sound. "He said he was going to sue everybody you'd ever worked with—including me."

"He can't do that," Nora said, though, of course, she had no idea whether or not he could.

"Are you sure?" Dee sounded scared.

"I'll talk to Tom myself," Nora answered, before Dee could really get going.

"Oh, thank God."

"What else is going on there? Is the brouhaha dying down?"

"No," and to her credit, Dee sounded miserable about it. "Your housekeeper went on *Larry King Live* last night and said . . . terrible things about you."

"*Adele* said bad things about me?"

"A woman named Barb Heinneman said you'd commissioned an expensive stained-glass window from her and never paid for it. And your hair lady— Carla—she said you were a lousy tipper."

"Oh, for God's sake, what does that have—"

"The *Tattler* reported that guy in the pictures wasn't your first . . . affair. They're saying that you and your husband had an 'open' marriage and you both slept with tons of other people. And sometimes . . ." Dee's voice dropped to a conspiratorial whisper. "You did it in groups. Like in that movie, *Eyes Wide Shut*. That's what they wrote, anyway."

Nora's head was spinning. Honest to God, a part of her felt like laughing, it was that ridiculous. *Eyes Wide Shut? Group sex?* For the first time since this whole mess began, she started to get mad. She'd made mistakes—big ones, bad ones—but this . . .

This, she didn't deserve. As she'd heard in a movie once—this shit she wouldn't eat. They were trying to make her out to be some kind of whore. "Is that it? Or am I carrying some space alien's mutant child, too?"

Dee laughed nervously. "That's mostly it. Except . . ."

"Yes?" Nora drew the word out, gave it at least three syllables.

"There was a thing in Liz Smith's column this week, one of those gossipy hints she loves to make—you know the ones. It sorta made it sound as if someone was writing a tell-all story about you. An ugly one."

"That's hardly—"

"It's supposed to be by someone close to you."

Nora released her breath in a sigh. She wasn't surprised; she'd expected this, and yet still it hurt. "I see."

"And your housekeeper said you ripped up parking tickets and threw away jury summonses. Some guy on the city council said they were going to launch an investigation."

That was it. "Good-bye, Dee," Nora said, uncertain as to whether her assistant was still talking or not.

She hung up the phone and wrenched the cupboard doors open.

There they were: the cheap, yellow crockery plates she'd bought at a garage sale a lifetime ago. She picked one up, felt the heft of it in her hand. And hesitated. There was no point in making a mess—

Launch an investigation.

She wound her arm back and threw the plate. It went flying through the air and smacked the wall by the arch, shattering.

Like Eyes Wide Shut . . . *group sex.*

She threw another one. It hit with a satisfying smack.

Open marriage . . . lousy tipper.

Another plate flew.

There were bits and pieces of china everywhere now; dents in the walls, scratches in the paint. Nora was breathing heavily. And smiling.

She should have tried this years ago. It actually helped. She reached for another plate.

Ten-million-dollar lawsuit.

And sent it sailing across the room.

Just then, Ruby came running downstairs. "What in the he—" She ducked, flung a protective hand across her face. The plate brushed past her head and hit the wall. When the pieces clattered to the floor, she hesitantly looked up. "Jesus, Mom . . . if you don't like the plates, buy a new set."

Nora sank to her knees on the hard, cold floor. She laughed until tears leaked out of her eyes . . . and then she was crying.

She buried her face in her hands, ashamed to let her

daughter see her like this, but she couldn't seem to stop . . .

It was too much for her suddenly, all of it—Eric's illness, her career, her ruined reputation.

She felt lonely, and old. A woman who'd traded everything in her life for a treasured gold coin, and found that in a heavy rain, the gold had washed off, leaving an ordinary bit of copper in her hand.

She looked up at Ruby, saw her daughter through a blurry curtain of tears.

"Mom?" Ruby knelt in front of her. "Are you okay?"

"Do I look okay?"

"In that Courtney Love, presurgery, after-concert sort of way." She reached out, pushed a damp strand of hair out of Nora's eyes. "What happened?"

"A lady is suing me for fraudulent advice. And someone close to me—apparently a friend—is writing an ugly tell-all about my life. Oh, and don't be surprised when you hear that your dad and I engaged in group sex." She tried to smile; it was a dismal failure. "But don't you worry, I can get through this. I've been through worse. It's just a midlife tantrum. The only thing that matters is how much I love you."

Ruby jerked back, let her hand drop into her lap. "Oh, man . . ." she whispered.

Nora climbed awkwardly to her feet and hobbled to the kitchen table. She slumped onto a chair, plopped her casted foot on another one.

It occurred to her then, as she watched her daughter, who still knelt on the floor with her head bowed, that there was no silence more cruel and empty than the one that followed that simple declaration: "I love you."

She'd spent a childhood waiting to hear those words from her father, then an eternity waiting to hear them from her husband.

Now, it seemed, she was destined to wait again. And she'd thought things were going so well with Ruby . . .

"Would you like some coffee?" she said, pushing the newspaper aside. Her voice was calm and even, as if it were completely ordinary for them to be here together, amid a smattering of broken yellow china.

Ruby looked up at her. "Don't."

Nora saw that her daughter was crying; it confused her. "What is it, Rube?"

"Don't pretend you didn't say it. Please."

Nora had no idea how to respond. Ruby got up, turned, and went upstairs.

Nora heard each footfall on the steps. She couldn't seem to draw a steady breath. *What in the world just happened?*

Then she heard the steps again; Ruby was coming back downstairs. She walked into the kitchen, carrying a suitcase in one hand and a tablet of paper in the other.

Nora's hand flew to her mouth. "I'm sorry. I thought we'd gotten to the point where I could say that to you."

Ruby dropped the suitcase. It landed with a *thunk* that shook the thin windowpanes.

"Ruby, honey . . ." The endearment slipped out on a current of longing and regret.

"It was never about forgetting or forgiving," Ruby said slowly. Tears welled in her dark eyes, bled down her cheeks. "It took me so long to figure that out. And now it's too late."

Nora frowned. "I don't understand—"

"I love you."

Ruby's voice was so soft Nora thought at first she'd imagined the words, drawn them up from her own subconscious and given them the substance of sound.

"You love me?" Nora dared to whisper.

Ruby stood there, a little unsteady. "Just try . . . to remember that, okay?"

"How could I possibly—"

Ruby slapped a yellow pad of paper on the kitchen table. "I spent all of last night making you a copy of this."

Nora barely glanced at it; she was too busy watching Ruby. "What is it?"

Ruby backed up, stepped alongside her suitcase. "Read it," she said dully.

With a little shrug, Nora pulled the table close. "I might need my glasses . . ." She peered down at the paper, squinting.

In the interest of full disclosure, I must tell you that I was paid to write this article. Paid handsomely, as they say in the kind of restaurants where a person like me can't afford to order a dinner salad. Enough so that I could trade in my beat-up Volkswagen Bug for a slightly less beat-up Porsche.

I should also tell you that I dislike my mother.

No, that's not true. I dislike the snotty salesclerk who works the night shift at my local video store.

I hate my mother.

Nora looked up sharply.

Ruby was crying now, so hard her cheeks were bright pink and her shoulders were trembling. "It's an article for *C-Caché* magazine."

Nora drew in a sharp, gasping breath. She knew it was all in her eyes—the stinging betrayal, the aching sadness . . . and yes, the anger. "How could you?"

Ruby clamped a hand over her mouth, grabbed the suitcase, and ran out of the house.

As if from a great, unbreachable distance, Nora heard the car start up and speed away, sputtering through loose gravel.

It was quiet once more.

Nora tried not to look at the yellow pages, with their scrawled blue words marching across the even lines, but she couldn't help herself. Those horrible, hateful words leapt out at her.

I hate my mother.

She took a deep, deep breath, then looked down again. Her hands were shaking as she lifted the pad and began to read.

The story of us starts a dozen years ago, in a place few of you have ever seen: the San Juan Islands up in Washington State.

It was only a few sentences later that Nora began to cry.

* * *

Ruby made it all the way to the end of the driveway, then she slammed on the brakes.

She was running away again, but there was nowhere to hide on this one, no way past except through. She'd done a terrible, selfish thing, and she owed more to her mother than an empty house.

She put the minivan in reverse and backed down the driveway. Parking, she walked down the path, through the fragrant garden, and out to the edge of the bank. She would have gone to sit on her favorite rock, but her mother couldn't get there on crutches.

She *wanted* to be seen. When Mom finished the article, she would undoubtedly head for the porch; it was her favorite place. Then she would see her daughter, sitting out on the edge of the property.

She sat down on the grass. It was a beautiful summer's day. The islands were an endless mosaic of color—blue, blue sky, green forested land, silver, choppy sea.

She lay back on the grass and closed her eyes. The air smelled sweetly of grass and salt, of her childhood.

She knew she would remember this day for the rest of her life, and probably at the oddest times—when she was elbow-deep in sudsy water, washing the dinner dishes. In the shower, with the sweet, citrusy scent of her mother's favorite shampoo all around her, or holding the babies she prayed someday to have. At times like that, she would remember this moment, and all the others that had led up to it. In a very real way, this would be the beginning of her adult life; everything that grew afterward would be planted in the soil of what she and her mother said to each other right here.

She wondered if she would ever get over her shame, or if she would carry it with her always, the way she'd once been weighed down by anger.

Now Ruby would be the one sending gifts across the miles, leaving phone messages on machines, waiting, forever waiting, for an answer . . .

"Hey, Rube."

Ruby opened her eyes and saw her mother standing beside her. She was leaning awkwardly forward on her crutches. The sun haloed her auburn hair in brightness.

Ruby jackknifed up. "Mom," she whispered, finding that her throat was too tight to say anything more.

"I'm glad you came back. You can't get away from me so easily on an island, I guess."

Mom tossed the crutches aside and knelt slowly onto the grass, then sort of fell sideways into a sitting position. She set the article on her lap and stared down at it. The curled edges fluttered in the soft breeze. "I read every word you wrote about me, and I have to admit, it broke my heart."

Ruby wanted to curl up and die. She considered how far they'd come, she and her mom, the winding, shaded road that had taken them from then to now, and she ached for what her selfishness had wrought. If not for the article, Ruby would be laughing right now, telling her mother about the night before. Maybe they would have talked about ridiculous, girly things like wedding rings and bridesmaids and flower arrangements.

"I'm so ashamed," she said. "I knew those words would hurt you. In the beginning, that's what I wanted to do."

"And now?"

"I would give anything to take it all back."

Nora smiled sadly. "The truth always hurts, Ruby. It's a law of nature, like gravity." She glanced out at the Sound. "When I read your article, I saw myself. That doesn't seem like much, but I've spent a lifetime running away from who I am and where I came from. I never trusted anyone enough to be myself. When I started my advice column, I knew people wouldn't like *me*, so I made up Nora Bridge, a woman they could trust and admire, and then I tried to live up to that creation. But how could I? The mistakes I'd made—the woman I really was—kept me on the outside all the time, looking in at my own life." She looked at Ruby again. "But I trusted you."

Ruby squeezed her eyes shut. "I know."

"I was right to trust you, Ruby. I knew it when I finished reading. You listened and you wrote, and when it was over, you'd revealed *me*. From the girl who hid under the stairs, to the woman who hid behind the metal bars of a mental institution, to the woman who hid behind a microphone." She smiled. "To this woman, who isn't hiding now. You made me see *me*."

"I know I gave away all your secrets, but I'm not going to publish the article. I won't do that to you."

"Oh, yes you are."

Ruby wasn't surprised that her mother didn't believe her. "I'm making you a promise. I won't deliver it."

Nora leaned forward, took Ruby's hands in hers, and held them tightly. "I *want* you to publish this article. It's a beautiful, powerful portrait of who we are, and it shows who we can be, both of us. It shows how love can go wrong, and how it can find its way back to the beginning if you believe in it. What you wrote . . . it isn't a betrayal, Ruby. Maybe it started out that way, but why shouldn't it have? We had a long, long road to walk. And at the end of it, what I saw was how much you love me."

Ruby swallowed hard. "I do love you, Mom. And I'm so sor—"

"Sshh, no more of that. We're family. We're going to trample all over each other's feelings now and again. That's the way it's supposed to be." Nora's eyes were bright with unshed tears. "And now, we're going to go inside and call your agent. I'm appearing on *Sarah Purcell* with you."

"No way. They'll eat you alive."

"Let 'em. I'll be holding my daughter's hand for strength. They can't hurt me any more, Ruby. And I'm itching to fight back."

Ruby stared at her mother in awe. She was doing it again, changing before Ruby's eyes. She had a sudden glimpse of yet another woman altogether. "You're amazing."

Nora laughed. "It took you long enough to notice."

Chapter Twenty-five

I had my fifteen minutes of fame, and amazingly, when the clock struck the quarter hour, I was still famous. My mother and I had become, it seems, symbols that the world wasn't on such a fast and ugly track, after all. It makes sense, when you think about it. We live in a time when the evening news is laden with one depressing story after another.

Sadly, none of it surprises us anymore. We sit in our living rooms, on our plush sofas that a decade's affluence has allowed us to purchase, and we shake our heads at the stories. Sometimes—boldly—we turn off the news or change the channel. What we rarely do is ask why. Who has declared that murder is more newsworthy than the heartwarming story of an elderly woman who delivers Meals-on-Wheels to local AIDS sufferers?

But, as Dennis Miller says, I'm off on a rant. It's just that I have seen firsthand that celebrity is not the utopia I'd imagined, and it has made me question my interpretations of the world around me.

Famous people have more money . . . and less freedom; they have more choices . . . and less honesty. Everything is a trade-off. And when we let the media choose our heroes for us, we are lost already.

What Mom and I discovered was that we are not as isolated—any of us—as we believe. People want good news as well as bad, and they loved the story of my redemption. Girl hates mother . . . girl learns to love mother . . . girl gives up career to keep from breaking her mother's heart.

People loved it. They loved me.

But most of all, they loved my mother. They heard the story of her whole life, laid out before them like a novel, and they cheered at what she had overcome. She became something more than a celebrity . . . she became one of them. An ordinary woman, and surprisingly, it made her more famous and more beloved.

I listen to her on the radio now, and I hear the responses. Every now and then she gets an angry caller, who labels her a hypocrite and a loser for abandoning her children.

The old Nora Bridge, I think, would have fallen apart at such a personal and accurate attack. No more. Now, she listens and agrees, and then goes on, talking about the gift of mistakes and the miracle of family. She hopes that people will learn from her bad choices. And she wraps that spell around them, the one only she can spin, and by the end of the show, her listeners are reaching for tissues and thinking about how to find their way back to their own families. The smart ones are reaching for the telephone.

There's no substitute for talking to the people you love. Thinking about them, dreaming about them, wishing things were different . . . all of these are the beginning. But someone has to make the first move.

I guess that's one of the things I learned this summer, but it's not the most important; it's not the thing I will hold close and pass on to my own daughter when the time is right. The truths I gathered on Summer Island were so easy; they were lying right there on the grass. I should have tripped over them. I would have, if only I'd opened my eyes.

As mothers and daughters, we are connected with one another. My mother is in the bones of my spine, keeping me straight and true. She is in my blood, making sure it runs rich and strong. She is in the beating of my heart.

I cannot now imagine a life without her.

I know how precious time is. I learned this from my friend, Eric. Sometimes, when I close my eyes, I see him as he once was, laughing, standing at the bow of his sailboat, looking forward to the rest of his life. I hear his voice in the wind, I feel his touch in the rain, and I remember . . .

Life is short. And I know that when Eric loses his battle with cancer, I will find the missing of him unbearable. I will reach for the phone then and call my mother, and her voice will bring me back to myself.

A daughter without her mother is a woman

Kristin Hannah

broken. It is a loss that turns to arthritis and settles deep in her bones. This I know now.

I left Los Angeles as a hard, bitter, cynical young woman with a huge chip on her shoulder. On Summer Island, I became complete. And it was all so easy. I see that now.

I went in search of my mother's life, and found my own.

"Do you think they'll be coming home soon?"

Dean didn't need to ask who Eric was talking about. In the three days since Nora and Ruby had left, he and Eric had speculated endlessly about their return. Dean knew that Eric often forgot their conversations on the subject. Sometimes, they would end one discussion and moments later Eric would ask the familiar question again. *Do you think they'll be coming home soon?*

"They'll be here any day," Dean answered. Although he always answered similarly, he wasn't so sure, and the uncertainty was killing him. It was Nora who called every night to talk to Eric; Ruby was always off somewhere, doing publicity or "taking a meeting." She'd talked to them only once, and although she'd said all the right words to Dean, he'd felt a distance blossoming between them.

She was famous now. It was what she'd always wanted, even as a little girl; she'd dreamed of being loved by strangers. He couldn't blame her for enjoying every minute of her newfound celebrity, and he couldn't help wondering if there would still be a place in her life for him.

Eric coughed.

Dean turned away from the window. For a split second, the sight of his brother shocked him. The past few days had been like that. Eric's decline had come so suddenly that sometimes, from moment to moment, Dean was caught off guard. Eric was so hollow, so shrunken; smiles were becoming rare. He seemed exhausted by the simple act of breathing, and the medications didn't stave off the pain for long.

"Can we go outside?" Eric asked. "I can see what a beautiful day it is."

"Sure." Dean ran outside and prepared everything. He set up a wooden lounge chair in the shade of an old madrona tree, placed it so that his brother could see all the way to the beach. Then he went back upstairs and bundled Eric in heavy blankets and carried him outside.

It was like carrying a small child; he weighed nothing at all.

Dean gently placed his brother on the chair. Eric settled back, sinking into the mound of pillows. He closed his eyes. "Man, that sun feels good on my face."

Dean looked at his brother, whose face was tilted up to catch the sunlight. What he saw wasn't a thin, balding young man huddled in a multicolored blanket... what he saw was courage, distilled to its purest essence.

"I'll be right back." He ran into the house and got his camera, loaded it with black-and-white film, and hurried back out into the yard. He started snapping pictures.

Eric's eyes fluttered open. It took him a minute to

focus, a few more to comprehend the silvery box Dean was using. Finally, he gasped and held up a weak, spotted hand. "Oh, God, Dino . . . no photos. I look like shit on a lounge chair." He turned his head away.

Dean eased the camera from his eye and went to his brother, kneeling down. "Come on, you put Tom Cruise to shame."

Eric turned to him. "I used to be a fine specimen of a man," he said, smiling crookedly. "And you wait until I look like something out of *Alien* to take my picture."

Dean stroked his brother's damp forehead. He could tell that Eric was tiring already. "I missed those years, pal. I don't want to miss these. I'll need . . . pictures of you."

Eric groaned. "Shit." He brought a hand up, rubbed his eyes.

"You know what I see when I look through this lens? I see a hero."

Slowly Eric opened his eyes and smiled. "I'm ready for my close-up, Mr. DeMille."

Dean finished the roll of film, then tossed the camera onto the picnic table, and lay down in the grass beside his brother.

"Do you think they'll be home soon?"

"Any day now." Dean rolled onto his side and looked up at his brother. "Ruby's famous now. Remember we saw her on *Entertainment Tonight* yesterday? It's what she always wanted."

"Yeah, well, I used to want to be an astronaut. Then I took a ride on some vomit-comet at the state fair."

"I think Ruby needed to be famous."

Eric scooted onto his side, groaning a little at the movement. He stared down at Dean. "You think *fame* is what she wanted?"

"I've seen the media up close. I dated a supermodel a few years back. It can be a pretty wild thing, everybody loving you."

"That's not love."

"Yeah," Dean said, but he didn't feel the truth of it in his bones.

"I know what love is, pal. She'll come back to you, and if she doesn't, she's too stupid to live."

Dean came up to a sit. This was the one subject they'd steered clear of, the thing Dean had never been able to ask and Eric had been too cautious to mention. But it had always been between them. At first, it had been the size of a boulder; now, it was a pebble. But always, it was there, nagging, waiting to be released. "What was it like between you and Charlie?"

Eric made a little sound of surprise. "You sure you want to go there?"

"Yeah."

A slow, heartbreakingly earnest smile transformed Eric's face, made him look almost young again. "I looked at Charlie and saw my future." He grinned. "Not that this seemed like a good thing at the time, mind you. I mean, I knew I was supposed to see my future on a body that held a uterus. I didn't want to be gay. I knew how hard it would be . . . that it would mean giving up the American Dream—kids, a house in the suburbs, my own family. It tore me up inside."

Dean had never thought about that, about what it really meant to be gay. To have to choose between who you were and who the world thought you should be. "Jesus . . . I'm sorry."

"I wanted to talk to you about it, but you were sixteen years old. And I was afraid you'd hate me. So I kept silent. Finally, what I felt for Charlie was more important than everything else. I loved him so much . . . and when he died, a huge part of me went with him. I wouldn't have made it without Nora. She was always there with me . . ." He closed his eyes. His breathing made a fluttering sound. Then suddenly he woke up, angled forward. "Where did I leave my eraser?"

Dean touched his brother's forearm. "It's on the kitchen table. I'll bring it to you."

"Oh." Eric immediately calmed down and sank back into the pillows. "Do you think they'll be here soon?"

Dean stroked Eric's forehead. "Any day now." When he heard his brother's breathing even out into sleep, Dean lay back in the grass and closed his own eyes. The hot sun felt good on his face, and if he tried really hard, he could almost pretend that this was an ordinary summer's day from long ago. That he and Eric were exhausted, sleeping on the beach after a day spent swimming in the cove . . .

He woke when a car drove up. "Hey, Lottie," he called out, waving sleepily. He didn't bother to get up. It felt so good to lie here with his eyes closed.

"Is that any way to greet your newly famous, still ringless fiancée?"

Dean's eyes snapped open. Ruby was standing beside him, arms akimbo, blocking out the sun's rays. He scrambled to his feet and swept her into his arms, giving her the kisses he'd been counting since she left.

She drew back, laughing. "Jeez, I'm going to have to make a point to leave *lots* in our marriage. Coming home is great." Taking his hand, she bent down to Eric, who was still sleeping. "Hey, Eric," she said softly.

Eric blinked up at her. "Hi Sally."

She frowned at Dean.

"He's getting pretty bad," he whispered. "Keeps forgetting where he is."

Ruby sagged against him. Dean anchored her in place with an arm around her waist. "We watched you and Nora on *The Sarah Purcell Show*. You were great."

Ruby grinned. "It was fun. In a reporters-following-you-into-the-bathroom-stall sort of way. Being famous is harsh. I turned down the sitcom offers."

"Really?"

"I took a book deal. A novel this time. I figured it was something I could do up here."

"Hey, guys!" Nora shouted, waving. She came beside them, limping on her brand-new walking cast. She touched Dean's shoulder. "How's Eric?"

Dean shook his head, mouthed *Not good*.

Eric's eyes opened again, focused. "Nora? Is that you?"

She knelt beside him. If she was shocked by how bad he looked, she showed no signs of it. "I'm here, Eric." She held his hand. "I'm here."

"I knew you'd be here any minute. Have you seen my eraser? I think Sally hid it."

"No, honey, I haven't seen it." Her voice was throaty. "But do you know what day it is?"

Eric looked at her. "Monday?"

"It's the Fourth of July."

"Are we gonna have our party?"

"Of course."

"With sparklers?" He smiled sleepily.

"You go ahead and sleep for a minute. I'll get your brother to start the barbecue."

"Dean's shitty at barbecuing. He drops everything onto the coals. You always let me cook the fish."

She stroked his forehead. "I know. Maybe you could supervise."

"Yeah." He grinned up at Dean. "Just take the meat off *before* it bursts into flames."

Nora leaned forward and kissed Eric's cheek. By the time she got to her feet, he was asleep again. When she turned around, Dean saw the moisture in her eyes. He reached for her hand, held it. The three of them stood there, holding hands in the middle of the yard for a long, long time. No one spoke.

Finally, Ruby said, "Let's get this party rolling."

Dean gave Nora a last, heartfelt look. "Thanks," he said softly. June hadn't yet rounded the bend into July, but this party was exactly what Eric needed.

While Nora and Ruby set the groceries and supplies out on the picnic table, Dean went upstairs and turned on the stereo. Music had always been a big part of their celebrations. He stuck the old-fashioned black speakers in the open window, pointing them toward the yard. Then he found the local golden-oldies station (none of them needed to be reminded now of the passing of time), and cranked the volume. For this one night, he would do his best to turn the clock back a dozen years.

As if in answer, the first song to blare through the speakers was Dire Straits' "Money for Nothing."

By the time he got back outside, Nora and Ruby had everything ready. The corn on the cob had been shucked and wrapped in tinfoil; the store-bought macaroni salad was in a pottery bowl and ready to be served; and the salmon was seasoned and layered in slices of Walla Walla Sweet onions and lemons.

The music changed. Now it was "Crazy for You" by Madonna . . .

Dean looped an arm around Ruby's shoulder and drew her close. They moved in time to the music. "God, this brings back memories."

She pulled him away from the picnic table. "Dance with me."

He took her in his arms and danced back in time. If he'd closed his eyes, he would have seen the high-school gymnasium, decorated in glitter and tinfoil and tissue paper. He would have seen Ruby, wearing an ice-blue polyester dress with braided spaghetti straps, with her long hair flowing down her back.

Only he didn't close his eyes, didn't look back. From now on, he only wanted to look ahead.

When the music changed again, to Shaun Cassidy's "Da Do Ron," Nora limped out and started dancing with them. On the lounge chair, Eric was doing his best to clap along to the song.

They spent the rest of the day laughing, it seemed. They talked, they reminisced about the old days and spun dreams about the days to come. They ate dinner off paper plates balanced on their laps. Eric even managed a few bites of salmon. And when the darkness finally came to their party, they lit up the sparklers and shot off the fireworks.

Ruby stood at the bank, with her back to the Sound, and wrote RUBY LOVES DEAN in glittering white bursts of light. Beside her, Nora wrote I LOVE MY GIRLS and SUMMER ISLAND FOREVER. They were both grinning as they waved at Dean and Eric.

Eric turned his head. When their gazes met, Dean felt a clutch of fear. His brother looked hopelessly old and tired. "I love you, baby brother."

The world spiraled down to the two of them, sitting in this darkened yard. A silence swept in, snuffing out the music and the sound of the women's laughter. The sudden quiet felt endless, dark, and dangerous.

"I love you, too, Eric."

"No funeral. I want you guys to have a party, something like this, like the old days. Then throw my ashes off the *Wind Lass*. Maybe under the bridge at Deception Pass."

Dean couldn't imagine that, standing on the boat, watching gray ashes float on the surface of the choppy green sea, thinking about a pair of blue eyes that would never look at him again . . .

Eric's breathing grew labored. He closed his eyes. "I can't find the practice roster."

"I'll get it for you."

Eric opened his eyes. He didn't seem able to focus. "Get Mom, would you? I need to talk to her."

Dean froze.

"She's here, isn't she?"

Dean nodded quickly, wiping the tears from his eyes. "Of course she's here."

Eric smiled and leaned back into the pillows. "I knew she'd come."

"I'll go get her." It seemed to take Dean an hour to cross the small patch of lawn. As he walked, the sounds came back to him—the music, the laughter, the waves on the beach. "That's What Friends Are For" was playing on the radio.

"Come on, Dino." Ruby laughed, reaching for him. "You haven't written my name yet."

Dean couldn't hold out his hand. He felt as if he were unraveling, and the slightest movement could ruin him. "He's asking for Mom."

Nora immediately covered her mouth with her hand. A small gasp escaped anyway.

Ruby dropped her sparkler. It shot sparks up from the grass, and she carefully stomped it out with her foot.

In utter silence, the three of them walked toward Eric. Dean could hear everything now, down to the crushing of the grass beneath their shoes.

Ruby was the first to kneel beside Eric. She stared down at him, and Dean could see the tears in her eyes.

Eric smiled up at her. "You're unclenched . . ."

Dean frowned at the garbled words; amazingly, Ruby seemed to understand. "I am," she said softly, leaning down to kiss his cheek.

"You take care of my brother."

"I will."

Eric sighed and closed his eyes again. Dean moved in close to Ruby, took her hand and squeezed it.

"Oh, God," she whispered, and he knew she was wondering how she would possibly get past this. How would any of them?

Eric fell asleep for a few minutes, then opened his eyes, blinking hard. "Mom?" He looked around. There was an edge of panic to his voice. "Mom?"

Dean clung to Ruby's hand. The feel of her was a lifeline, the only thing that kept him steady.

Nora lowered herself to the chair, sitting on the edge beside him. "I'm here, honey. I'm right here."

Eric stared up at her, his eyes glassy and unfocused. "Dino came home . . . to me. I knew you would, too. I knew you wouldn't stay away. Where's Dad?"

Nora stroked his forehead. "Of course I came home. I'm sorry it took me so long."

Eric let out a long, slow sigh. Then he smiled, and for a split second, his eyes were clear. "Take care of Dino for me. He's going to need you now."

Nora swallowed hard. "Your dad and I will watch over him," she said in a throaty voice.

"Thanks . . . Nora. You were always my mom." Eric smiled and closed his eyes. A moment later, he whispered *Charlie, is that you?*

And he was gone.

Epilogue

DECEMBER

The chapel on Summer Island was a narrow, pitch-roofed, clapboard building set on the crest of a small rise. Even now, in the middle of a cold, gray winter, the building was cloaked in glossy green ivy. Ropey brown clematis vines framed the double doors; in a few short months, they would again produce a riot of green leaves and purple blossoms.

"I still can't believe you wouldn't let me fill the church with flowers."

Ruby laughed at her mother. They were standing in the tiny gravel parking lot adjacent to the church, waiting for the ferry to dock.

"Thank you, Martha Stewart, for that wedding-fashion update. This is exactly how we wanted it. There's only one decoration that matters to me."

"It's the dead of winter. You know there's no heat in the chapel." Nora crossed her arms. Her elegant green St. John knit suit set off the flawless ivory of her skin. There wasn't a breath of wind to upset her carefully arranged hair. Unfortunately, it was about thirty degrees out here—unusually cold for Christmas week.

To her credit, Nora tried to smile. "I wanted to plan this day for you. Make it perfect in every way."

Ruby's smile was soft and understanding. "No, Mom. You wanted to plan it for you."

"And that's my right, damn it." A quick smile tugged at her mouth. "Maybe Jenny will do it right?"

"That's a fight I'd pay to see—you and Caroline battling for control over Jenny's big day. You'd probably settle on a small service at the Vatican."

Nora laughed and moved closer. "I love you, Ruby," she said softly, then, "Oh, damn, I'm crying already."

Ruby started to say something, but the ferry honked its horn.

Within minutes, three cars drove up, parked side by side. The doors opened, and the rest of the gang appeared.

Caroline, looking as cool and elegant as a water flower, was in pale ice-blue silk. Beside her, Jere brought up the kids. They all belonged in a Ralph Lauren ad.

Caroline hugged Ruby fiercely, then drew back. Her eyes were full of tears as she smiled. "My baby sister in—" She frowned. "What are you wearing?"

Ruby posed. What had once been her dress of shame had become her wedding gown. "Isn't it great?"

Caroline's narrowed gaze swept her from head to foot, noticed the plunging neckline and the ankle-to-crotch slit up the side. "You didn't find that in *Modern Bride*."

"It's Versace."

Caroline grinned. "It certainly is. You look gorgeous." Jere came up beside his wife and took her hand. "Hey, Ruby," he said, settling Freddie on his hip. "You look great."

Ruby grinned. "I could get used to this."

Then Rand was there, wearing an elegant black tuxedo. Marilyn was beside him, holding their son. Lottie was there, too, wearing her frilly "town" dress and a big straw hat. The only concession she'd made to winter was a pair of oversized black snow boots.

Rand kissed Ruby, whispering, "Heya, Hollywood, you look like a princess," before he drew back.

"Hey, Dad." Ruby looked up at Marilyn, who stood back from the crowd. Ruby gave her a bright smile. "Hi, Marilyn—it's good to have you here. How's that beautiful baby brother of mine?"

Marilyn broke into a smile and moved forward. "He's great. You look fabulous."

After that, they all started talking at once, their voices climbing over one another.

Then another car roared into the parking lot. Dean stepped out of the car and slammed the door shut. In his black Armani tux, he was so handsome that, for a moment, Ruby couldn't breathe. He walked up to her and gave her a smile so slow and seductive that she felt heat climb into her face.

Gently, he took her hands in his. "Are we ready to do this thing?"

I've been ready all my life, she wanted to answer, but her heart was so full, she could only nod.

"Then let's go."

Together, they went into the church. Inside, an aisle separated two short rows of rough-hewn benches.

The altar was a plain wooden trestle table that held two thick white beeswax candles. Their flickering flames released the sweet scent of hand-dried lavender. A gold silk scarf decorated with a single red cross draped the width of the table. In the corner stood a small noble fir that sparkled with white Christmas lights.

The family found their seats and crowded in. Jere whipped out a video recorder and started filming.

Dean walked down the aisle alone and took his place at the altar.

"Are you ready?"

Ruby heard her father's voice and turned slightly. He came up beside her, offered his arm. She knew her smile was a little shaky, and that it was okay. She slipped her arm through his and let him guide her down the aisle.

At the altar, he stopped, then leaned down and kissed her cheek. "I love you, Hollywood," he whispered.

Her emotions teetered on the edge of control. It was all she could do to nod as he stepped back, leaving her standing beside Dean.

Directly in front of them, on the altar, was a big photograph, framed in ornate, gilded wood. The only decoration that mattered.

Eric.

In it, he was about fifteen years old and standing on the bow of the *Wind Lass*, half-turned back to face the camera. His smile was pure Eric.

Dean stared at the picture. He sighed, and she knew he was remembering. She slipped her hand in his and squeezed tightly, whispering, "He's here."

"I know," he answered, holding her hand tightly. "I know."

Father Magowan smiled at them. Sister Helen gave Ruby a quick wink, then waddled over to the organ and sat down.

"Dearly beloved, we are gathered here to celebrate the union of this man and this woman in holy matrimony." His rich, melodious voice filled the small chapel.

Finally, he came to "Who gives this woman to be wed?"

It was the only thing Ruby had requested of this service, that question, and when she turned around and saw her mom and dad standing together, she knew she'd done the right thing. It was a vision that would stay in her heart forever.

Rand looked down at Nora, who was weeping openly. He slipped his arm around her and drew her close. "We do," he said proudly, "her mother and I."

Caroline was crying now, too, and Ruby saw the way Jere moved closer to her, sliding his arm around her waist.

Ruby turned back to Dean, gazed up into his shining blue eyes . . . and forgot everyone else. The service kept going, words thrown into a silence broken only by the soft organ music.

". . . You may kiss the bride."

Dean stared down at her, his eyes moist. "I've waited a lifetime for this," he said softly. "I'll always love you, Ruby."

She saw it all in his eyes: her past, her present, her future. She saw tow-headed children playing in the cold, cold waters of Puget Sound . . . and Christmas dinners with lots of chairs at the table . . . she even saw them when they were old, their hair gone white and their eyesight dimmed, and she knew she'd never forget this moment.

"That's good," she said, grinning up at him, tasting the salty moisture of her own tears. She knew she was ruining the makeover her mother had paid for, but she didn't care.

He leaned down and kissed her.

Behind them, the family clapped and cheered and laughed out loud.

Suddenly Elvis—in full beaded white jumpsuit—pushed through the doors. The King ran a hand through his pompadour, gave a sneering little half smile, and burst into song.

He was all shook up.

KRISTIN HANNAH is the bestselling author of *On Mystic Lake*, *Angel Falls*, *Summer Island*, *Distant Shores*, *Between Sisters*, and *The Things We Do for Love*. She lives with her husband and son in the Pacific Northwest. Visit her online at www.kristinhannah.com.